NOIR

THE BIG BOOK OF NOIR

EDITED BY

LEE SERVER

ED GORMAN

MARTIN H. GREENBERG

CARROLL & GRAF PUBLISHERS, INC.

NEW YORK

First Carroll & Graf edition 1998

Carroll & Graf Publishers, Inc.
19 West 21 Street
New York, NY 10010

Library of Congress Cataloging-in-Publication Data is available.
ISBN 0-7867-0574-4

Manufactured in the United States of America

Contents

III: COMIC BOOKS

IV: RADIO & TELEVISION

FOREWORD

The present collection, by no means comprehensive, is a first and informal attempt to chart—through interviews, essays, and memoirs—the various strands of the noir vision in popular entertainment, from its vague beginnings in American pulps and European movie studios to the modern proliferation in mainstream cinema and fiction.

Noir is the French-derived term for a dark, pessimistic, and fearful world view as expressed in film, fiction, and other popular arts of this century. In its English-language adaptation the word was first attached almost exclusively to a loosely generic style of moviemaking. But the French film critics who coined the term in the 1940s had always been aware of the intersecting roots of the still-evolving format. "Film noir" was a direct play on *Série Noire,* a Parisian publisher's new line of grim thrillers and violent detective stories, most of them American in origin—the fresh form of tough literature by the likes of Hammett, Chandler, and Woolrich that grew out of the pulps of the 1920s and '30s (the line itself reflective of an older literary category dubbed *roman noir*).

The initial delineators of film noir saw at once the aesthetic and spiritual kinship between noir fiction and film. Indeed, it took only the reading of the credits on the average film noir to see the literal cross-fertilization at work: movies adapted from the hardboiled school of pop lit or scripted by the former pulpsters and hardboiled novelists themselves. With the popular acceptance of the noir style and perspective, aspects of the genre would spread to other creative realms. The poetic tough-guy cadences of a James M. Cain or Raymond Chandler first-person narrative, transferred to screen in the voiceovers and dialogue heard in films like *Double Indemnity* and *Murder My Sweet,* would in turn be echoed in an endless array of mystery and private-eye programs on 1940s radio, and eventually on the televised variations of the '50s and '60s. The rich, shadow-drenched visual style of film noir created by veterans of German Expressionism like Fritz Lang and Robert Siodmak would become a major influence on the look of crime comic books and superhero comic strips (and the graphic novels of more recent vintage).

The spreading influence of the noir aesthetic has continued to the present, and echoes and elements of noir are seen these days everywhere from music videos and magazine ads invoking classic noir iconography to the more substantial worlds of the movies and fiction exploring the darker corners of human experience. Whether perceived as a romantic/nostalgic category from out of the past or as the popular genre that best addresses the anxieties of the modern world, it is clear that the once disreputable and never more than loosely defined genre has attained a cultural significance and ubiquitousness that could never have been imagined by the creators of those original pulp novels and crime films a half century and more ago.

—The Editors

Courtesy of Kino International

Barbara Stanwyck, one of the great dark ladies of film noir, observes her latest victim (Kirk Douglas) in *The Strange Love of Martha Ivers*.

Introduction:

PAINT IT BLACK: THE FAMILY TREE OF THE FILM NOIR

RAYMOND DURGNAT

In 1946 French critics, having missed Hollywood films for five years, saw suddenly, sharply, a darkening tone, darkest around the crime film. The English spoke only of the "tough, cynical Hammett-Chandler thriller," although a bleak, cynical tone was invading all genres, from the *Long Voyage Home* to *Duel in the Sun.*

The tone was often castigated as Hollywood decadence, although black classics are as numerous as rosy (Euripedes, Calvin, Ford, Tourneau, Goya, Lautréamont, Dostoevsky, Grosz, Faulkner, Francis Bacon). Black is as ubiquitous as shadow, and if the term film noir has a slightly exotic ring it's no doubt because it appears as figure against the rosy ground of Anglo-Saxon middle-class, and especially Hollywoodian, optimism and puritanism. If the term is French it's no doubt because, helped by their more lucid (and/or mellow, or cynical, or decadent) culture, the French first understood the full import of the American development.

Greek tragedy, Jacobean drama, and the Romantic Agony (to name three black cycles) are earlier responses to epochs of disillusionment and alienation. But the sociocultural parallels can't be made mechanically. Late forties Hollywood is blacker than thirties precisely because its audience, being more secure, no longer needed cheering up. On the other hand, it was arguably insufficiently mature to enjoy the open, realistic discontent of, say, *Hotel du Nord, Look Back in Anger,* or Norman Mailer. The American film noir, in the narrower sense, paraphrases its social undertones by the melodramatics of crime and the underworld; *Scarface* and *On The Waterfront* mark its limits, both also "realistic" films. It's almost true to say that the French crime thriller evolves out of black realism, whereas American black realism evolves out of the crime thriller. Evolution apart, the black thriller is hardly perennial, drawing on the unconscious superego's sense of crime and punishment. The first detective thriller is *Oedipus Rex,* and it has the profoundest twist of all: detective, murderer, and executioner are one man. The Clytemnestra plot underlies innumerable film noir, from *The Postman Always Rings Twice* to *Cronaca di Un Amore.*

The nineteenth century splits the classic tragic spirit into three genres: bourgeois realism (Ibsen), the ghost story, and the detective story. The avenger ceases to be a ghost (representative of a magic order) and becomes a detective, private or public. The butler did it. *Uncle Silas, Fantomas,* and *The Cat and the Canary* illustrate the transitional stage between detective and ghost story. For ghosts the film noir substitutes, if only by implication, a nightmare society, or condition of man. In *Psycho,* Mummy's transvestite mummy is a secular ghost, just as abnormal as Norman is, at the end, Lord of the Flies, a Satanic, megalomaniac, hollow in creation. The film noir is often nihilistic, cynical or stoic as reformatory; there are Fascist and apathetic denunciations of the bourgeois order, as well as Marxist ones.

There is obviously no clear line between the threat in a gray drama, the somber drama, and the film noir, just as it's impossible to say exactly when a crime becomes the focus of a film rather than merely a realistic incident. Some films seem black to cognoscenti, while the public of their time takes the happy end in a complacent sense; this is true of, for example, *The Big Sleep. On The Waterfront* is a film noir, given Brando's negativism and anguished playing, whereas *A Man Is Ten Feet Tall* is not, for reasons of tone suggested by the title. *Mourning Becomes Electra* is too self-consciously classic, although its adaptation in forties Americana with Joan Crawford might not be. *Intruder in the Dust* is neither Faulkner nor noir, despite the fact that only a boy and an old lady defy the lynch mob; its tone intimates that they tend to suffice. The happy end in a true film noir is that the worst of danger is averted, with little amelioration or congratulation. The film noir is not a genre, as the Western and gangster film, and takes us into the realm of classification by motif and tone. Only some crime films are noir, and films noir in other genres include *The Blue Angel, King Kong, High Noon, Stalag 17, The Sweet Smell of Success, Jeanne Eagles, Attack, Shadows, Lolita, Lonely Are the Brave,* and *2001.*

The French film noir precedes the American genre. French specialists include Feuillade, Duvivier, Carné, Clouzot, Yves Allegret, and even, almost without noticing, Renoir (of *La Chienne, La Nuit du Carrefour, La Bête Humaine, Woman on the Beach*) and Godard. Two major cycles of the thirties and forties are followed by a gangster cycle in the fifties, including *Touchez Pas Au Grisbi* (Becker, 1953), *Du Rififi Chez Les Hommes* (Dassin, 1955), *Razziá sur la Chnouff* (Decoin, 1957), *Mefiez-vous Fillettes* (Allegret, 1957), and the long Eddie Constantine series to which Godard pays homage in *Alphaville. Fantomas,* made for Gaumont, inspired its rival Pathé to the Pearl White series, inaugurated by the New York office of this then French firm. *La Chienne* becomes *Scarlet Street, La Bête Humaine* becomes *Human Desire. Le Jour se Leve* becomes *The Long Night,* while *Pepe-le-Moko* becomes Algiers ("Come with me to the Casbah") and also Pepe-le-Pew. The American version of *The Postman Always Rings Twice* (1945) is preceded by the French (*Le Dernier Tournant,* 1939) and an Italian (*Ossessione,* 1942). The fifties gangster series preceded the American revival of interest in gangsters and the group-job themes. Godard was offered *Bonnie and Clyde* before Penn, presumably on the strength of *Breathless* rather than *Pierrot Le Fou.*

The Italian film noir, more closely linked with realism, may be represented by *Ossessione,* by Senza Pieta, *Caccia Tragica, Bitter Rice* (neorealist melodramas that pulverize Hollywood action equivalents by Walsh et. al.), and *Cronaca di Un Amore,* Antonioni's mesmerically beautiful first feature. The American black Western, which falters in the early sixties, is developed by the Italians. Kracauer's *From Caligari to Hitler* details the profusion of films noir in Germany in the twenties, although the crime theme is sometimes overlaid with the tyrant theme. *The Living Dead,* a compendium of Poe stories, anticipates the Cormans. The Germans also pioneered the horror film (*Nosferatu* precedes *Dracula*, *Homunculus* precedes *Frankenstein*). German expressionism heavily influences American films noir in which German directors (Stroheim, Leni, Lang, Siodmak, Preminger, Wilder) loom conspicuously (not to mention culturally Germanic Americans like Schoedsack and Sternberg).

The English cinema has its own, far from inconsiderable, line in films noir, notably, the best pre-war Hitchcocks (*Rich and Strange*, *Sabotage*). An effective series of costume bullying dramas (*Gaslight*, 1940), through *Fanny by Gaslight* and *The Man in Grey* to *Daybreak* (1947), is followed by man-on-the-run films of which the best are probably *Odd Man Out*, *They Made Me a Fugitive*, and *Secret People*. The also-rans include many which are arguably more convincing and adventurous than many formula-bound Hollywood cult favorites. The following subheadings offer inevitably imperfect schematizations for some main lines of force in the American film noir. They describe not genres but dominant cycles or motifs, and many, if not most, films would come under at least two headings, since interbreeding is intrinsic to motif processes. In all these films, crime or criminals provide the real or apparent center of focus, as distinct from films in the first category from noncriminal "populist" films such as *The Crowd*, *Street Scene*, *The Grapes of Wrath*, *Bachelor Party*, *Too Late Blues*, and *Echoes of Silence*.

1. CRIME AS SOCIAL CRITICISM

A first cycle might be labeled: "Pre-Depression: The Spontaneous Witnesses." Examples include *Easy Street* (1917), *Broken Blossoms* (1919), *Greed* (1924), *The Salvation Hunters* (1925). Two years later the director of *The Salvation Hunters* preludes with *Underworld*, the gangster cycle that is given its own category below. The financial and industry-labor battles of the thirties are poorly represented in Hollywood, for the obvious reason that the heads of studios tend to be Republican, and anyway depend on the banks. But as the rearmament restored prosperity, the association of industry and conflict was paraphrased in politically innocent melodrama, giving *Road to Frisco* (1939) and *Manpower* (1940). (Realistic variants like *The Grapes of Wrath* are not noir.) *Wild Harvest* (1947) and *Give Us This Day* (1949) relate to this genre. The former has many lines openly critical of big capitalists, but its standpoint is ruralist-individualist and, probably, Goldwaterian. The second was directed by Dmytryk in English exile, but setting and spirit are entirely American.

Another cycle might be labeled: "The Somber Cross-Section." A crime takes us through a variety of settings and types and implies an anguished view of society as a whole. Roughly coincident with the rise of neorealism in Europe, this cycle includes *Phantom Lady*, *The Naked City*, *Nightmare Alley*, *Panic in the Streets*, *Glory Alley*, *Fourteen Hours*, *The Well*, *The Big Night*, *Rear Window*, and *Let No Man Write My Epitaph*. The genre shades into Chayefsky-type populism and studies of social problems later predominate. European equivalents of the genre include *Hotel du Nord*, *It Always Rains on Sunday*, *Sapphire*, and even *Bicycle Thieves*. If we include the theft of bicycles as a crime, which of course it is, albeit of a no melodramatic nature. The American weakness in social realism stems from postpuritan optimistic individualism, and may be summarized in political terms. The Republican line is that social problems arise from widespread wrong attitudes and are really individual moral problems. Remedial action must attack wrong ideas rather than the social setup. The Democratic line is a kind of liberal environmentalism; social action is required to "prime the pump," to even things up sufficiently for the poor or handicapped to have a fairer deal, to be given a real, rather than a merely theoretical, equality in which to prove themselves. Either way the neorealist stress on economic environment as virtual determinant is conspicuous by its absence, although the phrase "wrong side of the tracks" expresses it fatalistically. It's a minor curiosity that English liberal critics invariably pour scorn on the phrases through which Hollywood expresses an English liberal awareness of class and underprivilege.

Two remarkable movies, *He Ran All the Way* and *The Sound of Fury,* both directed by victims of McCarthy (John Berry, Cy Enfield) illustrate the slick, elliptic terms through which serious social criticism may be expressed. In the first film, the criminal hero (John Garfield) holds his girl (Shelley Winters) hostage in her father's tenement. The father asks a mate at work whether a hypothetical man in this position should call in the police. His mate replies: "Have you seen firemen go at a fire? Chop, chop, chop!" A multitude of such details assert a continuity between the hero's paranoid streak ("Nobody loves anybody!") and society as a paranoid (competitive) network. Similarly, in *The Sound of Fury,* the psycho killer (Lloyd Bridges) incarnates the real energies behind a thousand permitted prejudices: "Beer drinkers are jerks!" and "Rich boy, huh?" His reluctant accomplice is an unemployed man goaded by a thousand details. His son's greeting is: "Hullo father, mother won't give me ninety cents to go to the movies with the other kids," while the camera notes, in passing, the criminal violence blazoned forth in comic strips. When, sick with remorse, he confesses to a genteel manicurist, she denounces him. An idealistic journalist whips up hate; the two men are torn to death by an animal mob, who, storming the jail, also batter their own cops mercilessly.

Socially critical films noir are mainly Democratic (reformist) or cynical-nihilistic. Republican moralists tend to avoid the genre, although certain movies by Wellman, King Vidor and Hawks appear to be Republican attempts to grasp the nettle and tackle problems of self-help in desperate circumstances (e.g., *Public Enemy, Duel in the Sun, Only Angels Have Wings*).

However, certain conspicuous social malfunctions impose a black social realism. These are mostly connected with crime, precisely because this topic reintroduces the question of personal responsibility, such that the right-wing spectators can congenially misunderstand hopefully liberal movies. These malfunctions give rise to various subgenres of the crime film:

(a) Prohibition-type gangsterism. It's worth mentioning here a quiet but astonishing movie, *Kiss Tomorrow Good-bye* (1949), in which Cagney, as an old time gangster making a comeback, corrupts and exploits the corruption of a whole town, including the chief of police. His plan—to murder his old friend's hellcat daughter (Barbara Payton) so as to marry the tycoon's daughter (Helena Carter) and cement the dynasty—is foiled only by a personal quirk (his mistress's jealousy). The plot is an exact parallel to *A Place in the Sun* except that Dreiser's realistically weak characters are replaced by thrillingly tough ones. (Its scriptwriter worked on Stevens's film also.) Postwar gangster films are curiously devoid of all social criticism, except the postwar appeal of conscience, apart from its devious but effective reintroduction in *Bonnie and Clyde.*

(b) A corrupt penology (miscarriages of justice, prison exposés, lynch law). Corrupt, or worse, merely lazy, justice is indicted in *I Want to Live, Anatomy of a Murder,* and *In the Heat of the Night.* Prison exposés range from *I Am a Fugitive from a Chain Gang* to

Dassin's brilliant *Brute Force* and Don Siegel's forceful *Riot in Cell Block 11*. Lynching films range from *Fury* (1936) through *Storm Warning* (1951) to *The Chase* and, of course, *In the Heat of the Night*.

(c) The fight game is another permitted topic, the late forties springing a sizzling liberal combination (*Body and Soul, The Set-Up, Champion, Night and the City*).

(d) Juvenile delinquency appears first in a highly personalized, family motif concerning the younger brother or friend whom the gangster is leading astray. The juvenile gang (*Dead End,* 1937) introduces a more "social" motif. *Angels with Dirty Faces* combines two themes, with sufficient success to prompt a rosy sequel called *Angels Wash Their Faces,* which flopped. The late forties seem awkwardly caught between the obvious inadequacy of the old personal-moral theme and a new, sociology-based sophistication that doesn't filter down to the screen until *Rebel Without a Cause* and *The Young Savages*. Meanwhile, there is much to be said for the verve and accuracy of *So Young So Bad* and *The Wild One*.

Rackets other than prohibition are the subject of *Road to Frisco* (1939), *Force of Evil* (1947), *Thieves Highway* (1949), and, from *The Man with the Golden Arm* (1955), drugs.

The first conspicuous postwar innovation is the neodocumentary thriller, much praised by critics who thought at that time that a documentary tone and location photography guaranteed neorealism (when tardily, disillusionment set in, it was, of course, with a British variant—*The Blue Lamp*). In 1945 a spy film (*The House on 92nd Street*) borrowed the formula from the *March of Time* news series, to give a newspaper-headline impact. The most open-air movies of the series (*The Naked City, Union Station*) now seem the weakest, whereas a certain thoughtfulness distinguishes *Boomerang, Call Northside 777,* and *Panic in the Streets*. The cycle later transforms itself into the *Dragnet*-style TV thriller. Several of the above films are noir, in that, though the police (or their system) constitute an affirmative hero, a realistic despair or cynicism pervade them. A black cop cycle is opened in Wyler's *Detective Story* (1951), an important second impetus coming from Lang's *The Big Heat*. The cop hero, or villain, is corrupt, victimized, or berserk in, notably, *The Naked Alibi, Rogue Cop,* and *Touch of Evil*. These tensions remain in a fourth cycle, which examines the cop as organization man, grappling with corruption and violence (*In the Heat of the Night, The Detective, Lady in Cement, Bullitt, Madigan,* and *Coogan's Bluff*). Clearly the theme can be developed with either a right or left-wing inflection. Thus, the post–*Big Heat* cycles of the lone-wolf fanatic cop suggests either "Pay the police more, don't skimp on social services" or "Give cops more power, permit more phone tapping" (as in *Dragnet* and *The Big Combo*). The theme of a Mr. Big running the city machine may be Democratic (especially if he's an extremely WASP Mr. Big) or Republican ("those corrupt Democratic city machines!") or anarchist, of the right or the left. If a favorite setting for civil rights themes is the Southern small town, it's partly because civil rights liberalism is there balanced by the choice of ultraviolent, exotically backward, and Democratic, backwoods with which relatively few American filmgoers will identify. *Coogan's Bluff* depends on the contrast of Republican-fundamentalist-small town with Democratic-corrupt-but-human-big-city. The neodocumentary thrillers created a sense of social networks, that is, of society as orgnizable. Thus they helped to pave the way for a more sophisticated tone and social awareness that appears in the late forties.

A cycle of films use a crime to

inculpate, not only the underworld, the deadends, and the underprivileged, but the respectable, middle-class, WASP ethos as well. *Fury* had adumbrated this, melodramatically, in the thirties; the new cycle is more analytical and formidable. The trend has two origins, one in public opinion, the second in Hollywood. An affluent postwar America had more comfort and leisure in which to evolve, and endure, a more sophisticated type of self-criticism. Challengingly, poverty no longer explained everything. Second, the war helped Hollywood's young Democratic minority to assert itself, which it did in the late forties, until checked by the McCarthyite counterattack (which of course depended for its success on Hollywood Republicans). These films include *The Sound of Fury,* the early Loseys, *Ace in the Hole, All My Sons* (if it isn't too articulate for a film noir), and, once the McCarthyite heat was off, *The Wild One, On the Waterfront,* and *The Young Savages.* But McCarthy's impact forced film noir themes to retreat to the Western. Such films as *High Noon, Run of the Arrow* and *Ride Lonesome* make the fifties the Western's richest epoch. Subsequently, Hollywood fear of controversy mutes criticism of the middle-class from black to gray (e.g., *The Graduate*). *The Chase, The Detective,* even *Bonnie and Clyde* offer some hope that current tensions may force open the relentless social criticism onto the screen.

2. GANGSTERS

Underworld differs from subsequent gangster films in admiring its gangster hero (George Bancroft) as Nietzschean inspiration on a humiliating world. If *Scarface* borrows several of its settings and motifs, it's partly because it's a riposte to it. In fact, public opinion turned against the gangster before Hollywood denounced him with the famous trans-auteur triptych *Little Caesar, Scarface,* and *Public Enemy.* To Hawks's simple-minded propaganda piece, one may well prefer the daring pro- and contra-alternations of *Public Enemy.* The mixture of social fact and moralizing myth in pre-war gangster movies is intriguing. Bancroft, like Cagney, represents the Irish gangster, Muni and Raft the Italian type, Bogart's deadpan grotesque is transracial, fitting equally well with the strayed WASP (Marlowe) and the Eastern European Jews, who were a forceful gangster element. It's not at all absurd, as NFT (Noir Film Theater) audiences boisterously assume, that *Little Caesar* and *Scarface* should love their Italian mommas, nor that in *Angels with Dirty Faces,* priest Pat O'Brien and gangster Cagney should be on speaking terms. Nineteen-twenties gangsters were just as closely linked with race loyalties as today's Black Muslim leaders—the latter have typical gangster childhoods, and without the least facetiousness can be said to have shifted gangster energies into civil rights terms. It helps explain the ambivalence of violence and idealism in Black Muslim declarations; dialogues between "priest" (Martin Luther King) and advocates of violence are by no means ridiculous. Disappointed Prohibitionist moralists found easier prey in Hollywood, and the Hays office, and cut off the gangster cycle in its prime. A year or two passes before Hollywood evolves its "anti-gangster"—the G-man or FBI agent at his own game. *Angels with Dirty Faces* (1938) combines Dead End kids (from Wyler's film of the previous year) with gangster Cagney. When he's cornered, priest Pat O'Brien persuades him to go to the chair like a coward so that his fans will be disillusioned with him. By so doing, Cagney concedes that crime doesn't pay, but he also debunks movies like *Scarface.* In 1940 *The Roaring Twenties* attempts a naive little thesis about the relationship between gangsterism and unemployment.

Between 1939 and 1953 Nazi and

then Russian spies push the gangster into the hero position. A small cycle of seminostalgic gangster movies appears. A unique, Hays code–defying B feature, *Dillinger* (1945), is less typical than *I Walk Alone* (1947). This opposes the old-fashioned Prohibition-era thug (Burt Lancaster), who, returning after a long spell in jail, finds himself outmoded and outwitted by the newer, nastier, richer operators who move in swell society and crudely prefigure the "organization men" who reach their climax in the Marvin-Gallagher-Reagan setup of Seigel's *The Killers. The Enforcer* is another hinge movie, putting D.A. Bogart against a gang that, while actually Neanderthal in its techniques is felt to be a terrifyingly slick and ubiquitous contra-police network. *Kiss Tomorrow Good-bye* and *White Heat* are contemporary in setting but have an archaic feel. *The Asphalt Jungle* is a moralistic variant within this cycle rather than a precursor of *Rififi* and its gang-job imitations (which include *The Killing* and *Cairo*, a wet transposition of Huston's film.)

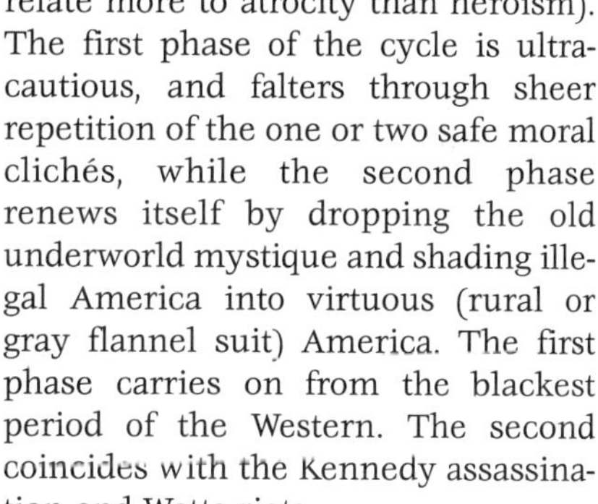

The next major cycle is keyed by various congressional investigations, which spotlight gangsterism run big-business style. "Brooklyn, I'm very worried about Brooklyn," frowns the gang boss in *New York Confidential* (1954); "It's bringing down our average—collections are down two percent." An equally bad sequel, *The Naked Street*, handles a collateral issue, gangster (or ex-gangster?) control of legitimate business (a tardy theme: during the war Western Union was bought by a gangster syndicate to ensure trouble-free transmission of illegal betting results). Executive-style gangsterism has to await *Underworld U.S.A.* and *The Killers* for interesting treatment. For obvious reasons, the American equivalent of *La Mani Sulla Citta* has still to be made. *Johnny Cool* is a feeble "sequel" to Salvatore Giuliano.

Instead, the mid-fifties see a new cycle, the urban Western, which takes a hint from the success of *The Big Heat*. A clump of movies from 1955 to 1960 includes *The Big Combo, Al Capone, The Rise and Fall of Legs Diamond, Babyface Nelson, The Phenix City Story,* and *Pay or Die.* Something of a lull follows until the latter-day Technicolor series (*The Killers, Bonnie and Clyde, Point Blank*). With or without pop nostalgia for the past, these movies exist, like the Western, for their action (though the killings relate more to atrocity than heroism). The first phase of the cycle is ultra-cautious, and falters through sheer repetition of the one or two safe moral clichés, while the second phase renews itself by dropping the old underworld mystique and shading illegal America into virtuous (rural or gray flannel suit) America. The first phase carries on from the blackest period of the Western. The second coincides with the Kennedy assassination and Watts riots.

3. ON THE RUN

Here the criminals or the framed innocents are essentially passive and fugitive, and even if tragically or despicably guilty, sufficiently sympathetic for the audience to be caught between, on the one hand, pity identification, and regret, and, on the other, moral condemnation and conformist fatalism. Notable films include *The Informer, You Only Live Once, High Sierra, The Killers, He Ran All the Way,*

They Live by Night, Cry of the City, Dark Passage, and a variant, *The Third Man. Gun Crazy* (*Deadlier Than the Male*), an earlier version of the Bonnie and Clyde story, with Peggy Cummins as Bonnie, fascinatingly compromises between a Langian style and a Penn spirit, and, in double harness with the later film, might assert itself as a parallel classic.

4. PRIVATE EYES AND ADVENTURERS

This theme is closely interwoven with three literary figures, Dashiell Hammett, Raymond Chandler, and Ernest Hemingway. It constitutes for some English critics the poetic core of the film noir, endearing itself no doubt by the romanticism underlying Chandler's formula: "Down these mean streets must go a man who is not himself mean . . ." This knight errant relationship has severe limitations. The insistence on city corruption is countered by the trust in private enterprise; and we may well rate the genre below the complementary approach exemplified by *Double Indemnity* and *The Postman Always Rings Twice,* in which we identify with the criminals. The genre originates in a complacent, pre-war cycle, the *Thin Man* series (after Hammett) with William Powell and Myrna Loy, being both sophisticated and happily married (then a rarity) as they solve crimes together with Asta the dog. The motif is transformed by Bogart's incarnation of Sam Spade in the misogynistic *Maltese Falcon,* and the bleaker, lonelier, more anxious Hemingway adventurer in *To Have and Have Not.* In the late forties Chandler's Marlowe wears five faces—Dick Powell's, Bogart's, Ladd's, Robert Montgomery's, and George Montgomery's, in *Farewell My Lovely* (*Murder, My Sweet*), *The Big Sleep, The Blue Dahlia, Lady in the Lake,* and *The High Window* (*The Brasher Doubloon*). An RKO series with Mitchum (sometimes Mature) as a vague, aimless wanderer, hounded and hounding, begins well with *Out of the Past* but rapidly degenerates. The series seeks renewal in more exotic settings with *Key Largo, Ride the Pink Horse, The Breaking Point,* and *Beat the Devil,* but concludes in disillusionment. In *Kiss Me Deadly, Confidential Agent,* and a late straggler, *Vertigo,* the private eye solves the mystery but undergoes extensive demoralization. In retrospect, films by well-respected auteurs like Hawks, Ray, Siegel, and Huston seem to me to have worn less well than the most disillusioned of the series, Dmytryk's visionary *Murder My Sweet,* prefiguring the Aldrich-Welles-Hitchcock pessimism. *The Maltese Falcon,* notably, is deep camp. Huston's laughter deflates villainy into the perverted pretension of Greenstreet and Lorre, who are to real villains as Al Jolson to Carmen Jones. In the scenes between Bogart and Mary Astor (a sad, hard, not-so-young vamp with more middle-class perm than "it"), it reaches an intensity like greatness. Huston's great film noir is a Western (*Treasure of the Sierra Madre*).

5. MIDDLE-CLASS MURDER

Crime has its harassed amateurs, and the theme of the repeatable middle-class figure beguiled into, or secretly plotting, murder facilitates the sensitive study in black. The thirties see a series centering on Edward G. Robinson, who alternates between uncouth underworld leaders (*Little Caesar, Black Tuesday*) and a guilt-haunted or fear-bourgeoisie (in *The Amazing Dr. Clitterhouse, The Woman in the Window, Scarlet Street, The Red House,* and *All My Sons*). Robinson, like Laughton, Cagney, and Bogart, belongs to that select group of stars, who, even in Hollywood's simpler-minded years, could give meanness and cowardice a riveting monstrosity, even force. His role as pitiable scapegoat requires a little excursion into

Nightmarish imagery devised by director Anthony Mann and brilliant noir cinematographer John Alton.

psychoanalytical sociology. Slightly exotic, that is un-American, he symbolized the loved, but repudiated, father/elder sibling, apparently benevolent, ultimately sinister, never unlovable—either an immigrant father (Little Rico in *Little Caesar*) or that complementary bogey, the ultra-WASP intellectual, whose cold superior snobbery infiltrates so many late-forties movies (Clifton Webb in *Laura*). The evolution of these figures belongs to the process of assimilation in America, Robinson's fifties and sixties equivalents include Broderick Crawford, Anthony Quinn, Rod Steiger, and Vincent Price. The theme of respectable eccentricity taking murder lightly is treated in *Arsenic and Old Lace, Monsieur Verdoux, Rope,* and *Strangers on a Train.* The theme of the tramp corrupting the not-always-so-innocent bourgeois is artistically fruitful, with *Double Indemnity, The Postman Always Rings Twice, The Woman in the Window, The Woman on the Beach,* and, a straggler, *Pushover.* *The Prowler* reverses the formula: the lower-class cop victimizes the DJ's lonely wife. The theme can be considered an American adaptation of a prewar European favorite (cf. *Pandora's Box, La Bête Humaine*) and the European versions of *The Postman Always Rings Twice.* The cycle synchronizes with a climax in the perennial theme of Woman: Executioner/Victim, involving such figures as Bette Davis, Barbara Stanwyck, Gene Tierney, Joan Crawford, and Lana Turner. Jacques Siclier dates the misogynistic cycle from Wyler's *Jezebel* (1938), and it can be traced through *Double Indemnity, Gilda, Dragonwyck, The Strange Love of Martha Ivers, Ivy, Sunset Boulevard, Leave Her to Heaven, Beyond the Forest, Flamingo Road, The File on Thelma Jordan, Clash by Night, Angel Face, Portrait in Black,* and *Whatever Happened to Baby Jane?* A collateral cycle sees woman as grim heroic victim, struggling against despair where her men all but succumb or betray her (*Rebecca, Phantom*

Lady). Many films have it both ways, perhaps by contrasting strong feminine figures, the heroine lower-class and embittered, the other respectable but callous (like Joan Crawford and her daughter in *Mildred Pierce*), or by plot twists proving that the apparent vamp was misjudged by an embittered hero (as Rita Hayworth beautifully taunts Glen Ford in *Gilda,* "Put the blame on mame, boys . . ."). The whole subgenre can be seen as a development out of the "confession" stories of the Depression years, when Helen Twelvetrees and others became prostitutes, golddiggers, and kept women for various tear-jerking reasons. Replace the tears by a glum, baffled deadpan, modulate self-pity into suspicion, and the later cycle appears. Maybe the misogyny is only an aspect of the claustrophobic paranoia so marked in late forties movies.

Double Indemnity is perhaps the central film noir, not only for its atmospheric power, but as a junction of major themes, combining the vamp (Barbara Stanwyck), the morally weak murderer (Fred MacMurray), and the investigator (Edward G. Robinson). The murderer sells insurance. The investigator checks on claims. If the latter is incorruptible, he is unromantically so; only his cruel Calvinist energy distinguishes his "justice" from meanness. The film's stress on money and false friendliness as a means of making it justifies an alternative title: *Death of a Salesman.* This and Miller's play all but parallel the relationship between *A Place in the Sun* and *Kiss Tomorrow Good-bye* (realistic weakness becomes wish fulfillment violence).

6. PORTRAITS AND DOUBLES

The characteristic tone of the forties is somber, claustrophobic, deadpan, and paranoid. In the shaded lights and raining night it is often just a little difficult to tell one character from another. A strange, diffuse play on facial and bodily resemblances reaches a climax in Vidor's *Beyond the Forest* (where sullen Bette Davis is the spitting image, in long shot, of her Indian maid) and, in exile, in Losey's *The Sleeping Tiger,* where dominant Alexis Smith is the spitting image of her frightened maid. A cycle of grim romantic thrillers focused on women who, dominant even in their absence stare haughty enigmas at us from their portraits over the fireplace. Sometimes the portrait is the mirror of split personality. The series included *Rebecca, Experiment Perilous, Laura, The Woman in the Window, Scarlet Street,* and *The Dark Mirror.* Variants include the all-male, but sexually inverted, *Picture of Dorian Gray, Portrait of Jennie* (rosy and tardy, but reputedly one of Buñuel's favorite films), *Under Capricorn* (the shrunken head), and a beautiful straggler, *Vertigo.*

7. SEXUAL PATHOLOGY

In *The Big Sleep,* Bogart and Bacall, pretending to discuss horse racing, discuss the tactic of copulation, exemplifying the clandestine cynicism and romanticism which the film noir apposes to the Hays Office. Similarly, "love at first sight" between Ladd and Lake in *The Blue Dahlia* looks suspiciously like a casual, heavy pickup. In *A Lonely Place* and *The Big Heat* (and, just outside the film noir, *Bus Stop*), we see another basic equation: the hero whose tragic flaw is psychopathic violence meets his match in the loving whore.

The yin and yang of Puritanism and cynicism, of egoism and paranoia, of greed and idealism, deeply perturbs sexual relationships, and films noir abound in love-hate relationships ranging through all degrees of intensity. Before untying Bogart, Bacall kisses his bruised lips. Heston rapes Jennifer Jones in *Ruby Gentry,* and next morning she shoots her puritanical brother for shooting him. Lover and beloved exterminate each other in

Double Indemnity and *Out of the Past.* He has to kill her in *Gun Crazy* and lets her die of a stomach wound in *The Lady from Shanghai.*

Intimations of noneffeminate homosexuality are laid on thick in, notably, *Gilda,* where loyal Glenn Ford gets compared to both his boss's kept woman and swordstick. A certain flabbiness paraphrases effeminacy in *The Maltese Falcon* (the Lorre-Greenstreet duo repeated in the Morley-Lorre pair in *Beat the Devil*), and in *Rope* and *Strangers on a Train* (where Farley Granger and Robert Walker respectively evoke a youthful Vincent Price). Lesbianism rears a sadomasochistic head in *Rebecca* (between Judith Anderson and her dead mistress) and *In a Lonely Place* (between Gloria Grahame and a brawny masseuse who is also perhaps a symbol for a coarse vulgarity she cannot escape). Homosexual and heterosexual sadism are everyday conditions. In *Clash by Night* Robert Ryan wants to stick pins all over Paul Douglas's floozy wife (Barbara Stanwyck) and watch the blood run down; we're not so far from the needle stuck through a goose's head to tenderize its flesh in *Diary of a Chambermaid* ("Sounds like they're murdering somebody," says Paulette Goddard).

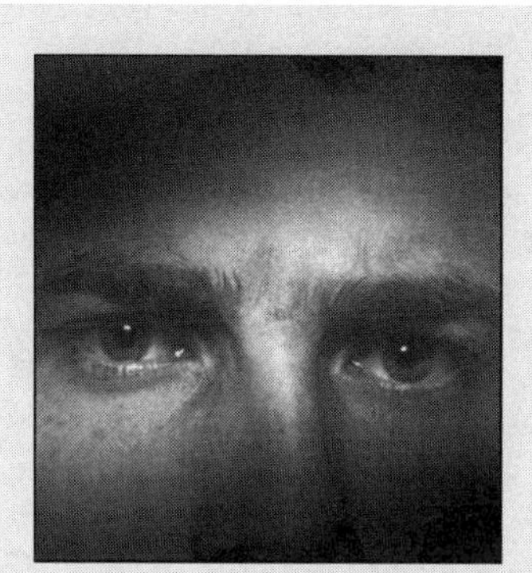

Slim knives horrify but fascinate the paranoid forties as shotguns delight the cool sixties. Notable sadists include Richard Widmark (chuckling as he pushes the old lady down the stairs in her wheelchair in *Kiss of Death*), Paul Henreid in *Rope of Sand* (experimenting with a variety of whips on Burt Lancaster's behind), Hume Cronyn in *Brute Force* (truncheoning the intellectual prisoner to the strains of the Liebestod), Lee Marvin flinging boiling coffee in his mistress's face in *The Big Heat;* and so on to Clu Gulager's showmanlike eccentricities in *The Killers* and, of course, Tony Curtis in *The Boston Strangler.*

8. PSYCHOPATHS

Film noir psychopaths, who are legion, are divisible into three main groups: the heroes with a tragic flaw, the unassuming monsters, and the obvious monsters, in particular, the Prohibition-type gangster. Cagney's *Public Enemy* criss-crosses the boundaries between them, thus providing the moral challenge and suspense that is the film's mainspring. Cagney later contributes a rousing portrait of a gangster with a raging Oedipus complex in *White Heat,* from Hollywood's misogynistic period. Trapped on an oil storage tank, he cries exultantly: "On top of the world, Ma!" before joining his dead mother via the autodestructive orgasm of his own personal mushroom cloud. The unassuming monster may be exemplified by *The Blue Dahlia,* whose paranoid structure is almost as interesting as that of *Phantom Lady.* Returned war hero Alan Ladd nearly puts a bullet in his unfaithful wife. As so often in the late forties films, the police believe him guilty of the crime for which he is nearly guilty. The real murderer is not the hero with the motive, not the wartime buddy whom shellshock drives into paroxysms of rage followed by amnesia, not the smooth gangster with whom the trollop was two timing her husband. It was the friendly hotel house-detective.

On our right, we find the simple and satisfying view of the psychopath as a morally responsible mad dog deserving to be put down (thus simple, satisfying films like *Scarface* and *Panic in Year Zero*). On the left, he is an ordinary, or understandably weak, or unusually energetic character whose inner defects are worsened by factors outside his control (*Public Enemy, The Young Savages*). These factors may be summarized as (1) slum environments, (2) psychological traits subtly extrinsic to character (neurosis), and (3) a subtly corrupting social morality. In Depression America, the first explanation seems plausible enough (*Public Enemy,* with exceptional thoughtfulness, goes for all three explanations while insisting that he's become a mad dog who must die). In 1939, *Of Mice and Men* prefigures a change of emphasis, and in postwar America, with its supposedly universal affluence, other terms seem necessary to account for the still festering propensity to violence. Given the individualism even of Democratic thought, recourse is had to trauma, either wartime (*The Blue Dahlia, Act of Violence*) or Freudian (*The Dark Corner, The Dark Past*). A second group of films, without exonerating society, key psychopathy to a tone of tragic confusion (*Of Mice and Men, Kiss the Blood off My Hands*). A third group relates violence to the spirit of society (*Force of Evil, The Sound of Fury*). A cooler, more domestic tone prevails with *Don't Bother to Knock,* with its switch-casting (ex-psychopath Richard Widmark becomes the embittered, kindly hero, against Marilyn Monroe as a homicidal babysitter). This last shift might be described as antiexpressionism, or coolism, with psychopathy accepted as a normal condition of life. Critics of the period scoff at the psychopathic theme, although in retrospect Hollywood seems to have shown more awareness of American undertones than its supercilious critics. *The Killers, Point Blank,* and *Bonnie and Clyde* resume the "Democratic" social criticism of *Force of Evil* and *The Sound of Fury.* A highly plausible interpretation of *Point Blank* sees its hero as a ghost; the victims of his revenge quest destroy one another, or themselves. The psychopathy theme is anticipated in pre-war French movies (e.g., *Le Jour se Leve*) with a social crisis of confidence, a generalized, hot violent mode of alienation (as distinct from the glacial variety, à la Antonioni). With a few extra-lucid exceptions, neither the French nor the American films seem to realize the breakdown of confidence as a social matter.

9. HOSTAGES TO FORTUNE

The imprisonment of a family, an individual, or a group of citizens, by desperate or callous criminals is a hardy perennial. But a cycle climaxes soon after the Korean War with the shock, to Americans, of peacetime conscripts in action. A parallel inspiration in domestic violence is indicated by *The Petrified Forest* (1938), *He Ran All the Way,* and *The Dark Past.* But the early fifties see a sudden cluster including *The Desperate Hours, Suddenly, Cry Terror,* and *Violent Saturday.* The confrontation between middle-class father and family, and killer, acts out, in fuller social metaphor, although often with a more facile Manichaeanism, the normal and abnormal sides of the psychopathic hero.

10. BLACKS AND REDS

A cycle substituting Nazi agents and the Gestapo for gangsters gets under way with *Confessions of a Nazi Spy* (1939). The cold war anti-Communist cycle begins with *The Iron Curtain* (1948), and most of its products were box-office as well as artistic flops, probably because the Communists and fellow travelers were so evil as to be dramatically boring. The principal exceptions are by Samuel Fuller (*Pickup on South Street*) and Aldrich (*Kiss Me Deadly*). Some films contrast the good American gangster with the nasty foreign agents (*Pickup on South*

Street); *Woman on Pier 13* links Russian agents with culture-loving waterfront union leaders and can be regarded as ultraright, like *One Minute to Zero* and *Suddenly*, whose timid liberal modification (rather than reply) is *The Manchurian Candidate. Advise and Consent* is closely related to the political film noir.

11. GUIGNOL, HORROR, FANTASY

The three genres are clearly first cousins to the film noir. Hardy perennials, they seem to have enjoyed periods of special popularity. Siegfried Kracauer has sufficiently related German expressionist movies with the angst of pre-Nazi Germany. Collaterally, a diluted expressionism was a minor American genre, indeterminate as between film noir and horror fantasy. Lon Chaney's Gothic grotesques (*The Unknown, The Phantom of the Opera*) parallel stories of haunted houses (*The Cat and the Canary*), which conclude with rational explanations. Sternberg's *The Last Command* can be considered a variant of the Chaney genre, with Jannings as Chaney, and neorealistic in that its hero's plight symbolizes the agonies of the uprooted immigrants who adapted with difficulty to the tenement jungles. The Depression sparked off the full-blown, visionary guignol of *Dracula, Frankenstein* (with Karloff as Chaney), *King Kong* (with Kong as Chaney!), *Most Dangerous Game, Island of Lost Souls,* etc. (the Kracauer-type tyrant looms, but is defeated, often with pathos). Together with gangster and sex films, the genre suffers from the Hays Office. After the shock of the Great Crash, the demoralizing stagnation of the depressed thirties leads to a minor cycle of black brooding fantasies of death and time (*Death Takes a Holiday, Peter Ibbetson*). The war continues the social unsettledness that films balance by cozy, enclosed, claustrophobic settings (*Dr. Jekyll and Mr. Hyde, Flesh and Fantasy, Cat People*). A postwar subgenre is the thriller, developed into plainclothes gothic (*The Spiral Staircase; The Red House; Sorry, Wrong Number*). *Phantom Lady* (in its very title) indicates their interechoing. A second Monster cycle coincides with the Korean War. A connection with scientists, radioactivity, and outer space suggests fear of atomic apocalypse (overt in *This Island Earth, It Came from Outer Space,* and *Them,* covert in *Tarantula* and *The Thing from Another World*). *The Red Planet Mars* speaks for the hawks, *The Day the Earth Stood Still* for the doves. *Invasion of the Body Snatchers* is a classic paranoid fantasy (arguably justified). As the glaciers of callous alienation advance, the Corman Poes create their nightmare compensation: the aesthetic hothouse of Victorian incest. *Psycho* crossbreeds the genre with a collateral revival of plainclothes guignol, often revolving round a feminine, rather than a masculine, figure (Joan Crawford and Bette Davis substitute for Chaney in *Whatever Happened to Baby Jane?*). The English anticipations of the Corman Poes are the Fisher *Frankenstein* and *Dracula.* With *Dutchman,* the genre matures into an expressionistic social realism.

The sixties obsession with violent death in all forms and genres may be seen as marking the admission of the film noir into the mainstream of Western pop art, encouraged by (a) the comforts of relative affluence, (b) moral disillusionment, in outcome variously radical, liberal, reactionary, or nihilist, (c) a post-Hiroshima sense of man as his own executioner, rather than nature, God, or fate, and (d) an enhanced awareness of social conflict. The cinema is in its Jacobean period, and the stress on gratuitous tormenting, evilly jocular in *The Good, the Bad and the Ugly,* less jocular in *Laughter in the Dark,* parallel that in Webster's plays. Such films as *Paths of Glory, Eva,* and *The Loved One* emphasize their crimes less than the rottenness of a society or, perhaps, man himself.

I: FILM

Courtesy of Kino International

One of director Fritz Lang's great wartime thrillers, *Hangmen Also Die,* starring Brian Donlevy.

Fritz Lang Remembers

GENE D. PHILLIPS

High above Beverly Hills, beyond Benedict Cañon Drive, Fritz Lang lives in a splendid, secluded home overlooking Los Angeles. Lang's place in film history is equally high. His departure from Germany in 1933 in the wake of the rise of Hitler had been cited as marking the end of the Golden Age of German Cinema; and four decades after he left Germany, in 1973, Lang's spirit so pervaded the Sorrento German Film Encounter of young German filmmakers that it awarded him a special prize for his achievement as the best German film director.

Now an octogenarian, Lang is still very much an imposing figure and speaks with a ring of authority in his voice grounded in a lifetime of experience. At the same time he is gracious, good-humored, and patient in providing an interviewer not only with fresh anecdotes about his career but with additional details concerning incidents that he has talked about before. Listening to Lang reminisce, one is put in touch with one of the genuine pioneers of motion picture history who has had a lasting influence on the development of the medium. For, as the industry grew, he grew with it and helped it to become an art form by becoming a film artist himself. As one cinema historian has put it, the movie industry will never again see giants like Fritz Lang.

Let's begin by talking about your early life since there is very little written about it. You were born December 5, 1890, the son of a Viennese architect who wanted you to be an architect too.

I ran away from home to become a painter and went first to Brussels and then to Bruges and there I saw my first film. I forget what the title of it was—it was a film about the French Revolution or some such thing. Then I went to Paris and traveled through Marseilles and on to Asia Minor, the South Seas, Africa, China, Japan, and Russia for almost a year. I lived by painting postcards and drawing cartoons for newspapers. Then I went back to Paris and started to work there in a private art school. Then the First World War broke out and I left Paris on the last train and escaped to Vienna. When I came back to Austria in 1914 I was drafted into the Austrian Imperial Army and in 1915 I was sent to war.

At the Front you were wounded and decorated.

I was shot in the shoulder in Italy and went back to Vienna. I was rather unhappy because as a lieutenant I didn't have enough money to live on. Then one day I was sitting in a café in my uniform (there were several decorations on it) and a man came up to me and offered me a job, and I asked him very haughtily who he was. His name was Peter Ostermeyer and he was a director of the Red Cross Theatre. The play which he was producing was about an Austrian lieutenant who was captured by the French and then was saved by his servant (every officer had a man who helped him). I asked him what I would be paid and he said 750 kronen. Now as a lieutenant I was getting only 120 kronen, so you can imagine what this meant to me. Sometimes—very seldom—I get a bright idea, so I said to him, "That is very little," and he responded that he couldn't pay me more than one thousand! So naturally I agreed. Then he developed another problem: he was planning for me to play a German officer who appeared only in the second act, but because of my Viennese dialect he had to give me the main part.

How did you make the transition from the stage to working in films?

The play met with some success and I met someone with whom I had worked before writing scripts who introduced me to Erich Pommer, who had his own production company, Decla-Bioscop. When Pommer first saw me he looked at the monocle which I was wearing (because my right eye has always been not as good as my left) and said, "I don't want to have anything to do with that son of a bitch. I don't like his looks." But since he had already promised to talk with me, we met one evening after the show and we talked together until 4 A.M. He gave me a job in the script department as a script doctor.

I understand that you worked on several scripts in this period but were sometimes dissatisfied with the way that they were filmed.

In 1919 I told Erich Pommer that I wanted to direct my first film; it was my own script and it was called *Halb-Blut* (*Half Breed*). I still wrote some screenplays for other directors, however, such as *Pest in Florenz* (*Plague in Florence*), which was directed by Otto Rippert the same year. I next directed *Der Herr der Liebe* (*The Master of Love*, 1919). Then I did *Der Goldene See* (*The Golden Lake*), the first part of a projected four-part series of features with the overall title of *Die Spinnen* (*The Spiders*), and *Hara Kiri*, whose plot was based on the famous opera *Madame Butterfly*.

***It was then that you were offered the direction of* The Cabinet of Dr. Caligari.**

It was first given to Erich Pommer, not to me, and Erich wanted me to do it. So I read it over and said, "Erich, an audience will not understand an expressionistic film of this kind with distorted perspectives, etc., unless you devise a scene at the beginning of the film in which two people talk in a normal way in a realistic setting so that the audience is aware from the outset that the story is being told by a mad man." Erich accepted this idea but he had to take the film away from me because the exhibitors wanted to have the second part of the *Spiders* series. So instead of shooting *Caligari* I made *Das Brillanten Schiff* (*The Diamond Ship*, 1919), which turned out to be the last part of the series to be filmed.

At this point you left Decla-Bioscop.

I was upset about the whole situation and when I got an offer from the Joe May Company, my one-year contract with Erich Pommer was over, so I took it. I first wrote scenarios for Joe May's company, and it was there that I met my later wife, Thea von Harbou, who was also writing scripts for Joe May.

Courtesy of Kino International

Anna Lee in Fritz Lang's *Hangmen Also Die.*

She had written a book called *Das Indische Grabmal* (*The Indian Tomb*) and together we wrote a film script based on it which was very long and so was to be filmed in two parts, to be presented on successive evenings. Joe May, his wife, and his daughter read it and were very enthusiastic about it. I was supposed to direct it, but eight days later Mrs. von Harbou came to me and said, "Look, I have very bad news for you. Joe May says that you can't direct the picture because he wouldn't be able to get enough money to make such a big film if the director is as young as you are." The truth is that Joe May wanted to direct the picture himself.

***Interestingly enough, you were to make a sound version of this story in 1958, but at this time May directed the silent version and had you direct* Das Wanderne Bild (The Wandering Image, *1920*).**

Erich Pommer offered to rehire me, and Thea von Harbou said, "I will help you write a screenplay especially for you to direct"—*Der Muede Tod* (*Weary Death,* 1921), which was to become known abroad as *Destiny.* That was my first big success—but not right away. When it was first shown in Berlin the newspaper critics, for reasons that I have never been able to figure out, tried to kill the picture. One of them said the film made the viewer weary of watching it. After two weeks it was withdrawn from the cinemas in Berlin; but it went on to open to the most unbelievable reviews in Paris and elsewhere. One of the Paris critics said, "This is the Germany that we once loved"—this was right after World War One, remember. Then the film was rereleased in Germany and became a world success. Everything in life has a sunny side. Douglas Fairbanks, Sr. bought the American rights to the picture for $5,000 but he had no intention of releasing it there. He liked the technical effects and he had them copied for his famous film, *The Thief of Bagdad.* Naturally, because he had more money and greater technical facilities at his disposal, he improved on the tricks and made them better than we were able to do.

The Thief of Bagdad *was directed by Raoul Walsh. Did you meet him at the time?*

I never traveled around meeting other directors. I wasn't haughty in this respect. It is just that all my life I have been so involved in my work that I guess one could say in general that, whenever I had to balance my private life and my profession, my profession always won out.

Your next big success in Germany was* Dr. Mabuse, der Spieler (Dr. Mabuse, the Gambler, *1922).

It was a thriller about an archcriminal and the public liked it for that. Nevertheless it was also a picture of how crime was rampant in Germany after the First World War. The film reflected the demoralized atmosphere of Germany at the time, with the despair and vice attendant on the loss of the war. It was the kind of atmosphere in which a man like Mabuse could thrive. I saw the master criminal after World War One as a version of the superman which Nietzsche had created in his writings.

In his book* From Caligari to Hitler *Siegfried Kracauer suggests that your film of the Siegfried legend in the two parts of* Die Nibelungen *(1924) also incorporated the idea of the superman, and that its pageantry foreshadowed that of the Nazi rally in Leni Riefenstahl's* Triumph of the Will *(1935).

I would like to make a remark about this book. In my opinion this book is wrong about a lot of things and it has done a lot of damage, I feel, particularly among young people. When I made my films I always followed my imagination. By making *Die Nibelungen* I wanted to show that Germany was searching for an ideal in her past, even during the horrible time after World War One in which the film was made. At that time in Berlin I remember seeing a poster on the street which pictured a woman dancing with a skeleton. The caption read: "Berlin, you are dancing with Death." To counteract this pessimistic spirit I wanted to film the epic legend of Siegfried so that Germany could draw inspiration from her past, and not, as Mr. Kracauer suggests, as a looking forward to the rise of a political figure like Hitler or some such stupid thing as that. I was dealing with Germany's legendary heritage, just as in *Metropolis* I was looking at Germany in the future and in *Frau im Mond* (*The Girl in the Moon*) I was also showing Germany in the age of the rocketships.

Die Nibelungen *was the first film made by UFA, the federation of film studios in Berlin. How did you find working with Erich Pommer when he became the production chief of UFA?*

Erich Pommer in my opinion was the only real producer that I ever worked with in my life. He always discussed things with me instead of just issuing commands from his office. In fact we never said "You *must* do this or that" to each other throughout our entire lives. He came to me while I was making the second part of *Die Nibelungen* and said, "I was thinking about the scene in which the Huns come over the hill. It will cost a lot of money for all of the extras that you want to use. Is it really necessary?" I told him that I would think the matter over and the next day I said to him, "Look, we can't compete with American films when it comes to these massive scenes anyhow; so let's drop this scene from the shooting schedule." "I have been thinking it over, too," Erich said to me, "and I think we should go ahead and shoot the scene just the way that you envisioned it." Tell me one American producer who would react that way. UFA had us take the picture to the United States for release there because it was a tremendous success all over Europe, but we did not meet with the same kind of success in America. After all, what do people in Pasadena know about Siegfried fighting with dragons?

But your trip to the U.S. gave you the inspiration for* Metropolis *(1926), did it not?

Erich and I were considered enemy aliens and for some such reason we couldn't land in New York on the day that the boat docked there but had to wait until the following day to disembark. That evening I looked from the ship down one of the main streets of New York and saw for the first time the flashing neon signs lighting up the street as if it were daytime. This was all new to me. I said to myself, what will a big city like this, with its tall skyscrapers, be like in the future? That started me thinking about *Metropolis.*

Metropolis *enhanced your reputation both in Germany and abroad.*

But after I finished the film I personally didn't much care for it, though I loved it while I was making it. When I looked at it after it was completed I said to myself, you can't change the social climate of a country with a message like "The heart must be the go-between of the head (capital) and the hands (labor)." I was convinced that you cannot solve social problems by such a message. Many years later, in the fifties, an industrialist wrote in the Washington Post that he had seen the film and that he very much agreed with that statement about the heart as go-between. But that didn't change my mind about the picture.

Yet young people today take the film very seriously.

In the later years of my life I have made it a point to speak with a lot of young people in order to try to understand their point of view. They all hate the establishment and when I asked them what they dislike so intensely about our computerized society they said, "It has no heart." So now I wonder if Mrs. von Harbou was not right all the time when she wrote that line in *Metropolis* a half century ago. Personally I still think that the idea is too idealistic. How can a man who has everything really understand a man who has very little?

I believe that Stanley Kubrick paid tribute to* Metropolis *in naming his 1968 film 2001 because your film takes place in the year 2000.

That never occurred to me, especially since I don't recall that any specific year is ever mentioned in *Metropolis.* In any event, another thing that I didn't like about the film afterwards were scenes like the one in which a worker is pictured having constantly to move the hands of the giant dial. I thought that that was too stupid and simplistic an image for a man working in a dehumanizing, mechanized society. And yet years later when I was watching the astronauts on television I saw them lying down in their cockpit constantly working dials just like the worker in my film. It makes you wonder.

The Girl in the Moon *(1928), your last silent film, was also a science fiction story.*

My technical advisers on this film were Willy Ley, who is dead now, and Professor Oberth, who became a Nazi. Ley, however, became a rocket expert in the United States. I am told that

Courtesy of Kino International

Brian Donlevy in *Hangmen Also Die.*

some of the people who saw the moon landings said that it was exactly as I showed it in my film—the early part of the film showing the launching of the rocket expedition and their landing on the moon, not the later parts of the story, of course.

The Girl in the Moon *came right at the dawn of the sound period.*

When I finished it, UFA wanted me to add sound to portions of it—sound effects for the rocket going off, etc. One of their executives had been in New York and had seen the first sound picture there and was very enthusiastic about it. I, on the other hand, felt that sound would kill the style of the film. So UFA told me that they would break their contract with the Fritz Lang Film Company. My lawyer said to me that I had to live up to all of my obligations to UFA, otherwise I couldn't win my case. This went on for seven months and I had to give up to UFA my chief actress, my three architects, and several other people. I was very disgusted with filmmaking and wanted to become a chemist. Just at this time an independent producer who did not enjoy a very good personal reputation constantly came to me asking me to make a picture for him. I always turned him down until finally I said to him, "I'll make you a proposition: I will make a picture for you provided that you have nothing to do with it but give me the money to make it. You will have no right to cut anything or to change anything; the film must be finished and exhibited to audiences exactly as I made it." This film was *M*.

M *(1931) was your first sound picture and many think it your masterpiece.*

It is difficult for me to choose which is my best film, but I like *M*. I discovered Peter Lorre, who had been working in improvisational theatre before he came to Berlin where I saw him, and I chose him for the key role of the child murderer in what was to be his very first film.

Did you have any problems working with him?

The only difficulty that I had with him was that he insisted that he couldn't whistle. Now in general I am not interested in the music that is used in a movie. Having a musical background for a love scene, for example, has always seemed like cheating to me. But the mournful whistling of the murderer in *M* was crucial since it helped establish his sinister character. My wife offered to whistle on the soundtrack for Lorre but it didn't seem to me to fit properly. Then the cutter volunteered and he was not right either. I am a musical moron who can't carry a tune but I decided to dub the whistling myself. It was off-key and turned out to be just right since the murderer himself is off balance mentally. This was a lucky accident which I couldn't have planned; so, you see, I don't take credit for everything that turns out right in my pictures.

After the Nazis banned your last German film,* The Testament of Dr. Mabuse, *you left Germany and made one film in France,* Liliom *(1933), before being signed by David O. Selznick to come to Hollywood.

I was under contract to MGM for a whole year without having gotten a project launched. At the end of the year the studio wanted to end the contract. Eddie Mannix, who was the representative of L. B. Mayer, liked me and I said to him, "Look, Eddie, I was the most famous director in Europe and you just can't kick me out without my even making one picture." He asked me what property I would like to make and I told him that I had found a four-page synopsis of a story by Norman Krasna about lynch law and mob rule, and he accepted the idea. So Barlett Cormack and I wrote the screenplay.

You have usually worked on the scripts of your films, though you rarely have received screen credit for this.

I began my career in films as a scriptwriter and have always collaborated on the scripts that I was to direct, except when my agent failed to get such a clause in my contract. I think of the director as the basic creator of a film. Dudley Nichols, a wonderful man and a fine screen writer, always said that the script was the blueprint for the film and that it was up to the director to fill it out. But once shooting had started I never made any substantial changes in the script. I might change a line that an actor couldn't express properly, but I never changed an idea.

What was your daily routine when you were shooting?

At the end of the day at around 6 P.M. I would look at the rushes from the previous day's shooting. I would arrive home around 8 P.M. and have dinner. Afterwards I sat down at my desk and worked over the scenes for the next day. When you have a seven-page scene to direct you take the script and work out the camera setups and blocking on the plan of the set that you have in front of you. You decide how many shots you will take from each camera angle and arrange to do them all together before going on to the next camera setup because the lighting has to be adjusted each time you shift your camera angle. The next day I would than rehearse the actors until each one knew what to do and then I would begin shooting. The two hours that I spent each evening in this kind of preparation saved two hours on the set next day and consequently could cut as much as a week or more off the shooting schedule.

Producers should have been grateful for this. Why, then, did you have difficulties with some of them? In a recent interview, for example, Joseph L. Mankiewicz, the producer of your first American film,* Fury *(1936), said that he sold Louis B. Mayer on having you direct "his" film and that you did not get along with him. I am sure there is more to the story.

I wonder sometimes if it serves any purpose to rake up these old arguments. Still, one likes to have the facts straight. To begin with, I was a cofounder of the Screen Directors Guild and therefore a black sheep in the eyes of executives like L. B. Mayer. As for *Fury,* Mr. Mankiewicz came late to the project. It was I who chose the subject and worked on the script before shooting began, as I pointed out a moment ago. During the course of shooting he became the producer. I encountered a great lack of cooperation from various quarters while I was making that picture. In the evening I would check out a new set before I went home only to find the next morning that it had been dismantled, allegedly because some of the parts were needed elsewhere in the studio. If I needed a car with four doors, I got one with two doors—or vice versa. Finally, when we finished shooting the film, Mr. Mankiewicz wanted us to change the ending. Can you imagine Spencer Tracy, after finishing his stirring speech to the judge, immediately turning away to hug his girl? Mr. Mankiewicz, however, got his way.

How was* Fury *received by the public? Since MGM considered you a "black sheep," did they promote the picture properly?

The studio was sure that *Fury* was going to be a flop. When Mr. W. R. Wilkerson, the publisher of the *Hollywood Reporter,* asked a studio executive if MGM had any new pictures of interest, the latter said no. Mr. Wilkerson pressed the executive to let him attend a sneak preview of *Fury* and he was told, "Don't bother to go and see it. It's a terrible movie and it's all the fault of the German son of a bitch with the monocle, Fritz Lang. Let's play poker instead." But Wilkerson knew of my reputation in Europe and insisted on going to the preview. When the preview was over it was clear that the film was a great success and Mr. Mankiewicz asked everyone that he saw in the foyer of the theatre if they really thought it was a good picture. I had gone over to the Brown Derby restaurant with Marlene Dietrich after the preview and Mr. Mankiewicz came in a bit later. When he came up to me I did a stupid thing: he offered me his hand and I did not shake it.

Does it really bother you when a producer or someone else that you have worked with makes less than kind remarks about you in an interview?

It used to, but a friend of mine told me that you cannot work in this business for a long time without making some enemies. What someone says about you today will be forgotten tomorrow by most people who read it, my friend pointed out; so there is no point in making an issue of it. Besides, I have from time to time received recognition for my work and that makes it easier for me to forget the unpleasant things.

One accolade that you received was from some old-timers out west who registered their surprise that a European director could capture the authentic flavor of the Old West in pictures like* Western Union *(1941).

The answer to that is simple. I never believed for a moment that the Old West as pictured in the Western movies which I saw ever existed. The legend of the Old West is the American counterpart of the Germanic myths like that which I embodied in *Die Nibelungen.* A director of any nationality, therefore, can create this legend on the screen that we know as the Old West since it is something that people have built up in their imaginations. What probably impressed those gentlemen who wrote to me, I suppose, were the little realistic touches that I put into a film like *Western Union.* Such as when Randy Scott pats his horse on the back to reassure it, or when Scott flexes his fingers, which are still healing from some burns, before he goes into a gun battle to see if they are all right. That is the kind of thing real cowboys do.

During the Second World War you made several anti-Nazi movies, such as* Man Hunt *(1941) and* The Ministry of Fear *(1943), the latter based on Graham Greene's novel. Greene has told me that he was disappointed that the psychological dimension of his novel was not more evident in the film. How did you feel about the script?

I have always admired Graham Greene, and when I came back to Hollywood from New York, where I had signed the contract, and read the script, I did everything I could to get out of making that picture; but Paramount wouldn't cancel the contract. That was one of the times that my agent had failed to get a clause in my contract that allowed me to work on the script.

In addition to your war films you also made some thrillers in the forties like* Woman in the Window *(1944). That was a screenplay that you did work on.

As the story originally stood, a lonely man, a professor (Edward G. Robinson), meets an attractive girl and goes home with her. He has no affair with her; in fact he may never have even considered that possibility. Suddenly her boyfriend comes in and attacks the professor, who kills the man with a big pair of scissors while defending himself. Because he is an involuntary murderer, everyone in the audience at this point would have wanted him to get off. Then another man (Dan Duryea) tries to blackmail him and he kills this fellow too, and finally commits suicide. I personally felt that an audience wouldn't think a movie worthwhile in which a man kills two people and himself just because he had made a mistake by going home with a girl. That's when I thought of having him wake up after he had poisoned himself to discover that he had fallen asleep in a chair at his club. As he leaves the club he recognizes the hatcheck boy as the blackmailer in his dream, the porter as the man he killed in the girl's apartment, etc. He stands looking into a store window at the portrait of a woman when another girl comes up and asks him to go with her, just as Joan Bennett had done at the beginning of the picture. Robinson is scared and runs away shouting, "Not on your life!" So I was able to end the film on a healthy laugh instead of just grimly winding up a story with three deaths in it.

Scarlet Street *(1945) had the same trio of stars as* Woman in the Window: *Joan Bennett, Edward G. Robinson, and Dan Duryea. Did you have censorship problems with the movie because Duryea, who had been conning Robinson with Bennett's help, goes to the chair for killing her—when in reality Robinson did it?*

The studio worried about that, but I pointed out that Robinson is punished more by living with his guilt than he would have been by going to jail. At the end of the film he is a man driven by the Furies, at his wit's end. Interestingly enough, not one review complained that an innocent man had to go to the chair for a crime he did not commit. But the reason that no one commented on it is possibly not because they were aware that he had done a lot of other things that would have justified his death, but because they simply did not like his character. If this is so one wonders if the morals of the average moviegoer have eroded over the years.

Why is* Scarlet Street *your favorite among your American films?

I cannot really say why, any more than I could tell you earlier why I liked *M*. Somehow a certain film just seems to click, have all the right touches, and turn out the way I hoped that it would. This is difficult when there are obstacles to one's creative freedom.

The greatest obstacle to your working in America was, of course, when you were blacklisted during the era of Senator Joe McCarthy and the Un-American Activities Committee.

I was on the list, but I was never a member of the Communist Party, though I had friends who were. Someone from the American Legion went to the front office and said, "We have no proof that Lang is a Communist, but we know that he has friends who are. We suggest that you investigate him before you let him make another picture for you." The front office doesn't investigate people; the easiest way out was just not to let them work anymore. So I didn't get a job for a year and a half. Then one day Harry Cohn, the top executive at Columbia, said to me, "Fritz, is there any truth in this business about your being a Red?" "On my word of honor there isn't," I replied. With Cohn's support I was hired by an independent producer to make *The Blue Gardenia* (1952), and then Cohn asked me to make *The Big Heat* (1953) at Columbia.

It has been suggested that your films often deal with the duality of human nature, man's capacity for good and evil, and that this has never been more vividly displayed than in* Scarlet Street *and* The Big Heat: *one side of Gloria Grahame's face is permanently disfigured by Lee Marvin when he throws hot coffee in her face in the latter film.

I knew perfectly well at the time that you can throw coffee at someone and not leave a scar at all. So I put in a shot showing the coffee overboiling on the stove before Marvin picked up the pot. That made it more believable.

***I have often wondered if you were drawn to doing* While the City Sleeps *(1955) because it deals with a homicidal maniac, as did* M.**

While the City Sleeps was actually based on a real murder case somewhere in Chicago; I read in the papers that the killer wrote on a mirror, "Catch me before I kill more." That is what drew me to the story.

Your last American film before visiting Germany again was a picture called* Beyond a Reasonable Doubt *(1956). Is there a connection between* M *and that film in terms of the anti-capital punishment theme?

The theme of my later films in America is that not everyone who does wrong is considered a criminal by society or themselves. In *Beyond a Reasonable Doubt* you have a woman (Joan Fontaine) who finds out that her lover once killed his mistress, but she doesn't turn him in until she falls in love with someone else. What would you call behavior like that? Ultimately I don't like to dwell on the thematic implications of my films, to explain what they mean. Sometimes they have a very personal meaning for me and I have never given an interview about my personal life. All I have to say I have said in my films and they speak for themselves.

Marlowe's Mean Streets

THE CINEMATIC WORLD OF RAYMOND CHANDLER

WILLIAM F. NOLAN

Sputtering neons. Cracked sidewalks. Shadowed, dark-mouthed alleys. A drumbeat of rain laying a wet cat-shine on the pavement. Bums in slouch hats clutching paper-sacked wine bottles. Tall buildings like brick-and-glass tombstones looming overhead. A checkered taxi cruising for fares. The heavy rumble of a truck, muted car horns, the mournful night cry of a police siren.

A tall figure emerges from the shadows. Brim-down fedora, belted trenchcoat, .38 Smith & Wesson Special in a shoulder holster, and a battered gray coupe waiting at the curb. A shamus. A private dick. Hard knuckles and a smart lip. Independent. A loner. No wife or kids. He's Marlowe—Philip Marlowe—and this is his domain, his hunting ground, his urban jungle. He's where he belongs, alone, walking the mean streets.

Marlowe was born in the pages of Raymond Chandler's first novel, *The Big Sleep,* in 1939; but he had his roots in a variety of hard-edged pulp fiction novelettes written for *Black Mask* and *Dime Detective* that featured tough detectives named Mallory and Dalmas and Carmady. They were all Marlowe prototypes, men of honor who followed a strict code of personal morality, who couldn't be bluffed or bought off, who could stand up under a police grilling, and who knew how to take a punch and deliver one. They were tarnished knights, without armor. Too much booze, too many cigarettes, too many lonely hours in cramped apartments and dusty offices. Tough, cynical, but inwardly romantic. With a dark past and a dubious future.

They all converged within the character of private investigator Philip Marlowe, who would star in seven of Chandler's classic crime novels and reach a vast global audience on radio, in films, and on television.

Moviegoers first met him in 1944, via Dick Powell's powerful portrayal in *Murder, My Sweet*—but Marlowe actually made his screen debut two years earlier.

Well, he did and he didn't. In July of 1941, on the advice of his agent, Chandler had sold RKO film rights to his second novel, *Farewell, My Lovely,* for a flat fee of $2,000. The studio needed plot material for its ongoing "Falcon" series and promptly converted Chandler's novel into a sixty-three-minute programmer, *The Falcon Takes Over,* starring George Sanders as the suave amateur crime-solver.

One critic described it as "a six-reel potboiler made on a shoestring budget," pointing out that the film had "little to do with Chandler. It is set in New York, where the Falcon resides in an elegant townhouse, attended by his valet, and assumes a general air of world-weary anglophilia."

The film *did* retain several of Chandler's characters, and its basic storyline is taken from his novel, but little else remains. Marlowe had been totally erased.

A second cheaply produced B-series quickie, *Time to Kill,* based on another Marlowe novel, *The High Window,* appeared in the same year, 1942. This time the crime-solver was detective Mike Shayne (a creation of writer Brett Halliday). Fox paid Chandler $3,500 for screen rights, adapting it for Lloyd Nolan as Shayne, who delivered the scripted wisecracks with a brisk toughness. The film was watered-down Chandler, thin and forgettable, and Philip Marlowe and his mean streets were nowhere in sight, yet, in the persona of Shayne, at least his ghost was present. By 1943, badly in need of money, Chandler himself turned to scriptwriting, but he was not being paid to bring Marlowe to the screen. Instead, he'd been hired to adapt a James M. Cain novella, *Double Indemnity,* for director Billy Wilder. When Paramount was unable to obtain the services of Cain (who was busy on another film), they settled for Chandler, paying him $750 a week for the job.

He was anything but happy with his new assignment. Things had started off sourly in Wilder's office. Upon reading Chandler's first batch of script pages, the director tossed them back to him: "This is crap, Ray. You don't know a damn thing about writing for the screen, but I'll teach you. We'll work together on this baby."

At fifty-five, with four novels and more than twenty published crime stories to his credit, Chandler had never collaborated with anyone, and deeply resented his forced association with this brash, opinionated young director. But he needed the money, and he also needed to learn the craft of screenwriting. Therefore, with gritted teeth, he reported to Wilder's studio office each morning to carve out the script.

Raymond Thornton Chandler had traveled a long and twisting road from his early life in Europe to the gates of Paramount in Hollywood . . .

Philip Marlowe appeared very late in Chandler's life, and had he been financially successful in his many business ventures it is unlikely that he would ever have turned to detective fiction.

Born in Chicago in 1888, Chandler was descended from Quaker colonists who had come to Philadelphia in the sixteenth century from England and Ireland. At seven, after his parents divorced, the youngster was taken to England with his mother, where they lived with relatives. He eventually attended London's Dulwich College (in American terms, a private secondary school for upper-middle-class boys) from 1900 to 1905, receiving the balance of his education in France and, later, from a private tutor in Germany.

Of this early period, Chandler commented: "I had the qualifications for a pretty good second-rate poet. My first poem, composed in 1907, was published in *Chambers' Journal.* I was fortunate in not acquiring a copy."

At eighteen, the precocious youth took a British Civil Service examination, earning the third-highest grade in a group of six hundred.

"I went to the Admiralty," related Chandler, "but found it so stultifying that I resigned after six months. This horrified my family, and I took refuge in Bloomsbury. I managed to survive by turning out copy for *The Westminster Gazette* and *The Spectator.* Like all young nincompoops, I found it very easy to be clever, nasty, and precious." The outbreak of World War I seemed to answer Chandler's need to find himself as an individual; he enlisted in the Canadian Highlanders and saw action in France. During this service, a shell landed squarely on his bunker; Chandler was the only man to emerge alive from the explosion. By the time he was discharged, he had earned a pair of medals.

"I headed for the States after the war," he declared, "arriving in California in 1919 with a thick British accent and a thin wallet. I worked for twenty cents an hour on an apricot ranch, then switched to a fifty-four-hour-a-week job stringing tennis rackets. They gave me $12.50 a week."

Chandler grew restless. He amazed a bookkeeping instructor by completing a three-year course in just six weeks—which led to a succession of dreary office jobs.

After his mother's death in 1924, Chandler (who was then thirty-five), married Pearl (nicknamed "Cissy") Hurlburt Pascal, a divorcee, who was eighteen years his senior. The age gap made no difference in their genuine and enduring love for one another.

"I detested business life," Chandler admitted, "but in spite of this I became an officer in half a dozen oil corporations. The depression knocked them all out, and I took to the road, wandering aimlessly up and down the Pacific Coast."

In these wanderings, Chandler picked up a copy of *Black Mask*, the detective pulp, and discovered a new world of writing. Here, he felt, was honesty and clean-cut, honed prose. He determined to break into the field. For five months he worked on an eighteen thousand-word, massacre-brimming novelette, "Blackmailers Don't Shoot." The story was promptly accepted, a check for $180 was dispatched to Chandler, and the novelette was printed in a 1933 issue. Therefore, in his mid-forties, Raymond Chandler began a new career.

His greatest influence was, of course, *Black Mask* regular Dashiell Hammett, whom he called "the ace performer."

"Hammett took murder out of the Venetian vase and dropped it into the alley," said Chandler. "He was spare, frugal, hard-boiled, but he did over and over again what only the best writers can ever do at all: he wrote scenes that seemed never to have been written before."

***

From 1934 to 1938 Chandler turned out fifteen tight-lipped crime novelettes. By the close of 1938 he had finished his first full-length novel, *The Big Sleep*, which introduced Philip Marlowe to the reading public.

"I was going to call my detective Philip Mallory," he said. "But my wife came up with Marlowe. It stuck."

Published in 1939, Chandler's book luridly echoed the pulps in its unrestrained violence (six bloody deaths). Its overly complex, tangled plot tended to annoy rather than intrigue the casual reader, but the Chandler magic was there, lighting every page. By the climax, when Marlowe's bitter thoughts on death are revealed, the cumulative power of the narrative exerted its hypnotic effect ("What did it matter where you lay once you were dead . . . You just slept the big sleep, not caring about the nastiness of how you died or where you fell"). Here was a book to remember.

Chandler's second novel, *Farewell, My Lovely*, appeared in 1940. This fast-paced, keenly characterized Marlowe adventure was proof positive of the author's ability to fashion permanent literature, however specialized, from the field of perishable pulp fiction. As stylized as a Russian ballet, *Farewell* presented the seedy milieu of low-life crime with cunning exactitude. Images and descriptions were diamond-sharp: "He was a windblown blossom of some two hundred pounds with freckled teeth and the mellow voice of a circus barker . . . the kind of cop who spits on his blackjack every night instead of saying his prayers." Or: "She was a blonde to make a bishop kick a hole in a stained glass window." Or: "The old woman smiled at me, a dry tight withered smile that would turn to powder if you touched it."

Here, in this dank subworld of corruption that Chandler illuminated, the grimy guns-and-gangsters atmosphere was so real you could feel the grit between your fingers. "You gotta play the game dirty or you don't eat," snarls a crooked cop (and Chandler reveled in exposing crooked cops). Marlowe suffers at the hands of gangster and cop alike, but as he muses after one such encounter: "You can take it. You've been sapped down twice, had your throat choked and been beaten half-silly with a gun barrel. You've been shot full of hop and kept under it until you're as crazy as two waltzing mice. And what does all that amount to? Routine."

Chandler was a self-taught expert in many fields relating to his profession: he knew police procedure, and poisons, and how a human being can be killed. And he knew slang, the honest kind that hard men used. Nothing annoyed him more than academic criticism on this subject. "It is very difficult for the literary man to distinguish between a genuine crook term and an invented one. How do you tell a man to go away in hard language? Scram, beat it, hit the road . . . All good enough. But give me the classic expression actually used by Spike O'Donnell of the O'Donnell brothers of Chicago, the only small outfit to tell the Capone mob to go to hell and live. What he said was, 'Be Missing.'"

In 1943, working with Billy Wilder on the Cain *Double Indemnity* project at Paramount proved so frustrating to Chandler that he listed a variety of complaints in a typed document delivered to the producer in charge of the film. In part, it stated:

> Mr. Wilder is at no time to swish under Mr. Chandler's nose, or to point in his direction, the thin, leather-handled malacca cane which Mr. Wilder is in the habit of waving around . . . and Mr. Wilder is not to give Mr. Chandler orders of an arbitrary or personal nature such as "Ray, will you open that window?" or "Ray, will you shut that door?"

Wilder was cautioned to "ease off" on his collaborator and the matter was settled, although Chandler declared (in a letter to his British publisher) that working with Billy Wilder was "an agonizing experience that has probably shortened my life."

The script was completed in September of 1943 and the film was released the following year, earning high marks. Barbara Stanwyck played the scheming blonde who lured insurance man Fred MacMurray into murdering her husband. Chandler's dialogue was singled out for special praise, while the screenplay itself was nominated for an Academy Award.

"Overnight, I've become Paramount's golden boy," Chandler reported. "After *Indemnity,* they signed me to a long-term contract, and suddenly I'm pulling down a grand a week!"

***

Over the course of the next two years, under his new contract, he worked on a pair of undistinguished films for Paramount: *And Now Tomorrow,* a gauzy soap opera starring a fluttery Loretta Young, and *The Unseen,* supernatural hokum based on a second-rate British mystery. On the latter, Chandler totally reworked a script by Hagar Wilde, adding "numerous British bits."

At this point, Chandler admitted that he was frustrated by the Hollywood system telling a friend that

> once you find out how films are really made you'll be astonished that any of them can be good. Making a fine motion picture is achieved with immense difficulty: It's like painting "The Laughing Cavalier" in Macy's basement with [the janitor] mixing your colors.

Meanwhile, over at RKO, Philip Marlowe was about to take his first walk on Hollywood's mean streets. He would be portrayed by Dick Powell, who had been previously trapped in a serious of insipid song-and-dance films. Now Powell would effectively establish his new tough-guy persona in a classically executed film noir version of *Farewell, My Lovely* titled *Murder, My Sweet.* (In fact, he would turn out to be the only actor to play Marlowe on film, radio, and—later—on television.)

The mood here was pure Chandler, and the shadowed night spaces of the urban jungle were alive with menace. John Garfield had originally been slated to play Marlowe, but it's hard to imagine how he could possibly have matched Dick Powell's edgy, whip-smart performance. Before *Murder My Sweet,* Powell had been described as "an Arkansas farmboy who got into show business because his voice was too sweet for calling hogs, and who never got the hay out of his hair." As Marlowe, he had made a decisive break with his earlier screen image; Chandler provided the bridge to a new Powell career.

Early in 1945 Paramount studio heads discovered that their top star, Alan Ladd, was due to report for army service—and that they had only a few weeks to get him into a final film before his departure. Producer John Houseman found that Chandler was in a state of writer's block at the 120-page mark on a new novel. He talked him into converting this into an original screenplay, *The Blue Dahlia,* to star Ladd. It was shot section by section, as Chandler handed in his pages, and in order to produce the ending, Chandler risked his life by resorting to alcohol. ("I can only finish it drunk!") Since drinking was a severe health problem at this point in his life, Chandler had the studio provide two limousines on standby alert outside his home in case he needed instant medical aid. He worked with six secretaries (in relays of two) in order to get out the final pages. The result was a script good enough to win Chandler another Academy Award nomination.

In the summer of 1945, fully recovered after his alcoholic bout with *The Blue Dahlia,* Chandler accepted an assignment from MGM to script his first Marlowe film, *Lady in the Lake,* to be based on his published novel. The MGM executives were excited: who better to put authentic Marlowe onscreen than the man who had created him?

Chandler was nervous and uncertain about the job, and he shocked his producers by discarding much of the book, generating new material they didn't like. "You're ruining your own novel," they told him, but Chandler persisted. Bored with poring over material he'd already written as prose, he plunged ahead in new directions.

By September, his final screenplay at 195 pages (which would have run for three hours!) proved to be radically different from the novel MGM had paid him to adapt. They quickly hired a second writer.

"By God," vowed Chandler, "I'll never do another screenplay from one of my own books. It's just turning over old bones. Let somebody else have a crack at Marlowe. At least, he'll be in fresh hands."

And Chandler proved to be right. In 1946, when William Faulkner and Leigh Brackett adapted Chandler's *The Big Sleep* for director Howard Hawks at Warner's, they turned out a film noir classic, a brooding piece of dark cinema that returned Philip Marlowe to the screen in ideal form. Humphrey Bogart delivered a stellar performance, playing Marlowe with cynical wit and riveting intensity. In fact, there are many Chandler buffs who claim that his is the ultimate portrayal of Chandler's knight in a trenchcoat.

Late in 1945, for a blistering essay in *The Atlantic Monthly,* Chandler attacked the studio system. Because of its obvious, uncaring contempt for the screenwriter, Chandler claimed that most of the industry's product was decidedly inferior, citing (in prime Chandler style)

> asinine musicals about technicolor legs and yowling nightclub singers . . . "psychological" dramas with wooden plots, stock characters, and that persistent note of fuzzy earnestness which suggests the conversation of schoolgirls in puberty . . . comedies in which the gags are as stale as the attitudes . . . and historical epics in which the male actors look like female impersonators and the lovely feminine lead looks just a little too starry-eyed for a babe who has spent half her life swapping husbands.

Despite serious misgivings about his ability to create anything "decent" for the screen, in 1946 Chandler was working on another suspense film script, *The Innocent Mrs. Duff,* when his contract with paramount expired. Incensed by this published attack (which had shocked Hollywood), the studio declined to renew Chandler's contract, cutting him off in midscript.

"I'm actually relieved," he declared. "Now I can get back to my novels."

In this pre-television era, radio ruled the air, and Chandler's detective had already been heard at the microphone in the person of Dick Powell, redoing his Marlowe role for a 1945 Lux Radio Theatre dramatization of *Murder, My Sweet.*

During the summer of 1947, NBC presented Chandler's character in a series format as *The Adventures of Philip Marlowe,* starring Van Heflin. The show was well received.

That same year saw the release of MGM's film *Lady in the Lake.* Robert Montgomery not only played Marlowe, he also directed. He chose to tell the story from Marlowe's perspective, via the "seeing-eye" camera, a very awkward, artificial approach. Since the camera *was* Marlowe, Montgomery was seen only as a reflection in mirrors. Understandably, audiences were annoyed and confused.

Chandler had liked *Murder, My Sweet* and *The Big Sleep,* but he detested *Lady in the Lake.* "They even got Marlowe's first name wrong," he complained. "They spelled it with an extra 'l'—as 'Phillip'—on his office window. What a godawful mess!"

Despite all this, the film made money, and as a result Hollywood decided to forgive Chandler for his scathing criticism and take him back under its financial wing. Based on a five-page screen outline, he was able to set up a truly incredible "hands-off" deal with Universal for his next script.

He would write it at home, sans studio interference, at a salary of $4,000 a week, and no one at Universal would be allowed to see any of the pages until he had completed the final script. He would also retain all print rights.

"I've pulled off the sweetest deal

in town," he bragged to a friend. "No writer has ever been able to wrangle a contract like this."

Which was true. In just four years, from his shaky $750-per-week start at Paramount, Chandler had reached the top of the ladder. He was suddenly the envy of every scriptwriter in the industry.

He called his new project *Playback,* a suspense thriller that had nothing whatever to do with Philip Marlowe. Much of the action takes place in Vancouver, British Columbia, and deals with a mild-mannered Canadian detective, Jeff Killaine, who pursues—and falls in love with—a victimized young woman on the run from a North Carolina murder.

During this same period another Marlowe novel, *The High Window,* was being filmed at Fox under Chandler's first manuscript title, *The Brasher Doubloon,* which was the name of the rare missing coin at the heart of the action. (Chandler's editor at Knopf had warned him that if he published the novel under its original title, book buyers would read the second word as "brassiere" and confuse it with female lingerie. Chandler thought this was ridiculous, but he finally settled for *The High Window.*)

In 1941 Fox had paid him $2,000 for the screen rights. Now, with the project in final development, they signed a mustached George Montgomery, a former boxer and stuntman, to portray Chandler's detective. The resulting film (released in 1947) drew strong critical fire. The *New York Times* called it "plodding and conventional," adding that "Montgomery lacked conviction" as Marlowe. Another review claimed that the picture "completely violated the spirit of Chandler." Certainly Montgomery's flat, low-key performance totally lacked the solid believability of Powell and Bogart.

By the time Chandler completed the final draft of his original screenplay in 1948 (the same year in which a new CBS Marlowe radio series starring Gerald Mohr made its debut) the studio heads at Universal decided to consign *Playback* to the shelf. They felt that the script lacked a dynamic hero and that shooting on Canadian locations would prove too costly. With this frustrating rejection, Chandler considered himself "out of the film-writing game."

He had moved from the Los Angeles area to the beach town of La Jolla, north of San Diego, to a home that overlooked the ocean. His wife, Cissy, was weak and ill, requiring constant care, and as he said, "I have my books to write."

However, he was lured back to the cinema world for one last job by director Alfred Hitchcock, who felt that Chandler was just the man to write the script for his new thriller, *Strangers on a Train.* He would be paid $2,500 a week to adapt Patricia Highsmith's novel to the screen.

The plot revolved around two strangers who meet on a train. Bruno Anthony hates his father, while Guy Haines wants to rid himself of an unfaithful wife. They agree to "swap" murders, on the assumption that neither will be suspected of the other's crime. Chandler was dubious about the project. His bitter opinions about Hollywood had not softened. Hitchcock, who refused to take no for an answer, flew from Los Angeles to San Diego and hired a limousine to take him to La Jolla. The legendary director prevailed in his pitch; Chandler agreed to tackle the project. Their honeymoon was a short one. Chandler was soon complaining in his correspondence about Hitchcock's constant suggestions regarding the script. "He's always ready to sacrifice dramatic logic for the sake of a camera effect," Chandler declared. "Hitch directs the whole film in his head before he knows what the story is."

The personal relationship between writer and director grew

strained, with Chandler asking him: "If you know exactly how you want it done, why did you hire me?"

Story conferences were another problem. Chandler insisted that Hitchcock travel to his home in La Jolla for each script discussion. On one particular afternoon, as the portly director clumsily exited the limo, Chandler was watching from a screened window. He turned to Cissy and said in a loud voice (which Hitchcock heard clearly): "Look! Here comes that fat bastard again."

This marked Hitchcock's last trip to La Jolla. In December of 1950 Chandler was off the film. His replacement was Czenzi Ormonde. She scrapped much of the original screenplay under Hitchcock's direction—although Chandler retained co-credit on the final shooting script. He wrote an angry letter about the fact that "a Hitchcock picture must be all Hitchcock. Any signs of another style must be obliterated . . . even if this means making [the story] quite silly . . . My script was far better than [the one] they finished with. But it had too much Chandler in it."

This project marked the end of Raymond Chandler's involvement with the film industry. In all, he had worked on eight screenplays. Aside from financial rewards, he felt that he had largely wasted his time, and that he had failed to match the distinction of his prose with his script work.

He now labored on what would turn out to be his most ambitious Marlowe novel, *The Long Goodbye.* Chandler was attempting to create a work of literature that would transcend the mystery genre, and it took him two years to complete the book to his satisfaction.

The Long Goodbye first surfaced in England in the autumn of 1953, and did indeed earn exceptional critical praise. However, when the novel was published in the U.S. in 1954 it was released as another Philip Marlowe mystery thriller, albeit one with (as the dust jacket proclaimed) "a deeper cut and a quieter overtone." The failure of the novel as breakthrough literature—and much more importantly, the death of his beloved wife, Cissy, at the end of 1954—sent Chandler into a severe downward spiral.

In February of 1955 he carried a loaded gun into the bathroom of his home in La Jolla and attempted to kill himself. He'd been drinking, and the shots went wild.

"Ray was in a deeply depressed emotional state," a friend reported. "He needed to find some kind of escape, and decided to return to his British roots by moving to London. He knew that over there, at least, he'd be accepted as a serious novelist and not as just another mystery writer. This afforded him the stability he needed and restored some of his self-confidence."

But the "good life" in London didn't last long. Chandler's drinking soon got out of control. His British friends were embarrassed for him, becoming concerned about his wild, obviously self-destructive behavior.

He also began a manic pursuit of women, reverting to his pre-Cissy days when he had earned the reputation of a "skirt chaser." San Diego columnist Neil Morgan, who knew Chandler during this period, recalled: "Ray talked a lot about remarriage, and actually proposed to several women. But nothing happened. He either changed his mind or was rejected. Women found him alternately charming and boorish. His need to possess them was overwhelming. When they sought more conventional male company he fell into sullen depression and took refuge in alcohol."

In 1958, having returned to the U.S., Chandler found a task to challenge him, at least on a temporary basis. He consulted with the producers of a new *Philip Marlowe* television series for ABC, supervising the scripts and offering detailed advice on how to present Marlowe to TV audiences. Philip Carey starred in the title role as

Chandler's tough-but-romantic detective. The show lasted for just six months, and Chandler was once more adrift.

From time to time over the years he had attempted other types of fiction outside the detective genre, but (as he put it) "all they want is Marlowe, Marlowe, Marlowe, so I guess I'm stuck with the guy."

Indeed he was. His publisher was pressing him for a new Marlowe novel, but Chandler lacked the stamina for another major effort. Instead, he appropriated the basic plot and several of the characters from the aborted screenplay he'd written for Universal, reworking this material into a Marlowe adventure, and using the same title. He managed to carve out fifty thousand words, which was less than half the length of his previous novel. But even this proved to be exhausting, unnerving work.

Playback was published in 1958; it was received by critics as a minor effort. Mystery reviewer Anthony Boucher summed up the general reaction: "The mountain has delivered forth a mouse."

However, the author was past any concern with negative reviews; his health was rapidly declining under constant assaults of alcohol, and the act of writing became more and more difficult.

Chandler's death, at seventy, in late March of 1959, spurred fresh interest in his work. Over the next two decades four more Marlowe films were produced. The first of these, *The Long Goodbye,* retained Chandler's title, but radically altered his plot as well as his conception.

Defending her controversial approach to this novel, screenwriter Leigh Brackett claimed that the character of Marlowe was an outdated throwback to an earlier era, and that such a man could not function successfully in the 1970s (the film was released in 1973). Thus, she scripted him as confused and ineffectual, an eccentric loner unable to adjust to modern society. Elliott Gould played a fumbling, weak-voiced Marlowe in a film that outraged Chandler buffs and proved a box-office dud.

Two years later, with its original book title restored, Chandler's second novel, *Farewell, My Lovely,* was remade as a darkly textured film noir vehicle set in the 1940s, rendered with careful attention to period detail. It offered moviegoers a welcome return to "Chandler country." Robert Mitchum's expertly orchestrated performance as Chandler's tarnished knight blended perfectly with the brooding mood established by director Dick Richards.

Ideally, this film should have climaxed Marlowe's screen career, but British producer-director Michael Winner had other ideas. He launched into a disastrous 1978 remake of *The Big Sleep,* staging the action against a contemporary British locale. The result was bizarre and off-putting. As one disgruntled critic wrote:

> The new Philip Marlowe not only dresses impeccably, but has a tasteful bachelor pad in Morpeth Terrace near Westminster Cathedral . . . Here is a film entirely devoid of atmosphere or personality, thoroughly torpid and banal.

A bored Mitchum sleepwalks through his role, his eyes at half-mast, obviously aware of his mistake in reprising Marlowe for this undercooked British turkey.

The picture took vital hits. *Newsweek* headed their review: "The Big Yawn," while *Time* did them one better with "The Small Snooze."

In his *Raymond Chandler in Hollywood,* Al Clark was clearly stunned at Winner's attempt to remake the Howard Hawks version of Chandler's novel, which has long since established itself as a classic in the genre. Clark commented on Winner's "disregard for another director's past glories," declaring that "the original screen version of *The Big Sleep* has become more of a yardstick than the novel itself and every scene in the [new] film that is also in Hawks' version seems positively supine by comparison."

Chandler's detective was next seen, in yet another British production, in the 1980s on television (cable in the U.S.), when cool-eyed Powers Boothe essayed Marlowe for a five-part series, *Chandlertown*. This new effort, however, failed to reignite film interest in Chandler's detective.

Thus, the 1978 remake of *The Big Sleep* stands as the last theatrical motion picture made from a Chandler work. One hopes for a revival. In fact, Chandler's moody novelette "Red Wind" would make a dandy film. I'd happily write the script for this one.

Whatever their fate on screen, the works maintain their classic status: *The Big Sleep; Farewell, My Lovely; The Lady in the Lake; The High Window; The Little Sister; The Long Goodbye;* and *Playback* continue to sell steadily around the world. In them, the lone detective in the rumpled trenchcoat still prowls his mean streets, moving through the menacing night shadows of Los Angeles in pursuit of personal justice.

Thanks to Chandler's genius, Philip Marlowe is immortal.

We can all be grateful for that.

A Walk on the Wilder Side:

BILLY WILDER AND THE HOLLYWOOD NOIR MAINSTREAM

WILLIAM RELLING, JR.

I subscribe to the notion that among the functions of any artist is to behave subversively within whatever society he or she happens to reside. That's one of the reasons I'm such a fan of Bob Fosse's 1974 film "bio-pic" of Lenny Bruce (and, in fact, a big fan of Lenny himself, gone lo these three decades now). In particular I get off on the courtroom scenes wherein Dustin Hoffman, as Lenny, attempts to justify his work, and indeed his very existence, by shouting to the judge (and repressive American society at large), "You need the deviate! Don't shut him up! You need that madman to tell you if you're blowing it—and the harder you come down on the deviate, the more you need him!"

I've been tempted to shout back, during any of the dozen or so times I've seen the movie, "Absolutely!"

Why society needs a deviate is probably obvious to anybody reading this essay, so I won't go into that. I'd rather speak to the method of deviancy (is that a word?) and the ability of certain artists to maintain a high level of functional subversion within a repressive, conservative environment for a long period of time. A truly remarkable and enviable artistic achievement.

That's what's sad about artists like Lenny Bruce, when they cannot (usually because of their own self-destructive natures) maintain their quixotic function for more than a handful of years. It's also what's so cool about somebody like Billy Wilder, who was able to keep it up for decades.

Man. To spend close to half a century raking in vast piles of movie studio bucks and Oscar statuettes, to achieve the level of fame that he possesses, to be revered as one of the true giants of world cinema—all the while making some of the darkest, nastiest, most cynical and subversive motion pictures ever produced?

Is that great, or what?

* * *

I've always found it curious that most films noir, for all the influence purported to be possessed by the genre to this very day, weren't A-list pictures from A-list studios. It's curious, but it's not surprising, given that then, as now, major Hollywood studios didn't (and don't) see a lot of mass-market entertainment value (i.e., profits) in grim stories featuring as their protagonists cynical, disillusioned (if not outright sociopathic) loners with bleak pasts and even bleaker futures. "Hey," shouts MGM in 1950, "to hell with these depressing, doom-laden downer endings! That crap's for RKO! America wants more *Anchors Aweigh!"*

I'm talking about noir's heyday, during the 1940's and fifties, before the *Cahiers du Cinema* crowd had a chance to slap on a name that would umbrella movies with as little in common as, say, *Kiss Me Deadly* and *Gaslight.* That's why it's fortunate for us noir-philes that big-timers like Alfred Hitchcock and John Huston and Michael Curtiz and Howard Hawks possessed the inclination, and the clout, to make stuff like *Spellbound* and *The Asphalt Jungle* and *Mildred Pierce* and *The Big Sleep.* Movies with lots of moody lighting and less-than-virtuous characters and a healthy streak of fatalism—and from big studios like Warner Brothers and Paramount. Thank God, because otherwise all we fans would have to warm our anthracite hearts is Edgar G. Ulmer.

It was pretty subversive of Hawks and Huston and those other big-timers, wouldn't you say, to sneak that stuff through? And none of 'em was sneakier at it than Billy Wilder.

***

Wilder seems to have come by his cynical streak naturally, having started off as (a) an Austrian-born Jew who reached adulthood around the time that Adolf Hitler was taking over and, consequently, had to flee his native country to keep from being tossed in a concentration camp, and (b) a writer. In other words, he knew well what it felt like to be treated like dirt—politically, ethnically, and vocationally.

After working as a journalist for a time in his native Vienna, he got involved in motion-picture making. He wrote or co-wrote scripts for a number of popular German pictures, and finally co-directed a film called *Mauvaise Graine* (a k a *Bad Blood* or *Bad Seed,* depending on your source) in France in 1934. After that he came to Hollywood as part of a huge influx of German and Austrian filmmakers who were fleeing the Nazis. These included such future noir notables as the Siodmak brothers (Curt and Robert) and Fritz Lang, among others.

By the late 1930s Wilder and his partner, Charles Brackett, were the hottest screenwriting team in town, working for such notable directors as Ernst Lubitsch and the aforementioned Howard Hawks. Eventually Wilder was able to parlay his success as a writer into his first directing gig, *The Major and the Minor* (1942). He wrote, produced, and directed movies for the next forty years.

If you study Billy Widler's movies, you'll discern a pattern to many of the stories he chose to tell. The bare bones of that story go something like this: a likable if not especially morally upright character (or characters, as in *Some Like It Hot*) becomes involved in some deception that is ethically slippery if not outright illegal.

The character's (or characters') reason for perpetrating the deception varies from movie to movie: Franchot Tone's attempt to avoid being executed for espionage by General Rommel in *Five Graves to Cairo;* Fred MacMurray's lust for Barbara Stanwyck in *Double Indemnity;* Kirk Douglas's keen ambition to return to a big-city reporter's job in *Ace in the Hole;* hack screenwriter William Holden's quest for "security" in *Sunset Boulevard;* Jack Lemmon's and Tony Curtis's desire to keep from being rubbed out by George Raft in *Some Like It Hot;* Lemmon (again) pimping his way up the corporate ladder in *The Apartment;* Lemmon (yet again) agreeing to go along with Walter Matthau's scam as a means to get back Lemmon's trampy ex-wife in *The Fortune Cookie.* Those are just the better known examples of Wilder's paradigm. Even in his first Hollywood directorial effort, *The Major and the Minor,* everything in the plot evolves from a deception: Ginger Rogers is a struggling actress who's so broke she has to try to pass as a teenager in order to get a cheaper train fare home from New York City.

The lesson of these stories is always the same, namely that when one practices deception, one has a way of entangling one's self in a pretty sticky web. The price one pays to extricate one's self is also always dear, but in the end the price must be paid. When the story is a comedy—*The Major and the Minor, Some Like It Hot,* even *The Fortune Cookie*—everything works out more or less happily. Or, at least, nobody dies.

Not so with stuff like *Double Indemnity, Sunset Boulevard,* and *Ace in the Hole,* in which the central characters pay for their deception with their lives. How's that for bleak?

***

That those three films fit well into the noir category has been determined by many whose critical acumen is probably more unassailable than my own. Both Alain Silver and Elizabeth Ward, in their informative and fascinating if flawed tome *Film Noir,* and Ephraim Katz, in his *Film Encyclopedia,* list all three as noir. (Katz adds *The Lost Weekend,* but I'm with Silver and Ward on leaving this one out, for reasons I'll get to presently.)

Calling *Double Indemnity* and *Ace in the Hole* noir is kind of a slam dunk; they're films that practically define the genre. To me, *Sunset Boulevard* (which I state here and now, for the record, is my favorite movie of all time) is more of a gothic horror story than a noir story, since my personal definition of noir demands that as a key component of the plot there has to be (or have been) some crime committed. Which, I suppose, lets *Sunset Boulevard* slide in, since Norma Desmond actually does murder Joe Gillis. (This is why *Lost Weekend* doesn't meet my criteria; dipsomania dramatized so graphically may be tough for an audience to watch, but it ain't against the law. I suppose you could argue in that case that it also cuts out *Ace in the Hole,* since there's a question whether Kirk Douglas could actually be charged with criminal wrongdoing concerning the death of a man whom he's helped keep buried alive—and I think he could—though it's a question that's rendered moot when Douglas himself croaks. But I digress.)

So—does Billy Wilder deserve an honored place in the pantheon of noir directors? No question. But, as I say, he shouldn't be an admirable figure to us noir fans just because he chose to play in our park a few times. Why we should admire him is that mainstream Hollywood—and, by extension, mainstream America—found his grim art so embraceable.

Double Indemnity made money for its studio, Paramount, and garnered a great deal of critical acclaim at the time of its release, even though it wasn't a monster hit. It did, however, manage to score seven Academy Award nominations. (Though it lost most of the Oscars to Paramount's biggest hit of that year, *Going My Way,* which to my thinking might be better retitled *Go Figure.* Leo McCarey, who picked up the statuette, a better director than Billy Wilder? I'm afraid not.)

Sunset Boulevard was a hit, though it played much bigger in New York and Los Angeles than it did in what's euphemistically called "Middle America." And it did even better come Oscar time, scoring eleven nominations and winning two. That *Ace the the Hole* tanked, critically and commercially, suggests Wilder may have pushed the envelope a bit too far, the movie being easily the grimmest and most cynical of the three.

But, as they say in Hollywoodland, it did get made, and that counts for something. The case can also be presented that what Wilder learned from his *Ace in the Hole* experience was to subvert his noirish inclinations even further, in the service of comedy. This led to the biggest commercial successes of his career, including *Some Like It Hot, The Apartment,* and *The Fortune Cookie,* all of which possess clear noir underpinnings in addition to (or, rather, complementing) their scathing humor.

But Wilder's philosophy, as bleak as anything espoused by Robert Aldrich or Sam Fuller, from *Double Indemnity* all the way through *Fortune Cookie,* doesn't alter much. He still believes that most human beings are, at core, greedy, venal, self-serving shits. How can you not love the guy for getting away with that for as long as he did?

And how did he manage it? Beats me. But he did.

Robert Siodmak in Black and White

JEAN PIERRE COURSODON

The case of Robert Siodmak is one of the puzzling paradoxes of the American cinema. A talented filmmaker with an unquestionable flair for film noir, he made more films in that particular idiom than anyone else around—yet few, if any, rank with the masterpieces of the genre. Another paradox is his reputation. Little has been written about him, and he is thus, in a sense, a "neglected" director, but some of his films (*The Spiral Staircase, The Killers*) were very favorably received when first released, and have been widely considered "classics" of the genre ever since, while other less prestigious items were rediscovered by diligent researchers in the sixties.

Siodmak's career falls into four chronological-geographical periods: German (1929-34), French (1934-39), American (1940-51), and European (mostly German) from 1952. He started in the film business by writing German titles for American films, and according to Jack Edmund Nolan in his 1969 *Films in Review* career article on Siodmak, "learned the rudiments of directing" by "making one new silent film out of two old ones." a chore at which he toiled from 1926 to 1928. He then independently co-produced and co-directed the legendary *Menschen am Sonntag* with Edgar G. Ulmer, which led to a series of directing assignments for Erich Pommer at UFA. It is interesting to note that one of his UFA films, *Stürme der Leidenschaft,* dealt with what was to become Siodmak's dominant theme in his American period, a man's infatuation with a treacherous woman, leading him to his destruction. The sixth of Siodmak's UFA pictures was to be the last, as it was denounced by Goebbels as an attempt to corrupt the German family by showing that there could be such a thing as marital discord under the Third Reich. Siodmak, who was a Jew, saw the writing on the wall, and like Fritz Lang at about the same time, although probably less hastily, fled to France. There he directed several comedies and one operetta before he was able to handle more congenial dramatic material. The theme of *Mollenard,* in which Harry Baur played a man harassed by a shrewish wife, is quite similar to that of his later *The Suspect,* with Charles Laughton. *Pièges,* his last film made in France, has quite a reputation, and *Cargaison blanche,* a semidocumentary exposé of the white-slave trade, is remembered as quite daring for its time (Siodmak reportedly called it "a dirty movie").

Although Siodmak's American period consists of about two dozen films in a variety of genres, his reputation rests almost entirely on a small group of melodramas in the film noir idiom: *Phantom Lady, The Spiral Staircase, The Killers, Cry of the City, Criss Cross, Thelma Jordon,* to which one may add a couple of cult items like *The Suspect* and *The Strange Affair of Uncle Harry,* which do not quite belong to the genre. His earliest efforts in the genre (*Phantom Lady, Christmas Holiday, The Spiral Staircase*) are his most debatable ones, although some critics hold them in high esteem.

Phantom Lady would deserve little more than passing mention had it not been extravagantly praised by a number of critics, notably Jack Edmund Nolan, Charles Higham, and Joel Greenberg in *Hollywood in the Forties,* and Tom Flinn in a *Velvet Light Trap* article reprinted in *Kings of the Bs.* Produced by Joan Harrison, who had been the producer of several Hitchcock films, *Phantom Lady* has little that recalls Hitchcock aside from a wrongly suspected protagonist. The plot, based on the traditional search for the missing witness who can save an innocent, is more farfetched and improbable than even an average "B" thriller has any right to be, and nothing that takes place in it is ever quite convincing. One must take particular exception to the claim that *Phantom Lady* is a character study. The three principals (a man convicted of murdering his wife and sentenced to death; his secretary, who secretly loves him and fights to exonerate him; and the real killer, a psychopath) are utterly devoid of any kind of personality, and they never behave in an even remotely credible fashion. The husband is so bland and uninteresting, he reacts so feebly and so dumbly to everything that happens to him, that it is difficult to work up any kind of interest in him or his plight. The killer is introduced only in the second half of the movie, and no attempt is made to elucidate his twisted psychology and motivations. What saves *Phantom Lady* from utter boredom is an occasional set piece: a trial scene exclusively composed of shots of the spectators with the voices of the judge, attorneys, and accused off; a night scene in which a girl follows a man through empty streets and on an elevated subway platform; an intensely expressionistic (and totally arbitrary) sequence in which Elisha Cook, Jr., who lusts for Ella Raines, takes her to a dive where a Dixieland band is playing after hours, and performs a drum solo that can only be described as orgasmic. Siodmak may have had fun while filming, but these eccentric flourishes, which have prompted recent enthusiasm, are too superficial to pull the film out of the trashy confines in which it was conceived.

The Spiral Staircase, made at RKO under the aegis of Dore Schary, was a more expensive, more ambitious, and perhaps even worse picture. Wretchedly scripted, poorly paced, indifferently acted, and clumsily directed, it is watchable solely for its consistently superb photography by Nicholas Musuraca. The script is thoroughly dishonest, without the redeeming features of cleverness or efficiency. All the trappings of a third-rate mystery are dragged in: red herrings, pseudo-clues, meaningless "hints" painstakingly misleading or ambiguous characterization . . . but almost every cheap trick played upon us is soon exposed for what it is through its own ineptness or absurdity. The heroine, who is often referred to as a deaf-mute in discussions of the film, is actually merely mute (the result of a childhood trauma), an excuse for the other characters to talk at her incessantly (most of the overabundant "dialogue" is addressed to the poor girl), thus conveniently making the necessary plot points that more inventive writing and direction would have found other ways to establish. This basic contrivance is characteristic of a film that is all gimmickry, both in story and in direction.

Immediately after *The Spiral Staircase,* Siodmak was hired by producer Mark Hellinger to direct *The Killers,* one of his best pictures and his most famous one, for Universal. It was also at Universal that he made, two years later, the underrated *Criss Cross,* arguably his masterpiece. *The Killers* and *Criss Cross* are closely related thematically. In both films the hero (played by Burt Lancaster) is in love with a woman who is involved with a gangster, who drags him into a life of crime, and who eventually betrays him. The two plots, indeed, are basically the same; the hero takes part in a robbery with the girl's gangster boyfriend (her husband in *Criss Cross*), she talks him into double-crossing the gang and running away with her and the loot, but it turns out to have been *her* scheme to double-cross *him.* Both films, moreover, make extensive use of flashbacks (a series of overlapping flashbacks in *The Killers;* an extended one that makes up more than half the running time in *Criss Cross*). In both cases, the structure emphasizes the hero's helplessness and the inevitability of his fate, which appears sealed from the very beginning. *The Killers* begins (after the famous introductory Hemingway scene of the two gangsters in the diner) with the hero fatalistically awaiting his murderers in his furnished room. In *Criss Cross,* Siodmak established the triangle situation in an opening scene, immediately follows it with Lancaster's driving the armored truck on his way to the planned robbery, and from there goes into the flashback, with the hero's voice-over comments on the chain of events that led to his involvement with the gangsters.

One of the reasons for the earlier film's inferiority is the artificiality of its flashback construction and the inevitable clumsiness with which it is at times handled. The device of reconstructing a character's past from interviews with witnesses and participants is not particularly well suited for this type of crime story. The position of the flashback in *Criss Cross,* on the other hand, although arbitrary from the point of view of narrative continuity, is structurally most effective, as it both generates suspense and conveys the feeling that all the events in the flashback inevitably lead to and culminate in the imminent robbery.

Criss Cross is more successful, too, in its depiction of the hero's relationship to the woman who is to be his nemesis. The Ava Gardner character in *The Killers* is sketchy, although the actress's allure is more than sufficient to make the hero's attraction to her credible. She is little more than a prop used in engineering his doom, and the relationship is never really developed. In *Criss Cross,* the two were married and divorced before the action begins, and the relationship is picked up when he returns from a two-year stretch in the army. The film is particularly successful, at the beginning of the flashback, in suggesting the hero's obsession with his ex-wife, his firm determination to avoid meeting her thwarted by the irresistible attraction that pulls him to the places where she might be found. Their relationship is a paradoxical but not uncommon mixture of mutual attraction (largely but not exclusively sexual) and radical incompatibility, a contradiction neither knows how to deal with and which eventually causes their destruction. Although she lures him back only to betray him, she is as much of a victim as he is, her treachery a consequence of her feelings of insecurity. She is a cold, calculating femme fatale in the best film noir tradition, yet we can't help feeling sorry for her at times (for example, the scene in which she reveals to her ex-husband that her new one deprives her of all freedom and beats her up sadistically), even when she uses her helplessness as a tactical weapon. Yvonne De Carlo's limited range as an actress seems to help the characterization. The mechanical way in which she takes direction, her clockwork matching of one gesture or move to each sentence she speaks, which makes her look like an automaton even in moments of strong emotion, bring out the character's insincerity as well as the lack of subtlety of her scheming.

Although fatalism is the keynote of the genre, few films noir have been as insistent as *Criss Cross* in their depiction of the hero's own ensnarement in the web of his destiny. In one of the film's best scenes, Lancaster and De Carlo, who have secretly met at his house, are intruded upon by her husband (Dan Duryea), who has been tailing her. Forced to explain the gangster's wife's presence at his place, Lancaster claims that he wanted to talk over a plan to rob the armored truck he drives, so that she could tell him if her husband might be interested in the job. He had made no such plans, at least consciously, but the fortuitous situation gives the fictitious project reality. To prove his earnestness to the skeptical gangster (Duryea plays cat and mouse with Lancaster somewhat in the way Kirk Douglas did with Robert Mitchum in *Out of the Past,* an intensely fatalistic, doomed-hero film noir which may have influenced *Criss Cross*), he grows increasingly specific and convincing, so that there won't be any way to back out of the situation later on. Thus the hero manages to fashion his own doom while being a victim of circumstances.

Siodmak's best noir films have been praised for their location work (the Bunker Hill section of Los Angeles in *Criss Cross;* New York City in *Cry of the City*), although the places are more often suggested than actually shown. The contrast between location shooting and studio scenes is at times jarring; but there *are* moments of authenticity. Thus, in *Cry of the City,* a brief scene shot on Eighth Avenue at Eighteenth Street is of no particular visual or dramatic interest, but it affords a rare glimpse of the real thing in a Hollywood film of the period: the wind is blowing newspapers about, an old man walks by and spits, Eighth Avenue looks just as forlorn as it ought to.

Aside from the credible New York atmosphere, *Cry of the City* is weak on story, strong on characterization. Its plot never seems to come into focus and becomes quite dull at times (there are long stretches involving a clichéd Italian mama worrying about her good-for-nothing boy, or the boy meeting with his girl in a church). The protagonist, however, beautifully played by Richard Conte, is a fascinating character. A small-time hoodlum with an irresistible but sadly misapplied charm, he is clever enough to get himself out of trouble most of the time, but not enough to keep out of it altogether, or to prevent trouble from catching up with him and eventually engulfing him. He is a victim, but at the same time a ruthless predator, and the film maintains a rather remarkable objectivity about him. A doomed hero from the very beginning, he has our sympathy—as most movie criminals on the run do—but no attempt is made to gloss over his antisocial and ultimately self-destructive behavior. It is so clear that he is headed for destruction, and that no other option is really open to him, that we almost feel relief when he eventually gets killed, but the feeling involves neither a sense of pity nor a sense of justice done. The eschewing of both pathos and moralizing is the film's most unusual feature.

Conte's performance tends to steal the show from Victor Mature, the film's nominal star, yet Mature is remarkable, too, as the cop who pursues Conte with a doggedness verging on neurotic fanaticism. All the characters they meet in the course of their brief game of cop and robber are (with the exception of the already mentioned mother and girlfriend) incisive, sometimes fascinating sketches, with at least two performances standing out: Berry Kroeger as a menacing crooked lawyer, and the gigantic Hope Emerson as a masseuse whose specialty is to torture rich old ladies to get their jewels. Towering over Conte in their memorable first scene together, she starts giving him a massage, proceeds almost to strangle him, then later fixes him a huge breakfast that she devours herself while he watches. (This extreme instance of Siodmak's flair for monstrous couplings—like that of Laughton with Rosalind Ivan in *The Suspect*—may be seen as an exaggerated statement of his apparent belief in the basic grotesqueness of couplings in general.) The most visually striking moment in the film is a deep-focus shot through the glass door of Emerson's massage parlor; she comes from a back room and proceeds toward the camera, turning on light after light as she walks across three successive rooms, and looming increasingly large.

Exceptionally, there was no treacherous heroine in *Cry of the City;* the character was back, however, with a vengeance in *Thelma Jordon,* a late entry in the noir genre and Siodmak's last notable picture, at least in the United States. Again, the woman is involved with a crook and uses an honest man who has fallen in love with her. Played by Barbara Stanwyck, who by then had run up an impressive record of such roles, she is considerably more devious and deceptive than the Ava Gardner of *The Killers* or the Yvonne De Carlo of *Criss Cross.* She lies constantly, yet with a sprinkling of truths that create an appearance of sincerity, and she very convincingly justifies her lies after they are exposed, so that, having secured renewed confidence from her victim by her confessions of treachery, she can continue scheming and deceiving even more brazenly. The spectator, despite a thorough familiarity with this type of heroine, is often in doubt as to whether she is sincere or not, and is likely to be as dismayed as her lover when he realizes the full extent of her treachery.

Thelma Jordon is dramatically uneven, and its moments of visual brilliance are infrequent, but the relationship is convincingly portrayed, with Wendell Corey perfectly cast as the assistant D.A. who sacrifices everything—family, job, reputation—for the woman he loves. The premise, although somewhat farfetched, is conducive to efficient suspense, and is typical Siodmak: when Thelma's wealthy aunt is murdered in unclear circumstances and Thelma is tried for her murder, her lover maneuvers to be put in charge of the prosecution, then proceeds to weaken his own case and covertly do the defense's job in order to secure an acquittal. He thus finds himself in one of those uncomfortable situations Siodmak delights in creating for his characters (although, in fact, the characters implicate themselves), his predicament recalling Lancaster's in *Criss Cross.*

Three scenes stand out. In the opening, a very drunk Corey has been telling a colleague about his marital problems when Stanwyck arrives to report a burglary (an imaginary one, it turns out; she lies from her very first moment on screen). They talk, he takes her home, and his fate is sealed. Corey is outstanding throughout this long sequence, first in projecting sarcastic bitterness and self-pity with drunken candor, then in handling the character's response to his growing attraction to the woman. Later, when the two are about to fix the murder so that Thelma won't be suspected, they are disrupted by a caretaker's coming through the garden toward the house to check why the lights went out, and their neat panic as they frantically scramble to prevent the irreparable is electrifyingly depicted. The third scene is purely a stylistic flourish. When Thelma is being escorted from the jail to the courthouse across the street for her trial, the camera follows her in one continuous moving shot through a crowd of journalists and excited bystanders, and up an equally crowded staircase (Siodmak had a definite liking for staircases, and not only spiral ones, as also shown, for example, by the closing scene of *The Killers*).

Siodmak was so closely associated with film noir that it is not surprising his American career ended at about the time the genre died out after 1950. Besides the six pictures discussed in this essay, a few minor efforts are also related to the genre, the most curious of which is *The Dark Mirror,* an extravagantly contrived story about twin girls, one good, one evil, that is thematically interesting for, in effect, splitting the two-faced, treacherous heroine of Siodmak's major films into two distinct persons. (He had already directed a good-twin-bad-twin story two years earlier for the same studio, the camp item *Cobra Woman,* which, despite its utter silliness, may have been of more than routine interest to him.) Throughout *The Dark Mirror,* uncertainty first about which twin is good and which bad, then about which twin is which, is sustained with teasing perversity. In an almost obligatory scene, the bad twin, impersonating the good one, visits the latter's lover and asks him if he could really tell her kisses from her sister's. When he answers that deep down in his heart he could (or words to that effect), the irony becomes almost overwhelming. This titillating toying with the idea that the person one loves (desires) may be someone else is really what films like *Criss Cross* and *Thelma Jordon* are about, and the twin contrivance, through its very exaggeration, may help us better understand the nature of the attraction the male protagonists in these films feel for the women who deceive them.

Only very remotely related to the genre (since it is set in turn-of-the-century London) is *The Suspect,* which Siodmak has called "the best story I have told." Although Charles Laughton's performance as the long-suffering husband and Rosalind Ivan's as the shrewish wife are memorable, and the film as a whole well directed and suspenseful, it remains a minor work that doesn't really stand repeated viewings. It is the most Hitchcock-like of Siodmak's films, but the Hitchcock it brings to mind is that of the television series rather than the motion-picture masterpieces (or even minor works).

There is little else worth mentioning in Siodmak's Hollywood career, except his last American film, *The Crimson Pirate,* a joyous romp that has absolutely nothing in common with the rest of his work. (Burt Lancaster, whom Siodmak had directed in his first screen appearance, had developed a liking for Siodmak and offered him the assignment when he produced and starred in this humorously acrobatic buccaneer yarn.) Siodmak did not return to the United States after the filming of *The Crimson Pirate* (which was made in Spain and England). The rest of his career belongs to the history of the German film, although he made a few pictures in France and one in England, and directed one last American production (made in Spain), the curious and not totally negligible *Custer of the West,* his only Western. However, it is mostly, if not exclusively, for the handful of fine films noir discussed above that the viewer should be urged (to quote the phonetic transcription of the director's name displayed on his most often reproduced photograph) to "see odd Mack."

Marc Lawrence: THE LAST GANGSTER

LEE SERVER

Marc Lawrence has been in a hundred and fifty movies. Maybe two hundred and fifty, who can say? Some of those pictures he never heard of even when he was making them. His was one of the familiar faces in the floating repertory company of big-studio Hollywood. He was a trained New York actor, wise in the precepts of Stanislavsky, but he played whatever was going—cowboys, hillbillies, pirates. Cecil B. DeMille cast him as an Indian brave in *Unconquered,* kind of a reach for a guy with a Bronx accent, though Boris Karloff played the Big Chief in the same film. Most of the time he was the movies' hardest working hoodlum, a ubiquitous presence in mean streets cinema, the guy with the snap-brim fedora and the snub-nosed .38, the cruel-looking thug with the pock-marked skin and the dead-eyed glare. *I Am the Law. Homicide Bureau. Racketeers in Exile. Little Big Shot. San Quentin. Invisible Stripes. Johnny Apollo. Dillinger. This Gun for Hire. Key Largo.* Underworld parts were his bread and butter, few did them better. No one ever did more with less, in some of those bottom-of-the-barrel productions. Hack screenwriters should have kissed his ring. He could make one-word lines like "Sure . . . " and "Yeah?" sound like monologues crafted by Odets.

He—or his agent—liked to keep the checks coming in. They turned down nothing. Not *Yokel Boy, Abbott and Costello in the Foreign Legion,* or *Love, Honor and Oh, Baby!* He was always better than he had to be, even in *Yokel Boy.* But when you gave him a part that was not bad to begin with, like Cobby, the weasel middleman in *The Asphalt Jungle,* he could be electrifying. And all the while he worked on the stage. His performance in the London production of Arthur Miller's *A View from the Bridge* was that year's theatrical sensation. Burton and Brando paid homage. It was a crazy sort of career.

And it got crazier. The postwar witch-hunters put him in their gunsights. The House Un-American folks hauled him onto the witness stand, asked their Un-American questions. He shot back at them with hard-boiled wisecracks, like they were the D.A.'s office and he was a guy named Lefty, like it was a scene from *Invisible Stripes* or something. He spoke one of the few laugh lines of the whole miserable misadventure. *"I joined,"* he said, *"because I heard it was a good place to meet broads."* They brought him back, squeezed a few names out of him. He regretted it at once but there was no chance for a retake. The turmoil put him in a sanitarium, shot up on tranquilizers. He watched friends like John Garfield drop by the wayside. He had to "have a tomorrow" and fled America for a peripatetic existence in Europe. Italian producers, pleased to have a genuine Hollywood gangster in their presence, starred him in Cinecitta crime pictures, one with an inexperienced Sophia Loren. Then Rome became Hollywood on the Tiber and the Via Veneto became crowded with old pals and old enemies too. He returned to America after a while, began a second career as a director, taking the helm on TV shows like *M Squad, Lawman,* and *The Roaring Twenties.* In the sixties and seventies he commuted between Europe and the States, working both sides of the camera. He was the Nazi trying to drown Dustin Hoffman in *Marathon Man.* He was a caricature of his own archetypal hood in *The Man with the Golden Gun* (two days' work, four weeks cooling his heels in sunny Thailand). He guest-starred on the tube, stealing scenes as capos and tough-talking operators in countless private-eye and cop shows. Kept working. And as he looked toward his ninetieth birthday the jobs still came. Up to Canada to play Carlo Gambino in HBO's *Gotti.* Over to Barstow for a part in *From Dusk till Dawn,* Tarantino on him like a dog in heat, pumping for movie lore.

Marc Lawrence lives in Palm Springs, "death's waiting room," he calls it. The temperature is roughly 190 degrees on the late summer afternoon when I phone to tell him I'm in town. "Get your ass over here!" he says. His house is a few minutes from downtown, past the fabulous fifties steakhouses and motels on Palm Canyon Drive, turn left at the local nudist camp, and climb the pale brown hillside. He comes to the front door, taller than expected—he was so often hunched over in the movies, scheming, or going eye to eye with tiny stars—and younger-looking too, a very vigorous eighty-six year-old. "How are you, ya fuck . . . " We enter a spacious main room, big glass doors at the far end looking out on a swimming pool and a large wedge of endless desert sky. "I was robbed, did I tell you that? A couple of drug addicts. They sprayed my eyes with something, took some money. Fucking bastards. I've got a gun now." On the walls and shelves are artifacts of an eclectic life story—Etruscan pottery acquired during his Roman exile and a painting by friend Henry Miller sharing space with a lobby card for *Nazi Agent,* a 1942 Conrad Veidt-starrer about twins spying for Hitler.

We sit down with some drinks. We talk. One subject leads to another, ranging over the memories of seven decades in show business. You want movie lore? Pick a name. "Bogie was a mensch . . . We were making *San Quentin* together. He said, 'You know, Marc, I hate to talk fast in a scene because I start to lisp.' He wanted me to tell him if I heard him start lisping his lines. So I said, 'I'll watch it for you.' I gave him the okay for every line he said. I'm a young kid in this fucking gangster thing, trying to be a tough guy, and this guy says, 'Watch my lisp.'" Abbott and Costello: "I did three pictures with them. Costello was a clever little guy, but pushy. He was the star and wanted everybody to know it. Bud Abbott was a very sweet guy, very lonely. Didn't have all those Italian hangers-on like Costello. Bud invited me to his house. I didn't know him really. I thought there would be other people, but it was just my wife and myself and Abbott and his wife. A nice guy. A lonely man."

He saddens at a recollection of his wife. She died not long ago and they had been married for over fifty years. "I found out she'd been lying to me all those years," he says with mock indignation. "She lied about her age. I thought she was younger than me. All this time I was living with an older woman." Friends have set him up on dates. Later, at dinner, he recounts in great detail a recent one-night stand, a tale hilarious, poignant, and obscene.

At nightfall we climb into his white Lexus and drive to a restaurant,

Courtesy of Marc Lawrence

Marc Lawrence with Marlon Brando, on the set of *Guys and Dolls*.

Melvin's, a Palm Springs landmark. Sinatra enjoys his prime rib there and Garbo once slept in the attached hotel. The restaurant's owner, a friend of Marc's, is out of town this night but the majordomo and staff know who's who and greet him effusively. His picture is on the wall of fame, a flashlit pose with Hugh Hefner, a few frames down from the shots of Frank and Barbara and a grinning ex-president. "That was a crazy night with Hefner. Have you ever been to that house of his?" Marc holds court and tourists at the next table wonder who he is. People recognize him, he says, but it's mostly like the old American Express ad: the face looks familiar but I don't recall the name. He remembers a night in New York, getting his shoes shined on Seventy-sixth Street, two guys walking by. "One guy stops, says, 'Hey, you're a movie star? I seen you in the movies!' I throw my chest out, a big shot. Then the other guy takes a look. 'Movie star?' he says, 'You're too fuckin' ugly to be a movie star!'"

The earliest film I can remember seeing you in is* Desire, *the part of Marlene Dietrich's driver in the opening sequence. It wasn't much of a part but I guess it couldn't have been a hardship opening doors for Dietrich.

My dear fellow, the reason why I got that part was they were using some second-unit footage that was shot in

Paris and the guy in the footage looked like me. I was just a piece of the furniture to Dietrich. I met her many years later in Rome and that time we sat down and talked. It was the summertime but she wore gloves, I remember. Those legs crossed up high. Very nice. When I had done *Sergeant Madden* for von Sternberg he invited me to a party he was throwing in her honor. She never showed up. Terrible for von Sternberg, humiliating night for him. I said to her, "That party he had in your honor back then, why didn't you show up?" She just giggled, "Oh . . . I might have forgot." On *Desire,* the thing that impressed me was when John Gilbert came to visit her. Marlene and Gary Cooper meant nothing to me, not at that time. But Gilbert was the legend of my boyhood growing up in the Bronx. He won the war for me in *The Big Parade.* There was John Gilbert, standing right next to me—I almost fainted. Holy shit. The guys back in the Bronx won't believe this!

Once they typecast you as that New York thug you never stopped working.

The same part, over and over, same wardrobe.

I think you said they didn't even change your name from one film to the next.

Yeah, I was always playing somebody named Lefty. I played more damned Leftys. Jack Warner once threw a fit in a screening room, said I played a goddamn guy named Lefty in every Warner Bros. picture they released!

Harry Cohn liked you, though; you played even more of those parts at Columbia.

He was pals with Johnny Roselli, a big goddamn mobster. This is the guy the CIA once hired to knock off Castro. Anyway, he was sitting with Harry Cohn at the studio, watching some rushes. It was a scene I was in, and Roselli said to Harry—Harry's wife told me this—he whispered to Harry, "You know, that kid up there, he's pretty good, acts like the real thing. He could be one of the mob." And from that I became a legend with Harry Cohn. He loved me. Cohn loved tough guys. All that gangster shit.

But you did get friendly with some real-life mobsters, didn't you—like Bugsy Siegel?

Benny Siegel and I belonged to the same club in Beverly Hills. We always nodded to each other, like rival gangsters, never talked much. One time I said to him, "You got a nice tie," and he took it off and gave it to me . . . I did some pictures with his girlfriend—what's her name?

Virginia Hill?

No, no . . . Wendy. Wendy Barrie . . . he was crazy for her.

That was before Virginia Hill.

Virginia Hill was a mob bookkeeper . . . a carrier for the mob, carried money. I knew Virginia. I saw her here and there, once in Zurich, many years later. She wasn't a beauty. Four of us went out one night. She was seeing a movie actor, John Carroll, and I had a girl, and we went back to Benny's place on Tower Road when he wasn't there. Rudolph Valentino's old house. I never told Benny that I had been to his house, getting laid.

Did the real gangsters like the way you guys were portraying them on the screen?

Of course! Shit, yes. Jimmy Cagney. Eddie Robinson. Hey look, fellas, that's us! Pretty good! They loved it, copied the gestures, the clothes. The time I met "Lucky" Luciano in Italy, I swear to God, I thought he was imitating me. He had that "dead look." Eyes looking at you cold, dead, without blinking. What's he doing, imitating Marc Lawrence? It was during the blacklist, all that shit, and I didn't give a fuck who he was. Meant nothing to me. Leave me alone, get off my fucking back. I didn't want to be bothered with him, I had my own problems. And Lucky says to me, "I want to hear New York talk." He'd been deported from the U.S. The schmuck is homesick. He wants to hear New York talk, that's what he was hungry for. So I talk New York talk. I had lunch with him at Capri. He had seven or eight guys with him, sitting around the table. And he carried on like King Farouk—if he laughed, everybody laughed. He had a little dog named Bambi. I said, "Bambi, from the Disney picture?" He said, "Yeah, I like dat fairy tale."

You knew all the movie tough guys, of course. You and John Garfield started out together in New York, right?

We worked together in New York. We did a Eugene O'Neill thing, I don't remember the name of it, he was the son, I was the father. I was accepted into the company, Julie wasn't. Didn't make any difference to Julie, what the hell. It didn't take anything away from his talents, he went on. Always enthusiastic. Julie was a very sweet kid. That's what made him a star. Sweetness, the enthusiasm of life. The witch-hunters got him, right through the heart.

You go along with those people who say it was all the aggravation from the investigations that killed him?

Sure, it killed him. But he died while fucking a girl. That can kill you too.

***Before, we were talking about a guy I've always found kind of interesting, Lawrence Tierney. You did his breakthrough picture—*Dillinger.**

Oh, Jesus Christ, Lawrence Tierney. Very talented actor. But what a temper, terrible temper! He was kicked out of two countries.

Ha! What do you mean?

Thrown out, couldn't go back. Spain and England. When he was drinking in those days . . . when he was drunk he got violent, completely unpredictable. you didn't know what the hell he was going to do. A lot of people were afraid of him because of that . . . He's a nice guy now and a marvelous actor. Did a picture a little way back, the gangster thing [*Reservoir Dogs*] and he's wonderful in it. I remember that first story we did, *Dillinger*. We had Max Nosseck, a German director. A very short guy. And Tierney was playing Dillinger and after the first three days I wondered why the hell they had hired this kid. I didn't think he had anything. I didn't feel the danger behind this guy. And then he does a scene where he's got to shoot somebody at the telephone. And he does it, gives it nothing . . . bang bang. And Max Nosseck comes flying up to him, this little guy reaches his waist, and starts screaming at him, "What the fuck is that . . . bang bang? You know how to shoot a guy, you stupid fuck? You shoot a man you go—BANG BANG! Stupid!" And Tierney comes alive. "What you say, you cocksucker? Say that again, you son of a bitch!" And for the first time in the whole fucking picture he was a terror. Fucking beautiful. Little Max screaming brought him out of his shell.

You worked everywhere, from MGM to PRC. You've got credits at seven different studios in 1941 alone. Did you have a favorite place to work?

You were with royalty when you worked at Metro. The others were more like factories, you went to work, did your job. Columbia was my place for many years. Warner's always seemed the strangest place to work. It was in the Valley and it was so hot you felt like you were in a foreign country. But the atmosphere had more to do with who you were working with. I thought more about the director than the studio. They ran the show their own way, someone like Dieterle, wearing his gloves on the set, von Sternberg, Fritz Lang. Some people were easy to work with, some were a pain in the ass . . .

You did* Cloak and Dagger *for Fritz Lang. They didn't give you a lot of lines but that fight scene with you and Gary Cooper was unforgettable.

Six days shooting that. That was one line in the script. One line—"so and so has a fight with so and so." It took six days, Lang had it worked out for these intense close-ups—the hands, the face, fingers in the eyes, the nose—as these two guys tried to kill each other. I said to Gary, "I'm a fan of yours, I hate doing this, Gary, putting my dirty fingers into your beautiful nose, your lovely eyes . . . " He was such a sweet, gentle guy. And Fritz would go, "Harder! With the fingers, harder!" Six fucking days of this. Fucking Germans, they know how to torture. Fritz Lang loved this kind of scene—technical, visual. He wasn't interested in the people. In a way he was a little monster, Mr. Fritz Lang. Screaming, violent screaming at Lili Palmer, in German . . . There were a lot of directors who like to browbeat actors. Shake them up. Like the rabbi hits you on the knuckles—"Do it right!" Same thing. Lang did it with me. Just once. I said, "Mr. Lang, please . . . show me what you want. Show me just how you want me to do it, please." He did it, loved it. And I imitated every fucking gesture back at him. When you compliment a director like that they get so pleased and proud. I learned that from Eddie Lowe. He said to me, "If you've got a director who's a problem, just compliment him, whatever he says. Tell him, 'Thank you for telling me this, it's wonderful. What a wonderful idea, I would never have thought of that. Brilliant. It's a pleasure to be in your presence!' Hahaha! Blow steam right up his ass. Blow it so high the guy is dizzy when you're through, and he doesn't care what you do in the scene he's so in love with what you fucking told him!

You did some great work with John Huston.

He was beautiful. Such spirit. He was half animal. He had an appetite for living.

Key Largo ***was the first one with him. Ziggy. One scene, but you come in there and take over.***

Yeah. Richard Brooks saw me in New York when I did a play by Irwin Shaw called *Survivors*. Louie Calhern was in it, and Louie and I got very good notices. Anyway, Brooks saw it and told John about me, that's how I got *Key Largo.* So I did that and then I was at Metro doing a picture called *Black Hand,* with Gene Kelly. And I ran into John there. He said, "Do me a favor. Help me with something. I'm doing a picture and I want to test two people who have never acted." One was Ludwig Bemelmans and one was Tom Reed. They were both writers. Bemelmans was a Viennese painter and writer, a funny man. Tom Reed was a big, tall guy, wrote some things, I don't know what he wrote.

Tom Reed did a screenplay with Huston years before. So you tested with them?

I go and do a scene with Bemelmans. I'm cueing him on the stage. I'm reading the lines of this character, Cobby. I look through the script to figure out who I'm supposed to be. It says he's just a runt of a man. He's dealing with these big, tough guys. Maybe he's got a chip on his shoulder—"Look, I'm just as tough as you . . . don't tell me what to do!" A short guy always fighting with bigger guys. I pictured this guy like a mosquito, bup bup bup, comes at you, pulls back, before somebody hits him. I'm on the set with Bemelmans. He's a cute little man, very warm, very Viennese. He said, "No man should work more than ten minutes a day." Hahaa! That was his credo. And he was falling asleep during the scene. I was off-camera. John pushed me into the scene, keep this guy awake. Tells me to keep the scene going. So I'm ad-libbing around this guy, bup bup bup. So John watches this shit and says, "Okay, Marc, I'm casting you for the part." I said, "You're crazy. This is supposed to be a short little guy, a little runt." He says, "No, you're gonna do it, that was great." So I was the first guy cast in *Asphalt Jungle.*

We were doing the picture and he wanted to play a joke. He wanted Marilyn Monroe to get naked under her coat for a scene when Louis

Calhern comes over. Open the coat up, "Hello darling!" and give him a shock. He asked me to go over, ask her to do it. And Marilyn would have, she was like a child. I told her, "It's not good, don't do it. Wear your slip and your brassiere, the joke will still work." John played jokes on everybody. He liked to have a good time. He didn't give a shit about directing.

But he made some of the greatest films of all time!

Sure. He couldn't help it.

Ha!

John was a guy who loved life. He had an appetite for the best of everything. Of course he would make the best movies too! But John enjoyed himself. He knew he had a limited time on earth and he wanted to do everything. And you could sense it. You knew his mind was going everywhere. I remember when I did *Kremlin Letter* for him. Small scene. I was supposed to talk in Russian. I played a psychiatrist, a spy-psychiatrist, and I was supposed to interrogate this character in Russian. I didn't see John yet, but they sent me a guy to teach me these Russian lines, an old actor named Feodor Chaliapin. He lived in Rome, just died recently, a lovely guy. He taught me the lines in Russian. Anyway, so I came to do the scene and John shows up. "Marc! How's your bride?" I hadn't seen him in nine, ten years. I'd been married for many years but he always said the same thing, "How's your bride?" So we greeted each other and he says, "Okay, kids, let's shoot the scene." No discussion, just get started with it. And we start the scene and I start talking Russian. And John's eyes go wide, he stops everything. "What the hell is this? You're not speaking English, kid!" And somebody explained it to John. He listened, very interested. "Wonderful. We do it in Russian. You're quite right. Action!" He didn't give a shit. He was there to have fun.

Bogart said to me—we were having lunch, he was talking about *Beat the Devil;* I was supposed to be in that, I don't know why I didn't do it—"That son of a bitch Huston lost me a million dollars on that picture." And he says, "You know what? If that son of a bitch walked in here right now and asked for another million, I'd give the son of a bitch another million."

You got caught in the middle of the whole blacklist nightmare.

Yeah. We're gonna talk about that shit now?

You don't want to talk about it?

No, ask! What do you want to know? What it was like? It was like a stab in the back. You're still breathing, but you can feel that knife and you can't get the thing out of your back.

You tried to joke your way out of it with the investigators, told them you went to Party meetings to meet women. But you really weren't political, were you? You said you didn't even vote.

But they didn't give a fuck. They were out to destroy, out for control. You think they thought these Hollywood schmucks were going to take over the government? What's funny is I get to Rome and everybody thought the Commies were gonna take over Italy any day, for real, and nobody cared about your politics there. There were Communists, Fascists—who gave a fuck? One of the directors was head of the Communist Party. This was 1951 and the Commies were supposed to come in any day. Nobody wanted to own anything because they thought it would all be taken away. The producers wanted to give me an apartment in payment for a picture instead of money. I didn't want it. I didn't want the Commies throwing me out of my own apartment!

John Garfield came to see you after he had testified.

I'll remember it the rest of my life. To comfort me. He went through shit with these guys but he came over to comfort me. And I was too fucking impatient to be comforted. I told him all the jokes I would tell very badly to the committee. I said, "What are you going to do? Why don't you go away from here? Why don't you go to Europe?" And I remember his pause. And he says, "I don't know . . . I don't know, Marc, I don't know." Last time I saw him. He died. And I was the one went to Europe. I knew I had to have a tomorrow. If you have nothing to look forward to, you die. So I went to Europe, and maybe it saved my life, I don't know . . . You have no idea, kid, what that atmosphere was like. You had to be there.

Obviously a lot of the pain you felt in that period has never gone away.

No, never . . . Where would it go?

The Making of *The Naked City*

MALVIN WALD

Just as in baseball, the chief aim of almost everyone in show business is to score a hit. *Webster's New Collegiate Dictionary* defines a hit as something that is "conspicuously successful" or "a stroke of luck."

The Naked City was a solid hit. In 1948 the British Film Academy nominated it for the award as the best film of the year, along with such classics as Olivier's *Hamlet* (the winner), Rossellini's *Paisan,* and Carol Reed's *The Fallen Idol.* The following year I received an Academy Award nomination from the Hollywood Academy of Motion Picture Arts and Sciences for best-written story; the cinematographer, William Daniels, and the film editor, Paul Weatherwax, won Oscars for their contribution to the film's success.

As the definition suggests, there is also a stroke of luck in any success. *The Naked City* came together at the right time. It was the first film completely shot by a Hollywood producer in New York City using the skyscrapers, streets, and bridges, as well as natural indoor sets of homes and offices. Years later it became the source of a very successful police television series of the same title. *The Naked City* TV series in turn gave birth to a rash of imitations, which can still be seen nightly on the small screen.

Another stroke of luck leading to production of *The Naked City* originated in Brooklyn, the so-called dormitory borough of New York, which was to be the scene of the movie. When I was seventeen years old, I was a junior at Brooklyn College. As an avid reader of the tabloids, two of my journalistic heroes were Mark Hellinger and Walter Winchell, the Butch Cassidy and Sundance Kid of William Randolph Hearst's *Daily Mirror.* Both of these esteemed columnists encouraged readers to mail in contributions. I did so and had some of my adolescent quips printed in both columns. Word spread around my college campus, and I was invited to write a humor column for the school newspaper, *The Pioneer,* a space occupied two years before by a star football player named Irwin Shaw.

Shortly after World War II, I found myself as a young Air Force veteran in Hollywood, and I met Mark Hellinger, then a producer at Universal-International Studios, doing his first independent production, Ernest Hemingway's *The Killers.* I recalled my contributions to his column, and Hellinger asked casually, "Did I pay you for them?"

"No," I replied. "But making your

Courtesy of Marc Lawrence

Malvin Wald, screenwriter of *The Naked City*.

column got me started as a writer." My career up to date had been a modest one with screen credits on five long-forgotten films: *Ten Gentlemen from West Point, The Powers Girl, Two in a Taxi, The Underdog,* and *Jive Junction.* My collaborator on *Jive Junction* was a prolific young writer named Irving Wallace, my first friend in Hollywood, who was thrilled to receive his first screen credit.

Hellinger was not satisfied with my reply. He reached for his wallet and offered to pay for those long-ago gags. I steadfastly refused. This irritated Hellinger, famed for his generosity as the fastest check-grabber in the West. "Look," he said, "I'm in debt to you and I don't like that. Here, take some money so I don't have to feel like a heel."

Again I refused. Then he had a bright idea. "Since you're so damned stubborn," he said, "let's make it a business deal. Sell me an old story. Maybe it will be lucky for both of us." He told me how he had just purchased a story from an unknown writer named Patterson and was assigning Richard Brooks to write the screenplay of what turned out to be a splendid film called *Brute Force.* I frustrated Hellinger further by insisting that I wouldn't sell him an unsold story because it probably wasn't very good. But I had a new story approach that excited me very much. This intrigued the old reporter in him, and he questioned me carefully.

I explained that I had just spent almost four years in the Air Force, mostly in the First Motion Picture Unit of the Army Air Forces, where screen personalities such as Ronald Reagan, Alan Ladd, Arthur Kennedy, George Montgomery, Kent Smith, and even Clark Gable were involved in making documentary and training films. Other talents who passed through our unit were directors William Wyler and John Sturges, and writers Norman Krasna, Nedrick Young, Edward Anhalt, Robert Carson, and Jerome Chodorov. One of the most talented of all was a young writer-director of documentaries named Ben Maddow, who was later to write such outstanding films as *Intruder in the Dust* and *The Asphalt Jungle.* Ben had worked in New York in documentary films and asked me if I had seen any. I confessed that my training was in playwriting, and I knew little about documentaries.

Ben also discovered a similar ignorance among the other young army writers, and he organized a series of lunch-hour screenings of the early works of Robert Flaherty, John Grierson, and Joris Ivens. I was greatly moved by the techniques and artistry of Flaherty, considered the "father of the American documentary," and applied his approach in some thirty documentary and training films I wrote during the war. It was an ironic footnote that in 1948, when *The Naked City* was nominated for an Academy Award, one of my four rivals for the Oscar was the great Robert Flaherty for *The Louisiana Story.*

Hellinger listened patiently to my

story about Ben Maddow, Robert Flaherty, and the documentary film and asked what this had to do with Hollywood. "At last," I said triumphantly, "you've hit on the big question. Why doesn't Hollywood leave its sheltered studios and go out in the world and capture the excitement of a city like New York in a feature film, instead of using painted backdrops or street sets on back lots?"

Hellinger considered this carefully and said, "Okay, you may have something there, but where's the story?"

"The story," I replied, "is in the files of the New York Police Department's unsolved cases."

"What has Manhattan Homicide to do with a semidocumentary film?"

I explained that in combining the artistic documentary technique of Flaherty with the commercial product of Hollywood, a safe subject matter should be used—murder, a police story. I admitted that I had never written a crime story before and knew very little about murder detection. However, I pointed out that in the Air Force I knew nothing about flying P-51s, or assembling portable radar sets, or gunnery on the B-29s, or ditching B-17s at sea, or launching guided missiles. But I soon learned about these complex subjects by being assigned to technical advisers who taught me enough to write acceptable scripts. I wanted to do the same thing: have the New York Police Department advise me on scientific crime detection—with the accent on homicide.

Hellinger agreed to finance a one-month research trip to New York Police Headquarters. He knew William O'Dwyer, the mayor of New York, and he thought he could arrange it. The month spent with those hard-boiled New York City cops was an eye-opener. They did not greet me with open arms. I felt like a criminal suspect as the various detectives eyed me with cold appraisal. They brusquely informed me that they harbored little affection—or respect—for Hollywood screenwriters, especially those who wrote murder mysteries based on the books of Dashiell Hammett or Raymond Chandler. In too many fictional movies, police detectives were shown as lazy, comic characters, who wore derbies indoors and spoke out of the side of their mouths like ex-cons. They were portrayed as hopelessly inefficient buffoons and bunglers who could not find a sailor in the Navy Yard without the help of Sam Spade or Philip Marlowe. In most films, they were unable to solve even the simplest murder without the assistance of the wise-cracking private eye and his leggy blond secretary. And this in the face of the fact that not a single murder had been solved by a private detective in the last quarter-century.

"Look, friend," said one detective, "we don't look upon ourselves as heroes. We're hard-working civil servants trying to support families on $80 or $90 a week. We've paid our dues pounding beats as patrolmen and earned promotions to detective the hard way."

"We're no glamor boys," pointed out a neatly dressed lieutenant. "But we solve most murders and arrest the killers. And we hope to dodge enough bullets to stay alive and collect our pensions."

They started to give me an informal third-degree. No rubber hoses or bright lights. Just the names of a few current murder movies they had seen—and hated. I hadn't written any of the films, but still I started to sweat—a kind of guilt-by-association feeling for the writers who did. Finally I confessed: many Hollywood writers had gotten trapped in the excitement of their stories and had been careless with the truth. I promised to try to avoid that pitfall—and write an honest film about police detectives, if it ever got produced.

I started making the rounds of all the bureaus and offices of the police department concerned with homicide, picking up a little knowledge of law. Then I started to run into problems. My first obstacle was the elderly warden of the files, Inspector Joseph Donovan, who had a definite anti-Hollywood bias. He said he would cooperate with me but within the extent of the law, meaning that he would allow me to read the solved cases only. I explained that I could go to any newspaper morgue for the solved cases. It was the files of the unsolved cases that fascinated me—the anonymous tips to the police, statements of dying men. As he argued with me, I detected a touch of Brooklyn accent in his Irish brogue. I asked him what street he lived on in Brooklyn. Puzzled, he told me and I named the nearest cross streets. I then explained that I was from Brooklyn. His attitude softened as he called various police officials and said he had a lad from Brooklyn doing some research.

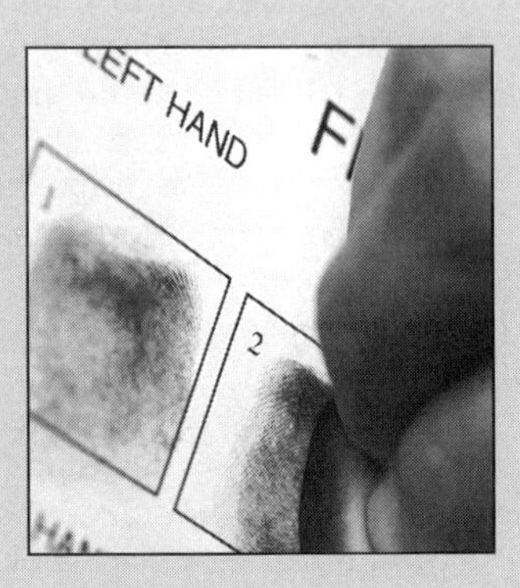

In the course of my wanderings, I learned that the police academy, then located in the Borough Hall district of Brooklyn, had a one-week refresher course for detectives. I wanted to sit in on the homicide courses, but was advised that no civilian was ever admitted. I finally tracked down Deputy Chief Cutrayne, who was in charge of the academy. He advised me that the academy was none of my business. Besides, it was located on some tiny street in Brooklyn and I would never find it. As a native of Brooklyn, I recalled that the street was something like Pineapple Street, and I assured the chief that I knew where Pineapple was. It was right next to similarly named streets—Lemon, Orange, etc. The indignant chief was certain that I was making this all up, so I made a deal with him. If I was wrong, I would stop annoying him. If I was right, I would go to the academy. We sent for a map of Brooklyn. I pointed to the area where I knew the police academy was located—and sure enough, there was a series of single-block streets—Pineapple, Lemon, Orange. The chief okayed a pass for me to go to the academy. What he didn't know was that I had worked two years in the Brooklyn Post Office. I had memorized the Brooklyn City Scheme and knew the names and locations of every street in Brooklyn—a mass of trivia ingrained in my mind for many more years.

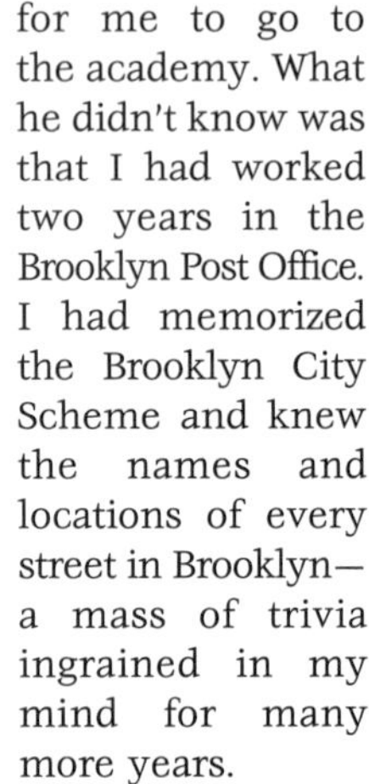

After my refresher course at the police academy, I watched the police at work questioning criminal suspects in the morning lineup, and I interviewed detectives from the homicide squad, which investigates all murders. I spent several uncomfortable hours at the city morgue watching the medical examiner and his assistants perform autopsies on recently arrived corpses. I sniffed lethal poisons in the test tubes of the city toxicologists. I peered at bullets through the double-barreled comparison microscopes of the ballistic experts. I examined the spectrograph machines of the technical research laboratory. At the Bureau of Criminal Investigation, I met the "silent detectives," the files of criminal records. These records included the fingerprint files and the "rogues gallery," a file of criminal photographs categorized according to height and modus operandi.

When I returned to Hollywood, Hellinger demanded to know what story I had created out of all that research. I told him, to his amazement, that I had at least a dozen good stories. After all, there were eight million people in New York City, and, as Hellinger was later to say in final narration of the film, there are "eight million stories in the Naked City and this is just one of them."

Hellinger as a journalist had written about a thousand short stories for the Hearst press, and all of them had O. Henry endings, surprise twists. I knew that's what he wanted, and among the stories I told him was one about a beautiful blond model, Dot King, who was found slain—her murder unsolved. I had seen some inside information in the files about this case, never revealed to the press, and I had a notion of how the crime might be theoretically solved—by using bits and pieces of other cases. Hellinger was excited because he had been in on that case. He and Winchell were riding with the police one night when the homicide call came. He had visited the murder apartment and had seen the corpse—and he had known the victim when she was alive.

"Write up an outline," Hellinger ordered, "but try and make the lead character a part that Jimmy Stewart can play." Mark and Jimmy had a gentlemen's agreement to work together some day. But as I sat down to my typewriter, a funny thing happened. Instead of a thirty-five-year-old detective, my leading character turned out to be a sixty-five-year-old veteran with an Irish brogue. Hellinger was annoyed. Where in the world would we find a sixty-five-year-old star? "Right here in Hollywood," I replied. "A recent Academy Award winner in *Going My Way,* Barry Fitzgerald." Hellinger was dubious. "We'll never get Fitzgerald for a crime picture—not after he just finished playing a priest."

But, being a long-shot player, Hellinger sent for Mr. Fitzgerald and his agent. "Mr. Fitzgerald, I know you are a busy man, but I have a young writer with the crazy idea that you might consent to play a detective in a script he wants to write."

"A detective?" Fitzgerald's bushy eyebrows shot up. "Why would you be thinkin' that I would want to play a detective?" Hellinger tossed me a gloomy look and indicated for me to answer the question. I reminded Fitzgerald that when he was a working actor in Dublin as a young man, many of his fellow countrymen emigrated to New York and became cops. Some of them advanced to the ranks of detective, and a few became inspectors and deputy chiefs. Then I reeled off the names and ages of the department's top brass—and all were Irishmen of Mr. Fitzgerald's age.

He conceded that was a logical point, but then he asked, "Doesn't a detective do a lot of runnin' and shootin'?"

"Not necessarily," I replied. "His main job is investigation and interrogation, sitting across the desk from a suspect and trying to get at the truth in the criminal's black heart. And that's mostly talking."

Fitzgerald nodded thoughtfully. "Ah, that I could do," he agreed, "but I still want to know about the runnin' and the shootin'."

"For that," I explained, "we have a young detective, an actor like Don Taylor, who played Pinky in *Winged Victory.*"

Fitzgerald meditated for a moment, then turned to Hellinger. "And when would you be shooting this film?"

Hellinger held his breath. "We were thinking about next summer."

Fitzgerald smiled, "Well, now," he said, "I think that would be lovely, seeing as how I would be free then. Mr. Hellinger, if you've a mind, you just got yourself an actor."

And with that, the Irish Oscar-winner walked out of the room, with his agent trailing behind him. For a moment there was silence between Hellinger and me. Then he looked at me and grinned. "I'll be damned," was all he said.

***

It took me a week to complete an outline to Hellinger's satisfaction. But then, after reading it, doubts suddenly overwhelmed him about the entire project. At the time I was working for Hellinger, Richard Brooks was also employed by him as a writer on the screenplay of *Brute Force*. After Hellinger's death in 1948, Brooks wrote about Hellinger in *Screen Writer* magazine (March 1948):

> Mark lived in two distinct demi-worlds. In one world, he was secretive, suspicious, frantic, fearful. It was a world overwhelmed by jealous, greedy punks who were constantly trying to find a way to destroy him. Big executives were, he often complained, conniving against him, pulling off secret deals against him, planning to push him out of the movie business. Somebody or other was trying to grab all the glory away from him, make him appear a fool. He greeted each day as though catastrophe were about to befall him.

What concerned Hellinger was the way I wrote the outline in a bastard form—using the documentary-style presentation of a divided page with one half for the visuals, the other half for the narration, for the semidocumentary form. I then would resort to full-page treatment for the dramatic sections. The new form frightened Hellinger. He had never seen it before, but I explained it was common practice in the world of documentaries.

Then Hellinger revealed to me what he felt was a secret and made me swear I would never repeat it in his lifetime. "Look, Pappy," he said, "I'm basically a writer, always will be. So when I assign a writer to a script, I become the collaborator. In other words, I am the co-author. Now, here you come along with a brand-new technique which I don't understand. So I can't possibly collaborate with you, as I do with my other writers. Therefore I can't have confidence in your script because I am not personally involved."

I was crushed. "All right," I asked, "what do you want to do—abandon the project?"

"No," he said slowly, "I love what you've written. I'm absolutely intrigued by the way you treat the city—the kind of romantic Walt Whitman-type narration you're throwing in. I want you to do a treatment in this cockamamy style of yours—but I want you to know you're on your own. When the treatment is finished, if it's any good, I'll get Ben Hecht or John O'Hara to do the screenplay. That way you'll be guaranteed story credit at least." That was fine with me. From a few jokes in a column, I had parlayed my way into a screen treatment assignment.

When I finished the treatment, Hellinger sent for me and said, "Let's forget about Ben Hecht or John O'Hara. Hecht's from Chicago, O'Hara's from Pennsylvania. Do you think you can manage the New York scene all right in a first-draft screenplay by yourself?" I assured Hellinger I could. I was born in New York City, had gone to college in Brooklyn, did social work at a settlement house on the Lower East Side in the shadow of the Williamsburg Bridge (which was to be the setting for the spectacular chase at the end of the film), had been a reporter on a Brooklyn newspaper, and had been a Broadway song-plugger covering the radio stations, the jazz joints on Fifty-second Street, and the nightclubs in Harlem.

I did the first draft and the second draft. By that time six months had elapsed since my first conversation with Hellinger. Hellinger sent for me one night at his mansion in Hollywood. His wife, the former Gladys Glad, once called "the most beautiful woman in show business" but now a fading beauty, seemed to stay clear of bright lights and walked in shadows. She left us alone, and Hellinger told me he had read my script, was fascinated by my semidocumentary approach but was worried about production problems. How can you shoot a film on the streets of New York and keep the crowds away? (I explained that the cops would exercise crowd control.) How about the proposed chase on the bridge? Autos used that bridge to get from Brooklyn to Manhattan. (Shut off that section of the bridge and use the lower section; besides, there were three other bridges spanning the East River.)

Finally, Hellinger confessed his real fear. He recalled to me that he had been a writer and then a staff producer under Jack L. Warner at Warner Brothers and produced such Humphrey Bogart successes as *The Roaring Twenties, They Drive by Night,* and *High Sierra.* He left Warner Brothers once to do an independent film at Twentieth Century Fox with Jean Gabin and Ida Lupino. It was called *Moon Tide* and had artistic pretensions. But it was a flop, and when Warner took him back into his studio, he crowed that Hellinger was merely a staff man, couldn't do anything good on his own. Now Mark was on his own again with Mark Hellinger Productions at Universal-International Studios. His first film, Hemingway's *The Killers,* was out and seemed to be a hit. His next two films, both written by Richard Brooks, *Swell Guy* and *Brute Force,* were seemingly also destined for commercial success.

"Why," he asked me, "should I stick my neck out with experimental films when I'm doing so well in what I know best?"

"I'll tell you why," I replied. "Because at heart you're a gambler. You've gambled on horses, and you've gambled on cards. Why not really shoot for big stakes and gamble with your career?"

"But if I flop again," Hellinger protested, "Jack Warner will make me the laughingstock of Hollywood. He hates my guts, even though he says he's my pal."

"Mark," I said, "remember years ago when you wrote sketches for the Ziegfeld Follies, when Broadway musicals consisted of sketches and chorus girls kicking up their legs. Then along came Rodgers and Hammerstein, and they revolutionized musical theatre with *Oklahoma,* which included a ballet scene. Well, ballet is like the documentary film, conceived by artists but later converted to commercialism."

I argued that Hellinger as a creative Hollywood producer could help advance the film world in a small way. But Hellinger protested that he was not in the business to experiment. How did I know that it would work out? My reply was that one producer—the New York-based Louis de Rochmont—had already succeeded in 1945 with a semidocumentary called *The House on 92nd Street,* shot mostly in New York City. In a month or so he would be out with a similar film, *13 Rue Madeline,* shot in Paris, and was planning *Boomerang,* to be filmed in Connecticut. Thus there was ample precedent for going all out, turning the island of Manhattan into a film studio.

Hellinger shook his head. De Rochmont was famous as the man who made the *March of Time* semidocumentary shorts. He was a veteran, expert at shooting on location. Hellinger was a Hollywood studio man. He was adamant. He was not going to produce *The Naked City.*

(The original title of the film was "Homicide." Then one day, I chanced across a book of photographs called *The Naked City* by Weegee, a celebrated crime photographer. Hellinger bought the rights to the title for a thousand dollars, and this was to give rise to a whole series of subsequent titles with the word *naked* in them—such as *The Naked Prey* and *The Naked Jungle.* On the ridiculous side, a nudist colony in the Midwest became famous as "The Naked City.")

Hellinger told me honestly that he had a half-dozen other scripts that he preferred to mine, all ready to go.

Furthermore, he reminded me that he was an independent producer, doing his own financing. It was not wise for him to take risks; he had to play it safe with scripts that he was sure of. Sorry, Pappy, *The Naked City* was to go on the shelf—the fate of two out of every three scripts in studios.

I took a vacation and when I returned Hellinger called me. He had surprising news. He had changed his mind! He had given my script to his *Brute Force* director, Jules Dassin, who disagreed with Hellinger and thought there was a picture there, and it should be made. But what was needed was a final shooting script, and a top screenwriter to do it. Hellinger submitted the script to one of the best in Hollywood, Albert Maltz, famed short-story writer, playwright, and novelist and screenwriter of three of the finest films of that era—*This Gun for Hire, Destination Tokyo,* and *Pride of the Marines.* Much to Hellinger's delight, Maltz agreed to accept the assignment. Maltz's decision to do the script elated me, too. One moment I had been told the script was dead and now it was being brought back to life at the hands of an artist whose work I had long admired.

The finished result was what I had learned to expect from Maltz—highly dramatic, exciting, preserving my original intent but bringing a fresh outlook and new shadings of plot and character.

During the summer of 1947 when the film was being shot in New York I heard all kinds of rumors. The police were not cooperating in holding off the crowds at the one hundred and seven locations. City bureaucrats were holding up production, and payoffs had to be made to cut red tape. Hellinger had suffered a heart attack. The film went about a half-million over budget. When Hellinger returned to Hollywood in the fall, I stayed away from him, figuring I was the cause of his trouble by selling him on the idea of shooting a film entirely on location. Then one day while visiting the studio, I was spotted by his secretary. She urged me to see Hellinger, who was wondering why I was avoiding him.

When I went to his office, I told him about the rumors I had heard and how much he had suffered making the film. Mark nodded soberly. He always wore a blue suit, a blue shirt, and a white tie, a kind of standard uniform reminiscent of the underworld figures he knew so well. He looked especially somber that day. "Yes," he said, "I suffered making that film. But you don't do anything great without suffering, and we have a great film here."

"Wonderful," I said with a sigh of relief. "I'm glad it turned out well. Do you think you can put me on the preview list so I can see it when it comes out?" Hellinger stared at me. "What do you mean—wait until the preview! You originated this thing—you with your cockamamy split-page, semidocumentary treatment. You're going to see the picture right now! I'm running it off for Howard Duff [who played a featured role in the film] and Ava Gardner."

I was thrilled with the work Dassin had done as a director on the film. After the showing, I went to congratulate him. There was one question I had for him. I recalled a scene in which the killer, Ted DeCorsia, is poised in flight on the Williamsburg Bridge and looks down—and there two hundred feet below can be seen people leisurely playing tennis in white clothing.

"Boy," I said, "you were lucky to have those people in white clothes playing below the bridge."

"Lucky," snorted Dassin indignantly, "I planted those tennis players there—they're extras!"

***

On December 16, 1947, Hellinger called me and swore me to secrecy. He was having a sneak preview of the film at the Loyola Theatre in

Inglewood, California. I was to go there but tell nobody. My wife and I went and were dismayed that the audience laughed at some of the opening documentary scenes. "Don't worry," Hellinger told me the next day, "we'll cut some of those scenes. It will be all right."

According to the papers, on his way out of the theatre, Hellinger had turned to Frank McFadden, his publicist, and said, "That's my celluloid monument to New York. I loved it." In a way, *The Naked City* was to be a monument to Hellinger because less than a week later, while viewing the recut film at his home on a Saturday night, Hellinger had a heart attack and collapsed. He died the next day—at the age of forty-four.

Hellinger's friends in the press responded to his death, and the early reviews reflected it. *The Naked City* was heralded as an immediate hit. The *Hollywood Review* called it "A 4-Star Hellinger Monument"; the *Hollywood Reporter,* "A potent tale told with a master touch"; *Box Office Digest* referred to it as a "Smash Big Money Hellinger Hit." "Toweringly impressive," said *Hollywood Variety.* "A pulse-pounding thriller. It should come pretty close to paying off its negative cost on Broadway alone." New York *Variety* predicted, "It can't miss at the box office . . . The word of mouth . . . should be phenomenal."

The New York opening at the Capitol Theatre of March of 1948 was preceded by a barrage of raves from Hellinger's journalistic contemporaries—Walter Winchell: "One of the most thrilling moving pictures ever made"; Ed Sullivan: "Mayor O'Dwyer says it's the greatest picture ever written about New York City"; Quentin Reynolds: "The greatest motion picture Mark Hellinger ever made . . . I loved it." Most of the New York critics were equally enthusiastic. Whether it was because of the film technique or the recent death of the beloved Hellinger, the critics generally responded with superlatives.

I was delighted when Alton Cook commented in the *World-Telegram,* "The picture is about the most faithful version of actual police methods." That was what I had promised the police at headquarters, and I was glad to see that one critic felt it had been achieved. Howard Barnes in the *Herald Tribune* was more critical than his colleagues and assayed the script as "fairly honest" and characterized the film as a melodrama "which depends upon suspense for most of its impact." Archer Winsten in the *Post* was the only critic to pay special attention to the contribution of the director and the writers and their origins as New Yorkers. He called the film fascinating, rich with emotion and-"very eloquent-very inside stuff." Bosley Crowther, the most distinguished of New York critics, complained in the *Times* that the subject matter was limited but praised the roaring "Hitchcock" end and assessed the film as a vivid job that came off as "spontaneous and unrehearsed."

The film boomed at the box office, grossing $1,600,000 in its first month of national release in April. *Consumers Union* in its national poll of critical evaluations determined that seventy percent of the film critics of America had rated the film excellent, twenty-five percent good, and only five percent fair—with an overall rating by the magazine of excellent.

So much for anatomy of a hit. But what happened to the creators? The producer had died. The director, Jules Dassin, soon found himself a political exile in the early days of McCarthyism and switched his career to Europe, where his reputation as director of *The Naked City* preceded him. He achieved even greater fame as the director of *Rififi* in France and of *Never on Sunday, He Who Must Die,* and *Phaedre* in Greece. Albert Maltz and I were nominated by our peers for the first Writers Guild Award in two categories: best written American drama and screenplay that deals most ably with problems of the American scene.

Photoplay magazine selected *The Naked City* as one of the ten best pictures of the year, and, as was the custom, invited the writers to attend the awards banquet. At the time of the awards Maltz, as one of the "Hollywood Ten," was on his way to a federal penitentiary for contempt of Congress during the House Un-American Activities hearings. The editors of *Photoplay* were embarrassed. They could not refuse to invite Maltz, but they saw to it that he and I were seated out of sight of the photographers, behind a palm tree, near the kitchen. That was nearly thirty years ago, and it was the first and last time I was to meet Albert Maltz. But as I recall it now, the rest of the banquet room was enthusiastically responding to the introductions of the stars who were being honored, and there sat Albert Maltz, one of America's most gifted writers, quietly sipping champagne, on his way to prison for defying Congress and pleading his First Amendment rights. If the scene were New York and not Hollywood, it could easily have been one of the "eight million stories of The Naked City."

Daniel Mainwaring:

AN INTERVIEW

TOM FLINN

Daniel Mainwaring (pronounced Man-a-RING) wrote both the original novel (*Build My Gallows High*) and the screenplay for *Out of the Past.* He alone is responsible for the thematic density of the film in which such ultimate noir elements as betrayals, the femme fatale, and the "frame-up" are combined with reckless abandon. After completing *Out of the Past,* Mainwaring, in spite of a brush with Hollywood's witch-hunters, went on to script three films that represent the perfect cinematic realization of the burgeoning middle-class paranoia of the fifties. The first of these was *The Hitchhiker* (1953, directed by Ida Lupino) in which Kansas desperado Emmett Meyers (William Talman) systematically terrorizes two average family men (Edmond O'Brien and Frank Lovejoy) on a fishing trip.[1] The second was *The Phenix City Story* (1954, directed by Phil Karlson) based on the real-life struggle of Alabama attorney general John Patterson against the ruthless, entrenched power of the vice rings that controlled Phenix City. The third was *Invasion of the Body Snatchers* (1957, directed by Don Siegel), a marvelous marriage of *film noir* paranoia, political hysteria, and a science-fiction premise. In addition to this trilogy (which exhibits a remarkable consistency of tone), Mainwaring wrote *The Lawless* (1950) for Joe Losey, as well as *The Big Steal* (RKO, 1949), *Baby Face Nelson* (1957), and *The Gun Runners* (1958) for Don Siegel.

The following remarks that pertain to *Out of the Past* and RKO were excerpted from comments Mainwaring made when he appeared at a seminar on the gangster film held at Northwestern University in the summer of 1972, a project sponsored by the University of Illinois in conjunction with The American Film Institute and supported by a grant from the National Endowment for the Arts in Washington, D. C. Mainwaring prefaced his remarks with a short biographical statement:

I went to Fresno State . . . In the early twenties I worked as a crime reporter for the *Los Angeles Examiner* . . . In 1935 I got my first job in the industry as a publicity man at Warner Brothers. Working in publicity you got to see and learn more about picture making than the writers did. I didn't escape from the publicity racket until 1943. Bill Thomas of Pine and Thomas, who made very small and very bad pictures at Paramount, gave me my first real screenwriting job. I wrote six pictures in one year, all of which I'd just as soon forget except *Big Town.* At the end of the year I fled to the hills and wrote *Build My Gallows High.* Bill Dozier, head of RKO, bought it and me with it. Warren Duff, an ex-Warner's writer, produced, Jacques Tourneur directed, Robert Mitchum, Kirk Douglas, and Jane Greer were the stars. On the advice of Gallup's audience research, RKO changed the title to *Out of the Past.* I stayed at RKO until 1949. Howard Hughes dropped my option when I refused to work on *I Married a Communist.* He used that project to get rid of a lot of writers, directors, and actors. If you turned it down, out you went.

You'd written some mystery novels in the thirties. Did you sense different interests and different themes in this novel in the forties?

Well, *Build My Gallows High* was a different kind of book, entirely different. First I had a detective named Robin Bishop and I got sick of him. Bishop got married and then got awfully soft and I got fed up with him. I changed to Humphrey Campbell, who was a tougher one. With *Build My Gallows High* I wanted to get away from straight mystery novels. Those detective stories are a bore to write. You've got to figure out "whodunit." I'd get to the end and have to say whodunit and it would be so mixed up I couldn't decide myself.

What changes did you make from the novel?

Well, I haven't read the novel since about '46, but basically it was the same, although there were more characters in the novel.

Was it told from Bailey's point of view?

From his point of view. The novel opened in Bridgeport where he ran a gas station and the guy came looking for him. All the stuff in the mountains, the Tahoe and Bridgeport stuff, was in the novel. Much of the novel took place in that little town and along the river. The fishing scene was in the book. That was one of the things that sold the book to pictures, the gimmick of the kid using a casting rod to pull the guy off the cliff. Warren Duff fell in love with that and bought the book.

The Mexican stuff was in there too. I had been to Acapulco a couple of years before I wrote the book. It was just a little bitty town, not like it is today. There were very few cafés, and one hotel. I used to sit in this little café across from the movie house, and all day long there would be music blasting from the loudspeakers, so I thought I'd use that in a story some day, which I did.

The scenes in San Francisco, however, took place in New York in the book. We switched to San Francisco because we wanted to shoot there. We did change the ending. At the end of the novel Bailey is killed by Whit's men, not by Kathi and the police.

The title *Build My Gallows High* is from a poem and I never could find it again. It was a Negro's poem and I saw it somewhere. I happened to read it and jotted it down.

Did you write the screenplay alone?

I wrote the first draft, and Duff wasn't sure about it. All I had done were those pictures for Pine and Thomas. When I finished and went on to something else, Duff put Jim [James M.] Cain on it. Jim Cain threw my script away and wrote a completely new one. They paid him $20,000 to $30,000 and it had nothing to do with the novel or anything. He took it out of the country and set the whole thing in the city. Duff didn't like it and called me back. (Frank Fenton had worked on it for a while.) I made some changes and did the final. But that's the way things used to work. You'd turn around and spit and some other writer would be on your project.

What were some of the changes you made?

Originally we used a trick. The first script had the deaf and dumb boy as the narrator. We started with a shot of a stream with the boy fishing. Two guys came along and one said to the other, "That's the kid who used to work for that son of a bitch Bailey." Cut to a closeup of the kid and a shot of the stream as raindrops begin to fall. Then you hear the voice of the kid saying, "He wasn't an SOB," and he told the story. Well, it flashed back twice, and it just didn't work.

At what stage did Jacques Tourneur work on the film?

After the script was completed.

Did you have any script conferences with him?

No.

Did you go on location?

Oh, I went up there but I didn't do anything. I just went up to look around. I had some time off. I liked it up there, and I just drove up to see what they were doing.

Did you like the way Tourneur handled the film?

He did what was in the script—very much so. One thing I didn't like was that mother (Ann's mother) in Bridgeport.

***At one point I was struck by a similarity to* The Maltese Falcon.**

Well, don't think I haven't swiped from *The Maltese Falcon* often.

The thing that struck me was when Mitchum went in to see Douglas and said, "We have to have a fall guy."

That was right out of *The Maltese Falcon.* Chandler swiped from Hammett, I thought I could too.

How do you interpret that last business with the deaf boy? Are we supposed to think that the boy is purposely lying to her so she will go on to a better life?

Yes.

Even with the two people from the small town getting together and going away, it's not much of a happy ending because all of the interesting people are dead.

Well, the front office said, "Jesus, you can't end it with them dead there. You've got to put something on it." Nowadays they would have ended it right there with both of them dead.

Why did you choose not to stage the scene in which Kathi shoots Whit?

It was staged, but it worked out better the other way. There was a scene when Whit came back from Reno with the money and she shot him, but we found it was more effective if we stayed on Mitchum, and he walks in and finds the dead man.

The first time I ever saw the film they were showing it to some people on the lot. When Mitchum walked in and found that body lying there, all those people who worked on the lot said, "Oh no, not another one."

When you were doing the script, did you know that Robert Mitchum was going to play Jeff Bailey?

When I finished the script I took it down to Newport where Bogart was living. He was going to do it, but Warner's wouldn't let him. So then we took Mitchum. He had already done *G.I. Joe,* which was a beauty. He was fine, though he looks a little fat.

That was just before his trouble with the law.

He smoked marijuana all the time on the set.[2] He had a vicious sense of humor. The executive producer on the film was a guy named Robert Sparks, a very nice guy, dignified and sweet. Sheilah Graham, the commentator, came on the set to see Mitchum, and she was talking to him when a drunken dress extra came up and started pestering Mitchum. Finally Mitchum had to tell him to get the hell out of there. Graham said, "Who was that?" Mitchum replied offhandedly, "That's a very sad story. That's our executive producer, Robert Sparks. He's an alcoholic." Sheilah was busily taking notes the whole time, but luckily the publicity man overheard and afterwards he took her aside and said Mitchum was kidding. Well, she wouldn't believe him and finally had to be taken up to Sparks's office to meet him.

How did they decide what actor would play what part? Did they have readings or did they just say, "Well, Rhonda Fleming is available?

Rhonda Fleming was under contract. Mitchum was under contract. Jane Greer was under contract. They fit the parts so we used them. They [the studio] had to pay them anyway.

Had Jane Greer made many pictures before this one?

No, I think this was her first big role. Warren Duff decided to use her. They tested her and she was fine. She was in *The Big Steal* next.

How did you get along with Duff?

He was a sensitive man and a fine producer to work for. [Dore] Schary didn't like him. When Schary came to RKO he fired him. Schary didn't like *Out of the Past* because it had been bought before he came. He didn't like anything that was in progress at the studio when he got there. He tried to get rid of all of them. He just threw them out without any decent publicity.

One thing I noticed was that there are a lot of small towns in your films, and these small towns turn out to be not very safe places.

Small towns are miserable places. Farmers I know up in the San Joachim Valley have been trying to put out a contract on [Caesar] Chavez to get him knocked off for organizing the migrant workers. They're sweet people.

[1] *The Hitchhiker* was released by RKO during the Hughes regime. Mainwaring's name was taken off the film so Hughes (who had fired Mainwaring from RKO) would release it.

[2] Nick Musuraca, the cameraman, was not aware of any pot smoking on the set.

Out of the Past

TOM FLINN

In the development of any art movement (or film genre) there comes a point well after the initial breakthrough has been accomplished when the themes and ideas that marked the development of the style or genre reappear in countless elaborations, producing works of greater complexity if less originality than those that defined the style or initiated the genre. Usually termed "decadent" or "baroque" by historians, these later efforts are frequently dismissed as "more of the same" at the time they are produced, though they often seem more interesting in retrospect than the "classic" works they followed. The bleak, pessimistic style/genre called film noir that developed in Hollywood during the 1940s, initiated by such landmark films as *The Maltese Falcon* (1941) and *Double Indemnity* (1943), did not escape the sort of artistic evolution (and concomitant value judgments) described above, and the time is surely ripe for a reappraisal of some of the late-blooming "noirs" of the forties. It would be hard indeed to find a better example of the "baroque" phase of film noir than RKO's *Out of the Past* (1947, directed by Jacques Tourneur), a veritable motherlode of noir themes and stylizations.

Closely based on *Build My Gallows High,* a crime novel by Daniel Mainwaring (under the pseudonym of Geoffrey Homes), *Out of the Past* is a direct descendent of the hard-boiled school of detective fiction, owing a particular debt to Dashiell Hammett's *The Maltese Falcon.* Although there are many superficial similarities in plot, it is the moral ambiance of Hammett's novel (and Huston's film) that provides the most obvious link with *Out of the Past.* In contrast to the traditional detective yarn, the emphasis in these hard-boiled works is not on "whodunit." Murder is never just a clearcut puzzle to be solved by clever sleuthing. The problem in the last act of hard-boiled drama is to find an explanation people will buy, and, more important, someone to take the rap and satisfy the conviction-hungry police. Both *The Maltese Falcon* and *Out of the Past* contain scenes where the protagonists openly discuss choosing a fall guy from their midst, scenes in which the ostensible hero and ostensible villains appear to be motivated by the same sort of pragmatic cynicism.

In considering the style/genre of film noir the archetypal importance of the detective hero and the attractive villains of *The Maltese Falcon* can hardly be overemphasized. Certainly Robert Mitchum's chain-smoking detective, garbed in trenchcoat and dark hat is the iconographic equivalent of Bogart's Sam Spade,[1] while Whit Sterling (Kirk Douglas in *Out of the Past*), though he lacks the picturesque bulk of Caspar Gutman (Sydney Greenstreet in *The Maltese Falcon*), shares Gutman's status as an aristocrat of crime. When confronted by their respective detective adversaries, Sterling and Gutman admire the operatives' laconic good sense and show their admiration by speaking to them as equals, rather than adopting the superior tone they use when addressing their underlings. Similarly, Kathi Moffat (Jane Greer in *Out of the Past*), although hardly as genteel as Brigid O'Shaughnessy (Mary Astor in *The Maltese Falcon*), shares Miss O'Shaughnessy's ability to slip chameleonlike from one guise to another, no matter how incriminating the situation. Thus in both films, the protagonist, when confronted by the "performance" of his femme fatale, remarks in mocking admiration, "You're good, you're very good" (Bogart to Astor), which is escalated to "You're wonderful, you're magnificent" (Mitchum to Greer)[2] An interesting example of the baroque elaboration of characters in *Out of the Past* is provided by the presence of Meda Carson (Rhonda Fleming), a second femme fatale whose "Junior League patter" with Mitchum displays the same sort of surface gentility that characterized Hammett's Brigid O'Shaughnessy.

Whatever its similarities to *The Maltese Falcon* in moral tone, characters, and confrontations, *Out of the Past* is structurally and stylistically very different. Where *Falcon,* although based on a novel, is playlike in its relatively close adherence to the unities of time and place, its paucity of locations, and its linear narration, *Out of the Past* is novelistic in its episodic expansiveness, its exotic locales, and its complex narrative form. Stylistically, *Out of the Past* is characterized by a significant use of location shooting that skillfully combined with studio footage yields a more realistic appearance than the studio-bound look of *The Maltese Falcon,* while avoiding the inexpressive verism of such "documentary" features of the same period as *Call Northside 777.*

Perhaps *Out of the Past*'s most striking departure from *The Maltese Falcon* is its episodic five-part structure. Like John Brahm's *The Locket* (RKO, 1948), *Out of the Past* has a plot that might easily be described as Byzantine. The first episode, which was filmed on location in the mountain resort town of Bridgeport, California, sets the realistic tone for the rest of the film. After a series of mountain vistas behind the credits, the camera pans across a road to a highway sign covered with familiar names—Reno, Los Angeles, Bishop—which anchor the film in the "real" world. Next comes a shot with the camera actually mounted on the back of a dark convertible behind a black-clad stranger who cruises slowly down Bridgeport's main drag, stopping at the gas station run by Jeff Bailey (Robert Mitchum).[3] Getting no information as to Bailey's whereabouts from the deaf-mute boy attendant (Dickie Moore), the stranger crosses the street to the diner where the garrulous proprietress provides him with all the local gossip he needs to locate Bailey. Does this sound familiar? With good reason, since this opening is very reminiscent of "The Killers," Hemingway's famous short story that Robert Siodmak had just filmed (from a John Huston script) in 1946. Yet there are important differences, not the least of which is the fact that the forces from Jeff Bailey's past are not bent on his immediate destruction.[4] Informed of the stranger's arrival by the boy, Jeff returns from a mountain lake where he has been fishing with his girlfriend,

Ann (Virginia Huston). Jeff confronts the stranger, who turns out to be Joe Stefanos (Paul Valentine), a former acquaintance, in a subtly choreographed scene (shot by Tourneur in largely one take) in which the actors' icy breaths underline the menacing import of Stefanos' summoning Jeff to meet his boss, Whit Sterling, at Lake Tahoe. At nightfall Jeff, who has in the meantime donned a trenchcoat (an important iconographic clue that he is about to resume his former profession), picks up Ann,[5] who will drive with him to Tahoe and return his car to Bridgeport.

During the trip to Tahoe Jeff narrates the pertinent details of his past to Ann in a far-flung flashback that ranges from New York to Acapulco, San Francisco, and Los Angeles. This extended flashback, which forms the second major segment of *Out of the Past,* is bathed in the fatalistic modulations of Mitchum's baritone commentary. The text he reads is the same sort of colorful, first-person narration that was so important to Hammett (in the Continental Op novels) and Chandler (in nearly everything he wrote) and which became a staple device of film noir, an outstanding feature of such films as *Double Indemnity, Murder My Sweet, Criss Cross,* and *Sunset Boulevard*.[6] The stories and situations in these films differ substantially, but the mood created by the narrator, be he Fred McMurray, Burt Lancaster, William Holden, or Robert Mitchum, is always the same—a mood that translates into a vision of a cool, harsh world ruled by an inexorable fate, a world view just a half-step away from the bleak, irrational universe of the existentialists.[7]

Jeff begins his story in New York where as Jeff Markham he worked as a private investigator. Whit Sterling, a big-time gambler, hires Jeff and his partner, Fisher (Steve Brodie) to locate Kathi Moffat, Sterling's mistress, who has run off with $40,000 after putting one shot out of four in her "protector." The flashback opens in Sterling's apartment (all the New York scenes are studio interiors) during the initial meeting between the still-convalescing Sterling and the detectives. Sterling's man Friday, Joe Stefanos and Jeff's partner, Fisher, quickly discredit themselves, Stefanos with an emotional outburst against the newspapers, and Fisher with an ill-timed wisecrack ("A dame with a gun is like a guy with a knitting needle"), thereby disqualifying themselves from the special, touchy understanding developing between Jeff and Sterling. As interpreted by a smiling, gracious Kirk Douglas, Sterling is clearly no ordinary hoodlum. He may cheat on his income taxes, or turn a blind eye while Stefanos collects a bad debt, but he does have a code of sorts, a gambler's credo that can be reduced to "Don't welch on a bet or an agreement." Jeff accepts the case knowing the implacable nature of Sterling's desire to get Kathi back, but little realizing the sadistic drives that underlie Sterling's smooth exterior.

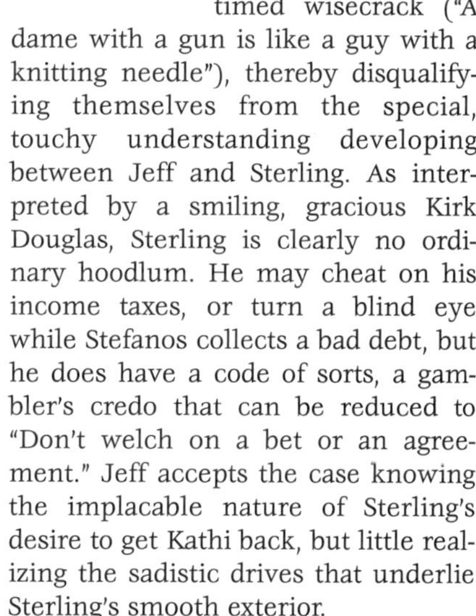

The only other New York scene, introduced by a closeup of a jazz trumpeter, takes place in a Harlem nightclub where Jeff interviews Kathi Moffat's maid. This curious encounter mirrors the moral ambiguities of the film. Jeff lies to the maid about working for Sterling and she lies to him about Kathi's destination. Yet, in spite of these deceptions and the obvious racial barrier (Jeff is the only white in the club), a kind of rapport develops between Jeff and the maid, who provides him with the information he needs about Kathi's vaccination and forty pounds of excess baggage. Tourneur filmed the interview in one shot with Mitchum's back to the camera, concentrating on the reactions of the maid and her escort.[8]

Jeff quickly traces Kathi's excess baggage to Mexico City and from there to Acapulco, where he finally catches up with her. Striding out of the Mexican sunlight in a white dress and floppy hat, Kathi is stunningly self-assured in the face of possible discovery. Intrigued by a veiled invitation, Jeff is tempted to dally with her, but his sense of duty propels him to the telegraph office, which, as fate and the Mexican custom of the afternoon siesta would have it, is closed. This excuse is all Jeff needs to begin a romance with Kathi. Typical atypical tourists, they loll in bars, visit the casino, tryst on moonlit beaches. The climax of their romance comes during a rainstorm that drives them to Kathi's bungalow, where, just as they start to get better acquainted, a gust of wind blows open the door, knocking over a lamp and plunging the room into darkness. After this sexual "bus"[9] the camera discreetly tracks toward the door. Next comes symbolic panning shot of the rain outside, followed by another straight cut to a shot of Jeff fully clothed getting up to close the door. The Breen-office-impose discretion of this dissolveless sequence cannot hide its metaphorical content. In spite of the complete lack of specific sexual details, no attempt is made to disguise the extramarital nature of the relationship between Jeff and Kathi, which in itself must have been quite daring in 1947.[10]

Kathi seduces Jeff's professional conscience by denying she took the $40,000 and by declaring her hatred for Sterling and what he has done to her. During the rainy night Jeff and Kathi decide to run away together. The next day, just as they are about to implement their plans, Sterling and Stefanos arrive to check up on Jeff, precipitating some forced but effective suspense before they depart, unaware that Kathi is still in Acapulco. Once Sterling has gone, Jeff and Kathi flee to San Francisco, where they live a shadowy existence in the urban half-world, patronizing dark cinemas and small out-of-the-way clubs.

Fate puts an end to their metropolitan idyll when Jeff is spotted by his ex-partner, Fisher, at the racetrack. The fatalism of this chance meeting is underlined by its setting in front of the payoff windows at the track. Fisher, who has been retained by Sterling to find Jeff, immediately begins to shadow the couple. Jeff and Kathi split up, agreeing to meet at a mountain cabin after Jeff has shaken Fisher. But Fisher follows Kathi and interrupts their reunion with a blackmail demand. Kathi panics, shoots Fisher, and flees, leaving Jeff with the corpse and thoughtlessly forgetting her bankbook, which shows an incriminating balance of $40,000. Shattered by this strange sequence of events, Jeff drifts to Bridgeport, changes his name to Bailey, and opens the gas station.

The flashback ends as Jeff reaches Sterling's Tahoe estate. The short but crucial third section of *Out of the Past* occurs there as Jeff confronts first Sterling and then Kathi. As affable as ever, Sterling welcomes Jeff back to the fold, informing him of a job he can do to make up for the one he bungled. Jeff is extremely suspicious of this "opportunity" and finds little comfort in the fact that Kathi has evidently regained her position as Sterling's mistress. But the "job" Sterling outlines, getting important documents from a slippery tax lawyer in San Francisco who has saved Sterling one million dollars and now threatens to turn him in to the IRS, seems simple enough and Jeff is in no position to refuse. Kathi meets with Jeff furtively in his bedroom, but he is uninterested in her explanations and rejects her attempt at a rapprochement.

San Francisco is the setting for the fourth and most complex episode. Jeff's contact there is Meda Carson, secretary to the blackmailing lawyer, Leonard Eels. Jeff has been told that he is simply supposed to break into Eels's office and steal the documents, but his suspicions are aroused when Meda takes him to Eels's Fulton Street apartment for cocktails. By this time Jeff has figured out that Eels is on the spot and endeavors as best he can to warn the hapless lawyer. After dropping Meda at Eels's office, Jeff ignores her instructions and waits for her to come out. When she does, she is carrying a valise that Jeff figures contains the tax records he was supposed to steal. He hurries back to Eels's apartment, but Eels is already dead. Jeff drags Eels's body to a neighboring apartment that is being painted (shades of *Crime and Punishment*) and hides the corpse in a closet. Then he heads for Meda's apartment, where he finds not Meda, but Kathi, who is phoning the manager of Eels's apartment building, asking him to check up on Eels, thus insuring prompt discovery of the body. Needless to say, she is somewhat taken aback when the manager reports that the apartment is empty and even more disturbed when Jeff confronts her. Believing that the entire scheme has backfired, Kathi confesses that Meda has taken the documents and left an affidavit, which Kathi signed, stating that Jeff murdered Fisher, thus giving him a motive to kill Eels. In another dramatic long take Kathi momentarily switches sides and tells Jeff that Meda has deposited the records in the office of a North Beach gambling club owned by Sterling. Acting quickly, Jeff bursts into the club and makes off with the incriminating tax records. Next he makes a deal to exchange them for the affidavit, but the agreement is queered when the police, led by the apartment manager (who has finally located Eels's body), arrive at Eels's office building just as Meda is about to retrieve the affidavit. Now wanted by the police for the murder of Eels and Fisher, Jeff flees to San Francisco to hide out in the mountains near Bridgeport.

The concluding section of *Out of the Past* oscillates between Bridgeport and Tahoe. Jeff sends the deaf-mute boy to Sterling's Tahoe estate to arrange a meeting, but Whit is not there. Kathi is, however, and she sends Stefanos to follow the boy and kill Jeff. The result is a spectacular bit of action during which the boy pulls Stefanos off a forty-foot cliff with a perfect cast of his fly rod just as the gunman is about to shoot Jeff. In spite of the obvious gimmickry involved in Stefanos's death, his death has an essential rightness about it since the black-clad hoodlum is clearly out of place in the wilderness along the East Walker River. That night Jeff visits Tahoe himself, where he meets with Sterling and Kathi, demanding that Sterling provide him with a way out of the country and turn Kathi over to the police for the murder of Fisher. Facing a sure prison term for tax evasion, Sterling agrees, slapping and threatening Kathi into compliance in the film's first graphic display of the sadistic side of his nature. Jeff then drives to Bridgeport and says goodbye to Ann before returning to Tahoe, where he finds Sterling's body decorating the living-room floor. Kathi is now in charge, and she ordains that Jeff run away with her. With all the hope of clearing himself gone, Jeff is trapped. When Kathi goes upstairs to get her things, he calls the police. As their car nears a roadblock, Kathi, realizing what Jeff has done, shoots him and dies herself in the fusillade of machine-gun fire that rakes their car as it plunges into the barrier.

The film ends with a studio-imposed coda in which Ann is relieved of her romantic obligations to Jeff by the boy, who nods when she asks him if Jeff was really going away with Kathi.

The preceding plot summary, while necessarily dull, provides at least some notion of the labyrinthian nature of the film's story line. Of course, this is a characteristic *Out of the Past* shares with many other films of its era from *Passage to Marseilles* (1944) to *Nightmare Alley* (1948). What is interesting about *Out of the Past* is the way in which the complex plot structure is handled. The frame-up in San Francisco, for example, is done with no narration and a minimum of expository dialogue. The crucial scene in which the police arrive at Eels's office before the affidavit can be retrieved consists of a couple of quick long shots with no direct dialogue references and no explanation. The editing is often elliptical, Sterling's murder is not shown, nor do we see or hear Jeff call the police at the end, for the camera follows Kathi's preparation upstairs. The presumption in *Out of the Past,* as in the horror films Tourneur directed for Val Lewton, is that an alert and sensitive audience will fill in the narrative gaps.

Although he evidently did not work on the screenplay, Jacques Tourneur is responsible for much that is excellent about *Out of the Past.* In this case Tourneur was not so much an "auteur" as a "metteur en scene," but an examination of *Out of the Past* will demonstrate the importance of the director as interpreter. Tourneur's visual style, never as flashy or obvious as those of Anthony Mann or Robert Siodmak, suffuses *Out of the Past,* investing every scene with the right atmospheric ingredients. Although *Out of the Past* is just as much of a "shadow play" as any of the justly named films noir, Tourneur never lets the visuals overwhelm the actors, never resorts to extreme angles, or goes out of his way for an expressionistic effect, preferring to shoot crucial scenes in one or two shots rather than opting for more dynamic montage effects. Yet, with the aid of RKO's top cameraman, Nick Musuraca, Tourneur provides a wealth of memorable images: dark, dramatically lit interiors; stunning day-for-night shots of Mexican beaches; and clear, meticulous exteriors, all of which are well integrated into an atmospheric whole. Tourneur also deserves a lot of credit for his handling of young, inexperienced players, particularly the twenty-two-year-old Jane Greer in the crucial role of Kathi Moffat and Paul Valentine, who made his debut as Joe Stefanos. Valentine not only had the right size and look for his role, he was a ballet dancer and Tourneur made full and subtle use of his fluid, graceful movements.

More than most films noir, which typically feature a large gallery of superlative performances drawn from the seemingly inexhaustible ranks of Hollywood character actors, *Out of the Past* depends on the play of its youthful leads. Jane Greer, the youngest of the principals, managed her role with impressive skill, while Kirk Douglas, whose mannerisms had yet to become affectations, made Whit Sterling a character who is still refreshing after twenty-five years in the can. From a modern perspective Robert Mitchum is equally successful, though his stolid underplaying was greeting by exasperation from James Agee, who referred to Mitchum in typical "Timese" hyperbole as "Bing Crosby supersaturated with barbiturates." Agee in fact suggested that Mitchum confine himself to masculine pictures where he wouldn't have a chance to be "so very sleepily self-confident with the women that when he slopes into the clinches you expect him to snore in their faces." To a modern observer, especially one who has suffered through the likes of Donald Sutherland in *Klute*, Mitchum's performance seems anything but bland, but as he often did, Agee inadvertently hit on something important. The typical noir hero was, it seems, a cool, relatively impassive fellow not given to flights of fancy or passion. Compare Bogart's Sam Spade with Ricardo Cortez's interpretation of the detective as lounge lizard in the 1931 *The Maltese Falcon* and you find one of the cardinal reasons why the 1941 version is a film noir and the 1931 film is not. Only a few actors (Bogart was the foremost) had the presence and skill necessary to parlay this passivity into acting dividends without becoming locked in the frozen-face dead end of an Alan Ladd or a Lawrence Tierney[11] Mitchum, who clearly saw himself in this tradition ("I came into being during the era of ugly leading men started by Humphrey Bogart."), drew on his own resources and managed to make Jeff Bailey a fascinating sloe-eyed variant of the tough-guy hero.

It was Raymond Chandler with his British public-school education who stressed the chivalric aspects of the detective story and in Philip Marlowe created a moral hero who stood out in bold relief against a corrupt society. In comparison Jeff Bailey is a much more naturalistic detective, an extremely fallible sort of shamus, whose series of mistakes reads like an inversion of one of Marlowe's successful quests. Jeff's downfall starts when he accepts Sterling's dubious proposition. Then, having succeeded in his tainted quest, he can't resist the temptation to rescue the damsel in distress, who turns out to be one of the deadliest females since Morgan le Fay. Even if his motives are romantic and chivalric, Jeff, with his constant compromising of professional ethics, has as much or more in common with the doomed protagonists of *Double Indemnity*, *Criss Cross*, and *Sunset Boulevard* as with Marlowe. Mitchum, who even before his famous pot burst had earned the reputation of a "bad boy," recognized the anarchic aspects of his role and managed to invest something of his own nonconforming, independent spirit in Jeff Bailey, assuring his creation a unique spot in the sleazy gallery of film noir, a niche located somewhere between Philip Marlowe and Walter Neff (*Double Indemnity*), halfway between knight and knave.

In discussing *Out of the Past* I have endeavored as best I can to place it in the film noir tradition, stressing (and perhaps overemphasizing) the parallels to and borrowings from, other films. After several viewings it is a simple matter to break a film down into any number of elements, but it is another thing entirely to suggest the excellence of a film like *Out of the Past* with the mass of critical and historical verbiage involved in such an analysis, much of which contains its own built-in value judgments. One of the most pervasive and least questioned assumptions of aesthetics in the Western world since the Renaissance is the preeminent value of originality. Film critics, like their brethren in painting and music, are always looking for something new and criticizing, often unfairly, genre efforts like *Out of the Past* for not giving it to them. Admittedly the film industry had done much to foster this critical hunger for something new. With its blatantly cannibalistic practices, its odious remakes, its seemingly inexhaustible series films, Hollywood has numbed the critical palate for decades. The economics of the industry dictate that every success spawns a number of imitations and similar efforts. That's how film genres are born. The task of the critic is to wade through all the blatant rip-offs and lackluster follow-ups to find the occasional film like *Out of the Past* in which the generic elements are combined in a new pattern to create a film that can not only stand by itself, but that also resonates with the collective power of its iconographic, stylistic, and thematic components.

[1] I am amazed at the durability of the image of the trenchcoated tough guy that reappears in countless films, including Jean-Pierre Melville's *Le Samourai* (1967), a film replete with references to the American film noir tradition. *Le Samourai* in fact opens with a shot of Jeff Costello (Alain Delon) smoking alone in his room.

[2] These masculine tributes to feminine duplicity were among the favorite dialogue gambits of the era. Compare those cited with *Nightmare Alley* where Ty Power says: "You're good, you're awfully good, just about the best I've ever seen," or Bogart, again in *Dead Reckoning,* "You do awfully good."

[3] Nick Ray used a similar shot for the opening of *In a Lonely Place* (1950) and Joseph H. Lewis also had the camera mounted in the back of a car (a sedan this time) for the famous one-shot bank robbery in Gun Crazy (1949).

[4] The opening sequence of *Out of the Past* is clearly more realistic than that of *The Killers* (which was shot in a studio) and demonstrates the trend toward location shooting and surface realism evident in the late forties.

[5] Jeff just stops outside Ann's house and honks his horn, a gesture that indicates his status as an outsider in Bridgeport, where he remains a tight-lipped mystery man, accepted only by Ann and the deaf-mute boy.

[6] When Mr. Mainwaring indicated (in the interview that precedes this article) that his original plan was to have the deaf-mute boy narrate the story, the seminar broke up in laughter. But, in view of the fact that *Sunset Boulevard* was very successfully narrated by a dead man, an interior monologue by a deaf-mute is not by itself unfeasible, although the double flashback structure would have been cumbersome to say the least.

[7] Camus especially was influenced by American tough-guy literature, particularly by Horace McCoy's *They Shoot Horses Don't They,* which was extremely successful in European literary circles.

[8] While it is difficult to commend (or blame) a director for casting a black as a domestic, Tourneur, who allowed black actors from Sir Lancelot in *I Walked with a Zombie* (1943) to Rex Ingram in *Stars in my Crown* (1950) a considerable amount of dignity, handled the scene with his usual sensitivity.

[9] The shock effects ("busses") used in the Lewton unit horror productions (of which Tourneur directed the first three).

[10] Not that extramarital affairs weren't common in Hollywood films of the forties. They were. What is rare about the situation in *Out of the Past* is its explicitness (Ann asks Jeff if he has ever been married before and he replies negatively) and its duration (the narration leads us to believe that Jeff and Kathi were together for months, if not longer). The Breen office undoubtedly passed the film because both participants in this illicit relationship get killed.

[11] The success of Alan Ladd, Lawrence Tierney, Gregory Peck, and others demonstrates the increasingly minimal demands placed on masculine emoting.

From the Nightmare Factory:

HUAC AND THE POLITICS OF NOIR

PHILIP KEMP

The bourgeoisie, wherever it has got the upper hand . . . has left remaining no other nexus between man and man than naked self-interest, than callous "cash payment" . . . It has resolved personal worth into exchange value.

—Marx and Engels,
The Communist Manifesto

It has often been observed that the key period of American film noir—roughly 1945 to 1954—coincides neatly with the years of the great anti-Communist witch-hunt, of HUAC (House Committee on Un-American Activities), McCarthy, and the blacklist. Noir, with its pervasive atmosphere of fear and paranoia, its sense of hopeless fatalism ("Fate or some mysterious force," muses the hero of *Detour,* "can put the finger on you or me for no good reason at all"), presents an oblique response to the political climate of those years. Less often considered—and less easy to delineate—is the political *content* of the cycle: noir as statement, rather than as response.

Where Danger Lives, one of the lesser-known noir movies, was made by RKO in 1950. Robert Mitchum, a surgeon at San Francisco Hospital, becomes infatuated with one of his patients, an attempted suicide, played by Faith Domergue. She evades his suggestions of marriage, talking of an elderly father "living on borrowed time." Mitchum confronts this obtrusive parent (a regrettably brief appearance from Claude Rains, silkily malignant), who turns out to be Domergue's husband. They quarrel; Rains hits Mitchum with a poker, Mitchum knocks him down and seemingly kills him. The guilty couple take off, heading for the Mexican border. En route Mitchum displays progressive signs of delayed concussion, and Domergue's behavior grows increasingly unstable. Finally, holed up in a sleazy border town, he realizes that she must be psychotic, and that it was she who murdered Rains. He accuses her; she tries to kill him, but is gunned down by the police.

If the plot of *Where Danger Lives* seems familiar, it may be because much of it anticipates *Angel Face,* made two years later—also for RKO—by Otto Preminger, in which Mitchum's ambulance driver gets entangled with the even more lethal Jean Simmons. Simmons's cool, accomplished performance easily outclasses the relentless pouting of Domergue, and indeed *Angel Face* is by some way the better movie of the two. Though both

Mitchum and Rains make the most of their roles, and Nicholas Musuraca—after John Alton, probably the finest noir cinematographer—casts some atmospheric shadows, *Where Danger Lives* is minor-league noir at best. Nevertheless, it remains an intriguing film for two reasons, neither of which has much to do with its artistic quality. First, because it can be read, without any strain on the text, as a dramatic exposition of the Marxist dictum quoted above. Secondly, because it was almost certainly never intended as any such thing.

Mitchum, we learn from the start, is a dedicated and selfless doctor, working fifteen hours at a stretch, making up bedtime stories ("Things looked pretty bad for Elmer the elephant") for the children in his ward. In fact, the only unselfish people who appear in the film are the staff of this public hospital—among them Mitchum's girlfriend, a figure of angelic forbearance played by Maureen O'Sullivan (wife of John Farrow, the film's director). But already the lure of the cash nexus threatens to rupture the world of socialized altruism. A young patient accuses Mitchum of being about to "go away."

> NURSE (*with hint of reproach*): I told him you were leaving us, doctor—to go into private practice.
> MITCHUM (*embarrassed*): Well, I won't be going for a couple of weeks . . .

And enter, on cue, Domergue, incarnation of the acquisitive instinct, to lure him into a world of gaudy nightclubs, where the patrons sip cocktails out of coconut shells. Just in case we should find this acceptable face of capitalism superficially attractive, however, the film loses no time in exposing the ugly impulses that lie behind it.

In his confrontation with Mitchum, Rains expounds the basis of his marriage to Domergue: a textbook illustration of "personal worth resolved into exchange value." Margot married me for my money. I married her for her—youth. We both got what we wanted—after a fashion." This revelation offers Mitchum his last chance of escape, back to O'Sullivan and social responsibility. He stays, and is drawn into the exchange of violence that precipitates him into the shadowland of venality.

From here on in, Domergue's values rule. Mitchum, gripped by creeping paralysis of his social conscience ("My whole left side's beginning to get numb"), has abdicated control. They fell southward, through a society deformed and corrupted by the lust for cash. In Fresno, a used-car dealer (a fine portrayal of chortling rapacity from Tol Avery) swiftly sizes up their situation and forces them to swap their plush limousine for a rickety truck. Passing through a small township, they collide with a drunken Mexican, and to avoid questions buy him off with the connivance of the kindly, white-haired local doctor. Thirty miles from the border, they are arrested—because Mitchum has no beard. The town is holding a Whiskers Week, a pretext to con $25 out of unwary passers-by.

And so finally to the border town of Nogales—a city of dreadful night where the mercenary instinct has supplanted all other human impulses. A cigar-chomping pawnbroker (a statue of blind justice on ironic display among his stock) allows them $1,000 on Domergue's $9,000 bracelet, and passes them on to the next-door theatre manager, who in turn hands them over to a seedy impresario prepared to smuggle them across the border for $1,000. ("American dollars—cash.") When Mitchum protests, the pawnbroker materializes to clinch the deal: "Young fella—how *are* things back in San Francisco?" The circle of venality is complete. Only with the death of Domergue, dark angel of avarice, is Mitchum set free, waking in a clean white hospital room to O'Sullivan's forgiving smile.

A nightmarish interrogation scene from *T-Men,* directed byAnthony Mann, screenplay by John C. Higgins.

It is my determination to make RKO one studio where the work of Communist sympathizers will be impossible.
—Howard Hughes

In 1950 RKO, Cinderella of the Hollywood majors, lay in the erratic grip of Howard Hughes. That same year shooting began on *Jet Pilot,* surely the least Sternbergian of Sternberg's movies, in which John Wayne as a U.S. airman persuades Janet Leigh, bizarrely cast as his Russian counterpart, of the superiority of the American way of life by flying her to Palm Springs and feeding her on steak.

Jet Pilot, planned as the *Hell's Angels* of the jet age, was a project especially dear to Hughes's heart, and by all accounts this "right-wing camp on a comic strip level" (as Andrew Sarris described it) closely reflected his political outlook. As far as anyone knows, Hughes never voted in his life, impartially regarding all politicians, Republican or Democrat, as commodities to be purchased when they could be of use. Only one cause ever engaged his interest: anti-Communism. According to his chief of staff, Bill Gay, Hughes "felt that Communism versus free enterprise was such an important issue in our time. It was one of the few issues in his life that he felt strongly about." Strongly enough not only to fire the writer Paul Jarrico, who had taken the Fifth Amendment before HUAC, but to remove his credit from *The Las Vegas Story,* a vapid Jane Russell vehicle, and, when the Screen Writers Guild arbitrated in Jarrico's favor, to fight the Guild through the courts, and win.

Yet this was the man whose studio could produce, simultaneously with *Jet Pilot,* a film so deeply critical of capitalist values as to border on

Dennis O'Keefe (left) goes undercover as a government agent on the trail of counterfeiters, in *T-Men*.

Marxist allegory. It might be imagined that a routine thriller like *Where Danger Lives* would simply have been beneath the boss's notice—but in this case, apparently not. Hughes took a close interest in the career of Faith Domergue, one of his less successful protégées, and this picture marked the final attempt to establish her as a popular sex symbol.

If Hughes seems an unlikely exponent of socialism, the same could be said of those directly concerned in making the film. The director, John Farrow, was a Catholic, devout to the point of excess. Holder of an LL.D. from Loyola University. (California), author of *Damien the Leper* and *Pageant of the Popes,* he was made Knight of the Holy Sepulchre in 1937 for his services to the church. "The house was always filled with priests," his daughter Mia recalled. "To some extent he looked down on Hollywood."

The screenplay of *Where Danger Lives* was written by the English-born Charles Bennett, who scripted several of Hitchcock's best British movies (*The Man Who Knew Too Much, Sabotage, The 39 Steps*). During the war he worked for the FBI and U.S. Naval Intelligence. Leo Rosten, on whose story Bennett's screenplay was based, was the successful and prolific author of *Hollywood: The Movie Colony, The Movie Makers, The Joys of Yiddish, and The Education of Hyman Kaplan,* among much else. His view of the witch-hunt years was expressed in a

1956 article in *Look*: "The record of what the party henchmen *tried* to do in the movie colony makes an appalling story. They lied, they deceived, they manipulated, they cheated . . . They used the psychological tactics of the Gestapo and the political tactics of the gutter . . . The scars they left on Hollywood are deep and tragic." He was, of course, referring to the Communists.

Rosten was also at one time Special Consultant to the U.S. Secretary of War. Neither he, Farrow, or Bennett ever attracted the attention of HUAC, and all three continued to work in the movie business throughout the blacklist years.

None of which, admittedly, rated as conclusive disproof of leftist tendencies, and it would be tempting to concoct a Le Carré-esque scenario, with Soviet moles from U.S. Intelligence infiltrating Hollywood for propaganda purposes. Tempting, but implausible and in any case superfluous. For one thing, no closet Marxist drip-feeding subversive attitudes into the studio product would ever, at a time of rabid anti-Red scares, have dared mount so blatant an assault on the capitalist ethos as *Where Danger Lives.* The very stridency of its polemic attests to the innocence of its intent. For another, the body of film noir offers far too many similar, if rarely so thoroughgoing, examples of left-wing slant to be credibly attributed to a handful of individuals.

We are interested to see if there existed something that might be called a "structured sensibility," that is a complex of both conscious assumptions and taken for granted, half-articulated assumptions about art and politics which a number of people held in common.

—Jim Cook, Alan Lovell,
Coming to Terms with Hollywood

It's clear that defining the political stance of a group of films as amorphous as film noir is a problematic undertaking. Noir, most critics agree, is less a genre than a matter of mood, styling, and atmosphere shared by a number of movies made at a particular juncture—economic and technical—of cinematic development. There is considerable disagreement over which films can be admitted into the noir canon. Raymond Durgnat, in his trail-blazing article in *Cinema,* provocatively included *King Kong* and *2001* in his list. Other, stricter taxonomists have preferred to rule out all films in color, or made after 1955, or with happy endings.

As for noir's politics, many writers would deny that it has any. In Colin McArthur's view, "The meanings spoken by the film noir are not *social,* relating to the problems . . . of a particular society, but *metaphysical,* having to do with angst and loneliness as essential elements of the human condition." Certainly a political slant, of any kind, can't be demanded as a prerequisite component of noir, and the idea of a right-wing noir movie involves no contradiction in terms. (*Pickup on South Street* comes to mind, though Fuller's film is ambiguous in its ideology, as well as tackier specimens like *I Was a Communist for the FBI.*) But even if explicit political statements are rare in film noir, it can be argued that most of these pictures share a set of implicit, perhaps even inadvertent attitudes to society that readily lend themselves to interpretation as left-wing.

There were of course avowed leftists, of various shades, among the writers and directors of film noir, and many of them introduced socialist views into their work, if not necessarily with the express aim of advancing the cause. As Abraham Polonsky put it, "I don't ask myself, 'Now what are the social issues I have to realize here?' There's a Marxian world view behind my films, not because I plan it that way. That's what I am." Most of them fell victim, one way or another, to McCarthyism: some recanted

(Rossen, Dmytryk), some were blacklisted (Howard Koch, Albert Maltz, Polonsky), some driven into exile (Losey, Dassin), some self-exiled (Welles, Huston). But attitudes that would seem, on the face of it, to derive from equally leftward thinking frequently recur in noir movies made by people with no known left affiliations. If we reject the notion of some vast, clandestine network permeating every Hollywood studio, we seem to be faced with only one other option: that for nearly a decade one aspect of American filmmaking was pervaded by a set of political assumptions so widely held as to have become virtually undetectable both by those who expressed them and those who virulently opposed them.

To develop this thesis thoroughly would need a volume of detailed analysis beyond the scope of an article. But we can perhaps isolate a few notably recurrent themes. These themes are almost wholly negative in scope—not suprisingly, given the inherent pessimism of the noir cycle. Descriptive rather than prescriptive, film noir explores the symptoms of a deformed society, but rarely suggests remedies. (Much the same could, after all, be said of *Das Kapital.*)

1. Pecunia voncit omnia. "Has money completely lost its power? Is everyone now dominated by love?" demands Claude Rains in *Rope of Sand,* pained by Burt Lancaster's refusal to cooperate. Of course it hasn't, and everyone isn't. Lancaster, ennobled by his love for Corinne Calvet, is a weird aberration. Elsewhere, as always in noir, the "callous cash payment" rules supreme in a society cankered by greed. Most noir protagonists, and most of the supporting players too, are motivated, like Robert Young in *They Won't Believe Me,* by an "obsessive desire to stay in the money at all costs."

The corrosive power of money is a common enough theme, not only in Hollywood cinema. But where film noir differs is that it portrays single-minded cupidity as standard, the element in which everyone swims. A 1930s gangster—Cagney, Muni, or Robinson—might be ruthless in pursuit of loot, but against him there stood the regular citizen, honest and industrious, supporter of the forces of law. The big businessmen of Capra's populist comedies were obdurate and grasping enough, but the little capitalists, the small investors, would rally round and smilingly save the day. *It's a Wonderful Life,* epitome of Capra's work, even includes its own noir sequence in James Stewart's nightmare vision of Pottersville; but the episode is explicitly canceled out by the closing scene, with its celebration of communal solvency.

2. Class warfare. Class, in pre-war Hollywood movies, was largely a source of comedy. The rich were shown as stuffy and uncomfortable, ripe—if they were lucky—for liberation through a blast of down-to-earth proletarian good sense. Working-class nouveaux riches who aped the manners of the wealthy were mocked for their pretensions, and in most cases secretly yearned to revert to their natural, unbuttoned ways.

In noir, class is no joke. It functions as an instrument of oppression, a cause of hatred and violence. *The Locket,* directed by John Brahm from a screenplay by Sheridan Gibney, furnishes a mordant parable of the wealth-based class system, and the moral and psychological distortion inflicted on those who live in it. Laraine Day is traumatized by a childhood incident when, as the daughter of a servant in a rich household, she was falsely accused of stealing by her mother's snobbish employer. The resultant kleptomaniac obsession infects her sexual relationships, causing the death of two men, the breakdown of another, and finally her own mental collapse. The locket of the title symbolizes the wealth and social privilege to which Day believes her looks and intelligence entitle her, and which she will steal and murder to attain.

3. Land of the free-for-all. Noir depicts a society largely devoid of any communal sense, where the cult of individualism and the deification of free enterprise have eroded belief in loyalty to a general good. Anyone who underestimates the ferocity of the prevailing self-interest is liable to suffer for it. "I wasn't low or dirty enough," Barry Sullivan laments in *The Gangster.* "I should have smashed the others first. That's the way the world is." In the 1930s, heroes on the run, such as Paul Muni in *I Am a Fugitive from a Chain Gang,* could usually hope to meet a few people who, out of common humanity, would help them. In *They Live by Night,* Farley Granger rashly assumes as much, and dies.

Social conscience scarcely exists in noir. It's assumed that witnesses (a whole string of them in *Phantom Lady*) can be bribed, suborned, or warned off with barely a token protest. *Kiss Tomorrow Goodbye* has Cagney effortlessly buying up an entire townful of officials. Only fools stand up for their principles, as Rita Hayworth, the lady from Shanghai, tells Orson Welles: "Everything's bad, Michael. Everything. you can't escape it or fight it. You've got to get along with it, deal with it, make terms." The nadir of this self-serving logic is attained with Billy Wilder's acerbic *Ace in the Hole,* where virtually everybody furthers personal ends at the expense of a man dying wretchedly in a subterranean crevice.

These are generalized thematic statements, attempts at a distillation of an overall ethos, and exceptions to all of them can easily be cited from this film or that. It's worth bearing in mind, though, Paul Schrader's caveat that in film noir, "the theme is hidden in the style, and bogus themes are often flaunted ('middle-class values are best') which contradict the style." The final reel, for example, may be pushing the message that crime doesn't pay; the protagonist may have wound up dead or in custody, an underling may trundle on to toss a sop to the Hays Office—"We got the whole gang rounded up, Chief." But all those petty chiselers, hustlers, and con men we met along the way are, we know, still out there making a living. A pretty slimy one, maybe, but a living all the same.

When you see a little drop of cyanide in the picture, a small grain of arsenic, something . . . which destroys our beliefs in American free enterprise and free institutions, that is Communistic.

—Rupert Hughes,
Screenwriter, HUAC witness

The paradox is evident. On the one hand a Hollywood running scared, frantic to purge itself of the least taint of leftist connections, with studio bosses eagerly (Howard Hughes, Louis B. Mayer) or reluctantly (Dore Schary, Sam Goldwyn) rooting out alleged subversives, egged on by a pack of Commie-hunters that included HUAC, the American Legion, and a chorus of journalists. And on the other hand those same studios producing, right through the hysterical years, an uninterrupted flow of pictures that could easily—had anyone wanted—have been denounced for disseminating anti-American, left-wing propaganda. Films that negate not only what Hollywood claimed it was doing, but what it wanted to do.

The factors involved here—social, political, and cultural—are clearly too complex, and too ambivalent, to allow for simple explanations. There's certainly no single answer, and possibly no wholly satisfactory answer. One aspect of the puzzle, though, must bear on the peculiarly circumscribed preoccupations of HUAC itself. For all the loudly professed alarm at the idea of Communists insinuating propaganda into Hollywood movies, the actual content of any given film seems to have been the last thing members of the committee wanted to consider.

Initially, when HUAC first turned its attention to Hollywood in 1947, a few films were subjected to perfunctory examination. These consisted mainly of such well-meaning attempts at solidarity with the Soviet war effort as *Days of Glory, North Star,* and *Song of Russia*—about as subversive, most of them, as *Mrs. Miniver.* The novelist Ayn Rand, prominent member of the Motion Picture Alliance for the Preservation of American Ideals, assured the committee that *Song of Russia* must be Communist propaganda, since it featured smiling Russians. Ginger Rogers's mother, the formidable Mrs. McMath, testified that her daughter had turned down the title role in a projected version of Dreiser's *Sister Carrie* because it was "open propaganda." Walt Disney related how the Screen Cartoonists Guild had tried to make Mickey Mouse follow the Party line, but failed to cite any cartoons where he thought that this had been accomplished.

In 1951, when HUAC launched its major series of investigations into the movie business, committee members evinced even less interest in what those they interrogated might have put into their movies. By now the committee was totally obsessed with the grotesque ritual of "naming names," whereby each witness confessing to past or present involvement with Communism was required to prove contrition by identifying fellow transgressors. These people could then in turn be subpoenaed, and so it went on. No other form of evidence

Bertolt Brecht, co-author of the brilliant screenplay for *Hangmen Also Die,* was one of the first "unfriendly witnesses" called to testify in the postwar HUAC investigations. He gave brief responses and then fled to Germany.

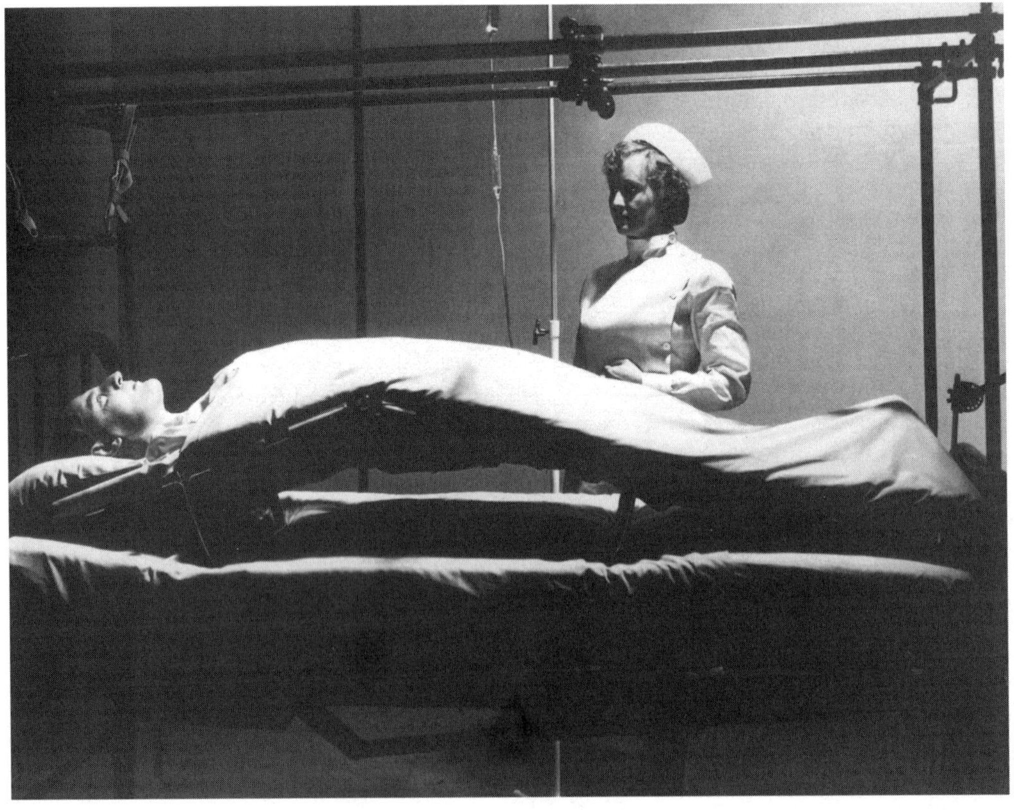

seemed, in the committee's view, to be worth bothering about.

When Elia Kazan, most famous of the recreants, confessed to one-time party membership and named former associates, he appended to his testimony a detailed account of the films he had made, defending each against possible charges of left-wing sentiments. Thus, on *Gentleman's Agreement:* "It won an Academy Award and I think it is in a healthy American tradition, for it shows Americans exploring a problem and tackling a solution. Again it is opposite to the picture which Communists present of Americans . . ." No one, though, had asked him to provide such a list, and the committee, apart from a formal word of thanks, ignored it. As far as they were concerned, Kazan had repented and offered up his quota of names, and that was all they wanted of him.

By the same token, those films subjected to boycott or picketing by such bodies as the American Legion or the Catholic War Veterans were rarely, if ever, singled out for alleged subversive content, but simply because they had provided employment for people who should have been denied it. *Born Yesterday* was widely picketed by the Catholic War Veterans, not because it might have infected its audience with un-American ideas, but for starring Judy Holliday, who was suspected of having been sympathetic to Com *munism. *Born Yesterday* was released in 1950, two or three months after *Where Danger Lives,* which nobody had dreamt of picketing.

As a country and a culture Americans were, during the cold war, governed by the questions they didn't ask.

—Victor S. Navasky,
Naming Names

In *The Interpretation of Dreams* Freud suggested that, especially under conditions of psychological stress, the "manifest content" of a dream serves as "the distorted substitute for the unconscious dream-thoughts, and this distortion is the work of the ego's forces of resistance . . . The dreamer can no more understand the meaning of his dreams than the hysteric can understand the connection and significance of his symptoms." Those thoughts that the ego refuses to countenance will be played back by the unconscious, disguised as the innocuous fictions of a dream—or a nightmare.

In her 1956 study of the impact of Communism on Hollywood movies, Dorothy B. Jones found little evidence of any Communist influence at all in the post-1945 period. This was partly because she limited her survey to films in which members of the Hollywood Ten were directly involved, but also, as she explained, because "the films of the Ten during [the post-war] years were, with a few exceptions, escapist Hollywood fare"—thus assuming as axiomatic that "escapist Hollywood fare" must be devoid of political content. It could be argued that, on the contrary, standard Hollywood product such as thrillers, romances, and gangster movies offers far more effective conduits for political ideas than overtly didactic films.

The term "escapist," too, begs a lot of questions. As Michael Wood observed in *America in the Movies,* "It seems that entertainment is not, as we often think, a full-scale flight from our problems, not a means of forgetting them completely, but rather a rearrangement of our problems into shapes which tame them . . . We should perhaps . . . ask, not how so many interesting meanings crept into flawed and ephemeral films, but how these films could possibly have kept such meanings out." Somewhere between Wood's "taming rearrangements" and Freud's "distorted substitutes" may lie a facet of one possible resolution of the paradox of film noir.

During the decade immediately following the Second World War, America underwent a prolonged trauma that, in an individual, might have been diagnosed as paranoid schizophrenia. Certain subjects, certain modes of expression, came to be seen as threatening, and were declared taboo. A whole alternative tradition of American political thought was subjected to a savage repression from which, despite the partial resurgence of the 1960s, it has never fully recovered. Doubt, dissatisfaction, the left-wing habit of healthy skepticism were declared un-American and equated with treason. Socialism was deleted from the national curriculum.

These repressed thoughts and feelings, denied overt expression, resurfaced in the California dream factory, outlet for the collective unconscious. Just as a submerged sexuality can be detected in the novels of such public Victorian writers as Dickens and Trollope, so a submerged socialism bubbles just below the restless, swirling surface of film noir. (And in both cases, probably, the phenomenon is more easily discerned today, with historical hindsight, than it was at the time.) For a while, the dream factory had unwittingly set up a slightly disreputable, wholly owned subsidiary: the nightmare factory, through whose pale windows the spectre that, a century earlier, had haunted Europe could now do the same for America.

From this viewpoint, film noir can be seen as a riposte, a sour, disenchanted flip side to the brittle optimism and flag-waving piety of much of Hollywood's "official" output of the period. All those patriotic parades along Main Street had their sardonic counterpart in the mean streets; the brighter the lights and the louder the drums *here,* the darker the shadows and the more hollow the echoes *there.* The last and darkest phase of film noir, characterized by Paul Schrader as "the period of psychotic action and suicidal impulse," coincides with the height of the anti-Communist obsession, and the decline of the cycle follows closely on the fall of McCarthy. As the hysteria loosened its grip, the national psyche no longer needed the countervailing subconscious fantasies—or, at least, not that particular kind.

Evaluations are always provisional, and perhaps they're really only testimony.
—Raymond Durgnat

Noir, alone among the cinematic categories, is an ex post facto historical construct, like the Middle Ages. People who filmed Westerns, or comedies, or biopics, knew that that was what they were doing; but nobody who made a film noir during the cycle's key period thought of it as such. (Outside France, the term didn't enter common parlance until the mid-sixties, and only such late entries as *Chinatown* or *Night Moves* were planned as self-consciously noir movies.) Hence, perhaps, the innate elusiveness of noir, in which lies much of its fascination. It evades explanation, just as it evades definition. A cinematic black hole, it seems able to ingest any amount of critical theory without losing its lean and hungry look.

Noir also—as witness this article—tends to raise more questions than it answers. "There is something very important about the idea of film noir, whether or not we are able to completely pin it down." (The quote, and the hint of desperation, come from Spencer Selby's study of noir, *The Dark City.*) Perhaps even more than most other cinematic styles, film noir depends for its impact on nonverbal, essentially visual effects, where form far outstrips content. Attempts at reinterpretation are less likely to arrive at firm conclusions than—with luck—to open up fresh perspectives for exploration. There's still no shortage of secrets lurking in those rain-washed shadows.

If You Don't Get Killed It's a Lucky Day

A CONVERSATION WITH ABRAHAM POLONSKY

LEE SERVER

Long after all the old political ideologies have been replaced by the uniform worship of a big ball of tinfoil, the consequences of the Hollywood Blacklist will still be felt. Who knows the great movies that might have been? Case in point: Abraham Lincoln Polonsky, a colorful character and original talent who fell victim to the movies' postwar purge. A lawyer, professor, little-known novelist, and radio writer, he came out of nowhere in 1947 to deliver the dynamic, richly detailed original screenplay for John Garfield's "fairy tale of the streets," *Body and Soul.* He made his directorial debut the following year with a compelling and unique film noir called *Force of Evil,* a crime drama about the numbers racket and brotherly love. *Force of Evil*'s complexity, its intellectuality, the showy dialogue that was like hard-boiled free verse, all signaled the arrival of an audacious new filmmaker. By all odds, a series of great movies should have followed this tremendous one-two punch. But it didn't happen. Suspected of harboring radical thoughts, Polonsky was run out of the business and his name did not appear on another film until 1968 and the Richard Widmark cop drama *Madigan,* directed by Don Siegel. He then returned to his long-vacant director's chair to make a strikingly original Western, *Tell Them Willie Boy Is Here,* with Robert Redford and Robert Blake. A career resumed, but there was no getting back those twenty years in the blacklistee's underground. *Force of Evil* remains his greatest achievement. At the age of eighty-seven Abe Polonsky is still in possession of a legendary wit and way with a good line of dialogue.

How are you doing?

This is too early for me. I've been lying in bed and wondering whether it's worth it to take another breath.

I've had those days.

Oh, you have it philosophically, I'm talking factually. You must remember I'm 150 years old. So all right, I'll stick around for your sake. What are we going to talk about?

I heard you and Bernard Herrmann were friends as little boys?

Yeah, we grew up together. We were friends forever. Later, when I was blacklisted, he denied he ever met me.

Oh no!

My feelings would have been hurt, but

luckily I didn't have any by then.

A lot of people found him rather difficult to get along with.

Benny? He never was difficult with me. We were old friends. His frustration was that he wanted to be an English lord, with painted pigeons flying around. Or at least to become conductor for the New York Philharmonic. But his dreams never came true.

The first time you went to Hollywood you were still working as a lawyer, right?

I was working at a law firm back east and I came here with a client, Gertrude Berg. She was going to write a screenplay during time off from the radio. She was going to write for the male version of Shirley Temple, a young man called Bobby Breen. You remember him?

I've seen him in some movies, unfortunately.

In any event, we came here and she wrote the screenplay, and I lived in style with my wife. That was in 1937. And then I came back as a writer and I was offered a five-year contract by Paramount Pictures. This was a week before I went overseas for the O.S.S., where I served in France. I went and talked to the general of the O.S.S. and he said sign the contract, it makes a good cover story for you. And I hopped planes—army planes—back and forth between coasts, and we got Paramount to issue a story saying that I was going overseas to cover the air war. So it was after I returned from the war alive that I showed up at Paramount for my five-year contract.

You wrote* Golden Earrings *for Marlene Dietrich.

She kissed me for that. *Golden Earrings* was ostensibly about the Gypsies in Europe, but by the time they got done with the film it was just a bunch of jokes. I was walking around the lot with a writer friend. I saw Alan Ladd standing on a box, doing an intimate love scene. We ran into Marlene Dietrich on the lot and she gave me a little kiss and she congratulated me. I said, "That's it?" So then she gave me a kiss that lasted two and a half weeks.

When did you and John Garfield get hooked up?

I was at Paramount and I had an assignment that was never made. I'd come in and have lunch with my friends and then leave. Enterprise Productions was just a couple of blocks away. They had a small studio with just one or two soundstages as I recall. A writer I knew was working on a boxing story for John Garfield and he was having trouble with it, trouble with censorship, and he got discouraged and took a job at Paramount. He told me, "Why don't you go talk to Garfield about a boxing story." And so I called up Garfield and walked over to see him. And in the two blocks I walked I made up the story. The story that became *Body and Soul.* It was no big deal.

So you pitched the story to them verbally when you got there?

Yeah. And they were very pleased and said, "Will you sit down. We're going to call a meeting." And while I sat down to wait I worked out the story. There was a meeting of the top brass, [David] Lowe and [Charles] Einfeld, and I pitched the story to them and they were very pleased with it. I then thanked them and got up and went to the door. Einfeld said, "Where are you going, Polonsky? We want you to write this story?" I said, "Sorry, I'm under contract to Paramount." By the time I walked back to Paramount, Louie, the guard at the front gate, told me, "They want you in the front office." And the front office informed me they had already lent me to Enterprise Studio.

So you went to work for John Garfield.

I went to work for John Garfield. And my world changed. It wasn't like Paramount. Working for him, I was perfectly free to write it the way I felt like it. He said, "Write it." And I consulted with him as the need came up. We saw each other every day, had lunch together—they had a very nice, small lunch room at Enterprise, with a good cook. It was very amiable. He liked this story. He was from New York and I was from New York, and it was a typical New York story. I came from the East Side, and in those days boxing wasn't the way it is now. There were gyms all over town, and boxing matches every week. Boxing was important to the kids in the neighborhood, poor kids. You could go in to the gyms and train and every week or so there was a boxing match and maybe you made ten dollars. And maybe if you were good you went on from there. Or you dreamed about it. Garfield liked this story I was writing.

When did the director, Robert Rossen, come on board?

Rossen was hired after the screenplay was finished. He had directed one picture before that. And they hired him because he had talent. And he was a radical. So they hired him.

Was it important that he shared Garfield's political views?

Garfield was sympathetic to lefties, you know. He had been in Group Theatre. But he really had nothing to do with politics. He liked to play cards and go out with girls. Also act. A marvelous actor. He was a trained actor and he came prepared. I directed him later, and I can tell you he was absolutely marvelous to work with-sensitive, gifted, and prepared.

***Did you watch Robert Rossen directing* Body and Soul?**

Yes, because I had to make sure he didn't write lines. He had promised not to write a single line without permission but he started slipping pieces of yellow paper to the actors. One of them showed me, and so Rossen was called into the office by Garfield and fired. His lawyer came and worked it out, he promised not to do it again, and he didn't.

So I guess you didn't get along with Rossen?

Nobody got along with Rossen, don't you understand? He was a very disagreeable person. Now I can get along with a disagreeable person, just as I can get along with an agreeable person . . . but in a different way. I learned a lot from him. He knew his business and went about it. He put energy into his work. Put energy into his directing. A lot of people don't do that. I was on the set every day, watching, and learning. That was why I thought it would be possible for me to direct a picture. And I did. And I watched Jimmy [James Wong] Howe, the cameraman. I was a friend of his, and he had been a combat cameraman during the war and so he used a lot of the techniques he learned in combat when he shot the film.

I understand the ending of* Body and Soul *was a matter of dispute. Rossen wanted an unhappier ending?

The film had a happy ending only in the sense that instead of selling out, he doesn't. If you call that a happy ending, I don't know. That's when I had a fight with Rossen. I mean a dispute with Rossen. Because Rossen wanted him to get shot and killed and end up in a garbage can when he left the ring because he had broken the rules. But I said that was stupid. It ends with him defying the bad guys but you don't have to take it to the next step and show what happens.

***How did you come to move into the director's chair for* Force of Evil?**

Hollywood, like everywhere else in the United States, is very impressed by success. *Body and Soul* made money. It was a hit. When it was a hit, I was a hit. I had never directed anything. But I figured I could do it. And I could. I knew that was where the fun was. The director spends the money. And it's harder to replace him. You can get rid of him, but it's a very expensive hobby. Getting rid of the writer is cheaper. With a director, the picture's started, you see, so the best thing is to go on with what you have. You hardly ever change directors.

So you went and asked Garfield if you could direct a picture?

I had spoken of directing, and he said, "Do you want to direct the next project?" And I did. He said, "Okay, do it. But, remember, it has to be a melodrama." And I had no problem with that. I knew what I wanted to do once he said "Do it." I had this wonderful book, *Tucker's People*, which is a melodrama indeed. But it was a long, long book, drawn out, with lots of characters and it would be my job to make it work as a movie.

Ira Wolfert wrote it. Did you know him?

Wolfert was a pretty famous guy, a famous reporter. He had written a prize-winning book called *American Guerrilla in the Philippines.* And he had covered Dewey's war on the rackets in New York. I met him and his whole family, and I brought him out here. He lived at the beach in the house of a friend of his called Donald Ogden Stewart. And we met every day to talk over the book and how I wanted to make the picture.

You collaborated on the screenplay?

No, he couldn't write a screenplay to save his life. I sent him home after we finished talking. I said, "If you want to write a screenplay, go ahead and write it. But, remember, I'm writing this screenplay." That's it. He died not long ago. A good writer. The picture has a lot from the book in it. But the picture is mine. It represents my way of telling the story, my language, not Wolfert's. I gave him a co-writing credit because we worked on the script, talking it over. I didn't have to do it. But I thought because I was going to be the director I could spare a credit and I thought it would be fair to give it to him.

It's a very unconventional screenplay in many ways—the literary quality of the dialogue and the voice-over narration.

I made a deliberate attempt to make an experimental film, if I could. And I did.

The movie doesn't make it easy for the audience. You don't tell them "John Garfield is bad. Thomas Gomez is good." They have to think for themselves how they feel about these people. Gomez presents himself as his brother's moral antithesis, but he's very self-deluding.

Of course he's deluding himself. "I'm not a crook like Tucker!" No, he's a smaller crook, as his brother tells him. Everyone is self-serving. Except the girl and she knows a little too much, anyhow. For a shy young lady she's very experienced, isn't she? Well, that's part of the story too. You don't make a story about a noble person. You make a picture about a corrupt society in which people sometimes show elements of character which you didn't expect them to have. In the end, Garfield is going to go against Tucker. But what Garfield wants is revenge for his brother's death. He doesn't want to go over to the other side, he just wants revenge.

You don't feel his character had changed?

He is changed because he got his brother killed. But the change isn't from being bad to being good. This is the story of the love between these two brothers.

What did Garfield want to know about the character as he played him?

I had a very interesting discussion with him. He read the script and he said, "Hey, it's a little intellectual, isn't it? It's about a lawyer." And I said, "Yeah." He said, "It's really not my field." I said, "It's your field, don't worry." I went out to a secondhand pawn shop and I got a Phi Beta Kappa key and a gold chain and a watch. And I went to Garfield and I put them on him. He looked at himself in the mirror and said, "Got it." That's an actor!

Did you spend a lot of time thinking about the look and the technical aspects of the film? The style of photography you wanted.

I had a very famous cameraman, George Barnes. And he had been shooting sixty-year-old female stars so they would look thirty years old. That makes for very soft lighting, you know? We did a day's shooting. He lit it quite softly and I said, "That's not the look I want." He said, "Well, tell me the look you want." I did not know how to describe it because I didn't know film or lights. So I went out and got the Edward Hopper paintings and showed them to him. He said, "Oh . . . single source lighting." And that was that. Then, I thought it was important that we shoot those things we did in New York. To have that bridge was very important. But all that stuff we got looked great: Trinity Church, the buildings, everything. New York is my city and no one had to tell me what to shoot. We had no problems, either. Bob Aldrich was my assistant director and he made sure it all went well. The police cooperated. Everybody was paid off.

What was the reaction to* Force of Evil *when it came out?

Well, the film was praised, but it didn't get very good distribution. Its reputation has built up through the years. It wasn't like *Body and Soul,* which was a hit from the moment it emerged. This was darker, a little more brutal, dealt with more complex material and so on. *Body and Soul* was a fairy tale of the streets, right? Poor boy makes good. But this was nothing like that—no one makes good in this picture.

You sound like you were happy directing. I suppose you thought that was what you'd be doing from then on.

I certainly did. But I got interrupted.

When did you first feel the heat of the political witch-hunt?

It was around by the time I did *Force of Evil.* It was in the air. It was part of the cold war. The blacklist was already happening to people. It was inevitable that it was going to happen to me too unless I changed my position, which I wasn't about to do. So . . .

You seem to have taken it more philosophically than some.

I'm not a panicky type of person. I was in the O.S.S. during World War II. If I'm a panicky kind of person, is that the kind of job they're going to give me? That doesn't mean I don't feel sad. When I feel sad, I do what everybody else does, I fall down on the ground and hope for the best.

You wrote under the table during the blacklist. What features did you write?

I did *Odds Against Tomorrow,* with Harry Belafonte. Harry Belafonte approached me with this book. The heist in the story depends on one of the characters being black, but the character in the book is a kind of cowardly, creepy-crawly type of person. That's not the kind of person Harry's going to act. So I rewrote the whole story, wrote the script, and gave it the character it has in the film. Now the Harry character is strong and good opposition for the racist, Robert Ryan character. I worked for Harry on many projects. The Amistad story that was just made into a movie? We had that all prepared forty years ago. I researched it all at a library in Harlem.

But Harry could never get anybody to film it.

How much of a secret would it be that you were doing the script? Did Robert Wise know, for instance?

Harry put the name of a young black writer on the script. But people knew. Wise tells how he came to meet the Afro-American who did the screenplay "and it turned out to be you." It's a very good picture. Well directed and acted. And the dialogue was great. I can't praise my work enough! I was just given public credit for it, by the way, forty years later.

They didn't use the term film noir at the time you were making* Force of Evil, *but you've probably heard it often enough since then. Why do you think there were all these dark, pessimistic films in this period?

I don't know what inspired it. They were just melodramas, with perhaps a more intensive tone running underneath. If you want an answer, think of what had gone on. An extraordinary, terrible war. Concentration camps, slaughter, atomic bombs, people killed for nothing. That can make anybody a little pessimistic.

The Novel and Films of *Night and the City*

PAUL DUNCAN

In 1937, Gerald Kersh was the assistant editor of *Courier* magazine. He was paid a pittance and couldn't afford anywhere to stay, so publisher Norman Kark allowed Kersh the luxury of sleeping in the editorial offices. It was indeed a luxury because the preceding years had seen Kersh sleeping rough on park benches and in seedy Soho establishments—the settings that would inspire his best writing. Then things changed: Kersh sold his manuscript of his third book, *Night and the City,* to Michael Joseph (book one was withdrawn the day it was published due to libel action from three uncles and a cousin); he got married to Alice Rostron; moved into a proper London home; received respectable reviews for the book (published March 1938); and began to work regularly, and prolifically, for newspapers and magazines.

After the Second World War (Kersh deserted from the Coldstream Guards to become an American colonel and ended up at the liberation of Paris), on his first trip to America, he sold the film rights to *Night and the City.* In a letter to his brother Cyril, a noted newspaperman on Fleet Street, he wrote, "As you know, Hollywood bought *Night and the City* for $40,000. This makes me the world's most highly paid writer: all they are using is the title. At $10,000 a word, had I written *War and Peace* I'd not only be immortal but own General Motors in the bargain . . . when they showed me that script I told them to have it suitably perforated and hang it in a tramp's lavatory . . . "

Was Gerald Kersh justified in writing this? Had Hollywood chewed up his characters and ideas and regurgitated a mess of a film? Or was the City of Light capturing the spirit, mood, and message of the book? Let's take a closer look . . .

As one reviewer put it, "This novel of the London underworld has something of the realism of a Hogarth picture and the satire of a Swift. Pimps, prostitutes, panderers, petty crooks, and odd characters move about in low joints and nightclubs, fleecing and being fleeced by each other."

The novel begins with a description of American Henry sauntering down a Soho street in his sharp suit and brimmed hat, flicking coins, cultivating a Hollywood accent, and talking in terms of dollars instead of pounds. This is ponce (pimp) Harry Fabian, born in the gutter and never to leave it. He lives on the immoral earnings of Zoë, his girl, a lovely streetwalker of twenty-three who, at present, can make money easily.

They live on Rupert Street, and their marketplace is Leicester Square. Their money is spent in nightclubs on whiskey at £2 a bottle and chocolates at twelve shillings a pound. Harry has a wide circle of confederates; Figler, for instance—"Looking at him, you had an impression of a large quantity of something soft poured into a smallish black suit with a pin-stripe, and overflowing at the wrists and collar." Figler makes his living by long-firming, buying on credit and selling for cash, then starting another firm when the first one goes bust. Harry and Figler join forces to promote all-in wrestling contests—a dirty game, because neither trusts the other, and neither is interested in fair play or the sport.

The two other major characters are lovers: Adam, a young sculptor having a hard time expressing his art because he can't make ends meet, and Helen, a decent girl, presently a dance hostess, but plunging down the slippery slope to prostitution. Their lives are intertwined with Harry's in a way that bodes ill for Cupid's arrows.

Despite the pose and the patter, Harry Fabian is basically a loser. He's a small-time criminal trying to break into the big time. He thinks he's a contender, but the ring's too small for him, and Harry ends his fight half-Nelsoned, thrown over the ropes and in a messy pile on the ground. He walks around not knowing his number's marked—everyone else knows he's doomed, they see through him straight away. As it says in the novel, ". . . he fools nobody as completely as he fools himself . . ."

The power of the novel comes from the way you understand how Helen is at first attracted to Harry, then corrupted by him. At the end of the novel, Harry's ideas about money, his predatory view of people, overpowers Helen's love for Adam. Helen allows the physical pleasures of life to blot out the emotional ones. She becomes a fool.

There have actually been two film adaptations of Kersh's novel, the first in 1950—starring Richard Widmark and directed by Jules Dassin—and the second in 1992—starring Robert De Niro and directed by Irwin Winkler. I'll discuss each movie in turn.

Coming toward the end of the postwar spate of Spiv films, Dassin's *Night and the City* opens with Harry Fabian on the run from an unnamed, unseen man. In fact, throughout the film, the impression is that Harry is constantly ducking and diving through the seedy, rain-soaked streets of nighttime London's Soho. At one stage he says, "All my life I've been running. From welfare officers, thugs, my father . . ."

Harry Fabian tries to make a few bob here and there, always charming/wheedling money out of others. But the more money he gets hold of, the quicker it seems to slip through his fingers. Harry even tries stealing from his lover, Mary, a fellow American who sings at the Silver Fox nightclub. He feels guilty about it, sure, but he needs the money, his life is in danger. Mary looks at a photo of them together on a small boat, remembers the old days when they were normal people. What happened to Harry to change him from clean-cut college kid to sweating hustler? We never find out.

Adam, a sculptor in the novel, a toy designer in the film, describes Harry as being "an artist without an art," who has "no way of expressing himself." This is the point. Harry is a bundle of energy and ideas, a spontaneous, charming man, a confidence trickster who has no focus. We see him touting for business, tricking American businessmen into going to the Silver Fox, where luscious, vivacious showgirls will persuade them to buy ludicrously expensive wine and cigarettes. What these girls do outside the club is their own business.

However, he finds his focus at a

wrestling bout. Gregorius the Great, a legendary undefeated wrestler, is outraged at the clowning antics of modern so-called wrestlers. He extols the virtues of proper Greco-Roman wrestling. Gregorius is also the father of Kristo, London's biggest wrestling promoter. Harry has a brilliant idea—he persuades Gregorius to help him set up Greco-Roman wrestling in London, knowing that Kristo will never touch him.

But Harry needs finance. He gets it through the scheming Helen Nosscross, wife of fat Phil, the owner of the Silver Fox. Helen is waiting for her husband to die, so that she can inherit all his money and possessions. Phil is infatuated with her, but she won't allow him to touch her. Fed up with his advances, Helen turns to Harry to get her a license for her own club—in exchange, he'll get the money for his wrestlers. He can't get a real one so, unbeknownst to her, he orders a forged one to ensure he gets his money.

From the opening shot Harry is doomed. He was born a loser, and you know he'll die one too. Because of this, the film takes on the aspect of tragedy. His "friend" Phil says at one point, "You've got it all, but you're a dead man, Harry Fabian. A dead man." Harry has no friends to rely on. "Nobody can help you." And he is ashamed of betraying the woman who loves him. "You're killing me," Mary says, "and you're killing yourself." Harry is contorted by all these schemes, these selfish acts, and blind to the effects they have on others. If only he'd stop and think, listen to other people, then he'd travel more slowly to his doom, perhaps even see it in time to avoid it.

Then it all goes wrong. Phil withholds the finance. Gregorius dies after a tortuous and gripping fight with The Strangler. Kristo wants Harry dead. In the end, hunted through the city throughout the night, Harry, at last stops and reflects, "I was so close, then everything fell apart. I've stopped running." In his final moments, he performs one selfless act, but it's too late.

Harry was never close to anything—he was always going to die.

Harry's is a desperate life, vividly realized by Jules Dassin, director of *Naked City* (1948), *Thieves' Highway* (1949), *Rififi* (1954) and *Topkaki* (1964), and photographer Max Greene. The film lacks the biting language of Kersh's novel, but it makes up for it by using postwar London's atmospheric ruins to best effect. The noir camerawork is some of the finest this side of *The Third Man* (1949), utilizing exaggerated lighting, sharp angles, and wide-angled lenses—every bead of sweat can be picked out on Richard Widmark's face. The performances are first-rate, especially Francis L. Sullivan's subtle portrayal of Phil, and Stanislaus Zbyszko's emphatic and dignified Gregorius.

The more recent film version moved everything to New York, switched wrestling to boxing, and presented Harry as an ambulance-chasing attorney-at-law. "Harry Fabian—Defender of Worms," one character comments. It's a streetwise reworking of Dassin's film rather than Kersh's novel, and its intention seems to be to make Harry more of a lovable dreamer who fails rather than a shyster lawyer who get his comeuppance.

The Irwin Winkler–directed film starts promisingly enough with a speeding ambulance, the camera following a pair of walking legs, the owner of the legs (Harry) outsmarting a couple of muggers, and Harry entering Boxers, a bar owned by Phil Nasseros. Everyone knows and likes Harry, laughs at his jokes—he's a character.

In this film, Harry is having an affair with Phil's wife, Helen. Again, as in the previous film, she requires a liquor license to leave Phil and start her own bar. This time, when Harry delivers a fake license, he is wracked with guilt and shame. Later, when she finds out what Harry did and she loses the bar ("Are we even? Are we even?" Harry asks her, bleeding on the ground with multiple gunshot wounds), she still forgives him. What an angel! Can I have one, please?

There is no sense of doom and despair, only of incompetence and a man out of his depth—a porpoise basking in shark-infested waters. Without a hard edge to the film, no noir, nothing seedy, no tragedy, the film falls flat. Ultimately, Harry only has himself to blame. "You let everybody walk all over you. You can't even promote a pillow fight."

It's interesting to note that the people in the film are quite respectable/well-to-do, upper middle-class, well-dressed, not short of money. They are people who have something, but are greedy enough to want a lot more. This doesn't have the same air of desperation as the original film, where the characters need to survive as well as succeed.

By the time we get to the dénouement, and Harry gives his "I'm a dead man, I'm so tired of running" speech, although we may sympathize with him, we only do so if we are still awake.

The end has Harry survive his wounds, making plans to move to California with Helen, and being driven away in the ambulance that has been chasing him throughout the movie.

So did Hollywood chew up Kersh's characters and ideas and regurgitate a mess of films? Well, they basically did what they always do—took the bits they liked (Fabian) and fashioned their own ideas. Irwin Winkler, working from Richard Price's script, missed the mark because for his film to work we had to know and care about Harry—this doesn't happen. Jules Dassin, working from Jo Eisinger's screenplay, crafted a superb fall into the depths of hell—the tenth ring, maybe? Whatever you think of the movies, the irony is that, even with a greater tolerance of sex and violence within our society, Kersh's 1938 novel is still dirtier, grittier, and darker than the films. It is not about one man who is corrupt, but about how that man can corrupt others. That, I think, is the real essence of noir.

Phil Karlson:

DREAMS AND DEAD ENDS

JACK SHADOIAN

In a decade of hard, ugly crime films, no director made harder, uglier, less visually ingratiating ones that Phil Karlson. The fifties' sternest moralist, his films lack the fun and romantic rebelliousness of Fuller's and the brisk, chilly agitation of Don Siegel's. A plain, seemingly graceless stylist, his rather unpalatable movies, full of rabid, sloggingly orchestrated physical pain and psychic damage, picture crime as a monstrous, miasmal evil, divesting it of any glamour it ever had. He is the key figure of fifties violence, specializing in foreground placement of smashed, bloody faces. Karlson's movies are grueling, disenchanted journeys through suffering, and their violence is disturbingly infectious, since the necessity for counterviolence is always expressed. His heroes stagger dully about as life's punching bags, until they can't take it anymore and go haywire, striking out in a reasonless frenzy. Karlson and Fuller share a nightmare vision of the American status quo and a desperate hope that it can be purged of its evil. Fuller wants to rid America of its bourgeois hypocrisy and ideological divisiveness. Karlson wants it made safe for a normal, decent life. His stress is almost always (deceptively) local—the family, the community, the town, the individual. Fuller is the more flexible of the two, can roll with the punches and crack a smile. For Karlson, criminals are the lowest scum on earth, and crime must be thoroughly destroyed. His hatred runs deep, and his cheap, sleazy, action movies are dead serious assaults upon the audience's automatic receptivity to screen "entertainment."

I will deal briefly with what I consider to be Karlson's three best works in the fifties. All three illustrate the repositioning of the genre's conflicts that is typical of the fifties and, in sequence, form a triptych of progressive horror and hopelessness.

In the first, *99 River Street* (1953), the emphasis is on individual infection. The hero's melodramatic race against time is one we are pretty certain he will win. The film is dark—not a single scene in daylight—but the hero's journey is of the archetypal Aeneas-through-the-underworld-for-his-own-and-everybody's-good kind. There's light at the end of the tunnel. The action is emotionally charged, and the film has a hothouse eroticism. In *The Phenix City Story* (1955), a whole community is diseased, and the hero cannot prevent the loss of significant lives. His race against time is nearly lost, and the community nearly sinks away in a bog of corruption and apathy. Its visual look vacillates between capturing, openly and candidly, the depressingly banal ugliness of a real, medium-sized American city and a dramatic deployment of a thick, stark, noir night world. *The Brothers Rico* (1957) shows that all is lost. The hero acts, but clearly far too late. The infection has spread to national proportions. The film has a fresh, clean, spacious, well-scrubbed look; the camera is reserved and distant. We have emerged from the tunnel into a radiant facade of vast geographical extent. The film culminates in a dark, cramped candy store on New York's Mulberry Street, but its convictions about what the world is really like lie elsewhere.

99 River Street takes place in New York. Its hero, Ernie Driscoll, is an ex-prizefighter with a damaged eye. Barred from the ring, he drives a cab for a living. A heavy pall of lost hopes hangs over his marriage. The discovery of his wife's unfaithfulness throws him into a bitter rage, from which he is distracted by a plea of help from Linda James, an actress friend who claims she has just killed a man. It turns out to be a trick—she has used Ernie to help her perform in an audition. He socks a few theatre people and they put out a call for his arrest as a publicity prank. The actress, contrite, seeks him out. Together, they find his wife's dead body stashed in his cab, placed there by her lover, Victor Rawlins, who has killed her and wishes to frame Driscoll. After working his way through some hostile entanglements with Rawlins's underworld acquaintances, Driscoll, with Linda's help, tracks Rawlins down before he is able to escape the country and beats him to a pulp. He and Linda marry and look forward to successfully managing a gas station.

The film is about so many things that it is difficult to decide which is uppermost. Its general theme is that one must accept one's limits. Its general method is a narrative that keeps clotting with betrayals and deceptions that the viewer, too, is victimized by. Its central metaphor is Driscoll's bad eye, which looks and looks but does not see. Its bias is that sophistication is deadly, that one must descend to the primitive.

99 River Street opens with a hard-slugging boxing match. We watch the action, aware of the obscene disproportion between the announcer's relish and the bloody images. Soon, a voice-over tells us that we are watching one of the "Great Fights of Yesterday." A slow-motion replay takes us by surprise. We are told that the challenger for the title, Ernie Driscoll (John Payne), has "never been knocked off his feet" and that his eye is so badly cut he can't see. He is "fighting on instinct alone." The camera pulls back to reveal we have been watching TV. It pulls back further to show us, from behind, the head of a man. He has a scar over an eye, which twitches involuntarily. He watches the screen intently, almost not hearing a voice that reminds him of his dinner. It is Ernie Driscoll, watching his own self getting destroyed; he is fascinated, mesmerized. The camera reverses after a female hand clicks the TV off, and we are shown the full setting from behind the TV—Mr. and Mrs. Driscoll's apartment, dinner waiting on the table.

Ernie's obsession with his past

seals him off from his reality. The visual confusion perpetrated on the viewer is the truth about Ernie's life. He could have been the champ; that he never made it haunts him. He thinks of himself as that person he can never again be. His wife Pauline (Peggie Castle) works in a florist shop and has a similar syndrome. In her mind, she married a "pug" instead of going on in show business. She says to Ernie, "I could have been a star." Ernie reminds her that she was "just a showgirl." They are separated from each other by their fantasies. Ernie would like to patch up their marriage, but the opening sequence tells us he is too psychologically crippled to do so. It is too late anyway, since his wife, as we soon learn, has transferred her emotions to someone else—a slick, erotically persuasive thief. She has helped him steal some jewelry and plans to flee with him to France as soon as the stones are fenced. He kills her.

99 River Street is a film full of "I could have beens" and "ifs." Ernie and Pauline aren't young kids, yet they still believe that the big chance is there for them to grab. The present is a quagmire; all possibility lies in the past. Life is pervaded by myths. Ernie insists on believing in his marriage when it is evidently dead; Pauline, prodded by her past dreams, thinks she can run away. Victor Rawlins (Brad Dexter) thinks he can escape to France. Linda James (Evelyn Keyes) thinks she can be a great actress. The disease that goes by the name of the American Dream infects all the characters. As Ernie tells Linda: "A chance at the top. It's the most important thing in the world." This is a fantasy the film destroys and then rebuilds in altered form. The film gives Linda and Ernie a new life only when they recognize that their fantasies are impossible. The future is closed only to big dreamers. Dreaming big dreams is what has closed it off so fast.

The gangster/crime genre documents America as a failure. The experience of failure, as reflected in the progression of its films, is cumulative. *99 River Street* gives us an America that has worsened in time. Its myths are used up. The frontier is closed; there is no space left. America is prematurely middle-aged and must face its middle-aged problems. The two people who try to escape it, Victor and Pauline, cannot. There is nowhere for them to go. They can't go west, so choose to head for France, the old world. This is, of course, a desperate backtracking, a return to the seat of the corruption. But it was only a delusion anyway that we were ever free of the corruption from which we sprang. Victor makes a great effort to board a ship that's in dry dock. There is no way of escaping the corner we have backed ourselves into. Ernie battles Victor on a plank that connects the ship to the land, high above the ground. The extreme long shot is a symbolic tableau. We're stuck in the middle of the bridges we have built. The fight is never finished; the police drag Ernie away and calm him down, and we are kept at a distance that implies the futility of it all. The future has no room for high expectations. Ernie and Linda's talents and ambitions are put under the pressure of real situations that they cannot adequately handle. An immense effort of will barely earns them enough time, and the intensity of the effort burns their unreasonable dreams away.

In *Pickup on South Street* Richard Widmark's Skip McCoy has a lot of brash charm and exhibits more than a trace of the appealing hyperactivity of the thirties gangster. In *99 River Street* John Payne plays his glum, drab dupe with a rigid sorrow and despair. He is a powder keg of tensions that he can't release. Ernie Driscoll's life is pure hell, and there is no legitimate way he can break out of it. His wife tells Victor that he "broods about things" and is dangerous because "suddenly he explodes." Ernie is vaguely aware of his dilemma. When his wife leaves him, he tries to be a fighter again. "I gotta hit," he says. He takes a long look into a mirror, trying to decide who he is, and chooses to go back into the ring. He's got murder in him. He even roughs up his friend Stan (Frank Faylen), the film's voice of reason. Stan keeps advising him to take it easy, but that's easier said than done. When life punishes you, you want to punish it back. Ernie Driscoll has to learn to be reasonable the hard way, by a purgation of his anger and pride; he has to learn through his gut and not his head. The bland, settled Stan can't do him any good. He's got to beat his way to a peace of mind, and the violence he both inflicts and receives is a form of self-therapy, the stinging pain that is necessary for him to feel at the death of his old self. As is common in the fifties, it is the woman Linda's loyalty that is instrumental in his change.

Linda's problems are analogous. She thinks she is a great actress, but both of her "performances" in the film tell us she is not. The first, in which she fooled Ernie, and the audience, into thinking she has killed a man, is by far the more complex. Karlson plays on all the shifting relations among theatre, life, and film. We have a sense that Evelyn Keyes, the real actress of the film, does remarkably well, but we are not quite sure by the end what "remarkably well" even means. Linda is using Ernie as a prop in her audition, but we (and Ernie) don't know this. We know she is an actress, but we think she is being real. Yet Karlson stresses the *theatricality* of her response, which is fine in the theatre but extremely mannered in the cinema. Karlson follows her movements in a very long take and in medium close-up. It is a grotesque tour de force—strained, exaggerated, brutally revealing. But whose tour de force is it—Evelyn Keyes's or Linda James's? The transposition of theatrical skills onto the movie screen, where they seem glaringly inappropriate, makes us feel there is something wrong. Yet Linda James is an actress, and it is possible, maybe even likely, that she would maintain a role even under such circumstances, as a way of dealing with her fear. Ernie believes her and so do we, but not because we are really convinced. When Karlson reveals it as a hoax, we are startled, but also understand why we were "bothered" by the performance. It really wasn't very good—or, however acceptably it might have worked on a stage (like the one it is on), it was deafeningly unsubtle for the screen. When Linda drops back into being Linda, she naturally becomes "realer" than ever—at that point in the film, an obnoxious opportunist. The point isn't simply that she is not a great actress but that in trying to be one she treats people badly. Later in the film, she gives a performance in a real situation, when her life and Ernie's are on the line. In a waterfront bar, she tries to seduce the killer, Victor Rawlins, by coming on as the sexiest broad of all time. It is a lousy performance, and Victor doesn't bite. She finally drops the act and names Pauline, and that rattles him. All her acting gets her nowhere; it is the touch of reality that reaches him. When Ernie's vision blurs during the fight with Victor, it is clear that he can never be the champ he wants to be. Similarly, Linda's failure with Victor, in a situation that is a matter of life and death, suggests that *her* talent is more limited than she has thought. The American myth of success dies hard, but die it must, if the society is to become less self-destructive and more mindful of the nature of reality.

The themes of *99 River Street* are distinctly interrelated with its visual strategies. The deceptions of Linda's first performance, and of the boxing match that seems real, are perceived as realities before they are exposed as shams. They are the realities of characters who cannot see reality as it is. That the audience is tricked as well suggests that these characters' flaws are not unusual; reality has become difficult to perceive. It is as though we are watching the world through Ernie Driscoll's shattered optic nerve. No character in the film has an adequate knowledge of reality, and they often share with the viewer the problem of seeing things clearly. It is impossible to distinguish reality from facade because their merging has become the basis upon which life is lived. Christopher (Jay Adler) wears glasses. When Victor comes to demand the money, Christopher behaves as though Victor's threats are not a reality that could affect him. Victor raps his face, knocking his glasses off, after which Christopher sees he must comply. Mickey (Jack Lambert) has a nervous habit of putting his glasses on and taking them off, a means of changing his own reality as well as seeing things literally, but he mistakes who Driscoll is and is prevented from double-crossing Christopher. He beats Driscoll up for no reason. When Driscoll starts beating *him* up and asking questions, he responds with a look of disbelief. The brutality of both question-and-answer sessions is of the classic "I'll make ya talk" kind, except that neither character knows what is going on or why he is being asked questions that are apparently absurd. The old situation is given a new twist by a reality that fails to correspond to one's assumptions about it.

Christopher runs a pet store as a front for his fencing racket, but it is not an old-style front—mask and reality, black and white. His legitimate and illegitimate work are visually integrated. Trophies and awards decorate the walls of his back room. When we first enter it, Mickey is there, in white uniform, grooming a dog. Christopher is busy out front nursing a pup. He is a character who seems remote from his own evil. Karlson must have liked the irony of Christopher nursing a puppy. He used this unexpected image to convey his violence. As the nipple is forced into the squealing pup's mouth we feel the vast extensiveness of violence in the world of the film. Nothing is free from it. What should be handled tenderly is brutalized.

The novelties of *99 River Street* cannot be understood except as part of a general context of the questioning of reality common to its period. The film can no longer assume that there is a static reality out there to be recorded. The difficulties the characters experience come from a loss of instinct that renders all perception of reality uncertain. Ernie's confused groping is paradigmatic. It is the older figures only who feel certain about anything—and their knowledge is either mistaken or useless. Stan shakes his head after Ernie departs. Pop, the fight manager (Eddy Waller), shakes his head after Ernie leaves the gym. Christopher shakes his head after Victor's departure, implying both that Victor's a hopelessly ignorant punk to think he can outsmart him and that he doesn't have the brains to stay away from women. He knows certain things for sure.

Accompanying the insecurity is a view of the past as a golden age—an age of faith, hope, trust, decency, and a shared sense of reality. Ernie recollects Pauline's beauty and her happy laughter. He tells Linda, "When I was a kid I thought I'd grow up and meet a girl who would stick in my corner no matter what. Then I grew up. Things aren't the way you think they're gonna be when you're a kid." Pop warns Ernie that what the new managers think of is 33 1/3 percent of the cut, and that's all; they won't even bother to wash the resin out of his eyes. But there is no turning back the clock, and future hopes cannot merely be a reprise of past ones. The world has changed, and since the nature of reality can only be known by what men picture it as being, we can see how and in what ways it has changed by the evidence on the screen. Even as it points to a happy future, the film does not depart from its premise that the nature of things is difficult to perceive. It simply alters its tone toward the comic. The presentation of the images continues in the same vein. We see a boxer's gloved hands in practice and we think "Ernie," remembering that he had decided to start boxing again. We know it can't be, since that would go against the meaning of the film, but the image tells us nothing. The camera moves to show us Pop and Ernie watching the boxer. Now we know. Ernie mentions his new business and a partner. The camera moves to show us Stan, talking very businesslike. We think, "Him? But where's Linda?" The camera pans slightly to the right to show us Linda talking with Stan and make clear that she, after all, is the partner—as we had assumed until the image tricked us into momentarily thinking otherwise.

The genre has obviously shifted its assumptions and content over a period of twenty-five years, but its basic purpose and structure are still intact. Ernie Driscoll has to be separated from and put in opposition to his society, and the kind of individual assertion he makes carries those qualities that are in conflict with the status quo. The gangster is not now the center of interest. He is an aspect of society that people get mixed up with and require violence to get clear of. The hero's violence against the gangster resembles the old gangster's violence against the society, but there are new distinctions made about violence in the fifties and *99 River Street* is not content to leave them implicit, as most films of the period do. The problem of seeing clearly is connected to the problem of feeling clearly. The script makes explicit at the beginning and at the end that "there's something critical the matter with Driscoll's eye" and that he is "fighting on instinct alone—yes—on instinct alone." Violence based on instinct is good; it represents a basic will to live, to be human. Violence that is mechanical, impersonal, cerebral, staged—Christopher's, Mickey's, Victor's, the violence of the theatre and of the boxing ring—is bad. It cannot be fought on its own terms, but with guts and feeling. The fifties hero, most often, uses his fists and hands. There is only one shot fired in the film that hit its mark—Victor shoots Driscoll, but it doesn't stop him. Victor kills Pauline with her scarf, in a pervertedly erotic manner. Ernie bangs out a future for himself with good old-fashioned knuckle power. Since the police are associated with the rest of society, and are in fact chasing after an innocent man—the only one who can enact a true justice—they are pictured as irrelevant when they are not in fact unpleasantly obstructive. They have no knowledge of what has occurred, and proceed mechanically. At the end, they show up in a swarm when everything's over. In *The Phenix City Story* they are dangerous.

In June of 1954, Albert A. Patterson, the Democratic candidate for attorney general of Alabama, was shot dead outside his law office. It looked likely that he would be elected, and his ambition once in office was to prosecute the syndicate that controlled the vice industry in Phenix City and put an end to a notorious corruption that had lasted over a hundred years. *The Phenix City Story* (1955) is a generic dramatization of the actual events leading up to Patterson's murder and the subsequent calling out of the National Guard. Like many cold war films it exacerbates some horrible actuality to a state of generalized paranoia. The point of the film is not to make us feel bad about vice in Phenix City but to warn us of our deadened sensibility.

The film's situation is a metaphor for the erosion of American values (read: human values) and our mechanical acquiescence to an enveloping and deep-rooted corruption. In an atmosphere of bland, accepting conformity, we cannot see the evil in our midst and how it is poisoning us. As Patterson (John McIntyre himself says early in the film to vice lord Rhett Tanner (Edward Andrews), "I don't think at all. I don't want to. More relaxin'—and *safer.*" He tells his son, just returned from Germany, not to get exercised over the state of things and that "we live a long way from Fourteenth Street." It is an attitude that leaves us unprepared to deal with criminal syndicates, delegations from outer space, and Communists. To ward off these dangers, an eternal vigilance is required. (The reporter, Ed Strickland, informs us that the syndicate still exists a year after the attempt to smash it and is trying to come back.) Unfortunately, however, we are a society of sleepwalkers. It takes the genre's mainstay, the outsider, to take things in hand. It is John Patterson (Richard Kiley), who comes back to America after living in Germany, who spearheads the movement against Tanner. Fighting Tanner, the police, the political machine, his apathetic community, and his own ideals and feelings, he is the center of the film's conflicts. Coming from the outside into an old struggle between established vice and powerless virtue, the currents of the situation jolt him with a fresh impact. The murder of his father makes him see what needs to be done. He finally unknots himself by acting on his emotions and tries to strangle Tanner.

The Phenix City Story is one of Karlson's most savage films. It has a raw, documentary atmosphere, all the more menacing for seeming authentic. Like all of his crime films, *The Phenix City Story* is a version of American Gothic, its use of sleazy natural locations and its string of petty, cowardly, ugly gangsters giving crime a harrowing and horrifying feel. Nothing is prettied up in this movie, or caricatured. And there is no explicit commentary from Karlson. There is no need. The crime and corruption he shows are so repellent he is free to objectify himself, to blend his moral fervor completely with the material. As late as 1975, the film has university audiences cheering for the National Guard (unlikely, but true). It has no humor at all.

Karlson brings to his film an element of sordid horror. His environments are noisy, crowded, fetid. The sky over Phenix City is gray and dismal. The musical number at the Poppy Club is an anti-number, coarse, unprofessional, talentless. A dead child is thrown from a car onto a lawn. Voters, men and women, are beaten up at the polls and stagger into the street, dripping blood. The "heroine" gets killed, as does her pleasant young suitor. A crippled lawyer is shot in the mouth. One almost can't believe what is happening on the screen; the horror of it suffocates. We are not shown reality; we are assaulted by its dramatic recreation. We are made to see by being made to feel. At last, when the tide begins to turn against the criminals, the viewer must face the horror of his own lust for retaliation. The film exposes us, our own capacities, much more than it does the "reality" of Phenix City. We are bombarded into an awareness of our own condition. The film doesn't just expose what people preferred to ignore, it exposes the fact that people were ignoring.

The Phenix City Story is a message to the American citizen. As one interviewee says, if you shine a light on a rat "it will run for cover" (and it might run into city hall). This is not enough; one must beat the rats to death, and since they are always ready to come back, one must keep on beating them, ceaselessly. The movie makes you want to kill and robs you of the satisfaction. That it arouses the urge is a credit (discredit?) to its power. We, as viewers, have to be pulled back with the force that Zeke (James Edwards) uses to pull John back from strangling Tanner. Zeke's biblical remonstrances are well taken but frankly unwelcome. A true justice requires that Tanner die. The film allows us, like John Patterson, to live through a healthy anger as a form of vengeful release, despite our theoretical adherence to the laws of a democracy and our abhorrence to the shedding of blood. We must not kill, but to be made to want to kill should rouse a citizenry to take up a strong, if less dramatic, fight against crime or against its own numbness. The film is not cathartic. We leave concerned, angry, full of pent-up antagonism. Our frustrations are relieved only when John finally starts socking people around, unable to stick by his rational convictions. But he doesn't sock hard or long enough.

The Phenix City Story implies that without John Patterson's courage and eventual plunge into irrationality, conditions would have remained the same. The strong, extraordinary, honest men are few. The average American citizen is unkindly pictured. Good men turn away, morally lethargic; others are corrupt or indifferent. A parallel is made with Germany, from where John has just returned upon finishing his work prosecuting Nazi war criminals. Things were safer in Germany; the "war" here is more hellish. We are in the grip of a dictatorship of evil. John finds it hard to believe what he has come back to and finds the apathy even harder to understand. The police and the politicians are all bought off. The syndicate is, in effect, a mirror of the society. The *good* people say, "Let's get out of here, the cops are coming." John's father becomes the necessary sacrifice to the community. His martyrdom is garishly staged at night. Shot in the mouth, point-blank, he climbs out of his car and lugs himself down the street on his crutches. He staggers, but remains upright long enough to project a shocking image of destroyed integrity to the people slowly gathering. When he falls, it clinches our attitude for good, yanks us into the film with an appetite for action.

Karlson's confused heroes must batter their way out of their stagnant rationalism. John, like other Karlson heroes, is not only ordinary but rather hard to get behind because of his ambivalent position and the ease with which he takes certain notions for granted. He doesn't read the situation correctly, imagining that rational, democratic principles of law and justice can be applied. It is only when his father is killed and the rest of his family threatened that he realizes that conditions are too severe to be fought rationally and that he must let his true anger run its course. Karlson arranges his films to give his heroes a taste of humility, to make them confront their static assumptions and unrealistic shortsightedness (Eddie in *The Brothers Rico,* the Jeffrey Hunter character in *Key Witness*). They become as problematic as what they fight against. His characterizations are nonheroic and therefore nonassuring. The rage of his heroes is terrifying and forbidding but is preferable to self-delusion and ignorance. By giving way to it, they reach their humanity and cut a path for human goals. That their credibility, and the credibility of what they accomplish, is discreetly suspect is the sign of an honest pessimism that refuses to be crowded out.

Much is made of the events being true. The film does exert a fascination from being based on fact. But the power of *The Phenix City Story* rests not on its "reality" but on its being a well-made fiction making imaginative use of the genre's structure and elements. The opening fifteen minutes of stilted "real life" interviews should make any viewer thankful for what follows (an hour and a half of that would be too depressing for words). The film moves into gear only when Karlson takes over, superimposing on the actual material a blatantly fictional style (its blatant movieness accentuated by the news interviews that precede it), coaxing convincing performances from his actors (however sincere, the real people of Phenix City are awfully dull), and beginning the rhythmic buildup with a climax in mind. Incidents are tied together like a closely wound spring and dramatic pressure is gradually increased. However timely and "true," *The Phenix City Story* is a triumph of craftsmanship, of artistry, of economy of means. Karlson gives us just what we need to know about what Phenix City looks and feels like, enough to understand how Fourteenth Street came to be and why it continues, and why it has to be destroyed—and he does it swiftly and vividly.

Despite the apparent victory of John Patterson, the film leaves us emotionally astir. There has been too much horror, too many innocents killed and wounded. Phenix City has a long way to go; the cleanup is a long-term proposition. The newsreel footage of the gambling machines being smashed and burned is gratifying to an extent but is, visually, a spectacle of destruction similar to what has preceded. The oppressive evil of Fourteenth Street lingers in the memory, and there are ominous hints that the corruption is controlled by people we never see on the screen and who remain unconvicted. Moreover, the film insists that we carry away with us a concern about our own personal and social realities, the facades of which need to be penetrated by the eye and annihilated by our feelings. The genre has assumed the task of awakening us to ourselves.

The Brothers Rico, not surprisingly, is about a man who is completely out of touch with everything and the disasters that condition creates. The dark, dank, claustrophobic world of *99 River Street* was humanized by pain, suffering, and feeling. Its black mazes were charged with heated action and ultraexpressive camera work. Its stylized, Gothic treatment of locales, its nocturnal frissons, made it heavy with atmosphere. Each scene boiled under exact, intense pressures. Where *99 River Street* sizzled on top, *The Brothers Rico* (1957) sizzles underneath, and the sound is almost inaudible. Its pressures are invisible, often unseen within the image. The score of *99 River Street* was loud and obtrusive; the score of *The Brothers Rico* is minimal and unemphatic. The film presents its material with a mordant matter-of-factness. With calm and restraint, it lets the situation build to a *sickening* point, and we experience the horror of its clean, bright, ordered, undramatic world without being shown anything that is conventionally horrifying. The visual look of the film implies that the more evenly and fully you illuminate, without distorting, the world through light and shadow and unusual angles and compositions, the more horrible it becomes. It looks sane, pleasant, and healthy (unlike the world of *99 River Street*), but its condition is now cancerous. *The Brothers Rico* is typical of the genre in the fifties in that while it works on an immediate level—the syndicate is evil and must be crushed—it embodies much larger concerns.

The Brothers Rico is about Eddie Rico (Richard Conte), a former syndicate accountant who has been out of touch with the world of crime for three years and underestimates its heartlessness. The deaths of his two brothers, Johnny and Gino, finally provoke him to fight the organization led by Sid Cubik (Larry Gates), his uncle, whom he mistakenly trusts. He succeeds in killing Cubik, and the syndicate, with its head chopped off, will presumably breathe its last when the D.A. (never seen) starts prosecuting using Eddie's testimony. Karlson has in Richard Conte the perfect actor for the part—a family man who runs an honest, successful laundry business in Florida, a character with no obvious "hero" flair but who nonetheless looks like a gangster and promises, despite his well-mannered composure, to be successful when goaded into action. He and his wife Alice (Dianne Foster) in their ten-year marriage have been unable to have a child (two miscarriages), and his brothers' danger interferes with a long-awaited adoption procedure. The film implies that only when the syndicate has been smashed is there any hope for children and families, and the conclusion shows the adoption carried through. Eddie's lack of awareness contributes to both brothers' deaths—the price he pays for his obtuseness. Without their deaths, however, he would have not had the resolve to kill Cubik. Nonetheless, the terrible due exacted for his blindness, the character's helpless grief, and his belated vengeance have a Euripidean pain and implacability.

Eddie Rico is a recognizable modern American man. He typifies the culture's middle-class norm. He represents a credible facsimile of our desires, wishes, attitudes, and capabilities. He is a respected man who has put a shady and economically insecure past behind him. His secretary "sirs" him, his wife obeys him (albeit with a sense of irony), he speaks and acts with authority. In the course of the film, this at first commanding figure loses all his conviction and is ruthlessly exposed.

The film opens with a shot of Eddie and his wife sleeping peacefully in bed. The light of dawn shines softly through an expensive picture window, illuminating their modern bedroom. The phone rings, waking Eddie, and he gets up to answer it. The syndicate wants him to hide a fugitive. His wife asks where his loyalty lies, precipitating a mild but, we are given to understand, long-established domestic conflict. The sequence continues through Eddie reassuring Alice that "nothing's going to happen," taking her amorously to bed—after which they both wake up chipper and less tense—the reading of a letter from Eddie's mother, and Eddie's morning preparations prior to leaving for work. Their relationship is warm, loving, sexual, but the atmosphere since the phone call is tense, and the commonplace conversation and activity (Eddie shaving, she playfully biting his back, he pulling her into the shower) have both a forced quality and an undercurrent of the ominous. Karlson establishes in the long (and odd) sequence an intimacy, what seriously threatens it, and Eddie's obliviousness to the danger. This quiet, slow opening, with its long, relaxed takes, is characteristic. *The Brothers Rico* bides its time. The pace of the movie is in keeping with the now-subdued nature of organized crime.

The film is divided into about ten long sequences, all of which involve Eddie (he is present in the frame at least ninety-five percent of the time). Brief linking shots and scenes provide transitions for Eddie to bring one established conflict to bear upon another. Toward the end, the sequences shorten, the editing accelerates the film's tempo (there is even a montage of Eddie eluding the organization's dragnet), and the film is suddenly over before we know it. This curious method is antithetical to the demands of action cinema, with its typically blunt exposition and careening, continuous activity. Karlson wants to put Eddie through a series of encounters so we may discern his character and see him gradually abandon his false assumptions. The true climax of *The Brothers Rico* occurs at the hotel in El Camino when Eddie realizes that he has been used and that he is powerless to prevent Johnny's execution. After this, Karlson seems to lose interest; the tragic potential of the film is exhausted, and all that remains is for Eddie to mop things up, rather miraculously. There is some effective action—the banging of Gonzales's head against the sink is a devastating piece of brutality, especially since the wait for violent action has been a long one, Phil shot in the eye—but both climax (the killing of Cubik) and anticlimax (Eddie and Alice at the orphanage) are unusually swift and abrupt, implying that Karlson has already said what he had to say and is just routinely bringing things to a close. In any case, the moral problems of Eddie

Rico are at the center of the film.

As the oldest brother, with his own prosperous business, Eddie naturally assumes he knows what is right and that his younger brothers are overreacting and haven't sized up the situation properly. They try to warn Eddie that the syndicate wants their heads, but Eddie insists that Uncle Sid (indebted to their mother for his life and something of a substitute father) would never betray the Ricos, his adopted family. He uses the same line on both brothers: "Did I ever steer you wrong?" and causes, or at least accelerates, the deaths of both. He advises Gino to go back to St. Louis, as Sid wants. Gino knows it's a one-way ticket but is caught trying to flee the country. When Eddie defends Sid, Johnny (James Darren) sends him away with: "Maybe I'm gonna die. You've got even bigger problems—you're gonna live." Upon returning to the hotel, Eddie discovers that Johnny was right and that Sid's treachery, however unthinkable, is a fact.

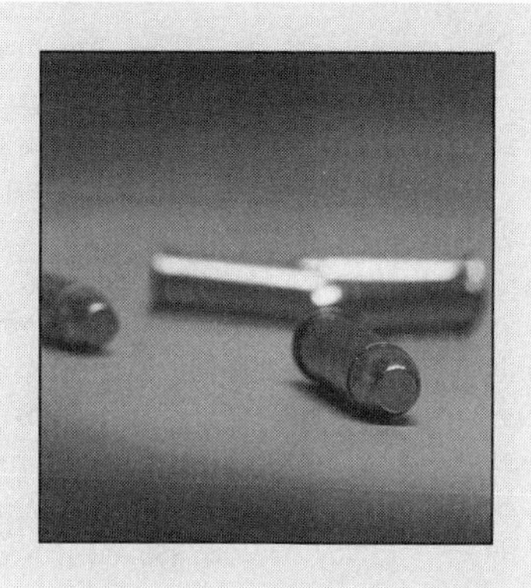

Eddie is understandably self-assured. He is a self-made man, with $100,000—"clean" money—in the bank. He has age and experience on his behalf. He drives a fancy convertible. He is living the American dream, oblivious to the realities of the American nightmare and to the truth about himself. In the long conversation with Cubik it is easy to see how he gets duped. Cubik almost convinces the audience with his gentle manner and white hair. We are made suspicious, but discreetly. As Eddie enters Cubik's suite, the camera glides in long shot to pick up the space, the elegance, the slightly ostentatious decor. Most of the talk is in close-up and two-shots, creating an intimacy between the two men. (The decor, however, which the characters naturally ignore, continues to function for the audience as a distraction in counterpoint to the conversation, keeping it on edge and making it question the development of the scene.) Cubik is apologetic, sincere; he calls Eddie "son," says "I believe in families," and of Mama Rico: "I worship her." There is no apparent reason why Eddie should not trust him. Cubik's strategy is impeccable. He smoothes a path to his own ends, doing most of the talking, controlling the situation. He subtly flatters Eddie by treating him as his equal. As men of the world who understand things as they are, they can understand each other. Eddie is putty in his hands. He follows Cubik all around, and the camera tracks with Cubik's movement. The audience even wonders if Cubik isn't on the up-and-up until, after Eddie leaves, we see Gino being beaten up in a room down the hall. At this point we know for sure what Eddie doesn't and must wait in frustration until he discovers the truth in a painful way.

Eddie is a man suddenly confronted with a lot of decisions to make, a man who has retreated into a complacent frame of mind and must now face some unpleasant truths. One of the advantages of the B movie is that it is possible to construct situations of moral and psychological ambivalence for the hero that no star of A features would tolerate. One cannot imagine a Wayne, a Tracy, a Cooper, a Gable agreeing to enact a character so played upon, so confused about his loyalties, so helplessly agitated sitting out his brother's death in the hotel at El Camino, so victimized by external pressures and internal guilt, about which he has only the dimmest awareness. Also, an ignorant hero is a foolish one. Richard Conte as Eddie appears confident, manly, and competent, but these qualities in the service of folly and vanity are considerably less positive. What draws the viewer to Eddie is the insecurity behind the confident exterior. He is a hero who does not know what to do and from whom a great deal is demanded by, in turn, his wife, Gino, Cubik, Malix, his mother, Johnny, the sheriff, Gonzales. They freely offer either their advice as to what he should do or their opinion of his character. Eddie is too strong to pity, but his difficulties gain our compassion. He is finally forced to make a choice he himself confesses should have been made twenty years ago.

The Brothers Rico exposes why that decision was never made and why it has become too late to make it. To put it bluntly, it is because America is living a lie, as the life of Eddie Rico demonstrates. Eddie thinks he can start life anew by denying his past. He covers up his guilt by a naive and unenlightened belief in his innocence. He is a basically good man who foolishly thinks he is a pure man. Eddie may have quit the rackets, but he is smeared with its dirt. His cleanliness, precision, order, and efficiency are shown as compulsive. His business is a laundry. We see him shower and shave. His wife goes to hand him the soap on the sink, thinks better of it, and opens a fresh bar. His convertible gleams, vividly reflecting his and Gino's images while they talk. Gino wears a dark suit and looks a bit disheveled. Eddie sits trim, stiff, and tight-lipped in a light suit behind a white wheel. His office has a gleaming sterility; everything is spanking new and clean and perfectly, geometrically arranged. When he disturbs some of Malix's clothing in an argument, he smoothes and pats it back to neatness.

Eddie also thinks he is infallible and that he is better and wiser than other people. When he gives advice, he expects people to take it. He has figured the world out like a good rationalist. Everything he does in the name of reason is shown to be profoundly, humanly ignorant. He ignores his mother's fears as expressed in the letter—sees it as part of the potpourri of aches and grumbles that aging mothers give vent to in letters to their children. He responds to his wife's fear by likening her to a "superstitious peasant from the old country." Gino's fear earns him this rebuttal: "Feelings like that are for old women." It is not that Eddie doesn't have feelings, anxieties, or instincts; he has just cut himself off from them and from his emotional roots in family. He thinks Cubik is family because he can't *feel* Cubik. Cubik makes *sense* to him, as one successful man would to another. He tells his mother that Gino is a "crazy" kid, and, as for Johnny, that it is necessary to "put some sense into his head." When Johnny tells him that he's "got a *feeling*" about Cubik "this time," Eddie counters with: "What must I do to make you *understand?*" Eddie's unnatural control over his feelings, his body, his tone of voice, his marriage (his wife runs to fetch his slippers and kneels to put them on), his life is an unconscious effort to deny that he is part of the corruption. His mother's uncooperative irrationality and lapse into religion irritate him but Cubik's ritzy suite and rational assurances impress him. Eddie Rico is a modern man, a machine. He thinks he is in charge of himself and of his life, but he doesn't know what either is anymore. At one point, someone asks him how he likes Florida and he replies, automatically, but revealingly, "It's a great life."

When he learns the truth, he tell his wife, "I gotta get it out of my system." It is a confessional speech but he never seems to break out of his psychological pattern. It does not shatter him. His response is deliberate and rational, a ritual transformation from wrong to right reason that does not involve his emotional depths. Unlike other fifties heroes, he is incapable of getting in touch with himself. He is too stamped by the way things are to change. When he goes after the organization, it is a decision, not a burst of uncontrolled feeling. The movie lets us know from the beginning that Eddie will not be carried away and, as we would wish, carry us away. The movie works on the strategy of our getting the message very early and Eddie getting it very late. By the time Eddie acts, our faith in him has been so undermined that we can't put much stock in what he does. An idle exchange between Eddie and one of his truck drivers early in the film says it all. The driver notices Eddie arriving to work in the morning and asks, "Little late, aren't you?" Eddie replies, "I guess I am."

The prosperous, inhuman syndicate is a symbol of aspects of American life that sever man from man, children from parents, brother from brother, man from woman. One assumes that Eddie has gotten Gino and Johnny into the organization (and then pulled out himself). Uncle Sid is a substitute for the father long dead and gone. Eddie has left the Italian ghetto of New York for sunny Miami. He is removed from his mother, who still gets by—despite a crippled leg—running a store on Mulberry Street. He is a proper son, expiating the guilt of his emotional detachment and real unconcern in typical ways. He sends Mama a new refrigerator (which looks absurdly inappropriate in her old-fashioned decor) and a big TV to keep Grandma—deaf, feeble, and unable to understand a word of English—amused. He advises his mother to send Grandma to a rest home. His mother refuses, despite the difficulty of caring for her. His mother, too, is confused—a victim of the modern world. She admits that she doesn't know right from wrong anymore and doesn't know what to do. But she lives amid realities, unlike Eddie. Her home is a haven of religious, human values, two steps away from the dark violence of the city. Eddie's mental suburbia keeps him insulated from the realities of both good and evil.

The phone call that interrupts his sleep suggests that Eddie's past is very much alive and that his meticulous and meticulously run laundry business was begun with dirty money. Once he starts after Johnny he runs into several people who know him, remember him, and deal with him on the basis of past associations. One particularly revealing moment occurs in the hotel at El Camino, La Motta (Harry Bellaver), Cubik's man who runs the town, tells Eddie to cook it about Johnny's execution—it is a foregone conclusion. Eddie, who has just realized that he has been used by Cubik like a dog on a leash to discover Johnny's whereabouts, is still moaning and cursing Cubik. La Motta, impatient with Eddie's unreasonableness, says, "You listening to me, or am I just talking to my own shadow?" At that point, Eddie, who has been on the bed the whole scene, gets up and sits in the chair La Motta has comfortably occupied all the while. The switch in position unites them. Eddie's earlier protest that his role in the rackets had never involved killing has been punctured by La Motta's "You knew what was going on, so don't start playing holy with me now." The fact that Johnny is Eddie's brother doesn't impress La Motta either: "So, he's your brother. We're all brothers, aren't we? Did that ever stop anything?" Eddie's situation tugs at our sympathy, but his naiveté is distressing. He later assumes responsibility for all the disaster, saying, "It was my fault," but he does it in a perfunctory way that is very much in character. The script's clincher, though, is when Johnny, overjoyed at just becoming a father, bubbles over the phone to Eddie, "Congratulations! You're an uncle." There is only one other uncle in the film—Uncle Sid Cubik—and the phone call is to set up Johnny's execution, moments later.

It seems that Karlson can't end the film with Eddie sitting on the bed, not particularly crushed, but immobile, after Johnny's execution—the point at which the film perhaps should end. This being so, he nonetheless appears to have tried to modify the upbeat conventions he has to follow. La Motta tells Eddie that he can scream his head off if he wants but that "it changes nothing." That is what we are made to feel.

For one thing, when Eddie boards the plane with Gonzales to be taken back to Cubik, we really don't know what frame of mind he is in. It is possible that even after all that has happened he has simply given up and will return to his business, still the "property" of the syndicate but a little wiser and less smugly know-it-all. Even when Gonzales mentions Gino's death Eddie seems to take it in, and settles back in his seat. It is only later made clear that the deaths of his brothers has finally made him want to act on his emotions, however futile the results might be. But the context in which his heroism is placed is overwhelmingly pessimistic. On their first and only meeting, Gino snaps at Eddie, "It was too late what you told me." Eddie says to his wife that he tried to prevent his brothers' deaths "but it was too late." His wife replies, "It was always too late." Mama, looking straight at Eddie, says, "My boys are dead. What's there to live for?" When Eddie replies, "There's a new life ahead, for all of us," Mama doesn't look at all convinced. The deaths of Johnny and Gino cannot be undone. Johnny's assessment is accurate: Eddie's problem is that he is going to go on living.

The film's emphasis is that nothing can change. The conventional structure of such a film is made curiously lopsided. Almost all the film is devoted to slowly waking Eddie up. Then there is a rapid ending in which we are told things can change. It happens too quickly, though, that there isn't enough time for the viewer to get adjusted to the switch in position or to savor it properly. It seems a perverse application of formula. One wants a real encounter between Eddie and Cubik, wants Cubik torn limb from limb. Eddie just shoots him. We don't even get a reaction shot, giving us Eddie's emotion, something implying a sense of release, of accomplishment. But given the film, it almost has to be this way. To make a big deal out of the ending, to let us feel Eddie's emotions, would be false to both theme and characterization. We understand why Eddie has been so cold and controlled a hero. In the world of *The Brothers Rico* to have made Eddie suffer would have been beside the point. What good would groveling and agonizing do? We are no longer in a world where those responses would make any difference. The film gets *us* mad. We want Cubik *more* killed. We fill in the emotions it is not possible, or not convincing, for the character to have.

We are given a character who basically doesn't change. The film plays on the viewer's frustration. Everything theoretically works out right, but we are left, as in *The Phenix City Story,* dissatisfied. The effect is to undercut the patterns of conventional illusionistic cinema. The usual prolonged action of car chases, gunplay, and suspense is kept to an absolute minimum. Malix, Johnny's wife's brother, who at last agrees to help Eddie bust the syndicate in court, is made priggish and unlikable. The new start provided for Eddie and Alice is a qualified one, and it is qualified by everything the film shows us is the truth about America. The coda, with Eddie and Alice adopting the child, is of course comforting but is awkwardly handled. The film seems aware that what we must be shown about Eddie is his newly gained humanity. He says he is "worried" about the adoption going through, and he has forgotten that his wife has the letter from the D.A. that he is fumbling for in his jacket. This is a different, humanized Eddie, a far cry from the blindly confident automaton who started the film. We have been shown, however, an entire country, from East to West, tied in corruption and evil, and the memory of that cannot be effaced by ten seconds of goodwill and lighthearted pleasantries.

America is one big happy family—the syndicate, which functions as a metaphor for our way of life. It is juxtaposed against the Rico family, which it destroys. Cubik calls Eddie "son" and Eddie accepts him as a father. Phil, Cubik's right-hand man, refers to Eddie as "Eddie boy." Even La Motta calls Eddie "son." From his luxurious suite in Miami's Excelsior Hotel, Cubik runs the complex, inhuman (Eddie twice calls Cubik "animal"), impersonal network of crime, a large, perverse family that is bound together by fear. It is the family, and the business, of all the brothers Rico who have left Mulberry Street to get up in the world. It is the new structure that binds human beings together, replacing the family, the neighborhood, and ties based on feeling. The film implies that just about everybody belongs to it or might as well belong to it. Eddie travels from Miami to New York and across to California. Everywhere he goes, the syndicate is there—at airports, in cabs, hotels, banks, on the streets. Cubik has a pipeline to the D.A.'s office. There is not a city or a town where he has not placed someone. One excellent shot in a hotel lobby showing two identically dressed men with curious looks on their faces synthesizes the film's paranoia—we are not told one way or the other, but the effect of the shot is to make us think that one of them is syndicate, the other not. There is no way, though, of telling which.

The syndicate follows Eddie's trail to Johnny. Karlson creates out of the geography of the whole country a closed universe. Eddie can go anywhere in the U.S., but he's trapped. Once part of the syndicate, you are owned by it forever. The film does not explain how so many people became involved. One is left to infer that at some point or another, either with or without your knowledge, you become indebted, either directly or indirectly, to something the syndicate has a hand in. Then you are obliged for life. La Motta and Gonzales arrange for Johnny to get killed with utter nonchalance. If they disobey, they are dead, so it is nothing even worth thinking about. A moral sense is a luxury they can ill afford. La Motta is not hideously evil, he's just resigned, and it is his absolute acceptance of the situation that gives us the shivers. Gonzales is his echo: "You can't buck the system." La Motta orders dinner while Eddie holds his head. Organized crime may have had its origins in the urban ghettos, but has come a long way since. It is not tied to any nationality. Gonzales is, presumably, a Mexican-American, and Cubik is made deliberately nonnational. He can't be typed, and he is given no history. All we have is his name, which suggests the hard, angular, rectilinear surfaces of the world the film shows us we live in. The only environment in the film that is distinguished from the rest is Mama Rico's—warm, comfortable, cluttered, a hodgepodge of rich wallpaper, old lamps, unpreten-

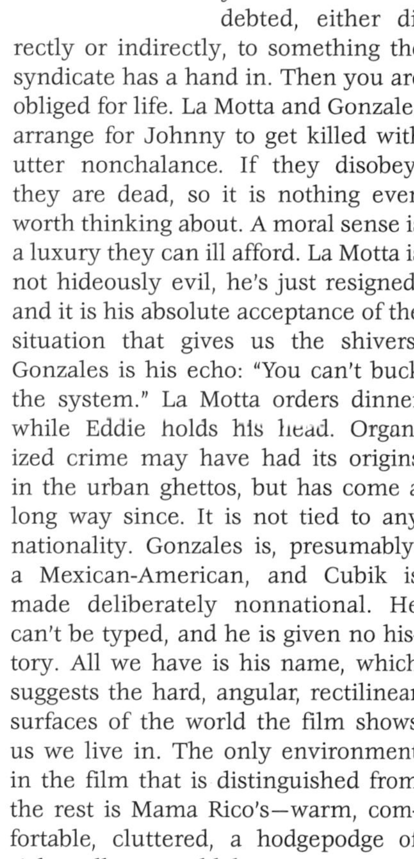

tious chairs and couches, rounded, tactile shapes. The store that is a home, the home that is a store.

What shot after shot suggests about the rest of the world is its severely ordered and clean appearance, its characterless neutrality and modernity, and its mechanical hardness. Cubik's suite is a precisely laid out and chicly incongruous blend of tile, glass, wood, expensive drapery, and Japanese silk screens. Eddie's home and office are equally immaculate and designed. The film is full of long hallways and rectangular doors. Eddie and Gino drive up to a white, glistening beach beneath geometrically swaying rows of palm trees. The interior of the Phoenix Airport—its floor being swabbed to a sparkle by a lone, unobtrusive black—appears as an uncannily logical arrangement. Its men's room features an array of sinks and urinals in rigid, glittering formation. Eddie stops his car beneath a mechanical stop/go sign that seems to have been included only to amplify a view of existence that isn't really lived but rather keeps clicking in and out of place. People walking in the film—at airports, on streets—have a stiff, somnambulant quality. The facade, whether it is the interior of a bank or a hotel lobby, is always one of order, smoothness, imperturbability. *The Brothers Rico* contains very little violence because crime isn't like that anymore. It doesn't show its face. Crime is Sid Cubik, pretending to be all heart but heartless underneath. He is the bureaucracy and the technology that have taken over. At El Camino, Eddie tries to reach Cubik by telephone and can't. Realizing he has been betrayed, he shouts, "My dear Uncle Sid!" and smashes his fist into the telephone. Sid Cubik is a telephone.

Karlson records the American landscape with a diabolical equanimity. We see the environments as actual and authentic, but in the context of the film we see them with a fresh perspective. They are the rot-disguising fronts and facades we live among, and that makes them more sinister than any diagonalized dark alley. Karlson's sobriety constitutes his most lethal critique. A visual opportunist like Aldrich would have invested the Phoenix Airport with a special filmic excitement. Karlson refuses to make it any more or less interesting than it is. It is just there, like everything, like crime, and crime is everywhere. Verisimilitude is being used for special ends. The film's method does not allow us to ask whether its view of America is true; it is so clear-sighted, level-headed, and undramatic that we accept it as true. We cannot undermine its effects by citing impatience, hysteria, an idiosyncratic shooting style. It makes us confront the accuracy of what it depicts. It is as clear and unmistakable as daylight, and it uses its audience's vision as an X-ray.

The Brothers Rico is so unsentimental (compared to earlier fifties films) that it cannot end without making it explicit that the values of the old world are irrevocably destroyed. All it can do is to suggest (unconvincingly) that there must be a way of living in a syndicate-image society without succumbing to the grossly evil nature of a syndicate as such. That is all that seems possible toward the end of the fifties. Cubik is forced to come down to Mulberry Street in person to search for Eddie and is destroyed there, at the place of his origins. But Mama too is crushed, her values violated by Cubik's treachery, her sons murdered. It is through the old grandmother, however, that Karlson suggests the permanent passing of an old way of life.

She is in two scenes. The first (a comic scene) has her watching the TV Eddie has sent, a big, large-screen monster that sticks out like a sore thumb in the surroundings. Grandma loves it and watches it all day. She mistakes Eddie for Gino and is vaguely aware that his presence is a special event. She babbles in Italian, and Eddie dredges some up for the occasion. Eddie and Mama, after the formalities, leave her glued to the TV. She is the old world on its way out, eased out by the great modern distraction, television. Near the conclusion there is a briefer, gloomier version of this scene. Eddie, escaping Cubik's men, runs into the store on Mulberry Street. He passes Grandma, still sitting in front of the TV, on his way toward his mother with the news that Gino and Johnny are dead. Eddie pauses for a moment to exchange a formal greeting with Grandma and hold her hand, which she extends. He moves toward the rear of the frame, back to camera, to face his mother, and when he lets go of Grandma's hand, her arm travels in a lazy arc across the bottom of the frame in the foreground. She mumbles something afterward, but that is the last we see of her. The movement of her arm is a gesture of farewell. It droops listlessly out of the frame and may be read as expressing the death of the old world.

The Ricos may go on living, but not on Mulberry Street. The new Rico—Johnny's son, Antonio (named after the father)—is born on a California farm and will not have a Rico for a father. The legitimate line stops there, since Eddie must adopt. It is all over for the Ricos, and for a particular chapter of American social life. The film takes perhaps an ambivalent position on its disappearance. In a sense it had to go, but its going involves a human loss. From the evidence the film gives, however, there in nothing to replace it except the world we have been shown, ready to resume its course after the ripple has died down. The shop on Mulberry Street may close, but there will be a new tenant for the suite vacated by Cubik at the Excelsior Hotel.

Unlike the old days, the defeat of the villain (and the success of the hero) does not seem to resolve anything. Simple resolutions are out of the question in a world in which the conditions of humanity are so precarious and our perceptions of reality so confused. There are no clear labels on anything, and we leave the film disturbed. We haven't conquered noir's jitters, merely pushed them below the surface. *The Brothers Rico* is as true to the life of its period as *D.O.A.* was to its. It gives us the surface, and looking at it gives us the jitters. There is no cure for these jitters and the unease we feel toward the film's matter-of-factness and its unsatisfying conclusion we must carry with us back to life, creating an echo chamber between film and reality. The world outside the film is more entrenched than the world of the film, and it is too set in its ways for us to make it any different. After all, if the movies can't do it for us, it is a sign that it can't be done.

Courtesy of A.I. Bezzerides

The screenwriter of *Kiss Me Deadly*, A. I. Bezzerides, seen here on a film location.

The Thieves' Market:

A. I. BEZZERIDES IN HOLLYWOOD

LEE SERVER

A. I. Bezzerides is a California native of Greek descent, a former truck driver and electrical engineer, and the author of two hard-boiled novels, *The Long Haul* and *Thieves' Market,* both turned into movies (*They Drive by Night* with George Raft and Humphrey Bogart, and *Thieves' Highway* with Richard Conte and Lee J. Cobb) in the 1940s. He has written thirteen produced screenplays, most of them tough, quirky thrillers with notably anarchic heroes.

His best film, *Kiss Me Deadly,* was derived from a Mickey Spillane bestseller, but Bezzerides, given free reign by producer-director Robert Aldrich, subverted the source material to create something else again, an unhinged, apocalyptic masterpiece. Its unique style mixed savagery and allusion, allegory and deadpan satire. Praised at the time by the French New Wave, the film was a decided influence on Truffaut's *Shoot the Piano Player* and Godard's *Alphaville* and *Made in USA*.

In his screenplay, Bezzerides takes Nietzschean Neanderthal Mike Hammer on a violent, postatomic quest for the "Great Whatsit," a Pandora's box of deadly attraction, crossing his path with a gallery of the corrupt and the crazy: a dimwitted murderess, a mythology-spouting scientist, a thieving autopsy surgeon, an escaped lunatic, and a nymphomaniac ("Whatever it is, the answer's *yes!*"). The explosive isotopes in Pandora's box are Bezzerides's final, existential punch line: the quest leads only to oblivion.

Bezzerides lives in Woodland Hills, in the San Fernando Valley, with his wife, Sylvia Richards, who has also written for the movies (*Ruby Gentry, Possessed*). Most mornings he heads for a nearby diner, Ryons, where he'll have breakfast and, somehow ignoring the clatter of silverware and conversation around him, will work on his latest writing projects. It's at Ryons where he agrees to meet me one morning, telling me to look for the "good-looking bald guy with glasses."

I arrive a little early and start scanning the tops of heads. A waitress tells me "Buzz" hasn't shown up yet. She offers to point him out when he arrives, but there's no need. Bezzerides spots me as he comes through the door and begins talking at me from across the floor as if we saw each other every day. He is a powerfully built man in his late seventies, grizzled, with thick shocks of white hair sticking out of his open shirt. A ripe Saroyanesque personality, he converses like a force of nature, roaming through subject matter and chewing it up—politics, religion, race, producers, and car repair. His free association—very free at times—doesn't make him easy to interview, and it's obvious he doesn't have much interest in the films he's signed his name to. Too many compromises, too much interference. Bezzerides had plenty of talent; others had the power. "Obligations," he says, made him take most of his movie and TV assignments. The producers got more than their money's worth out of Bezzerides, a writer with the energy and disposition to give his all to any project. They only occasionally made good use of it. Too often efficiency, not artistry, was all they wanted—"Don't do it good, do it today." But that, any Hollywood veteran will tell you, is an old story.

Tell me how you came to work in the movies?

Writers never understand: producers are the goddamnedest crooks you ever saw. And they think that writing is *shit*.

I wrote a book about truckers called *The Long Haul*. Warner Bros. wanted to buy it and they offered $1,500. I said, "Gee, that doesn't seem like much to buy the movie rights." I was very naïve. So the agent said, "We'll see if we can get more." And we went to Warner Bros. to see Mark Hellinger, the producer. As we walked into his office, Hellinger took something off the table and put it underneath something else. I saw the title, *They Drive by Night*. Well, the agent got them up to $2,500. I thought, "Well, if that's all we can get, I need the money." I was working as an engineer at that time. Then I read in the trades that Warner Bros. is making a picture about truckers and so forth, based on *The Long Haul*, and it's going into production. So that's when I find out that they'd already done a script. Jerry Wald's written *They Drive by Night* using my novel and using the ending of another story, *Bordertown*. They used it without permission, before they even bought it. A writer at the studio said to me, "You must have made a killing on *The Long Haul*." I said, "I got $2,500." "$2,500?" he says. "You could have gotten $100,000 out of them." They were about to make a picture called *The Patent Leather Kid*, but George Raft couldn't lose his potbelly and couldn't fit into the boxing trunks. They had a cast ready to go and no picture, so Wald did the trucking story. The script was done before they bought the story. They were lying to me.

But Warner Bros. put you under contract?

Yeah, they hired me. I had been working as an engineer, writing on the side. I'd written two novels, *The Long Haul* and *Thieves' Market*. They were based on things I'd seen with my father or on my own. I worked with my father, trucking, going to the market to buy produce. There was corruption and they'd try to screw you. When he was selling grapes, the packing house would screw him on the price and then sell to New York for an expensive price. When I was trucking I wouldn't allow it. A guy tried to rob me in such a blatant way I picked up a two-by-four and I was going to kill him.

I studied to be an engineer and I worked as an engineer at the Department of Water and Power. But then I went to work for Warner Bros., at $300 a week, and that was the end of my working as an engineer.

They put me on a picture called *Juke Girl*. Ronald Reagan and Ann Sheridan. I worked with a guy named Ken Gamet. He didn't like what I did with the thing. He had fallen for all the stereotype forms for "B" pictures. He didn't know the subject. He was a Hollywood character and hadn't gone through anything like this story. But I had been involved in that scene, I knew about people wandering into a town to pick crops. So I could write reality, and he couldn't. He hadn't been exposed to that reality. And we had some problems working together. He couldn't admit that he had something to gain from my point of view. And this is where a lot of writers go wrong, defending their egos.

So you didn't have any trouble adapting yourself to writing in screenplay form?

I had a certain visuality. When I was a kid, before I thought of being a writer, I used to look closely at things. I noticed a lot. I was very observant. And I began taking pictures with a camera when I was a kid, and endlessly took pictures. So I had no real problem writing for the movie camera. Dick Powell, when he had become a producer, wanted me to direct for him. He thought I wrote very visually. I turned him down. I just wanted to write. I'm sorry I did now. I think I could have directed all right.

Tell me about the writer's life at Warner Bros. in that period.

Jack Warner thought you had to create from nine to five. He'd be at the window when you got in late and you'd get a note or some such thing. He thought you could create at a certain time and then stop. But it doesn't work like that. You're creative at home, when you're driving in your car, it could be any time. But he could never understand it. I remember him walking in on us shooting craps on the floor in the writer's building. Steve Fisher, Frank Gruber, and me and some of the others shooting craps and we hear Warner barge in. *"Who's winning?"* he'd say. He didn't like it, but he couldn't really stop it.

Jack Warner was always saying something stupid. Warner would make these ridiculous dumb jokes in the executive dining room and all the producers would laugh and laugh and laugh. The writers ate at their own table. They didn't like to associate with producers. Nobody wanted them around, picking your brain. They'd take your ideas. Even take your conversation. I remember one day at the writers' table sitting next to Jerry Wald. I was working with him and we were talking about it, and Wald says, "Jesus Christ, Buzz, that's a cliché." And I say, "Jerry, everything is a cliché. You're born, you live, die, all clichés. It's what you do with the clichés that's important." A couple weeks later at the writers' table, somebody's talking about a meeting with Jerry Wald. Jerry wants some old bit in the script, and writer told him it's the oldest cliché in the book. And what did Jerry say? "Life's a cliché! You're born, you live . . ." That's a producer for you.

***Why didn't you get screen credit for* Action in the North Atlantic?**

Because of John Howard Lawson. *Action in the North Atlantic* was basically a piece of propaganda for our alliance with Russia. I was put on it to fix it. There were scenes in there . . . one with Bogart and the girl, and one with Raymond Massey and his wife, that were so out of context in their propagandistic way that the actors couldn't even act them. I polished every scene in that picture. I was entitled to credit. But when it came to arbitration, Lawson was so strong in the Guild that I couldn't get it. They protected their own.

I knew a lot of them working at Warner Bros. The Hollywood Ten guys. I used to drive three or four writers home every day, and one of them was Albert Maltz. We'd start driving and Maltz would say, "Tell me about your background. Tell me about so and so . . ." And I thought he was interested, and I'd start to tell him some story. But the moment I got to his house, he got out, with my story dangling. He didn't care what I was saying, he just wanted someone to occupy his mind till he got home. But I got back. Next time I'd be telling a story, I didn't let him out of the car. I kept driving around in circles near his house till I was finished.

And I worked with Alvah Bessie on something called *Baby Marine.* They had me break in Alvah. And we had a scene with a truckload of recruits, and a soldier's opening a cake he got from his mother. Alvah says,

"Let's do this scene like this. The kid takes a piece of cake and walks all the way over to the one black soldier and gives it to him. We'll show he's not prejudiced." I said, "How about we have him open his cake and say, 'Fellas, dig in', and you show whites, blacks, chicanos all helping themselves, instead of making a big point of it? Your way is labored." But he couldn't see it. He wanted to do things like that over and over. I couldn't work with him and I quit the picture.

And Alvah Bessie used to be one helluva writer, before the Spanish Civil War. After that he had to prove every day what he believed in.

It was at Warner Bros. that you became friends with William Faulkner? He lived with you for a while, didn't he?

Faulkner lived at my house. He was fond of me, considered himself a member of the family. He was making $300 a week and he was starving on it. He was sending the money home. That was one of the reasons why he stayed with me. He'd been drunk so often that no producer would hire him any more. But Warner Bros. hired him, and Warner boasted that he had the best writer in the world for "peanuts."

The first time I met Faulkner I was still working as an engineer. My wife and I were having dinner with some friends at the Pig 'n' Whistle. We saw Faulkner sitting at a table with his girlfriend. I recognized him instantly and I had to go over to him. I said, "I don't usually go around knocking on people's doors, but I've read all your books, everything you've written, and I think you're a great writer." And he shot up and said, "Thank you, suh!" We shook hands and I went back to my table, very embarrassed.

Four years later, I'm at Warner Bros. and I'd been there a few months when who do I see coming down the aisle between the secretaries but Faulkner. He had a pipe in his mouth and he had a way of walking leaning way backwards. Well, I see him and he sees me. I say, "Do you remember me?" He says, "Yes, suh, I do. What are you doing here?" I said, "I'm a writer." (Laughs.) I said, "What are you doing here?" And he said, "Uh, I'm a writer, too."

We talked. I asked him where he was staying. He was living at a hotel. He was going to catch a cab home and I said I'd take him home. And then we went to the endless places where he went to get drunk. And he could get *drunk,* man. I had to take him to the hospital, to dry out. Then I'd take him home, and he'd be very shaky.

One time he was in bad shape, asking me to get him a bottle of rum. I didn't want to, but if I didn't he said he was going to drink a bottle of hair tonic he had. So I went to get it. But first I took the hair tonic and hid it in a hole under the sink. I didn't have the nerve to empty it because he'd been snapping the blade out that he used to clean his pipe. I said, "Hey, what are you doing with that thing?" He said, "Oh . . . I'm gonna cut my agent's balls off."

I went out and when I got back with the rum he was passed out on the floor. He had found that goddamned bottle of hair tonic. I got him up and I told him again what the doctor had said, that if he didn't stop drinking like that he was going to kill himself. I left him alone for a few minutes and when I came back he had disappeared with his two bags. I yell, "Bill, Bill, where'd you go?" I ran out to look for him. He was outside the hotel, lugging his two bags up the hill. I caught up with him and said, "What the hell are you doing?" He said, "Gonna have a heart attack." So I held him, knocked the bags out of his hands, took him in my arms and tried to get him back to his room. And he was struggling with himself. I asked him what he's doing. He says, "Trying to get down." But it was his own collar he's pulling on, not mine. So I started laughing and he was laughing. He was something, all right.

He wrote *A Fable* in my house.

He'd by typing away in the middle of the night. Worked right on the typewriter, typed all night. I walked in on him, asked him what he was working on there in the middle of the night. He said, "Oh . . . on a novel." "Well . . . what's it about?" He said, "Oh, it's about Jesus Christ coming to earth during the World War." I laughed. I said, "I have to ask you a terrible question. Who the hell gave you entry to write about Jesus Christ?" Well, he gave me a look that told me it was the last time he'd talk story with me. But he finished the book and it was a stinker, one of his lousiest books.

What did he think of his movie work?

He had a contempt for it. Get the paycheck, that's all. Sometimes he'd think he would do it for the art. He wanted to do *Pickwick Papers.* And he wrote *The De Gaulle Story,* at four hundred pages. And that was a bunch of shit.

Faulkner and I were put together on a script at Warner's, to polish a picture called *Escape in the Desert.* We sat in the office and sat and sat and sat. I didn't want to start writing for fear of embarrassing him. I wanted him to start and then we could pitch in together. But he didn't say a word. Finally, I got exasperated and I said, "Hey, Bill, we got to write!" And he turned and looked at me and said, "Shucks, Buzz, it ain't nuthin' but a *moom picture."* So, screw him, I decided to start trying to write. And I started and finally he began to think of things. There was a scene in there where the Nazis are in the desert and he thought of a bit where a rattlesnake jumps out and frightens them. That was Faulkner's scene. And Warner read it and didn't want to shoot the scene. He said it would frighten pregnant women and give them spontaneous abortions. I said to Warner, "If you can guarantee *that,* you'll have a big hit." Jack didn't get it. He said, "No, no, they'll sue us."

But Howard Hawks was always trying to give Faulkner work. And Faulkner didn't do anything with Hawks, really. Bill's contribution would be little bits here and there. But the continuity of a script, he couldn't do it. The screenplay form was alien to him. He was musclebound with his talent. He needed prose so he could run off with it.

He loved Hawks, though, got along with him very well. You know why? Because they could sit there together and not say anything. Commune in silence. Hawks would ask a question and they'd have a few drinks. Faulkner would be "thinking" and after a long while he'd finally nod his head and say, "Uh-huh."

What did you do after leaving Warner's?

When I ended with Warner's I went to Paramount. I was supposed to work with John Houseman. But nothing we worked on ever got made. I respected John but we had trouble getting anything finished. Houseman was the kind of guy who'd tell you what to do and not listen to any of the problems. He only wanted his ideas, even if they didn't work.

At MGM we worked together on a picture called *Holiday for Sinners.* We did another one when he went to RKO. I did *On Dangerous Ground* for him and Nick Ray. And they left me completely alone during the writing of that one. But on the structure he wouldn't let me have my way. I told them, "You've got a beginning to this story, and an end to this story that gives meaning to the body of the story. You must use the beginning and the ending." We start with the cop in the city being called up for his violence. He's a vicious cop, vicious to criminals because he can rationalize it. Criminals are criminals to him, they're not people. So he's sent out of the city for his behavior, out to the mountains. And he gets involved with the blind girl and her brother, who has killed someone. And she tells him about her brother, and he gets some insight into this kid who's committed a crime. She's made him think. And when he confronts the kid at the edge of the cliff, he says, "Look, I'm not going to hurt you. I have to arrest you, but don't be afraid." But the kid is afraid, of the policeman's power, of what he represents, and the kid tries to escape and falls to his death. And now we have the end, and the cop must go back to the city, the city filled with violence. And the cop knows that violence is in him and it's going to be a struggle for him. But he's a better cop already, because the memory of that kid and what his presence did to him—made that kid die—has given him insight. But they wouldn't do it. They wouldn't do it that way.

They ended it with him going back to the blind girl.

It ruined the structure. They wouldn't listen.

One critic I read said Ray shot it or cut it to imply a "miracle."

Oh, shit.

But it's still a very good picture.

The beginning and the ending ruined it for me. But it was a helluva picture. Bob Ryan was perfect. Houseman again; he could have controlled the situation, because Ray wasn't that sure of himself. But there was no way to talk to them.

These nonwriters think they can do what they want to a carefully constructed script and it won't turn into a piece of crap. They're wrong. But nobody tells them that. Fox bought another novel of mine, a book called *Thieves' Market.* They didn't want to use the original title because "San Francisco objects to it." So, *Thieves' Highway.* So who cares? I said okay. Then the director, Julie Dassin says, "For the prostitute, I want Valentina Cortesa, so rewrite it for her." He was going with her. We were going to have Shelley Winters, who would have been perfect. This Italian, Cortesa, what would she be doing in this story? I said, "But . . . Julie!" But I rewrote it. And we go to the meeting with Zanuck—and already the picture is getting fucked up before that.

So we go to Zanuck's office. He's got a yes-man standing there, lips puckered to kiss Zanuck's ass. And Zanuck goes like this—holds his hand out, and the flunky immediately puts a Coke in his hand. I said, "Hey, how about me?" (Laughs.) And Zanuck said, "Get him one too."

Now in my story the father is dead at the beginning. The kid starts trucking because he's trying to make his father's life valid. The first thing Zanuck says is, "I want a new beginning. I want the father still alive. He's crippled, that's why the kid's trucking." It was bullshit. But I said, "Yes, Mr. Zanuck." I write another beginning, this revenge business. The picture didn't do real well. There were good things in it, but it wasn't the picture I wanted to do, it wasn't the story I wanted to do. I had the producer's chickenshit changes, the director's girlfriend, and Zanuck's ideas. I only knew that story from my life, my book, my script. But that didn't matter. Oh, I tell you, once you give in a little bit you're finished.

I worked on a lot of things people wanted fixed or rewritten. I did a lot of things with Bob Aldrich. I did *Sirocco* for Bogart. There was a script that was no good, and Curt Bernhardt asked me to rewrite it. It was for Bogart's production company. Bogart and Bob Lord were partners. So I start rewriting the thing. And three days into it, as I'm turning in pages, Lord calls me in. He says, "I'm firing Curt." I said, "Why?" He said, "Don't ask me why." I said, "Look, I'm on this job because of him. So I don't know if that'll work out with him fired. I'm upset about this." So Lord kept him on. And then Bernhardt got some guy from Germany in to work with me. And he did nothing. But he'd lie back, and as I finished a scene he'd say, "It's wonderful how you can take my ideas and put them in the script." But I didn't care. The picture got made. I worked with what I had. This was one of—what's his name—Zero Mostel's first things, and there were scenes between him and Nick, the little Greek, and how could you resist writing a comic scene for them?

It's a pretty depressing picture, though. Especially the ending, Bogart knowingly walking to his death, the Arab throwing the hand grenade in on him.

It was that character's fate. You knew he was doomed. They didn't give me any problem with it. I got along okay with Bogart. He wasn't very involved creatively. He knew me, trusted me because I'd worked on *Action in the North Atlantic* that he was in.

Can we talk about* Kiss Me Deadly*? I think it's your best screenplay.

I knew Bob Aldrich when he was an assistant director. We were going to do a picture, a Western, for Burt Lancaster. I had just started working on it. And we're going to lunch-Lancaster, Aldrich, and some other people. And Burt was grabbing my arm, telling me all sorts of shit that had to be in the picture. And there was so much crap. He didn't know his ass from a hot rock. So I said, "Burt, why don't you stick to acting and leave the writing to the writer." Well, he looked at me. And after lunch I went to my office and packed my stuff. I knew I was fired and I wanted to beat the message.

Bob called me, asked me "Why'd you do that?" I said, "He's telling me what to do and I can't write with somebody doing that."

And later, when Bob was directing and he wanted me, he knew the best thing was to let me alone. He gave me the Mickey Spillane book *Kiss Me Deadly,* and I said, "This is lousy. Let me see what I can do." You give me a piece of junk, I can't write it. I have to write something else. So I went to work on it. I wrote it fast, because I had contempt for it. It was automatic writing. You get into a kind of stream and you can't stop. I get into psychic isolation sometimes when I'm writing.

How long did it take to write?

About three weeks. I wrote at home, day and night. On some things I'm fast. On some things I'm slow. I do a lot of drafts, over and over. I copy and then I edit, cross out. Writing is hard, and sometimes you only discover what you're looking for by hard work, writing and rewriting.

What made you decide to change the contents of the Pandora's box from drugs to radioactive material?

People ask me—or they asked Aldrich—about the hidden meanings in the script, about the A-bomb, about McCarthyism, what does the poetry mean, and so on. And I can only say that I didn't think about it when I wrote it. These things were in the air at the time and I put them in. There was a lot of talk about nuclear war at the time, and it was the foremost fear in people's minds. Nuclear arms race. Well, I thought that was more interesting than the dope thing in the book. The Pandora's box references related to these characters, and the same with the poem by Rossetti.

I was having fun with it. I wanted to make every scene, every character, interesting. A girl comes up to Ralph Meeker, I make her a nympho. She grabs him and kisses him the first time she sees him. She says, "You don't taste like anybody I know." I'm a big car nut, so I put in all that stuff with the cars and the mechanic. I was an engineer and I gave the detective the first phone answering machine in that picture. I was having fun.

It's a truly nihilistic film . . . every character seems intent on self-destruction.

It was not too long after Hiroshima.

The threat of nuclear war hanging in the air. And we did it. It didn't come from the cosmos. My mother—not a political animal—listened to the McCarthy hearings, and she shook her head and said, "What are they doing to this beautiful country?" Look at it today, where you don't dare drink the water or walk across the soil. You can't breathe the air. You can't eat the food they're growing. Man's doing it all to himself. He'll go around killing millions of innocent people and rationalize it. I think man has been programmed long, long ago so that he self-destructs. And it's finally paying off. But there are certain shits in our society who don't care because they think they will be above it all when it happens. They think they can escape their destiny, but they can't.

Anyway, I was just writing. The Pandora's box was just a substitute for the dope. When you opened the box a little, it radiated. When the girl flings it open, it blazes. Dramatic.

The Mike Hammer character is unusually brutal for a Hollywood movie of that time.

The character in the book is that way. I just heightened his natural violence. I tell you, Spillane didn't like what I did with his book. I ran into him in a restaurant and, boy, he didn't like me.

But the brutishness seems typical of several of your protagonists—the Ryan character in* On Dangerous Ground, *Mitchum in* Track of the Cat, *Richard Conte in* Thieves' Highway. *Their violence is obsessive, unsympathetic.

Those characters fit those stories, that's all. I don't sympathize with their violence. But it is more interesting to write. Violence, traumatic events, these are the feelings that go deep. Under hypnosis, you don't remember pleasant things, always tragic things. Joy passes. Fear and anger don't pass. They sink into your genes.

Kiss Me Deadly *was considered another B movie here. Were you aware of how well received it was in Europe? It made Aldrich's reputation with the critics there.*

I hadn't realized how seriously they had taken it. Somebody from one of the French movie magazines tracked me down in my hotel in France. I don't know how he found me. And he wanted to know about *Kiss Me Deadly* and about Aldrich. They asked me this, that, how certain things got into the picture. I told him, "I *wrote* it." He couldn't believe it wasn't Aldrich. The poem, the bomb. I laughed. I said, "Aldrich directed it, but I wrote it." I was embarrassed. He said, "For many years we have thought of this New Wave picture as Aldrich's. But it is you." I couldn't believe what went on there. Truffaut, for Christ's sake, thought it was one of the best pictures made. I was awed.

One time I went over to visit a friend of mine, Nancy Nicholas. There was a big camper sitting outside her house when I got there. And in the kitchen there was a young guy drinking coffee. He was French. Nancy introduced me, said I was a writer. He asked me what I wrote. He wasn't too thrilled by it all. And I said I'd written a picture some of the French seemed to think was all right. "Oh yes?" he says. "What's that?" I said, "Oh, it was a crappy little picture, *Kiss Me Deadly.*" And he shot up fast. "*Kiss Me Deadly!*" And he goes out and gets his friend, and they both come back and stare at me. I said, "What are you so excited about? It's a piece of junk. I heard you French liked it, but . . . " They just kept staring at me with their mouths hanging open.

Aldrich took credit for everything, of course, when they asked him about it. But it's funny . . . a couple of months before he died he called me. He told me he'd been wondering how the hell he had shot *Kiss Me Deadly* in twenty days. So he had taken out the script and reread it. He said, "Now I know. It's all there. It's in the script."

The Welles Touch:

CHARLTON HESTON ON ORSON WELLES

JAMES DELSON

H**ow did the* **Touch of Evil** *project come to be produced?

It was submitted to me in December of 1956 by Universal, for whom I had made a successful comedy called *The Private War of Major Benson.* Since its release I had finished *Ten Commandments,* done a play in New York, and I was loafing over the holiday when Universal sent the script.

"It's a good enough script," I said, "but police stories, like Westerns and war stories, have been so overdone that it really depends on who's going to direct it." I told them I'd put it down and call them later.

They told me that although they didn't know who was going to direct it, Orson Welles was going to play the heavy. "You know, Orson Welles is a pretty good director," I said. "Did it ever occur to you to have him direct it?" At that time, Orson had not directed a picture in America since *Macbeth.* They were a bit nonplussed, but they got back to me in a couple of days and said, "Yeah, well that's a very good idea. A startling idea."

At this time, was Welles considered a cult figure at all?

About *Citizen Kane* he was. There was a rich preoccupation with the idea of Welles as a rebel, I guess, but they brought him in on the picture. He totally rewrote the script in about seventeen days, which I knew he would, and didn't object to.

He got a solo writing credit for it.

Well, he deserved it. He gives you your value. He has a reputation as being an extravagant director, but there are directors who have wasted more money on one film than Orson has spent on all the pictures he's directed in his career.

Nonetheless, people say, "Oh, you can't hire Orson because he's extravagant." Mike Nichols went farther over budget on *Catch-22* than Orson has spent on all the films he has directed, put together. In my experience, in the one film I made for him, Orson is by no means an extravagant director. As I recall, we had something like a forty-or forty-two-day shooting schedule and a budget of slightly under a million dollars, and we went a couple of days and about $75,000 over the budget. Now that really is not an outlandish, horrifying situation at all. The difference between that film *with* Welles and that film *without* Welles would be remarkable. His contribution as an actor, of course, was incredible. I would say the only major error that Orson made in the film was his conviction that he had to conceal something: the fact that his part was the best part in the film, as he had rewritten the script. In fact, it was evident anyway—I knew it. *Touch of Evil* is about the decline and fall of Captain Quinlan. My part is a kind of witness to this.

I agree that he wrote the best part for himself, but you're one of the three or four actors who have worked with Welles without being dwarfed by him, physically in terms of screen persona, or dramatically in terms of just plain showmanship. In watching the film recently, this is one of its aspects that I noted most carefully, knowing that this point would come up. I was looking to see how you would handle yourself when the famous Wellesian scene-stealing took place. In the scene where Joe Calleia "finds" the sticks of dynamite in the shoe box, Welles is playing it up, but you, through the opposite means, subduing every gesture and restraining yourself, manage to hold your own, which is a feat.

Well, I am happy to subscribe to the thesis that I can stand on equal ground with Orson in a scene, but that doesn't change the fact that Orson is party to that part, and that the film is *about* Captain Quinlan, really. But that's the way it should be. That's the story. I play a man who's looking for his wife, really.

Actually, I have Orson to thank for the fact that the part is as interesting as it was, because it was his idea to make it a Mexican detective. I said, "I can't play a Mexican detective!" He said "Sure you can! We'll dye your hair black, and put on some dark makeup and draw a black moustache, sure you can! We'll get a Mexican tailor to cut you a good Mexican suit." And they did, and it's plausible enough, I suppose, I play a plausible Mexican. As a matter of fact, it doesn't contribute to the stereotype of the sombrero Mexican lazing around in the shade.

Did Universal agree to let Welles act in the film so long as he directed it?

They imposed on him, for budget reasons. They were willing to take a chance on him directing, but only on that budget.

Was casting begun immediately upon the signing of Welles?

No. The first thing was his reworking of the script. He wanted it to be set on the Mexican border, and they wouldn't go for location work at that time. You must remember that this was sixteen years ago. Welles found an entirely acceptable substitute in Venice, California.

It was more than acceptable. Remind me not to visit Venice, California. Welles achieved a new low in ramshackle buildings, locations, and degeneracy. In searching for locations, and other preproduction work, did you play an active part?

Not *nearly* the amount I do now. I was consulted about things, but did not really participate on a serious level. I helped in things like casting. I had approval.

Was there anybody cast who you were either exceeding pleased or displeased over?

I thought all of the casting was marvelous. There was some uncertainty over the casting of the girl, who was played by Janet Leigh.

I guess she was very big at that time.

The studio wanted to use her very much. This casting was, in fact, almost imposed, and . . . as a matter of fact, it turned out better than I thought it would. I thought she was quite good. I don't think Orson was terribly upset about it. All the other casting I had approval on and, as far as I know, Orson made all the other castings.

There were some fine performances, especially Joe Calleia. I think it's one of the very best pieces of work he did in his whole career.

I thought the cameos were a nice touch.

Orson got his cronies to do them. Joe Cotton and Marlene Dietrich were fun, yeah.

Orson Welles as director. That's the dream of many fine actors. What is it that makes him special to work with?

He's exciting. He makes it fun.

Then why is it that he can't get the money to make films? He makes films that are literate, and as close as one can get to pure cinema, both in terms of artistic achievement and entertainment. I'm sorry. That was a rhetorical outburst. We were talking about how Welles works.

Film acting is not often very interesting. Even if you have a fascinating part with four or five major scenes, which is unusual, those scenes don't take up half the running time of the film, or the shooting time of the film, either. The bulk of your day is . . . well a good case in point is a scene from *Skyjacked,* where I came out of the flight deck and went into the john, where I saw the scrawled message saying that the plane was being skyjacked. I didn't say anything. I looked at Yvette [Mimieux], and in the course of that look, what they describe as a "charged look," I had to show "problems, what am I doing here, what are all these carryings on," and also "I'm involved in some kind of complicated relationship with this girl, and I'd really rather not be flying with her. All things considered, but on the other hand . . . " That's about all there is to the first shot. No lines . . . That was my first day's work on the picture. That's all there was to the first day. That's not all they did, but that's all I did. You understand the motivation, you've read the script, you know the importance of establishing the thing with the girl, but still it's really not the most marvelous day's work you've ever done. Orson has the capacity as a director to somehow persuade you that each time is indeed the most important day in the picture, and that's kind of marvelous, and I applaud it.

Is he this way with all the actors? Minor scenes as well, bit parts?

I think so, yes.

Can we talk about the first shot? The famous first shot?

This first shot in *Touch of Evil* is, as I said, technically one of the most brilliant shots I have ever seen in any film. Among film buffs it has become a classic shot.

It's in all of the books.

Is it? Is it in some books? Well, for the record, it begins on a close-up insert of a bundle of sticks of dynamite, and it pans up just enough to apprehend an unidentifiable figure dashing out of the frame. As the pan continues, you see in the middle distance a couple coming out of the door of a bar, and going even deeper into the background, and turning around the back of the building and disappearing. Led by the couple's exit, the camera pans down the alley in the direction in which the figure holding the dynamite has fled, on the near side of the building, going in the same direction. You see the figure (and of course now you can't possibly identify him) dart behind the building. Following with the camera, but still too far away to tell who he is, he lifts the trunk of a car and puts what is obviously a bomb into the car, slams the lid, and disappears into the shadows just as the camera, now lifting above the car, picks up the couple coming around the other side of the building and getting in the car. You establish him as a fat political type and her as a floozy blonde type. And they carry on—there's enough awareness of their dialogue to establish a kind of drunken nonchalance.

The camera booms up on a chapmain boom as the car drives out of the parking lot and out into the street. The boom sinks down, picks up the car, and picks up me and Janet Leigh walking along and talking. The camera then moves ahead of both us and the car, the car's progress being to some degree impeded by foot traffic, so as to keep us more-or-less in the same context. But first you pick up the car and then us walking, and in the course of our movement you establish that we are just married and honeymooning. All the time, on the sound track you hear the ticking of the bomb.

By this time we get to the border station and have a little dialogue that established me as a government official. We go through the Mexican station, and then through the U.S. station, and the car does too, and there's a little carrying-on that makes it clear that this fellow is a guy with some political clout . . .

And the girl says, "My watch is awfully loud, I think I hear something ticking."

No. "There's this ticking in my head" . . . she's drunk. Then the car zooms past us out of shot, we now being in the United States, and there's some dialogue to the effect that we've just been married and I haven't kissed her in an hour and I pull her into my arms and kiss her and of course as our lips touch the car explodes off screen. That's quite a shot.

That is called Orson Welles.

It took all one night to shoot, as indeed it might. And the spooky thing about night-shooting, night exteriors, is that when the sun comes up, that's all, you've got to quit. And we were shooting in Venice and we . . . Oh, I don't know, laying the shot was incredibly complicated. The boom work with the Chupman boom was the major creative contribution. The men who ran the boom had a *terribly* difficult job, but they finally were getting so it was working well enough to do takes on it, and we did two or three or four takes, and in each take the customs man, who had just one line, would flub his line.

Oh Christ.

Cause he'd see this great complex of cars and lights and booms bearing down on him from three blocks away, and they'd get closer and closer, and finally there they would all be, and he would blow his line. I will concede that Orson did not do a great deal to stimulate his . . . Orson said, "Look, I don't care what you say, just move your lips, we can dub it later. Don't just put your face in your hands and say 'Oh my God, I'm sorry.' "And of course the fellow never did get the line. He finally managed to blow the line impassively. He just stood there moving his lips impotently.

At which point Welles gave him a medal and his walking papers. At this time, were you beginning to take a creative interest in the technical aspects of the films you were working on?

Well, you begin to, if you have any brains, the first time you work on a film. This was the first film on which I was quite as aware of the enormous creative composition of the camera, which is not surprising since Russ Metty was the cameraman. I sat and watched Orson fiddle with sequences with his cutter, and it was a very learningful experience.

That's the kind of experience that most of us would give our shirts for.

Yeah, it's valuable.

Is he a perfectionist?

No.

In terms of just putting things right?

I think that's the last thing Orson is. He probably has a larger measure of talent, whatever the hell that means, than anybody else I've ever met, but a perfectionist he is not. He can get an *incredible* idea about how to solve a scene, or a piece of casting, or a bit of writing, or an editing problem. But rather than polish it to perfection, he is likely to substitute still another idea that is nearly as good or maybe better. But, I would say, he is disinclined to sandpaper.

Does he get a lot of coverage? I know Sam Peckinpah sometimes uses eighteen or nineteen cover shots on one setup.

No. Now, mind you, at the time I made *Touch of Evil* I wasn't as sophisticated an observer of the mechanics of film-making as I am now. But, nonetheless, in my memory . . . well, the first shot is . . . what I've said to you. There is no cutting to that. They just got the slate off it and that's the first three minutes of the film.

The studio likes that kind of thing. [Both laugh.]

Was Welles doing any rewriting when the film was being made? Or was he working straight through?

Not once we started shooting. I think that's one of the reasons *Touch of Evil* could be said to have turned out better than *Major Dundee*. Sam had to attempt to undertake his rewrite while shooting the film. Orson undertook his and accomplished it before shooting.

How would you describe the working relationship you had with him during the film?

Enchanted. Orson seduces you in a marvelous way. You know he's one of the most charming men in the world, if it's important to him to be charming. He is, at *minimum,* interesting—but it it's important to him to enlist your support and cooperation, he is as charming a man as I have ever seen.

And was he so with the rest of the crew as well would you say?

Oh yes. See, that's an important thing. Orson elicits remarkable support from his companies, he asks a lot from them, his crews too, but he jokes with them and recognizes what they're doing, their contributions, and it works *marvelously.* They put out a great effort for him.

It shows in the fact that he got tiny performances, one-scene performances, that are memorable.

Yeah, that's it. Sam, on the other hand, *requires* your commitment, and that's not quite the same thing as *eliciting* your support. Because you can choose not to deliver your commitment. Personally, in my own style of work, I prefer working as an individual film actor, in a somewhat more detached manner. I think you tend to get into a hothouse atmosphere. You're living in each other's laps anyway, and it's long days, and I frankly prefer a little more detached and cool relationship. But you've got to do it the way the director wants. In both the case of Sam, who demanded it and required it, and Orson, who elicits it, that's the way you go. But some people won't make that kind of commitment to Sam.

On individual scenes when you'd be working with Welles—would he say do this and this and this and this—in a way some directors will—or is he a director who will let you create and then say "Well, maybe this and maybe this?"

By and large, assuming the contribution of professional actors . . . in my experience on forty films the complexities of the mechanics of filming and the creative problems they present tend to preoccupy a director to a large degree. A good actor is likely to have a fairly free hand in the shaping of his—certainly of his character, possibly of the scene as well. I'm not speaking of a Wyler or Stevens or Lean, but most directors, even directors like those I've mentioned, who work in *incredibly tiny detail* in altering facets of a performance, they often tend not to do so in acting terms, if you follow me. I think Wyler, for example, has an absolutely *infallible* taste for a performance. If he says it's right—it's *right.* There's just no question. But I don't think he's particularly empathic with actors.

Orson probably taught me more about acting than any film director I've worked for. Which is not to say I necessarily did my best film performance for him, but he taught me a great deal about acting—the whole, acting generically. He's both specific in technical details and in broad concepts about acting, and I found it an enormously stimulating experience.

The scenes you did with Welles—did you find those to be your most difficult scenes?

The most difficult?

The most difficult, or the most draining, I would say. It's really the word I would use. Draining would also mean that when you were finished with them you probably felt the most satisfied.

I recall performing in the whole picture, doing the whole picture, as being as satisfying creatively as anything I've ever done. I don't recall it as being—the part was not an enormously difficult part. There was never a scene that you look on as a major jump—you know, a barrier that somehow you have to clear. Like the dagger speech in *Macbeth.* Or Antony's suicide. They were scenes that you did with as much creative juice as you could call on at that time. Orson helps you quite a lot.

The sequence with the shoe box is a brilliant scene. It's also brilliantly directed and photographed, again because the camera is constantly moving in that scene.

That's about thirteen pages. That was the first day's work on the picture. And Orson deceived the studio, and he conned them, because the scene was scheduled for three days of shooting, which is about reasonable, which would be a little over four pages a day—which is a respectable day's work in an "A" picture. He, in fact, had rehearsed the scene in his home with the actors over a Sunday or two. He proceeded to lay out the scene in terms of *one* shot with a crab dolly, that encompassed all the eight or nine performers who had lines in the scene. The action ranged through two rooms, a closet and a bathroom, and, as I said, thirteen pages of dialogue. It was quite a complex shot, with doors having to be pulled, walls having to be pulled aside—very intricate markings, inserts on the shoe box, and things like that. All of which were in one shot.

When you're shooting, the production office is informed when the camera turns over the first time, when the first print is made, and so on. And of course we never turned a camera until way . . . Lunch went by, and uneasy little groups of executives began to huddle about in the shadows, not quite willing to approach Orson but increasingly convinced that they were on the brink of disaster, cause we hadn't turned a camera and it was, by now, three or four o'clock in the afternoon. Finally, at about 4:30, we turned. And of course it was tricky. We did several takes—seven or eight takes. Finally we got a print, just before six o'clock. And Orson said, OK, that's a print. Wrap." He said, "We're two days ahead of schedule. We go to the other set tomorrow."

The executives must have been down on their knees.

Everybody thought it was marvelous. Of course he never did that again, you see, but they always thought he *might.*

It's a brilliant idea.

Just great. They never gave him any trouble again after that. They thought "My God, he did three days' work in one shot!"

The little touches that he adds from scene to scene. Were they all in the script? The things like Akim Tamiroff's hairpiece, which was a running gag throughout the whole film.

That was not in the script, no. And of course, I wasn't in those scenes, so I don't know how they were created, but I know they weren't—it wasn't in the script. The scenes are put together in a very loose atmosphere that makes for that kind of creativity.

Was there any ad-libbing in terms of dialogue?

Orson has a marvelous ear for the way people talk. One of the many things I learned from him was the degree to which people in real life overlap one another when they're talking. In the middle of somebody's sentence you will, in fact, apprehend what he's talking about and you will often start to reply through his closing phrase. People do that all the time. Orson directs scenes that way—to a larger degree than most directors do.

There's a marvelously counterpointed scene in *Lady from Shanghai* in which the people sit in the dark—obviously he doesn't want a visual image to intrude—and you hear two conversations interwoven. He likes that, and I do too. I think it's very valuable, and I've tried to use it in scenes myself since. He not only changes dialogue, as . . . dialogue is changed all the time on film. It's some of the most creative work in putting a scene together.

All of Hawks.

Pardon?

All of Hawks had to be written on a daily basis.

It goes on all the time. Sure. Orson is, as I said, a very instinctive, intuitive creator, and he would restage whole scenes. I mean put them in different places. We were shooting in this crummy hotel in Venice, and at three o'clock in the morning—in the middle of night shooting—we were down in the basement of this old hotel, peeing in a drain in the corner of this old basement, and he said, "Gee, these pipes and this boiler. That's marvelous. You know this—we should do the scene with Joe Calleia here—where he shows you the cane."

He zipped up his fly and said to the first assistant, "Get Joe Calleia down here." They said, "Jesus, Orson, we were gonna do that scene on Friday, they've got it set up at the studio." He said, "That's terrible. That's no place. We're going to do it down here. We'll do it right now." And they said, "Well, we've got to finish this scene." He said, "I can finish this scene in one shot. It'll take you an hour to get Calleia out of bed. Get him down here and I'll have this scene finished by then." And he did.

That's beautiful.

And it is better there.

Cause that is the turning point of the film.

It's a great scene. And part of the reason it's good is he . . . Here's Joe Calleia getting up out of bed in the middle of the night, and staggering down to Venice. They take him down in this stinking basement and they give him the cane, and they say, "Joe, now do it." And he says, "What-what-what???" "The scene." "Where?" You know, and it's marvelous.

which in
of love; if I have
I return again
not with the time
water

Spy vs. Spy:

JOHN HUSTON AND *THE KREMLIN LETTER*

PETER RICHARDS

After more than twenty years, *The Kremlin Letter* is still one of the least popular and least revived of John Huston's films. In his 1980 autobiography, Huston rather disingenuously claims that he expected the film to be a big box-office hit, but it was in fact a $6-million catastrophe. The worst year, financially, that Twentieth Century Fox ever had was 1970—despite the release of *M*A*S*H* and *Patton,* two of the biggest hits in company history, and the ongoing success of a third smash, *Butch Cassidy and the Sundance Kid,* released at the end of the previous year. And even then, *The Kremlin Letter* was one of the bigger flops.

It was also a major critical failure. In *An Open Book,* Huston noted wryly that the film was well received in France, where he was not normally in the vanguard of critical enthusiasms, but British and American reviewers gave it a near-unanimous thumbs-down. The veteran British critic Dilys Powell tendered a brief rave, merely noting that it was a skilled thriller; in *Sight and Sound,* John Russell Taylor proffered the sort of praise that puts most serious film enthusiasts right off (more or less saying it was too, too madly amusing, my dears). Virtually the only detailed examination of the film at the time was in the short-lived British magazine *Monogram,* whose critic, Richard Collins, compared it with Jacobean melodrama and hailed it as one of Huston's finest and most disturbing achievements. The eminent director Jean-Pierre Melville gave it unstinting praise, but so few people saw *The Kremlin Letter* anywhere that his perceptive comments went for little. In subsequent years, an assortment of film guides—Halliwell, Maltin, Shipman—have been uniformly hostile, though in the *Time Out Film Guide* of 1989, Chris Peachment does call it "possibly the clearest statement of Huston's vision of a cruel and senseless world in operation."

It's the harshest of Huston's films. After its failure, he was rarely asked about *The Kremlin Letter,* but remarks before its release, taken with the fact that Huston (unusually for his later years) also takes script credit with his longtime personal assistant Gladys Hill, suggest it was a very personal project for him, an expression of horror at the wickedness and cynicism of the world. *The Kremlin Letter* is set very precisely in the winter of 1969—in other words, a few months after it was actually made—but it's a film full of the past. There is, however, absolutely no nostalgia. This is a movie in which people lie a lot. It's less a lament for the old days than a cold-eyed differentiation between types of violence and evil. It is ab solutely characteristic of Huston in that it's both a group movie and a grail movie. This time, the false grail being pursued—one whose existence may be as illusory as that of the Maltese falcon or as fragile as the treasure of the Sierra Madre—is a letter that a Western spy chief has been duped into signing, unambiguously committing the United States to aid Russia in a secret mission aimed against China's burgeoning nuclear capability. The letter has gone missing in Moscow and the group must find it.

This group is no Hawksian band of no-nonsense professionals facing bravely up to daunting odds. The spies seeking the Kremlin letter are killers, perverts, torture specialists; they run drugs, they kidnap children, they murder and rape the defenseless. These are not the brave opponents of totalitarianism of Huston's *We Were Strangers,* nor the bumbling conmen of *Beat the Devil,* nor even the frightening but compassionately observed thieves of *The Asphalt Jungle.* Even the new player—a younger man brought in at the last minute, through whose eyes we acquaint ourselves with the team—is a most ambiguous and disturbing figure. This is Charles Rone, a hero figure from the machine age, a man who "speaks eight languages without an accent," an expert in karate, an unemotional and uninvolved intellectual with a supercilious attitude for just about everyone. In the way this character is treated, we see a validation of one of Huston's most oft-repeated precepts—that casting is a good ninety percent of the job of directing actors.

The film did not succeed in making a movie star out of television's Patrick O'Neal, but he was exactly the right actor for this part. In most of his best movie roles, O'Neal was cast as a cold-hearted smoothie, occasionally downright villainous (as, say, the android expert who designed and built *The Stepford Wives*), but more often as a ruthless careerist; one remembers him as a snobbish naval man in *In Harm's Way,* as the oleaginous, bogusly apologetic second-in-command to Richard Widmark in *Alvarez Kelly,* or, indeed, as the aloof film director in *The Way We Were* who seems to be partly based on John Huston. But now and then, these unlikably self-assured men have their more human side, and O'Neal managed to be touching, as well as debonairly funny, in both *A Fine Madness* and *The Secret Life of an American Wife,* playing seemingly unflappable executive types gradually revealed as flounderers in an American Dream setting turned nightmarishly sour.

This, in a very different tone, is what we get in *The Kremlin Letter.* Commander Charles E. Rone, U.S.N., arrogant and supremely self-confident ("I am a superior blend of intellect and physique, of athlete and scholar"), is forced to join the group under duress and does little to conceal his contempt for it. He has no loyalties—seemingly not to his job in the navy (from which he is brutally dismissed at the start of the film), certainly not to any individual (he witnessed the deaths of his parents and brothers when a boy, leaving him without ties and apparently without emotions), and presumably also not to the Richard Nixon America that requires him to kill and cheat and become a male prostitute. He does his loathsome job as a professional, but gradually he grows to hate it, for it requires a cruelty far beyond the self-protecting solitude he has wrapped himself in—and it is this hatred that marks him out, just barely, as a notch above his companions in espionage.

Callous as Rone is, he is gradually revealed as a man of feeling—something he may have forgotten about after years of functioning more as a machine (he has a photographic memory) than as a human being. He doesn't show it to the others, but we can tell he has some pity for Erika (Bibi Andersson), the wretched prostitute whom he is required to seduce because she has married his KGB opponent, Kosnov (Max von Sydow); and he grows to love B. A. (Barbara Parkins), the strange girl whom he himself brings into the obscene game when her father (Niall MacGinnis), an old-time group member, proves too ill to join in. This love is Rone's undoing, for it is the one thing that prevents him from being as heartless as either the Russian spymasters of various factions opposed to him or the terrifying colleagues on his own side. Gradually, this superefficient modern man learns that he is, in fact, the old-fashioned one on the team, precisely because he does see things in terms of "sides"; the others are all simply out for money and are ready to abandon or betray at any time, as they have done countless times in the past.

With one exception. *The Kremlin Letter* turns out to be a Huston film with *two* grails. If the letter itself proves to be a false grail (of which more anon), the other is all too real: for this "true" grail is nothing less than a human being. Throughout the film, we keep hearing about a dead man named Sturdevant—once the mastermind of the group, the man who trained most of its members, a sadistic and conscienceless killer, a torturer, a traitor, a pimp, a drug smuggler, and "as an individual spy, *sans pareil.*" After double-crossing both sides in the cold war once too often, and finding himself an anachronism in the mechanized world of post-World War II espionage, Sturdevant eventually blew his brains out in Istanbul in 1954. Or so we're told. What Rone gradually learns is that this dead man casts his shadow over almost all the other main characters-working for both the U.S.A. and U.S.S.R., Sturdevant had both been a benefit and a hindrance, not only to his fellow group members, but to both Kosnov (who betrayed him) and to the latter's rival in the Russian bureaucracy, the urbanely westernized Alexei Bresnavitch (Orson Welles). It won't take any ardent thriller fan more than a moment to figure out that Sturdevant is still alive, but Huston makes us wait and wait before he reveals himself.

We wait, in fact, until we realize that the Kremlin letter itself is the most offhand of Macguffins. The letter's existence proves to have no diplomatic importance whatever, for it transpires at film's end that it is in Peking. But did it ever have any political significance? We realize quickly that Polakov, the freelance spy dispatched to Moscow in the first scene to recover the letter, is in fact the man who caused the letter to be written and signed in the first place—for no reason more elaborate than that he knew that its recovery (expected to be a simple matter) would pay him enough money to retire on. But in the film's second sequence Polakov is already dead, having poisoned himself rather than submit to torture by Kosnov. By the end of the film, we find that the actual function of the letter has been simply to smoke out Kosnov and place him in a position of vulnerability. Finally isolated from his army of subordinates, alone and defenseless, Kosnov is left facing Sturdevant, who exacts a grisly revenge for the latter's past treachery and for his slaughter of so many over the years.

And who is Sturdevant? The revelation of his identity puts one in mind of another politically important letter, Edgar Allan Poe's purloined one, which turned out to have been in front of everyone's eyes all the time. Sturdevant is, in fact, the person he should most logically be, the one spy in the film who has indeed been *sans pareil,* i.e., the most ruthless and least susceptible to human weaknesses. This terrifying man is the one who has seemed the most good-humored—the irritatingly cheerful Ward (Richard Boone). This wrinkled, drawling good ol' boy, forever offering nuggets of cracker-barrel philosophy and absolutely unfazed by any turn of events—suggesting for all the world a Will Rogers character transplanted to a James Bond movie—is on no one's side; and yet he is, in an utterly unsentimental way, the one most bounded by loyalties, the one most defined by the past. He smiles constantly, he occasionally displays charming manners, he reproves Rone for his condescension and is quite fearless. Yet he is remote from human contact save once—surprisingly, when he displays huge, unfeigned enthusiasm for a performance of the Bolshoi. Other members of the group may pride themselves on their ruthlessness, but have their assorted Achilles' heels: sexual longings, greed, various forms of sensual gratification. Ward needs nothing. Except his revenge.

It is wholly unsurprising that a John Huston film should prefer individual talent to the machinations of a soulless bureaucracy (be it American or Russian). But what is so chilling is that the representative of the individualist ingenuity and courage that Huston films always prize should be, in this instance, perhaps the most evil man in the entire Hustonian oeuvre. In a world where there is no heroism, where there are no principles, where pain and death are so inevitable that all that seems to matter is who inflicts and who receives them, the least of all the terrible evils available would seem to be the evil that is practiced for some sort of recognizably human motive, however awful it may be. As inhumanly as Ward/Sturdevant manipulates his appalling group, he does, in his final confrontation with Kosnov, seem to have a disgusted awareness of what the betrayals of the past really mean. Rather than talk about his own sufferings, he talks instead about a large number of men we have never heard of before, victims of other Kosnov purges. It genuinely does seem to be for them, as well as for himself, that he exacts his horrid vengeance. Both horror and contempt are in his voice as he tells Kosnov, "You seem to like to hear men scream . . . "

And we shouldn't forget his remarks early in the film, when, as Ward, he is asked by the unsuspecting Rone about the legendary Sturdevant: "Sturdevant was a fraud . . . he was a con man and a coward." Just more deception? Or a real self-hatred? Richard Boone's finely judged performance gives us room to speculate. Certainly, he is a man who knows himself, and has no egotism about what he knows. We have no reason to suppose that he likes himself any more than he likes anyone else. Huston characters die when they don't face the truth about themselves (Alonzo Emmerich, Daniel Dravot, Fred C. Dobbs) but become heroes when they do (no wonder he made a film about Sigmund Freud). Charles Rone, though, faces up to the realization that he is a man of emotion and conscience, only to be confronted at film's end with the cruelest of its many serpentine twists: love for B. A. has made him a decent human being again, but now it must once more make him a killer.

The group has needed a base in Moscow and for this reason has taken over the apartment of a family named Potkin. The head of this family is a Russian official at the United Nations, a very nervous functionary whose loyalties shift awkwardly between Kosnov and Bresnavitch. To blackmail him into acquiescing, the group does two things. They kidnap his homely wife and nine-year-old daughter, and they hire a lesbian to seduce his other daughter, an eighteen-year-old art student in New York. Kidnapped himself (but only briefly) Potkin, in anguish, is forced to watch a film of his daughter's seduction and hands over his Moscow apartment for fear of depravities being visited upon his other daughter and his wife. He is freed (and his decision to reveal all to Bresnavitch causes the downfall of the group), but the wife and children are kept under lock and key. Bresnavitch captures B. A. and kills the other in the group; Rone escapes but discovers that Ward is not only really Sturdevant, but Bresnavitch's partner in treachery. But Rone is powerless to act with B. A. a prisoner in Moscow. To free the girl he loves, he must aid Ward by claiming that he is dead, and to sever all remaining links with the dreadful affair of the Kremlin letter, he must obey Ward's final order and murder the Potkin family. The film ends with him pondering this ghastly order as he boards a plane to return to America. His unspoken pain finds a sardonic outlet on the sound track over the film's closing images, as the scream of a jet engine drowns out all other noise.

***

It is ironic that John Huston's most savage film about a group of adventurers should, in itself, be a get-together for many old colleagues. The movie is, like its plot, full of reverberations from the past. Huston is reunited with many key workers from other films: cameraman Ted Scaife, editor Russell Lloyd, sound expert Basil Fenton-Smith. The role of Bresnavitch is taken by his old friend Orson Welles, while the NATO spy chief known as Sweet Alice is played by one of the men who gave Welles his start in the theatre, Micheál MacLiammóir. MacLiammóir's rich enunciation and large frame recall Sydney Greenstreet, but when we see him perched nonchalantly in a train seat, dark glasses hanging over his nose and too-small hat barely covering his large head, he also looks unmistakably like an older version of Huston's *Beat the Devil* scriptwriter, Truman Capote. The casting of Max von Sydow and Bibi Andersson as Kosnov and Erika inevitably suggests the conjugal tortures of Ingmar Bergman's movies.

The casting of Patrick O'Neal may have been partly as a compensation for his having lost the male lead in Huston's earlier *Reflections in a Golden Eye* to Marlon Brando; the actor's path and Huston's had indirectly crossed elsewhere, for O'Neal gave an excellent performance in Otto Preminger's *The Cardinal,* the movie that established John Huston as a character actor, and had earlier starred on Broadway as the male lead in Tennessee Williams's *The Night of the Iguana,* which Huston filmed in 1964 with Richard Burton in the part. Farther down in the cast list of *The Kremlin Letter,* it is a pleasure to find Huston reunited with the ravaged-faced Marc Lawrence, the chatty Ziggy of *Key Largo* and, even more memorably, Cobby, the small-time Mr. Big with ambitions, in *The Asphalt Jungle.*

And Huston himself contributes a trenchant cameo as the old-time admiral who dismisses Rone from the navy at the film's start. Cannily, Huston uses his one scene to articulate the central theme of the movie, the conflict between one's duty and one's personal or moral loyalties. Rone's intelligence work has, in the admiral's simple view, rendered him disloyal to his uniform: "Only officers of the United States Navy are allowed to wear that uniform. There was a time, legend has it, when men even died for it."

In the appalling world of *The Kremlin Letter,* women and children die as well as men, but not for a uniform, and not for a flag. They die for reasons they cannot understand, at the hands of people they do not know, so that an absurd game can be carried on in the name of patriotism, in order to make the corrupt powerful and the treacherous wealthy. Of course the film flopped at the box office. Within the confines of a popular movie genre, it presents a scathing critique of our senseless world with a clarity too painful for acceptance. As Jean-Luc Godard remarked in a different context, the ostrich is always a popular creature.

Courtesy of ENMU

Leigh Brackett with Howard Hawks, director of *The Big Sleep*.

From *The Big Sleep* to *The Long Goodbye*

LEIGH BRACKETT

The screenwriting job on *The Big Sleep* fell into my lap out of a clear blue sky. I had had only one previous film job, and damn glad to get it, on a ten-day wonder at Republic (it was two days over schedule), which was nothing upon which to build a giant reputation. But I had a hard-boiled mystery novel published that year, Raymond-Chandler-and-well-water but done with love. It set no worlds afire, but Harry Wepplo, who was then at Martindales in Beverly Hills, saw to it that a copy of the book got into the stack of thrillers that Howard Hawks was in the habit of buying every month or so. Hawks liked my dialogue and called my agent. He was somewhat shaken when he discovered that it was Miss and not Mister Brackett, but he rallied bravely and signed me on anyway, for which I have always been extremely grateful.

I went to work in a daze. A great Chandler fan, a great Bogart fan . . . I couldn't believe it. All this, plus one hundred and twenty-five separate and distinct dollars per week, all the money in the world even with take-outs. I'd have done it for nothing.

And there was William Faulkner. *The* William Faulkner. How was I, a no-where writer with four years of pulp behind me, going to collaborate with him?

I needn't have worried. The morning I checked in, Mr. Faulkner, immaculate in country tweeds, greeted me courteously, handed me a copy of the book, and said, "We will do alternate sets of chapters. I have them marked. I will do these, you will do those."

And so it was. Mr. Faulkner worked alone in his office, I worked in mine. I never saw his script, he never saw mine. Everything went in direct to Mr. Hawks, who was somewhere else. Beyond a couple of conferences, we never saw him. That is his way of working, and it has been known to drive good screenwriters straight up the wall. Most producers breathe constantly down a writer's neck. Howard Hawks sits down with you for a series of chats, giving you all his thoughts on what kind of story he wants, how it ought to go, etc., and then retires to Palm Springs and the golf course, leaving you to come up with a script the best way you can. This makes some writers feel rudderless and unhappy. Faulkner, of course, had worked for Hawks before and knew the routine. I had no experience anyway, so it didn't bother me. I had always done my work alone in a room with the door shut.

Actually, writing the script of *The*

Big Sleep presented even me with very few problems. The book was good, and it was contemporary; the war was on, but even so the idiom of 1939 was not far behind us. We were still living it, still speaking the same language. We updated the book in a few minor ways, such as the references to red stamps. Considering the rushing about done by Marlowe in his car, gasoline rationing and all, I don't think we even took that too seriously. Most important, though we didn't think about it then, the concept of the private eye, the tough, incorruptible, good-bad man who worked for justice by his own hard unsentimental light, was still fresh and exciting.

Along with Marlowe, we had the wealthy old man, Sternwood (one of Chandler's finest characters, and the scene in the orchid house is a masterpiece), the beautiful and oversexed daughters, the handsome no-good gambler, the sympathetic hood, a sufficiency of unsympathetic ones, sexy ladies, solid brutality, high life in low places, and suspense all along the way. How could we lose?

True, the plot was so tangled and complicated that we all got more or less lost in it. But it only got that way if one paused to look too closely. Otherwise, the sheer momentum of the action carried one along, and why quibble? I think we may have straightened out one or two kinks but I couldn't swear to it. I did witness the historic occasion upon which everybody began asking everybody else who killed Owen Taylor, and nobody knew. A wire was sent asking Chandler, and he sent one back saying, "I don't know." And really, who cared?

We never had a final script. Hawks went into production with the temporary. He shoots a lot of stuff ad lib—as does any creative director, getting an idea for a good scene and letting it play—which ran an already long screenplay into far too much footage. Jules Furthman was called in for a rewrite to cut the remaining, or unshot, portion into a manageable length.

The film, as everyone knows, was a hit and has gone on to become a classic. Bogart was the ideal Marlowe. Hawks's fastpaced direction, crisp and unerring, raced the story along from one exciting moment to the next. Audiences came away feeling that they had seen the hell and all of a film even if they didn't rightly know, in retrospect, what it was all about. Again, who cared? It was grand fun, with sex and danger and a lot of laughs, done with a professional expertise that made it fairly glitter.

That was *The Big Sleep*. Now we go forward twenty-five or so years, and Elliott Kastner has acquired rights to *The Long Goodbye*. Would I like to work on it? Indeed I would.

I hadn't read the book in years. I read it, and realized at once that this would not be another easy job.

The first problem was obvious. *The Long Goodbye* is an enormously long book. Done as is, it would come out a minimum of four hours' running time, and most of that talk. Ergo, it must be cut, and heavily.

Second problem, cut what and where?

This entailed endless rereadings, and it seemed that the deeper one dug, the more one analyzed, the more the problems multiplied.

Structurally, the book is awkward. Chandler is in effect telling two stories, so that you have first the Marlowe-Terry Lennox-Sylvia story, and then you have the Marlowe-Eileen Wade-Roger story, the two hung together by an involved and tortured chain of coincidences.

While the same criticism can be levelled against *The Big Sleep* as well, there is a difference. In *Sleep* the stories are better integrated, and Chandler never gives the reader time to consider the holes in the connective tissue. In *Goodbye* he gives far too much time. Moreover, in *Sleep* he was telling a tale, an entertainment; he didn't ask us to believe it. In *Goodbye,* he did. He wanted us to feel that these were real people in a real society, with real loves and hates, and therefore suspension of disbelief was that much more difficult.

Technically, the books differ greatly. *Sleep* is brisk and extroverted, a succession of cinematic scenes. Marlowe's stream-of-consciousness is manageable, easily translatable into dialogue. *Goodbye* is endlessly introspective, with long passages of subjective philosophical comment that are impossible to translate. Where the action in *Sleep* is swift and full of excitement, in *Goodbye* it is almost nonexistent in the physical sense—the complicated progression of the overlapping stories slows to the point of dragginess. There is nothing wrong with this at all. Chandler wasn't trying to do *The Big Sleep* over again. He was doing something quite different, making a different set of comments on life and truth and love and friendship. But what a reader will hold still for, savor and enjoy, on the printed page, is one thing. Putting it into visual form is quite another; audiences begin to squirm.

In addition, *The Long Goodbye* is a depressing book. It was written at a sad time in Chandler's life, and the sadness shows through. Everyone, to the point of monotony, is rotten, hopeless, corrupt, psychotic, alcoholic, suicidal. Terry's quixotic gesture of belated heroism is so buried under the exigencies of plot, and much of that self-contradictory, that it doesn't come off, and the final meeting between Marlowe and Terry is unsatisfactory and unresolved—as I suppose Chandler might have been saying that most human relationships are unsatisfactory and unresolved, but nonetheless . . . Eileen Wade's confession and death come through, at least to me, as pure corn, which I didn't believe for a moment. Nor could I believe the sequence where she killed Roger and tried, ridiculously, to pin it on Marlowe.

Courtesy of ENMU

Leigh Brackett, screenwriter of *The Big Sleep* and *The Long Goodbye.*

Now, to all of us—Elliott Kastner, Jerry Bick, Brian Hutton (our then director-to-be), and myself—another problem began to be apparent, probably the biggest one of all.

Time.

Twenty-five years had gone by since *The Big Sleep.* In that quarter-century, legions of private eyes had been beaten up in innumerable alleys by armies of interchangeable hoods. Everything that was fresh and exciting about Philip Marlowe in the forties had become cliché, outworn by imitation and overuse. The tough loner with the sardonic tongue and the cast-iron gut had become a caricature.

Also, in twenty-five years, the idiom had changed.

By Chandler's own definition, Marlowe was a fantasy, not a real man in a real world. He existed only in the context of the Raymond Chandler world especially invented for him, with its stylized corruptions, its stylized characters who represented attitudes, not people, its stylized orchestrations of violence. Take away that context, and who is Marlowe?

Time had removed the context.

The Los Angeles upon which Chandler based his literary world is as dead as Babylon. The characters with which he peopled it were never drawn from life anyway, but from the films of the twenties and thirties; shadow-play hoods and gamblers, madcap heiresses and tough cops. They don't make movies like that anymore. We don't speak that language anymore. We've got a whole new generation and a whole new bag of clichés—just as phony but different. The private eye is alive and well on television, but he exists in a new context and the corruptions he fights have new faces.

So we were all in agreement, pretty much at the beginning, that a lot was going to have to be changed, but we weren't sure what or how. One thing we did know. We had our Marlowe . . . Elliott Gould, a very Now actor with a talent and a style all his own. Whatever he did with the part, he was not going to be Humphrey Bogart. From there, it was only a short step to the corollary. If you could have Humphrey Bogart, just as he was then, to do the Marlowe bit again, *he* wouldn't do it the way he did it in the forties. He couldn't, without being a parody of himself.

The Long Goodbye was not going to be another *Big Sleep* no matter what we did with it.

The first script was a compromise, and like most compromises, an abortion. We tried to keep the "flavor" of the original, the true Chandler touch, while streamlining and trying to inject a little excitement. But we got involved with a plot of premise that simply did not work: the idea that Terry Lennox had plotted, planned, and premeditated Sylvia's murder, framed Roger for it, split for Mexico when something slipped up, and simply waited to reappear, knowing exactly what everybody was going to do to clear him; Marlowe would do thus-and-such, Eileen would obligingly murder her husband, and etc. This resulted in a succession of false scenes that creaked and groaned toward an ending that nobody liked. And we still had far too many characters. Our only achievements were two: Terry Lennox had become a clear-cut villain, and it seemed that the only satisfactory ending was for the cruelly diddled Marlowe to blow Terry's guts out, partly to keep Terry from getting away with it all, partly out of sheer human rage. Something the old Marlowe would never have done. He would have set Terry up somehow, got somebody else to pull the trigger. At least one critic went into a frothing fit over this blasphemy. But it seemed right, and honest. Chandler's Marlowe operated in his own peculiar world. Bogart's Marlowe perforce operated within both Chandler's world and the restrictions of the code then governing motion-picture morality. Being free of both in the seventies, we felt that we could be bold.

There ensued one of those long delays at the top level, which involved yet another delay due to having lost Mr. Hutton to another commitment. The project sat, as far as I was concerned, for several months—during which time I did a lot of thinking. The bad premise that had hampered us was easily remedied. And after having grappled with them repeatedly and without joy, there were some characters I felt I could lose: the Too Rich Old Man, his Gorgeous Oversexed Daughter, the dutifully corrupt and sinful, idle Valley types exemplified by Dr. Loring. In other words, tell the Roger Wade story and forget the rest. It was all we had room for. I discussed this by letter with Elliott and Jerry.

Then Robert Altman came on the scene and said, "I see Marlowe the way Chandler saw him, a loser. But a *real* loser, not the fake winner that Chandler made out of him. A loser all the way." And things began to fall into place.

Chandler himself characterized Marlowe as a "loser" vis-à-vis a society where money was the measure of success. But he showed you that the things Marlowe gained by losing—independence, pride, honesty, and the ability to say no, to be his own man—were wealth far and above the dirty dollars he might have made by selling out his integrity. Which is a premise, I think, that few will quarrel with. This is what we all liked in Marlowe, what we admired: the man in the mean streets who was not himself mean, a folk hero in a snap-brim hat and trenchcoat.

We did not contravene these tenets. Gould's Marlowe is a man of simple faith, honesty, trust, and complete integrity. All we did was strip him of the fake hero attributes. Chandler's Marlowe always knew more than the cops. He could be beaten to a pulp, but he always came out on top one way or another. By sheer force of personality, professional expertise, and gall, he always had an edge. We said, "A man like this hasn't got an edge. He gets kicked around. People don't take him seriously. They don't know what he's all about, and they don't care." So instead of being the tough-guy, Marlowe became the pasty.

The story line of the Roger Wade portion of the novel was greatly simplified. Much of it would have been unusable in any case because of the World War II time frame involved in the original relationship between Eileen and Terry. Much of it made very little sense anyway, on close examination. We relieved Eileen of all crimes except adultery, simplified motives all round, made the murder of Roger a suicide, gave the gambler a satchetful of money to tie things together, and stayed with the brutal ending. And Marlowe was a loser. The girl didn't walk out on him, she just didn't know he was there. He didn't even win a fight. He was a man out of his time, clinging to outworn ideals of honesty and fair play, only to find out that, in Chandler's own words, the man who tries to be honest looks in the end either sentimental or plain foolish. The ending is Marlowe's reaction of rage not only against the betrayer Lennox, but against the hatefulness of a world that permits this to be true.

Those were the basics of the script, the mechanics. From there Robert Altman took off, and the view from the camera became uniquely and brilliantly his own, turning the whole thing into a satire on the genre itself.

In its first release, the film was greeted, by some critics, with the tone of outrage generally reserved for those who tamper with the Bible. This seems just a bit silly to me. I'm an old Chandler fan from way back, probably farther back than a lot of the critics. He was a powerful influence on my own work in those years. But I don't feel that any sacrilege was being committed. And I doubt that Chandler himself would have regarded every aspect of his work as Holy Writ.

I think he might even have liked Altman's version of *The Long Goodbye.*

Courtesy of Kino International

Barbara Stanwyck, classic femme fetale of *Double Indemnity, The File on Thelma Jordan,* and *The Strange Love of Martha Ivers.* Seen here with Van Heflin.

Kill Me Again:

THE RISE OF NOUVEAU NOIR

STEPHEN HUNTER

In 1972, then film critic Paul Schrader wrote a seminal essay of the dark and mesmerizing postwar American cinema of deceit, murder, and betrayal known as film noir. He broke it down into three phases, the last of which, the "manic," had just ended—or so he thought. He didn't know, of course, that he himself would write the last great film noir of the "manic" phase, *Taxi Driver,* in 1976.

He also didn't know that there was a fourth stage yet to come, one that has blossomed of late into full, gnarled bloom. It might be called the "ironic" stage, or as some have christened it, "nouveau noir." It took root in 1981 and has now reached maturity in the works of John Dahl, the latest of whose films, *The Last Seduction,* has just opened.

Ironic noir is the antithesis of manic noir. Manic noir, whose two highest accomplishments were *Taxi Driver* and, before that, *Kiss Me Deadly,* Robert Aldrich's jazzy spin on the Mickey Spillane novel, celebrated the last pure product of America: craziness. They were by definition over the top and took as their protagonists men who lost control. In *Taxi Driver,* Robert De Niro's Travis Bickle shot his way into the American subconscious as a twisted version of Arthur Bremer, who would inspire an equally twisted John Hinckley. The movie ended in an excess of massacre as Bickle, under a Mohawk haircut and spattered with blood, blew away everything that moved in a New York brothel, convinced it was his messianic role to cleanse the world.

Nothing so impolite would happen in ironic noir. It's not about screwballs, psychos, gun people, or anything. It doesn't celebrate craziness, but rather another pure product of America: movies. In fact, it has the cool, detached humor of a good movie review, which in a sense it is. It's sublimely self-aware—as opposed to the genuine spontaneity of the original noir works—as directed by young men who are completely conscious of everything they do. Their primary goal is to do a film that both celebrates and parodies the genre. They lack the reflexively pyrotechnic drive of such noir greats as Billy Wilder (*Double Indemnity,* 1944), Joseph Lewis (*Gun Crazy,* 1950), or Rudolph Mate (*D.O.A.,* 1950), and, of course, they've seen too much film noir.

If you asked Wilder, Lewis, or Mate or any of the others about film noir, they'd say, "Huh?" Then they'd have the unit publicist kick you off the set. Ask John Dahl about film noir (I did), and he says, "Well, the three greatest influences on my work were . . ." and then proceeds to discuss with clinical detail three films—*Double Indemnity* and *Sunset Boulevard* by Wilder, and *A Place in the Sun* by George Stevens (not exactly a film noir but, courtesy of Theodore Dreiser, about a murder)—and how he set about to recreate their impulses.

That's not necessarily bad; it is necessarily inescapable. One of the real changes in film culture over the past, say, thirty years, is the sense in which it's turned in upon itself. The first few generations of sound movies were made by men who were pioneers as much as they were artists. They were flying by the seat of their pants. Most came from stage or newspaper backgrounds, most worked under intense studio pressure (the studios being literal factories that turned two hundred "units" a year), and most just did what worked without thinking about larger meanings until later. They were eminently practical men, and in their interviews they tended to make fun of the earnest young intellectuals who asked Big Questions.

Why did you shoot the concluding sequence from Hell on Four Wheels *through the reflection of the broken mirror? Was it to indicate Bill's advanced state of psychosis?*

Er, no. I saved about $8,000 that way. We had a whale of a cast party with that money.

That sort of thing.

Yet given the helter-skelter nature of its inventors, film noir nevertheless has such a coherence to it you wonder if it was engineered by a single brilliant mind, or at the very least a learned committee.

There are many explanations for its emergence as the dominant film mode at the end of World War II. The most common is that it somehow reflected postwar exhaustion and pessimism. We had just won a giant victory and what did we win? Yet another war with yet another ominous superenemy, this time made all the more potentially lethal by the possibility of nuclear extinction.

Add to this the infusion of refugee technicians (cinematographers, lighting technicians, makeup artists) who had no homeland to return to—the emergence of a protocounterculture in the rigidly conformist fifties—and you get a cinema with a dark streak, satiny, existential, full of doomed suckers and smart ladies.

I favor a more literary explanation: that film noir was a decade-late cinematic extension of the literary movement called "hard-boiled." That genre had reached its full flower in the thirties with the diamond-hard prose of such geniuses as Dashiell Hammett, James M. Cain (both of whom hailed from Maryland), and the great Raymond Chandler. They all but reinvented American prose before the war by somehow desentimentalizing it. They refused to see the city as a world of glittery possibility, but instead as a neon-lighted sewer where death was hiding in an alley. When that sensibility eventually reached the movies, it took the form of film noir, with its concentration on squalid little tales of death without redemption.

Why did noir die, or at least go into eclipse, sometime in the late fifties? One reason may have been utterly stylistic, reflecting the ancient question scholars of the genre argue: is noir a philosophy or a look, a content or a style?

If it's a style, then the death of black-and-white filmmaking in the late fifties pretty much explains things. Somehow, noir didn't work in color. It lost its meanings. Just look, say, at Robert Siodmak's brilliant *The Killers* of 1946. The vivid cascade of blue-gray shadings, the exquisite placement of shadow on faces, the use

Van Heflin and Kirk Douglas in *The Strange Love of Martha Ivers.*

of lighting (as in the gun flashes that illuminate the dark as Swede's hand slips off the bedpost, signifying his surrender to death)—all give the movie a visual distinction that exactly communicates its view of a fate-haunted, doomed universe.

In 1964, Don Siegel, a great director, remade (and reinvented) the movie with an especially hip cast that included Lee Marvin and Clu Gulager as the killers, John Cassavetes as the betrayed quarry (played by the young Burt Lancaster in the original), and as ace bad guy, in his last film, Ronald Reagan. Subtract the weirdness that attends any movie with Ronald Reagan as a bad guy, and the movie still doesn't work. It's shot in almost pastel colors against generic studio backgrounds, and it feels feather-light and silly. It needed a much darker palette to give its weighty themes density.

Another reason for the demise of film noir was television. The ubiquitous made-for-TV movie came along halfway through the sixties to take over the economic stratum—that is, the B movie niche—that had been the exclusive province of film noir. By the mid seventies, there were no B movies anymore; they had moved entirely to television, and the studio product tended to be big-budget and demographically driven. A film like *Taxi Driver* (1976) was something of a fluke, ramrodded home by a tough producer (Julia Phillips), a brilliant young director and star (Martin Scorsese and De Niro), and Paul Schrader's exceptional script. That *Taxi Driver* exists at all says more about the unique momentum that talent develops (in this case Scorsese's) than about the systemic acceptance of the genre.

So noir was dead, or at least exiled to television. Then, in 1981, Lawrence Kasdan all but reinvented it with *Body Heat,* making stars out of William Hurt and Kathleen Turner in the process. *Body Heat* was the first ironic noir, and it established the pattern to come. It was both a film noir and a parody of a film noir. Immensely assured, it took place in two zones: the literal, where it was really happening, and the ironic, where it was echoing in our minds with associations to other films.

Of classic noir themes, it was a reiteration of the "black widow" or "femme fatale" variant—the frightened male fantasy about the sexually voracious and predatory female who used men to advance her ends, then spits them out and moves on. Turner, tawny as a leopard and just as fierce, wrapped Hurt around a Popsicle stick and seemed to enjoy every second of it. But the lines were so campy with double entendre and cynicism, they could never have been uttered in a literal noir. "You're stupid," she purrs to him. "I like that in a man."

The noirs that have followed are almost all in that film-savvy tradition.

Quentin Tarantino, in particular, is a moviemaker so arch you can see each of the five thousand movies he's seen spinning behind his eyes as he works. *Reservoir Dogs* is a treasure trove of noir tough-guy conventions, but for true devotion to the cult, consider the even denser *Pulp Fiction* in terms of the movies that invented it and the classic noir themes it plays with: there's the couple on the run (Tim Roth and Amanda Plummer) from *Gun Crazy* and *They Live by Night;* there's the hit-man couple (John Travolta and Samuel L. Jackson) from *The Killers* I and II; there's Bruce Willis as the boxer getting even with the fixer (John Garfield in *Body and Soul*); there's Uma Thurman as the femme fatale (*Double Indemnity, The Postman Always Rings Twice*), almost luring poor Travolta into Big Trouble; there's Ving Rhames as the Big Boss (Richard Conte in *The Big Combo,* Louis Calhern in *Asphalt Jungle*). Is this a movie or a film-school class?

Of course, Tarantino dumps all this into the Cuisinart of his own sick imagination, pushes the No. 10 button, and the whole thing comes out sliced, diced, mulched, and crushed into something that's entirely old but feels entirely new.

Of the eighties and nineties noirs, only one feels utterly isolated from the ironic mode: Carl Franklin's brilliant *One False Move,* which could be called "country noir." This film feels so fresh and powerful it seems to have been made by a director who's seen no other movies, though it too cleaves to classic themes (couple on the run, plus one; small-town sheriff against big-time criminals).

The Dahl films fall somewhere between Tarantino and Franklin. They're not so playful and allusive that they become catalogs. They do, however, pay genuine homage to what's come before and in some way comment ironically on that work. They're also not nearly so violent as either Franklin or Tarantino. Dahl is attracted to the menace and the plot twists of noir, but not to the gut-wrenching, modern violence of either Tarantino or Franklin.

Kill Me Again was a private-eye caper, somewhat undone by the fact that the private eye who should have been played by a Bogart clone was played by a twenty-two-year-old kid (Val Kilmer). *Red Rock West* was a classic innocent-man-in-the-wrong-place tale, in which a drifter (Nicolas Cage) is taken to be a hit man, and people keep giving him money to kill other people, until the real hit man shows up. Complications ensue.

The Last Seduction is by far Dahl's most accomplished film, and it, too, is built around a classic theme, the femme fatale. In fact, the movie feels in some sense like a remake of *Body Heat,* though moved to a cold-weather clime (a small western New York town). Linda Fiorentino plays a wife who's stolen $750,000 from her mildly abusive husband (Bill Pullman), money that the couple had earned by selling stolen hospital cocaine to street dealers.

What kind of a woman is she? Let's put it this way: she'd give Medea the willies. She takes off for Chicago, but instead lies up in Beston, New York, and begins a casual affair with a somewhat defenseless claims adjuster (Peter Berg). Berg is the sucker, the Hurt analog. She jerks him this way and that until she finally sees a use for him and sends him on his way, even as she's being stalked by her husband who, mildly and suprisingly, only wants half the money back.

The great kick in the movie isn't the plotting or the surprises (not as well done as in *Body Heat*) but the

Guns and shadows: timeless ingredients of film noir.

guilty pleasure of sharing Fiorentino's manipulations. She's the point-of-view character (in *Body Heat,* it was Hurt). The true seduction in the film isn't hers of him, but its of us—it makes us feel the subversive joy of using and destroying another human being. And it mandates that we smile while we do it.

That would have been impossible in the old noirs, where evil was eventually punished. In the fourth-stage world of irony and metaphor, there's no room for such outdated concepts as good and evil.

True Confessions

JON L. BREEN

Does this dialogue sound familiar?

"I saw this great movie—"

"Yeah, but the book was better."

In one sense, a book—assuming it's a good book—almost has to be better than the movie. Novels provide depth of character and detail that is hard to duplicate in an adaptation. On the other hand, the two media are so different, comparisons are unfair. Only in relatively short, objectively written, and dialogue-driven novels that can be filmed scene-for-scene—*The Maltese Falcon,* say—can a virtual equivalent be achieved, and even then there are as many differences as similarities.

John Gregory Dunne's 1977 novel *True Confessions* is a rare example of a very good book that was made into an even better film. Scripted by Dunne and wife Joan Didion and directed by Ulu Grosbard, the screen version was released in 1981 to decidedly mixed reviews. In an unusually strong year—the Oscar nominees for best picture were *Reds, Chariots of Fire, Raiders of the Lost Ark, On Golden Pond,* and *Atlantic City*—it got no awards attention and fared only modestly at the box office. Still, to some observers it is one of the great films of the eighties, a classic of latter-day film noir that provides almost a textbook of effective print-to-film adaptation. Comparing the film to the novel, I didn't so much feel regret at what had to be left out as marvel at how what was left was conveyed more briefly and pointedly.

Some writers hate the idea of trying to adapt their own work for the screen, perhaps for good reasons. In most cases, it may be better for the adaptor not to be too close to the original source material. But the presence of the original author as one of the co-adaptors is one key to the artistic success of *True Confessions*—obviously what Dunne wanted to say about L.A. and Catholic-Church politics didn't change, so the two versions are thematically of a piece. Also, when favorite snippets of dialogue and character points didn't work where they appeared in the original novel, Dunne and Didion were able to use them in other contexts.

Why is the story so firmly in the noir/dark suspense tradition? With one exception, every single character, whether crook or cop or whore or priest, is corrupt. This does not mean the characters are unsympathetic—certainly both Spellacy brothers, cop Tom and priest Des, especially in the film, are very believably human and likable. The single exception to the corruption in both versions is Monsignor Seamus Fargo, a crotchety old priest who plays irritating conscience for the other Catholic clergy. He tells Des, "You have a mind like an abacus. You do everything, in fact, but feel. And it's the unfeeling ones that bring the Church into disrepute."

The present-day chapters that begin and end *True Confessions* are narrated in the first person by retired L.A. cop Tom Spellacy, with the main part of the book set in the mid-forties told by an omniscient third-person narrator. As the novel opens, Tom is having lunch with his old partner, Frank Crotty. The pair reflect on the changes in the city—for one thing, their old colleague, black cop Lorenzo Jones, is now the mayor. (Jones, based on longtime L.A. mayor Thomas Bradley, does not appear in the film.) The chapter flashes back to memories of finding the body of Lois Fazenda, dubbed in the papers "The Virgin Tramp," a nickname Tom comes up with himself to get irritating *Herald-Express* reporter Howard Terkel off his back. Fazenda, a young woman whose oddly bloodless body is found in two pieces on a vacant lot, is clearly based on the Black Dahlia, a notorious forties murder case.

Tom and brother Des grew up in the Boyle Heights section of Los Angeles, a tough Irish Catholic enclave at the time. Tom, the elder, had been a navy boxer who joined the police force following a failed pro career. He also once worked as a car thief for a finance company, demonstrating the thin dividing line that sometimes separates law enforcers and law breakers. His wife, Mary Margaret, who talks to an imaginary saint, Saint Barnabas of Luca, is in a state mental institution in Camarillo. Their daughter, Moira, who weighed 161 pounds at age thirteen, became a nun. They also have a son, Kev, who is in the religious supply business and has both a wife and a girlfriend.

Monsignor Desmond Spellacy, the younger brother, is pastor of Saint Mary's of the Desert in Twenty-nine Palms in the present-day story. He has been there for twenty-eight years. During the period of the novel's main action, he is chancellor of the archdiocese, a mover and shaker in the community, right-hand man to Hugh Cardinal Danaher, "A combination lightning rod, hatchet man, and accountant." His tactlessness as a chancellor causes pastors to complain about how much time he spends "in country-club locker rooms buttering up the fat cats of the archdiocese." During World War II, he had gained fame (and a star spot on a War Bond tour) as the Parachuting Padre.

The cardinal and the monsignor had real-life models. According to a June 22, 1997, *Los Angeles Times* review of Monsignor Francis J. Weber's *His Eminence of Los Angeles* by California State Librarian Kevin Starr, Danaher is a "thinly disguised" version of James Francis Cardinal McIntyre, "with McIntyre's chancellor and priest-of-all-work, Monsignor Benjamin G. Hawkes, appearing as Monsignor Spellacy . . . whose priestly vocation had long been lost in his rise up the ecclesiastical ladder and in his toadying to the wealthy and the prominent."

The novel is more of a procedural than the film—a police procedural, with departmental politics a prominent feature, and a Catholic Church procedural, with archdiocese politics closely examined. As the police try to solve the Virgin Tramp case, the church's problem is what to do about Jack Amsterdam, "[c]hief construction contractor for the archdiocese and pillar of the community," whose shady business practices and dubious associations are beginning to make him an embarrassment, leading to a decision to phase him out.

Tom also has an Amsterdam connection. Before coming to the robbery-homicide division, he had been a member of Wilshire Vice, where he was the bagman for Amsterdam's prostitution sideline, collecting payoffs in exchange for laying off the houses. When Tom shot and wounded a robber who held him up while he was sitting in a parked car registered to Brenda Samuels, a madame working for Amsterdam, his recovered wallet proved to have $1,100 in it. The resultant cover-up brought a jail sentence for Brenda but a transfer for Tom. The novel suggests Des was involved in covering Tom's part, but Tom is uncertain Des was aware of Amsterdam's involvement.

In both the book and film versions, Tom eventually solves the Virgin Tramp murder, though the solutions are entirely different. Though Amsterdam is not the murderer, there is an Amsterdam *connection,* real in the film, manufactured in the novel. Out of his hatred for Amsterdam, who has brought on Brenda's suicide, Tom is determined to charge the builder for the crime, satisfied to ruin him even if he knows the charges can't stick. In doing so, he brings multiple scandals to light—though not involved in the crime, Des had known the girl—and effectively ruins his brother's ecclesiastical career.

It's the same story with the same ending, but the different ways of getting there on the page and on the screen are fascinating. That the film is finally a more effective telling of the story is due not just to the skill of the screenwriters and director Grosbard but to the extraordinary cast that was assembled. Robert De Niro and Robert Duvall, arguably the best and most versatile screen actors of their generation, play Des and Tom respectively. Charles Durning plays Jack Amsterdam, a somewhat shadowy figure in the novel, who appears in many more scenes and is a much more striking and fully developed figure in the film. Kenneth McMillan is Tom's partner, Frank Crotty; Cyril Cusack, the somewhat ruthless and cynical cardinal; Burgess Meredith, the noncorrupt Monsignor Fargo; Ed Flanders, the slick lawyer Dan Campion; and Rose Gregorio is Brenda. All are perfect choices.

All of the detail about Tom's family life in the book's prologue is jettisoned in the film, with the action beginning with him driving to the desert church, summoned there by Des. The dialogue at the church is truncated considerably, but Des's anecdote about the daughter of a parishoner who is leaving the nunnery to become a professional bowler is reproduced in the film almost word for word. In an example of reusing favorite lines in different contexts, Des of the film refers to the Irish as having more hemorrhoids than other people—in the novel, another character credits *Mexicans* with having more hemorrhoids. Both versions segue from past to present with Des's revelation to Tom that he is terminally ill.

The screenwriters' choices reflect not just the need to compress but to provide interesting visuals. The funeral scene of the novel's second chapter becomes a much more pictorially interesting wedding. Film scenes of the cardinal attending a Mexican fiesta, feeling "such a fool" while wearing a huge sombrero, and playing croquet are not in the novel. The Virgin Tramp's tattoo, on her lower abdomen in the book, is moved to her hip in the film so that it can be used as a visual clue without incurring an X rating. The stag film in which the tattoo appears leads to the movie's solution, not necessarily more ingenious or plausible than the book's but more interesting in motion-picture terms.

Though the theme and the basic story line remain the same, some of the elements are interestingly reshuffled. In the novel, there are at least three women in Tom's life—in the film, there is only Brenda. The wife of the screen Tom is not hospitalized in Camarillo but has simply left him, taking along her tuna-casserole recipe ("her one dish!"). The mental failings of Tom's wife, Mary Margaret, in the book are attributed to his elderly mother in the film. The "let's-play-carnival" joke ("You sit on my face and I try to guess your weight") comes from a crank caller to the police in the book, from a prostitute in Brenda's employ in the film. A crack about mistrusting a priest whose eyes twinkle is made by Monsignor Fargo in the film but by the cardinal *about* Fargo (whose eyes never twinkle) in the novel. The name Leland K. Standard is used in both versions, but the characters are entirely different. The banquet that provides an important scene late in both versions if Monsignor Fargo's retirement party in the book, the awarding of Catholic Layman of the Year to Jack Amsterdam in the film. The latter scene and the opening wedding of Amsterdam's daughter in the film show how the character's role was wisely expanded for the film, resulting in Durning's memorable performance—some of the dialogue about the pregnant bride comes from a scene much later in the book about the daughter of lawyer Dan Campion.

While most scenes from the book are shortened for film, on at least one occasion the opposite happens: an argument at the crime scene over how many stretchers are needed for a body that has been cut in half, only a passing allusion in the book, becomes a memorable comic scene in the film.

On repeated viewings, the film version seems a virtually perfect piece of storytelling, aided by the focus and compression of a careful and faithful adaptation. The more rambling novel is a splendid work itself, though marred by two anachronisms. Des could not have won an exacta at Del Mar, since that exotic form of wagering was not available at California race tracks in the forties. While only racing buffs might have noticed that gaffe, many more surely would do a double-take at Tom's appearance on a radio call-in show, complete with seven-second delay, a genre and a technology that did not exist in forties radio.

In either version, *True Confessions* is a remarkable work of crime fiction, with an intriguing plot, deeply involving characters, and insights into the workings of two disparate institutions: the police and the Catholic Church. Both reward the consumer with a memorable experience. But if you had to choose only one of them, I'd head for the video store.

The Black List: Essential Film Noir

LEE SERVER

Here is an admittedly idiosyncratic selection of one hundred titles that will provide the aspiring fan of dark film with a solid foundation in the noir vision through the decades and around the world.—L. S.

American Friend. 1977. U.S./France/Germany. Wim Wenders's great adaptation of two Highsmith Ripley books (one used with permission, one without). Savory supporting roles for iconic auteurs Nick Ray and Sam Fuller.

Angel Face. 1953. U.S. As he did with *Laura,* Otto Preminger imparts an aura of sleazy chic to another story of the murderously petulant and rich.

Asphalt Jungle. 1950. U.S. Huston's masterpiece, perhaps *the* great film about professional criminals.

Battles Without Honor and Humanity. 1973. Japan. Kinji Fukasaku's stunning yakuza shoot-em-up, starring great tough guy actor Bunta Sugawara.

***Big Combo.* 1955.** U.S. Director Joseph H. Lewis and D.P. John Alton create one of the last great studio shadow-plays. Though the look was old-school classic, the film has a daring new perverseness: homosexual henchmen and Jean Wallace, hooked on cunnilingus.

Big Knife. 1955. U.S. Hollywood eats its own, with help from Clifford Odets. Jack Palance is miscast, over-the-top, and marvelous as the sensitive, doomed "John Garfield" movie star.

Big Sleep. 1946. U.S. An elegant thriller full of the behavioral charms of Hawks's comedies; dark when it has to be but this Chandler adaptation has as much in common with the *Thin Man* series as it does with *The Maltese Falcon.*

Bird with the Crystal Plumage. 1969. Italy. The headiest application of pure cinema style since Welles's *Touch of Evil;* loose use of a Fredric Brown storyline.

Black Book. 1949. U.S. The French Revolution as film noir. Directed by Anthony Mann.

Blood and Black Lace. 1964. Italy/Germany. Mario Bava's influential *"giallo"* reduces noir to pure sensation and mise-en-scène, in luridly dazzling colors.

Blue Velvet. 1986. U.S. David Lynch's blithe perversity and general wackiness make the noir clichés seem new again. Jack Palance Award goes to: Dennis Hopper.

Born to Kill. 1947. U.S. One of the most underappreciated of the classic era noirs. Not until Mitchum's Max Cady would there be a noir creation to match Lawrence Tierney's Sam Wild for pure márociousness.

Branded to Kill. 1967. Japan. The bizarre, dreamlike adventures of a rice-sniffing Japanese hit man, from legendary maverick director Seijun Suzuki. You've got to see it to believe it, and even that may not convince.

Bring Me the Head of Alfredo Garcia. 1974. U.S./Mexico. Peckinpah's ugly south-of-the-border noir, with alter ego Warren Oates amazing in the role of a lifetime. One of the great ones.

Burglar. 1956. U.S. David Goodis adapted his own bleak Lion paperback, with first-time director Paul Wendkos's imaginative direction bringing to mind the early Kubrick. Shot at actual Atlantic City locations that couldn't look seedier with the usually greasy Dan Duryea as a surprisingly effective tragic hero.

Cape Fear. 1962. U.S. Robert Mitchum as the most frighteningly believable of great movie villains. Poor Gregory Peck makes a weak case for the side of "Good."

Casque D'or. 1952. France. Jacques Becker's sordid and tender classic of crime and the lower depths in 1900 Paris.

***A Certain Killer.* 1967. Japan.** Stark, intense tale of a kamikaze turned hit man.

The Chase. 1946. U.S. A very loose adaptation of Woolrich/Irish's *Black Path of Fear.* Enigmatic Hollywood figure Arthur Ripley directs with a real flair for Cornell's paranoid lyricism and nutty logic.

Chinatown. 1974. U.S. Writer Robert Towne's amazing, colorful, literary script is the star of this Roman Polanski-directed classic of noir romanticism. Faye Dunaway's heroine and John Huston's villain are superb; Nicholson's 1970s raffishness seems—sacrilege!—a weak link.

Le Circle Rouge. 1970. France. A twisting, inventive gangster caper from Jean-Pierre Melville. The most satisfyingly pure storytelling of his career.

City of Industry. 1997. U.S. In the midst of post-*Pulp Fiction* self-consciousness and slacker noir came this straightforward, compelling dark thriller of a Palm Spring jewel heist gone wrong and a long trail of revenge. Harvey Keitel makes an impeccable noir hero.

Le Corbeau. 1943. France. Savagely cynical Clouzot film of poison-pen letters in a wartime village.

Crime Wave. 1953. U.S. Shot in less than two weeks by André de Toth, the film is dynamically staged, fast and furious. Sterling Hayden as the toothpick-chewing cop gives another great performance. Could he be the echt noir star after all?

Criss Cross. 1949. U.S. By all odds noir's hottest-to-trot couple, Burt Lancaster and Yvonne De Carlo reduce even an armored-car robbery to its aphrodisiacal properties. Robert Siodmak, the most committed of noir stylists, directs every scene like it was his last.

Crossfire. 1947. U.S. By the time of this one, film noir had reached beyond the pulp mystery for its source material, comfortably combining the whodunit and the message picture. Every scene in the film looks like it was shot at two in the morning.

Cry of the City. 1948. U.S. Richard Conte, a noir second-stringer, here gives his most charismatic performance in another lush Siodmak urban jungle.

Dark Mirror. 1946. U.S. Noir expanding, from touch-guy pulp to ladies' magazine fiction. Olivia De Havilland as twins, one homicidal, one sort-of-good.

Dark Passage. 1947. U.S. David Goodis's first crime novel becomes a glossy vehicle for Bogart and Bacall. Prison breaks, mean streets, penthouse apartments, plastic surgery, moonlit South America, the kitchen sink. With the famous "subjective camera" first half hour.

Detour. 1945. U.S. Denying reality, Edgar Ulmer shoots this no-budget PRC quickie like he's Fritz Lang at UFA; results: a masterpiece. The boxed-in production only intensifies the sense of doom in a claustrophobic road movie. Award for Least Likely Murder Weapon: the wrong end of a phone cord.

Les Diaboliques. 1955. France. Henri-Georges Clouzot beats Hitchcock's *Psycho* by five years with this similarly tricked-up, sleazy, and erotic thriller.

Double Indemnity. 1944. U.S. James M. Cain, Raymond Chandler, and Billy Wilder combine to create what is perhaps both the most emblematic and most perfect film noir. Fred and Barbara as cold-blooded killer couple opened the floodgates to film noir decadence.

Le Doulos. 1962. France. Jean-Pierre Melville's gray-black tribute to forties Hollywood noir, starring Jean-Paul Belmondo and Serge Reggiani. From the celebrated Série Noire novel by Pierre Lesou.

Face/Off. 1997. U.S. Underneath the hyperbolic style and comic-book disdain for reality, this is a classic "double" theme with true noir resonance.

Fallen Angel. 1945. U.S. An underrated noir masterwork from Otto Preminger, his sordid, small-town follow-up to the glamorous *Laura*. Dana Andrews gives his greatest performance as the down-at-heels con man.

Jack Palance in *Sudden Fear.*

Farewell My Lovely. 1975. U.S. A wonderful, elegiac forties recreation, with a magnificent Mitchum as the ultimate battered romantic noir PI. Chandler actually declared Cary Grant to be the perfect actor to play Philip Marlowe, but here he got the actor his prose deserved.

Five Against the House. 1955. U.S. Nearly all of Phil Karlson's fifties crime films are full of grit and dark surprises, and this casino robbery caper (precursor to *Ocean's Eleven*) is no exception.

Force of Evil. 1949. U.S. Abe Polonsky's self-consciously literary noir tragedy of brotherly love-hate and the numbers game. A very original looking and sounding movie from a great new talent, unfortunately thwarted by the blacklist.

Full Contact. 1992. Hong Kong. One of the toughest and most entertaining of the dark crime dramas from Hong King in the late eighties. Directed by Ringo Lam, starring Chow Yun Fat,

Courtesy of Kino International

John Ireland as a killer, Sheila Ryan as a dame in distress in *Railroaded*, directed by Anthony Mann.

and with a fiendishly showy bad-guy turn from Simon Yam.

Funeral in Berlin. 1966. U.K. The anti-Bond spy films of the sixties were clear descendants of the forties film noir, with their ambiguous heroes, femmes fatales, and rain-soaked urban jungles, as in this tour of a seedy East Berlin, derived from Len Deighton.

Get Carter. 1971. U.K. Michael Caine as a London Mafia soldier gone back home to settle a few scores. Still the best and hardest-boiled British crime film.

Gilda. 1946. U.S. Noir romanticism at its peak, with a lush Rita Hayworth as the good-bad girl in dreamlike Buenos Aires.

Graveyard of Honor and Humanity. 1975. Japan. Wild yakuza thriller about a lunatic drug-addict mobster rushing to oblivion.

The Grifters. 1990. U.S. A horribly miscast John Cusack as the taciturn young confidence trickster shackles Donald Westlake's superb script, a twisty-turny narrative, wonderfully structured, from a Jim Thompson paperback.

Gun Crazy. 1949. U.S. *L'amour fou* as represented by two of Hollywood's more forgettable also-rans (John Dall, Cathy O'Donnell), elevated to mythic status by Joseph H. Lewis's wild, intense direction. The one-take bank robbery scene is, of course, legendary.

Hell's Island. 1955. U.S. What would have been a backlot black-and-white cheapie in the forties is now tarted up with lurid colors: scenes look like Gold Medal and Pop. Library covers sprung to life. Great fun from Phil Karlson.

High and Low. 1962. Japan. Kurosawa brings his gravitas and ineffable poetry to an Ed McBain kidnap melodrama. Magnificent.

His Kind of Woman. 1951. U.S. A dark, conventional, tough Mitchum actioner subverted by an amiable, *Beat the Devil*-like hipster comedy. Some people hate it, some of us think it's a one-off masterpiece. Key scene: Bob irons his money.

House of Bamboo. 1955. U.S. Sam Fuller in Japan. Gangsters, undercover cops, betrayal, a shootout in the sky. Wonderful, intriguing script, and absolutely stunning Cinemascope stagings.

House of Strangers. 1949. U.S. Richard Conte and Susan Hayward are an oddly erotic pairing in this Joseph Mankiewicz-directed drama. Another example of the noir style casting its net into unexpected areas.

I Died a Thousand Times. 1955. U.S. The original version, *High Sierra,* gets all the attention, but this widescreen/color remake is infinitely tougher. A great vehicle for a simmering Jack Palance, and dynamic Cinemascope compositions from director Stuart Heisler.

I Wake up Screaming. 1941. U.S. Deft, entertaining light noir thriller with a just-blossoming Betty Grable in the lead. Novelist Steve Fisher based the Laird Cregar character, "Cornell," on fellow pulp scribe C. Woolrich.

In a Lonely Place. 1950. U.S. A major rewrite on Dorothy Hughes's novel, directed by Nicholas Ray: Bogart is a cosmopolitan Hollywood screenwriter with a dangerous temper. Adult, imbued with a curdled romanticism, unpredictable and unforgettable.

Johnny Angel. 1945. U.S. The ordinarily workmanlike Edwin L. Marin follows cinematographer Harry Wild onto the trendy noir bandwagon, producing a lushly atmospheric revenge thriller set in an expressionistic backlot New Orleans.

Key Largo. 1948. U.S. Rather than downplay the stage-bound nature of the source material, director John Huston chooses to showcase it. The result is a talky but wonderfully intense, theatrical experience.

The Killer. 1989. Hong Kong. John Woo's international breakthrough, a deliriously cinematic tale of a compassionate hit man, played by Chow Yun Fat.

The Killers. 1946. U.S. Fractured storytelling becomes a staple of forties film noir with this dark, complex crime drama that takes over both the flashback structure and the elaborate, expressionist visuals of *Citizen Kane.*

The Killing. 1956. U.S. With one eye on *The Asphalt Jungle,* Stanley Kubrick hires Jim Thompson to adapt this racetrack robbery suspenser by another paperback pro, Lionel White. Awkward around the edges, but greatly entertaining, with a marvelously fatalistic Sterling Hayden and that ponderously ironic but very satisfying ending.

King of New York. 1990. U.S. The sometimes sloppy Abel Ferrara here puts it all together for a sumptuous, very cool crime epic. Faster, harder, and more efficient than the similar but often simple-minded De Palma/ Stone version of *Scarface.* The central violent set piece—beginning with the raid on the nightclub—is as good as any action scene in the genre.

Kiss Me Deadly. 1955. U.S. Scripter Bezzerides and director Aldrich turn Spillane's Manichean universe upside down with equal parts irony and anarchy. The hero is now a stupid, sadistic divorce dick, the dames are poetry-spouting psychos, and the MacGuffin is an A-bomb in a suitcase. Superb.

The Kremlin Letter. 1970. U.S. Huston caps the spy-movie era with this magnificent, outrageous tale of depraved adventurers trying to scam the Soviets. Outstanding scenes: the Acapulco lady wrestlers, and any containing Richard Boone.

Lady from Shanghai. 1948. U.S. Orson Welles's kiss-off to estranged wife Rita Hayworth, casting her as a treacherous killer.

Laura. 1944. U.S. Noir goes high style in Otto Preminger's worldly production of Vera Caspary's bestseller.

Maltese Falcon. 1941. U.S. Film noir as a genre really begins with John Huston's utterly inspired and faithful filming of Hammett classic.

Ministry of Fear. 1944. U.S. Underrated, atmospheric Lang adaptation of great Graham Greene novel.

Murder, My Sweet. 1944. U.S. Director Edward Dmytryk gives Chandler's second novel a hermetic, shadow-drenched atmosphere not seen since the heyday of German expressionism. A turning point for the genre.

Narrow Margin. 1952. U.S. Efficiently

intense direction from Richard Fleischer. A B classic.

Night and the City. 1950. U.S. Haunting portrait of a doomed hustler by Richard Widmark; amazingly seedy London locations.

Night of the Following Day. 1968. U.S. Hubert Cornfield's Frenchified adaptation of Lionel White's *The Snatchers* is like J. P. Melville meets the Actors Studio. Though bordering on unintentional parody, it's great fun, especially Brando versus Boone.

Odds Against Tomorrow. 1959. U.S. Icy, well-crafted noir directed by Robert Wise from William McGivern novel. Robert Ryan, as a close relative of his *Crossfire* killer, plays a rabid racist on a caper with cool cat Harry Belafonte.

Out of the Past. 1947. U.S. Argu-ably the great film noir—complex, sexy, haunting. Robert Mitchum as the hep chump of a private eye achieves greatness.

Phantom Lady. 1943. U.S. Sloppy storytelling in the second half, but earlier moments—the train station, the nightclub—are seminal noir set pieces from Robert Siodmak.

Pickup on South Street. 1953. U.S. Sam Fuller's explosive, tabloid masterpiece of pickpockets, Commies, and battered broads.

Point Blank. 1967. U.S. Richard Stark's first Parker novel gets cool modernist treatment from director John Boorman; with the great Lee Marvin.

Pulp Fiction. 1994. U.S. Tall tales from the mean streets. At its worst (the Harvey Keitel sequence), overconfident juvenilia; at its best, reignites the glories of yarn-spinning.

Purple Noon. 1958. France. Chic, beautifully filmed adaptation of Highsmith's first Ripley novel. Noir under a warm Mediterranean sun.

Railroaded. 1947. U.S. A spare beauty from the team of Anthony Mann and John Alton, with a superb John Ireland as a sultry, fetishistic gunman who polishes his bullets.

Rear Window. 1954. U.S. Extraordinary ode to Peeping Toms by Hitchcock. From Woolrich pulp story.

Rififi. 1954. France. Hollywood exile Jules Dassin directed an innovative, idiosyncratic, and hard-as-nails caper.

Le Samorai. 1967. France. Melville's influential, gorgeously austere classic, with Alain Delon as the iconic, icy hit man.

Second Breath. 1966. France. Dishonor among thieves, and a terrific highway robbery.

Shadow of a Doubt. 1943. U.S. Magnificent, nuanced Hitchcock classic of a killer coming home to his small town; Teresa Wright is sublime.

Sonatine. 1993. Japan. Contemplation, nihilism, and machine guns as yakuza gang hides out at the beach.

Stranger on the Third Floor. 1940. U.S. Often credited as the "first" film noir; with uncredited script work by Nathanael West.

Street of No Return. 1989. France/Portugal. Fuller's last film, an adaptation of an old David Goodis novel, is loony, stylish, and sublime.

Sudden Fear. 1952. An overripe melodrama with Joan Crawford, Jack Palance, and Gloria Grahame as the *menage a trois* from Hell. The romantic scenes are as scary as the violence.

Sunset Boulevard. 1950. U.S. Billy Wilder's staggering Hollywood Gothic. A kind of melding of Chandler and the Brothers Grimm.

Sweet Smell of Success. 1957. U.S. Shimmering James Wong Howe photography and deliciously stylized dialogue in this exposé of Winchell-era Broadway.

Taxi Driver. 1976. U.S. Paul Schrader's own "psychological memoir" brought to hellish life by Scorsese.

Third Man. 1949. U.K. Noir as international intrigue with a script by Graham Greene and Joseph Cotten's naive pulp writer based on James Hadley Chase.

Too Many Reasons to Be #1. 1997. Hong Kong. Wild, dark gangster craziness.

Touch of Evil. 1958. U.S. Orson Welles's phantasmagoric tribute to a genre he helped invent.

Touchez pas au Grisbi. 1954. France. Jacques Becker. Superb study of the "criminal code" with a brilliant Jean Gabin.

Two Men in Manhattan. 1959. France. Melville's jazzy, offhand tribute to New York and two decades of B movies.

Underworld USA. 1961. U.S. One of the last great black-and-white studio noir/gangster films. Written and directed by Sam Fuller.

Venus in Furs. 1970. U.S./U.K./Germany. The rare film to capture on film what Woolrich could convey in print: the illogic and woozy paranoia of a waking dream.

Vertigo. 1958. U.S. Hitchcock's *ne plus ultra,* making use of most of the important noir motifs in one awesome work of art.

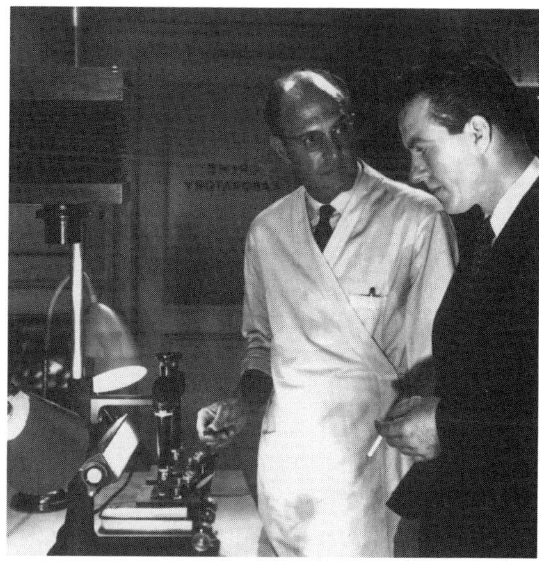

Hugh Beaumont as a police detective in the classic B noir, *Railroaded.*

Violated Women in White. 1967. Japan. Koji Wakamatsu's feverish take on the Richard Speck murders.

Where the Sidewalk Ends. 1950. U.S. Tough, pulpy script by Ben Hecht; lush, glamorous staging by Otto Preminger.

Woman in the Window. 1944. U.S. Greasy Dan Duryea and treacherous tart Joan Bennett make a wonderfully sleazy couple in Fritz Lang's, and Nunnally Johnson's "dream" of temptation and its consequences.

II: FICTION

SONY
SONY
SONY
STAND-UP
TRAGEDY
CRITERION CENTER

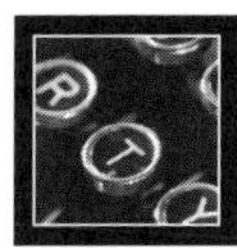

The Last Days of Cornell Woolrich

I. CORNELL GEORGE HOPLEY WOOLRICH

BARRY N. MALZBERG

At the end, in the last year, he looked three decades older. The booze had wrecked him, the markets had wrecked him, he had wrecked him; by the time friends dragged him out in April to St. Clare's Hospital where they took off the gangrenous leg, he had the stunned aspect of the very old. Where there had been edges there was now only the gelatinous material that when probed would not rebound.

Nonetheless, if the booze had stripped all but bone it had left his eyes moist and open, childlike and vulnerable. That September in the open coffin, surrounded by flowers sent by the Chase Manhattan Bank, he looked young; he looked like the man who in his late twenties had loafed around the ballrooms and written of the debutantes.

There were five names in the guest book, Leo and Cylvia Margulies of *Mike Shayne's Mystery Magazine* leading off. Leo died in December 1975 and Cylvia divested herself of the publication about two years later.

He died in print. The April 1968 *Escapade* had a story, and *Ellery Queen's Mystery Magazine* had taken his stunning "New York Blues" to publish it two years later; that novelette had been written in late 1967. Ace Books had embarked upon an ambitious program of reissue that brought *The Bride Wore Black, Rendezvous in Black, Phantom Lady,* and others back into the mass market. Truffaut's *The Bride Wore Black* was in production. The Ellery Queen hardcover mystery annual had a story. Now, more than a decade later, he is out of print; an item for the specialty and university presses, an occasional republication in an Ellery Queen annual. Ace let the books go a long time past: poor sales. There are no other paperbacks. The hardcovers—what few copies remain—are for the collectors.

"It isn't dying I'm afraid of, it isn't that at all; I know what it is to die, I've died already. It is the endless obliteration, the knowledge that there will never be anything else. That's what I can't stand, to try so hard and to end in nothing. You know what I mean, don't you? . . . I really loved to write."

His mother, Claire, died in 1956. Shortly thereafter his own work virtually ceased. A novel—never published—was found with his effects; it had been rejected all over New York in the early sixties. A few short stories for *Ellery Queen* and *The Saint Mystery Magazine*. His relationship with his mother had been the central—it is theorized that it was the only—relationship of his life; they had lived together continuously for her last fourteen years. When she died he lived alone in one room on the second floor of the Sheraton-Russell Hotel in Manhattan surrounded by cases and cases of beer cans and bottles of whiskey, and invited the staff to come up and drink with him and watch television. Sometimes he would sit in the lobby; more occasionally he would take a cab to McSorley's Tavern in the Village. The gangrene that came from an ill-fitting shoe and that, untreated, turned his left leg to charcoal, slowly, from early 1967 to April 1968, ended all that; he would stay in his room and drink almost all the time and stare at the television, looking for a film from one of his novels or short stories that came on often enough and usually after 2 A.M.; between the movies and the alcohol he was finally able to find sleep. For a few hours. Until ten or eleven in the morning, when it would all start again. At the end he had almost none of his books left in the room: he had given them all away to casual visitors. Bellboys. Maids. The night manager. An employee of his literary agent. He could not bear to have his work around him anymore.

"I got $600 from Alfred Hitchcock for the movie rights to 'Rear Window.' That's all that I got; it was one story in a collection of eight that was sold in the forties by the agent H. N. Swanson for $5,000; he sold *everything* for $5,000; that's why we all called him five grand Swannie. But that didn't bother me really; what bothered me was that Hitchcock wouldn't even send me a ticket to the premiere in New York. He knew where I lived. He wouldn't even send me a ticket."

The novels were curiously cold for all of their effects and mercilessly driven, but the characters, particularly the female characters, who were the protagonists of many of them, were rendered with great sensitivity and were always in enormous pain. That was one of the mysteries of Woolrich's work for the editors and writers who knew him: how could a man who could not relate to women at all, who had had a brief and terrible marriage annulled when he was twenty-five, who had lived only alone or with his mother since . . . how could such a man have had such insight into women, write of them with such compassion, make these creatures of death and love dance and crumple on the page? Some theorized that the writer could identify with these women because that was the terrible and essential part of him that could never be otherwise acknowledged. Others simply called it a miracle: a miracle that a lonely man in a hotel room could somehow create, populate, and justify the world.

"I tried to move out. In 1942 I lived alone in a hotel room for three weeks and then one night she called me and said, 'I can't live without you, I must live with you, I need you,' and I put down the phone and I packed and I went back to that place and for the rest of her life I never spent a night away from her, not one. I know what they thought of me, what they said about me but I just didn't care. I don't regret it and I'll never regret it as long as I live."

He began as a minor imitator of Fitzgerald, wrote a novel in the late twenties that won a prize, became dissatisfied with his work and stopped writing for a period of years. When he came back it was to *Black Mask* and the other detective magazines with a curious and terrible fiction that had never been seen before in the genre markets; Hart Crane and certainly Hemingway were writing of people on the edge of their emotions and their possibilities, but the genre mystery markets were filled with characters whose pain was circumstantial, whose resolution was through action; Woolrich's gallery was of those so damaged that their lives could only be seen as vast anticlimaxes to central and terrible events that had occurred long before the incidents of the story. Hammett and his great disciple Chandler had verged toward this more than a little; there is no minimizing the depth of their contribution to the mystery and to literature, but Hammett and Chandler were still working within the devices of their category: detectives confronted problems and solved (or more commonly failed to solve) them, evil was generalized but had at least specific manifestations. Woolrich went far out on the edge. His characters killed, were killed, witnessed murder, attempted to solve it, but the events were peripheral to the central circumstances. What I am trying to say, perhaps, is that Hammett and Chandler wrote of death, but the novels and short stories of Woolrich *were* death—in all of its delicacy and grace, its fragile beauty as well as its finality.

Most of his plots made no objective sense. Woolrich was writing at the cutting edge of his time. Twenty years later his vision would attract Truffaut, whose own influences had been the philosophy of Sartre and the French *nouvelle vague*, the central conception that nothing really mattered. Nothing at all . . . but the suffering. Ah, that mattered; that mattered quite a bit.

"I wasn't that good, you know. What I was was a guy who could write a little, publishing in magazines surrounded by people who couldn't write at all. So I looked pretty good. But I never thought I was that good at all. All that I thought was that I tried."

Inevitably, his vision verged toward the fantastic; he published a scattering of stories that appeared to conform to that genre, at least to the degree that the fuller part of his vision could be seen as "mysteries." For Woolrich it all was fantastic: the clock in the tower, hand in the glove, out-of-control vehicle, errant gunshot that destroyed; whether destructive coincidence was masked in the "naturalistic" or the "incredible" was all pretty much the same to him. *Rendezvous in Black, The Bride Wore Black, Nightmare* are all great swollen dreams, turgid constructions of the night, obsession, and grotesque outcome; to turn from these to the "fantastic" was not to turn at all. The work, as is usually the case with a major writer, was perfectly formed, perfectly consistent; the vision leached into every area and pulled the book together. "Jane Brown's Body" is a suspense story. *The Bride Wore Black* is science fiction. *Phantom Lady* is a Gothic. *Rendezvous in Black* was a bildungsroman. It does not matter.

"I'm glad you liked *Phantom Lady* but I can't help you, you see. I can't accept your praise. The man who wrote that novel died a long, long time ago. He died a long, long time ago."

At the end, amidst the cases and the bottles and the empty glasses, as the great black leg became turgid and began to stink, there was nothing at all. The television did not help, the whiskey left no stain, the bellhops could not bring distraction. They carried him out to St. Clare's and cut off the leg in April and sent him back in June with a prosthesis; the doctors were cheerful. "He has a chance," they said. "It all depends upon his will to live." At the Sheraton-Russell they came to his doors with trays, food, bottles, advice. They took good care of him. They helped him on his crutches to the lobby and put him in the plush chair at the near door so that he could see lobby traffic. They were unfailingly kind. They brought him into the dining room and brought him out. They took him upstairs. They took him downstairs. They stayed with him. They created a network of concern: the Woolrich network in the Sheraton-Russell.

In September, like Delmore Schwartz, he had a stroke in a hotel corridor; in September, like Schwartz in an earlier August, he died instantly. He lay in the Campbell funeral parlor in a business suit for three days surrounded by flowers from Chase Manhattan.

His will left $850,000 to Columbia University (he had inherited money; the markets didn't leave him much) to establish a graduate creative writing program in memory of Claire. He had been a writer of popular fiction, had never had a serious review in the United States, had struggled from cheap pulp magazines to genre hardcover and paperback. Sure he wanted respectability; a university cachet. Sure. Why not? Who wouldn't?

"Life is death. Death is life. To hold your own true love in your arms and see the skeleton she will be; to know that your love leads to death, that death is all there is, that is what I know and what I do not want to know and what I cannot bear. Don't leave me. Don't leave me.

"Don't leave me now, Barry."

II. "CON"

DON YATES

He was a friend, and I was not prepared to lose him. Somehow you never even consider the death of certain people, as if in your book they aren't subject to mortal wearing down and eventual defeat. Con Woolrich, despite his long and intimate familiarity with disillusionment and despair, was that kind of friend.

It was probably because I did so often consider the way he lived, somehow coping with his bleak view of existence and still surviving, that I deceived myself into thinking that he was among the toughest of the people I knew. But I was wrong. Things caught up with him, and in the autumn of a year now more than three decades distant, he died.

The last time I saw him was in July of 1968, in New York City, in his room at the Sheraton-Russell, at Park Avenue South and Thirty-seventh Street. I had been out of the country for a year, and when business took me to New York, I gave him a call. I was unaware then that, months earlier, as a direct consequence of his dogged disinclination to give any reasonable attention to the care and feeding of his body, he had let a foot infection fester and had lost his left leg, above the knee, by amputation. In July he was sick and dying, but I didn't know any of this.

So when I strolled into the lobby and found him waiting for me in a wheelchair, I was surprised. A few minutes later, upstairs, he dramatically disclosed the results of the operation, pitching off the prosthetic leg with a gesture and a curse. I wanted to try to play down the seriousness of his loss because that was what he seemed eager to hear. But I was deeply concerned. And he was clearly terrified beyond words of what was happening to him. I didn't comprehend it then—only later: death had moved into that lonely hotel room with him.

I first encountered Cornell Woolrich in April of 1961, at the Mystery Writers of America annual banquet at the Astor in New York. After the dinner formalities we met in someone's hotel room upstairs and soon we were a party of six on the town. It was a long and glorious evening, the first of many nights, over the next seven years, that I would spend doing the rounds of nightspots with him, with this lonely writer who would never let you say goodbye until daylight was in the street. That night he asked me to call him Con.

Thereafter, when circumstances brought me to New York, I'd give him a call at the hotel—first the Franconia, later the Sheraton-Russell—and we would set out, in the first of the evening's numerous taxicabs, to visit some of his favorite places. I won't be able to forget the unconcealed pleasure he communicated over the phone whenever I called to say I was in town and had the night free. It was the pleasure of a child. His few close friends must have come to recognize that special joy in him.

But what was hard always came later, when I would make a move to leave. Farewells were difficult, painful, and it always seemed that our friendship was washed up when I left him. I think I see now that he was afraid to be left alone.

It seems, too, that he was always trying to get away somehow. Back in the fifties, friends told me, he had a habit of disappearing from his hotel for months at a time. Few people had any notion of where he went. When he came back, it was evident that he hadn't escaped anything.

I think he detested the inside of a hotel room, with a visceral hate that perhaps no one can ever comprehend. And he made a hotel room his only home on this earth. During the time I knew him he had given up the struggle to get away from that room and, now abandoning the course of his flight, he planned to come out to Michigan for a visit, to the quiet small town where I lived then. But the plans fell through, for reasons I never knew. He had sent a letter saying, "Write back, and give me the name of the best hotel in Lansing, so I'll know where to make my reservation when I'm ready to come out. I imagine around Thanksgiving would be a nice time. It's not too cold out there then, is it?" We had wanted him to stay with us, in our big old rambling house that had plenty of room, but he insisted on the hotel arrangement. He never came. Perhaps the futility of switching one hotel room for another finally defeated the idea.

In an admirable bio-bibliography on Woolrich, Francis M. Nevins, Jr. included a separate bibliographic section dealing with Spanish-language films based on Woolrich stories, which is subtitled "Woolrich in Argentina." There's irony and a generous dose of coincidence in this for—I don't know if anyone else is aware of it—Woolrich very nearly went to Argentina for an eye operation in January of 1965. His right eye had been failing in 1964, and when I returned very briefly to New York from Buenos Aires—where I was spending a year of a research project-we got together once more.

He said he needed an operation. He claimed he had heard there were good eye specialists in Argentina. I told him he was more than welcome to be our guest. Things began to bog down when he found he needed to renew his passport. And when I couldn't free myself from business engagements long enough to take him around to the places he needed to go-his eyesight was poor, and he wouldn't go out on the street alone-he slowly let the air out of the project. Later, in the States, he was operated on successfully for cataracts.

The last attempt we made to get together away from New York occurred in the spring of 1966. I invited him again to come out to Michigan, and he seemed enthusiastic. But this time it became clear to me that he was perfectly poised in indecision—over wanting to leave his room, and fearing to leave it.

This time he wrote, "I thought I'd make it for the Decoration Day weekend, say, by June 1. Should I give up my pad here and just keep going after my stopover in Lansing? Give me some advice. I'm not secure. Should I take a chance? I'm not happy here. I'll have to get a new passport if I do shove off, though. I want to come by Trailways Bus. Give me the chance I need, give me the shove I need. Rig up a schedule of some kind, of theirs, and send it on to me. Exact time and stopovers and changes and so forth. Funny how helpless you can get, like a kid almost."

This time the plans foundered because the Trailways line didn't serve Lansing. That was his explanation.

In November of that year—November 28th it was—he sent a Christmas card with the laconic message: "Hello, pal. Sometimes I miss you. Sometimes I don't. Cornell."

There's probably no one who knows all the battles Con fought in that hotel room—what they were about, what it was that kept him hanging on, grappling with his own demons—much less how he managed to maintain enough equilibrium to keep writing anything at all. But in the spring of 1967 I had a glimpse into one of the dark pits. It was a story that would have sounded like a nightmare of his own invention had he not told it to me the way he did.

That time he was not well, and we stayed in his room. It was a long, confusing night, but the account Con gave stays with me. It was a nightmarish narrative, telling about his being followed, persecuted by a man who lived in his hotel. He said that his pursuer lived on the same floor, down the hall, and that this man, whom everybody else trusted, was after Con Woolrich for something that Con couldn't learn the nature of. When he left his room he was sure that the man would come into the room and search it. What he was searching for, Con never knew. He never caught the man in his room, but lived in mortal fear of this man discovering something.

He said the man had women in his own room, which was apparently some kind of condemnation of the fellow. He said that everybody else thought that he was a fine chap, but gradually, by talking to the administration, to the bellboys, to the staff, he managed to work up some opposition to the fellow and in the end managed to have him evicted from his room. He said he saw him later, in a restaurant, and the man acted very friendly then to him.

The way he told the story, it seemed to me as real as anything else in his life. Of course, it's the kind of chilling concoction that he would devise for so many of his stories. It may have been that he worked with the theme too long, and somehow it passed from the pages that emerged from his typewriter into his own existence. It made no sense. He said that he knew the man was elusive, and he could never pin him down and find out what he was doing. But he understood that something "real" had been after him for a long time and it had terrified him.

The last recollection I have of Con Woolrich is that of the last night I spent with him—the night of July 17, 1968—barely two months before he died. And that night there were no recriminations when, long after midnight, I said I had to leave.

I'd brought along a collection of my Woolrich and Irish books and I asked him if he'd sign them. I had them in a big shirt box, from the dry cleaner's, that I'd wrapped up and brought with me. That was my last request. He said, "Oh sure, I'd be glad to do that." He said, "You can pick them up tomorrow." There was not the bitterness in our parting that there had been on so many nights before, when he seemed terribly angry and disappointed and let down because I was going to leave him alone.

So we said goodbye. I came back the next morning, and there were the books, waiting for me downstairs. I checked through them, and they were all signed, in his very distinctive and fluid hand. All the Woolrich books were signed as by Woolrich, and all the Irish books were signed as by Irish. It was to be a last gesture, a final expression of his sense of friendship with me.

Weeks passed. Finally, at home in Michigan, on the night of September 19, 1968, it suddenly occurred to me that I hadn't called Con in a long time and he hadn't called me. So at 9:35 P.M., according to my telephone bill, I placed a call to his hotel at the

Sheraton-Russell in New York City.

The operator answered, and I said, "May I speak to Cornell Woolrich please?"

There was a long pause—too long a pause. Immediately I sensed that something was wrong.

She said, "Are you a friend of Cornell Woolrich?"

And I said, "Yes I am. Could I speak with him, please?"

She said, "Well," as if searching for words, "something's happened. Mr. Woolrich has been found unconscious, and he's just a minute ago been taken in an ambulance to the hospital."

I was, of course, dumbstruck.

I said, "I'll call back tomorrow and see what information you can give me."

I called back the next day, and she was able to give me the name of the doctor who was treating him. I called the doctor, and he said that Woolrich had suffered a stroke and was unconscious.

I said, "Well, I'll call you back again and find out how he's doing."

The days passed, and I called, learning only that he remained in a coma. On the 25th of September, six days after he lost consciousness, he died.

It seems sad and ironic to me that the last manifestation of our friendship was my call to him at an instant when he was in great need, but when it was impossible for me to do anything for him. I missed his last words by perhaps a minute or two. And that was the end.

I believe he was an enormously gifted writer, and it may be that a necessary part of his gift was the fact that he was a haunted man as well. At times I got the feeling that he thought he was living in some kind of uneasy, controlled dream. There always seemed to be an expression in his eyes—sometimes immensely painful—that never completely disappeared. It is clear to us all now that the essence of what he lived found its way into what he wrote.

Sometime later I composed an acrostic poem that, taking the first letter in each line, reads down: "William Irish." I tried to suggest in it the view of life that he seemed to have adopted. It is a bleak but sincere tribute to my lost friend, Con Woolrich.

We Are as Flies . . .

Who of us can claim
to steer his fate?
I know full well that such
is not our choice.
Laughing, always near in
mocking wait,
Lurk lethal, playful gods
who mute our voice.

I have shown the random deep
that draws
A life away from peace
down sombre trails,
Making man the dupe of
unknown flaws.
In all I've written, see how
doom prevails.

Read the signs. With hope
we wait our hour,
Inherit chaos, and our noblest aim
Shatters, broken by our
lack of power,
Held naught by players who
ignore their game.

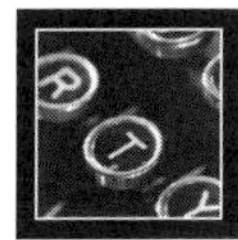

My Friend Fredric Brown

WALT SHELDON

The late Fredric Brown, with whom I was associated in an innocent age long ago, taught me more about the craft of writing fiction than he ever meant to, and certainly more than I would admit to at the time. He did this by dropping little gems of observations that I gathered up and tucked away in my mind, more out of tidiness than any realization of their value. I was to understand much later how helpful they really were.

Fredric Brown wrote mainly what I suppose we must call mystery novels, though they were never conventional whodunits or standard private-eye capers. His output still fills a long shelf in many a library, and it includes, in addition to the mysteries, several science fiction novels, at least one novel of no particular genre, and numerous short stories enshrined in anthologies. There was always something both wry and merry about a Fredric Brown mystery, even if it was also apt to be tough and fast-moving. John D. MacDonald once wrote me, after reading something of Fred's that he ought to be called Fredric *Brawn*.

John had never seen Fred in the flesh, or he wouldn't have said that. Short, slender, ginger-haired, and with a skin that freckled and burned easily, Fred struck most people as exceptionally mild. He had an absolute contempt for grooming or sartorial harmony. In Taos, New Mexico, where we both lived the good freelance life in the late forties, and where, granted, everyone wore what he damned pleased, Fred used to go around in a checked wool hunting shirt and a black homburg left over from somebody's diplomatic corps, seeing nothing strange in this combination. Whenever he went to the big city to call on editors he would camouflage himself in a more-or-less conventional suit and tie, but still manage to look like someone from another world, another dimension, floating through the scene, his eyes quizzical, a smile held in leash upon his lips, as if he found everything he beheld constantly amazing and just a touch absurd.

***

Small and almost fragile as he was, Fred was far from timid. He would, for example, hold his own against aggressive drunks, nearly always bigger than himself, who had a way of picking on him in barrooms. There was a Hollywood actor who once visited Taos and who, after a lot of drinking, began to excoriate the town and its residents, pretty much as an attack on Fred himself, who was nearby and handy as a target. Fred looked up at him mildly and said, "If you hate this place so much, why don't you move here?"

That was Fred—always the switch, the reversal, the transposition, the odd angle. Koestler speaks of this business of looking at things in some unexpected way in *The Act of Creation.* It was one of Fred Brown's favorite techniques. It is beautifully exemplified in one of his short stories where an asylum inmate, applying for release, swears he no longer thinks he's Napoleon—and the lie-detector registers a lie. There's been a flaw in the time continuum, you see, and the poor fellow really is Napoleon.

Or take Fred's Theory of Villainy. Once I said to him I needed a model for an antagonist in one of my stories and was trying to think of someone I really hated. "Wrong," he said. "Base your villain on someone you like. That'll give him some sympathetic traits and make him much more believable."

Fred's characters—villains, heroes, bit players—were always interesting and three-dimensional on his pages, though he seldom described them in great detail or went very deeply into their minds or backgrounds. They all had something of Fred himself in them. They were mostly plain folks with undemanding tastes. His heroes had strong sex drives and he delighted in writing sexy scenes in a day when editors and the post office blanched at that sort of thing. In one wild yarn, Fred hung his whole theme on a spaceman losing his temper and telling a Venusian to go four-letter-word himself, which the Venusian promptly did with pleasure because that was the normal reproductive way of the Venusians.

***

Any self-respecting sophisticate or bon vivant would have said that Fred's tastes, in general, bordered on the execrable. He liked the cheap, sweet wines of skid row—really preferred them—and wouldn't have appreciated a vintage Bordeaux if you'd given him one. A pot of beans suited him as well as capon with truffles. He bought pictures to hang for their frames. He attended college, he had a first-class intellect, and he read voraciously, but he lidded his mind to anything he considered pretentious or fancy. He considered French fancy and was infuriated by writers who would throw bits of it into their work on the—to him—snobbish assumption that everybody read French. In one of his stories he had a Frenchman saying, "*Viola!*" instead of "*Voila!*" It slipped by the proofreader, too. It wasn't an accidental transposition; he thought "viola" was some kind of expletive in French. When I pointed out the error he was completely unabashed and, as far as I know, promptly forgot his small mistake forever.

Fred was also above most data that might lend verisimilitude to a tale. In his crime stories he often made up his own police procedures because he couldn't be bothered to find out how it was done in real life. It was always sufficiently convincing, however, because it always seemed logical. In a way it reflected his view of the world, which seemed to be: "Well, if things aren't exactly this way, they *ought* to be."

He knew little about science, yet he wrote good science fiction. His was not the kind with a lot of scientific background—though he admired that kind—but his basic ideas, which always had some kind of twist to them, would always startle you and make you think. "Nobody cares," he'd say, "whether your spaceship operates by rockets or mice on a treadmill. They care about the people inside." If he needed a scientific principle to explain how something marvelous was happening he'd invent it and give it his own name. His Martians "quirtled" instead of using speech; a "wavery" was an intelligent creature made up of electromagnetic waves. It was almost as though he were kidding earnest science fiction.

I think that was it. He kidded everything else that was earnest. He liked, however, to make a distinction between science fiction and fantasy. In the introduction to *Angels and Spaceships,* a collection of his pieces, he wrote, "Fantasy deals with things that are not and cannot be. Science fiction deals with things that can be, that someday may be." That's about as clearly and succinctly as I've seen it put.

His stories, of whatever specie, all have an unmistakable Fred Brown twist. Boy astronaut falls in love with girl astronaut, as they are marooned in space. Only trouble is they are and must forever be in space suits. Even his mysteries, though in realistic settings, had a touch of the fantastic. In *The Night of the Jabberwock* the denizens of Alice's looking-glass world seem to appear again. Noticing that several people named Ambrose had disappeared—among them, Ambrose Bierce—Fred wondered if someone could be collecting them and wrote *The Ambrose Collector* [published as *Compliments of a Fiend-ed.*].

***

The ordinary given an offbeat twist—that was Fredric Brown's stock-in-trade there in the lovely art colony of Taos, New Mexico, high in the clear air, among adobe walls hung with strings of scarlet chile peppers and mottled ears of Indian corn. I'd come there first, then Fred, then Mack Reynolds, a big, amiable pipe-smoking bear of a man who wrote science fiction and general articles. We three were our own colony. We were never well received by the town's main art colony because we actually made money at what we did, and that just wasn't very arty.

We never got in with the group whose doyenne was Mabel Dodge Luhan, the heiress who had married a Taos Indian, and who surrounded herself with what I can only think of as dippers into the arts. Fred, Mack, and I would occasionally pay homage to the memory of D. H. Lawrence, who had long ago lived in Taos, by going out into the hills where his ashes were supposed to be scattered, and where we would picnic on sandwiches and wine and try to evoke his ghost. Once there was a stirring in the underbrush and an old goat appeared. Fred stared at it, then at us. "Ghost, not goat, gentlemen," he said. "You're simply not quirtling clearly."

We called upon D. H. Lawrence's widow, Frieda, sister of Manfred von Richthofen, a warm, delightful, and unpretentious lady who made us welcome. Fred later said to us he didn't believe the picture she showed was of her brother, the Red Baron and Germany's greatest World War I ace. He'd seen plenty of World War I movies, he said, and he knew all German pilots had mustaches and looked mean.

The three of us would often meet in a local bar in the early afternoon. That was because Mack and I wrote in the morning and Fred wrote at night. The reason he wrote at night was that he hated to write and kept putting it off all day. He would insert white paper with carbons into his typewriter and start right off with the final draft of whatever he was doing. No outline, no detailed plot, not so much as a scribbled note to keep him from giving a brown-eyed character blue eyes later on. Fred, who was an excellent chess player, wrote as he played chess, not knowing *exactly* what the next move would be, but with the general plan of attack firmly in mind. In chess he was positively sadistic. He would cackle with glee as he took your pieces then hounded your king across the board. He hated to have you resign because he wanted to taste the blood of the final coup de grace, which he mispronounced "koo-de-grah," deliberately, I think.

With a work in progress Fred would move along laboriously at the rate of two or three pages a day, but those pages would come out of his machine clean and ready for the printer. Between sentences he would get up, pace, gaze out of the window, and look for excuses not to write. His cheerful wife, Beth, whom he rightly adored, would save asking him to do household chores until this time because she knew he'd readily duff into them just to keep from getting back to the typewriter. Sometimes he'd sit and play his flute to the howls of Duchess, his neurotic weimaraner, whom he wrongly adored.

***

Fred could always find an idea for a story somewhere and never systematically went about gathering grist for his mill. He hated plans and he hated rules. Of fiction he'd say, "There are no rules. You can write a story, if you wish, with no conflict, no suspense, no beginning, middle, or end. Of course, you have to be regarded as a genius to get away with it, and that's the hardest part—convincing everybody you're a genius."

Fred was a genius of sorts, I suppose. He was a compulsive storyteller, and made up stories or bits of stories in his every waking moment. Wherever he went he would look at something or somebody—a bus driver, a woman with a baby carriage, a boy on a bicycle—and say to himself, "What if?" And then he'd be off on a fine fugue of ideas, chortling as each fell neatly into place.

His own neuroses, as far as he recognized them, went into his stories. "Better therapy than a psychiatrist," he'd say, "and one hell of a lot cheaper."

For his own pleasure, Fred read far outside the genre of his works. "Writers always read above themselves. I read James Joyce, Shakespeare, Tolstoy, and lots of others I think were giants. But I wonder who the giants read? God, I suppose, though I haven't checked any of his works lately . . . "

He'd often start with nothing but a title. One day someone (it may have been I) said to him Taos was a far cry from civilization, and he seized on that and wrote a mystery novel called *The Far Cry,* laid in Taos, which was one of his best. On another occasion, he said he had a title but no story for it yet. The title was *I'll Cut Your Throat Again, Kathleen.* I had a story to fit his title and he sold me the title for five bucks. When my story was published the editor of the magazine had changed the title to *Blood on My Hands.* Fred gleefully refused to return my five bucks.

***

Fredric Brown delighted in contradictions and paradoxes, and he himself sometimes seemed to be a cluster of irreconcilable opposites. Penurious over a lousy five bucks, he was generous with larger sums to friends in need. Impatient with social niceties, he was nevertheless basically courteous to all people at all times. Wrapped up in himself and his craft, he could be outgoing at gatherings he deigned to attend. Fragile, he could be strong, and was certainly physically brave. Uninterested in tomcatting, he still had a powerful sex drive. Capable, I suppose, of high artistic purpose in his work, he chose to turn out what probably in the long run must be regarded as froth, though it was delightful froth, and in judgments of this sort one can never be sure. Maybe he'll be "rediscovered" someday. I hope so.

I know there must have been a dark and secret Fred—I suppose there's a dark and secret anybody—because he had his own symptoms of inner turmoil. A quiet and private drinker, Fred, in later years, gave up his beloved cheap wine for stronger spirits that got to him more quickly. He never showed outward symptoms of being bombed, but, when he was, he wasn't quite the same inside. He turned into an ordinary earthling who couldn't see the delightful twists lurking in almost any situation, waiting to be recognized.

I've presented Fred's aphorisms as I recall them, possibly misquoting slightly in a few cases, but, I hope, retaining the spirit of what he said or thought. Fred's mind was never small and was more likely to be ridden by bug-eyed monsters from out of space (BEMs, we used to call them) than by hobgoblins of consistency. He made these remarks of his, or tossed them off now and then in his writings, and if you knew Fred—knew the rest of him—they added up to a kind of philosophy and, on the side, a course in the craft of writing fiction. He was devoted to that craft; he built his life upon it.

I have often wondered whether Fredric Brown would have flourished in today's literary climate. The sex scenes he used to slip into his books so gleefully would be Sunday School stuff today. The astounding world of the science fiction of his era is already here, and the only way to write about it is as straight adventure or pure nonfiction. Paradoxes are accepted as the norm, doublethink is commonplace, and the filching of watermelons—to say nothing of homicide—is so readily forgiven and unpunished that it's no fun anymore. Violence? No fiction can match the stuff every day in the news. These real happenings, often enough, aren't as logically motivated as fiction would have to be in order to seem plausible. Fiction, because it's too neat, seems increasingly artificial.

I think Fredric Brown would have translated this ironic twist into a delightful tale of some sort by his peculiar talent for reducing almost anything to its ultimate absurdity. By doing this he produced fine entertainment while throwing a little light on truth as he saw it—and I think he saw it as absurd, like everything else—but, anyway, to do all this, I say, is purpose enough for anybody's life.

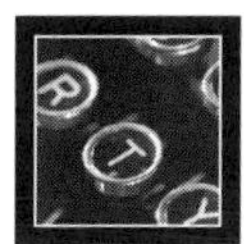

Warning! Warning! Hitchhikers May Be Escaped Lunatics!

STEPHEN KING

When a sign like this appears by the side of the road in the nightmare world of Jim Thompson, no one even comments on it . . . which may be one of the reasons that Thompson's work is still worth reading some forty years after it first began to be published. When first released, his novels appeared almost exclusively as paperback originals, just a few more titles in a flood of fiction unleashed by the popular new "pocketbook" format. Most of the others published in the late forties and fifties have long since been buried in the dustheap of the years, but Thompson is still being read . . . more now than when he was alive and in his prime. We are, in fact, in the midst of a small Thompson revival: almost all his novels are in print in paperback; two collections of three novels each are available from Donald Fine under the title *HardCore,* and a book of his uncollected prose, *Fireworks,* has been issued.

Amazingly, almost all his books hold up as "good reads." More amazingly, two or three (*Pop. 1280, The Grifters,* and *The Getaway* would be my nominees) hold up as "good American novels of their time." And one, this one, remains as timeless and as important as it ever was. *The Killer Inside Me* is an American classic, no less, a novel that deserves space on the same shelf with *Moby-Dick, Huckleberry Finn, The Sun Also Rises,* and *As I Lay Dying.* Thompson's other books are either good or almost great, but all of them pale before the horrifying, mesmerizing story of Lou Ford, that smiling good ol' Texas boy who would rather beat you to death with clichés than shoot you with a .41 . . . But if the clichés don't do the job, he is not afraid to pick up the gun. And use it.

Before Kerouac, before Ginsberg, before Marlon Brando in *The Wild One* ("What are you boys rebelling against?" "What have you got?") or Yossarian in *Catch-22,* this anonymous and little-read Oklahoma novelist captured the spirit of his age, and the spirit of the twentieth century's latter half: emptiness, a feeling of loss in a land of plenty, of unease amid conformity, of alienation in what was meant, in the wake of World War II, to be a generation of brotherhood.

Jim Thompson, author of *The Killer Inside Me.*

> The subject suffers from strong feelings of guilt . . . combined with a sense of frustration and persecution . . . which increase as he grows older; yet there are rarely if ever any surface signs of . . . disturbance. On the contrary, his behavior appears to be entirely logical. He reasons soundly, even shrewdly. He is completely aware of what he does and why he does it . . .

Lou Ford digs the above quote out of a psychology text by "a guy . . . name of Kraepelin" as his story winds toward its inevitable conclusion. I have no idea if Mr. Kraepelin is real or another product of Thompson's imagination, but I do know that the description fits a lot more people than one mentally disturbed deputy sheriff in a crossroads Texas town. It describes a generation of killers, from Caryl Chessman to Lee Harvey Oswald to John Wayne Gacy to Ted Bundy. Looking back at the record, one would have to say that it also describes a generation of politicians: Joe McCarthy, Richard Nixon, Oliver North, Alexander Haig, and a slew of others. In Lou Ford, Jim Thompson drew for the first time a picture of the Great American Sociopath.

It's not that Lou Ford is a killer without a conscience; it would be almost comforting if he were. But Lou Ford *likes* people. He goes out of his way to help Johnnie Pappas, son of the Central City restaurant owner and the local wild child. And when Lou breaks Johnnie's neck and hangs him in his jail cell to turn murder into something that looks like suicide, he does it with great and genuine sadness.

Yet when Lou leads Elmer Conway into the trap he has carefully constructed, and when Conway gets his first good look at the bait in that trap—the bludgeoned, grisly body of a prostitute named Joyce Lakeland—Lou begins to laugh, taking an extraordinary, vicious pleasure in both the battered woman and Conway's reaction to her.

> I laughed—I had to laugh or do something worse—and his eyes squeezed shut and he bawled. I yelled with laughter, bending over and slapping my legs. I doubled up, laughing and farting and laughing some more. Until there wasn't a laugh in me or anyone. I'd used up all the laughter in the world.

That Thompson was largely ignored by both the general reading public and the critics of his day can be taken as a foregone conclusion, I think, from the above sample of Thompson's nitro-and-battercy-acid style. In a year (1952) when Ozzie and Harriet were America's favorite postwar couple and Herman Wouk's *The Cain Mutiny,* a novel about the ultimate victory of rationality over cowardice and insanity, was the winner of the Pulitzer Prize for literature, no one really wanted to deal with this picture of a murderer so happy in his work that he laughs and farts before shooting the bewildered and drunken

Elmer Conway to death with six bullets at point-blank range.

Nor does Thompson allow us the comfort of believing that Deputy Lou Ford is a mutant, a sport, an isolated aberration. In one of the classic passages from the novel, Thompson suggests just the opposite, in fact—that there are Lou Fords everywhere:

> I've loafed around the streets sometimes, leaned against a store front with my hat pushed back and one boot hooked back around the other—hell, you've probably seen me if you've ever been out this way—I've stood like that, looking nice and friendly and stupid, like I wouldn't piss if my pants were on fire. And all the time I'm laughing myself sick inside. Just watching the people.

The fact is, we've all seen guys who fit the description exactly, right down to the goofy smile and the CASE gimme cap tilted back on the head. The honest—if a little dopey—eyes, the sincere smile. We just know that the first thing out of this fellow's mouth is going to be "Howya doon?" and the last thing out is going to be "Have a nice day." Jim Thompson wants us to spend the rest of our lives wondering what's *behind* those smiles (and if you think the smiling villains don't exist, take a good close look at a picture of Ted Bundy or John Wayne Gacy, two real-life Lou Fords.) In Jim Thompson's world, the signs warn of possible escaped lunatics instead of crossing wildlife, and Deputy Barney Fife is a raving psychotic.

There's nothing elegant in *The Killer Inside Me.* In fact, one of my chief amazements on rereading it was how much Thompson got away with (or how much Lion Books let him get away with) in an era when showing a woman in a bra was verboten in American movies and you could—theoretically, at least—go to jail for owning a copy of *Lady Chatterley's Lover.*

Thompson is not crude because he knows no other way to write; in fact, he twits more elegant writers who stretch their vocabularies more to say less:

> In lots of books I read, the writer seems to go haywire every time he reaches a high point. He'll start leaving out punctuation and running his words together and babble about stars flashing and sinking into a deep dreamless sea. And you can't figure out whether the hero's laying his girl or a cornerstone. I guess that kind of crap is supposed to be pretty deep stuff—a lot of book reviewers eat it up, I notice. But the way I see it is, the writer is just too goddam lazy to do his job. And I'm not lazy, whatever else I am. I'll tell you everything.

He does, too, including some things we're not sure we wanted to hear once we've heard them. And he tells us in amazingly blunt, no-holds-barred language.

For instance:

"The next son-of-a-bitch they send out here is going to get kicked so hard he'll be wearing his asshole for a collar."

"Well, whenever it gets too bad, I just step out and kill a few people. I frig them to death with a barbed-wire cob I have."

"[*She's*] One of those girls that makes you want to take off your shoes and wade around in her."

"Why, pardner that's . . . [*as*] easy as nailing your balls to a stump and falling off backwards."

And my own favorite among Thompson's assortment of picnic *crudités*: "There'd be all sorts of things to attend to, and discuss . . . even the size of the douche bag to take along on our honeymoon!"

Some of these vulgarities are harsh enough to be startling even to readers who have become relatively inured to rough talk; they must have really "laid them by the heels," as Lou Ford likes to say, in 1952. Leslie

Fiedler suggests in *Love and Death in the American Novel* that language itself is far less important than the *spirit* with which that language has been imbued, and even after all these years, the language Thompson employs to tell Deputy Ford's story has a kind of starey, socketed ugliness that rasps across our minds like stiff wire bristles. There is nothing pornographic in it, however; quite the opposite. In his introduction to Thompson's work (which is printed at the front of all the Black Lizard editions of Thompson's novels), Barry Gifford observes:

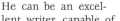

> He can be an excellent writer, capable of creating dialogue as crisp as Hammett's, descriptive prose as convincing as Chandler's. But then, all of a sudden, there will come two or three successive chapters of throwaway writing more typical of the paperback original Trash and Slash school of fiction.

This is a perfectly fair assessment of most of Thompson's books. The reason, I think, is the same one even such good line-by-line writers as John D. MacDonald, David Goodis, and Donald E. Westlake (who spent that period writing under only God and Westlake himself know how many names) sometimes lapsed into fits of hackery: the big paperback machine was hungry, it needed to be fed, and the pay was so low you had to write a lot of prose to make a living wage. Books were often written in a month, sometimes in two weeks, and Thompson himself boasted that he had written two of his titles in forty-eight-hour stints (if one judges by quality, one of those two must have been the infamous *Cropper's Cabin*). There was little time to rewrite, and none at all to polish. The news that Joseph Heller would, two decades later, labor for seven years to produce a turkey like *Something Happened* would have caused these speed-writers to boggle with amazement.

But I would argue there is little or none of the salami writing of which Gifford speaks in *The Killer Inside Me.* In this one book, Thompson's muse seems to have led him perfectly. Every one of Lou Ford's casual country vulgarities is balanced—and outbalanced—by some pithy and un-settling comment on the human condition. Such comments run the risk of being of little use to the story . . . of being, in fact, the negative image of the meaningless clichés with which the smiling Lou belabors the people he doesn't like ("It's not the heat, it's the humidity," "The man with the grin is the man who will win," etc., etc.). Instead, they have exactly the same startling, empty-socketed effect as Ford's vulgarities. Again, the language has been imbued with a tone that lifts it considerably above Thompson's rather pedestrian use of words.

"Why'd they all have to come to me to get killed?" Lou Ford complains suddenly in the midst of his tale. "Why couldn't they kill themselves?" Up to this point, Ford has been narrating, rationally and completely, the story of how the vagrant he ran out of town in the book's first chapter has returned to haunt him. Into this rational account, like a human skull rolling out of the darkness and into the lamplight, comes this paranoid, put-upon, Poe-esque shriek.

When this vagrant later sees the

body of Amy, whom Lou has already murdered, he goes into a fit of horror that strikes Lou not as pitiful or frightening but as extremely funny . . . and such is the power of his skewed vision that it strikes us funny as well.

> Did you ever see one of those two-bit jazz singers? You know, trying to put something across with their bodies that they haven't got the voice to do? They lean back from the waist a little with their heads hanging forward and their hands held up about even with their ribs and swinging limp. And they sort of wobble and roll on their hips.
>
> That's the way he looked, and he kept making that damned funny noise "Yeeeeee!", his lips quivering ninety to the minute and his eyes rolling all-white.
>
> I laughed and laughed, he looked and sounded so funny I couldn't help it.

I laughed too, God help me. Even as I was trying to imagine what Lou Ford must have looked like to a man on the edge of his own death at the hands of a maniac and knowing it, I laughed. It *did* look and sound funny.

In *The Killer Inside Me,* Jim Thompson sets himself one of the most difficult tasks a fiction writer can hope to perform: to create first a sense of catharsis with and then empathy (but not sympathy; never that; this is a strictly moral novel) for a lunatic. The passage above is one of the magical ways in which he achieves his end.

In a book that fairly bristles with painful ironies, we are not really surprised to discover that the motto of Central City, the Texas town where all this mayhem takes place, is "*Where the hand clasp's a little stronger.*" It is a motto a fellow like Lou Ford can take to heart. Especially when it's *his* hands, around your neck.

Writing about the modern hard-boiled detective story, Raymond Chandler once said, "We've taken murder out of the parlor and given it back to the people who do it best." Thompson has gone that one better in *The Killer Inside Me;* Lou Ford is not only the sort of man who "does it best," but the kind of man who can do nothing else. He is the bogeyman of an entire civilization, a man who kills and kills and kills, and whose motives, which seemed so persuasive and rational at the time, blow away like smoke when the killing is done, leaving him—or us, if he happens to be the sort who kills himself and leaves the mess behind with no explanation—with no sound but a cold psychotic wind blowing between his ears.

At one point Lou tells us a story that seems to have no bearing at all on his own. It is the story of a jeweler with a fine business, a beautiful wife, and two lovely children. On a business trip he meets a girl, "a real honey," and makes her his mistress. She is as perfect in her way as his wife: married, and willing to keep it that way. Then the police find the jeweler and his mistress dead in a motel-room bed. A deputy goes to the jeweler's house to tell his wife, and finds her and both of the kids dead. The jeweler has shot them all, ending with himself. The point of the story is Lou Ford's judgment of the jeweler, chillingly brief and to the point: "He'd had everything, and somehow nothing was better."

Thompson, by the way, went on to write a very good novel called *The Nothing Man.*

Okay. Enough. It's time to get out of your way and let you experience this amazing piece of workmanship for yourself. I have explored the story in more depth than is my custom when writing introductory notes such as this, but only because the story is strong enough to do so without spoiling that experience. No amount of introductory material or postmorteming can prepare you for this work of fiction.

So it's time to let go of my hand

and enter Central City, Jim Thompson's vision of hell. Time to meet Lou Ford, the nothing man with the strangled conscience and the strangely divided heart. Time to meet all of them:

> Our kind. Us people. All of us that started the game with a crooked cue, that wanted so much and got so little, that meant so good and did so bad. All us folks . . . all of us. All of us.

Amen, Jim. A-fucking-men.

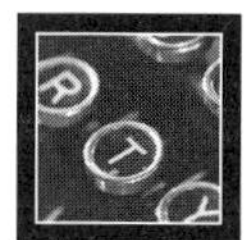

The Golden Harvest:

TWENTY-FIVE-CENT PAPERBACKS

ED GORMAN

I still remember buying it.

I could hardly forget. It packed the same charge of anxiety as purchasing one's first teenage beer.

The woman behind the counter of the place then called Horak's—now called the Neighborhood Tavern—peered down at me and said, "Pretty racy stuff, ain't it?"

Or at least that's what I think she said. Whatever formulation of syllables she used, the point was this: I was a fourteen-year-old Catholic-school boy in a working-class Irish-Czech neighborhood and this just wasn't the sort of thing kids my age were supposed to be buying.

But I would not be dissuaded. I put down my quarter and a penny for tax and she took it.

Outside, shut of the woman, I got my first good glimpse of it there in the new spring sunshine.

Gold Medal Book number 663 was *Death Takes the Bus* by Lionel White.

This was the first of probably twenty novels I read by White. While nobody would accuse him of being a great stylist, he was a great, deft plotter (I think Donald Westlake made the same point somewhere) and his "bus" ride certainly proved it.

I can't define exactly what drew me to the book. The sex, such as it was, was great; so was the violence. It seemed, unlike the books I'd read up till then, real. More like the street-gang violence I'd come to know personally, and less like the heroic stuff of cowboy movies.

But ultimately it was White's people that made me start roaming the secondhand stores for more of the man's books. None of his innocents were quite innocent and none of his hoods were entirely bad. And none of them had many answers. Life was a curse, White seemed to be saying, and no matter what you did, you never got out with much of anything resembling dignity or meaning. A year later, when I discovered Hemingway, I found some of the same themes, and while Hemingway was the greater artist, of course, it was easier for me to identify with White's people. They hung out in grubby bus stations and prowled gray streets, much as I did. Not even the romance of war saved them.

That was my first Gold Medal Book.

Within a month I probably owned fifty of the things, mostly bought used for a nickel each. I lined them up along my bedroom window. They all had yellow spines with black type and the

Gold Medal medallion at the bottom. On the basis of their wisdom, and a few other suspicions, I came to the early conclusion that life was a sinkhole and that these guys knew it. They didn't pretty-up that fact and could even, once in a nasty while, rub your face in it. Marcus Aurelius and Céline had nothing on these guys in the despair department.

What I didn't know at the time was that much of these men's work derived from Hammett, Chandler, and James M. Cain—or some complex combination thereof. But it's too easy to dismiss the best of the GM writers as simply derivative. And wrong too.

They filled in the details about life in the fifties the way no other group of writers did. For the most part—and again I make reference here to the best of them—they wrote about the people and places I knew. The taverns. The barbershops. The whores. The pathetic, scared little men. The predators.

Only recently have I realized that people such as Vin Packer came not from crime fiction but from the realists and naturalists such as the vastly undervalued John O'Hara.

But now let's take a look at some of the writers I read back in those days, at least a few of whom you might want to search the used bookstores for.

Note that I pretend to no special wisdom; what follows is merely my opinion as to who were the primary players in the Gold Medal fifties, and how their work has fared over the past three decades.

PETER RABE

Probably the most original of the GM writers. This is not to say that he was the "best" necessarily, or even that he was always even very good. But there is great hard sorrow and real ingenuity in his best work. Someday he will be recognized as being at least as important a crime writer as Jim Thompson or David Goodis. He could even handle black comedy, as he demonstrated in *Murder Me for Nickels.*

Mandatory reads: *Kill the Boss Good-by, Anatomy of a Killer,* and *The Box.*

JOHN D. MACDONALD

Where most GM writers set their stories in the working class, John D. generally dealt with the middle class. His heroes tended to be engineers, businessmen, construction managers, and civil servants rather than the drifters and ex-cons of most noir. He was a thundering moralist, a seductive stylist, and a very sly observer of our shortcomings, both as individuals and as a citizenry. Despite writing millions of early mediocre words to support a young family, he was the best crime writer of his generation. Sure Travis McGee was a Rotarian version of a hippie, but the later books, informed as they were with John D.'s own health problems, are moving and occasionally profound utterances about a man facing his own extinction.

Mandatory reads: *Slam the Big Door, The End of the Night, One Monday We Killed Them All, Soft Touch,* and *Dead Low Tide.*

MALCOLM BRALY

Braly spent a good deal of his rather short life in prison and wrote, as his fifth novel, the classic *On the Yard.* Earlier he wrote three Gold Medal originals that were among the best things the company ever published. There was an almost numbing sadness in all Braly's work, and a hopelessness redeemed only by a certain nutty laughter. Read anything you can get by him. *It's Cold Out There* is probably my favorite, however, with its cast of crazed losers and grinding air of desperation.

CHARLES WILLIAMS

Line by line, Williams was the best of all the Gold Medal writers. He has not found an audience the way Thompson and Goodis have because they are more appropriate to our era—splashy in their effects, titanic in their feelings. Williams was quiet and possessed of a melancholy that imbued each of his tales with a kind of glum decorum. John D. always claimed that Williams was one of the two or three best storytellers on the planet and I certainly wouldn't disagree. He was probably at his best in his books set at sea.

Mandatory reads: *Hell Hath No Fury, The Big Bite, Aground, Dead Calm,* and *Scorpion Reef.*

DAN MARLOWE

Another writer who hasn't gotten his due. He probably did more with the pure hard-boiled story than anyone since Rabe, giving his tough guys true interior lives. Health problems interrupted his career at midpoint. He may have been the most exciting of all the Gold Medal writers. His best stuff just explodes every thirty pages or so. I always thought of Marlowe as an uncle of mine, always in a working-class shirt with Camels in the pocket, tavern whiskey on his breath, and a weary, knowing gleam in his eyes. He's a nice, cold treat.

Mandatory reads: *The Name of the Game Is Death, Strongarm,* and *One Endless Hour.*

JIM THOMPSON

Yes, I agree, he was upon occasion a genius; but he was also a stupendously lousy craftsman. It is a credit to his vision (and I'm serious) that he was able to convey his particular truth despite some of the most sloppy, incoherent writing I've ever stumbled across. That said, I think that Thompson deserves most if not all the adulation he's getting today. He was a thoroughgoing original, a kind of Okie version of Graham Greene, all shifting ironic morality and honky-tonk remorse. And just as most of Greene's darkest books had unexpected comic moments, so, too, do Thompson's. A couple of his books break my heart every time I read them, his operative moods seeming to be pity and despair. Your education as a writer, reader, or would-be human is incomplete until you've read the basic Thompson library.

Mandatory reads: *The Killer Inside Me, Texas by the Tail* (I'm well aware, thank you, that everybody thinks this book stinks; I happen to love the damned thing), *Savage Night* (his best organized and most nimbly rendered novel), and *Pop. 1280* (his masterpiece).

DAVID GOODIS

Goodis didn't write novels, he wrote suicide notes. Like Thompson, he didn't always take a lot of care with his books. He's the only writer I know who can make Cornell Woolrich's yarns seem sane and logical by comparison. But, like Woolrich, he was a sad, suffering guy and he was able to get that sadness and suffering down on paper. And that's why he survived. For a writer as introspective as he was, he had a nice reportorial knack. He gave us hellish glimpses of the inner-city ghettos of the forties and fifties. He was the poet of vacant lots and abandoned buildings and bars where guys take turns going outside to puke. Just thinking about him bums me out and I'm not kidding. He seemed to be one of those guys who never knew a moment's peace or joy and that's never much fun to contemplate.

Mandatory reads: *Nightfall, Cassidy's Girl, The Burglar,* and *Dark Passage.*

WADE MILLER

Some feel that Bob Wade and Bill

Miller did their best work for publishers other than GM; others feel that four or five of their GMs are the strongest of their entire careers. Who cares. These two were past masters at mood, pace, and people. HarperCollins reissued four of their Max Thursday private-eye novels in beautiful trade paperbacks, and after rereading them all, I realize that they've been in the front ranks all the time . . . it's just that nobody ever gave them proper credit. As for their GMs, I'd say my favorites are *South of the Sun, Devil May Care* (which reads in places like a collaboration between early Ray Bradbury and Cornell Woolrich—maybe it's all the great Mexican stuff), and *The Girl from Midnight.* But don't just read their GM books. Read virtually everything.

Mandatory reads: *Kiss Her Goodbye* (a powerful straight novel), *Badge of Evil* (which was the basis for Orson Welle's *Touch of Evil*), and *Pop Goes the Queen,* which is a screwball murder mystery about a hapless couple who win a radio quiz show back in 1947. This book works a lot better for me than those antidepressants I've been known to take.

DONALD HAMILTON

I had always suspected that Jack Kennedy was a wienie and when I read that he preferred Ian Fleming to Donald Hamilton, I was sure of it. For me, Hamilton's first six Matt Helm novels are some of the best espionage books written in this half of the century. Hamilton has never been given his due for the psychological tension of his books (masterly, dark, and constantly surprising), or the wry rococo language of their telling. He is a pure storyteller of the first rank. Just by carefully reading the first pages of *Assassins Have Starry Eyes,* you'll see what I'm talking about.

Mandatory reads: *Death of a Citizen, The Wrecking Crew, Line of Fire,* and *Assassins Have Starry Eyes.*

VIN PACKER (MARIJANE MEAKER)

Like John D. MacDonald, Vin Packer was obviously fond of John O'Hara. Her novels—early on, rather dark fables about the small-town South of the World War II era; later, hipper but no less dark fables about New York City—are novels of manners as much as they are crime tales. She was always reliable and many times brilliant in a nervous kind of way. Her major characters usually had secrets they desperately wanted to keep from those closest to them, and these secrets frequently became the basis for the books. In the late fifties, Gold Medal began packaging her as a mainstream writer whose books just happened to include crime. And that was fair. She was one hell of a writer. *Something in the Shadows* is one of the most breathtakingly cunning crime tales I've ever come across.

Mandatory reads: *Alone at Night, Intimate Victims,* and *The Damnation of Adam Blessing.*

GIL BREWER

Certainly the most uneven of all the primary GM players. In his memorable remembrance of Brewer, Bill Pronzini draws a portrait of an alcoholic who hastened both the end of his career and the end of his life. Brewer's early specialty was the "jailbait" novel—nice ordinary guy who starts bopping his baby-sitter and then ends up robbing a bank with her. Charles Starkweather redux but with a sexy sixteen-year-old babe playing Charlie. John D. once said that most crime stories are really "folktales" and when you read Brewer, you know just what MacDonald meant. At his best, he hooked you in the first paragraph and never let you go. For me, his one true masterpiece was *A Killer Is Loose,* a strange, nightmarish story about a guy who goes out for a drink one sunny morning and winds up being a hostage of sorts to a man who is shooting people at random. Fine piece of work, with the pith and punch of a barroom anecdote well told. A genuinely scary book.

Mandatory reads: *The Red Scarf, The Three-Way Split,* and *A Killer Is Loose.*

***

> *There's a difference between those earlier pulp writers and [me]. It deals directly with the difference between the novels of plot and the novels of character*
> —*Warren Murphy*

Murphy's right. After coming back from World War II and wanting a more realistic kind of popular fiction that spoke to veterans, a new generation of writers decided to bring some of the qualities of mainstream into pulp fiction.

This was evident almost from the start with Gold Medal. Such early John D.'s as *The Damned, Dead Low Tide,* and *Murder for the Bride* quietly announced that here was a new kind of fiction. No big revolution, you understand, but certainly a more realistic portrayal of life and people in the United States.

Not all writers took this path, of course. Some still tilled the older fields, but not without distinction. This is the next group we'll look at—writers more generally concerned with plot than people.

DAY KEENE

This guy almost always gets bad press in pulp circles. Yes, he wrote too fast; yes, he wrote too much, but he managed to do some first-rate work. His biggest writing problem was that the faster he wrote, the more flamboyant and unlikely his plots became, to the point that you sometimes wondered if he wasn't spoofing some of his own work. But when he was good . . . He had a mean, true feel for fallen men and women, even a sympathy for them, and in his best books he told compelling stories about working-class people trying to make some sense of existence, a slant that the best of his hundreds of early pulp stories also took. One of his last novels was *The Carnival of Death,* which, despite the title and despite its throwaway publisher, was a reasonably fresh look at carnival life. At the end of his career he made the transition to mainstream and wrote four modest bestsellers, all fashioned more or less on the model of *Peyton Place.*

Mandatory reads: *Framed in Guilt, Home Is the Sailor,* and *Murder on the Side.*

HARRY WHITTINGTON

It pains me not to put Harry up in the first tier, but I can't because most of his people were types rather than individuals. Several exceptions come to mind, notably the folks in *Rampage* and *Saturday Night Town,* but overall Harry was much better with plotting than psychology. But let us not be unappreciative—you could make the same claim about Saki and de Maupassant and (everybody get his gun out now and point it at Ed), Roald Dahl. Harry was one of the wonderful campfire storytellers who came out of the pulp era and survived several decades after because he'd learned how to adapt to changing audience demands. He was always readable and on occasion of the very first rank. He was also, as a guy, one of the great charmers of all time. Early in life he got the notion that he was F. Scott Fitzgerald reincarnated and the notion never quite left him. But he was the good Fitzgerald, not the bad Fitzgerald—garrulous, charitable, witty.

Let me note here that I frequently change my mind about Whittington. Most likely, he really does belong in the first rank.

Mandatory reads: *Brute in Brass, Strip the Town Naked* (as Whit Harrison), *A Night for Screaming,* and *Desire in the Dust.*

EDWARD S. AARONS

Pure, old-fashioned pulpster, true, but a very sleek, cunning writing machine. I loved the Sam Durrell spy books. Sure, they were long on cold war paranoia and self-righteousness, but they were also damned good adventure novels. Aarons was capable of writing place description just about as well as anybody, except maybe Donald Hamilton or John D., when he was really cooking. A writing student of mine once asked me what I really, really thought of her work, and I said, "It's really, really well written but it really, really doesn't go anywhere." I gave her a couple of Sam Durrell novels and she said, "God, are you kidding?" and I said, "Huh-uh." A week later she had had a religious conversion, called me up, and said, "These books are really trash, but I see what you're talking about." Trash to her maybe; great lurid fun to me.

Mandatory reads: *Assignment-Suicide, Assignment-Treason,* and *The Art Studio Murders* (a very winsome fair-clue traditional mystery circa 1950, originally published under the pseudonym Edward Ronns).

BRUNO FISCHER

Bruno Fischer, one of the first of the Gold Medal authors.

Time has not been generous to much of what Fischer wrote. He came out of the old "spicy" pulps and some of that showed up in his style a couple of decades later. But at his best, in maybe half a dozen books, he showed a true mastery of the suspense novel that combined a James M. Cainian sexual tension with a very good eye for the everyday setting. His people were invariably ordinary, suddenly set upon by dark forces. Like Whittington, he probably belongs in the first tier, especially considering the fact that his last novel, *The Evil Days,* was one of the truly important books of the seventies. Well into his sixties, he helped reshape the contemporary mystery novel.

Mandatory reads: *The Bleeding Scissors, Murder in the Raw,* and *The Lady Kills.*

LIONEL WHITE

While White's people were interesting, it was usually their situations rather than their personalities that drew you in. What White could really do was plot caper novels that rivaled those of W. R. Burnett himself. The first GM novel I ever read, as I mentioned earlier, was White's *Death Takes the Bus.* I stayed up on a seventh-grade school night until maybe 2, 3 A.M., mesmerized. White always grabbed me that way. He knew just when to wrap a scene fast, just when to wrap a scene slow. And he knew just when to put the twist in. If only he'd done a little more with some of his people . . . Stanley Kubrick filmed his books, as did several other notable directors. His most nail-biting book of all is *The Money Trap,* which seemed to have an enormous impact on the generation just before mine. I've seen several famous writers rewrite *The Money*

Trap several times. It is one dazzling sumbitch of a book.

Mandatory reads: *The Snatchers, Flight into Terror,* and *Hostage for a Hood.*

MARVIN ALBERT

Here's another guy who wrote too much too soon but who could sometimes work on a very high level of old-fashioned pulp. His Tony Rome books are wonderful old-fashioned pulp, and his caper novel, *The Looters,* is right up there on the level of Lionel White. He did everything—men's adventure, Westerns, even the "jailbait" novel, his *Devil in Dungarees* (as by Albert Conroy, 1960) coming just as the cycle was (you should forgive the expression) petering out. But, God, I haven't praised him enough. Go out and find yourself a copy of a GM book called *Driscoll's Diamonds* (1973). It's one kick-ass adventure novel, let me tell you, and shows Albert at his absolute best (oh, yeah: he published it under the name Ian MacAlister). He was also the then-king of the novelizations. He did a lot of them. He also had five or six international bestsellers under his own name, and while they were eminently readable, I sort of prefer a lot of the stuff he did while cranking at top speed. He did some of the moodiest pulp stuff in GM history.

Mandatory reads: *My Kind of Game* (Tony Rome), and under the name Albert Conroy, *Nice Guys Finish Dead* and *The Chiselers.*

ROBERT COLBY

Another guy who probably belongs on the first list. He wrote one of the great GM novels, *The Captain Must Die,* and several other good ones. He also wrote one of the all-time-great crime novelettes, "Paint the Town Green." He's a real writer, a sturdy psychologist, an excellent plotter.

Mandatory reads: *The Star Trap, Murder Times Five,* and *The Captain Must Die.*

***

This list could go on for several more pages, but it's got to stop somewhere, so I guess I'll pull the plug right here.

There are a number of other GM writers worth reading—Bernard Mara (the pen name of literary writer Brian Moore); Stephen Marlowe (one of my favorites, even if his last GM editor didn't like his stuff); John Trinian, who wrote mostly about ex-cons (because, it was said, he was one himself); Richard S. Prather, who, page for page, probably gave me as much enjoyment as any writer of my youth; Michael Avallone and his alternate-universe take on private-eye conventions, another man who was a favorite of my misspent youth; John McPartland, who wrote anxious little books about anxious failed men and their anxious failed lives, and who, despite a tragically early death, left us one true minor masterpiece, *No Down Payment,* which also became the truest movie about the fifties I've ever seen (including *Rebel Without a Cause*); William Campbell Gault who, while not a GM writer as such, did several fine Joe Puma Adventures for Fawcett; and people such as Gardner F. Fox and his eerie take on Jack the Ripper, *Terror Over London;* and James O. Causey, whose three novels curiously anticipated the direction crime fiction would take in the seventies, especially *The Baby Doll Murders,* which also had the single most erotic GM cover of all time (I guess I like sullen, pouty babes in white silk slips).

Little of GM was art of any kind, though some of it was, I think, minor art. A lot of it was slapdash and completely predictable; and some of it was even laughable.

But the best of it, the books I've discussed here, represent a very important period in the development of the contemporary crime novel. Such modern stars as Lawrence Block published with GM even before the fifties were quite over. Donald

Westlake came along a few years later with his Stark books (he said somewhere that he intended the early Starks for GM, but that they turned him down and the books were published by Pocket). Harlan Ellison, Kurt Vonnegut, W. R. Burnett, and Jim Thompson were included in the next wave of sixties GM writers.

GM is gone now, fit company mostly for an old man's reveries, and yet I think the best of it is worth your time and trouble in looking up.

I had a ball with a lot of it and you will too.

Two reputable dealers with extensive GM catalogs are:

Pandora's Books, Box 54, Neche, North Dakota, 58265.

R. C. Holland, 302 Martin Drive, Richmond, Kentucky 40478.

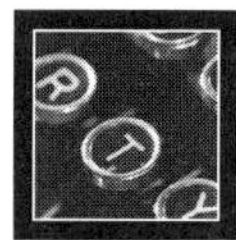

Forgotten Writers:

GIL BREWER

BILL PRONZINI

I don't like the *Murder, She Wrote* TV show.

I don't like it because it gives a false and distorted picture of what it's like to be a mystery writer. Dear Jessica effortlessly produces a couple of novels that become instant best-sellers. Critics and readers adore them, every one. Film and play producers flock to her door, offering huge amounts of money. She attends fancy New York parties and everyone knows her name, everyone praises her work. Small towns, ditto. Foreign countries, ditto. Her agent is a prince; so are her U.S. and foreign publishers. She has no career setbacks, no private demons. She writes when she feels like it, which isn't very often, and never has to worry about money. Her life is full of adventure, romance, excitement, joy. It is the kind of life even royalty envies.

Well, bullshit.

You want to know what the life of a working mystery writer is *really* like? Gil Brewer could tell you. He could tell you about the taste of success and fame that never quite becomes a meal; the shattered dreams and lost hopes, the loneliness, the rejections and failures and empty promises, the lies and deceit, the bitterness, the self-doubts, the dry spells and dried-up markets, the constant and painful grubbing for enough money to make ends meet. He could tell you about all of that, and much more. He would, too, if he were still alive. But he isn't.

Gil Brewer drank himself to death on the second day of January, in the Year of Our Lord nineteen hundred and eighty-three, at the age of sixty.

> . . . Last year [1981] I nearly croaked; not through drinking, but because I had an infected lung, emphysema, heart failure and pneumonia—all at the same time. It was a rough go at the hospital. Then nearly a year of sobriety and I figured I was ready for work, when things went to pot again. . . . I'm ashamed of all the evil damned things I've done when drinking. [But] I'm straight now, and must remain so, because one more drink and Gil Brewer goes down the slot.

Sure, it's a cliché. Look at all the writers who have destroyed themselves with alcohol. Poe, Stephen Crane, O. Henry, Jack London, Sinclair Lewis, Dorothy Parker, Fitzgerald, Faulkner, O'Hara. And Hammett. And Chandler. And hundreds more. So does it really matter that a minor mystery writer named Gil Brewer also drank himself to death?

Damned right it does.

It matters because he was a gentle, sensitive, vulnerable man who felt too deeply and cared too much.

It matters because he produced some of the most compelling noir softcover originals of the 1950s.

It matters because he understood and loved fine writing and hungered to create it himself, to just once write something of depth and beauty and meaning.

It matters because of the writer he might have been with a little luck, encouragement, and the proper guidance, for in him there was a small untapped core of greatness.

It matters because if it doesn't, then nothing does.

> . . . For all my seemingly sometimes rattlebrained manner, I am actually deathly sincere and serious about my writing . . . Am only happy—my only real happiness—at the machine.

Gil Brewer was born in relative poverty in Canandaigua, New York, in November of 1922. He dropped out of school to work, but retained a thirst for knowledge and a love of books; he was an omnivorous reader. At the outbreak of World War II he joined the army and served in France and Belgium, seeing action and receiving wounds that entitled him to a VA disability pension. After the war, he worked at a variety of jobs—warehouseman, cannery worker, bookseller, gas-station attendant—while pursuing a lifelong desire to write fiction.

His early efforts were not crime stories but mainstream and "literary" exercises. He sent some of these to Joseph T. Shaw, the former editor of *Black Mask,* who had become a successful literary agent in the forties. Shaw liked what he saw and encouraged Brewer to keep writing, though with a more commercial slant to his work.

> I began as a "serious" writer, and came close, but married and had to have money so switched to pulp. I was with Joe Shaw at that time. I sold shorts to *Detective Tales,* etc. Shaw had my entire career planned. I tried writing a suspense book to see if I could do it, and wrote one single-spaced in five days. Then I wrote *Satan Is a Woman* and Gold Medal bought it and asked for more—Dick Carroll and Bill Lengel—and Joe said to me, "You've already got another one [finished]. The five-day book, *So Rich, So Dead.*" So GM published that. Then I wrote *13 French Street* and was off to the races.

Fawcett was the first and best of the softcover publishers to specialize in original, male-oriented mysteries, Westerns, historicals, and "modern" novels. Their Gold Medal line was in its infancy (the first GM titles appeared in late 1949) when they bought Brewer's first two novels in 1950; but GM's success was already guaranteed. They had assembled, and would continue to assemble, some of the best popular and category writers of the period by paying royalty advances based on the number of copies printed, rather than on the number of copies sold; thus writers received handsome sums up front, up to three and four times as much as hardcover publishers were paying. Into the GM stable came such established names as W. R. Burnett, Cornell Woolrich, Sax Rohmer, MacKinlay Kantor, Wade Miller, and Octavus Roy Cohen; such top pulpeteers as John D. MacDonald, Bruno Fischer, Day Keene, David Goodis, Harry Whittington, Edward S. Aarons, and Dan Cushman; and such talented newcomers as Charles Williams, Richard S. Prather, Stephen Marlowe, and Gil Brewer.

What the Fawcett brain trust and the Fawcett writers succeeded in doing was adapting the tried-and-true pulp fiction formula of the thirties and forties to postwar American society, with all its changes in lifestyle and morality and its newfound sophistication. Instead of a bulky magazine full of short stories, they provided brand-new, easy-to-read novels in the handy pocket format. Instead of gaudy, juvenile shoot-'em-up cover art, they utilized the "peekaboo sex" approach to catching the reader's eye: women depicted either nude (as seen from the side or rear) or with a great deal of cleavage and/or leg showing, in a variety of provocative poses. Instead of printing a hundred thousand copies of a small number of titles, they printed hundreds of thousands of copies of many titles so as to reach every possible outlet and buyer.

They were selling pulp fiction, yes, but it was a different, upscale kind of pulp. On the one hand, the novels published by Fawcett—and by the best of their competitors, Dell, Avon, and Popular Library—were short (generally around fifty thousand words), rapidly paced, with emphasis on action. On the other hand, they were well-written, well-plotted, peopled by sharply delineated and believable characters, spiced with sex, often imbued with psychological insight, and set in vividly drawn, often exotic locales . . . the stuff of any good commercial novel, then or now. Thanks to writers such as Gil Brewer, the best of the Gold Medal novels are the apotheosis of pulp fiction—rough-hewn, minor works of art, perfectly suited to and representative of their era. What has been labeled as pulp since the early sixties is not the genuine article; it is an offshoot of pulp, or a mutation of pulp, reflective of the "new world" that has been created by the technological and other sweeping changes of the past twenty-five years. The last piece of true-pulp-as-art was published circa 1965.

Readers responded to the Gold Medal formula with enthusiasm and in huge numbers. It was common in GM's first few years for individual titles to sell up to five hundred thousand copies, and not all that unusual for one to surpass the one million mark. Brewer's *13 French Street,* published in 1951, was one of those early million-copy bestsellers, going into eight separate printings and many overprintings.

Yet *13 French Street* is not his best novel. A deadly-triangle tale of two old friends, one of whom has fallen mysteriously ill, and the sick one's evil wife, it has a thin and rather predictable plot, and too much of the narrative takes place in the house at the title address. Nevertheless, it has all of the qualities that give Brewer's work its individuality and power. The prose is lean, Hemingwayesque (Hemingway's influence is apparent throughout the Brewer canon), and yet rich with raw emotion genuinely portrayed and felt. It makes effective use of one of his obsessive themes, that of a weak, foolish, and/or disillusioned man corrupted and either destroyed or nearly destroyed by a wicked, designing woman. And it has echoes—especially in the use of Saint-Saëns's *Danse Macabre* as a leitmotif—of the haunting surreality and existentialism that infuses his strongest work.

With the success of *13 French Street,* Brewer was indeed "off to the races." Over the next nine years, Fawcett's editors bought and published a dozen more of his novels, nine under the Gold Medal imprint and three under their Crest imprint, generally reserved for hardcover reprints. All but one were contemporary suspense novels; the lone exception is Brewer's only Western novel, *Some Must Die* (1954), an excellent variation on the theme of good people and bad thrown together and entrapped by the elements. (The cover art and blurbs for *Some Must Die* were carefully crafted to give the impression that it was modern suspense rather than Western suspense. Brewer's readers weren't fooled, though; *Some Must Die* sold the fewest copies of his early books.)

Despite some lurid titles—*Hell's Our Destination,*—*And the Girl Screamed, Little Tramp, The Brat, The Vengeful Virgin*—Brewer's fifties GM and Crest novels are neither sleazy nor sensationalized; they are the same sort of realistic crime-adventure stories John D. MacDonald and Charles Williams were producing for GM, and of uniformly above-average quality. Most are set in the cities, small towns, waterways, swamps, and backwaters of Florida, Brewer's adopted home. (The exceptions are *Some Must Die* and *77 Rue Paradis* (1954), which has a well-depicted Marseilles setting.) The protagonists are ex-soldiers, ex-cops, drifters, convicts, blue-collar workers, charterboat captains, unorthodox private detectives, even a sculptor. The plots range from searches for stolen gold and sunken treasure to savage indictments of the effects of lust, greed, and murder to chilling psychological studies of disturbed personalities.

Probably the best of his Fawcett originals is *A Killer Is Loose* (1954), truly harrowing portrait of a psychopath that comes close to rivaling the nightmare visions of Jim Thompson. It tells the story of Ralph Angers, a deranged surgeon and Korean War veteran obsessed with building a hospital, and his devastating effect on the lives of several citizens of a small Florida town. One of the citizens is the narrator, Steve Logan, a down-on-his-luck ex-cop whose wife is about to have a baby and who makes the mistake of saving Angers's life, thus becoming his "pal." As Logan says on page one, by way of prologue, "There was nothing simple about Angers, except maybe the Godlike way he had of doing things."

Brewer maintains a pervading sense of terror and an acute level of tension throughout. Although the novel is flawed by a slow beginning and a couple of improbabilities, as well as an ending that is a little too abrupt, its strengths far outnumber its weaknesses. Two aspects in particular stand out: one is the curious and frighteningly symbiotic relationship that develops between Logan and Angers; the other is a five-page scene in which Angers, with Logan looking on helplessly, forces a scared little girl to play the piano for him—a scene Woolrich or Thompson might have written and Hitchcock should have filmed.

A Killer Is Loose—in fact, all of Brewer's early novels—was written at white heat and almost entirely first-draft. This accounts for their strengths, in particular the headlong immediacy of the narratives, and for their various weaknesses. It seemed to be the only way Brewer *could* write: fast, fast, with black coffee and cigarettes and liquor to help him get through the long sleepless periods, and pills to help him come down afterward.

> I batted out those Gold Medal books for so very long, never taking more than two weeks on one, and once wrote one in three days—in fact more than one—and often in five or six days—and they all sold. I possibly thought it would continue forever, poor fool that I am, but with never any encouragement toward better stuff, except on one occasion I recall that didn't work.

***

The fifties was Brewer's decade; satisfied with his work or not, he was a commercial success. In addition to his books for Fawcett, he sold suspense novels to Avon, Ace, Monarch, Bouregy. He continued to write short stories, too, under his own name and such pseudonyms as Eric Fitzgerald and Bailey Morgan, and placed them with most of the digest-sized mystery magazines of the time—*Manhunt, The Saint, Pursuit, Hunted, Accused*—as well as with numerous men's magazines. His new agent (Joe Shaw died in 1952) sold film rights to four of his GM books: *13 French Street, A Killer Is Loose, Hell's Our Destination* (poorly filmed as *Lure of the Swamps*), and *The Brat*. Almost everything he wrote found a publisher. And almost every one of his novels, if not every one of his short stories, had more than a little merit.

Outstanding among his non-Fawcett books of the fifties, and two of his best overall, are *The Red Scarf* (Mystery House, 1958) and *Nude on Thin Ice* (Avon, 1960). The former title has an interesting history. It was inexplicably rejected by Fawcett and other paperback houses, and eventually sold to the lending-library publisher, Thomas Bouregy, for a meager $300 advance; it was Brewer's second and last book to appear under Bouregy's Mystery House imprint—the first was *The Angry Dream* (1957)—and his second and last U.S. hardcover appearance. After publication of *The Red Scarf,* Fawcett's editors had a sudden change of heart and decided the book was worthwhile after all: they bought reprint rights (presumably for much less money than they would have had to pay Brewer for an original) and republished it as a Crest title in 1959.

The Red Scarf is narrated by motel owner Ray Nichols. Hitchhiking home in northern Florida after a futile trip up north to raise capital for his floundering auto court, Nichols is given a ride by a bickering and drunken couple named Vivian Rise and Noel Teece. An accident, the result of Teece's drinking, leaves Teece bloody and unconscious; Nichols and Rise are unhurt. At the woman's urging, he leaves the scene with her and the money—and it is only later, back home with his wife, that he discovers Teece is a courier for a gambling syndicate and that the money belongs to the syndicate, not to either Teece or Rise. While he struggles with his conscience, several factions begin vying for the loot, including a Mob enforcer, the police, and Teece. There are some neat plot turns, the various components mesh smoothly, the characterization is flawless, and the prose is Brewer's sharpest and most controlled. Anthony Boucher said in the *New York Times* that the book is the "all-around best Gil Brewer . . . a full-packed story."

Nude on Thin Ice is a much darker and more surreal novel. Set primarily in the Sandia Mountains of New Mexico, it has a deadly triangle plot reminiscent of *13 French Street,* though much different in execution. The three main characters are drifter Kenneth McCall, the lonely widow of one of his old friends, and a strange and exotic nymphet who enjoys posing naked on ice for men and their cameras. Half a million dollars in cash and an implacable lawyer named Montgomery also figure prominently, as does explosive violence both expected and unexpected. What makes the novel memorable is its brooding narrative, its mounting sense of doom, and an ending that is both chilling and perfectly conceived. The narrator, McCall, is one of Brewer's most striking creations—weak and immoral on the one hand, so sadly tragic on the other that the reader cannot help but empathize with his fate.

At least some of the nightmare, existential quality of *Nude on Thin Ice* can be attributed to Brewer's increasing dependency on alcohol and sleeping pills. By 1960 he was living a private nightmare of his own.

His success had begun to wane. Overexposure, a slowly changing market, the darkening nature of his fiction . . . these and intangibles had led to a steady decline in sales of his Gold Medal and Crest originals after the high-water mark of *13 French Street,* to the point where Fawcett decided to drop him from its list. In his world-by-the-tail decade, he published twenty-three mostly first-rate novels under his own name, fifteen of those with Fawcett; between 1961 and 1967, he published a total of seven mostly mediocre novels—one last failure with Gold Medal (*The Hungry One,* 1966) and the other six with second-line paperback houses (Monarch, Berkley, Lancer, Banner).

In the late fifties he and his wife, Verlaine, had moved out west. It was not a good move for Brewer. In Florida he had had a coterie of writer friends, among them Harry Whittington, Frank Smith (Jonathan Craig), and Talmage Powell. In Colorado and New Mexico, he missed their counsel and support when he began selling less and drinking more. There was also the fact that he was beginning to be strapped for money; he had lived high off the hog in his salad days, saving and/or investing little. Financial worries combined with the professional frustrations to lead him into protracted binges. More than once he entered a clinic to dry out, only to backslide again after his release. A major crash of some kind was inevitable; it happened in 1964.

> . . . I was drowning in alcohol and drugs, [and then came] the bleary morning I awakened to a tall, cold glass of vodka on the bedside table, left the house for breakfast at a friend's, and was warned loudly by an echoing voice on a corner to "Turn back—go home," which I ignored, only to, an hour later, total a creamy Porsche and pick up 8 broken ribs, 28 fractures, torn lung, etc., in the process. Then the wild, rather ribald, hallucinatory hospitalization . . . peopled with Bozo the Clown, Rhinemaidens, and other happenings that could only be described as otherwordly or science-fictional; a mad doctor, a hospital nightclub, etc.—the beginning of a transfer to hell during which, for a time, at least, I turned out novels and stories, all the while in the very depths of the pit.

With medical help, he hauled himself out of the pit and he and his wife eventually returned to St. Petersburg, Florida. He was still able to write as well as ever, but his once-flourishing markets, both for novels and short stories, were then dead or dying or had passed him by. He had no marketable skills except those of the professional fictioneer, yet he couldn't sell his own variety of suspense novel and he couldn't afford to take the time necessary to write the serious fiction he yearned to do. He had only one choice, as he saw it: to descend kicking and screaming into hackwork.

He wrote half a dozen sex books under house names for downscale publishers. He wrote stories by the dozens, mostly for the lesser men's magazines, only now and then placing a crime short with *Alfred Hitchcock's Mystery Magazine* and the lower-paying digests. In the late sixties he wrote three novelizations of episodes of the then popular Robert Wagner TV series *It Takes a Thief;* published by Ace in 1969 and 1970, these were the last novels to appear under his own name. He wrote four Gothics as by Elaine Evans for Lancer and Popular Library. On an arrangement with Marvin Albert, he wrote two of the Soldato Mafia series published by Lancer under Albert's Al Conroy pseudonym. He ghosted an Ellery Queen paperback mystery, *The Campus Murders* (Lancer, 1969); a Hal Ellson suspense novel, *Blood on the Ivy* (Pyramid, 1971); and five of the novels about the Israeli-Arab war purportedly written by Israeli soldier Harry Arvay. (He had a chance to take over ghosting of the *Executioner* series as well—what would have been a major source of income—but while his one effort pleased the publisher, it did not please Don Pendleton.)

He hated every minute of this type of work, but he always—or almost always—did the best possible job with the material he had to work with. And at this stage of his fading career, he always—or almost always—delivered as promised and on time.

> . . . I keep hoping for a [subsidiary] sale of some kind; something that might complement the exemplary qualities of my work, ahem. [I'm] up one minute when possibilities of movie rights, or perhaps reprint rights on some lost seed throng my konk, and down the next on Realization Flight 110, knowing that publishers simply are lethargic, fickle, disoriented-and-one-track-oriented . . . Ah me. (Ah Me's a Chinese philosopher with rancid breath who appears as a ghost at my shoulder—

he's from back in 3,000 BC—and forever bids me to go with the tide.) Or maybe better yet, woe is me. At times I do feel exergued. Rats, how I ramble. The notorious Griffin, me, once again, with that dazzling old blue hope, ready to whoop it up at the party, hypostatic, ineffable, even, you might say, but unable to partake of the inducive viands and nectar because of insuforial earth-worms called editors who are, after all, so fucking hidebound, shade-eyed and ponderous it makes me scream—in agony. In agony.

By 1976 through 1977 even the hack-work was beginning to dry up, the assignments—and the sales—fewer and farther between. He was drinking heavily again—so heavily that he and his wife agreed to separate. They continued to live in the same building, however, in separate apartments. Verlaine also continued to lend moral support, and as much financial support as she was able from a job of her own.

Brewer managed to keep turning out short stories for *Hustler, Chic,* and similar magazines, as well as occasional novel ideas and proposals . . . until the drinking once more slid out of any semblance of control. It not only affected his ability to write, it put him in dangerously poor health. He knew something had to be done, and he did it: he voluntarily joined AA.

The program seemed to work for him, at least for a while. Eventually he was able to return to work on a regular schedule. When his agent wrote to tell him that the Canadian publisher Harlequin was looking for mysteries for its new Raven House line, the prospect of once again writing suspense fiction under his own name energized him; he promised to come up with an idea, fifty pages, and an outline. But he soon realized that he was not as attuned to crime fiction as he had once been.

> Tried valiantly to read some contemporary suspense stuff, so I'd be up on how character was handled. Tisk. It coddled my fidgeting brain. Awful. Sparse and futile . . . So many writers are taking old writers' plots these days, like Raymond Chandler's yarns, and rewriting them. I just don't go that way. Perhaps I'm stupid, but it seems a sloppy damned way to make a buck.

And so he couldn't seem to get his head into a book for Harlequin. He had what he felt was a good idea: a novel about the world of bisexuals and homosexuals called *The Skeleton.* The problem lay in putting the right words down on paper.

> Suppose you've been wondering why I seem to have been so bloody lax about this Harlequin project. The fact is I had a small relapse—no drinking, or anything like that, just an inability to read one of the [Raven House] books so I could get the formula down pat. Was trying too hard, obviously. Hope you'll excuse any screwy letters dashed off during this hectic interim. Seem to be getting back in place now, for the most part, though my concentration isn't perfect—but believe I'll be at work soon. I have these spells, as you know . . .

More time passed, and he still couldn't write *The Skeleton* proposal. At length he shelved it in favor of a new novel concept, one that excited him tremendously because it was the sort of serious work he longed to do, and intensely personal and therapeutic as well: an imaginative-autobiographical novel about his alcohol-and-drug abusing days in the early sixties. The title was to be *Anarcosis.*

> It'll be written in sequences of dream-reality, with the dream as reality and the reality as dream . . . It peregrinates all over the U.S. and ends with that bedeviled incarceration in a mental institution back in '64 . . . a big sweep of both subjective and objective shocks, strung with startling characters who, phantom-like, pre-destined and Martian in appeal, connect with me in one way or another—traveling hospitals on the highways of America, a besieged trip to Mexico on sleeping pills and bourbon, various alky wards includ-

> ing the one I call Insanity Ranch in New Mexico, a pack of dogs chasing me at four o'clock in the morning in Albuquerque when I planned to walk to California, and many crazy, firefly incidents that send me screaming through the blinding tunnel of daymare into my own private Gehenna—to survive, or so it seems, anyway. There are dialogues with internationally celebrated dead such as Jack London, Arnold Bennett, Lytton Stratchy [sic,] and numerous others, political figures and men and women in the arts; psychic adventures with tortuous conflict, and, at the end, a promise of another book to come called *Man on Tape* . . .

He had telephone discussions about the project with his agent, who was impressed enough at its potential to write to the Fine Arts Council of Florida in an (ultimately futile) effort to get Brewer a grant that would ease his financial burden. As excited as Brewer was about the project, however, he had trouble writing it. This led to another, albeit brief and different setback.

> . . . I was on a valium binge. There's been no drinking, but that pill thing was evil—all done for good now. No more of that—ever! No more of anything except life, work, recovery. Recovery from a lifetime of knowing I knew as much as the gods, was, in fact, perhaps, one of them—and all I want to do is write. Write with the knowledge now that I know nothing. Helpless, hopeless exactitudes.

He managed, finally, to get thirty-five pages of *Anarcosis* written to his satisfaction and sent them to his agent in February of 1978. The regretful evaluation was that it was "just short of unreadable . . . uncontrolled, hallucinatory dynamism," and it was the agent's suggestion that Brewer rethink it and rewrite it in a more coherent and commercial fashion. The agent also suggested that because of Brewer's financial straits, it would be best if he devoted his immediate energies to short stories for such well-paying markets as *Hustler,* or the long-overdue Harlequin proposal.

At first Brewer balked at this advice.

> . . . I am going to devote all my energies to *Anarcosis.* I cannot, so help me, face another pulp project—at least, not now. It turns my stomach. It has given me diarrhea; the very thought of it, the attempts to turn a plot again, again, again! I cannot do it.

It was not long, though, before he relented. He had no choice; as always, he was living hand to mouth—mostly on a VA disability pension and a Social Security pension. He forced himself to complete the fifty pages-and-synopsis of *The Skeleton.* Then, encouraged by his agent's favorable response, he wrote a portion-and-outline for a second mystery, *Jackdaw.* After that was delivered, he agreed to take on a massive rewrite-and-ghost job—an original manuscript bought by a minor paperback house of which there were two different, unacceptable versions, one of 426 pages and the other of over 1,100 pages. He was to rework the mish-mosh pair into an intelligible, publishable book.

The project was a disaster from the beginning. He had long, violent telephonic clashes with the book's editor that eventually, after months of labor and psychic drain, forced him off the job with only nominal payment. As if this bitter pill wasn't enough to swallow, Harlequin rejected *The Skeleton* portion, after holding it for several months, because although they felt it read entertainingly and "would surely make a good mystery novel," the bisexual/homosexual content was deemed unacceptable. *Jackdaw* was not bought either, for more obscure reasons.

These, combined with continuing frustrations with *Anarcosis,* were the final straws.

By mid-1979 Brewer was again drowning in booze. In 1980 one of his writer friends wrote sadly to another, " . . . Gil has drunk the tops off all the vodka bottles and is writing very little, alas." Brewer's redescent into the depths of alcohol and despair continued into 1981, when he nearly died of several different ailments. Then, with Verlaine's help, he managed to lift himself out of the pit for the final time. He rejoined AA; he tried once more to put his life back together.

> I no longer drink and attend AA meetings regularly. Last eve a head cheese in the organization suggested I'd be a good speaker. I told him he'd have to wait till I have some front teeth replaced—three have fallen out, God help me [and] I can't afford to go to a dentist.

In late April of 1982 he wrote an abject, rambling, five-page letter to his agent.

> I'm hanging by a thread and practically living on noodles and rice with the way things are. The bloody Social Security disability pension and the VA disability pension could give out any time, and I'd be on the streets. I just skin by each month as it is, living like a hermit. Maybe grass, good green grass, I mean, would be a treat . . .
>
> All I know is, I must write. I love to write. I can sit at the mill again, and I can write the stuff . . . I've got to make money, but in return I'll deliver better goods than ever . . . I have so many terrific books in me! And I no longer drink, nor do I take any drug that would disrupt the scene. I'm sober and ready for work.

But it was too late. Over the previous several years there had been too much conflict, too many failures and missed assignments, and during the dark, alcoholic years of 1979 through 1981 there had been to many incoherent, angry, pleading letters, too many drunken phone calls. The agent said that his agency and Brewer were "moving in different directions" and wished him well; their thirty-year professional marriage was finished.

In August Brewer wrote Mike Avallone, asking Mike to help him find new representation.

> . . . Could you write a brief note to your agent and see if he'd be willing to take me on as a client? I must still have some rep: I've sold over 50 novels . . . about four hundred short stories and novelettes . . . have been published in 26 countries . . . I have some new, fresh material at hand, and would dearly love an assignment . . . All I need and want now is an agent, a good one, and a word processor. But at the moment I feel terribly lost and in limbo.

Nothing positive came of this, despite Avallone's efforts. And so, inevitably, Brewer plummeted into the pit for the final time. In December, shortly before Christmas, he placed one last telephone call to his former agent. He was so drunkenly incoherent that the agent had no idea of what he was saying or why he called.

Two weeks later, on the morning of the second day of the new year, Verlaine entered his apartment and found him dead.

That is not quite the end of the Gil Brewer story, however. The gods can be perverse sometimes—damned perverse. This is one bitter instance.

In the years since January 2, 1983, a French film company paid a five-figure advance for film rights to *A Killer Is Loose* and produced it in 1987. Two other early GM novels, *13 French Street* and *The Red Scarf,* were bought for reissue by Zomba Books in England; those two and a number of others were also reissued in France. Black Lizard has expressed interest in reprinting several Brewer titles here. And a number of his short stories were purchased for anthologies edited by the writer of these words. Gil Brewer is dead, but his career, by God, is not; new life has been breathed into it, and it is still on life support at the time of this writing.

> . . . I'm encouraged by how I feel toward really good stuff. It turns me on, as it always has—but I've always denied myself the pleasure of [such] work; forever tied up with one project after the other, facing the stricture of money needed . . . Everything in my plans hinges on money as a support; I'm tortured out of my

skull when the gelt is low . . .

And the drinking . . . I always imagined it a necessity for my work. I am a terrible fool.

AFTERWORD

The italicized passages in this piece were taken verbatim from letters written in 1977, 1978, and 1982 by Brewer to a number of individuals, primarily his agent and Mike Avallone. None of the letters were addressed to me personally; I had no correspondence with Gil Brewer, did not know him at all.

In retrospect I find this strange, discomfiting, because on numerous occasions from the late sixties to the early eighties I intended to write Brewer a letter; to tell him that I grew up reading his work, admired it, was in fact influenced by it in certain small ways. I *did* write similar letters to such other writers as Evan Hunter, Robert Martin, Jay Flynn, Talmage Powell—but never one to Brewer. In the mid-seventies I went so far as to track down his address and type it on an envelope, yet no farther than that. I don't know why.

I wish I *had* written to him, established a correspondence, gotten to know him a little. I might have been able to help him in some small way—bought some of his old stories for anthologies while he was still alive, maybe, or given him an assignment to write an original . . . something. It would have made absolutely no difference in the long run, of course. Just the same, I can't help feeling a bit guilty for my silence.

Maybe I'm a fool, too, in my own way.

Maybe we all are, us real-life working mystery writers . . .

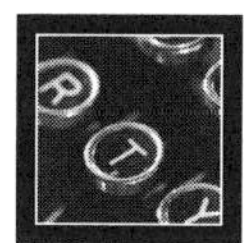

Harry Whittington

BILL CRIDER

Obsessed characters wracked by their passions—lust, greed, the desire for revenge—travel through the night world of cheap bars, back-alley dives, and backwoods swamps: crooked cops and honorable ones, bent private eyes and those who live by a strict moral code, the dishonest and the noble, the seeking and the lost. Harry Whittington has written about them all, and many more, in a career that has covered parts of five decades. Under his own name and as Whit Harrison, Hallam Whitney, Harry White, Kell Holland, Clay Stuart, Harriet Kathryn Myers, and Ashley Carter, to name just a few, Whittington has been almost the prototypical paperback writer, always delivering a solid story and breakneck pacing for the reader's money. He has written, in addition to his mystery and suspense novels, Westerns, historical romances, backwoods romances, "mainstream" fiction, love stories, and nearly anything else that can be read, with the exception of science fiction and fantasy. He has written for such now-forgotten paperback houses as Handi-books, Uni, Phantom, Carnival, Venus, Original Novels, and Graphic, as well as for such famous houses as Fawcett Gold Medal, Avon, Pyramid, and Ace.

Whittington was particularly suited to the emerging paperback market of the early 1950s because of his ability to produce saleable fiction at a rapid pace. After the sale of his first softcover original, *Slay Ride for a Lady,* to James Quinn's Handi-books in 1950, he wrote and sold twenty-five paperback originals in the next three years. Whittington tells about these years in an interview with Michael S. Barson in Billy Lee's *Paperback Quarterly* (Volume 4, Number 2), explaining that "Gold Medal was the prestige paperback line" and that they also paid the best advance ($2,500), while allowing writers to keep all foreign and movie rights. Gold Medal, after buying *Fires That Destroy* in 1951, naturally got to see most of Whittington's books before other publishers, and as Ashley Carter he continues to write for Gold Medal today, thirty-six years later, continuing the popular Blackoaks series. Other publishers in the early 1950s did not pay as well as Gold Medal, and Whit-tington recalls receiving a $750 advance for each of his Handi-books novels, while Ace paid him $1,000 each for *Drawn to Evil* (1952) and *So Dead My Love!* (1953). He had a unique arrangement with Mauri Latzen, whose firm owned Carnival, Venus,

Phantom, and Original Novels. He could submit a three-page outline at any time and receive a check for $375. After sending in the completed novel, he received another $375, and each reprinting brought an additional $375. Graphic, like Ace, paid a $1,000 advance.

Considering the size of the advances, a writer had to produce a large number of books if he intended to make a living at his typewriter, particularly if, like Whittington, he had a growing family to support. In a 1978 address to the Florida Suncoast Writers' Conference (portions of which are reprinted in *Paperback Quarterly,* Volume 2, Number 2), Whittington says that he "chose consciously to write swiftly and with spontaneity" and that he "sold as fast as [he] could write." He was trying to make a living, and he did not have time to spend six months waiting for the prestigious hardback houses to make a decision about his work. He needed to sell, and he needed the quick decisions of the paperback market, despite its lack of prestige. After all, Hardcover snob appeal is not everything, and when reviewers did begin to notice paperback originals, Whittington received excellent notices. Anthony Boucher, surely one of the shrewdest critics the field of mystery and suspense has ever known, was one of the first to devote regular space to paperback authors, and in his "Criminals at Large" column in the *New York Times Book Review* he called Whittington "one of the most versatile and satisfactory creators" of the paperback original. In a review of *You'll Die Next!* (Ace, 1954), Boucher wrote that Whittington was capable of "the best sheer storytelling since the greatest days of the pre-sex detective pulps."

Such comments were the result of Whittington's ability to produce books that combined fast action, clever plotting, and three-dimensional characters in a rapidly paced story. In his article "The Paperback Original," published in *The Mystery Writer's Handbook* (edited by Herbert Brean, Harper, 1956), Whittington writes, "It's as true in paperbacks as in trade editions—maybe even truer—that you must tell a vital, hard-hitting story; you've got to keep it moving and give it that old emotional pull." This was a lesson that Whittington had learned well, but there is more. The writer must also "[c]are. Make the characters come alive; get so involved in those people you're writing about that you yourself want to race right along beside them and see that they come out all right." All Whittington's best work involves characters the reader cares about, in situations which at first seem simple. The characters have goals that seem easily obtainable, but unexpected complications arise. Things suddenly get worse, and then worse still. Finally, when the character seems doomed or helplessly trapped, when it appears that things could not possibly get any worse, they do. A good example of this technique is found in Whittington's first paperback, *Slay Ride for a Lady* (Handibooks, 1950). Narrator Dan Henderson, an ex-cop framed for murder, is released from prison to find the wife of a criminal/political bigshot. He finds the woman almost at once, but then she is killed. Henderson is framed again, beaten to a pulp by vicious cops, and betrayed by a girl he trusts. He survives, even prevails, but there is no false happy ending such as some writers might provide. It just wouldn't

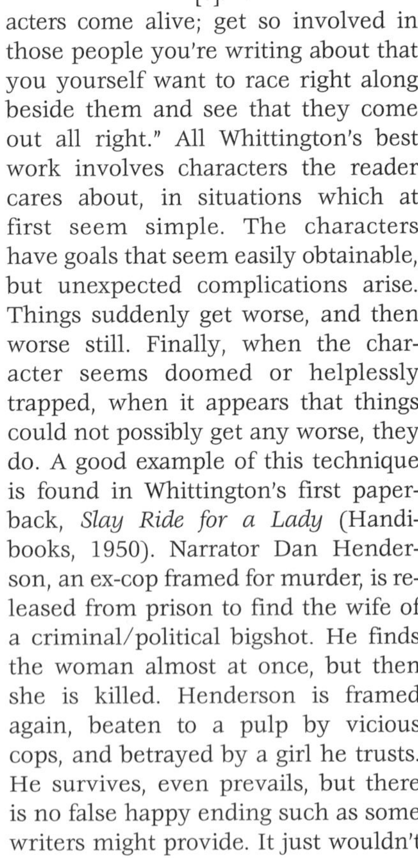

work in a story this hard-boiled, and though Whittington does believe in a happy ending most of the time, he avoids it here. In addition to refusing to provide the expected upbeat conclusion, Whittington throws in another unique touch. The murdered woman has a baby for whom Henderson feels a sense of responsibility. There is a memorable episode in which Henderson, chasing a murderer, blood pouring down his arm from a knife wound in his shoulder, pauses to feed the baby its milk from a bottle. Has any other hard-boiled hero ever done the same?

The device of the man framed for murder was one to which Whittington returned often and effectively, especially in two of his novels for Graphic, *Call Me Killer* (1951) and *Mourn the Hangman* (1952). The former combines the murder frame with amnesia as Sam Gowan, soft-boiled nebbish who is a far cry from Dan Henderson, wakes up in the office of a prominent businessman who has very recently been shot in the face. Sam is holding a gun and certainly appears to be a likely suspect in the murder. His situation is further complicated by the fact that he has been missing from home for some months and, as the reader eventually learns, has constructed for himself an alternate identity as "David Mye" while suffering from a loss of memory. Add to this a brutal cop named Barney Manton, who is determined to crack the case and pin the murder on Sam, no matter how illegally he has to proceed, and the result is a typical fast-paced Whittington story. In *Mourn the Hangman,* Steve Blake, a private eye working on a case involving a government supplier who is cheating on his contracts, is framed for the murder of his wife. He is pursued by the police, hunted by the bad guys, betrayed by his partner, and put through more twists and turns of plot than would seem possible. Like Sam Gowan, he hardly has time to eat or sleep as he tries to set things right.

Gowan and Blake are typical Whittington protagonists, but Whittington was anything but formula bound, as a look at another of his Graphic novels, *Murder Is My Mistress* (1951), demonstrates. The title is entirely misleading—there is no murder in the novel. That fact alone is enough to make the book different from the typical mystery paperback. And murder is no one's mistress. In fact, the book's main character is a woman, and the story is one of psychological suspense as it follows the life of Julia Clarkson, whose past catches up with her. Now a middle-class housewife, Julia had twenty years earlier been the companion of a criminal, Paul Renner. She informed on him to escape the life she was living, but now she learns that he has been released from prison and begins to fear for her life. He torments her with a series of "accidents," and her life and marriage deteriorate rapidly.

Another female protagonist, though a very different one, is Bernice Harper, the mousy secretary of *Fires That Destroy* (Gold Medal, 1951). Bernice kills and robs her employer, a wealthy blind man, and gets away with it. Well, almost. Whittington's killers never *quite* get away with murder, though they often come close. The punishments that Whittington sets up for them are always interesting and always grow out of their characters. The punishments are also always wonderfully ironic, as in the case of Bernice and especially in the case of the lawyer in the excellent *Web of Murder* (Gold Medal, 1958), one of Whittington's best and most cleverly plotted novels. The lawyer and his secretary, with whom he is having an affair, decide to kill the lawyer's wife. They succeed, but they are confronted with a cop much like Barney Manton from *Call Me Killer* (though this time the cop is an honest one). He is convinced that the pair are guilty of murder, but can he prove it? It would not be fair to tell, but it is not revealing too much to say that things—lots of little things—do begin to go wrong with the lawyer's beautifully planned "perfect" murder, leading to one plot surprise after another. Though each twist is carefully prepared for, each works to perfection, right up to the powerhouse conclusion.

A similar story, but one that does not work quite as well, is *The Humming Box* (Ace, 1956). The female protagonist, Liz Palmer, discovers a unique murder method and uses it to rid herself of the husband she no longer cares for, and of course to get his money. While not as strong a story as *Web of Murder*, this novel nevertheless has its moments, as Liz succeeds with murder only to be preyed on by a very slimy private detective before she meets her ironic fate.

Lethal women, though they figure prominently in Whittington's work, are not always the protagonists. Often they are secondary to the men who fall—and fall hard—for them. In *Satan's Widow* (Phantom, 1951), tough cop Barney Hodges falls for the widow of "Satan," a terrible but powerful man who, when alive, delighted in ruining people's lives. When Satan is poisoned, Hodges is certain the wife is guilty, though there are plenty of other suspects. He is so powerfully attracted to her, however, that he is determined to see that she is not arrested, no matter who he has to frame for the crime. Her guilt or innocence becomes irrelevant to him. There is a definite James M. Cain influence on this novel, and the sex scenes are fairly steamy stuff for a 1951 mass-market book. In *The Mystery Writer's Handbook,* Whittington says that *Satan's Widow* is a revised version of a serial, *Body in the Bedroom,* that he wrote for the King Features Syndicate. He sold the novel against his agent's and editor's better judgment, but it was reprinted in five foreign countries and earned its author a lot of money, "although everybody says it stinks." Whittington evidently liked the novel well enough to use a *very* similar plot in a much stronger book, *Drawn to Evil* (Ace, 1952), in which the tough cop, once more drawn irresistibly to the prime suspect—the dead man's wife—goes so far as to conceal evidence and frame another, less likely, suspect for the crime. How tough is this cop? Listen:

> I let him make his play. Before he got his knife out, I had a wad of shirt front in my fist. I jerked him off balance. When he spread his legs to steady himself, I drove my knee into his groin. Hard.
>
> I released him without even looking at him again. I heard something clatter on the floor. It must have been his long-bladed slap-knife. He wasn't going to need it for a while. Not while he writhed.

Despite the similarity of this novel to *Satan's Widow,* they are two distinct stories, with completely different ways of working out the various plot threads. Overall, *Drawn to Evil* is the more successful and satisfactory book, and it has a bang-up ending that can stand with the best of Whittington's work.

Another novel with a dangerously attractive woman is *A Night for Screaming* (Ace, 1960), which also brings in a framed man on the run. Mitch Walker is a former cop innocent of the murder of which he is accused, though naturally he can't prove it. He is pursued by his brutal former partner, Fred Palmer, and winds up on a wheat farm in Kansas. (How many suspense novels set on wheat farms can you name? Leave it to Harry Whittington to come up with a setting like this and to make it seem absolutely real.) The farm is owned by Mr. Barton M. Cassel and looks like a good place to hide from the law, except that the work is brutal, the pay is low, and when Mr. Cassel's wife, Eve, takes a liking to you, well, sixteen hours in the sun at manual labor might be easier. There are plenty of twists in the story, and the suspense, a Whittington hallmark, never lets up.

The man-on-the-run theme also figures prominently in *You'll Die Next!* (Ace, 1954), in which Henry Wilson, an ordinary guy married to a woman whose past he knows little about, is viciously beaten, receives a threatening letter, loses his job, is involved in a hit-and-run accident (as the victim), and is accused both of beating his wife and shooting a cop—all in the first fifty pages. In the *New York Times Book Review,* Anthony Boucher wrote, "*You'll Die Next!* is a very short novel, which is just as well. I couldn't have held my breath any longer in this vigorous tale whose plot is too dexterously twisted even to mention in a review." High praise indeed, especially coming from Boucher, but certainly justified in the case of one of Whittington's cleverest stories.

Whittington also dealt effectively with the theme of "one man against municipal corruption." A prime example is found in *Violent Night* (under the name Whit Harrison, Phantom, 1951). Coast Town is a hotbed of teen prostitutes, dope dealers, and gambling dens. O'Brian, an honest cop with an invalid wife, has to deal with his mistress's leaving him, suspension from the police force, a hired killer imported into town to murder him, and a dead teenage girl found beside the road with three poker chips in her shoe. No one but Whittington could deal successfully with so many plot threads in such a short (128 pages) book, while compressing all the events into the period of a single fast-moving night. He succeeds almost as well in *So Dead My Love!* (Ace, 1953). Jim Talbot, a New York private eye, is called home to Duval, Florida, by the man who got his conviction overturned and got him out of one of Florida's toughest prisons some years before. The man is now married to Talbot's former sweetheart, the very woman who got him into prison in the first place. It's Talbot's job to locate a missing man, and in doing so he must deal with a fat, nasty sheriff who likes things just as they are and his psychopathic deputy. The small-town southern setting adds spice to the plot.

In fact, Whittington is particularly good at depicting the small towns and rural areas of 1950s Florida, and readers should not overlook certain of his books simply because their titles do not suggest mysteries. For example, *Backwoods Tramp* (Gold Medal, 1959) might seem from its title and cover to be a sort of "cracker romance" along the lines of *Backwoods Shack* or *Backwoods Hussy* (both of which first appeared under the Hallam Whitney name), but it is instead a powerful suspense story. It does feature an archetypal southern poor white woman as a love interest, but it is really the story of Jake Richards, who is searching the swamp country for Marve Pooser, the man who engineered the robbery that cost Jake his job, his girl, and his reputation. Pooser is a psychopath any reader can hate, and Richards is a believable protagonist, no hero but a man who learns quite a bit about himself and his motives. By the end of the novel, Richards is able to face what he has become in his search for Pooser and to avoid becoming something worse.

A man who faces what he has become and doesn't even seem to care is the crooked cop Mike Ballard in *Brute in Brass* (Gold Medal, 1956). Ballard is at first a completely contemptible man, callous, indifferent to others, concerned only with himself and what he can get, no matter how he gets it. He always looks for the angle, the way to turn any situation to his own advantage. Little by little, Whittington reveals the reasons for Ballard's attitudes and surprises the reader by eventually eliciting sympathy for the man. Despite the book's strengths as a character study, however, it moves at the typical jetlike pace of any Whittington novel, a neat trick but one that Whittington pulled off with regularity.

Two more books that should not escape anyone's notice are *Married to Murder* (Phantom, 1951) and *Body and Passion* (as Whit Harrison, Original Novels, 1952). The former is the story of yet another cop framed for murder, one of Whittington's seemingly infinite and original variations on a single plot idea. The cop, Palmer, agrees to undergo plastic surgery and pose as the son-in-law of a wealthy New York woman in order to travel to Florida and help the woman's daughter, who is in some unspecified kind of trouble. Before he quite knows what is happening, he has had his appearance altered and finds himself sitting in the front seat of a car with a dead body in his lap, a body the old woman has been keeping in her freezer and whose dead face bears a striking and unsettling resemblance to the face Palmer now sees when he looks into the mirror. To top it off, when he gets to Florida, Palmer finds the daughter being kept as a virtual prisoner in her own house, held there in a drug-induced haze by none other than Palmer's larcenous and treacherous ex-wife.

Palmer's identity crisis, however, can't hold a candle to the problems of the protagonist of *Body and Passion*. He doesn't know who he is, and neither does anyone else. Two men, one a gangster and one an ambitious assistant district attorney, are trapped in a terrible fire at the gangster's hideaway cabin. Only one man survives, and he is so badly burned that there is no way to recognize him or even to take his fingerprints. (On the book's cover he is depicted as what cover-art critic Art Scott has called "the mummy in the tuxedo.") The D.A.'s parents want him to be their precious son, the mob wants to kill him, and the girl who loved the gangster wants him to marry her. But he simply can't remember his identity, despite living for a week both as D.A. and as gangster. And if that isn't enough, it turns out that a third man, a newspaper reporter who was spying on both the other men, has also disappeared on the night of the fire. The protagonist, X, as he is called throughout most of the story, does recover his memory, but Whittington manages to keep the reader guessing most of the way through this unusual suspense novel.

Because he has written over one hundred paperback novels, Whittington did not manage to come up with a winner every single time, which is not surprising considering the amount of work. After all, even Sandy Koufax lost a few ball games. Two books that don't quite live up to the author's usual high standards are *One Got Away* (Ace, 1955) and *Hot as Fire—Cold as Ice* (Belmont, 1962). In *One Got Away*, a man named Gosucki steals plans worth $1,000,000 from the government. Dan Campbell, who was assigned to watch Gosucki, tries to redeem himself by catching the thief, and in doing so travels from Chicago to Carolina to Indianapolis to Hawaii, while being pursued by his own agency. The chase elements and the race against time don't quite click in this one. *Hot as Fire* fails for different reasons, as a deep-freeze salesman tries to foil kidnappers who are keeping a dead body in a freezer he has sold them. It's a thin plot, a far cry from the incident-packed twists and turns of Whittington's best work.

According to Mike Barson's introduction to the interview for *Paperback*

Quarterly, Whittington "retired from the paperback field in disgust" from 1969 to 1975, "convinced he was demeaning himself" after writing a series of movie and television show "novelizations," Westerns, and nurse novels for little pay and even less prestige. One of these novels was, however, one of Whittington's biggest successes with readers if not in a financial sense. Whittington, who also did many of the lead novels for *The Man from U.N.C.L.E.* magazine, wrote *The Doomsday Affair* (*The Man from U.N.C.L.E. #2*) for Ace books. The book proved to be extremely popular with fans of the television series and drew more mail than any of Whittington's previous works. The book apparently sold well, but the sale did not particularly benefit the author, series books of this sort usually being on a work-for-hire basis and paying a flat fee instead of a royalty.

In 1975, Whittington began his comeback in the paperback field. As Ashley Carter, he took over Gold Medal's Falconhurst and Blackoaks series of slave/plantation historical novels and once more found himself a bestselling writer. Since that time he has written other historical works (*Panama,* Gold Medal, 1978), mainstream novels (*Rampage,* Gold Medal, 1978), and Westerns (six novels in Jove's Longarm series). Most of these books, though longer by far than the lean, mean novels Whittington wrote in the 1950s, nevertheless retain most of the virtues of the earlier works—clever plotting, fast pacing, and expert storytelling.

In spite of his well-deserved successes in the past twelve years, it is for his earlier work that readers of mystery and suspense fiction will remember Harry Whittington. He has said that his favorite writers at that time were Frederick C. Davis, Day Keene, and Fredric Brown, and that if there was any influence on his work it was James M. Cain. Readers might also note the influence of Cornell Woolrich, and Whittington encouraged would-be paperback writers to read Fitzgerald, Faulkner, Hemingway, Dostoyevsky, O'Hara, and Wouk in his article in *The Mystery Writer's Handbook.* He also mentioned Brown, Woolrich, Chandler, and Roy Huggins. Some of these writers are revered today, some forgotten; some are still in print, others not. For far too long Whittington's has been the latter case, his best works available only to those willing to spend long hours in dusty used-book stores, searching through stacks of crumbling paperbacks in the hopes, in the hopes . . . An enterprising publisher, Black Lizard Books, has done something to remedy this situation by bringing back into print a number of Whittington's mystery and suspense novels. The readers who buy these books will have a lot of pleasure in store, presented to them by a master of the suspense novel, who will provide them with a gallery of believable characters in incredibly tense situations, pushed to the extremes of their mental and physical abilities, plunged into despair but never quite losing hope, always struggling, always alive. Of the great paperback writers of the 1950s, Jim Thompson eventually attracted a cult following. John D. MacDonald went on to take his place on the hardcover bestseller lists. Harry Whittington, on the other hand, saw his best work fall into neglect. Let us hope that posterity will rediscover his books and recognize him as what he is: one of the true masters of paperback fiction.

CHECKLIST: HARRY WHITTINGTON

Backwoods Hussy (as Hallam Whitney)	(Paperback Library, 1952)
Backwoods Shack (as Hallam Whitney)	(Paperback Library, 1954)
Backwoods Tramp	(Gold Medal, 1959)
Body and Passion (as Whit Harrison)	(Original Novels, 1952)
Brute in Brass	(Gold Medal, 1956)
Call Me Killer	(Graphic, 1951)
The Doomsday Affair	(Ace, 1965)
Drawn to Evil	(Ace, 1952)
Fires That Destroy	(Gold Medal, 1951)
Hot as Fire—Cold as Ice	(Belmont, 1962)
The Humming Box	(Ace, 1956)
Married to Murder	(Phantom, 1951)
Mourn the Hangman	(Graphic, 1952)
Murder Is My Mistress	(Graphic, 1951)
A Night for Screaming	(Ace, 1960)
One Got Away	(Ace, 1955)
Panama (as Ashley Carter)	(Gold Medal, 1978)
Rampage	(Gold Medal, 1978)
Satan's Widow	(Phantom, 1951)
Slay Ride for a Lady	(Handi-Books, 1950)
So Dead My Love!	(Ace, 1953)
Violent Night (as Whit Harrison)	(Phantom, 1951)
Web of Murder	(Gold Medal, 1958)
You'll Die Next!	(Ace, 1954)

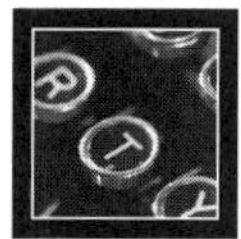

John D. MacDonald

ED GORMAN

The Damned *proved that you are a born mainstream novelist. Do you recall the circumstances under which the book was written, and were you aware it was taking your career in a slightly new direction?*

I was not trying to fit books into market slots. I wrote *The Damned* because I knew the locale and I was interested in what would happen if a lot of people got jammed up at the crossing. A lot of things would happen to them, and that is the definition of a story.

While the critics have always talked about how Travis McGee puts rather helpless women back together, female characters such as Laurie in* April Evil *are very strong in their quiet ways. You seem to like your strong female characters better than the weaker ones—or is that me misreading?

I think that most of us have a greater liking for strong and solid people than we have for the wimps of the world. With strong people you can tell where you stand. Nobody, of course, is too strong to ever be broken. And that is McGee's forte, helping the strong broken ones mend.

Soft Touch *was an interesting variation on your early work. Here we had the resolute war veteran—intelligent, forceful, capable—so familiar in your early books . . . yet here he goes bad. Your readers don't seem to mention that book quite as often as some of your others but it's an almost flawless performance. Is it one of your personal favorites?*

I think I would have a warmer feeling about *Soft Touch* had it not been made into a pretty sorry motion picture called *Man Trap.* I think the book worked fairly well, in that it almost did what I wanted it to.

What was it like, as a young family man, to embark on the hazardous career of freelance writer?

It was nervous, but not too bad. I had four months of terminal leave pay at lieutenant colonel rates starting in September of 1945, ending in January 1946. I wrote eight hundred thousand words of short stories in those four months, tried to keep thirty of them in the mail at all times, slept about six hours a night and lost twenty pounds. I finally had to break down and take a job, but then the stories began to sell. I was sustained by a kind of stubborn arrogance. Those bastards out there had bought one story "Interlude in India," and I was going to force them to buy more by making every one of them better than the previous one. I had the nerves of a gambler and an understanding wife.

What are some of your favorite memories of your early writing days?

Every sale had a kind of iron satisfaction about it. "I showed you guys." I remember standing in front of the downtown post office in Cuernavaca and opening a letter with $1,000 in it for *Louie Follows Me,* bought by Colliers. In late 1949 I wrote a long pulp novelette. My agent, Joe Shaw, asked me to expand it. I resisted, but complied. I hate puffing things. Cutting is fine. Everything can use cutting. But puffing creates fat. Gold Medal took it for their new line of originals. It was titled *The Brass Cupcake.*

What are some of your least favorite memories of that time?

Professionally, I do not recall any particularly bad memories. The book which just won't jell. The editor who gets fired when you have half a book in his shop. The clown who was taking my old pulp stories and changing the point of view and selling them to *Manhunt.*

You've mentioned, in several places, how much a part luck plays in a career succeeding or failing? How has "luck" helped you?

I began to learn my trade in late 1945. Had I begun ten years later, I would never have had the chance to earn while learning. The short-story market was sliding into the pits. Luck is being born at the right time. I had an agent who kept me out of Hollywood despite some pretty offers. I was lucky to have a man so wise. I decided against doing a series character in 1952. I had no good reason. It was just a gut feeling. I didn't start McGee until 1964. By then I could avoid being trapped in the series. Saying no was the purest kind of luck.

Which writers of your generation, suspense or mainstream, do you feel have been undeservedly neglected?

There are some, of course. Charles Williams comes to mind. I do not want to enumerate those who wrote too seldom or too short. Or who went into another line of work. That was their decision.

Would you share with us some of the books you feel you've learned a great deal from, both as a man and a writer?

Bronowski, *The Ascent of Man;* Tuchman, *A Distant Mirror;* Aries, *Centuries of Childhood.* I have made lots of these lists. They change from time to time.

The House Guests ***manages to portray an interesting family in a way that's sweet without being treacly. One senses that your family has helped you, in a variety of ways, be the writer you are today. True?***

My family has given me the support one might expect. Approval, backup, affection, respect.

The House Guests ***is also remarkable in one other way. You make the felines in your life assume almost human shape without resorting to any Disney tricks. I remember especially one of your lines: "A cat cannot abide being made to look ridiculous." Do you still get great pleasure from cats?***

The present cats in residence are Bogie, an eighteen-pound male neuter tiger, and Canella (Cinnamon in Spanish), a spayed tabby. They are the same age, four, and I believe they are related.

When you look back over the past thirty years of writing, do you have any major regrets?

No regrets.

How did Travis McGee come into existence?

At the request of Knox Burger, then at Fawcett, I attempted a series character. I took three shots at it to get one book with a character I could stay with. That was in 1964. Once I had the first McGee book, *The Deep Blue Goodbye,* they held it up until I had finished two more, *Nightmare in Pink* and *A Purple Place for Dying,* then released one a month for three months. That launched the series.

Do you find a series character confining?

I do not find a series character confining. I do other kinds of books in between the McGee books. First-person fiction is restrictive only in that you can't cheat. The viewpoint must be maintained with flawless precision. You can't get into anyone else's head. The whole world is colored by the prejudices and ignorances of your hero.

Does Travis have any secrets we should know about?

No.

Will you describe a typical day for Travis when he's eighty-five?

Nope.

Do you recall your mood while writing* The End of the Night? *It's a much better book than* In Cold Blood, *yet it's also more despairing than Capote's work. The curious thing is that you dedicated it, rather cutely, to your cats.

I remember that when I wrote *The End of the Night* I was very curious about the social and political effects of the mind-altering drugs. This was a new force in our arena at the time I wrote the book. At that time my cats, Roger and Geoffrey, had the habit of napping on my big work table. They scruffed up my pages and left pad marks. So I dedicated the book "To Roger and Geoffrey, who left their marks on the manuscript." That sounds cute to you? How about the people who had no idea I owned cats? They thought I was talking about editors.

Whom do you read for pleasure these days?

I might as well tell you the titles of the books on my nightstand and on the table by the couch. *Fadeaway*—Rosen, *Table Money*—Breslin, *Something about a Soldier*—Willeford, *Hugging the Shore*—Updike, *Blue Highways*—Moon, *Plumb*—Gee, *A Perfect Spy*—Le Carre, *It*—King.

Would you tell us a bit about any works-in-progress?

In the fall there will be a book of letters called *A Friendship,* letters to and from Dan Rowan (*Laugh-In*) from 1967 to 1974. In the spring there will be a new edition in hardcover of *Slam the Big Door,* and a bit later, the twenty-second McGee, as yet untitled.

What would you like your epitaph to say?

He hung around quite a while, entertained the folk, and was stopped quick and clean when the right time came.

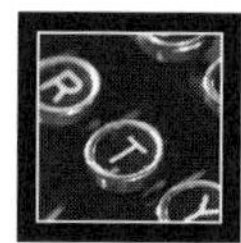

"I Kill 'Em Inch by Inch!"

STEVE HOLLAND

We said, "Don't pull your punches, Griff," so he's smashed into this terrible story with raw mitts . . . It's going to make your nerves shreak like rusty nails on glass . . . but it's all TRUE LIFE!

—cover blurb on *Some Rats Have Two Legs* by Griff, 1950

The blonde arches her back, exposing an acre of flesh and her long silky legs are curled up under her, the firm muscles of her thighs taut under sheer nylon. She eyes you coyly, provocatively. The lingerie she's almost wearing is see-through. Get a load of the new "Griff" screams the cover.

That two shillings in your pocket is burning a hole. You pick up the book and turn back the cover, arching the back of the blonde still more, and read:

> Raw, rough, real . . .
> Sizzling, scorching slices of True Life in this crime-ridden post war age . . .
> That's ace writer
> GRIFF
> No lily-fingered stylist, but by heck!
> That guy can write, and he makes his characters LIVE WITH YOU!
> "Rats are vermin all right. They breed in dirt. They spread plague. There are plenty of HUMAN RATS around the world right now, the mentally twisted kids who go around with knives, coshes and worse, assaulting the weak and unprotected, a thieving, scheming pest on society"

Are you sold on this book yet? Are you gonna let that money burn a hole? G'wan, get a load of the new Griff. Get a load of that dame on the cover.

You're hooked? So was I, even forty years later. The unnamed copywriter who penned the blurb to the Griff books knew how to sell them. So his spelling was enough to make your nerves "shreak", but by then your two shillings were on the counter and you were plunging into the raw world of racket-torn Chicago where the back-alleys swarmed with the two-legged rats of the title. Inside, author F. Dubrez Fawcett wove a chilling story of the rise and fall of The Kid, a runaway as tough as nails who does his running with the Paloni gang, becoming an expert with a cosh and rubber hose, only to fall out and take a knife to his one-time hero at the end of the story.

Some Rats Have Two Legs was typical of Fawcett's staccato death-rattle style, his novels ground out at the rate of one a fortnight straight onto the typewriter and straight into his publisher's raw mitts. Under the penname Ben Sarto he was already a bestseller, shifting fifty thousand copies of each novel; Griff followed closely with a print run of around forty thousand per title, which meant almost half a million copies in print by the time The Kid put the knife into Paloni's throat.

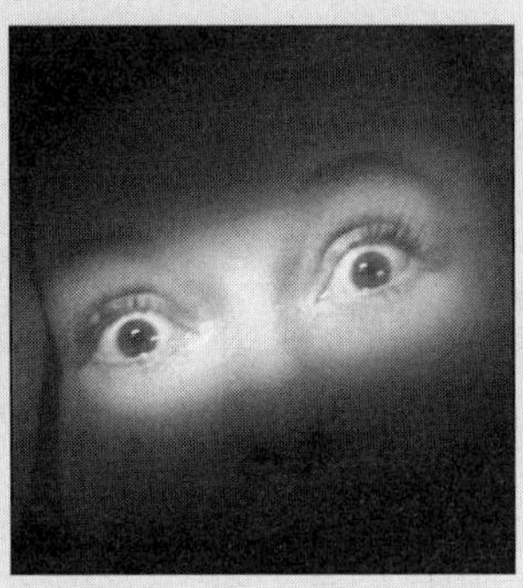

Both Sarto and Griff were published by Modern Fiction (London) Ltd., established in 1943 by Eddie H. Turvey and his wife Irene. Turvey had previously distributed British and American magazines to hawkers and marketstall holders ("24s gross, 2s1d dozen") from his address in Northview Parade, Holloway, in North London (the address was actually a pub called the Nag's Head), later expanding into printing and publishing tuppenny comics and children's pocket books from Tufnell Park Road ("opposite the Gaumont Cinema").

Modern Fiction's first adult titles appeared in 1945, two thirty-two-page romance novelettes by Eugene Glen, followed a couple of months later by a clutch of novels by George Stanley and the probably pseudonymous W. A. Sweeney. The British paperback boom was gathering steam. Paper had been rationed since 1940, and almost anything that appeared in print was being snapped up by a public starved for entertainment. The "mushroom" publishers appeared to fill the gap: small, tightly run paperback houses who churned out cheap, colorful entertainments. If American magazines and novels could not be imported, the mushroom publishers could supply ersatz American novels, written in racy pulp style and printed on any paper that was available. Britain's black-market economy could supply anything: ends of newspaper rolls were a favorite, and a number of small publishing ventures claiming their eight tonnes of paper per quarter never seemed to produce anything themselves, finding it more profitable to sell their quota to printers. Modern Fiction was not the first to exclusively distribute books "published" by their printers, and would not be the last. With their books printed by the Metropolitan Press, based in Denmark Street and a warehouse just around the corner in Morwell Street, off the Tottenham Court Road, Modern Fiction was in a prime position to supply the booksellers of Charing Cross Road and Piccadilly; in June 1946, *Miss Otis Comes to Piccadilly* became their first bestseller, and went back to the presses more than once.

***

"When Mabie Otis entered the room for the first time she drew the breath out of most men. She stood just under six feet tall and every inch was a dream. Her wide, slinky hips curved down into long, nylon-clad legs, their shape revealed by the tight-fitting skirt that clung to them when she moved. Her bosom was full but firm, her features small, and topping that breath-stealing body was a mass of peroxide hair.

And her voice was the huskiest a man could imagine; her chin dimpled when she smiled, revealing small white teeth. She carried herself with queenly aplomb, spoke commandingly, and knew she could turn a man's head at fifty paces. Only her eyes betrayed her. Light in color, as cold and expressionless as moonlit pools, the mascara on her lashes helped disguise but could not hide their coldness and the hint of feline cruelty that lay in them."

H. W. Perl's cover showed the gorgeous Miss Otis in a turquoise silk evening dress, poised like a catwalk model with legs as long as Broadway. While Cole Porter may have had his regrets, Eddie Turvey must have thanked his lucky stars. With the creation of Miss Otis and the titles that quickly followed, Modern Fiction could soon boast its first million-selling author.

When collectors talk of favorite writers, Ben Sarto is not likely to come into the conversation. In fact, it would come as no surprise if this is the first time you've heard the name. His books do not receive a mention in any of the reference works commonly associated with crime fiction, there is no learned entry in John M. Reilly's *20th Century Crime and Mystery Writers,* and only the statistical bleached-bones of a titles listing in Allen Hubin's *Crime Fiction: A Comprehensive Bibliography* that can say nothing about the books and the people behind them. Ninety-nine titles are listed in Hubin's book with an additional two titles in the *Supplement*. One hundred and one criminous novels? That's more novels than Edgar Wallace wrote (in fact, there were one hundred and five in all, with two books later retitled). Is your interest starting to be piqued even if only a little?

Sarto's creator, Frank Dubrez Fawcett, was born in Great Driffield on November 13, 1891. He joined the military publishers Gale & Polden Ltd. as an office boy in 1906, staying with them for two years, subsequently working as a newspaper reporter and advertising copywriter until in 1915 he joined the British Army, with whom he served in France. Wounded in Macedonia, he returned to England, where he reestablished himself as chief copywriter with Imperial Advertising and Dorland Advertising between 1924 and 1940.

Fawcett's first novel appeared in 1923 (coinciding with his marriage to Betty Harwood) when Federation Press published *Loose Love* under the name H. Dupres. Dupres became a regular with risqué novels of bohemian behavior with titles like *Shop Soiled* (1924), *A Bride from the Street* (1928) and *Too Much Love* (1929). Fawcett's publishers were Fred Mowl and Arthur Gray, who, as Federation Press and later Gramol Publications, were notable as "one of the worst-paying firms in Fleet Street, [specializing] in 'sensational' novels," (so noted Ernest McKeag, who was turning out novels for them under the name Roland Vane at an even more prolific rate than Fawcett at the time). Mowl and Gray play an interesting—if indirect—part in the Sarto story, and that of the mushroom publishers in general, as they established the seedy, low-life bestseller like no other publishers before them and launched upon an unsuspecting world the king of romance, Paul Renin. The success of Renin, Vane, and Dupres was the same linchpin upon which the mushroom publishers established their names and their astonishing sales figures.

Not that Fawcett was solely a purveyor of "sophisticated" paperbacks: in the 1930s he was published in hardcover at least twice; as a copywriter, he penned brochures for business firms of topics ranging from vitamins to fishing gear, later writing the daily "Detectographs" feature and "World's Strangest Stories" for the *Evening News.* He contributed stories and articles to *Punch, Blighty, Everybody's, Illustrated, London Opinion, the Sunday Express* and the *Guardian;* he was a book reviewer for *History Today* and *John O'London's;* his last published book was the *Cyclopaedia of Initials and Abbreviations* (1963), as distant from *White Slaves of Two Cities* (by H. Dupres, 1923) as his children's fantasy books set on the magical island of Ulla Gapoo were from *She Ruled with a Rod* (1946) and other Sarto epics.

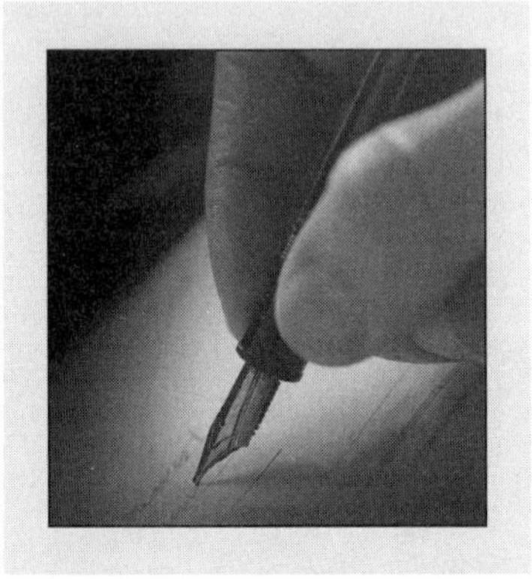

If Fawcett has any fame—and his name is all but forgotten these days—it has to be with Ben Sarto. A rough estimate of sales—and this is an educated guess only—has Sarto certainly selling at least five to six million copies of his books.[1] Whatever the true figure, Sarto was an astonishing success story, one that attracted the attention of other publishers immediately. The early Sarto novels were spine-thrillers exposing lawless racketeering from the hooch and hijacking of *Hi-Jacker's Lady* (1947) to the snatch rackets, white slavery, dope dealing, and gangsterism, set everywhere from New York's Bowery to London's Soho. Perhaps Fawcett's occasional focus on the Soho vice rackets brought the stories home to his readers harder than tales of some mythical New York that never quite matched the genuine article; perhaps the frenetic pace of his stories simply overwhelmed his readers. They were pure, concentrated entertainment.

Fawcett's gutter-slang style of storytelling dragged the reader in quickly, his characters swiftly drawn in confident strokes of his pen. That was the strength I found in Fawcett's books; while others were happy to regurgitate characters as thin as the paper they would eventually be printed on, Fawcett created intense characters with habits and flaws that gave them personality. That first Sarto gave us Giuseppe "Jews" Pelligrini, actually the main focus of Mabie Otis's debut novel: sallow, frightened "Jews" whose talent was for opening strongboxes but who had milk flowing in his veins rather than blood; fear gave him caution, and that saved his life long enough for a sequel. He loved his wife, which was unusual enough in this (British-invented) land of molls and showgirls. Or the Big Boss dope racketeer in *Duchess of Dope* (1948), Maso ("which he pronounced 'Mat-zo' and couldn't stand for folks who called him 'May-so'"). He deals colorfully with a colleague who wants out:

> "Perhaps he wants a bigger take-off" suggested Maso, showing his teeth in the usual grinning manner. "Perhaps he's getting too big for his boots. Zoom! I talk to him like twoerclock. Dazz-dazz-dazz. Then he apologises and is a good boy again, heh?"

Can't you just see what he's doing with his hands?

***

Ben Sarto quickly established himself with his white-hot narratives and sometimes elusive invented slang. So much so that Fawcett was tempted away from Modern Fiction by Thorpe & Porter and began writing Ben Sarto novels for Hermitage Publications. *Susie Comes to Soho* (1947) was almost parodic of his first title a year earlier (as was *She Talked with a Gun* (1950) of *She Ruled with a Rod*), although the West End slashing of Nancy O'Shane by a razor-wielding thug in the opening paragraphs buried any belief that this was going to be anything but Ben Sarto at his most ruthless. The action around Soho guaranteed a heap of two-bob sales at the bookshops and newsagents right on Modern Fiction's doorstep.

It was not an exclusive deal: Fawcett continued to pen new Sarto novels for his original publisher and by the early months of 1948 Sarto was boasting his first million sales, each title billed as his latest exposé, be it of the "West End plague-spots" (*Too Bad for Susie,* 1948) or "How stranded girls are trapped" (into white slavery in *Bodies Fetch Good Prices,* 1948). Call them stark, blood-curdling gangster epics as his publishers did or escapist fiction of the most unworthy and sordid as his critics did, but don't deny the power of Fawcett's writing as he wove tragedy and breathless action for his million-plus readers.

Then something happened. In May 1948 Modern Fiction published *I'll Get By* and for once Ben Sarto disguised another writer, William Newton, and a few months later Newton again donned the Sarto cloak for *There's Always a Dame* (1949). This time it seemed to galvanize Fawcett into action, taking out an injunction against Modern Fiction, claiming that the name was his and his alone—and he won. That seems to have been tied into a new deal Fawcett struck with Thorpe & Porter in 1948 for the exclusive publication of Sarto under the Beacon Books imprint. For three years Sarto remained with Beacon, the novels growing to 190-page epics of corruption and murder, although Fawcett did not burn any bridges and continued to write for Modern Fiction's (safely established) house name Griff, under which name he created a slew of hard-hitting yarns.

The first Griff title was written by Ernest Lionel McKeag, an editor of children's papers with the Amalgamated Press since 1923 who moonlighted for a variety of paperback publishers; most of his originals were spicy romance stories in the vein of Paul Renin, his most prolific nom de plume being Roland Vane. As Griff he turned on the heat as a tough American crime reporter (all British gangster novels were written by Americans according to the adverts). With *Rackets Incorporated* (1948) McKeag set the style of future Griff shockers, introducing Bill Truscott, a newshound with the *Tribune-Sun,* a sucker for blondes, and a magnet for trouble. That's Trouble with a capital T, which he runs into when he starts questioning Big-shot Killahan's moll, Susette Delaine, on the opening page; from there the book becomes a runaway express as beating follows murder follows double cross. Hot-headed Truscott later turned private eye, with Susette as his sidekick, reappearing in other Griff novels by McKeag that exposed the dope rackets and white-slave trading in his toughest yank reporter style.

Griff was a shared name, the second writer being William Newton, switching from the abortive attempt to establish himself as Ben Sarto the previous year. If anything, Newton turned in an even tougher, harder yarn than McKeag in *Come and Get Me* (1949). "Meat Kosky was dead before he hit the deck," wrote Newton. "The shrill, ear-piercing shriek which he had started to give petered out into a choking gurgle as the slim, icicle-sharp blade penetrated his grey matter." It may not be Pulitzer Prize material, but coupled with the leggy, shotgun wielding blonde on the cover it helped Griff pile on the sales.

If the early Griff novels trod the unsafe streets of a New York that their writers had never seen, Frank Dubrez Fawcett took things one step further into the sick heart of American vice and rackets. *Some Rats Have Two Legs* (1950) was set in Chicago, where *From Dance Hall to Opium Dive* (1950), which marked Griff's half a million copies sales, began. The latter followed Swell Matson, a murderer on the lam who picks up innocents in a Manhattan dancerie, turning them into dopeheads, but becoming an addict himself, which leads to his downfall. Most of the Griff titles—and most of the British gangster fiction of the time—were written to a standardized formula in which the bad guys inevitably became victims of their own depravity.

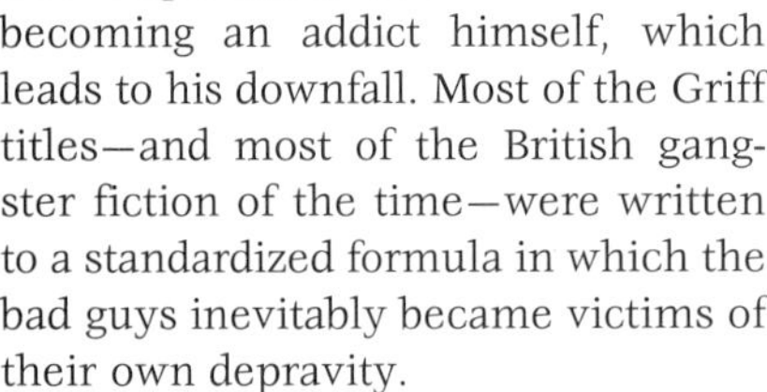

Fawcett was one of the few writers to twist the formula to his own ends. A speed writer he may have been, but for all the novels that poured from his typewriter, Fawcett produced some of the most original characters on offer. *Brooklyn Moll Shoots Bedmate* (1951) introduced Kinsey Target, coward, drunkard, killer; Kinsey staggered from one problem to another, caught up in the underworld, looking for easy money and only getting grief. Kinsey would reappear in two further Griff novels and one under the Hank Spencer house name, usually just out of the pen and heading straight into trouble—all written in a weird slang accent that Fawcett carried to extremes at times.

In comparison, *Eastern Men, Chicago Women* (1951) was a straightforward tale of a girl caught up in a Chinese-fronted dope racket in Chicago; *Crooked Coffins* (1952), an almost straightforward private-eye yarn, and *Too Tough to Live* (1952), a relatively straightforward morality play of a boy gone bad whose life ends at the switch of the electric chair. The latter, however, was made more interesting by an afterword that introduces Dr. Lewis Berg's *The Human Personality* as a source for creating the violent, boastful Martin Gott, who robs and murders his way through the book. That Fawcett was trying to achieve something a little more lasting is almost certain, but it was lost among the endlessly supplied gangster novels churned out by less thoughtful writers whose imaginations rarely leapt beyond the Bogartesque gumshoe or Hank Janson newshound.

Not that Fawcett was perfect; he still turned in formula pieces that, mixed in with other formula stories by other writers, tended to go unnoticed. The stories, even the less creative ones, did, however, still manage to shriek across the nerves: the magnificent, poisonous Vera Venner in *Devil's Daughter* (1952)—the first to feature Don Danby as the hero—was a character who lifted an otherwise average story and whose life ends in the final paragraph: "flames clung all about her, seemed to be lapping her with the caresses of torturing death." Even if the plots were repetitive, and the characters paper thin, you just had to read Griff for his wonderfully purple prose!

In March 1952 Ben Sarto returned to Modern Fiction with *Take What's Coming,* Fawcett still in control of the name and by now turning in books to Modern Fiction under various names at the rate of at least one a month. Fawcett himself claimed that he was writing a novel a fortnight, straight onto the typewriter without even a readthrough until the printer's proofs arrived, preferring to rise early in the morning and write solidly until midday without a break for breakfast, or even a glass of water. This strict regime, along with the popularity of both Sarto and Griff, must have helped Fawcett's sales for Modern Fiction hit a million books a year. That made him an attractive proposition to the newly founded Milestone Publications, which talked Fawcett into a new deal whereby, in 1953 through 54, he was producing a Ben Sarto each month for them. The Milestone Sarto novels concentrated on new adventures of the queenly Miss Otis.

Fawcett was expanding his repertoire: in November 1952 his study of Charles Dickens on stage, screen and radio was published by W. H. Allen as *Dickens the Dramatist* in hardcover; Modern Fiction published the nonfiction *You and Your Stars* by Madame E. Farrah; Coolidge McCann was resurrected for a single Western from Barrington Gray. Meanwhile, the beleaguered Scion Ltd. (some of whose best authors had jumped ship in mid-1952 to establish Milestone) tempted Fawcett to produce more two-shilling dreadfuls, although hidden away under house names rather than setting up an exclusive name under which he could establish a line to rival Sarto. Perhaps the very fact that Sarto had once again abandoned Modern Fiction was the reason. His Griff novels continued to appear: *That Room in Camden Town* (1952) saw him return to spivs and crime in the heart of London (a stage he'd used before as Ben Sarto); in *Demon Barber of Broadway* (1953), he moved the Sweeney Todd legend to the Bronx and introduced Rapier Codd, nicknamed Swordfish, a herculean private investigator pitched against a razor murderer; *Dead Bones Tell Tales* (1953) featured one Professor Porson, an osteologist whose reconstruction of skeletons helps bring criminals to justice.

It proved to be Fawcett's last Griff tale, and the series quickly sunk to average in the hands of others. The only late story of interest is *Liquid Death* (1953), which was totally different from every other Griff title. For starters it was written by John Russell Fearn, briefly taking a sabbatical from being Scion's science fiction yarnsters Vargo Statten and Volsted Gridban to bang out a couple of crime novels; its setting in Britain and its police investigation of a counterfeit coin racket was made even more atypical when Fearn gave the plot a scientific basis and created a machine for transmuting metals. It's an unusual book for Fearn, and an even more unusual book for Griff—but when a dozen or so writers share a name, the occasional rogue should be expected.

It proved to be the last of the series. With the fading out of Griff, publisher Eddie H. Turvey was trying to establish new bylines Hank Spencer and Blair Johns alongside other money-spinning schemes. By now Turvey's operation ran not only to publishing but also to printing and distribution. In the mid-1940s Barnardo

Amalgamated Industries Ltd. were the north London printers (and "publishers") of many of Turvey's more risqué novels under house names like Ramon Lacroix, which tapped the same "sophisticated" market as Paul Renin, Roland Vane, and H. Dupres. In 1950 C. M. & Co. was a semi-regular "publisher" for Modern Fiction-distributed novels—namely the printers Craig Mitchell of 525-527 Liverpool Road, Holloway N7, which became E.H.T. Printers Ltd. in 1952. From the same ad-dress you could buy success in love, money, and health for a mere shilling postal order, thanks to *The Book of the Zodiac,* which would be mailed to you in a plain envelope. By return of post the secrets of Zosines were yours, plus the secret supplement "You and Your DESTINY—How you can change it and mould YOUR OWN FATE." How many plain envelopes were mailed out from 1951 onward, or how many 3 shilling readings done by Modern Fiction's own astrologer Madame Patrice we shall never know.

The year 1954 saw Fawcett's last contributions to the Ben Sarto saga. The Hank Janson trial in early 1954 sent a red warning light through the paperback industry, and further trials in the months that followed proved that no one was immune from the steely eyes of the vice squad. Modern Fiction had come in for its fair share of problems with titles like *Trading in Bodies* (Griff, 1950) being destroyed at the insistence of the courts. The Sarto novels avoided obvious sexual innuendo, although clothes clung to creamy white bosoms and there was always plenty of leg on show from husky-voiced molls. The mushroom publishers stripped their lines of the toughest tough-guys and the blondest of blondes. Milestone published the last of the Miss Otis novels, Scion had collapsed, owing money to Luton-based printers Dragon Press, and Fawcett bailed out of Modern Fiction with *They Burn for Me,* his final Sarto. Perhaps his successful publication of a science fiction novel in hardcover (*Hole in Heaven* from Sidgwick & Jackson, 1954) prompted Fawcett to turn away from the cheapjack publishers. More likely, the pressure of producing some one hundred novels in eight years burned him out. At sixty-three years of age Fawcett retired from the paperback market.[2]

***

That wasn't the end for Sarto, or Modern Fiction. *Corpse in the Cabin* (1954) saw Sarto producing a slower-paced mystery, the unknown author mixing ex-boxer Nick Garth with a redhead and stirring up some heat (the same author had earlier penned at least one novel as Griff). Viper's Brood, also published that month, was set in New York's crime mile concentrating on the headaches faced by a homicide detective. It was a relatively low-key debut for Alistair Paterson, who was to become the most regular hand behind Ben Sarto over the next few years.

Paterson, an ex-editor at Scion, penned only one memorable character in his time at Modern Fiction, P.I. Gentle Hoggerty, created originally in the novel *Curves Can Cast Shadows* (1953) as Griff and star of at least three more Griff novels. Hoggerty returned after a two-year break to take a central role in *Dread* and *Fear* (both 1955), although in the latter it was as an undercover agent for the FBI; the same book contained the most blatant reference to Paterson's influence when a hood says thinly, "Mickey Spillane's on guard . . . " Spillane certainly inspired a number of Paterson's novels in both plot and language.

Paterson and our as-yet unidentified author seem to have shared the name over the next few years. The titles by "unknown" were, if anything, faster and tougher then Paterson's, a return to the fast pacing and violent action of the early fifties mushroom boom, although by then—1956 through 1957—the boom was long gone. Most surviving publishers had switched to reprint material, with only a few mushroom publishers clinging on the paperback original—Brown Watson, John Spencer, and Modern Fiction among the last. But last, unfortunately, it could not. In 1958 Modern Fiction published its final Ben Sarto Titles. These later books, produced in much smaller numbers than in Sarto's heyday, seem to be thinner on the ground,[3] and I've only come across a few of them—quickly absorbed into my collection, of course. Toward the end I have found one stray Victor Norwood tale—*Swamp Fever* (1957)—and learned of a curiosity in *Baby Moll* (1957), which credits Sarto on the cover, but J. A. Jordan on the title page. James A. Jordan was a prolific Western writer in the 1950s, in fact, a prolific everything writer, as I know of numerous romances and a number of gangster novels produced under the name Chris Wheatley. Perhaps further research will prove Jordan to be the mysterious "unknown writer" and solve another mystery.

Modern Fiction continued to publish into the 1960's but it was no longer the publisher of gangster fiction it had been. In the mid-1950's it turned its attention to the growing glamour market, the forerunner of today's men's magazines, establishing a popular line of nude photography magazines. Typical for the time, one or two pages of the magazines were usually (at least in the early days) dedicated to technical details of lighting, exposure times, and depth of focus, to prove that they were art magazines with studies of nudes for the dedicated photographer, not pornography.

The warehouse in Morwell Street no longer exists. Eddie and Irene Turvey disappeared, Frank Fawcett and Ernest McKeag are long gone, and all that remains of Modern Fiction is the usually tag-eared and well thumbed reminders of yesteryear, the novels of Ben Sarto and Griff, the toughest of gangster thriller writers, the exposers of rackets and crime. Griff was never the ace reporter the early books tried to tell us he was, nor had Ben Sarto personally investigated every den of vice or every corruption-ridden city he wrote about. But sometimes the books really did "shreak like rusty nails on glass." Shoddy production, poor editing, and the usually formularized style of writing didn't help and like that copywriter said: "You've got to be tough-skinned not to squirm." But take a look. There are gems, there are "sizzling, scorching slices of True Life" hidden away behind the provocative covers: the blonde arches her back, exposing an acre of flesh and her long silky legs are curled up under her, the firm muscles of her thighs taut under sheer nylon. She eyes you coyly, provocatively. The lingerie she's almost wearing is see through.

Get the lowdown from Ben Sarto. Get a load of Griff.

FOOTNOTES

Note: 2 shillings in old pre-decimal currency was worth about 25 cents.

[1] Not as many as one of Sarto's publishers claimed—the fifth Sarto novel claimed a sale of five million. Sorry, but there wasn't that kind of paper ration available, and if any evidence was needed, that book itself was printed on three different grades of paper alone! But if he was to have hit a million sale by the time his publishers claimed, he would have to be selling seventy five thousand copies per book—and the jump between one million and three million meant one hundred thousand per title.

[2] Fawcett continued to write, but outside the paperback field. He died in Beckenham on July 26, 1968.

[3] And lower in quality. By then, the rates of pay were also down from the average £1 a thousand words, which, in the late 1940s, meant a writer could make a good living if he was fast. Some would be able to earn £36 ($75 in 1949) a week when the average take-home pay was £7 ($14.50). TV writer Malcolm Hulke sold his first novel for the princely sum of £18 to Modern Fiction who published it as *The Dead Don't Cry* by Ben Sarto (1956). That's ten shillings a thousand words, or (taking inflation into account) about £300 ($500) today, for a thirty-six thousand-word novel, flat fee, no royalties. Perhaps it's little wonder that the later Ben Sarto novels are so poor.

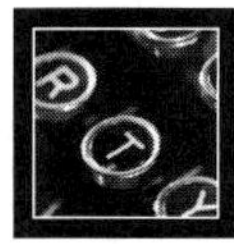

Lion Books:

NOIR PAPERBACK ICONS

GARY LOVISI

> It is the smell of death . . . The Oxnan Hotel stank with the stale odor of cheap whiskey, cheap two-bit racketeers, cheap unwashed women. But behind the rotting-front, behind the peeling-plastered walls, a big time syndicate did its filthy business. The payoff was in the millions.
>
> Edna Loomis—*and there was nothing cheap about her*—set out to get it all. Her method was simple . . . she used the weapon of her flesh. But she made one mistake. His name was Peone, of the drugged eyes and the slender knife. Edna Loomis was a beautiful, ambitious woman. Peone was a coked-up killer!

It comes right out at you, noir, hard-boiled, a crime and corruption ride on the hellbound train, and Lion Books, in the above example from *Blondes Are Skin Deep* (Lion number 62) by Louis Trimble, sets the locomotive on the tracks and stokes the furnace up high for the reader.

Noir and hard-boiled writing plunges us down to the depths, and during the 1950s tiny Lion Books was the undisputed king of noir and hard-boiled paperback publishing.

These days Lion is mostly forgotten, an obscure publisher of yesteryear, but in the 1950s it was big stuff. It began publishing in 1949, coincidentally the same year that its chief rival, Gold Medal Books, began publishing, but Lion published all these cool, incredibly hard-hitting paperback originals (PBOs) by some of the biggest names ever. Many Lion books have since become acknowledged classics.

Today, Lion Books are heavily collected, the original series of 225 books (numbered from 8 to 233 and published from 1949 to 1955) including such big-money items as the eleven Jim Thompson PBOs, including Thompson's hard-to-find classic first novel, *The Killer Inside Me* (Lion number 99). In nice shape this book can fetch upward of $500. The other ten Thompsons are each valued in the $100 to $300 range.

Thompson really epitomized the feel and mood of Lion's noir paperbacks. People on the skids, down in the lowest depths, going only lower and deeper into it in spite of how they tried to save themselves. There's no salvation here, only despair and gloom. No hope, no quarter, and these books told it all true, where every single character was a louse or worse. In fact, the books often portray situations where not even one single character is a normal, well-adjusted human being. It's a rough ride through hell, a hell of their own making. Jim Thompson was the best practitioner of the art in the Lion stable of writers, but he wasn't the only one. There were others, and some of them wrote books for Lion as good or better than Thompson.

David Goodis knew despair firsthand. His personal life was a noir disaster, and it came through in his books, including the four PBOs that he wrote for Lion. All Goodis books are excellent, with perhaps the most interesting being *The Dark Chase* (Lion number 133), a great tale of nonstop rage and revenge. The most difficult to find is *The Blonde on the Street Corner* (number 196), "The story of men and women on the skids!" This last one in fine condition can fetch upward of $200. It features, as do most of the Lion Books, incredible noir and hard-boiled cover art, tough gals, sleazy girls, bad guys, thugs, violence, and crime images, all suitably atmospheric in the best 1950s noir style. These books really are noir icons, and with their cover art herald a time when we all *thought* the world was a better place. But it wasn't—not for the people in these books. Not for a lot of real people living back then either. Another reason why these books were so successful was that they held truth and power in their pages. They told it like it *was*. And like it still *is*.

Of course, Lion published all types of books in its main series—two nonfiction books on baseball, quite a few Westerns, World War II novels, and even some science fiction. However, its mainstay was noir, hard-boiled crime, and Lion did it better than anyone.

Even Lion's other genre books had definite aspects of noir and hard-boiled attitude in them. For instance, its three science fiction end-of-the-world and disaster novels: *Doomsday* (number 148) by Warwick Scott, *The Deluge* (number 233) by, and get this, Leonardo DaVinci (actually written by Robert Payne), and *False Night* (number 230) by Algis Budrys all feature tough-minded survivors as heroes who battle in the ruins of a hostile and destroyed world merely to exist one more stinking day. Now, you can't get any more noir than that!

Lion's Westerns, with such outrageous titles as *Eat Dog or Die* (number 103) by C. William Harrison (which, by the way, shows an incredibly gruesome and sadistic cover of a man being hung), indicate its interest in (and one might even say obsession with) violence, war, crime, greed, corruption, and loss—many of the overriding themes of the noir and hard-boiled genre.

Nevertheless, it is for noir and hard-boiled crime that Lion Books is best remembered today, and we'll take a look at some of the best they had to offer now.

"Graft, murder, and his best friend's wife—a big city cop batters down the doors of hell." So proclaims the blurb on the cover of *Bodies Are Dust* (number 83) by P. J. Wolfson, and let me tell you, this book does not disappoint. For sheer noir despair and hopelessness, for the all-constricting feel of the rope around the throat, this book delivers. A crooked cop who thinks he's such a smart guy and knows all the answers loses it all over a woman. It's a hell of a ride. And it ends with a slam.

In the same vein, though even darker and more twisted, if that can be possible, is the incredible and sadistic novel of an honest cop torn apart by a depraved woman, *Sin Pit* (number 198) by Paul S. Meskil. This one's a chillingly twisted story that you will not be able to put down.

The Outward Room (number 26) by Millen Brand is a love story of despair in which a man falls in love with an insane woman. She's an escapee from a mental institution. A dark love story that actually has a happy ending, it's an early Lion, interesting because of the early noir influence. No later Lions will ever have happy endings again.

G. H. Otis (pseudonym of Otis

Hemingway Gaylord) wrote two brutally intense novels for Lion, *Bourbon Street* (number 131): "A loot-mad thug takes New Orleans apart," and *Hot Cargo* (number 171): "They carried 129,000 tons of explosive oil—and a TNT woman!" These two are tough and gritty noir-hard-boiled at its best, in the James M. Cain tradition, with characters out of Thompson, and full of corruption, crime, greed, double-dealing, and betrayal, all wrapped up in a nice sweet bouquet of lies. Must reading!

Meanwhile, in *Sin People* (number 159) by George Milburn, we see the lovely Mamie, bad-girl town harlot, go berserk. Let me tell you, what this little girl does to this town . . . The cover blurb proclaims: "Scandal, booze, and race hatred turned the townfolk into raging brutes," and that's only the good news! It's a brutal book.

Lion published books by a lot of perennially favorite authors, many from the pulp magazines, and others who are forgotten today. It also published fiction by big-name authors such as the two brutal noir crime novels by Richard Matheson, *Someone Is Bleeding* (number 137) and *Fury on Sunday* (number 180), and one by veteran horror master Robert Bloch, *The Kidnapper* (number 185), a noir crime horror masterpiece. Veteran pulpster Day Keene has two fine books in the series: *Sleep with the Devil* (number 204) and *Joy House* (number 210), and his buddy Fletcher Flora has *Strange Sisters* (number 215), a kind of lesbian-noir novel. R. V. Casill, known today on the literary high-end, slummed a bit with an early book in the Lion series, *Dormitory Women* (number 216), and crime writer Jonathan Craig stepped in with a nasty little shocker, *Alley Girl* (number 206).

Famed crime author Richard Prather, before he created Shell Scott, wrote two books for Lion in his early career: *Lie Down, Killer* (number 85), and, as Douglas Ring, *The Peddler* (number 110), a nasty novel about a low-life monster. Crime author Howard Browne had his classic noir novel *If You Have Tears* published by Lion as *Lona* (number 94) under his pseudonym, John Evans. Veterans such as Gerald Butler, *The Lurking Man* (number 81), and Gerald Kersh, *Prelude to a Certain Midnight* (number 98), also had excellent books representing them in the Lion series, the Kersh book with a stylish fog-enshrouded cover by Rudolph Belarski that captures the mood of noir perfectly.

Other Lion noirs of note are *The Hoodlum* (number 161) by Elaezar Lipsky, a retitling of his classic *The Kiss of Death.* Then there are the three fine hard-hitting novels by Benjamin Appell: *Brain Guy* (number 39), in which a tough crime boss has all the answers; *Dock Walloper* (number 166), about crime on the New York docks; and *Hell's Kitchen* (number 95), a tale of youth gone wild on crime. A noir icon himself, author A. I. Bezzerides even steps in with *Tough Guy* (number 153) and Frederick Lorenz has some worthy noir entries with *Night Never Ends* (number 193) and *The Savage Chase* (number 223).

David Karp wrote some incredible books. He's largely forgotten today but remembered by those who love great noir and hard-boiled work. He had four novels in the Lion series: *The Big Feeling* (number 93), *The Brotherhood of Velvet* (number 105), *Hardman* (number 119), and *Cry Flesh* (number 132). These are all worth reading.

Lion Books also tackled tough social topics, such as racial problems, usually in its own characteristically noirish fashion. Interracial love, sex, suspicions, and race hatred got an ample going-over in such Lion books as *How Sleeps the Beast* (number 45) by Don Tracy. The cover blurb tells us in three simple lines: "The man—NEGRO, The Girl—WHITE, The Payoff—LYNCH! Another book dealing with an interracial affair, or just plain lust, is *Luther* (number 114) by Roy Flannagan. There are also three interesting Curtis Lucas novels: *Third Ward, Newark* (number 80), whose cover blurb loudly proclaims: "A negro girl gets the jolt of her life" (some white men rape her); *Angel* (number 162), with a nice cover of an attractive interracial couple walking down a city street and getting "the look"; and *So Low, So Lovely* (number 91), a noir novel of despair among black people of the 1950s.

Almost every book that Lion published bubbles over and seethes with the style and mood of noir; it is always there somewhere. It is there in the text, in the cover art, in the title or blurbs, in the very look and feel of each individual book. Lion Books, like its rival, Gold Medal, published fine crime paperback originals now considered classics. And if Lion Books is not remembered today as it should be, the novels and authors it published certainly are. And that's a hell of a fine legacy for any publisher.

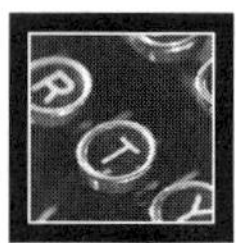

An Interview with Arnold Hano

GEORGE TUTTLE

The 1950s was the decade of the paperback original. They sold incredibly well, so well that they made deep cuts into the profits of hardcover publishers. Fawcett was the first paperback publisher to feature a line of originals with Gold Medal, but other publishers soon followed: Dell, Ace, Popular Library, and Avon. Another company to join the pack was Magazine Management, which started publishing a line of originals and reprints called Red Circle Books, an imprint later changed to Lion Books. Though Lion Books couldn't pay the rates that Gold Medal did, it still succeeded in publishing some of the best crime fiction of that period, including that of writers like Jim Thompson and David Goodis.

How was it able to publish top writers even though it didn't pay top rates? The main reason was that it had an editor who had an eye for quality and who wasn't afraid of buying material that might be a shade too sophisticated for the mass market, an editor named Arnold Hano.

Under Hano's guidance, Lion became a respected line, and in years to come, critics and scholars, first chiefly French and later American, would read Thompson, Goodis, and other Lion writers and marvel at their skill. These writers would be heralded as a major part of what is now called noir fiction. Though Thompson is often the focus of the praise, it should be noted that even if one were to exclude Thompson, Lion was still a key publisher of noir, with novels like David Goodis's *The Burgler* and *Black Friday,* David Karp's *The Big Feeling* and *The Brotherhood of Velvet,* Day Keene's *Sleep with Devil* and *Joy House,* Richard Prather's *The Peddler,* Frederick Lorenz's *A Rage at Sea,* G. H. Otis's *Bourbon Street,* and Robert Bloch's *The Kidnapper,* to name a few. As editor of Lion Books, Hano played an important role in providing a forum for this talent, and there is no doubt that without Hano some of this talent might never have come to light.

Besides his career as editor at Lion, Hano also worked at Bantam and had a long and varied career as a writer, writing both fiction and nonfiction, though most of his fiction was written under the pseudonyms Ad Gordon, Matthew Gant, Mike Heller, and Gil Dodge. Though Hano had a noteworthy career as a writer, this interview is limited to his work at Lion Books. At the time of the interview, Hano lived in Laguna Beach, California, with his wife, Bonnie. They are now retired and living in Costa Rica.

To begin at the beginning, how did you get the job at Lion Books?

I had left a job at Bantam Books where I was the managing editor from 1948 to 1950, and I guess I answered an ad. I don't really recall because I had never heard of Magazine Management, the publisher of Lion Books and a million other things. But I must have answered an ad since I couldn't have applied there for any reason other than a blind ad. So I was hired to be the editor in chief of what was to be a new line of paperback books that had actually already started and was called Red Circle Books, but when I saw Red Circle Books, I told my boss, Martin Goodman, that it didn't interest me. I didn't want to do a line of books like that. They were kind of tawdry "el cheapos." I won't pretend that I was putting out a literary product with Lion Books, but it was better than that. So we wrangled that around and came up with a concept that was more to my liking and then changed the name from Red Circle Books to Lion Books. That was in 1950, and I stayed there until 1954.

You mentioned Martin Goodman. Was he the typical profit-conscious publisher?

Well, it's hard to say. He was very much the businessman and the mass marketeer, but he was surprisingly more literate than a lot of people are giving him credit [for]. For instance, I could never beat him in a Scrabble match. So don't write him off. Though he did have his ideas as to what sold and he would much prefer that we began every Lion Book with some woman standing in front of a mirror admiring her breasts, he was probably talked out of that and he went along with my taste, oh, possibly ninety-five percent of the time. So again, not that I am a literary anything, but we were able to do things like *All Quiet on the Western Front.* We had a line of war and antiwar books that probably were the envy of the industry, William March's *Company K,* for example—we did a whole bunch of them, though names escape me now.

You had a lot of freedom at Lion Books?

I had a lot of freedom, yes. A lot of freedom and no budget.

Yes, that's one fact about Lion Books—other publishers had more money, but Lion still produced one of the most impressive lines of paperbacks to come out of the fifties.

We just went for books that I had known about at Bantam. I had known that they had not been snatched up by anybody else. So we did those and when we went into paperback originals, that made life easier because then we could compete better since most of the companies were still sluggish about doing originals.

Speaking of paperback originals, what kind of rates did Lion pay its writers?

We were paying $1,500 to $2,000 for a book, and we were paying it in two installments, at the end of three chapters or ten thousand words and an outline, and then the rest upon completion of the manuscript. We were at $1,500 at the beginning and moved to $2,000, but we never spent more than that.

That seems to be comparable to what most publishers were paying with the exception of Gold Medal.

Well for some reason, Gold Medal was paying on amount printed. I did a book for Gold Medal and they didn't base payment on sales. They based it on the size of the print order, and they printed something like four hundred thousand copies. So I got $4,000 for doing a Western novel for them.

I don't recall that title. Was it written under your own name?

No. Very few of those things were written under my own name. It was *Valley of Angry Men* and it was probably under Matthew Gant.

At Lion Books, isn't it true that you worked out the plots in advance?

We did. We would write synopses and hand them to writers and say could you give us a book like this? Now that was when we were just beginning to do our originals and I say we, I mean Jim Bryans, who was my assistant, and I, and he wrote most of those synopses. He was very good at that. For instance, two of the first novels Jim Thompson did for us were based on synopses. Now, I know this always arouses Alberta Thompson to a point of denial, but it's the truth. We gave him a synopsis of *The Killer Inside Me,* which he very artfully changed to satisfy his own style, but it was based rather loosely on a synopsis that Jim Bryans wrote.

Was it the same with David Karp?

David Karp to a lesser degree. I don't think we actually handed him a synopsis, although we may have. Dave would come in and since he was very good at plots, we would sit and work a plot out, like the one he did called *Hardman.*

***Switching to another writer, tell me about David Goodis, the author of* Dark Chase *and* Black Friday.**

David Goodis is somebody whom I never met, but whose stuff came in. I believe he was not represented by anybody. I think his work simply came in over the transom, but we liked it, welcomed it, and went with it. He was certainly one of the more interesting writers of the black suspense novel, the type of novel that the French love so well. I understand that he is a hero over there like Jim Thompson is.

It would probably be correct to say that you are a small hero over there yourself.

Well, I don't know about a small hero. They do ask me for comments once in a while. Somebody wanted me to go on a lecture tour and I said okay, what language? So that ended that.

A large number of the noir writers of the fifties came from Lion Books.

Well, apparently; of course, you have to understand we didn't know this was happening. We were simply publishing books and we did not think of categories. We didn't think that history later on would put a label on it. We were just looking for writers that appealed to us and appealed to me. So, thank you. I'm flattered. Jim, of course, before Lion Books, was publishing hardcovers, and though he did do a lot for us, he also did books for other publishers.

Of the various writers you handled, who did you respect most?

Jim Thompson. He became a very close personal friend and the whole family and Bonnie and I are still very close to Alberta and his three children. Jim and I stayed very close even when he was writing elsewhere, and then when Bonnie and I moved to the West Coast, the Thompsons followed soon after, so we continued our friendship. Jim remains very warm in my memory and I think that he was probably the most interesting writer we published and perhaps one of the most interesting writers of the 1950s and maybe in the whole psychological suspense genre. Jim was enormously talented. Not that we created that. He simply found in our publishing house a nurturing relationship. We liked what he did and we didn't question what he did. So he had something that he had not found elsewhere and would have to a lesser degree elsewhere.

Outside of the obvious classics by Thompson, Goodis, and Karp, are

there any other books that stick out in your mind?

Yes, Jay Thomas Caldwell and a book called *Me an' Ou.* It's about a black boxer who fought in the days of Henry Armstrong. Caldwell was a very, very talented young man who had been in prison and came out and wrote this dark look at a boxer who was manipulated by money forces. It was an exceptional first novel and I finally got to his agent a few years later and said, "Gee, I think we ought to get another book out of this guy. How about having him do something . . ." and I suggested an idea. The agent said, "Swell, I'll talk to him." But Caldwell had been shot to death that weekend in an armed robbery. So that was the end of a very, very promising writer. I wish that we had gotten back to him sooner or I wish somebody with money had gotten back to him and given him an out instead of crime. So, he sticks. It's hard to say who else.

To mention one more writer, how about Day Keene?

I like Day Keene's stuff very much. I like Fletcher Flora and a whole bunch of them, but I think that Jim and David Karp would be the most memorable. They were the ones in our house considered to be the best of our stable and probably more people liked Karp. Martin Goodman liked Karp's stuff better, but in no way did he ever try to slow me down to running with Jim's stuff the way we did. I believe Jim wrote nine books for us in the period of about a year, though they might not have come out that same year.

Thompson seemed incredibly loyal to Lion.

Even though he was about fifteen years older, I think he was a frightened boy in search of a father figure and he found it in Lion Books and I think that was more important to him than maybe making a buck elsewhere, although he would complain about not being able to make money. He was a self-defeating person, his drinking for one, and so it was not easy for him to go elsewhere. He'd go elsewhere, run into strange editors, strange publishers, and he couldn't handle that very well. Look what happened to him in Hollywood. I mean, he was absolutely the worst person in the world to go to Hollywood. His run-ins there got to be legend. Karp was more of a traditional writer and knew he could make it elsewhere and really wanted out from our publishing logo.

It seemed that Karp was trying hard to get into hardcovers, while Thompson seemed to be satisfied with Lion Books.

Jim was so embittered with his previous experience with hardcovers where he made like $500 from a book. When he came to us, he was very embittered about whatever it was that had gone on in his hardcover experience. He was really washing his hands of it then. Now today, I think he would be thrilled that *The Killer Inside Me* is coming out in a hardcover edition.

Why did you leave Lion Books?

I left Lion Books when Martin Goodman offered all of the editors a ten percent cut because of one of the recessions. I had an ex-wife and two kids and a new wife and ten percent removed my margin. Since I had been dabbling in freelance writing, I decided I would just try the freelance life. If I was going to starve, I would rather starve at my own rate.

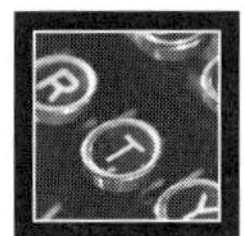

Mecca Spillane

MAX ALLAN COLLINS

When the plane landed at the Myrtle Beach airport, the case of nerves finally hit me. It wasn't the landing: coming from Muscatine, Iowa, to South Carolina took two flights that encompassed four puddle-jump landings and, except for the one that had woken me up (I hadn't slept much the night before), none of the landings bothered me, really. And the sight of blue ocean as the plane had gradually descended to come in for its landing had been tranquilly beautiful.

But as the plane rolled to a stop, and as I stepped out into the aisle of the plane, carrying a copy of Spillane's *The Body Lovers* (which I'd reread on the flight), it came to me: *you're about to visit Mickey Spillane.*

Now, I'd met Spillane before—almost exactly a year before, at the Bouchercon, mystery fandom's major convention, which that year had been held in Milwaukee; but the prospect of meeting him on his home turf suddenly overwhelmed me . . .

Spillane, of course, has always been sort of the black sheep of mystery fiction; and the Bouchercon I'd met him at had been, well, historically significant. Despite his being the best-selling mystery writer of all time, the prevailing attitude among his fellow mystery writers as well as much of so-called mystery "fandom," over the years, has been one of apparent disdain. Never mind that the popularity of his books had given mystery fiction a much-needed postwar shot in the arm; never mind that paperback originals virtually owed their existence to Spillane, as the pioneer Fawcett Gold Medal was expressly designed to provide the public with Spillane-style fare.

Courtesy of Mickey Spillane

Mickey Spillane, author of *I, the Jury* and *My Gun is Quick*.

But then, around ten years ago, several voices began to be heard in mystery fandom (mine among them) who admitted to liking Spillane (occasionally, over the years, a mystery fan would cop to reading a Mike Hammer story, and finding it "fun," if trash). Now, many consider him one of the major talents ever to write mysteries, placing him (and not the more critically acceptable Ross Macdonald) with Dashiell Hammett and Raymond Chandler as the third member of the Unholy Trinity of Tough Mystery Fiction.

Not that there still aren't plenty of critics around who despise Spillane—though most of them, now as then, obviously haven't read much or any of his work; even on the rare occasion a critic bothers reading Spillane before lambasting him, the criticism comes largely from surface reactions: his right-wing sensibilities, the sex, the violence. But the small camp of defenders of Spillane has grown to an army—now, at a Bouchercon, should someone glibly, smugly bad-mouth Spillane, another shall rise up and smite him. And about time.

Why should one of the most popular authors of the twentieth century need defending? Easy, as Mike Hammer might say: his subject matter and his approach were so hard-hitting, so individual, that Spillane repelled the more proper and staid among the Literary Establishment (and the Establishment in general, including Dr. Frederic Wertham and *Parents Magazine* and other unappointed arbiters of public morality). And it has taken time, and changing mores—plus the natural PR knack of Spillane himself, with such disarming tactics as funny self-parody beer commercials and the writing of award-winning children's books—to give him his rightful place as the living giant among mystery writers.

When, in the summer of 1981, it was announced that Spillane would be a guest at Bouchercon, I immediately called the con organizers to confirm it. They in turn asked me, as a contemporary mystery writer who had been one of the most vocal of Spillane's defenders, if I would mind serving as the official liaison between the con and Spillane. A tough decision for me to make . . .

Anyone who is a fan—a-dyed-in-the-wool fan like me—will know how nervous, how sleepless, the night before my first meeting with Spillane was. It is dangerous to make an idol of anyone; the actor or actress, the baseball player, the rock star, the author, famous as they might be, are human beings all. And occasionally they are lousy human beings who happen to be famous and/or talented. Even the best of them, inevitably, are human beings who have good days and bad, and on the day you come face to face with your idol, that idol might be having an exceptionally bad day, and snap your head off when you ask for a simple autograph. A friend of mine who was a fan of a famous cartoonist met his hero at a National Cartoonists Society affair where the cartoonist was apparently inebriated and gave his die-hard fan only a "Get away, kid, you bother me" for his trouble; to my friend's credit, he thought (and thinks) no less of the man for it. My friend was wise enough to understand that, where heroes are concerned, feet of clay come with the territory. I knew this, preparing mentally to meet the Mick. I also knew I'd had a recurring nightmare since I was age thirteen in which I finally met Spillane and he turned out to be a thoroughly nasty individual who told me to get the hell out of his sight.

Shortly after arriving at Bouchercon, my wife Barb accompanied me to Spillane's top-floor suite at the hotel in Milwaukee. I knocked, and Spillane opened the door. He seemed small to me at first. He waved us in, genuinely glad to see us, and treated me like an old friend, talking about how glad he was to "finally" get to meet me, telling me he'd read my books and liked them pretty well—"You're improving," he said.

I'm usually not at a loss for words, but I was tongue-tied, my brain overloading at the thought of Spillane sitting down and reading something I'd written.

Fortunately, Spillane took control, and immediately began spinning yarns, putting us at ease with his smile and his enthusiasm as he told us, as if we were kids sitting around a campfire, the stories that would make up his next three young-adult books. And he seemed larger than life now, big.

But not *too* big, as I was to learn over the next two days, during which time I hogged the chair next to Spillane whenever he held court (which was generally in the coffee shop downstairs; he avoided the bar, as he doesn't drink when he's working, and he saw the Bouchercon appearance as work since Miller Lite had brought him in for the affair). Spillane was "on," but in a most unpretentious, natural manner. I have been around a few celebrities in my time, but have seen none as friendly, open and down-to-earth as Spillane. It didn't take me long in Milwaukee to realize how lucky I was in having chosen Spillane as my hero.

At Bouchercon one afternoon, Spillane and I made up a two-man panel, which amounted to me interviewing Mickey in front of the assembled convention. And it went very well, though despite my best efforts to crack Spillane's defenses, many of the pat answers and patented anecdotes I had hoped to do end runs around got recycled as answers to my questions anyway. He charmed the con—conned the con, if you will—and even those who had come not liking his writing went away liking the man. He put up with an endless autographing session; he jawed hours on end with fans and fellow writers; he attended the evening movie showings and introduced *The Girl Hunters,* the movie in which he stars as Hammer ("That was me thirty pounds ago"). Then later, after an episode of the Mike Hammer TV series was shown, he stood and shouted good-naturedly to the audience, "I didn't write that!"

They loved him, and it is to the 1981 Bouchercon's credit that Spillane was invited, and for the first time ever put into direct contact with mystery fandom. I do not resent that Spillane was not the guest of honor, but rather a "special" guest (guest of honor was Helen McCloy). Crazy as it seems, considering the countless book autograph sessions Spillane has given (at drugstores and supermarkets, where the real people are), Spillane had never before attended a meeting of mystery fans and/or writers. And I think he got a kick out of it. I think maybe that cold shoulder given him in the early days by the more snobbish mystery fans and his fellow mystery writers (who were more than a little jealous of his success) had made him a little wary (he has never joined the Mystery Writers of America, for example). And I think it must've been a nice thing for him to come into contact with working pros in the mystery field (and I am just one of many) who admire him and appreciate what he has done for the genre—which is to say revitalize it, spawning everything in the hard-boiled area since, from James Bond to Dirty Harry to Magnum P.I.

After the Bouchercon, I kept in touch with Spillane—just before he'd gotten in a cab to go to the airport, he'd given me his home phone number. So, every once in a while, I would call him, every couple of months—usually when I had a reason to, such as to get his reaction to the new Mike Hammer TV movie. And I kept sending my novels to him as they appeared and he continued to say nice things about them—namely, that I was still improving.

Finally *he* called *me,* one Sunday afternoon. At his request, I'd sent him a copy of the manuscript of my new novel, *True Detective,* a long historical private-eye story set in the Chicago of the early thirties; my most ambitious book to date, I'd talked to him about it a lot during its writing, so he had asked to see it. And he called and told me he thought it was "terrific."

Allow me an understatement: this meant a lot to me. Back in Milwaukee, I had a couple of times asked Spillane to come down to our room to meet us before going to eat or whatever; his room on an upper floor couldn't be gotten to by elevator, because the top several floors were accessed only by a special key. But he never would—either we had to climb up to him, or simply meet him in the lobby. This confused me, but my wife straightened me out: "He's Mickey Spillane. He doesn't come to you. You go to him." Right. Nice as he is, as unpretentious as he is, Spillane the mountain was not about to come to me, the Mohammed. I came to accept this bit of wisdom on my wife's part and it helped me to understand why my letters didn't always get answered (though they were obviously read) and why I called him, but he never called me.

Only this once he did call me. To tell me I'd written a good book. Despite his seeming disdain for anything "literary," Spillane respects a good book and a writer for having written it, and this book had somehow opened a door. I wasn't sure I deserved that respect, but I took it—and I took the invitation to go down to Murrell's Inlet and visit him for a few days.

He greeted me at the airport; he wore a black T-shirt and white shorts and the Spillane grin. His grin disarmed me more easily than Mike Hammer taking a rod off a dame.

And the next two days were casual and comfortable, with Mickey driving me around the Myrtle Beach area, showing me the sights from the front seat of his "Carolina Cadillac" (a pick-up truck—his fabled white '56 Jag is seldom used), pointing out the development of condos and such along the ocean with a mixture of pride and sadness—sad to see civilization come knocking at his door, but pleased that this "neck of the woods" he'd spotted from a P-51 many years before has been found so desirable by others.

Much time was spent sitting around the Shipwreck Bar, a charmingly ramshackle affair built around some trees in Spillane's front yard (which also boasts a hammock). Spillane's son War, a successful charter fisherman, lives with his father, and is about my age, so we swapped some stories about playing in rock 'n' roll bands in younger days. Every few minutes, it seemed, a tourist or two would drop by, and be greeted by a friendly Spillane, handing out Miller beers to strangers as if to next-door neighbors. Also present was Spillane's long-time buddy Dave Gerrity, who lives nearby and who carries on an unending good-natured verbal battle with the Mick on every subject you can think of.

Gerrity is one of a group of satellite writers who sprang up around Spillane in the fifties, friends of Spillane's who sought his help, both in terms of teaching them to write and in landing publishing contracts. These include Charlie Wells (*Let the Night Cry,* Signet, 1953; *The Last Kill,* Signet, 1955) and Earle Baskinsky (*The Big Steal,* E. P. Dutton, 1955; *Death Is a Cold, Keen Edge,* Signet, 1956). Gerrity alone has made a reputation of his own, and his list of suspense novels includes the excellent *The Plastic Man* (Signet, 1976), and *Dragon Hunt* (Signet, 1965), the latter loosely based on a 1954 continuity in the Mike Hammer comic strip. A good, slightly tongue-in-check private-eye yarn worth searching out in the used-book bins, *Dragon Hunt* "introduces" private eye Peter Braid (in his only appearance to date), and includes a few appearances by Mike Hammer himself (Spillane is pictured with Gerrity on the back cover. The gifts of

Hammer as a character, a supportive cover blurb, and the basic comic-strip story show Spillane's generosity with his writer friends).

Conversation around the Shipwreck Bar often included anecdotes about the comic-book business. One of these had Spillane and Mike Roy walking along Broadway and spotting an open competition for "best painting." Spillane and Roy entered the gallery and Spillane said to Roy, "You can do better than these guys." Roy nodded thoughtfully, went home, and the next morning brought back and hung a painting, not yet dry, which took top honors—and the $1,000 grand prize. Another story involved the next-door neighbor of the comic-book studio, a theatrical producer, whose expensive sets were destroyed in a trucking accident; again, overnight, as a lark, and gratis, the comic-book artists got together and whipped up some sets for the producer, saving the day.

Spillane has a genuine affection for his comic-book years, when he was earning a good living as a writer, but without the attendant hassles of fame and controversy. He seemed anxious to show me the hand-colored stat of the original "Mike Danger" cover, never published, of the comic book he and Harry Sahle had put together about a tough private-eye. When the comic-book market fell through (due in part, Spillane says, to dwindling sales on the less-populated postwar army bases where, in wartime Pxs. comics had been big sellers), Spillane changed Danger to Hammer and the rest was publishing history.

He also seemed very pleased with the recently published paperback collection of the Mike Hammer comic strip, which I'd co-edited and written the introduction for. He remembered working with Ed Robbins, writing the Sunday pages himself, plotting daily stories for Robbins to script. (Spillane and Robbins are still friends—a fairly recent oil portrait of the Mick by Ed hangs just inside the front door of Spillane's home.)

Mickey Spillane in the 1990s.

There was more to the Spillane visit. I was allowed to sit in one of Spillane's three offices and look over various movie, TV, and radio scripts and several long fragments of Hammer stories Mickey decided not to finish. I looked through hundreds of 8-inch-by-10-inch stills of Mickey filming *The Girl Hunters* in England. In another office—kept locked by Spillane—I stood and stared at the original cover paintings of *One Lonely Night* and *I, the Jury*. Then there was the first evening when Spillane took me to a seafood place frequented more by the locals than tourists, and I took advantage of the gracious Spillane being waylaid by some autograph seekers and went over and paid the check, only to glance across the room and see Mike Hammer glaring at me. "Did I see you do something nasty?" he said to me on my return. I stammered. "Don't ever do that again," he said. I didn't. On Saturday afternoon I accompanied Mickey to a shopping mall, where at a sporting-goods store he bought two pairs of 3-D glasses for his son and himself, for an upcoming 3-D TV presentation. I couldn't resist asking if it was *I, the Jury,* the 1953 3-D movie version that Spillane despises. He just glowered at me affably. We then went to the mall's bookstore, where he checked to see how his new young adults book (*The Ship That Never Was*) was doing—they were sold out and had more on order, having sold five hundred copies already. That pleased Mickey.

Before I left Sunday morning, I asked Mickey if I could take a few foreign editions of his books home (he is the world's fifth most widely translated author, and two massive bookcases in his study are overflowing with proof of this) and he said, Take all you want. Like any good collector, I made a pig of myself, taking three Miller Lite bags of books home with me. I was afraid Mickey would be irritated with my enthusiasm, but he was only amused. In fact, he helped make my suitcase heavier by letting me have several magazines with Spillane stories I hadn't managed to track down (his only copies—"I'll know where they are if I need 'em") and some scripts based on his work, including both the 1953 *I, the Jury* script and the current remake, as well as the new TV movie and several TV scripts from the old Darren McGavin series, sent to him for approval back in the fifties and, in two cases, still sealed.

During the visit we had spoken several times about the possibility of a new Mike Hammer book—it's been over a decade since the last one—and Mickey, despite occasional protestations and claims of indifference to Hammer and the writing game, seemed to be on the verge . . .

On Saturday, when he was driving me around in his Carolina Cadillac, Mickey said to me, "What do you mean, you want to be 'your generation's Mickey Spillane'?" I said, just that: my ambition was to be the mystery writer of my generation, as he was of his.

"You can't be your generation's Mickey Spillane," he said ingenuously, "I'm still here. *I'm* your generation's Mickey Spillane."

He had me there.

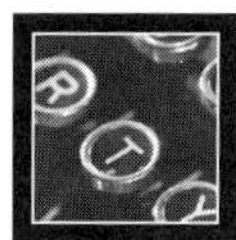

Série Noire

ETIENNE BORGERS

During the autumn of 1945, just after the end of World War II, the French publisher Gallimard launched a new collection of popular fiction. The idea was to translate the English and American novels of an emerging genre: the hard-boiled detective novel, popularized by such writers as Dashiell Hammett and Raymond Chandler. This genre—with its roots in the American pulps—was already thriving in the Anglo-Saxon countries, and Gallimard had already translated some notable hard-boiled American novels for its literary collections.

Gaston Gallimard gave editorial control of the new collection to Marcel Duhamel, a specialist in American literature as well as a skilled translator. Duhamel, a one-time member in good standing of the Paris Surrealist movement, was convinced that hard-boiled and even more pessimistic forms of crime fiction were the future of popular literature. For one thing, the Americans having just liberated France, Belgium, and other west European countries, things American had become much sought after, especially among European teenagers and young adults. For another, France had been deprived of any mystery or detective literature of Anglo-American origin since early 1940, due to the ban imposed by the German occupation on anything of British or American origin. This was applied to literature, films, music, and all other intellectual products. The hard-boiled and pessimistic mysteries were certainly selected by Duhamel because he valued them as literature, but it was also his intent to distinguish the new collection from a very famous French collection of mainly British and French novels—*Le Masque*. Published since 1927, *Le Masque* was devoted to the classic detective novel, typified by Agatha Christie, one of the most popular writers in the collection. *Le Masque* was a great success, with a rather sophisticated reputation for selecting good detective literature without vulgarity or cheap violence.

Gallimard would take a contrastingly revolutionary stand with the Série Noire: from now on, the police would be corrupt, heroes more brutal than the criminals, and private investigators would use and abuse all vices!

Words to that effect, a kind of manifesto and warning to the reader, were published on the jackets of the first volumes of the publisher's new collection.

Série Noire. "Black Series." This

evocative name was selected for the new collection by popular French poet Jacques Prévert. A play on the French expression *"une série noire"* used to describe a succession of bad events, the name was also reminiscent of *"littérature noire,"* the term for Gothic literature of English origin and its successors. With such a title the reading public would be duly warned that there would be no place for conventional mysteries in this new collection.

Wrapped in austere jackets—solid black background, no cover illustration, and perhaps only a tiny photo of some of the authors inside the jacket—the first volumes of the Série Noire arrived at French bookshops and magazine stands. The harsh, no-frills covers gave readers a clear indication of what type of literature they could expect from Série Noire.

The first two titles in the collection were by Peter Cheyney, a British writer who mimicked and exaggerated the American hard-boiled style. *La Môme Vert-de-Gris* (literally *The Oxidized Gal,* original English title: *Poison Ivy*) and *Cet Homme Est Dangereux (This Man Is Dangerous)* both featured Cheyney's FBI hero, Lemmy Caution. For a time, the average French reader was convinced that Cheyney was an American author, an impression reinforced by film adaptations with Lemmy played by an American actor living in France, Eddie Constantine. Fortunately, most of the early Série Noire releases were the work of the very best of the American hard-boiled and noir writers. Among the first thirty titles released, Cheyney appears seven times (due to the commercial success of the first two books), James Hadley Chase (another British author) five times, Raymond Chandler three times, and once apiece for Horace McCoy, Jonathan Latimer, Dashiell Hammett, James M. Cain, and W. R. Burnett. From 1948 onward, Série Noire would establish and maintain a tradition of selecting and publishing the best authors in the field, such as Jim Thompson (beginning with number 54 in 1950), Raoul Whitfield, William P. McGivern, Paul Cain, Dan Marlowe, Verne Chute, John D. MacDonald (number 97, 1951), Charles Williams (number 246, 1955), and Chester Himes (number 477, 1959), as well as purely commercial successes like Carter Brown (number 477, 1959), to name only a few from the extensive and impressive list.

Real mass success started during 1948, when each new title was assured a first printing of thirty thousand copies. There were then two new titles each month, a figure that would steadily grow to approximately one hundred new titles each year from 1966 to 1975. These figures were very impressive for the French publishing trade of the time. France had then a little over fifty-five million inhabitants and the French-speaking parts of Belgium, Switzerland, and Canada together added approximately ten million to the potential market.

The hard-boiled publications of Série Noire and its top authors soon became a center of interest for a new, emerging readership composed of university students, intellectuals, and modern literature buffs. These groups were variously attracted by the books' *"contestaire"* (antiauthoritarian) social content, the unblinking outlook on modern life (and death!) and its illnesses, and the distinctive literary qualities of the Noire authors. This new public, not afraid to claim real value for this form of popular literature, was added to the more traditional mass of readers more interested in action stories and light reading. Together, they gave Série Noire a special and unique readership. In the beginning, for most people, including Gallimard and Marcel Duhamel, Série Noire was intended as a new addition to the so-called *"littérature de gare"* (train-station literature). The expression had a negative implication and was used to describe novels that were badly written, outrageously appealing to the low instincts of readers—books to be read on a train ride and then forgotten. Duhamel's goals in this matter were, however, ambiguous. He knew that some of this hard-boiled literature was "real literature." On the other hand, he had to keep the books in the series accessible to its prime public, which barely ever entered a real bookshop, and had to keep giving his publisher high commercial returns. Looking back, we may say that he was highly successful in his editorial approach. He managed to keep the mass readers attracted to his *littérature de gare* marketing while bringing in the readers who could appreciate the novels of real value. This enlightened part of the readership would play an important role in the building up of the Série Noire's positive reputation, giving it the cult status it enjoyed by the end of the 1960s.

THE MAGIC OF THE "OLD BLACK LADY"

During the 1950s, nobody could suspect the place that Série Noire would eventually take in the history of French literature. In fact, with the intention of rivaling other low-quality pop-fiction lines, standards were low, with hacking and amputating of the original texts, as well as rewriting parts of the novels. It was the typical treatment given to popular literature of the lowest order. And yet, while Marcel Duhamel wanted to keep a mass public interested by trying to make all Série Noire novels fit a kind of mold, he was at the same time hunting for the best American authors, and using some first-class translators for selected novels, or appointing good writers such as the eclectic Boris Vian (poet, engineer, jazz musician, singer) to translate select books into French. The result of Duhamel's approach, at the least, was that even bad and mutilated translations were still efficient vehicles for the best hard-boiled and noir literature to reach a large audience. Eventually, the French public and the new generation of readers developed more discriminating tastes and began requiring better quality in the collection. Bad translations became less frequent and good authors received fair treatment. One of the best examples of this was Number 1,000 of the Série Noire, published in 1965: an emblematic novel from one of the new generation of American hard-boiled writers, *Pop. 1280* by Jim Thompson—one of the best novels of the time. Published as *1275 Emes* (1275 in this version not being a result of Duhamel's poor arithmetic but simply an adjustment because it was easier to pronounce in French), the novel was translated by Duhamel himself and for it he wrote a special introduction. A first-class treatment for a great author! Thompson's novel became an instant "*livre-culte*" in France.

Adding to the growing literary reputation of the collection from the sixties on was a surrealistic element imposed by Duhamel. Since the early days he had occasionally injected into the collection very interesting novels that were not of the genre promoted by Série Noire. They ranged from interesting and chilling psychological thrillers, preferably of the darkest noir imaginable, to Western stories, pure "black humor" stories, and other novels that were quite atypical of the series. One of the most famous of these was *London Express* by Loughran, a British writer. Two more "white sheep" were *Orgies Funeraires* (originally *The Coffin Things*) by Michael Avallone (number 1281) and *Donovan's Brain* by Curt Siodmak. This tradition of selecting atypical novels survives to the present day.

In the sixties and seventies, Duhamel and his collaborators maintained their flair for selecting the best American and British novels for Série Noire. This allowed the publishing of a new generation of first-class authors like Donald Westlake, Robin Cook (a k a

Derek Raymond), Joe Gores, Russel Greenan, Joseph Hansen, and many more.

When Marcel Duhamel died in 1977, the Série Noire catalog was the best anthology available for modern, nonclassic mystery novels. Robert Soulat, one of his assistants, would continue after him, maintaining the same editorial goals, until 1991, when a writer named Patrick Raynal was appointed the new director for the series in order to rejuvenate the Old Black Lady. The successors of Duhamel kept to his tradition of reaching for the best, adding to the existing hit list some of the top modern authors such as James Crumley, Loren D. Estelman, Timothy Harris, Walter Mosley, Donald Goines, and Marc Behm.

SÉRIE NOIRE IN A GALLIC TEMPO

Besides British and American authors, who were the prime targets of Marcel Duhamel, French writers also received attention in the collection. Through the years, French writers received increasing opportunities to have their work published in Série Noire, though translations from the Anglo-Americans did remain in the majority. Due to the strong association existing in the French reader's mind between hard-boiled and America, the earliest French authors in the series were obliged to publish under Anglo-Saxon aliases—in order to be credible! This trend went on until the mid-fifties.

The first Frenchman to join the ranks was "Terry Stewart" in 1948. Serge Arcouat, the real name of Terry Stewart, published *La Mort et l'Ange* (Death and the Angel) as number 18 in the collection. The novel took place in the States, to continue the deception that this was the work of an American writer.

More interesting was the contribution of Jean Amila (his first novel was signed with an Americanized John Amila.) The writer had already established a literary reputation when Duhamel asked him to write for the series. This excellent author gave very personal novels to Série Noire, books that contained a strong social consciousness and distinctly French content. Realistic and dealing with typical French problems, the world of Amila was essentially made of ordinary people rebelling against injustice and authority and facing tragic destinies.

The personal life of Amila, especially his youth, was certainly the basis for his vision of French society. Orphaned at an early age and placed into public institutions, he was the son of a French soldier who was executed by the French Army "as an example" after the 1917 pacifist rebellion of infantry troops during World War I (this historical horror was masterfully filmed by Stanley Kubrick as *Paths of Glory,* with a script by Jim Thompson). In *La Lune d'Omaha* (Omaha Moon), one of Amila's best noir novels, he used his repulsion for war to describe the story of an American soldier who deserts the army while the Allies are invading Normandy, and who, during a revisit to France after World War II, discovers that his name is in the American military cemetery there. Another typical and original work, Amila's *Jusqu'o plus Soif* (Ad Libitum), concerns a gang producing illegal liquor in Calvados (the French district of Normandy famous for its apple cider and very strong alcohol produced from fruits) and gives a ferocious description of the alcoholism raging in the French countryside (a real problem at the time).

Jean Amila was a very interesting author, producing well-constructed plots with provocative subject matter, from *Y'a pas de Bon Dieu!* (There Ain't any Good Lord), his first for Série Noire (number 53, 1950), to *Au Balcon d'Hiroshima* (From Hiroshima's Balcony), his last, published in 1985. He died in 1995.

A world apart was the work of Albert Simonin. His first novel in the collection, published in 1953, was *Touchez pas au Grisbi* (Don't Touch the Bread), which became an instant hit after receiving the Priz des Deux Magots literary prize. It was the only time that a noir or hard-boiled novel received an official literary prize in France. The first printing contained a preface by Pierre Mac Orlan, the famous populist literary writer. *Touchez* was innovative in its vivid use of authentic Parisian underworld slang. In a way, Simonin was continuing an old French literary tradition of the "*roman de mauvais garcon*" (local gangster stories featuring antiheroes who deliberately choose the underworld over normal society).

Strong plots, hard-hitting but controlled violence, well defined professional outlaws as the characters, and clear, direct writing were trademarks of the excellent novels produced by Simonin for Série Noire. His tough stories did not try to mimic the American books. His sombre underworld heroes and style of writing were distinctively French. Albert Simonin became one of the founders of the modern French hard-boiled novel, though his important impact is a little forgotten today in France. Not only an excellent writer, Simonin was also a very popular one until the end of the seventies. Of his seven novels published in Série Noire, the most successful was *Touchez pas au Grisbi,* which sold more than two hundred and fifty thousand copies, while the others sold within the eighty to one hundred thousand range.

Auguste Le Breton appeared in the collection for the first time in the same year as Simonin. The three novels he published in Série Noire are among the best he wrote in a long, varied career, with their realistic descriptions of the Mob and the French underworld, and a certain hard-hitting social content due to his own difficult youth. *Du Rififi chez les Hommes* (Clash among the Tough Guys), a tale of a falling out among thieves, issued in 1953, was totally written in French slang. American filmmaker-in-exile Jules Dassin adapted and directed it into a worldwide success under the same title.

At the end of the fifties, some of the best French hard-boiled and noir writers emerged. The top noir novel by Pierre Lesou was *Le Doulos* (The Finger Man) in 1957. The story about friendship, deadly mistakes, and lies, set in the French underworld, gave birth to one of the best French films noir, by Jean-Pierre Melville, one of the masters of modern French cinema.

Jose Giovanni, as a writer, was in tune with the same tradition revived by Albert Simonin. Giovanni himself had had a troubled past and served time in French jails. After his first writing, dealing with the inmates of a French prison, was published successfully by Gallimard, Marcel Duhamel recognized the potential of an emerging author and signed him with Série Noire. This move would give French hard-boiled literature one of its most creative authors. Giovanni's characters were memorable, his heroes most of the time on the wrong side of the law, trying to escape the repression of the police and a blind justice, to escape a world they didn't understand and in which they certainly didn't fit. Their destiny was inevitably tragic but they would always face it down without flinching. Giovanni created what is still among the most powerful characters in all French hard-boiled fiction. *Le Deuxième Souffle* (The Second Breath), his first book for Série Noire, masterfully adapted by Melville, is a remarkable work about the escape from prison and last score of an aging mobster. Other Giovanni works—*L'Excomunie, Classe tous Risques, Ho, Histoire de Fou*—remain among the best hard-boiled novels produced in French to this day. Later he abandoned the pure noir and hard-boiled crime novel to describe adventurers and offbeat characters in action novels that always maintained a tint of noir and expressed the same views about friendship, organized society, and the futility of achievement. Giovanni was attracted by the cinema from early on, and his first novels were all adapted to become successful films. He collaborated on scripts, from his novels and from those of other writers, and finally he became a director of a number of successful films. His films described adventures and crime plots similar to what could be found in his writings. Some of his films, like *Dernier Domicile Connu* and *Deux Hommes dan la Ville,* were well above average.

Interesting novels with a humorous tone were to be found in the series, as in the three books published by Pierre Paoli. One of these was *Les Pigeons de Naples,* from 1961, a ferociously funny book with a sinuous plot, Italian setting, and highly amusing secondary characters. An achievement! Another funny work was George Bardawill's one novel for Série Noire, *Aimez-vou les femmes?* (Do You Like Women?), also from 1961 and one of the most memorable books of the series. Bardawill mixed black humor, parodies of noir and hard-boiled writing, a pastiche of gore fiction and other nonsense in a first-class novel featuring a vegetarian author of fairy tales for young kids who lives a daytime nightmare. A classic.

After May 1968 and the student riots in the streets of Paris, culture and art were never the same in France. In the big changes that followed those events, a lot of new mystery and noir writers emerged with a distinct new vision of society, putting strong political and social content in their books. They were published in many collections, mostly by independent editors, but major publishing houses stepped in as well, seeing the changes occurring among young adults and the corresponding changes in their reading preferences. This was eventually known as the New-Polar movement, in opposition to the more tradition Polar (colloquial French for the mystery novel genre). An indirect result of all this was that in the seventies some of the best French contemporary authors appeared in Série Noire. At the same time, the collection maintained its success and sales by mixing these new writers with the more traditional authors in the catalog, French and foreign.

The top French author to come out of this decade was certainly Jean-Patrick Manchette. Writing in a very personal style, with interesting plots that often had political undertones, Manchette produced for Série Noire some unforgettable novels such a *L'affaire N'Gusto, Laissez Bronzer les Cadavres* (both 1971), *O Dingos, i chateaux!* (1972) and *Nada* (1973). He created a French private investigator, cynical and disenchanted, who appeared in two powerful stories strongly laced with black humor: *Morgue Pleine* and *Que d'Os!* (The Morgue is Full; So Many Bones!). He terminated his short career as a noir novelist in 1985, stopping dead after one last intriguing book, *La Position du Tireur couche* (The Position of the Lying-down Shooter), which described the trouble encountered by a hit man as he tries to stop his trade and return to his hometown. A novel about power and its corrupting influence, as well as about the loss of power, with a very elaborate construction of the chapters and events, it was Manchette's best book. Manchette continued to produce reviews of hard-boiled and noir novels, as well as very good and well-regarded essays about this type of literature, all published in specialized magazines. Jean-Patrick Manchette is definitely one of the great writers of French noir literature, with an unmistakable influence on many contemporary young authors. He died in 1995.

***

A.D.G.: three letters to designate one of the best French hard-boiled authors of the seventies. His first two novels in the collection described internal struggles between factions of the French underworld, partially based on actual events. He did not want to publish under his real name for fear of possible retaliation. Later, he produced some quite efficient novels full of direct action and evoking contemporary French reality. A.D.G. had a most evocative way of describing provincial towns, the countryside, the remote villages and their inhabitants. His very precise style, together with very well-constructed plots and provocative views of society and its disguised evils, made A.D.G. one of the most interesting French authors of the time.

La Nuit des Grands Chiens Malades is a real gem, mixing bravura, offbeat humor, and thrilling situations. Hippies installed in a small village are upsetting the locals, until a more serious problem arrives in the form of an organized gang. An unnatural alliance is formed between the citizens of the village and the hippies, resulting in delirious fun. Black humor could be found in *Cradoque's Band* (1972), an obvious salute to the great French writer Louis-Ferdinand Céline in its subject (lower-class life in horrible big-town suburbs) and the style of writing. Hard-boiled, cruel, with a touch of lyricism, *Pour Venger Pepare* (To Avenge Granddaddy) told of a merciless barrister tracking down some punks who had killed his grandfather during a holdup. With his right-wing anarchist view of modern society's problems, A.D.G. ensured that he would not receive his due as a first-class French author against the prevailing pressure of certain French literary bigots.

Equally individualistic was Jean Vautrin. From articles for the legendary magazine *Cahiers du Cinéma* to screenplays, documentaries, and feature film direction, the first part of his life was fully dedicated to the cinema, under his real name of Jean Herman. In the early seventies, at the age of forty, after losing confidence in the creativity left to authors of commercial films, and devoting time to the serious health problems of his son, he decided to dedicate himself only to writing. His first two novels were published in Série Noire under the name of Jean Vautrin. *A Bulletins Rouges* (With Red Bulletins), published in 1973, is set in a poor Parisian suburb of sterile high-rise housing blocks. In an atmosphere of fear, boredom, and criminality, a team of young workers serve as thugs for a local politician during an election campaign. A tale of dirty politics, murder, and tragedy. *Billy ze Kick* (1974) is a very original and personal novel by Vautrin, wherein a small girl of seven is living out one of the fairy tales her father has constructed for her. The book mixes realism and surrealism, and skillfully uses a blend of colloquial and slangy French.

With these and other noir novels, Vautrin quickly became one of the strong voices of the French Neo-Polar. He was known for his hyperactive characters and high-octane plots, telling his stories in a distinctive "nervous" style, through a rapid succession of events. In the background of many of his novels there are highly critical views of modern French society, which gives few chances to the weakest. A very active writer, Vautrin is one of the very few to have one foot in popular literature and the other in serious literature, receiving equal respect and popularity in both camps. In 1989 he received the Prix Goncourt, one of the most prestigious prizes for French literature, for a literary novel titled *Un Grand Pas vers le Bon Dieu* (A Giant Step Toward the Good Lord). His most recent novel, set in Mexico, *Le Roi des Ordures* (The King of Trash), revisits successfully the noir domain.

Another top noir writer who helped spark the Neo-Polar movement was Alex Varoux, creator in 1974 of two cop characters, Lou and Globue, totally offbeat heroes, real blunderers involved in funny plots. In other novels he featured kids and old folks.

The mid-eighties saw three newcomers with high talent joining Série Noire. First, Marc Villard, an accomplished author who gave some memorable novels to the collection. *Le Sentier de la Guerre* (Warpath)—1985—described a quest for identity with solutions found in the aftermath of World War II and its impact on the French generation of the time. *Le Roi, sa Femme, et la Prince* (The King, his Wife, and the Little Prince), published in 1987, its title from a French nursery rhyme, is a masterful novel mixing hard-boiled situations, dark lyricism, and black humor. In it, a young man searches for his father, an ex-rock 'n' roll star whom he finally helps to escape from a mental institution. Their escape and its tragic consequences make it one of the best novels published in the Série Noire during those years.

Also worth mentioning are two Villard novels featuring a police officer, with very realistic descriptions of Paris and excellent plots having losers as central characters: *La Dame Es une Trainée* (The Lady Is a Tramp) and *La Porte de Derriére* (The Back Door). Villard, through the years, proved to be a real master of the short-story form in addition to his writing of first-class novels.

The second author was Didier Daeninckx. Inventive plots taking place in small provincial towns gave the writer the opportunity to describe the economic crisis then hitting parts of France. Historical facts, authentic events, and political problems were skillfully mixed. He became one of the most popular Série Noire writers of the 1980s, with acclaimed novels such as *Meurtres pour Memoire* (Murders to Remember) in 1984, and *La Der des Ders* (That's Really the Last One). He wrote many novels for other houses in addition to the Série Noire and is considered one of the important newer authors of noir novels.

Third of the newcomers, but not the least, is Thierry Jonquet. He produced some of the real highlights of the Série Noire: *Mygale* (1984), *La Bate et la Belle* (The Beast and the Beauty, 1985), *Les Orpailleurs* (Golddiggers, 1993), and *Memoire en Cage* (Caged Memory)—stories of horror and vengeance, often told with a streak of black humor. In other novels, published elsewhere, he rendered French political situations with sardonic bite. Jonquet is certainly one of the most versatile and interesting contemporary French authors. *La Bate et la Belle* was selected by the publisher to become number 2,000 of the Série Noire collection. This was twice emblematic: as open confidence in the talent of Jonquet (for the historic occasion, only the best was to be selected) and as recognition of the wide acceptance of the modern French novel in the domain—the dark crime world of the Série Noire—that had once been reserved for American authors.

***

In 1995 Série Noire celebrated fifty years of existence. At this writing, the publication of number 2,500 is expected soon. Fifty years and three generations of French readers, emblematic appearances of Série Noire book covers in films of the French New Wave, numerous cinematic adaptations (more than six hundred) of Série Noire novels by international filmmakers, French TV adaptations, and countless essays and in-depth literary analysis of the best of the Série Noire authors—these are among the elements that have helped to raise this collection to mythic status.

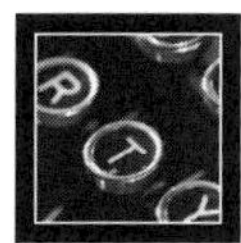

Lew Archer as Culture Maven

BURTON KENDLE

They watched with great dark eyes full of silent envy, as if Achilles was fighting Hector inside, or Jacob was wrestling with the angel.

—*The Way Some People Die,* 1951

Ross Macdonald's frequent classical and Biblical allusions come from the complex consciousness of private eye Lew Archer, the narrator and actual protagonist of eighteen novels and a handful of short stories published between 1949 and 1976*, or from the speeches of other characters who explain the enriching references to Archer *and* to the reader. The classical allusions ultimately stress the painful quest of a number of young men and some young women who emulate Oedipus or Telemachus, to discover their identities, a quest which often produces undesired answers. The biblical echoes underline a nostalgia for a lost Eden that was never really edenic, and the need to confront an inherited taint, amounting almost to original sin. The setting of a seedy boxing arena in *The Way Some People Die* seems to reduce the Trojan War and a spiritual struggle from the Bible to sordid popular entertainments and suggests both the deterioration of contemporary civilization from its heroic past and the possibility that the artists of the ancient world created myths to combat the corruption that has always been inherent in the human situation. But the modern world seems to have diminished even the capacity for tragedy that ancient drama once illuminated: "quite often nowadays the low-life subplots were taking over the tragedies" (*The Underground Man,* 1971). If actual ancient heroes were less heroic than their mythic versions and Eden was never as perfect as nostalgia demands, then man has always driven himself to create legends that soften such bedrock truths.

The Archer novels dramatize ingenious variations on these grim themes. The early *The Three Roads* (1948), which antedates the introduction of Archer, establishes many of Macdonald's key motifs. One stresses the often troubled but basically concerned and competent psychiatrists whose Freudian theories attempt, with some success, to explain the behavior of many characters. Another theme involves Macdonald's seeming obsession with the California coast as a false Eden:

> On an afternoon like this . . . it was hard to believe in sin and sadness and death. That cotton-batting surf didn't look much like cruel crawling foam.

> But, of course, it was and people suffered in California just as they did in other places—suffered a little more, perhaps, because they didn't get much sympathy from the weather.

The "cruel . . . foam" prefigures the many deaths by water in later books. The first Archer novel, the 1949 *The Moving Target,* begins the pattern: "The sea was cold and dangerous. It held dead men." And the implied unsympathetic sun shining on America's last paradise seems as pitiless as Camus's in *The Stranger.* Mother-son eroticism dominates *The Three Roads,* as it does in many later books. The protagonist suffers permanent blight because of his youthful introduction, immediately repressed, to his mother's sexuality. But mitigating the atmosphere of lethal sexuality that almost overwhelms the book is the nostalgia embodied in a recording of the "Pastoral" Symphony, whose "sweet rustic gaiety echoed forlornly" through an apartment building before "dying in the walled air." Both the creation of the music and the powerful response it evokes suggest something worth preserving in flawed humanity, however daunting the task.

The Oedipal theme survives intact even in Macdonald's last novel, *The Blue Hammer* (1976): "You were looking for a mother, not a wife," a final tribute to the aging boys who populate the books. *The Chill* (1964) reveals the most disturbing variation on this material, when Archer learns that a college dean (trouble in a recreated paradise) has passed his elderly and lethal wife off as his mother, with predictably horrific results. The significance of such a potentially overripe situation is less in the Oedipal echoes than in the skill with which it explodes the stereotype of the stern but principled dowager to reveal the tortured past of a disturbed woman. Both aspects of the character compel attention, as does the brilliant fusion of the two into a grotesque but still credible figure.

Writing at approximately the same time as John Cheever, who was creating his own flawed Edens, Macdonald frequently opens his books with images of California's beauty and implicit hope, which momentarily seduce even the worldly Archer, though he quickly undercuts his illusion: "you can imagine it's the promised land . . . Maybe it is for a few" (*The Wycherly Woman,* 1961). Sometimes a similar passage appears after the novel has already provided a context that belies or questions such edenic reveries: "I could smell the newmown hay, and had the feeling that I had dropped down into a pastoral scene where nothing much had changed in a hundred years" (*The Chill*). Elsewhere Macdonald alludes to the efforts of Marie Antoinette and her followers at Le Petit Trianon to recreate such a pastoral world and "play at being peasants" (*The Wycherly Woman*), an enduring but obviously doomed human aspiration. And the framed reproductions of Postimpressionist paintings in a faculty home offer yet another tempting illusion of Eden (*Black Money,* 1965).

A late novel like *Sleeping Beauty* (1973) presents a quasi-apocalyptical vision of a postedenic universe ("the end of the bloody world") devastated by oil spills, after hubris and greed and a predictably Daedalus-like inability to control his technology have pushed man beyond acceptable limits. *The Underground Man* focuses on the fires and mud slides resulting from a similar greed to develop land, an impulse partially stemming from a misguided attempt to return to nature and reestablish the bond that supposedly once linked man harmoniously with his environment.

Macdonald's atmosphere of despair goes beyond such ironic treatment of the nostalgic impulse to create a fictional world of beaten-down, middle-aged, and elderly characters whose liquor-tainted breath is an index to the pain of their existence (there are few abstainers in Macdonald's universe, including Archer). Such characters live either in mansions that signify old money and a futile attempt to continue moribund traditions that were corrupt at their source, or in "one-night cheap hotels," and seedy motels and apartment houses that reek of actual and figurative decay. Macdonald creates a large cast of rootless people who support themselves as the managers of these establishments and who infuse their pathetic stories into the mood, and often into the plot. Encounters with these people and other minor characters are like episodes in a fevered dream that fuses apparent accidents and coincidences into a relentless pattern of engulfing past and present sins. At times Archer seems a modern Dante, to whom he occasionally alludes, confronting embodiments of his own sins and weaknesses.

The books focus on young people, almost doomed by the past actions of parents and grandparents, desperately attempting to flee this blighted inheritance by solving the riddle of their identity. The young male in *The Instant Enemy* (1968) speaks for them all: "but I have to know who I am." The most extreme example of the tangled heritage of the past occurs in the same book when a woman reminds the confused Archer and the reader that the novel's troubled young questor for identity is the grandson, not the son, of another character ("she corrected me soberly"). The blight traps people into a nightmare of repeated mistakes and crimes that makes it, ironically, impossible to distinguish one generation from another.

Macdonald develops ingenious variations on this search for identity, from the young man in *The Galton Case* (1959), who learns that he really is the heir he thought he was impersonating (a discovery less happy than it sounds) to the girl in *The Wycherly Woman,* who eats compulsively to identify with her murdered overweight mother while she tries to protect her supposed father. Occasionally, Archer questions people's ability to absorb the truth: "I wished the boy a benign failure of memory" (*The Underground Man*). Thus, in *The Wycherly Woman,* Archer permits the real murderer, the girl's actual father, to hide the painful truth of her identity from her (the murderer briefly feels "back in Eden with the dew on the grass" when Archer allows him to kill himself). This novel typically creates the fevered atmosphere, if not the details, of both Greek legend and Jacobean drama. As he does in the surprising climax to *The Three Roads,* when the heroine protects the guilty male protagonist from the authorities, Macdonald allows Archer to develop a justice of his own that sacrifices legal criteria to deeper moral and psychological needs.

Competing with *The Wycherly Woman* for the most bizarre, yet touching variation on the theme of tainted parental legacy is *The Zebra-Striped Hearse* (1962), in which the murderer, a blighted young woman who has inherited her father's facial features, acceptable in a male, but ugly in a female, an appearance that makes her doubt his capacity to love her, commits a murder while wearing his coat, in a desperate, unconscious attempt to identify with him. The father is, predictably, guilty of more than bequeathing bad genes to her: "He got her so confused that she didn't know whether she was a girl or a boy, or if he was her father or her lover." Macdonald's father-seeking young men and women generally hover uneasily on the verge of adulthood as Archer watches anxiously, encouraging them to take the crucial steps: "his voice was low and I thought I heard the growl of manhood in it." Similarly, a girl must avoid becoming "a frozen woman, a daddy's girl" (*The Underground Man*).

Macdonald most powerfully fuses the image of a lost Eden with the quest for the father in *The Chill* (1963), which characteristically stresses the illusory magic of the California coast, though the familiar signs of sordid transience, the "service stations and . . . drive-ins offering hamburgers and tacos," gradually alter Archer's view, as does the inherited corruption of the past, which, perhaps permanently, dooms the sanity of a young girl he is trying to save. (The novels make no easy promises.)

The omnipresent fog, inevitable in a mountainous seaside area, not only can cause fatal pileups on the roads along which the characters, including Archer, dangerously, even suicidally, speed, but also suggests the shifting and precarious unknowability of the geographical and spiritual arena of the novel. Analogously, throughout his books, Macdonald's microcosmic imagery stresses the vastness of the moral and psychological worlds that are unfortunately dependent on man's frail body. As a suicidal girl hangs from the railing of a bridge, she looks "down over her shoulder into the depth of my lying and the terrible depth of her rage" (*The Underground Man*). With altered emphasis Macdonald endows natural forces with human attributes to suggest the lost harmony that once obtained between man and his world, at least in his imagination: "the sea was coughing in its sleep" (*The Blue Hammer*).

In *The Chill,* Macdonald's allusions to Zeno's view of the impossibility of traversing space, of arriving at a destination, perhaps of achieving in the context of the novel any final truth or justice show how his learning enriches the moral complexity of the narrative. Macdonald wittily leaves unresolved the analysis of Zeno that Archer overhears in a college hallway, so that the reader must speculate on whether Archer and the novel ever reach their intended goals of moral illumination. The college settings of a number of novels like *The Chill* play with the illusion, shared briefly by Archer, that retaining the best that was thought and said in the past will nurture those who commit themselves to an academic life ("the walls of books around me, dense with the past, formed a kind of insulation against the present world and its disasters. I hated to get up") and those who believe their educations will guide them once they leave these protecting walls. Besides its half-satiric, half-affectionate discussions of Zeno, *The Chill* dramatizes the impossibility of escape from the horrors of modernity and from the tormented individual pasts of the would-be escapees.

But *Black Money* (1965) offers the most devastating, yet most compassionate picture of academia. A new campus, built in "what had recently been the countryside," has uprooted the former orange groves, a sign of man's obsessive manipulation of his environment, and replaced them with trees that were "planted full grown," to create an alternative nature. A French professor, whose lust for a student precipitates the novel's disasters, is the definer and promulgator of a belief in "the luminous city . . . the world of spirit and intellect . . . the distillation of the great minds of past and present" from Plato through Augustine to "Joyce's epiphanies." The professor is the target of Macdonald's satire as much for his grandiloquence as for his lust (Archer, after all, experiences some of the same stirrings). And yet, however much the professor may pervert his learning to serve his desires, Archer senses the man's real, if sometimes unconscious, attempt to understand himself. The professor's frustrated wife, a former student and past victim of his seductive learning, is attracted to Archer, who is in turn attracted both to her and to the professor's current conquest. These sexual tensions create the strongest identification between Archer and a character, in this case a murderer, in any of the novels, though Archer manfully refrains from sexual involvement with both women. The vision of the luminous city is not only inadequate for survival in the real world but lethally dangerous: the novel's young male questor who commits himself to the vision follows a path of crime and self-destruction, and the women are permanently damaged. Yet *Black Money* reveals the power underlying the grandiloquence and presents an image of an outside world so grim that characters understandably seek a visionary alternative.

Archer, who makes many literary allusions and overhears many more, is himself the focus of an elaborate series of references. Though his name may suggest Sam Spade's inept partner, it also provokes a character in *Sleeping Beauty* to ask, "Where's your bow and arrow, Archer?" The Apollo the question ironically evokes played a variety of godlike roles, foreseeing the future, punishing evil-doers with plagues, and bringing back sunshine in the spring; such a combination of insight, retribution, and illumination suggests an exalted, perhaps satiric view of Archer's qualities as a detective. He himself is seemingly self-deprecating about his supposed lack of learning: in the short story "Gone Girl," he says, "If I had a classical education, I'd call her Junoesque," while in *Black Money* he claims he doesn't know the language as he teases the reader about the meaning of a Latin quotation. Many of the other characters and Archer himself struggle to define his role as detective and his professional ethics (in *Black Money* he calls himself a "semi-professional" man who's "working at not being a do-badder"). Possibly the most negative assessment comes from a character in *The Underground Man* who calls him an "auditeur," which by analogy with "voyeur" makes his calling sound perverted. His catalogue of a detective's qualities includes "honesty, imagination, curiosity, a love of people" (*The Zebra-Striped Hearse*), which counterbalances some less flattering self-assessments. What is crucial is not the components of the definition, but the constant impulse toward self-evaluation as both an individual practitioner and a member of a mysterious profession.

Though a number of critics and Macdonald himself have interpreted Archer as primarily a narrative device to give the reader some distance from the nightmarish world of the novels, Archer's rich consciousness is the real focus of the books. Superior to medieval monks who needed an actual memento mori to remind themselves of mortality and the ultimate issues, Archer automatically, and graphically, recognizes the skull beneath the skin of the people he encounters. A first-rate collector of facts and a shrewd rationalist, he nevertheless acknowledges frequent gestalts, which demonstrate the power of the unconscious hints and forces within himself. He responds to all sorts of signals and invitations from the breasts of a varied array of females: in the short story "Midnight Blue" he rather bizarrely perceives that "the tips of her breasts pointed at him through her blouse like accusing fingers." Sensitive to the way women touch themselves at emotionally charged moments, stereotypical in his belief in the relation of breast size to femininity, he is a close rival to Saul Bellow in his catalogue of female odors, usually pleasant ones. As excessive and even as offensive as some of this may be, it adds interest and complexity to Archer's consciousness. Though Archer defines himself as a Natty Bumpo, "a great tracker" (*The Zebra-Striped Hearse*), he seems less interested in trapping than in understanding his quarry. His constant speculations, sometimes self-contradictory within a single book, on coincidence, fate, and the causes of crime reveal the depth of his intelligence, whatever its source in experience or book learning. His frequent awakening by early morning birds attests to a harmony with the natural cycle that almost balances the horrors he witnesses. Few possessors of a University of Michigan Ph.D. in literature (earned in 1951) have demonstrated their learning as artfully as Macdonald.

* Kenneth Millar, the real man behind the pseudonyms, published most of the Archer novels as Ross Macdonald, one as John Macdonald, and four as John Ross Macdonald, but since the differing "authorships" don't affect the substance of the books, it is convenient in this discussion to attribute all of them to Ross Macdonald.

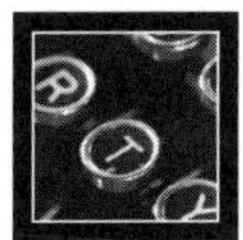

Fifteen Impressions of Charles Williams

ED GORMAN

1

"He was a hard luck kind of guy. He was much better than many writers who really made it. Not that he'd ever tell you, of course. He was genuinely modest, maybe even a little down on what he wrote. You could never be sure if he thought what he did was quite respectable. He was, after all, writing paperback originals and this was still the 1950s."

This is his agent, Don Congdon, talking on a late New York afternoon when autumn is giving bitter birth to winter.

2

> When she was through being sick, I wet a wash cloth at the basin and bathed her face while she leaned weakly against the bathroom wall with her eyes closed. She didn't open them until she was back on the bed. She took one long look at me and said, "Oh, good God!" and closed them again. She made a feeble attempt to pull her skirt down. I straightened it for her, and she lay still. I went out in the living room and lighted a cigarette. I could handle her all right, but if the police came by again and noticed those garage doors were unlocked, I was dead. It would be at least three more hours before it was dark.

This is from *Man on the Run*, November 1958, and in many respects the seminal Gold Medal Original, involving as it does, a) a falsely accused man trying to elude police, b) a lonely woman as desperate in her way as the man on the run, c) enough atmospherics (night, rain, fog) to enshroud a hundred films noir. In its simple, yearning, painful way, it is one of the best thrillers of its era. It has now been out of print for thirty years.

3

According to *Twentieth Century Crime and Mystery Writers* (second edition), Charles Williams was born in San Angelo, Texas, on August 13, 1909, was educated at Brownsville High School, Texas (only through the tenth grade), served with the United States Merchant Marine, married Lasca Foster in 1939, had one daughter, and died in 1975.

What it doesn't tell us is how he died. On that same late New York afternoon, his agent, Congdon, described the details, and it's now a month and a half later and I can't forget those details. Not at all.

4

In an exceptional essay on Williams, critic Geoffrey O'Brien noted: "Charles Williams is at face value the epitome of a macho adventure writer. his heroes are characteristically pre-occupied with hunting (*Hill Girl*), fishing (*River Girl; Go Home, Stranger; Girl Out Back*), athletics (*The Big Bite; A Touch of Death*), and, above all, sailing (*Scorpion Reef; The Sailcloth Shroud; Dead Calm*)."

Then O'Brien neatly goes on to point out that while the trappings of the book may seem standard blue collar—especially the early "hill" books-their real theme is "the hero's discovery that he knows nothing about women."

It is Williams's women we remember most, from the innocent girl in *Hell Hath No Fury* to the sullen and deadly Cathy Dunbar in *Nothing in Her Way* and the enigmatic Mrs. Langston in *Talk of the Town*.

No other power—not in Williams's world anyway—can match women's to redeem or destroy.

5

"It's actually kind of a funny story, how I met Charlie. In those days—this is back in the late forties—I was an editor at Simon & Schuster and his first novel came in over the transom; the writing was exceptionally good for a new writer but the plot was deemed by me and several others to be too commercial for hardcovers of that day, so the manuscript was returned to Charlie.

"Later, I left Simon & Schuster and joined the Harold Matson Company as an agent. I wrote a few writers whose work I had seen at Simon & Schuster to see if they would let me handle their work. Charlie sent me the same novel and I offered it to some other hardcover publishers, and it was turned down.

"Charlie suggested I throw it away, but I didn't. I put the manuscript on the shelf and a year or so later when Fawcett started their line of paperback originals, which they called Gold Medals, I remembered Charlie's work, sent it over to them, and they bought it immediately. I had difficulty reaching Charlie to give him the good news, but finally did. The novel, which was entitled *Hill Girl*, went on to sell two and a half million copies."

6

The French, more than any other people, love the suspense story. Gallimard, in its famous mystery-suspense series Série Noire, has kept most of Charlie's novels in print for many years. People such as Truffaut were interested in his novels and Jeanne Moreau and Belmondo starred in *Nothing in Her Way*, the first novel to be filmed.

"Hollywood was never as interested," says Congdon, "and the early paperback novels usually elicited contempt from most of the people out there, who thought they were 'pulp.'

"However, one of his novels, *The Wrong Venus*, did sell to Universal and Charlie was hired to write the screenplay. He was disgusted with that experience because the screenplay was pretty much rewritten for James Garner. He worked on a second screenplay of someone else's work, but it also turned out to be a poor film."

7

Not that during this period—1957–1958—the book career is moving along so marvelously either.

For some reason, the whole original paperback response to the suspense novel began to subside, and Charlie's audience shrank along with it. Sales simply weren't as big as they had been, with the exception of those writers who decided to do their suspense mysteries around a single detective or lead character, as John D. MacDonald did. Charlie was asked to do this, but he said it would bore him silly writing about the same guy each time.

Congdon and Williams went to Dell and Knox Burger with idea that Charlie's work ought to be in hardcover. Knox was willing to go along with a first hardcover printing if they could find a publisher and work out the appropriate arrangements. This was done with several of his novels, the first, *Scorpion Reef,* being at Macmillan.

They even talked to him about writing a series. Williams felt about series fiction much as he did about Hollywood.

Italy, Spain, and France—there Charlie is hot hot hot.

In the States, to Congdon, he says: "Sometimes I wouldn't mind giving it all up and just being a beach bum."

8

Charles Williams wrote in a definitive way about used car lots, drive-up restaurants, motels, gun shops, loafing, sex with women you don't trust, inhaling cigarettes on chilly mornings, people who just look stupid, loneliness, inadequacy, fear, acceptance, and dread.

He wrote a great deal about dread.

9

So Orson Welles, through this lawyer he had, buys this book of Charlie's and says he's going to make it into a film. Now Charlie had had several films made, but the idea was that Welles's standing and taste would be sufficient to expect that the film would be good. High hopes. Well, it did get made, but not all of it.

Jeanne Moreau, who was in the film, she said she'd seen early rushes and thought the film was a good one, but that Orson still wanted to tinker with it. And you heard on the talk shows from time to time about how more parts of it are getting made and soon now it will be done. But it was never released.

10

You see why I wake up this way? It's a dream I have.

I'm sitting there in the car watching her come out of that last bank and swing toward me across the sidewalk in the sun with the coppery hair shining and that tantalizing smile of Suzie's on her face and all that unhampered Suzie running loose inside that summer dress, seeing her and thinking that in only a few minutes we'll be in the apartment with the blinds drawn, in the semigloom, with a small overnight bag open on the floor beside the bed with $120,000 in fat bundles of currency inside it and maybe one nylon stocking, a sheer nylon, dropped by someone who didn't care where it fell . . .

And then in this dream she waves three fingers of her left hand and saunters on down the street, past me, and she's gone, and I'm trapped in a car in traffic at high noon in the middle of a city of 400,000, where two hundred cops are just waiting for me to step out on the street so they can spot me. I wake up.

Scream?
Who wouldn't

–*A Touch of Death*

11

In the early 1970s, his wife died of cancer. Charles Williams bought some land up on the border between California and Oregon and went there to live in a trailer. Alone.

"He'd call and he'd sound depressed," Congdon says, "and I'd say,

'Charlie, you sound really depressed, why don't you get out of there?'

"It rained all that winter and he didn't write much, couldn't get a new book going. Charlie felt that once decent weather came along, living close to the river where he could fish, that things would work out. But there were complications about building a house, so he sold the property and moved down to Los Angeles."

12

"Charlie worked on some screenplay with Nona Tyson, a friend, who was Steven Spielberg's assistant and secretary. Her support seemed to help Charlie start working again. He finished *Man on a Leash* and things looked as if they were going to be fine after all."

13

Charlie had one child, a daughter named Alison, and Williams was proud of her because she was especially bright.

14

"It was very strange," Congdon says. "So cold and purposeful. One morning I'm sitting in my office and I get a letter from Charlie and it says that by the time I read this, he'll have killed himself, which is exactly what he did.

"I couldn't tell you why, not for sure, and I would rather not speculate on it.

"Charlie was a smooth and polished writer, and he worked so hard on his books. He deserved more attention to his work in the United States, particularly in the film studios. He had the misfortune of writing suspense novels at a time when the public didn't seem to have as much interest in the genre."

15

Charles Williams wrote in a definitive way about pretty women, the way dust motes tumble in the sunlight, how pink a kitten's tongue is, how booze tastes when you're angry, how booze tastes when you're sad, and how booze tastes when you're alone in the woods and not thinking of anything special at all.

But mostly, Charles Williams wrote in a definitive way about all of us—brothers and sisters, fathers and sons, mothers and daughters, people unremarkable in any overt way, just fearful people finally, floating on daydreams and obstinate hope before the final darkness.

CHECKLIST: CHARLES WILLIAMS

The Big Bite . . . .(Dell, 1956)

Dead Calm . . . .(Viking, 1963) (hardcover)

Girl Out Back . . . .(Dell, 1958)

Go Home, Stranger . . . . .(Gold Medal, 1954)

Hell Hath No Fury . . . . .(Gold Medal, 1951)

Hill Girl . . . .(Gold Medal, 1951)

Man on a Leash . . . .(Putnam, 1973) (hardcover)

Man on the Run . . . .(Gold Medal, 1958)

Nothing in Her Way . . . .(Gold Medal, 1953)

River Girl . . . .(Gold Medal, 1951)

The Sailcloth Shroud . . . .(Viking, 1960) (hardcover)

Scorpion Reef . . . .(Macmillan, 1955) (hardcover)

Talk of the Town . . . .(Dell, 1958)

A Touch of Death . . . . . .(Gold Medal, 1954)

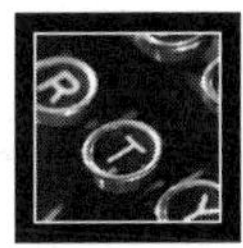

A Too Brief Conversation with Peter Rabe

GEORGE TUTTLE

I first contacted Peter Rabe in the fall of 1989. In that letter, I told him about how I'd admired his fiction and asked if he'd be willing to let me interview him for *Paperback Parade.* He wrote back, agreeing to the interview, and said he was very flattered. We set up a time, and I called. We talked for about fifty minutes.

The hardest part of preparing an interview for publication is typing up the transcripts. In this case, it took me almost three months. I would have finished sooner, but another project, work, and the holidays delayed its completion. But in January 1990, I had finished, and I sent the transcripts to Peter so that he could proofread and make changes. I also included some additional questions.

Because I didn't hear from Peter, I wrote him later that year, in May, and soon after, I received a letter from his companion of many years, Chris Nielsen. In the letter, Chris informed me that Peter had died on May 20 of lung cancer. The lung cancer was diagnosed in February.

I didn't know until Chris's letter that Peter had been ill. I couldn't help but think about all the questions I could have asked during that interview, but didn't.

The chance to talk to Peter was truly an honor. He was one of the most gifted writers of paperback originals, writing some of the best crime fiction to come out of the 1950s. Reviewers compared him to Hammett, and today's critics still discuss him as one of the greatest practitioners of the "roman noir." Recently, author Ed Gorman wrote, "Along with John D. MacDonald and Charles Williams, [Rabe] was one of Gold Medal's Holy Trinity. When he was rolling, crime fiction just didn't get much better."

I'll never forget our conversation. I wish it had been longer.

How did you get into the writing business?

By liking to write. I'd been writing for some time before I was published. It was an activity that I enjoyed.

***Gold Medal published your first three novels in rapid fashion, releasing them in successive months. Tell me about your beginnings at Gold Medal and the publication of* Stop This Man!, Benny Muscles In, *and* A Shroud for Jesso.**

There came a point in my writing when I decided I wanted to write for a particular market, the paperback market. I was living in Maine at the time and was doing a lot of winter reading of paperbacks. I felt that some were more boring than need be, and having the time and inclination, I started to write for publication in this market. The first one was what they eventually called *Stop This Man!* I had a former friend from college who had become an agent. So I sent the manuscript, and he sent it to Gold Medal, and Gold Medal bought it.

Actually the odd thing is that I had written and published something (*From Here to Maternity*) just before that novel, which had nothing to do with the paperback market or thrillers. So I enjoyed a two-punch turnover. First, with that first book, which was a book of humor with drawings, and then, in a very short period of time, a matter of six months, I sold this totally different thing, a crime novel. But that's how it started.

Then, liking the crime genre, I wrote several more. The next two . . . what were they called . . . ? You see, none of the titles were mine. Because of that, I have difficulty associating them with the titles given to them by the publisher.

***Yes, well, there was* Benny Muscles In . . .**

Benny Muscles In, for God sake, what a title [laughter], and then *A Shroud for Jesso.* Those were the next two.

Were they written in that order?

Yes, they were written in that order. Everything was written in the order that it was published.

Which writers influenced your crime fiction and your writing style?

No crime writers influenced my style. The writers that were meaningful to me came from a different area. For a while, I was very much taken with Hemingway. I always liked Faulkner, and there were European writers that I liked.

In other words, you were more influenced by mainstream writing rather than crime-fiction writing?

In crime fiction, I can't think of a particular author who influenced me. Maybe Dashiell Hammett, though I didn't consciously use him as a guide, and maybe some of the things [Erle Stanley] Gardner had written. I liked his illustrative kind of prose, which is just short of being overdone. So speaking of the crime scene, those two, who are very standard features in their field, they happen to impress me.

Gold Medal's editor Richard Carroll was very proud of you. It was self-evident that he thought of you as one of his biggest discoveries.

Yes, he was quite enchanted. That's true, and he had hoped, before he died, that I would do much better than I did.

What kind of man was he?

He was an old-time buccaneer type, an adventurous sort of person who'd like to recall stories of the war, in which he participated, and about fighting and drinking bouts in Hollywood when he wrote there. For example, he was very fond of telling the story of having written the movie *The Ape*, that starred Boris Karloff. Carroll wrote the script on a bet on a Saturday and a Sunday [laughter]. He liked telling stories like that.

What kind of an editor was he?

He was a very incisive and swift person, but he was open to dialogue. There was nothing particularly dictatorial about him. He was very explicit about what he liked and what he didn't like, so I liked working with him. He didn't give any guidance, as far as that goes, except for making very clear what his tastes were.

Did he ever give you much trouble in wanting rewrites or demanding changes?

No, not in the sense of giving me trouble. When he asked for rewrites, it was in very clear-cut terms: "Here's how it falls apart; here's where you left something undeveloped." It was that kind of an editorial relationship that he established with his writers, myself included. So there wasn't any trouble, and of his acceptance of manuscripts, there were no delays. On one of the better things I wrote, it took him three days to say yes.

Which book was that?

It's the one where the main character's name is Fell . . . I'll think of the title in just a minute. Oh, yes, I remember, *Kill the Boss Goodbye.*

As you said previously, Gold Medal retitled your novels. Do you remember any of your original titles before they were changed?

Well, I stopped trying to give them titles very quickly. I had titles such as . . . well, *Stop This Man!* I called *The Ticker.* The reason for that was eliminated by a rewrite, but that was the original title. Another one, *Benny Muscles In,* was originally called *The Hook.*

I went for brief titles. One they retained was also very brief, *The Box. A House in Naples* was my own title. The others, many of them, I didn't even bother giving them titles.

Gold Medal figured that the only advertising medium was the cover. So they retained contractually the right to do whatever they wanted with the cover, which included the title. On that basis and in view of the kind of titles they picked, I never gave a title after a while. I just identified them by a working title, which was usually the name of the main character.

Besides Richard Carroll, were there any other editors at Gold Medal that you worked closely with?

Yes, Knox Burger. He came after Carroll. We didn't have a close relationship. It wasn't even a good one, partly because of the deterioration of my work. He was fairly derogatory in his reactions, not in a mean sense, but in a very negative sense, just the same. He would, in contrast to Carroll, say, "I don't like this," just to paraphrase, and that would be it. He wouldn't say anything else. Unlike Knox Burger, Carroll would have then added what he did like or what was wrong. So my relationship with Knox Burger, as a writer relating to his editor, was a much more distant one, though I have been in touch with him on occasion on a personal basis and liked him quite well and like talking to him.

On a personal basis?

Yes, I found him a sensitive man and a charming person, not raucous like Carroll was. Carroll's hero would have been somebody like Errol Flynn, whereas Knox Burger was a much more thoughtful person.

A House in Naples *is one of your best books. How did you decide to write a book about the Italian black market?*

I don't know how that came about actually, because the way a book starts for me is with the fascination of [a] particular mood, the fascination with the particular situation a person finds himself in, or the curiosity about how a man handles a situation of a particular sort. Then in order to make that concrete and to give it a situational and personal garb, I will pick up on anything that happens to be along.

As far as the Italian setting is concerned, I had at the time poignant memories of when I had lived there. I simply used that because it was something that warmed me, but that is not how the book originated. Had I, at the time, been thinking about Maine, I might have put the whole situation in Maine.

In 1956, you wrote the first of five Daniel Port novels. One unique as-

pect of these books is that they don't read like the typical series. The books have a nonseries feel to them. When you created Port, were you intending to create a series character?

I intended to write a series, but I didn't intend to write Daniel Port as a series. I picked up on that being "the series," simply because it came along at that time. In other words, it was an arbitrary decision—it didn't grow out of my considerations of the character or of the themes I was pursuing then. It wasn't conceived of as a series. I simply decided at one point that I'd use this as a series character.

In* It's My Funeral, *Port goes to Hollywood. It's a very entertaining book, filled with fine touches of humor. Was it as fun a book to write as it is to read?

I found that book oddly difficult, but that had nothing to do with the book. Instead, it had to do with the fact that I was physically not well at the time. So I couldn't give you a good answer. It would be entirely contaminated by the physical circumstance I found myself [in]. I had the fascination for the theme. A fleeting one, it wasn't a particularly deep one. But I was so preoccupied with my own difficulties at the time that I can't really give you a great answer to the question you asked.

The Port novel I liked much better was the one that moves him to Mexico. I don't know the title. *The Chinese Millions,* I called it or something like that.

That would have been* Time Enough to Die, *the last book in the series and a favorite of mine. It seemed fitting that Port would end up in Mexico, so far away from his organized-crime roots.

Yes, if I would have continued the series, it would have been a turning point for him, far from his roots on one hand and with a new beginning on the other. But I didn't continue.

In 1958, you published your first non-Gold Medal thriller,* The Cut of the Whip, *for Ace. How did this come about?

It was rejected by Gold Medal. I think it was Knox Burger. It wasn't that bad of a book that they should have rejected it.

Some of the rejections I suffered were very much a function of neglect in writing. I, by temperament, write very fast, which made it very easy to jump the line and get very sloppy. Plus, I never read, again, what I have written, in many instances, and from a professional point of view, that is unforgivable.

Do you think if Carroll had lived longer you would have stayed in the writing profession?

I feel very sure that I would have become a better writer, a more consequential storyteller, and may well have stayed in longer. The reason I stopped was because of a combination of things. One thing was that I became very ill at the time with no prospect of recovery, which turned out to be wrong, but what that set up was some very deep disturbances. Out of those disturbances emerged a man who no longer felt like writing that sort of thing. Not to mention, at that particular time, the market changed radically, that was the end of the fifties and the beginning of the sixties, and from my point of view, it changed in such an arbitrary way that I simply couldn't adjust myself to the change.

***Just before that time, you sold your one and only hardcover thriller,* Anatomy of a Killer.**

That was rejected by Gold Medal and Abelard Schuman got the book after Gold Medal rejected it.

And then two years later, a paperback firm called Universal published* His Neighbor's Wife. *Was that too rejected by Gold Medal?

Oh, no, that I never submitted to Gold Medal. I wrote that as an absolute quickie, a quickie with pornographic overtones. This was when I was very short of money and simply had to knock something out.

Have you ever written under a pen name?

Yes, I have.

Is it anything that you'd like to mention?

No, absolute crap. It falls in the period that we've been discussing, the early sixties when I was quite incapacitated, very much in need of money, and needing it quickly. So then everything just deteriorated as far as the craft was concerned. I simply made an attempt to meet the demands of a quick market.

Soon after that, you took a break from writing and then you created your second series character, Manny DeWitte. Why did you venture into spy fiction?

I just thought it was fun. I think it was sort of a curiosity to deal with. I have no particular feeling for spy fiction, like a man like Le Carré who deals with the subject in considerable depth, or Deighton. I very much like his work. I just picked it as another area in which to frolic.

Kind of a lark. That's what the stories were like—light, entertaining, and not too serious.

Yes, but what really makes them fall short from my point of view is that they are sort of arched and I don't really care for that kind of story.

Arched?

Prettified, a very self-conscious humor.

Moving on to the final stage in your writing career, you returned to organized crime as a topic, and from this, two books came out,* War of the Dons *and* Black Mafia. *How did these two books come about?

I made an attempt to recapture a certain momentum that used to carry me in the past. My preoccupation with gangland settings was because they were rather meaningful to me in the past. I simply went back to them with the feeling that that would be easier than attempting something else. Most settings are simply designed by the writer, to sharpen, to accentuate, and, in some instances, to exaggerate the confrontive feelings and problems which we go through under even the mild crisis which most of us experience. This is why they were chosen, and also the gangland settings provide more leeway because there are less legal and psychological restrictions on the characters' actions. Because of this, they were not only inviting, but easier to write than, let's say, a good psychological novel which has to be much more tenuous in its treatment of things. So, at any rate, I went back to it mainly for reasons of familiarity.

Also, in the case of *War of the Dons,* I picked the setting because I was fascinated by a particular gangland family in New York, which in the book I called the Gallo brothers. And in the case of *Black Mafia,* the setting was chosen because blacks as a theme in this adventure-type fiction were very much in the foreground. Roundtree was doing the *Shaft* movies, for example. So it was entirely opportunistic. Any real interest in a black confronting our culture and then taking the violent recourse of entering organized crime was only secondary as a motivation, unfortunately.

Do you find antiheroes much easier to write than heroes?

Yes, very much so. The hero or the way I conceive the hero is very much a stereotype. Because of this, I find it a technical difficulty to write about the winner, the hero. I simply can't get in touch with the human being who is being that way.

When my focus is the antihero, I find I have much more of a feel, an intro in the reality of that kind of person's world or life. Even in the simplified and exaggerated version that they sometimes take in the kind of fiction we are talking about. So it is literally an inability to conceive of or to experience the hero type which has kept me from addressing myself to him in the fiction I have written. Whereas the antihero is much more a psychological reality for me. This determines its use and not any particular philosophical or moral theme.

Has your work in psychology influenced your fiction?

No, not in the least. But I think the kind of interest and focus that got me into psychology is the same one that got me into writing the way I wrote. I don't think that they are casually related, that one produced the other. They both come from the same kind of orientation and interest.

Looking back on your career, of all the books you have written, which is your favorite?

I don't know. I tend to be critical of myself in regards to things that I wrote in such haste, that I loathe to say, "This is best," since I see so many things I wish I had done differently. I think the Fell book, *Kill the Boss Goodbye,* is certainly one of my favorites and the one that came out in hardcover, *Anatomy of a Killer,* was another, and another one I also liked was *The Box.* So I'd say those three were the ones I liked best.

What about in terms of the covers? Were there any you fancied?

No, I don't even want to think about that. Of course, the covers went together with the titles. As I said, they had a contractual right to do what they wanted.

By the way, you asked about editors and I just want to mention an editor who was really working very closely with me, was very good to me, and helped me develop my craft as a fellow who I only remember by his first name, Hal. I think he was probably one of the best young editors in New York at that time.

When was that?

When I first started, around 1954.

How does it feel to be back in print again with Black Lizard Books?

I find it flattering. It's nice to be remembered through those republications. Frankly, I would have never expected them to be reprinted because I don't feel quite as convinced about them as the publisher is.

Well, you can't be objective about your own work.

If I can't be objective about my own work, it would be nice if my lack of objectivity went in the direction of thinking that I was the cat's whiskers [laughter].

Still, you've got some well-known fans in the mystery field, Donald Westlake, for example.

Yes, Westlake, my God, he's written such good things, and the reason why I take Westlake seriously in his praise is because he can be highly critical as well and is so. I received something in the mail just recently called *Murder off the Rack: Critical Studies of Ten Paperback Masters,* would you believe, and published by Scarecrow Press. In there, Westlake has written a critical essay entitled, "Peter Rabe." Now that is an excellent piece of work because he not only says what he likes and doesn't like, but he goes into the anatomy of his likes and dislikes in such a manner as to produce a thorough piece of literary criticism. You must look at it if you get the chance.

Did you ever have much luck selling the rights to any of your works to movies or television?

No, no luck. I signed contracts in that

regard, but nothing ever came of them.

The television work I did had nothing to do with my novels. I have written some things for the original *Batman* series. I've written outlines for other things, but I wasn't very successful.

***Was it from this work that you got the job of writing the novelization for the movie,* Tobruk?**

No, they were totally separate. I got the *Batman* job because I knew the chief writer, Lorenzo Semple, and I got the *Tobruk* job because my agent found that they needed somebody to do a novelization. At that point, my writing career was already on the skids or you wouldn't have found me doing novelizations of movie scripts. On the other hand, I found it a challenging piece of work to put the script into the form of a novel, an unexpected trial. The way the story jumps from one thing to another in the visual medium would leave enormous holes once it's put in print. The job took a great deal of writing that wasn't in the script. The script barely provided the skeleton of what you ended up with, which was a total surprise to me. So on that basis, as an exercise in the craft, I liked doing it, even though it wasn't my own story.

You plan to do any more writing in the future?

I have been writing, but I haven't been writing for publication. I don't know entirely why, but partly because I'm chicken, partly because I'm writing things that are quite different from what I used to write so I have no confidence that there would be an audience for it, and the main reason I haven't attempted to publish is because most of the things I have written are short stories and you know what the market for that is—zilch, especially in that they're not external-action oriented. I have moved from the story carved from the situational, the external, to the story where the action is more internal, psychological. That being the emphasis and the format being the short story, you don't really look for publication. Once I've enough and I have cleaned some of them, I might put them together and see if somebody would like to put them out.

You started your career when you were living in Maine. When did you move to the West Coast?

In the early sixties. I originally came here in order to get a slice of the pie in the television industry, which, of course, I didn't do very well [in].

Then you lived in Italy for a while.

Yes, in the late fifties.

***Your books reflect many of the places you have lived—for example, the Cleveland, Ohio, setting used in* Bring Me Another Corpse.**

I don't know why some places I've lived in I've used and others I haven't. In retrospect, there have been some very interesting places that I've been exposed to that I never utilized. I think it was a matter of chance. I don't think there was any particular pattern to the setting used. I don't think I used Spain, for example, which was very important to me, and I liked being there at the time.

When did you live in Spain?

In the early sixties. Before I came to California. And I lived in southern Germany sometime during the fifties. I never used that setting as far as I remember.

I think Germany was mentioned in one of your books.

Yes, one of the early ones, *A Shroud for Jesso*. There I used some settings which I remember from a town called Hanover, which was where I was raised, so that wasn't from when I lived in southern Germany. Those settings were from childhood memories.

As a matter of fact, some of the things that I described, like the landmarks, I found out no longer exist because of the war. There was a researcher at Gold Medal who checked things like that out.

Speaking of foreign countries, you've had good luck in having your books translated.

Yes. France, in particular, has been intrigued with some of the things I have written.

Have you ever read the translations and if you have, how do you feel about them? Are they true to your original work?

Yes, and they are surprisingly excellent. Especially the French ones.

Final note: We concluded our conversation talking about foreign languages. Besides English, Peter could speak German and French. Plus, he had a working knowledge of Italian and Spanish. Italian was his favorite language, though he felt that French is the best language for expressing content. After this short discussion, I told him that I'd send him this interview to proof and also said that I might need to ask some additional questions at a later date, to round off the interview. He said that was fine, and we said goodbye.

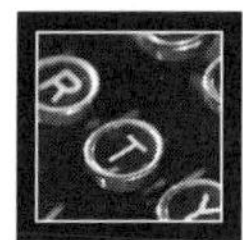

Dell First Editions

BILL CRIDER

Dell was a sort of Johnny-come-lately in the paperback original field. The first four novels from Fawcett Gold Medal were published in 1950. Avon, Graphic, and Lion soon followed right along with their own original novels, and in 1952 the first Ace Doubles appeared. That same year Ballantine began issuing books in paperback and hardcover simultaneously. But it wasn't until 1953 that Dell announced plans for its line of first editions.

Knox Burger headed up the line, and the emphasis from the beginning was on quality. Dell was the only line that really rivaled Gold Medal in that respect. Early titles in the series included *Down* (1E) by Walt Grove, *Madball* (2E) by Fredric Brown, and *The Bloody Spur* (5E) (later filmed and reprinted as *While the City Sleeps*) by Charles Einstein. All three are worth looking for, especially *The Bloody Spur,* an early serial-killer novel.

Writer, Bill Crider

There was a certain similarity between Dell First Editions and Gold Medal novels. Like Gold Medal, Dell relied heavily on suspense and Westerns, and Knox Burger brought some established Gold Medal writers (Walt Grove, John D. MacDonald, Charles Williams) to work for Dell. He got Donald Hamilton before Gold Medal. Everyone knows about Hamilton, MacDonald, and Williams (and if you don't, stop reading this and go out and buy all their books), but there are quite a few other Dell First Edition authors, now largely ignored or forgotten, who deserve to be much better known:

THOMAS B. DEWEY

Dewey's best work was in his series about the Chicago private eye known only as Mac, done for his hardcover publisher. But he wrote another series (which began with Popular Library and then moved to Dell), sexier and more lighthearted, about a Los Angeles private investigator named Pete Schofield. Unlike most of his paperback brethren, Schofield is married, and the banter between him and his wife, Jeanne, is sometimes a little tiresome. Too, the books lack the emotional resonance of those in the Mac series, but then they weren't intended to be taken seriously. If you're in the mood for a fast, funny, and suspenseful story, you could do worse. Try *Only on Tuesdays* or *The Girl with the Sweet Plump Knees.*

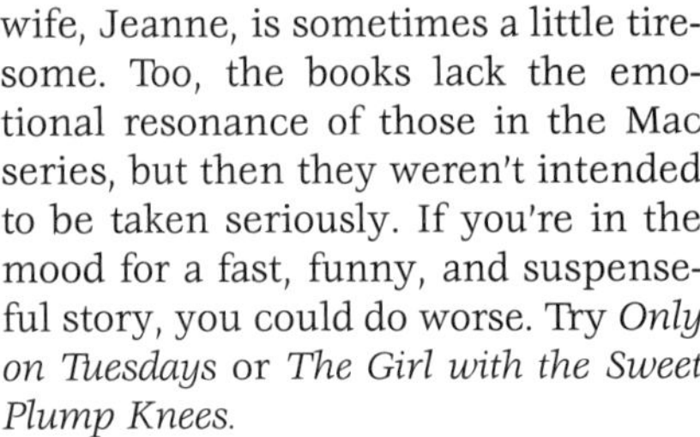

JACK EHRLICH

There aren't many paperback novels that feature parole officers, but Jack Ehrlich wrote three of them. All three feature Robert Flick, and all three are written with a remarkable emotional intensity. The first two are *Parole* and *Slow Burn.* (The third, *Girl Cage,* although an original, wasn't published as a Dell First Edition.) But as good as the Flick series is, a little novel called *Revenge* is even better. It's not quite in the same league with Jim Thompson's best work, but it's still an exceptional hard-boiled story of a madman, narrated in the first person with some of the same fervor that animated Thompson's *The Killer Inside Me.* Don't miss it.

HAROLD R. DANIELS

When the first Edgar for a paperback original was awarded, Daniels won it for a novel called *In His Blood,* a terrific little cat-and-mouse game with a point of view that alternates between the cops and the killer they're after. Any of Daniels's originals are worth reading. Look hardest for *The Girl in 304.*

ROBERT DIETRICH

You've probably heard of him under another name, E. Howard Hunt, who (as Dietrich) created probably the only hard-boiled series hero who's a C.P.A. As the blurb on the back of *Angel Eyes* puts it, "You might ask what a C.P.A. is doing assisting the D.C. police and chasing a murderer and racketeers." You might ask, but I'm not going to tell you. You'll just have to read one of the books in the series, preferably *End of a Stripper,* which contains some genuinely hard-boiled prose. But the title to look for is *Be My Victim,* a nonseries book of the kind I just can't resist: there's this small, corrupt Florida town (was there any other kind in the paperbacks of the 1950s?) presided over by a guy named Pop Seegar, who owns the whole town and the county it's situated in. Then along comes someone named Kendall, and, well, you can probably guess the rest, but Dietrich/Hunt does a dandy job of keeping things moving right along until the inevitable climax. It's the kind of book that reminds you that once upon a time, Hunt was a Real Writer before he got sidetracked into other activities.

WILLIAM FULLER

William Fuller was, if you believe Dell's cover copy, a merchant seaman, a hobo, a bit player in Western movies, and an infantryman in Guam, Leyte, and Okinawa. He also wrote a series of fast-paced novels about a drifter named Brad Dolan, whose paperback career begins in *Back Country,* when he rambles deep into backcountry Florida to a small, corrupt town where everything belongs to Ringo . . . Okay, I know what you're thinking. You're thinking you just read this synopsis up above, but you're wrong. That one was about a town that belonged to Pop Seegar, not Ringo, and Fuller is every bit as good at telling the story as Dietrich is. *Back Country* is the best book in the Brad Dolan series. *Goat Island* comes in second.

ROBERT KYLE

His real name was Robert Terrall, and he ghosted some entertaining Mike Shayne novels as Brett Halliday, but it's the Robert Kyle books that you should be looking for, especially the titles in the series about a private eye named Ben Gates. Paperback maven Art Scott has said (in *1001 Midnights*) that "Ben Gates' first-person accounts could perhaps be characterized as what you might expect from Archie Goodwin working solo." That should be enough to convince you right there. Look for *Ben Gates Is Hot* or *Some Like It Cool.* Kyle also did nonseries novels. Don't miss *Nice Guys Finish Last* (about harness racing) or *The Crooked City* (municipal corruption again).

JACK FINNEY

Finney's most famous Dell First Edition is undoubtedly *The Body Snatcher* (*Invasion of the Body Snatchers* in the movie version), and legions of readers know him for his science fiction short stories and his time-travel novel, *Time and Again.* But he also wrote *House of Numbers* for Dell, a prison-break novel that's a must-read for anyone who cares about original paperback suspense fiction of the 1950s.

JAMES MCKIMMEY

Here's a guy who seemed about to rival John D. MacDonald when it came to writing taut stories about ordinary people caught up in extraordinary circumstances, but then he disappeared from the paperback ranks. You can hardly go wrong by picking up any of his books, but try not to miss *Squeeze Play* and *The Long Ride.*

AL FRAY

Al who? I wish I could tell you more about him, but I don't know a thing. I have five books by him, three of them Dell First Editions, and they're all good—tough, knowing, and fast. *Built for Trouble* is reminiscent of Charles Williams, and *The Dice Spelled Murder* is about gamblers who take the suckers at convention hotels. I don't know who Fray was or where he went, but I wish he'd written a lot more books.

DAVID MARKSON

Like William Fuller, Markson held down a lot of jobs before producing his Dell First Editions. He was a logger, a reporter, and a paperback book editor, among other things. For Dell, he wrote two very good private eye novels featuring Harry Fannin. Both are in the Raymond Chandler/Ross Macdonald vein, and I highly recommend them. Look for *Epitaph for a Tramp* and *Epitaph for a Dead Beat.*

There's plenty of other great stuff in the Dell First Edition library. There's Morris L. West's first American title, *Kundu.* There's *The Deadly Mermaid,* a one-shot by James Atlee Phillips (Philip Atlee). Robert Donald Locke's *A Taste of Brass.* Henry Kane's *My Darlin' Evangaline.* If you're very lucky, you may run across one of them on a dusty shelf in a used bookstore somewhere. Don't pass it by.

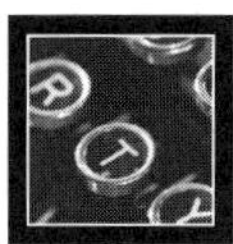

Interview with Donald Westlake

CHARLES L. P. SILET

Donald Westlake has written so many books over so long a period that it is almost impossible to remember them all. He even divides them into various categories when they are listed in the front of his latest works: novels, comic crime novels, The Dortmunder Series, crime novels, juveniles, Westerns, reportage, short stories, and anthology. *The Ax* mentions only thirty some books; he has written well over seventy—which he admits to—and that's not counting screenplays, so even this listing is incomplete.

Many of the crime novels also can be subdivided by series and Westlake has written many. The first were the Parker (no first name) books, which Westlake began writing under the pseudonym Richard Stark because he was writing too fast for his publisher to keep up with him. The Parker series begat one featuring Alan Grofield, a sometime associate of Parker's, but who basically had a nicer personality. John Dortmunder was created to pull off a caper that Parker would not do. Dortmunder is a long-suffering and dogged in ways that Parker is not. Mitch Tobin possesses a humanity that Parker will not allow himself to face.

Although initially he did not seek out the work, Donald Westlake is now also a highly regarded screenwriter. And after writing several movies, including a couple based on his own novels, his script for *The Grifters,* based on the classic Jim Thompson roman noir, won him an Academy Award nomination. The experience introduced him to Martin Scorsese, and Westlake is now working with the director/producer on other projects.

Donald Westlake was named Grand Master by the Mystery Writers of America.

You were president of the Mystery Writers of America. How did that come about?

I was part of the cabal to get Mickey Spillane the Grand Master, but other than that I've never had much to do with them. I guess it was another cabal to get me in.

The MWA presents both the Edgar Allan Poe Awards and the Grand Master awards and you have won both. What do you think these awards do for a writer?

I think the Edgar has become more meaningful. I started writing in 1960 and at that time the whole organization, the whole genre really, didn't mean anything. So I have to keep reminding myself that now it does. I don't know what the award does for sales, if anything, but I think what it does, which is almost as important, is that it adds credibility in the publishing world. Editors and publishers take it more seriously than they used to do. So it's valuable that way; they think you're more of a significant or serious person.

What's the value in bringing mystery writers together?

I think it's always a good idea. Shop-talk is a good thing in and of itself. It's sort of like watering a plant. Getting together is a good idea because it keeps your mind working, it lets you know what's happening. If you sit around with nine other writers and seven of them are doing serial killer novels, you may figure, "Well, maybe I shouldn't." But most of the shop-talk is good, and most of it is without envy and pettiness. I was on a panel with Russell Baker some years ago, and I said that the writers I knew had a distinct sense of themselves and were not really in competition with one another, so we could get along. Baker afterwards remarked, "You're very lucky, because with the writers I know backbiting is the order of the day." I haven't found that to be the case in the mystery field, and when the Western was a viable form, it was true there too, and in science fiction it's mostly true. The writers get along with each other; they like being together.

You have had a distinguished as well as prolific career in crime fiction. How did you get started?

When I was eleven years old I wrote a story about a gang killing in a nightclub. There wasn't a word in the story that I understood. Writers are always told write about what you know, but at eleven you don't know anything, except the movies and books you've seen and read. I sold a short story when I was twenty. I wanted to be a published teen-age author, but I missed it by a year.

Did you write professionally from then on?

No, I went to New York and had a lot of different oddball jobs, including one as a manuscript reader for the Scott Meredith Agency, which read amateur manuscripts for a fee, so they hire drifting no-goods like me to do the actual reading, although the letter would be signed by Scott Meredith. I used to say, "Aren't we engaged in mail fraud here?" I worked there for six months, and it was a learning experience because it was really at the commercial level of publishing. Also, because I was reading a minimum of forty short stories a week. I was learning all the mistakes writers make. After a while I had some short-story sales and decided it was time to go freelance to see what happens. Before I left, I did a mystery novel and brought it to the guy who was running that part of the office. I thought it had hardcover potential, but he said, "We'll try two publishers, if you want to waste the time, then we'll sell it to a paperback house." It was rejected with extreme prejudice by Simon & Schuster and then it went to Random House. Lee Wright, who's an incredible editor, called the agency and said, "I'm rejecting this book, but [there are] some things of interest in it, and I'd like to have a conversation with the writer." So I went over to pick up the manuscript at Random House and spent two hours talking to Lee, and it was agreed that I would rewrite the manuscript and she would look at it again. She eventually bought it. That was *The Mercenaries.*

And you did several more for Random House?

Lee was my editor for ten years, and I did eleven or twelve books for her, the first five of which were straight mystery novels. Then the sixth one I started was in the first person, and the guy's voice was comic. I called my then agent, who told me to drop the idea because he said, "You'll never get a paperback sale, you won't get any foreign sales, because nobody can translate comedy, and you're going to cut your income in half." But it was moving along pretty fast, and I decided just do it this once and get it out of my system, and I never went back. That book was called *The Fugitive Pigeon* [and] I still don't understand what it means, and it has sold five different times so far in paperback and did sell a lot of foreign.

You have been very successful with a number of series. The first was written under the pseudonym Richard Stark.

After *The Mercenaries,* I did a second book for Lee, but there's always been the belief in publishing that they can't publish more than one book a year from any one author. So I thought it would be interesting to have a pen name and to have another market, to aim for a paperback original this time. So I did this book with the assumption that the bad guy has to get caught at the end. I wrote it with Gold Medal in mind, but they rejected it. Then I sent it to Bucklin Moon at Pocket Books, who said, "I like this book and I like this character. Is there any way that you could change the book so that he would escape at the end and then you could give me three books a year about him." And I said, "I think so."

So that was the beginning of Parker?

Yes, but I had no idea that it was going to be a series, and I had not written it that way. I'd made Parker completely remorseless, completely without redeeming characteristics, because he was going to get caught at the end. So I wound up with a truly cold leading-series character, which was an interesting thing to do and to try not to soften him. In a series the guy's got to be around for years and the readers have to like him. But we came in here with this son of a bitch and we're going out with this son of a bitch. I felt that he had to remain true to himself.

Why did you decide to discontinue the Parker series?

I never did decide to discontinue them, I just ran dry. I was writing them regularly, and I started one more using a variation on an earlier one in which the gang goes into a building, something like a D & D building in New York where you've got wholesale jewelers, antique dealers, coin dealers on the upper floors. A lot of money in one building. The thieves would just go in, remove the building security-alarm system, and have the weekend to do the whole building. I started that and got sixty pages into it, and it just ran dry. I tried it a couple more times and nothing would happen. So I thought what's gone wrong is that I have domesticated Parker. He's now living with this woman, and he's not the character that he was. I have let him get soft, so let's start another book which begins with her getting killed. I tried that and it wouldn't work either. Eventually, the idea of the building I gave to Dortmunder, and there's a female character, who I had in the segment of the book when it was a Parker novel, and I made her a little kinder and gentler and in the same job.

Then in 1989 I tried again with another idea for a specific kind of oddball robbery of an evangelical meeting where people bring their love offerings or God offerings, and you've got a stadium full of cash. In fact, I did some of it when they were shooting *The Grifters,* and I got about half of it done, and it ran dry, and I really began getting tired of this. In 1991 or 1992, I showed it to Otto Penzler, and he had a couple little suggestions for ways to clean up what was done, but I was still stuck. Recently, I was between books and I told my wife, "I don't know what I'm going to do next," and she said, "Why don't you take a look at that Richard Stark novel," and I took a look at it and I finished it.

Your current series character is Dortmunder.

Well, Dortmunder. After I'd done about ten or eleven of the Parker novels, I was trying to think of something new for him. He handles frustration very badly, so it would annoy him if he had to steal the same thing several times because things would keep going wrong. I thought that's funny and useful, but I realized I've really got to be careful with this because the worst thing you can do with a tough guy is make him funny inadvertently, because then he isn't a tough guy anymore, he's just a jerk. So I didn't dare give Parker that job, because he wouldn't do it in the first place, and it would ruin him if he did. I still liked the idea of a guy having to constantly go back and do a robbery again in another way, so I needed another guy who couldn't be quite like Parker. He had to be more long-suffering. I was looking for a name, and in a bar I saw a German beer called Dortmunder Actien Bier and I said that's what I want, a guy whose "action" is wrong, and Dortmunder just has a nice gloomy sound to it.

You've had a lot of experience with the movies.

More in the last several years. I never sought it out. I think I would have but I didn't know how. I've always lived in and around New York, and I never wanted to spend more than a week or two in California, so I didn't know people or what you did. Then in 1970 or 1971, I got a phone call from a guy who said, "Hello, I'm Elliot Kastner and I'm a movie producer, and I think it's time for another *Rififi,* and you're the guy to write it." I thought, "What the hell was that?" I called my agent and he looked into it and said he's a guy who's produced a lot of movies, and the first movie he ever did was *Harper,* the screen version of the Ross Macdonald novel, and Bill Goldman had done that screenplay. So I called Bill and asked, "Who is this guy and why is he phoning me?" Bill said, "That's Elliot. He doesn't know anything about making movies, he knows how to make the deals, and if he calls you, that means you're about to be hot. If you'd like to get into the movie business, stick with Elliot. He will get the movie made with the wrong cast and the wrong director and the wrong budget, but he'll get it made, and you'll have a credit." Jerry Bick, an assistant of Elliot's, and I had lunch, and we talked about some script ideas. I suggested a story about a couple of New York City cops who have had enough, and with their knowledge, experience, and assets could pull a major robbery to get out and retire someplace. Out of that came *Cops and Robbers,* with the wrong budget, wrong director, and wrong cast, but a credit.

You did the script for Jim Thompson's* The Grifters, *which got you an Academy Award nomination.

I had read the novel years before, and so when they came to me as a result of my having done a thing called *The Stepfather,* I read it again and thought, "Jeez, this thing is not a Disney movie." When we met for the first time, before anything was committed, I said, The thing about this story is that it has a very harsh ending, but if it doesn't have that ending, it doesn't *have* an ending. I'll do this, but only if we all agree to keep the ending, and everyone agreed. I remember the first time Marty Scorsese, who was producing, saw a rough cut in New York, he turned around and he smiled at us and said, "Well, one thing for sure, we don't want to do test screenings on this. We wouldn't *want* to read those cards." We were never sure what people would come out of the theatre saying, but we went forward with it. When I went out to L.A. for the last week of rehearsal, Anjelica Huston, Annette Bening, and John Cusack all had the Black Lizard paperback, and they came running over to see why this and that had been cut—of course, it was all lines of theirs—but that's nice that they were defending the writer. Everybody had this feeling that we were doing something good. Back when I was working on the script, Marty said, "How's it coming?" and I said, "I'm doing damage on every page" and he sort of smiled and nodded. But I was doing damage on every page, which is what the story was about.

Stephen Frears, the director, likes the writer on the set during the shooting. Had you been on the set before?

I had with *Cops and Robbers,* which was unfortunately an unhappy experience. The director was a charming man—he's now dead—but as a director he believed in consensus, and it is the nature of the beast that a director has to be a dictator. It was rather chaotic, and since it was shot in New York, I would go home every night and say, "Oh God!" But the set on *The Grifters* was just terrific, and at the end of it I said that it was so nice to be in a boat in which everybody was rowing in the same direction instead of getting hit in the head by a lot of oars.

Isn't it frustrating to write scripts and then simply have them shelved?

Yes, horribly. You know you've done good things and you'd like to see them. The worse thing like that in the last several years is the work I did for Roberto Grimaldi, who owns the rights to Dashiell Hammett's first novel *Red Harvest.* He's had scripts done by tons of people—Bernardo Bertolucci did five. The German director Volker Schlondorff, who won an Academy Award for *The Tin Drum,* and I have been on a couple of doomed projects together, and Alberto came to us to do a script of the novel. We saw a couple of the other scripts and thought the wily Mr. Hammett has pulled the wool over these people's eyes. We saw how they were misled and how to do it right. At the beginning, Volker talked with Bertolucci and he said, "Forget it, he's not serious." Meaning Grimaldi. We did a couple of scripts, and it turned out that it was true. He's never going to get a movie made, and it has become a way for him to have lunch with people. I know that I've solved the basic problem with the novel, and I'm never going to see it.

You've had about a dozen of your books made into films. Generally, have you been pleased with the movies?

It's a variety. There's a great one, *Point Blank,* with Lee Marvin, which is from the first Parker novel. And there is a quite good one from *The Outfit,* another Parker novel, with Robert Duvall as Parker. It is a good, small movie with every B-movie actor you've ever thought of in it. And *The Hot Rock* is quite good. Then there have been others that are complete disasters, and a couple I've been warned away from, told if you see this movie, you're just going to tie up the suicide hot lines.

Has your experience in Hollywood affected your writing?

Very early on it did. Any time a novelist is affected by film it is for the bad. It's always a mistake. There was one book that I had to go back and completely rewrite to get *Casino Royale* out of it. There is a way of telling a story in a specific kind of episodic way that the movies do, and *Casino Royale* did, very well, but in a book it just looks as if somebody has dropped a manuscript and picked it up helter-skelter. All that writing screenplays has done is confirm me in how to write a novel. Movies are just the surface of things, what it looks like and what it sounds like. Where a novel is what it means as well. Even at their best there is still that sense in movie scripts of walking down a narrow corridor. With a novel there is the sense of entering a big room where you can go anywhere.

***Let's move onto your more recent fiction. What attracted you to Branson, Missouri, the setting for* Baby, Would I Lie?**

Friends of mine who spend part of each year there described it as a real desert for anybody who has anything to do with the life of the mind. They kept saying come on down to visit, which meant come down because we need somebody to talk to. So eventually we visited, and my wife called Branson an "irony-free zone." I thought there has got to be something here for me. I had already done this other book involving people from a newspaper like *The National Enquirer,* and those people are one hundred percent irony. So I felt to put the *National Enquirer* people together with Branson, Missouri, should be a learning experience for both sides.

What is it about the country western environment that attracted you?

I wasn't really interested until then. For me, the thing about a novel sometimes is that I get into its world. I got deeply interested in the whole Nashville/Branson tug-of-war, and I talked with some of the show-biz people, who are all very bright and very knowledgeable. For guys who spent thirty years on the bus with a bottle of Jack Daniel's in their hand, in Branson they can sleep in the same bed every night and play golf on Wednesday mornings. It's just a lovely retirement and more money than God.

***Smoke** is a crazy combination of sci fi and caper. Where did you come up with the idea for it?*

I was back in Anguilla for the first time in twenty years. I'd written my only nonfiction book in 1971 about their rebellion against independence. At resort places people will leave old paperback novels behind, and there was a copy of H. G. Wells's *Invisible Man* which I had not read for many years. I read it on the beach and thought that all this is about is how much trouble it is to be invisible. I kept thinking about it, because there is nothing else to do on the beach except read and think, and I felt there must be some fun in it or people wouldn't fantasize about it. I never intended to write *The Invisible Man*—I don't write science fiction—but if I did, what would it be like? The first thing I would do is make him a thief so that he would have some idea what to do with invisibility. The second thing I'd do would be to give him a girlfriend so there would be somebody to drive. I did the first chapter longhand down there and when I got back I looked at it. I liked the guy's style. I met a scientist years ago, a blue-sky thinker, whose job is to imagine impossible things. So I called him because I wanted to find a way to make this character invisible, and I suggested scientists who are working on melanoma, with pigmentation as the carrier, and that might be the way. He said, "It seems to me you've already got it."

Why does a tobacco company fund the research?

That sort of just grew. The whole tobacco thing was in the air. Then I read about the human genome project. I could hear some tobacco guy saying, This is for us. We've tried to make cigarettes safe for people; now let's try to make people safe for cigarettes.

***Tell me about* What's the Worst That Could Happen?**

It's different in one way: at the beginning of the book, he is the victim. He is stolen from. Then in his efforts to get this unimportant ring back, he keeps making more and more money. He's never made a profit before. In one of the earlier chapters, he comes home and says, as he drops $28,000 on the table, "I've got bad news, May. I didn't get the ring." He keeps on winning, but he keeps winning the wrong stuff. He's never been on a roll before. He gets a little lighter.

He takes on a large corporate type, too.

Somebody who is somewhere between Robert Maxwell and Rupert Murdoch. Not anybody in particular. The center of the character is Maxwell, because he was supposed to be an unimportant, dead, poverty-struck child, who instead got out of Eastern Europe to England and became Robert Maxwell. But he always had fun in life, since he wasn't supposed to be here, and he didn't give a damn anyway. That devil-may-care attitude I made the heart of this guy.

What is your latest book?

It is not comic at all. It is a downsizing novel, narrated by the guy who was downsized. It's called *The Ax,* no "e," because I say it's a no-frills book. It's very tough, it's very cold. In the book he says, "I know who the enemy is, the executives and stockholders, but there is nothing I can do to them that is going to help me at all. They're the enemy, but they're not the problem. The other people applying for the same job are the problem. And it is what he does about that.

Portions of this interview originally appeared as "What's the Worse that Could Happen?: An Interview with Donald Westlake," *The Armchair Detective,* 29:4 (Winter 1996), 394-401.

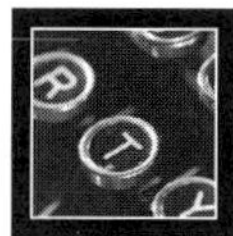

Chester Himes:

AMERICA'S BLACK HEARTLAND

JAMES SALLIS

In one early short story, Chester Himes writes of a black man who, because he will not step off the sidewalk to let a white couple pass, has his feet doused with gasoline and set on fire, consequently losing them. At the end of the story another white man becomes enraged when at a movie theatre he fails to stand for the playing of the national anthem, even though it is pointed out he has no feet.

A later story, "Prediction," opens with the black janitor of the city's Catholic cathedral sitting astride the public poor box with a heavy-caliber automatic rifle, waiting at the end of "four hundred years" while six thousand white policemen parade in the streets below. The ensuing massacre is described with characteristic intensity and shocking detail: rank after rank of policemen are mowed down; shards of bone, lariats of gut and dollops of brain spin through the air. A riot tank is dispatched and, unable to find a target, turns its guns on black plaster-of-Paris mannequins in a store window, then on the policemen themselves. Finally the black janitor's location is discovered. The tank turns to the stone face and stares a moment "as if in deep thought," then levels the cathedral. But his symbolic action strikes a resounding blow: "In the wake of the bloody massacre the stock market crashed. The dollar fell on the world market. The very structure of capitalism began to crumble."

These two visions, the naturalist-didactic and the apocalyptic, largely define Chester Himes's career and work. The first of the stories, in its limning of the ways in which white society makes demands on the black which that same society has assured he cannot fulfill, shares with the second a parabolic intensity common to Himes; each suggests, as do his later Harlem detective novels, that the forces of law and order only serve to amplify the disorder and chaos of American urban life. For Himes, the roots of our society are so thoroughly corrupt as to forbid anything approaching normal growth. And his interest from the first has been the individual human consequences of so distorted a society. If his people are monsters, misshapen, grotesque things, it is because the egg they formed in forced them to that shape.

In other respects Himes's naturalism underwent a progression unique to American letters. Reminiscent of Richard Wright and proletarian work of the forties, the early novels yielded, with their author's expatriation, to the serial exploits of a team of black Harlem detectives, Grave Digger Jones and Coffin Ed Johnson. These books proved quite successful in France and other European countries, while American publishers brought them out indifferently; many remained out of print for thirty years or more. Critics typically considered the Harlem books potboilers, pandering to excessive violence and grotesque characterizations, and not a few bemoaned the loss of a talented serious writer.

Himes did achieve brief celebrity in 1965 with *Pinktoes,* his satire of black-white (mostly sexual) relations, and in 1970 a popular movie was made from one of the Grave Digger/Coffin Ed books, *Cotton Comes to Harlem.* He then entered another phase with his two-volume autobiography (*The Quality of Hurt* in 1972, *My Life of Absurdity* in 1976) and a retrospective of shorter work (*Black on Black,* 1973). There was no new fiction, and despite the fact that Chester Himes is arguably among America's most powerful and original novelists, despite, too, a gathering critical acclaim, he remained largely unknown at his death in 1984. His work deserves and demands wider recognition.

***

"I got the story out of the American black's secret mind itself," Himes said.

Grave Digger and Coffin Ed prowl the streets in their beat-up, souped-up Plymouth, looking like "two hog farmers on a weekend in the Big Town," connecting with a broad network of junkies, stool pigeons, whores, and pimps, doing what they can to maintain law and order by bashing heads and making deals, in the interim shooting off their mouths and identical long-barreled, nickel-plated .38 revolvers on .44 frames. Grave Digger, the more articulate of the two, has smoldering reddish brown eyes, a "lumpy" face and oversize frame, and always wears a black alpaca suit with an old felt hat perched on the back of his head. Coffin Ed's face, disfigured by thrown acid in the first of the novels, has earned him a second nickname, Frankenstein, and he often must be restrained from impulsive violence by Grave Digger. The two live near one another, with their families, on Long Island. They share a considerable courage, a sure knowledge of street ways, studied flamboyance—and an abiding pragmatism. They know that nothing they can do is likely to have much real effect, and maintain order by improvisation, threat, and brutality, generally adding to the toll of bodies and confusion. Here is their first appearance, from *For Love of Imabelle* (also issued as *A Rage in Harlem*):

> They were having a big ball in the Savoy and people were lined up for a block down Lenox Avenue, waiting to buy tickets. The famous Harlem detective team of Coffin Ed Johnson and Grave Digger Jones had been assigned to keep order.
>
> Both were tall, loose-jointed, sloppily dressed, ordinary-looking dark-brown colored men. But there was nothing ordinary about their pistols. They carried specially made long-barreled nickel-plated .38-calibre revolvers, and at the moment they had them in their hands.
>
> Grave Digger stood on the right side of the front end of the line, at the entrance to the Savoy. Coffin Ed Stood on the left side on the line, at the rear end. Grave Digger had his pistol aimed south, Coffin Ed had his pistol aimed north, in a straight line. There was space enough between the two imaginary lines for two persons to stand side by side. Whenever anyone moved out of line, Grave Digger would shout, "Straighten up!" and Coffin Ed would echo, "Count off!" If the offender didn't straighten up the line immediately, one of the detectives would shoot into the air. The couples in the queue would close together as though pressed between two concrete walls. Folks in Harlem believed that Grave Digger

Jones and Coffin Ed Johnson would shoot a man stone dead for not standing straight in a line.

In a later novel, urged by their lieutenant to "play it safe" and avoid unnecessary violence, Grave Digger responds:

> We've got the highest crime rate on earth among the colored people in Harlem. And there ain't but three things to do about it: Make the criminals pay for it—you don't want to do that; pay the people enough to live decently—you ain't going to do that; so all that's left is let 'em eat one another up.

As H. Bruce Franklin points out in *The Victim as Criminal and Artist,* the varieties of violence inflicted on blacks by blacks, finally represented by the two detectives as much as by the criminals they chase, became Himes's persistent theme.

The Harlem novels were never true genre pieces, fulfilling few traditional expectations, and as they continued they withdrew ever further from preconceived notions of the detective story. Specific crimes are solved in the early books (albeit rather incidentally), but there is a progressive movement toward concentration on the scene itself, on Harlem as symbol, using the detective-story framework as vehicle for character and social portraiture. As this shift occurs, absurdities, incomprehensible events, and grotesqueries proliferate. The books close on greater disorder and confusion than they began with—a near-perfect reversal of Gide's description of the detective story as a form in which "every character is trying to deceive all the others and in which the truth slowly becomes visible through the haze of deception."

Himes did not plan this evolution; it grew quite spontaneously out of the material he was working with in the Harlem novels, and out of his own experience. *In My Life of Absurdity* he describes writing these novels:

Courtesy of The Targ Agency

Novelist Chester Himes, author of *A Rage in Harlem* and *Blind Man with a Pistol*.

> I would sit in my room and become hysterical thinking about the wild, incredible story I was writing. But it was only for the French, I thought, and they would believe anything about Americans, black or white, if it was bad enough. And I thought I was writing realism. It never occurred to me that I was writing absurdity. Realism and absurdity are so similar in the lives of American blacks one cannot tell the difference.

These trends culminate—there was a five-year delay between the final books—in *Blind Man with a Pistol.* Assigned to find the killer of a cruising white homosexual, Grave Digger and Coffin Ed roar through a landscape of crazy preachers, children eating from troughs, the cant of black revolutionaries, and a gigantic black plaster-of-Paris Jesus hanging from a ceiling with a sign reading *They lynched me.* Neither the original nor subsequent murders are solved; the sole connecting link is an enigmatic man (or men) wearing a red fez. Confounded and frustrated at every turn by politically protected suspects, payoffs, and neatly contrived "solutions," the two detectives halfway through the novel are taken off the case and assigned to investigate Harlem's swelling black riots. "You mean you want us to lay off before we discover something you don't want discovered?" Grave Digger asks point-blank. But he already knows; they all do, and the rest is little more than ritual dance.

Toward the novel's end, in a scene paralleling that of their debut in *For Love of Imabelle,* Grave Digger and Coffin Ed stand on the corner of Lenox and 125th shooting rats as they run from buildings being demolished. Their function, and efficacy, have been so abridged.

Meanwhile, a belligerent black man who wants no one to know he is blind, walking streets and riding subways by memory, has become involved in an argument with a gardener who thinks the blind man is staring at him. Soon involved as well are a white truck driver and a black clergyman who intervenes to preach against violence. Attacked by the truck driver, the blind man draws a pistol and fires, killing the preacher. He continues to fire as the subway pulls into the 125th Street station, then staggers up onto the street close behind the gardener and truck driver, where he is shot to death by white police watching Grave Digger's and Coffin Ed's display of marksmanship. Immediately the cry goes out that "Whitey has murdered a soul brother!"

> An hour later Lieutenant Anderson had Grave Digger on the radiophone. "Can't you men stop that riot?" he demanded.
>
> "It's out of hand, boss," Grave Digger said.
>
> "All right, I'll call for reinforcements. What started it?"
>
> "A blind man with a pistol."
>
> "What's that?"
>
> "You heard me, boss."
>
> "That don't make any sense."
>
> "Sure don't."

Thus the book ends on a familiar theme: having abrogated their authority, the lieutenant absurdly expects his detectives still to function. And just as Himes had discovered in his mythical Harlem a correlative for the absurdity of the urban black's life, so he found a final metaphor for the mindless ubiquity of violence against and within those same people.

***

Chester Bomar Himes was born July 29, 1909, in Jefferson City, Missouri, growing up chiefly there, in St. Louis, and in Cleveland, Ohio. His parents were middle-class, his mother a woman of dignity and iron will, his father a college instructor whose own will seems to have broken over the years, so that he wound up working at menial jobs. Himes attended Ohio State University for a time but was asked to leave following a fight in a speakeasy. He then worked as a busboy for Cleveland hotels, becoming involved with the hustling life, drinking, gambling. After two suspended sentences for burglary and bad checks, he was finally sentenced in 1928 to twenty to twenty-five years' hard labor at the Ohio State Penitentiary for armed robbery, serving seven years, five months of that sentence before parole.

It was in prison that Himes began to write. His first stories were picked up for publication rather promptly by black newspapers and magazines. Then in 1934 a short story titled "Crazy in the Stir," with a prison number as its only byline, appeared in *Esquire.* Two more of Himes's stories were accepted by *Esquire* before his parole in 1936, another six in later years.

The years following parole were difficult ones. Even with the sponsorship of Pulitzer Prize-winner Louis Bromfield, Himes was unable to find a publisher for his novel *Black Sheep.* Eventually he joined the river of blacks flowing toward Los Angeles and the wartime defense industry there, his work in the L.A. shipyards providing the setting (and no small part of the rancor) for his first published novel, *If He Hollers Let Him Go* (1945).

During the course of this novel, Bob Jones loses his girl, is demoted at the shipyard, suffers endless humiliation and insult, becomes entangled in a brawl, and is falsely accused of rape—finally having to enlist to avoid imprisonment. The story is told first-person. There's little real movement to it; structured around Bob Jones's enigmatic, terrifying dreams, the book moves through a train of situations and events reinforcing the sense of him and his destiny we have from the first. "I'm still here," he says at the end: hope and a man's life have been thus attenuated.

Himes's next novel, *Lonely Crusade* (1947), concerned fledgling Negro union organizer Lee Gordon, a man whose marriage is dissolving and who takes illusory refuge with a white mistress. The book is uneven, with lengthy discursive passages, a somewhat muddled plot, and a questionable upbeat ending. But it does track relentlessly the emasculating, *unmanning* effects of racism and is, more than any other of Himes's novels, a novel of ideas. Where Bob Jones was paralyzed by the ubiquity of his enemy, Lee Gordon is adamant in finding ground that allows struggle, in learning how to fight.

Upon publication, *Lonely Crusade* encountered misunderstanding and condemnation so nearly universal that Himes fell back into bitterness, losing all confidence in himself. He worked various jobs, first as a caretaker, then again as a porter and bellhop. In 1948 he gave an impassioned, brilliant address on "The Dilemma of the Negro Writer" at the University of Chicago. In 1952, following publication of *Cast the First Stone* and widespread attacks on it, Himes fled to Europe.

Cast the First Stone had been written sixteen years earlier, during and just after his prison experience, as *Black Sheep*, though the novel as published substitutes a white Mississippian for the original black protagonist. It combines graphic depictions of prison life with a story of the love between two men, Jim Monroe and Duke Dido.

Directly autobiographical in inception, *The Third Generation* (1954) focuses more on dissension within Negro families than on confrontation with white society, in this regard prefiguring the preoccupation of Himes's detective novels with "the infinite forms of violence perpetrated on blacks by blacks." The novel recounts the coming to manhood of Charles Taylor, son of educated, decorous Southern blacks, and the parallel disintegration of his family under the pressures of modern urban life and insidious racism. The parents are patently modeled on Himes's own: the father a dark-skinned trade teacher at Negro schools, gradually descending to manual work because of his wife's inability to accommodate colleagues and neighbors; the mother light-skinned and of genteel background, endlessly spurning her husband and showering her whole affection on their son. Sharing the melodramatic plot turns and acute psychological portraiture of preceding novels, *The Third Generation* represents Himes's most direct assault on the Negro middle class. "The American Negro, we must remember, is an American," Himes said in his address at the University of Chicago "the face may be the face of Africa, but the heart has the beat of Wall Street." One also is forced to remember Grave Digger and Coffin Ed with their comfortable homes and families out on Long Island, coming in to Harlem each day to commit mayhem against fellow, far less advantaged blacks in their enforcement of white men's laws.

Of the characters from *The Third Generation*, Edward Margolies has writen in *Native Sons:* "On the surface, rank bigotry seldom intrudes as the direct cause of their sufferings; they appear to be defeated by their own incapacities, weaknesses, blindness, and obsessions. But Himes makes clear that in order to understand them, one must understand the generations that preceded them, black and white: they are doomed not simply by their own psychic drives but by the history that created them and forced them into self-destructive channels."

With this restatement of Himes's determinism, the palpable beat of cataclysm, and specific focus on black community, we are moving close to the Harlem novels.

***

Just as the Harlem novels culminate in *Blind Man with a Pistol,* the earlier phrase of Himes's career climaxes with *The Primitive,* published the same year (1955) he began writing the detective books. In the story of Jesse and Kriss, a failed black novelist and a woman whose own wounds are just as mortal, Himes found a channel for his feelings about his rejection as a writer, and for an investigation of his obsession with the white woman and all she represented to him. *The Primitive* is easily the most closely structured and artistic of Himes's novels—"the most intricately patterned piece of fiction Himes ever produced," according to Stephen Milliken in his book-length study. In this novel, too, we find the profuse Rabelaisian humor central to the Harlem novels: Prior books had been irredeemably serious.

The narrative here, though, is anything but comic. Jesse and Kriss circle one another like dancers, first simply using one another to satisfy their own needs, then increasingly turning their feelings of failure and defeat upon one another, each in truth seeking his own destruction: the book ends with Jesse calling the police, having just killed Kriss. There's a marvelously sustained mood, a new intensity of characterization and physical detail, and fine, impassioned writing. This is a bleak book, one in which the external world and perceptions of it are increasingly bent to the shape of the characters' own doom.

Jesse is not so much a portrait of Himes himself, Milliken writes, as of "the man he believed he might easily have become had the sequence of misfortunes that overwhelmed him been just a little bit worse, if the screws had been tightened, ever so slightly, just a few notches more."

The Primitive was written in Majorca, where Himes lived in a series of ramshackle villages with a woman he'd met on the crossing.

> I wrote slowly, savoring each word, sometimes taking an hour to fashion one sentence to my liking. Sometimes leaning back in my seat and laughing hysterically at the sentence I had fashioned, getting as much satisfaction from the creation of this book as from an exquisite act of love. That was the first time in my life I enjoyed writing; before I had always written from compulsion. But . . . for once I was almost doing what I wanted to with a story, without being influenced by the imagined reactions of editors, publishers, critics, readers, or anyone. By then I had reduced myself to the fundamental writer, and nothing else mattered.

Distance had brought Himes one liberation and now, in the work, he found another. *The Primitive,* like Himes's other naturalist novels, is a biting, angry book, but there are also scenes of wild comedy: Jesse pursuing and effeminate male Pomeranian ("He takes after his Papa") through the apartment house, belt in hand; or stumbling drunkenly into and falling atop a white statue, thinking they're bound to call it rape. Jesse's self-awareness and irony suggest a new aesthetic remove from his material on Himes's part, and this sense of perspective is underlined by the continual counterpoint of TV, with its news and images of the external world, flooding into Jesse's and Kriss's closed-off world. (Among these images is a chimpanzee who announces historical events—including Jesse's trial and sentence—before they occur.) And that new freedom intimated by Himes, the simple joy in writing, in invention, more than anything else explains the Harlem novels.

***

Pinktoes, published in Paris in 1961, and in the United Stated in 1965, is something of a sport. Though it echoes the signature boisterous comedy of the Harlem novels and takes up yet again the author's disdain for the black middle class and fascination with interracial sex, there is nothing else like it in Himes's work. Centered around the activities of Harlem "hostess" Mamie Mason, who believes race relations (and her own social pretensions) are best served in bed, *Pinktoes* is a scattergun that misses very few targets.

Most of the novel concerns one of Mamie's parties and its aftermath for two men there, black leader Wallace Wright and Art Wills, soon to become (white) editor for a Negro picture magazine. Plot turns and scenes grow ever more grotesque and outrageous. When Mamie, because Art will not feature her in his first issue, tells his wife that he has proposed to a black woman named Brown Sugar, the wife goes home to mother. Word quickly gets around that white liberal husbands are fleeing their wives for brownskin girls and there's a panicked run on suntan lotion and ultraviolet lamps. A company that had been producing a skin lightener called "Black Nomore" prospers with its new product "Blackamoor." White women rush to kink their hair, dye their gums blue, redden their eyes.

The attacks in *Pinktoes* are savage ones, true—and unrelenting—yet in the conscious self-parody of his own obsession with interracial sex, and in the unbridled lampoonery of all he held in contempt, Chester Himes seems to have found a kind of deliverance from the pervasive bitterness and gravity of previous work. In this regard, *Pinktoes* may have helped complete what *The Primitive* began.

Two other books of this period are summings-up of a kind.

A Case of Rape, written in 1956 through 1957, was published in Paris in 1963 as *Une Affaire de Viol* and received English-language publication only in 1980 with a small run from Targ Editions; Howard University Press reissued it four years later.

The book springboards from the trial of four black expatriates for the rape and murder of a troubled white woman in Paris. In his postscript for the Howard University Press edition, Calvin Hernton notes that while Himes examines almost clinically the characters' individual motives, his ultimate concern is with the inhumanity of a morally degenerate world that allows a woman senselessly to lose her life and four men to be wrongly condemned. The men finally are condemned, not for specific guilt in the case under trial, but for their general guilt as black men; and the book's final sentence, "We are all guilty," echoing Dostoyevsky, is Himes's own final condemnation of society.

Run Man Run (1959, Paris; 1966, U.S.), Himes's only thriller without Grave Digger and Coffin Ed, lies somewhere between the early naturalist novels and the Harlem novels' stark intensity. Jimmy Johnson, a young black man who's witnessed the senseless, savage murder of two fellow night porters, is being methodically stalked by the murderer, a New York policeman named Matt Walker with a psychotic hatred of blacks. Himes said that he worked very hard to get everything just right in this book, even giving Walker his own alcoholic blackouts and character traits for greater verisimilitude. But as Stephen Milliken points out, what finally menaces Jimmy is not one sick man in a privileged position; it's "the national psychosis of racism fully exposed."

***

It seems clear now that the Harlem detective novels are not the anomalies they were first believed to be and, rather than breaking the line of Himes's development, significantly extended it. With them, recurrent themes fell into place, joining the dark vision of the earlier books to the turbulent comedy that surfaced in *Pinktoes.* Released from the twin burdens of autobiography and social significance (at least in any purely programmatic sense), Himes found the ideal vehicle for his particular gifts. The climate of suspicion, fear, and violence so much at the heart of the detective story mirrored Himes's own feelings about the black in American society and allowed him a kind of privileged expression. Grave Digger and Coffin Ed, men of ruthless action, supplanted the passivity of earlier protagonists, and Himes fully embraced life's fundamental absurdity. He had moved from finding to making, from the purely representational to a kind of epic poetry.

Yet the books began quite by chance. On a visit to Gallimard to drop off the manuscript for *Pinktoes,* desperate for money, Himes ran into Marcel Duhamel, who had translated *If He Hollers Let Him Go* into French and was then director of Gallimard's *Série Noire.* Duhamel asked Himes to write a detective story for the series and to Himes's protest that he wouldn't know how responded:

> Get an idea. Start with action, somebody does something—a man reaches out a hand and opens a door, light shines in his eyes, a body lies on the floor, he turns, looks up and down the hall . . . Always action in detail. Make pictures. Like motion pictures. Always the scenes are visible. No stream of consciousness at all. We don't give a damn who's thinking what—only what they're doing. Always doing something. From one scene to another. Don't worry about it making sense. That's for the end. Give me 220 typed pages.

Gradually, from an old confidence game called "the Blow," the book built itself by pure improvisation. After eighty pages Himes returned to Duhamel, who loved what he read and told him: "Just add another hundred and twenty pages and you've got it."

Himes had it, all right. That first novel was published in 1957 as *La Reine des Pommes,* winning the Grand Prix Policier the following year. And he went on to have it seven more times, in what's now called the Harlem cycle. These books are some of American literature's—make that world literature's—true treasures.

Excerpted from *Difficult Lives* by James Sallis (Gryphon Press, 1993)

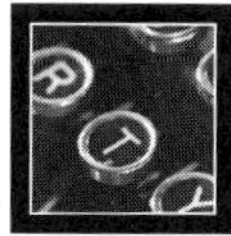

Donald Hamilton

ROBERT SKINNER

Paperback originals have often been the forum for fiction that was a little off the beaten track—wild, nihilistic, edgy, and even a bit experimental. Writers like Chester Himes, David Goodis, and Jim Thompson may be thought of as founding fathers of that school. It was a style of writing that couldn't be bothered with fancy cars and femmes fatales with unlikely names.

Among the many paperback heroes, Donald Hamilton's Matt Helm is one of the longest-lived and most successful in the history of the genre. It is worth noting as well that Hamilton's influence on other writers is pervasive. Crime writers as diverse as Loren Estleman, Bill Crider, Ed Gorman, James Sallis, as well as me, all consider him a primary influence on their writing.

Donald Bentgsson Hamilton was born in Uppsala, Sweden, on March 24, 1916. In 1924 he and his parents immigrated to America, where his father, a medical doctor, served on the faculties of Harvard, Johns Hopkins, and the University of Chicago.

Hamilton, in a recently published essay, says that he started school in his new homeland wearing something every Swedish schoolboy of his time carried as a matter of course—a small sheath knife. Horrified officials called his parents in for a consultation, and the knife disappeared. The experience was not lost on Hamilton, because two of the threads that run through his fiction are an affection for edged weapons and a disdain for bureaucracy.

Hamilton recounts that there was no dramatic turning point that caused him to be a writer. He began by keeping his kid sisters up at night telling scary stories "that I made up as I went along." In high school, he appropriated an old Underwood typewriter that his parents had stopped using and got himself a book on touch typing, a purchase he now says "was the best couple of bucks I ever invested." He knew at the time he wanted to write, but his father counseled, "That's fine, Donald, but you'd better have a way of earning a living, too." To that end, Hamilton enrolled at the University of Chicago, but he told *Collier's* in 1946 that his graduation was delayed a year because he was too busy "writing questionable fiction when [he] should have been writing incontrovertible facts."

Hamilton found his early inspiration in Dashiel Hammett, Hemingway, and Raymond Chandler, and some perhaps unwanted influence from Leslie

Charteris. Hamilton says, "I had to stop reading the Saint books . . . because I found that if I read one at night, everything I wrote next morning came out Leslie Charteris."

Hamilton joined the navy in 1942, was commissioned an officer, and spent the war at Annapolis doing chemical research. Two novels he wrote during that period failed to sell, but he cracked the lucrative slick magazine market in 1946 when he sold his first story to *Collier's.*

The sale was unexpected, since the editor kept sending it back for changes. "Between us," Hamilton says, "we rewrote that damn little love story seven times. When still another letter came from *Collier's* I thought we were just shooting for revision eight . . . but when I opened the envelope out fell a check for seven hundred and fifty dollars!"

Nineteen-forty-seven brought Hamilton's first hardcover sale, *Date with Darkness,* issued by Rinehart, and the publication of the novella "The Black Cross" in the influential *American Magazine.* As the titles suggest, each is classic noir, with unrelenting suspense, and a cast of characters who are rarely what they present themselves to be.

Hamilton's early preference for an essentially nonviolent protagonist (often a recently discharged or still-serving naval officer with no combat experience) who becomes more competent and dangerous as the menace heightens, suggests the strong influence of both John Buchan's *The Thirty-Nine Steps* and Geoffrey Household's *Rogue Male.* Another similarity may be seen in Hamilton's use of assassination as a plot element.

Hamilton's next triumph was *The Steel Mirror.* This story of an insecure chemist who becomes involved with a beautiful and enigmatic woman is noteworthy for the tension wrought by a cross-country car chase as the chemist tries to uncover the reason for the mysterious woman's flight, while protecting her from her unrelenting pursuers.

In 1953 Hamilton branched out and began to write Westerns. Even so, he continued to fall back on the idea of an Everyman pulled into trouble by circumstances beyond his control. As before, assassination would continue to be the impetus for the hero's involvement. *Smoky Valley* tells the story of John Parrish, an unassuming easterner who has gone west to recover from a bad wound received in the Civil War. Parrish's small size and his eastern sensibilities lead everyone in Logasa, New Mexico, to underestimate and even deride him. He bears this with quiet stoicism, because "he had become used to the way these people tended to dismiss as insignificant any man . . . unless he was at least six and a half feet tall and suitably wide to match." What the townspeople don't realize is that Parrish served as a captain of Union cavalry at the age of twenty. The ten years since the war have mellowed a reckless youth into a man of grim and quiet resolve who is about to turn the "smoky valley" on its ear.

Parrish is disturbed by the murder of the tough but elderly town marshal by men in the employ of cattle baron Lew Wilkison, but as he is about to marry town belle Caroline Vail and take her back east, he remains aloof. However, events occur that shake Parrish out of his complacency. He meets Judith Wilkison, the headstrong younger daughter of Lew Wilkison, and is intrigued by her forthrightness and cool disdain for Parrish's perceived indifference. Presently, Parrish recognizes that Caroline's supposed love for him is no more than a cold-hearted ruse to escape Logasa, and that her heart really belongs to George Menefee, a dissolute lawyer.

The final blow comes when the Pecos Kid, Wilkison's top gun, kills one of Parrish's young cowboys. This insult, falling so close to home, focuses the disquiet Parrish has felt at the marshal's murder into a cold rage.

Parrish tracks the hired gunslinger to a saloon, and, with ruthless effiency, kills him.

The death of the gunslinger immediately makes Parrish a lightning rod for local animosity against Wilkison, and results in an alliance among smaller ranchers. At the conclusion, Parrish transfers his affections to Judith Wilkison, who has stood beside him, gun in hand, through the worst of the danger.

Although Hamilton would publish only a few Westerns, the themes in this novel would carry over into the others. Of his five Westerns, three would feature as heroes transplanted easterners unused to the ways of the West, but fully able to deal with them. James McKay of *The Big Country* is a tough clipper-ship captain. Alexander Burdick, the hero of *The Man from Santa Clara,* is a photographer from Washington, D.C., who possesses an uncanny skill with a double-barreled shotgun and an almost suicidal relish of danger. Each has known or will experience romantic disappointments with women who were unworthy of them, and each finds true love with a two-fisted western gal.

The latter two of Hamilton's Western protagonists are true western cowboys, but they share the same quiet strength that enables them to vanquish their enemies and win the love of a good woman. Boyd Cohoon of *Mad River* returns from a term in prison to find his father and brother dead and his hometown in the grip of Paul Westerman, a power-hungry rancher. His tenacity and skill with a knife enable him to avange his family's deaths and resurrect his own tarnished reputation. Along the way he survives the perfidy of Claire Paradine, who promised to wait for him, and finds love with Nan Montoya, a dance-hall girl.

Chuck McAuliffe of *Texas Fever* takes over his father's cattle drive when the older man is murdered, and manages to both command the respect of his father's men and extract vengence from the outlaw gang that murdered him.

A particualarly interesting facet of *Texas Fever* is the character Amanda Netherton. Hamilton's Westerns invariably feature two women to whom the hero is attracted, and a defining moment in each of the first four books is when the hero discovers that the original object of his desire is unworthy of him. Amanda is an outlaw, but she is not without conscience. After sexually initiating Chuck and receiving a marriage proposal in return, she becomes so consumed with regrets about the path her life has taken that she commits suicide. The tragedy provides the impetus for Chuck's defeat of villain Jack Keller, and clears the way for his later marriage to "good" girl Jean Kincaid.

However, Hamilton's real western breakthrough was *The Big Country.* This story of an eastern ship captain who comes west to marry the daughter of a powerful rancher has a subtle brilliance to it. Jim McKay finds himself, against his will, embroiled in a land and water dispute between his prospective father-in-law, Major Terrill, and Old Rufus Hannessey.

Jim runs into trouble with his bride and her father when he seemingly avoids every opportunity to prove his manhood with guns, fists, and horses. Jim's impatience with western ways seems cowardly, but he stubbornly follows his own path, eventually realizing that Pat Terrill's doubts about his manhood make marriage to her an impossibility.

His growing friendship with Julie Maragon, Pat's best friend and owner of a crucial piece of land that both warring factions want because of the water that runs through it, eventually prompts Jim to purchase the land from Julie and make the water available to all. When Rufus Hannessey, not knowing of her sale of the land to Jim, kidnaps Julie, a violent showdown brews between Major Terrill and Rufus. Jim forces his way between the two factions, rescues Julie, and remains in Texas to marry her and build his own ranch.

The book was adapted into a mammoth Technicolor motion picture with an all-star cast that included Gregory Peck, Carroll Baker, Jean Simmons, Charlton Heston, Charles Bickford, and Burl Ives. The film was nominated for several Academy Awards, won awards for best musical score and best supporting actor (Burl Ives), and brought Donald Hamilton's name to the attention of the public like none of his previous books had.

Even during this particualrly fertile period in the Western genre, Hamilton continued to create memorable work in the suspense field. In 1955 he published the first of two books that may be thought of as the foundation for the Matt Helm series. As *Line of Fire* opens, gunsmith and expert marksman Paul Nyquist is lining up the sights of a scoped rifle on a gubernatorial candidate in the streets below. The report of the rifle that, strangely, only wounds the candidate, is followed by the unexpected entry of an innocent woman into the room. A gunman accompanying Paul tries to kill the girl, but Paul inexplicably kills him first. Paul gets the girl out of town and does his best to hide her involvement, eventually marrying her to insure her protection.

As the story unfolds, it becomes clear that Paul is in reluctant league with a gangster who is backing the candidate, and the attempted assassination was engineered to generate sympathy. It is clear that Paul despises the gangster, but there is a bond between them. Paul once saved his life during a hunting trip, but was injured, and rendered sexually impotent, during the rescue.

A sexually available moll who belongs to the gangster also enters the scene, and it is apparent that she has been trying, unsuccessfully, to "cure" Paul of his impotence for some time. It is also apparant that Paul is a borderline suicide, seemingly waiting for the right set of circumstances to push him over the edge.

This motley cast of characters becomes a volatile mix as Paul and the gangster head toward a dramatic showdown. Of perhaps more interest is the ambivalent romantic relationship that brews between Paul and the young woman he has saved from murder. The story ends on a hopeful note, but with Paul's impotence left unresolved at the conclusion.

A number of Hamilton trademarks are on display here. The hero's familiarity with guns and knives (Nyquist is Hamilton's earliest hero to use a blade), his sardonic, self-mocking first-person narration, and the moral ambiguity that hangs over virtually every character make the story perhaps one of Hamilton's most intriguing during this stage of his career.

The second of these "foundation" novels is *Assignment: Murder.* The novel opens as Dr. James Gregory, a mathematician with high-level government clearance, is shot while out hunting. Initially, he thinks that he has been the victim of a hunter who has mistaken him for an animal. However, after the third shot, it becomes clear that the hunter has been hunting him. Drawing on a reserve of strength he didn't know he had, Gregory fires his own rifle at the assailant, and kills him with a single shot, still thinking that his assailant is nothing but "a trigger-happy hunter." A federal agent named Van Horn who visits him in the hospital isn't so sure.

Gregory's next visitor is his wife, Natalie, who has just returned from Reno, where she went seeking a divorce. "She had been twenty when I married her," he says. "The whole thing had been a mistake, of course, but I could still think of arguments in its favor." It is evident from the conversation that follows that there is still a strong affection between the two of them.

Gregory's third visitor is Nina Rasmussen, the sister of the man who shot him. She comes in with a gun, but Natalie spoils her aim, and then knocks her out with a vase.

An idyll with Natalie follows while Gregory recuperates, but when a close friend and colleague on Gregory's atomic research project is found murdered and Gregory refuses to leave the project, Natalie decides to return to Reno and finish the divorce. Presently, her car is found wrecked, and she is missing. The deaths or disappearances of three others connected to Gregory's secret project add up to a conspiracy, both to Agent Van Horn and to Gregory himself.

Gregory eventually discovers that Nina Rasmussen and others are out to stop the research project by eliminating the scientists involved. In a move that presages the behavior of Matt Helm, Gregory ventures into the New Mexico wilderness, allowing himself to be captured. There, with the help of a hidden knife and several guns, Gregory manages to destroy the cell of domestic saboteurs. An interesting feature of the story is the tension created by his growing affection and admiration for Nina Rasmussen, and the ultimate necessity for wiping out her and her fellow saboteurs, which Gregory accomplishes with cold-blooded efficiency.

Nineteen-sixty is a watershed year, because it was then that Hamilton was tendered a fateful opportunity. Fawcett Gold Medal had, for some while, been successfully marketing Edward S. Aarons's *Assignment* series, which featured American espionage agent Sam Durrell. Durrell was an operative who worked overseas, usually in exotic locales. Fawcett was looking for a counteragent who would work against foreign spies within the boundaries of the United States. It was suggested that the new counterspy should be an assassin, since there was no more permanent way to counter the activities of a foreign spy than to kill him.

It is worth noting here that even though Ian Fleming had been publishing the James Bond novels since the early fifties, Bond was not yet well known in America, since none of the motion pictures had yet been filmed, nor had President Kennedy yet mentioned his affection for them to the press. In a very real sense, Helm predates Bond in the American imagination and, as critic Robin Winks has noted, stands up as a better creation, book for book, than Bond ever has.

Helm is introduced as a regular guy remarkably like Hamilton himself. He is happily married with children, an avid outdoorsman and hunter, and an accomplished writer and photographer. As his story opens, he and his wife are at a cocktail party in Santa Fe, New Mexico, when a woman he has not seen in fifteen years, known to him only by the code-name Tina, enters the room and gives him a secret recognition signal. Instantly, a solid citizen named Matthew Helm begins to die, and a deadly wartime assassin known as Eric rises from the ashes.

Within hours, Helm finds a young woman he met at the party dead in his study, but he is strangely unfazed by the discovery. "Already I had readjusted," he tells us.

> It happened that quickly. Three hours ago I'd been a peaceful citizen and a happily married man zipping my wife's coctail dress up the back . . .

> At that time, the death of a girl—particularly a pretty girl I'd met and talked with—would have been cause for horror and dismay. Now it was a minor nuisnace. She was a white chip in a no-limits game. She was dead, and we'd never had much time for the dead.

The compelling aspect of these first two dozen pages is the effortlessness with which Helm slips back into his half-forgotten patterns of behavior. He finds himself sizing up possible antagonists, and seems to relish the possibility of testing them in some kind of contest. We begin to realize that Helm has been kidding himself for the past fifteen years. He wanted to be an ordinary citizen, to forget his past, and live a normal life, but it's all disappearing before his eyes and ours. He's a predator, comfortable with the idea of killing, unbothered by the blatant face of death, and he's never been anything else. Helm narrates his story in such a reasonable tone, with occasional flashes of wry humor, that for a while we don't fully appreciate the impact of the change.

Tina reappears in Helm's study, identifies herself as an American agent, and explains that the dead woman was an enemy agent bent on the murder of an important atomic scientist, who happens to be Helm's neighbor. Suspicious, Helm neverthless agrees to assist her, and they leave in his pickup truck.

As they travel through the Southwest, Helm recalls more and more memories of his wartime life, allows himself to be seduced by Tina, and falls easily into the rhythm of a counterintelligence agent. We notice, and are disturbed by, his lack of resistance, particularly in the casual manner of his adultery.

At a certain point, Helm is confronted by his old boss, a man known to him only as Mac. Mac explains that Tina is working for the Russians, and that she was using Helm to get close enough to his neighbor to kill him. Mac, punctilious in both manner and speech, chides Helm for his gullibility. However, it is apparent to us, if not to Mac, that Helm was more than willng to be led astray.

With their cover blown, Tina and her associates decide to force Helm to commit their assassination for them, and to insure his cooperation, they kidnap his youngest daughter.

The final pages of this novel are remarkable for the depiction of Helm's mind as he ventures forth to kill his enemies. Provided with a fast car by Mac to get him where he needs to go, he walks around it, commenting, "It was the ugliest damn hunk of automotive machinery I'd ever had the misfortune to be associated with . . ." He provides us with a running commentary on the car for the next two pages, just as if he were a regular joe talking cars with a buddy, instead of a man about to dive willingly and cold-bloodedly into murder.

After reaching Santa Fe, he goes to rendezvous with one of Tina's associates, a man named Loris with whom he's already had a run-in.

> As I came up, he was saying something. His attitude was impatient and bullying. I suppose he was asking what the hell I was doing there, and telling me what would happen to me or Betsy if I was trying to pull something . . . I didn't hear the words . . . There was nothing he had to say that I had to hear . . . I took out the gun and shot him five times in the chest.

Soon, Helm finds Tina and systematically tortures her until she reveals the whereabouts of his daughter. He learns what he needs to know, but in an ending rife with dark irony, Helm is arranging Tina's bloody corpse to simulate a suicide when his wife walks in. Now the death of the citizen is complete. Horrified at the discovery that her husband isn't what she thought, Beth Helm leaves Matt, freeing him to return to a life that he now knows he should never have left.

In an era where paperback originals were seldom given credence as an art form and rarely reviewed, this stunning debut captured the eye of the dean of mystery critics, Anthony Boucher, who wrote in the *New York Times* that "Donald Hamilton . . . has brought to the spy novel the authentic hard realism of Hammett; and his stories are as compelling and probably as close to the sordid truth of espionage as any now being told."

Helm is, perhaps, the most single-minded and pragmatic secret agent in the genre. It isn't that Helm is incapable of tenderness or even regret, but more that for him, behaving like a professional at all times and in all ways pervades every facet of his character. It is, as Robin Winks explains, perhaps the only sustenance of "a man wishing he could find someone to believe in."

When an enemy female agent is killed while trying to assassinate him, he bends down to talk to her in her final moments:

> "I'm dying, aren't I?"
> "I should hope so," I said. "If not, we'll have to send my associate back to marksmanship school."
> After a shocked moment, she managed a little ghost of a laugh. "Thanks," she gasped. "Thanks for not feeling obligated to lie unconvincingly and tell me I'm going to be fine, just fine."
> "That bullshit is for amateurs," I said. "We're all pros here, aren't we?"

Helm often expresses admiration for a worthy opponent, as he does after outmaneuvering Jimmy Hanohano in *The Betrayers:*

> He licked his lips. "You . . . tricked me, haole!"
> It was no time to apologize. He didn't want my apologies. He wanted to know that he was dying at the hands of a man, not a kid who would weep over his kills.
> I said harshly, "I'm a pro, kanaka. I don't fight for pleasure, just for keeps."
> He showed me his big bright grin instead. "Too bad for you, man. You'll miss a lot of fun that way, a lot of fun . . ."
> Then the message got through to his brain at last and his face changed, and he pitched forward in the dirt of the cane field . . .. I'd never known him, but I was going to miss him anyway.

Very often the only kinship Helm can find is with an enemy. In *The Ravagers,* his attempt to disarm a female enemy armed with an acid-filled glass water pistol backfires, and she is badly burned and disfigured by the acid. The agent's accomplices are holding the daughter of Helm's love interest, and he knows that the only chance he has to rescue the daughter is to force the information from the injured woman. He offers a death pill in return for her cooperation:

> "I love you [, Helm]. You're almost as mean as I am."
> "Meaner," I said. "I'll come visit you in the hospital. See how you're coming with your left-handed Braille."
> I heard Jenny stir behind me. I guess she thought I was terrible, even though it was her child I was fighting for. She didn't count here. She didn't know how it was. She wasn't a pro, like the two of us.

It is a skillful and subtle replay of the end of his marriage. He and Jenny have fallen in love, but this exchange is sufficient to wreck the budding relationship.

Of all the women he meets during the course of his adventures, the two with whom he experiences anything close to a relationship are his enemies. The first is Robin Rostyn, whom he first meets in *Murderer's Row,* and the other is the Russian agent Vadya, who makes her debut in *The Ambushers.*

He duals with these women several times before, inevitably, losing them to violent death. Hamilton's subtlety of technique is at its peak on these occasions, as Helm gently leaks his sorrow, remorse, and anger from behind his stoicism, and acknowledges that anyone who gets colse to him may be used up by the violence swirling about him.

Like many of Hamilton's earlier protagonists, Helm has a fondness for edged weapons, even though he occasionally muses that "nowadays there's supposed to be something very underhanded and un-American about a knife." In another story in which he reveals some of his origins, he explains how he defended himself with a knife against a group of drunken college upperclassmen bent on hazing him. Helm explains:

> They could have gone and had their tight little fun anywhere they damned well pleased, except in my room at my expense. I made that quite clear to them before the action started . . . As far as I'm concerned, people can either stick to polite, civilized conduct, or I'll give them jungle all the way.

In 1977 Hamilton published what many feared was the last Matt Helm novel. *The Terrorizers* is somewhat unique in that, for a change, the object of Helm's pursuit is a gang of American terrorists with a leftist agenda. Helm, as he often does, manages to have himself captured by the gang, then waits for the opening he needs to turn the tables on them. When it comes, the battle Hamilton describes is a skillful choreography of violence. At the end, Helm stands alone in a roomful of people he has killed, noting that "when I let up on the trigger, the silence was frightening."

For the first time in his life the horror of the fight and the pain of his own wounds is nearly overwhelming:

> I was reluctant to move. I had a feeling that I would fall apart into a large number of little red squshy pieces if I tried to move. I was the last man alive in hell, a sinner myself knee deep in the burning blood of other sinners.

Now, at the end, the act of killing has become almost too much for him. As he comes to his senses enough to realize that the one person he has come to kill, the female leader, remains alive, he tells us, "I heard somebody say, "No. Go away, damn you. I don't want to . . . It's enough, go away." But once again, the predator in him, the professional, won't allow him to be defeated:

> The voice was mine. But nobody cared about what I wanted. I wasn't here to satisfy ny wants . . . I slipped the weapon out of the plastic case, took the caps off the scope . . . moved to the galley door . . . She was closer now. I opened the door. She saw me, stared at me, picked up the long skirts, and started to run back up the graveled road from the pier. I put the crosshairs in the proper place, applied easy pressure on the trigger,and let the weapon fire when it wanted to . . . After a while I had to sit down.

In the final scene, we find the hospitalized agent unsure of his future, and at least considering the possibility of a high-level desk job.

In the years following, Hamilton spent his time developing what might be thought of as his only "blockbuster" novel, *The Mona Intercept*. Reading it in the light of his earlier career, one can see virtually all of Hamilton's literary preoccupations at work. Women, both ineffectual and stalwart, are on display. Nonviolent Everymen driven to violence by criminal attack and bureaucratic indifference outnumber, but do not quite supplant ruthless government agents. There are also criminals who sacrifice themselves in a noble attempt to atone for their tragic flaws. The story seems to have everything but Matt Helm, and one almost wishes he was there. Even Robin Winks had reservations, stating in his book *Modus Operandi* (1982) that *The Mona Intercept* was "a possibly unwise experiment with substantially weightier fiction."

After a five-year absence, Matt Helm reappeared in *The Revengers*. Like *The Mona Intercept*, which preceded it, *The Revengers* is a large book with a plot more complex than the earlier stories, as are the books that follow it.

This new Helm (it's hard to think

of him as the original Helm, who would have to be in his late sixties by this appearance) is a bit different than the earlier one in that he is less ruthless, less willing to kill, and is a bit too sentimental about the women he meets. His love affairs, which often end badly for him, seem to take more out of him than his liaisons of the past.

His role in Mac's secret agency is changed now, too. Helm now appears more as a company troubleshooter than as Mac's favored and most skilled assassin. These books are a bit less fufilling than the earlier ones, if for no other reason than that the sheer size of them gets in the way of the thing Hamilton was best at—building suspense and maintaining it through the final pages.

For much of his career, Hamilton has produced a body of literature that is remarkably free of formula, and a protagonist who defies easy classification. That Matt Helm is a willing killer who also loves dogs and the heroic lore of his country is a paradox that continually kept him a fresh creation over several decades of time.

Andy East, in his *Cold War File* (1983), estimated that more than twenty million Matt Helm books had been published worldwide. The continued appearance of new titles and the retention in print of earlier ones suggests that the total may be half again as much as today. Hamilton's fully realized protagonist, crisp, taut dialog, and skilfully choreographed fight scenes make him one of the best of the Gold Medal writers and an enduring legend, both to readers and to the many writers who consider him an influence.

CHECKLIST: DONALD HAMILTON

Hamilton's early hardcover appearances were in relatively short runs, so finding any of them in a collectible state may be a considerable challenge. Paperback reprints, usually in Dell Mapback editions, may also be difficult to find in mint condition, given the quality of paper and glue bindings from that era. The same may be said of the Dell First Editions and the early Fawcett Gold Medal editions of his work. The value of paperbacks is volatile, and may differ widely from one dealer to the other.

All of the bibliographic data for this checklist was compiled by Raymond J. Peters.

Date with Darkness. New York: Rinehart, "R," copyright 1947 by Donald Hamilton.

The Steel Mirror. New York: Rinehart, "R," copyright 1948 by the Curtis Publishing Company. Copyright 1948 by Donald amilton.

Murder Twice Told. New York: Rinehart, "R," copyright 1947, 1949, 1950 by Donald Hamilton (includes the novellas "The Black Cross" and "Deadfall").

Smoky Valley. New York: Dell, April 1954 (Dell First Edition number 18).

Night Walker. New York: Dell, August 1954 (Dell First Edition number 27).

Line of Fire. New York: Dell, January 1955 (Dell First Edition number 46).

Mad River. New York: Dell, February 1956 (Dell First Edition number 91).

Assignment: Murder. New York: Dell, October 1956 (Dell First Edition number A123; later reissued as *Assassins Have Starry Eyes,* Gold Medal number k1491).

The Big Country. New York: Dell, April 1958 (Dell First Edition number B115).

Checklist: Donald Hamilton continued

Death of a Citizen. Greenwich, CT.: Fawcett, January 1960 (Fawcett Gold Medal number 957).

The Man from Santa Clara. New York: Dell, July 1960 (Dell First Edition number 817; later reissued as *The Two-Shoot Gun,* Fawcett Gold Medal number R2492).

The Wrecking Crew. Greenwich: Fawcett, August 1960 (Fawcett Gold Medal number 1025).

Texas Fever. Greenwich: Fawcett, September 1960 (Fawcett Gold Medal number 1035, later republished in hardcover by Walker, c1981 10 9 8 7 6 5 4 3 2 1).

The Removers. Greenwich: Fawcett, March 1961 (Fawcett Gold Medal number s1082).

The Silencers. Greenwich: Fawcett, February 1962 (Fawcett Gold Medal number s1194).

Murderer's Row. Greenwich: Fawcett, October 1962 (Fawcett Gold Medal number s1246).

The Ambushers. Greenwich: Fawcett, August 1963 (Fawcett Gold Medal number k1333).

The Shadowers. Greenwich: Fawcett, February 1964 (Fawcett Gold Medal number k1386).

The Ravagers. Greenwich: Fawcett, 1964 (Fawcett Gold Medal number k1452).

The Devatsators. Greenwich: Fawcett, 1965 (Fawcett Gold Medal number d1608).

The Betrayers. Greenwich: Fawcett, November 1966 (Fawcett Gold Medal number d1608).

Iron Men and Silver Stars (editor). Greenwich: Fawcett, 1967 (Fawcett Gold Medal number d1821; includes the first appearance of Hamilton's short story, "The Guns of William Longley").

The Menacers. Greenwich: Fawcett, 1968 (Fawcett Gold Medal number d1884).

The Interlopers. Greenwich: Fawcett, May 1969 (Fawcett Gold Medal number T2073).

On Guns and Hunting. Greenwich: Fawcett, September 1970 (Fawcett Gold Medal number T2299).

The Poisoners. Greenwich: Fawcett, March 1971 (Fawcett Gold Medal number T2392).

The Intriguers. Greenwich: Fawcett, January 1973 (Fawcett Gold Medal number M2659).

The Intimidators. Greenwich: Fawcett, March 1974 (Fawcett Gold Medal number P2938).

The Terminators. Greenwich: Fawcett, April 1975 (Fawcett Gold Medal number P3214).

The Retaliators. New York: Fawcett, August 1976.

The Terrorizers. New York: Fawcett, September 1977.

The Mona Intercept. New York: Fawcett, December 1980.

Cruises with Kathleen. New York: David McKay Company, 1980.

The Revengers. New York: Fawcett, November 1982.

The Annihilators. New York: Fawcett, August 1983.

The Infiltrators. New York: Fawcett, June 1984.

The Detonators. New York: Fawcett, July 1985.

The Vanishers. New York: Fawcett, August 1986.

The Demolishers. New York: Fawcett, November 1987.

The Frighteners. New York: Fawcett, May 1989.

The Treateners. New York: Fawcett, September 1992.

The Damagers. New York: Fawcett, November 1993.

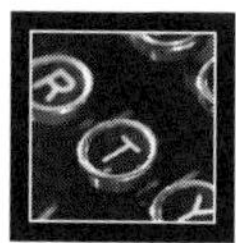

Highsmith's Ripley:
FROM VILLAIN TO VIGILANTE

NOEL MAWER

Have you ever wondered how the criminal mind works? Patricia Highsmith has. Her first novel, *Strangers on a Train,* focused on the pathology of a central character; and her only series character, Ripley, is a professional criminal. Some writers might make the hero charming—a bumbling crook, or a swashbuckling villain—but not Highsmith. Ripley is a thief, a murderer; he even takes risks in order to make it all more "fun."

Ripley undergoes some very interesting changes throughout the four-book series.* In his debut, he lives in a fantasy world, and Highsmith presents him as the unfortunate product of a corrupt society. By the fourth book, society is presented as a malignant force that makes criminal behavior an inevitability. A close look at this most unusual series, which began in 1956 and was last added to in 1980, shows Ripley's progression from a villain to a vigilante as the world in which he lives becomes even too evil for his taste.

The original Tom Ripley, in the 1956 *The Talented Mr. Ripley,* lives in a society that hardly touches him—that, in fact, he half created in his imagination. Tom is given a conventional fairy-tale orphan's background, complete with a sadistic aunt who belittled and humiliated him. Apparently as a result of this, Tom is lacking in self-confidence and drive, has identity problems, and creates his own imaginary world. Such a self-created world comes in later life to control him, and he loses his ability to tell real from imaginary. It is this invented "reality," coupled with Tom's weak sense of ego and contempt for the "real" Tom Ripley, which leads him first to attempt to alter his identity and finally to kill another human being with whom he has identified, actually assuming his identity.

Tom's great need to find an identity leads him to attempt to find it through "love": someone will love him, and he will lose himself in the identity of that person. He meets and seizes upon Dickie Greenleaf. "More than anything else in the world," Tom wants Dickie to like him, but in this Tom fails:

> In Dickie's eyes Tom saw nothing more now than he would have seen if he had looked at the hard, bloodless surface of a mirror. Tom felt a painful wrench in his breast, and he covered his face with his hands. It was as if Dickie had been suddenly snatched from him. They were not friends. They didn't know each other. It struck Tom like a horrible truth, true for all time, true for all the people he

> had known in the past and for those he would know in the future: each had stood and would stand before him, and he would know time and time again that he would never know them, and the worst was that there would always be an illusion, for a time, that he did know them, and that he and they were completely in harmony and alike.

Tom's disappointment finally results in murderous rage toward the would-be object of his love and identification, so he kills Dickie and finds after Dickie's death the identity that has eluded him: he assumes Dickie's name, his appearance, his voice, his manner, until it finally comes easier to Tom to be Dickie than to be Tom Ripley.

Tom Ripley's imagination has vast powers over the external world. It can cause "the whole city of New York" to "collapse with a *poof* like a lot of cardboard on a stage." But it does not have the power to give Tom Ripley self-confidence, or cause others to love or even like him. Since Tom could not get Dickie to love him, he killed him, and now he must go on killing in order to protect his new identity as Dickie Greenleaf. He has no doubt that these murders are justified; they are, after all, necessary to protect what simply is *due* him. In these latter respects, Tom becomes more the type, not of the psychotic in his world of delusions, but of the amoral, unfeeling psychopathic criminal—the type he will become in later novels.

Another development within Tom in this first novel is his increasing enjoyment, not only of his masquerade, but of the feeling of danger that goes with it. He has always chosen to "tempt fate," to "take a chance" whenever he can. After the first murder, "it was as if he were really inviting trouble, and couldn't stop himself." He thinks about taking risks and realizes that "risks were what made the whole thing fun" because "he was so bored." What had begun as a need to find a secure and acceptable identity has become a need for stimulation, for excitement to allay the boredom of life. For Tom, in whatever incarnation, cannot really feel very much. His overriding need is always to fill up the void that is Tom Ripley—with another's identity, with the stimulation of danger.

***

These latter elements are further developed in the second novel, *Ripley Under Ground* (1970). The recognizable traits of the psychopathic criminal, which have become evident in Tom by the end of *The Talented Mr. Ripley,* here dominate. Tom is no longer at the mercy of his imagination, and he is now Tom Ripley pretty consistently, and apparently satisfied with this. Tom now prides himself on his sensitivity, sincerity, and moral rectitude, while at the same time emerging as a moral Typhoid Mary. In the first novel, Tom murdered the person closest to him. In the second and third in the series, he becomes a malignant influence on those who are sucked into his orbit. In each novel, someone is driven to suicide through contact with him.

In *Ripley Under Ground,* Tom is a creator and part owner of a counterfeit painting racket. Bernard, the counterfeiter, becomes increasingly distraught over his own dishonesty, and Tom realizes that Bernard must die or he will expose the scheme and ruin everyone involved. When, after lengthy pursuit by Tom, Bernard kills himself, "Tom began to realize that he had willed or wished Bernard's suicide." Bernard has accused Tom of being the "origin" of the whole fraud, and Tom's response is to acknowledge—while deriding—the fact that people look upon him as "a mystic origin, a font of evil."

In this novel, Tom is less a prey to his fantasies, more secure in himself, but more in need of external stimulation to alleviate his boredom. Even some of his criminal activities, such as smuggling, cause him to experience "fatigue, contempt, boredom even." Only *danger* can alleviate this boredom, and the excitement of the dangerous game banishes all other concerns. Tom tells himself—and, as is usual with his imaginary constructs, *believes*—that he is concerned with ethics, with right and wrong. He even has feelings of sympathy for the wife of one of his murder victims. But Tom never really feels very much—including a sense of "right" and "wrong." He "saw the right and wrong, yet both sides of himself were equally sincere," because for Tom the actual reality is still that bottomless pit that is Tom's lack of identity—of any inner self. He is in constant—and increasing—need of stimulation to fill that void. And the more he fills it, the less he feels, and the more he needs. When the art collector first reveals that he is onto the forgeries, Tom does not know if he should feel anything or not: "Tom was unworried. Ought he to be more worried? He shrugged slightly."

Tom is fairly consistently self-confident, he is aware of his lack of a basic sense of right and wrong, but he is also becoming increasingly moralistic and self-righteous, and this characteristic manifests itself in his responses to French society. He thinks with scorn of "French bloody-mindedness, greed, a lie that was not exactly a lie but a deliberate concealment of fact." In Tom's observations about French society, Highsmith initiates the move toward depicting the actual society in which her protagonist functions. In *The Talented Mr. Ripley,* Tom lives in a New York City of his own imagination and in an Italian tourist wonderland. The natives are hardly noticed, and crime is not a significant enough occurrence to be commented on. In *Ripley Under Ground,* French society is full of greedy, dishonest people, and crime is a way of life—a business. Tom's new friend, Reeves Minot, is a smuggler by profession, and Tom's "business" interest is art forgery. Even murder is a business in this society, and the "honest" people are not really honest, cheating each other every chance they get. This is a different picture of society from that in the first Ripley novel, and this Tom is more confident but more criminal, more hardened. These changes will be developed in the next two Ripley novels, but with the added twist that Tom, while rarely seeing himself as evil (or even criminal), will become increasingly disgusted with criminal activity in society and will begin to direct his efforts *against* other criminals—and simply, he will tell himself, for the sake of foiling professional criminals. At the same time, he will continue to seduce and to destroy ordinary, innocent people—and still see himself as a decent, moral person. In the most recent Ripley novel, Tom does, in fact, see himself as the hero, fighting impersonal crimes in a corrupt society.

***

In *Ripley's Game* (1974), the focus is divided between Tom and his victim, Jonathan Trevanny, who seems to serve as counterpoint to Tom: against Tom's pretensions to ethics and morality is placed the genuinely ethical and moral Jonathan. And, while Tom always feels that he "understands" Jonathan, Jonathan *never* feels that he understands Tom. While Tom's "understanding" of Trevanny is always skewed, he yet is able to draw Trevanny into his schemes, and finally—while convincing himself that he is Trevanny's benefactor—to destroy him, both morally and physically. Tom's malignancy is stronger than the ordinary man's morality, just as, in society as it is seen in this novel, crime is stronger than honesty and the lives of criminals are worth more than the lives of ordinary citizens.

The Tom-Jonathan comparison is ubiquitous throughout *Ripley's Game.* Jonathan cannot manage the self-control to lie convincingly to his wife; Tom is still the master of invention, and one of his greatest inventions is his perception of himself as sensitive, ethical, and civilized. It is he who suggests pulling Jonathan into his and Reeves's criminal schemes, but when Reeves actually acts of the suggestion, Tom calls it "a dirty, humorless trick." Tom's luring Jonathan into crime is soon looked upon by him as an act of beneficence, and he both congratulates himself and feels some empathy with Jonathan, whom he can now view as just a murderer, like himself. As he did with Dickie Greenleaf, Tom identifies with his victim and feels the warmest of feelings for him—while never understanding that Jonathan both abhors and is mystified by Tom. Tom engages in crime to allay the boredom of his life—the boredom of being Tom Ripley. Jonathan has no need for stimulation and, in fact, after at first feeling "a bit euphoric" thinking of the money he will earn for his wife and child, is able to feel nothing.

To Tom, it is imperative that he see the rest of the world as no better than himself—as corruptible, as always having something to be ashamed of, as Jonathan must have felt once he became a murderer. Tom constructs a picture of himself as a heroic figure, kindly benefactor to Jonathan Trevanny, and moral superior to most criminals. He has the utmost contempt for large-scale, professional criminals, such as the Mafia, of whom he thinks as "more dishonest, more corrupt, decidedly more ruthless than himself." And because "the law couldn't get its hands on the bigger bastards among them," he, Tom, will become a vigilante, assassinating criminals whom the law cannot touch.

But, Tom's pretensions to moral righteousness aside, the society portrayed *is* growing more corrupt, at least within the context of the Ripley novels. Organized crime and random violence exist in a society in which governments do not seem to be "aware of the insane actions of some of their spies. Or those whimsical, half-demented men flitting from Bucharest to Moscow and Washington with guns and microfilm." This last is Tom's view, and in such a context Tom's "game" is relatively harmless, his claim to be a force for the good and the right almost credible. It is these claims and this eroding society that become dominant in *The Boy Who Followed Ripley* (1980).

The original Tom Ripley created his own reality. In *The Boy,* the deception is more often on the part of the environment, and Tom is at its mercy. The illusion of wilderness in the Grunewald Forest of West Berlin first leads Tom to wonder if *everything* is not an illusion, and then leads him to succumb to the deceptions of a gang of criminals and to fail to prevent the kidnapping of Frank (the "boy" of the title). External forces exert an unaccustomed control over Tom. After Frank's kidnapping, Tom feels that he "had never felt thus shaken by something that he himself had done, because in such cases in the past, he had been in control of things. Now he was anything but in control." Unlike the earlier, omnipotent Tom, this Tom becomes "tired of fretting over things he couldn't do anything about."

Tom once again identifies with the male figure in the story but this time seeks to *protect* his alter ego from the society that threatens both of them. No longer does he seduce the innocent into crime (Frank is a murderer before he meets Tom). And, this time, Frank's suicide seems to have nothing to do with Tom's influence. In this case, Tom's identification seems benign, a magnanimous, protective gesture. His perception of his righteousness grows as he opposes the professional criminals who try to kidnap Frank, and his perception seems (for a change) fairly close to reality. Tom initiates no evil, and the forces he is battling do seem more evil than he is. But the old Tom is still there, pursuing criminals finally for the ultimate good: the risk, the danger, the stimulation. And Tom Ripley the heroic crime fighter is still Tom Ripley who thinks like a criminal, anticipating the kidnappers at every turn-and succumbing to the foolhardy out of his abiding love of danger.

The old Tom Ripley is still with us, but the society in which he operates is now so rotten—*really* rotten—that the criminal with a "code" comes off as a hero. *Any* morality is superior to the total depravity into which most of society has sunk.

***

This view of society is not confined to the later Ripley novels. In *The Glass Cell* (1964), Highsmith depicts a naïve protagonist first victimized by criminals, then corrupted by the prison environment in which he is unjustly confined. That Highsmith's focus on society begins to usurp her earlier vision of isolated criminality is underlined by her using *The Glass Cell* as the one extended example of her creative process in her 1966 how-to book, *Plotting and Writing Suspense Fiction* (wherein she speaks of one of the "elements" of the story as "the deleterious effect of exposure to brutality in prison, and how this can lead to antisocial behavior after release"). Her next two novels, excluding the 1970 *Ripley Under Ground* and the 1974 *Ripley's Game,* continue the new interest in social forces: *The Terror of Forgery* (1969) depicts the effects of the alien view of criminality in Tunisian society on an American, and *A Dog's Ransom* (1972) is an obsessive portrait of a crime-ridden New York City that corrupts and destroys decent human beings. Three of Highsmith's four most recent novels (*The Boy Who Followed Ripley* is the exception) are set in the United States (and the latest Ripley novel ends there), and none focuses primarily on criminals. All (*Edith's Diary,* 1977; *People Who Knock on the Door,* 1983; and *Found in the Street,* 1986) depict a society in which most people are either obsessed with fanatical religious or political beliefs or are turned inward toward totally self-serving, socially irresponsible behavior. Both orientations can lead to criminality, and they do so in these books. The evolution of the picture of crime and society that occurs in the Ripley novels is consistent with the evolution occurring in Highsmith's other works. But while Ripley's perception of society seems to parallel Highsmith's, his perception of himself does not.

One must remember the irony: Tom Ripley may be right about the world, but he is still thoroughly lacking in insight into Tom Ripley. His motives are, ultimately, the strictly personal ones of his need for the stimulation of danger and, still, for occasionally losing his identity in a masquerade of some kind. These last Ripley novels are not works of social criticism. Patricia Highsmith remains the novelist of the psychological portrayal of criminal behavior. She simply has moved, over the years, toward a more social orientation—to a greater awareness of the effects of society on behavior.

* A fifth and final Ripley novel, *Ripley Under Water,* was published in the 1990's

The hardboiled and the female: in the world of noir they go together like gangbusters.

Not Herself Mean:

HARD-BOILED AND FEMALE, WITHOUT CONTRADICTION

DULCY BRAINARD

The history of female sleuths, which may have begun with Mary Magdalene or even Isis (both went in search of the body), is a venerable one. In modern fiction, it starts off with an impressive group of Victorian characters who investigated crimes committed close to their allotted place within the family or village. But in the last quarter of this century, the female sleuth left home for a wider world where, as professional private investigator, she applied herself in ways that carried her into the previously male-only class of detectives described as hard-boiled.

As a figure of fiction, the female PI entered the American scene abruptly and imperatively in the mid-1970s. Possessed of a well-developed stage presence from the start, she gained increasing authority in the following decade. Her type was vastly different from the genteel, friends—and relations—focused heroines created by Agatha Christie, Patricia Wentworth, or Carolyn Keene. Choosing mean streets over drawing room or kitchen, the woman PI takes cases that Lew Archer, Sam Spade, or Philip Marlowe could have signed on for, investigating crime along paths that these iconic forebears could easily have trod. Despite the common ground, however, the female PI has from the beginning done her work her way. She is not just another hard-boiled private dick in drag.

The honors for introducing the first fictional American woman PI generally go to Maxine O'Callaghan, whose southern California investigator Delilah West appeared in 1974 in *Alfred Hitchcock's Mystery Magazine,* although two years earlier in England, P. D. James brought out *An Unsuitable Job for a Woman,* starring secretary-turned PI Cordelia Gray.

The real beginning occurred a few years later and a few hours north when Marcia Muller introduced young Sharon McCone in her first novel, *Edwin of the Iron Shoes,* published by McKay Washburn in 1977. Very likely in early stages of gestation at that time and appearing first in 1982 were Sue Grafton's Kinsey Millhone, working in southern California's fictional Santa Teresa (*"A" Is for Alibi,* Holt, Rinehard & Winston) and, breaking the West Coast lock, Sara Paretsky's Chicago investigator V. I. Warshawski (*Indemnity Only,* Dial Press). These three pretty much owned the territory for the next six years or so and, while their ranks have been joined by a strong supporting contingent, they remain the three most powerful figures in the genre's female pantheon, characters whose widespread popularity lends heft to their stature as icons fairly representing their kind.

Although in their early adventures, both McCone and Millhone may have been softer boiled than in later stories (Warshawski started out abrasive and has stayed that way), these fictional women burst upon the culture as full grown as did Athena from the forehead of Zeus. The territory they expanded and staked had been partially cleared by a few literary antecedents, but these new figures were able to exert their powerful impact mainly because of the changes that had occurred in the land itself. The sociological, and specifically the gender-related, upheaval of the 1960s had made plausible for a wide readership the existence of a fiercely honorable, angry woman who could carry and use a gun.

The issue wasn't a change in the competency of women but involved a shift in perception that found women being willing—and to some extent allowed—to claim and hold on to their own authority. The powerful woman of the war years—or even the harsh frontier—tended to step out of her boots and into her pumps when times got better, turning away from the valor and accomplishments of hardship to fold up her capabilities and slip them into an apron pocket or one of her new kitchen appliances as a return to normalcy was accompanied by the seductions of the expanding economy. But underneath the trappings of a new and improved lifestyle swelled a cultural sea change that would crest in the 1960s. The social turmoil of that decade eroded the idea of a woman as accessory, home-based and compliant, and cleared the way for a woman who was motivated to be a citizen of the world as well as the hearth, someone who would choose to establish her own identity (and was willing to pay the high emotional price attached) rather than conform to the outline that a male-dominated society had prepared for her.

Crucial among the demands made by young women during that particular wave of feminism was the right to be outwardly angry. Once a woman could be angry in an expressive, active way, she could harness the power of that emotion, rather than sidestep or deny it, to serve others and even society. If her sense of honor was offended, she could stay angry and act to right the wrong she saw. It was with this new capacity particularly that a young woman could shoulder her way into the ranks of the hard-boiled detectives.

McCone, Millhone, Warshawski, and their later-born sisters are moved by the desire to right wrongs perpetrated upon others because their personal sense of honor is offended by such injustices. Although their approaches to detection can be different than those practiced by Marlowe, Spade, and Archer, the option to hold on to anger, to act upon it and keep it kindled as a source of power and determination rather than to transmute it (or turn it inward) is the quality that proves these women are full-blood relations to male noir icons.

VARIATIONS ON THE THEME

In "The Simple Art of Murder," written in 1950, Raymond Chandler delivers an acerbic, intelligent, and biased essay on American detective fiction. It is mainly a tribute to the groundbreaking work of Dashiell Hammett, that "ace performer," in Chandler's view, who wrote detective stories that, "made up out of real things," were not constrained by a "heavy crust of English gentility and American pseudo-gentility." Hammett, Chandler observes, gave murder "back to the kind of people that commit it for reasons, not just to provide a corpse."

It was here that he delivered his

famous description of the character and milieu of the hard-boiled male PI, invented by Hammett and further developed by himself, Ross Macdonald, and a host of others: "But down these mean streets a man must go who is not himself mean, who is neither tarnished nor afraid . . . He is the hero, he is everything. He must be a complete man and a common man and yet an unusual man. He must be, to use a rather weathered phrase, a man of honor, by instinct, by inevitability, without thought of it, and certainly without saying it. He must be the best man in his world and a good enough man for any world." He is also described as private, lonely, and proud, opposed to sham and pettiness, and possessed of a "rude wit."

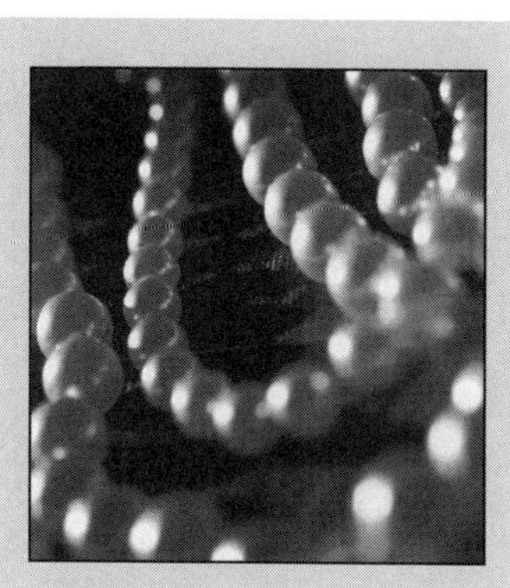

Half a century later in 1995, when the works of Chandler were reprinted in entirety by the Library of America, Joyce Carol Oates penned "The Simple Art of Murder: The Novels of Raymond Chandler" for the *New York Review of Books.* She effectively deflates Chandler's representation of Hammett's PI and his own as realistic and makes a clear case for them as figures of immense fantasy. As evidence, she cites the contrast between their allure for women and disdain of them; their contempt for wealth and privilege and their trafficking among the rich and powerful; their indifference to the opinions of others and the high regard in which others hold them; their ability to live in a gritty, urban, dog-eat-dog world but not be sullied or compromised; and, not least, their ability to survive all manner of physical insult.

The women who came to wear this mantle share much with these "good enough" men: distrusting society's conventions, they judge their behaviors by personal moral standards; they are suspicious of authority, tend not to have partners, and are congenitally inclined toward discontent rather than delight. That they are also fantasy figures is a given—that role and the assurance that they will triumph by the final pages is essential to the genre. But they also exhibit distinctly feminine responses to their situations. They take on cases for different reasons and arrive at conclusions via different paths.

In *Edwin of the Iron Shoes* and for quite a few novels to come, Sharon Mc-Cone does investigative for All Souls Legal Co-operative, a loosely knit organization of lawyers who work for little pay for clients with little to pay with. Right from the start, one of the notable characteristics of the female PI is evident: she's comfortable working in a network of relationships. Even those investigators who work on their own rely heavily on their relationships to accomplish their aims. Among these solo practitioners are Warshawski, Millhone, Carlotta Carlyle, the former Boston cop turned PI/cabbie and introduced by Linda Barnes in 1987 in *A Trouble of Fools* (St. Martin's), Sacramento PI Kat Colorado, Karen Kijewski's creation who appeared first in 1989 in *Katwalk* (St. Martin's), and Linda Grant's white-collar crime investigator Catherine Saylor, who investigates crime in California's Bay Area and was seen first in *Random Access Murder* (Avon, 1988).

Probably the most solitary of this group and consistently the angriest is Warshawski, but she'd falter seriously without the crucial succor of such continuing friends as Dr. Lotty Herschel and her downstairs neighbor, Mr. Contreras. In a similar way, Millhone, whose personal life is expanded by her reconciliation with members of her distant family, may have worked through husbands (two) and lovers, but her landlord Henry Pitts and tavern-owner pal, Rosie, are significant constants in her cases.

A mark of the male PI in the original mode is a contradictory relationship with women: he generally disdains them with an indifference that spills over into blatant misogyny, yet he is unceasingly alluring to them and is hard pressed to fend them off. He isn't described as any kind of hunk, yet he's depicted as irresistible to the opposite sex. The woman PI, on the other hand, possesses a much more ordinary sexuality. None of them is presented as drop-dead beautiful, although the six-foot-plus Carlotta Carlyle has a glamorous air. They are all possessed of healthy libidos and enjoy sex, but don't inspire fits of lust in every male who comes within sniffing distance. While some of the reasonable balance of love, sex, and business they exhibit may result from their being creatures of this quarter-century rather than an earlier one and some may be an effect of an apparent taboo against rape as an instance of the violence they encounter, for women, sex is a more integrated, less troublesome part of their lives. In their narratives, sex is usually included as an aspect of an ongoing relationship, not a display of desirability or prowess.

For women PIs, peripheral and/or significant relationships are more stable and more important too. McCone begins to break loose from All Souls to work on her own in her fifteenth appearance, *Til the Butchers Cut Him Down,* establishing her own agency, but she peoples it with friends and relations and settles her sights on her lover, Hy Ripinsky; her family too becomes increasingly important to her and her stories. Sandra Scoppetone's Greenwich Village PI, Lauren Laurano, first met in 1991 in *Everything You Have Is Mine* (Little, Brown) is in a long-term lesbian relationship with a psychotherapist; Susan Dunlap's southern California op, Kiernan O'Shaughnessy, who bowed in 1989 in *Pious Deception* (Villard) shares her lavish home with her young male housekeeper.

Children also figure prominently in the personal lives and cases of most women PIs, who are generally unmarried and childless. McCone's sixteenth case (*A Wild & Lonely Place,* 1995) is fueled by the PI's attachment to a kidnapped nine-year-old girl. Minneapolis PI Devon MacDonald, created by Nancy Baker Jacobs, debuted in 1991 in *The Turquoise Tattoo* (Putnam), a novel that, embracing racial politics, centers around a young boy who needs a bone marrow transplant. In Boston, Carlotta Carlyle has nearly adopted Paolina, whom she first met while participating in a Little Sisters program. Across the genre, children as subjects or triggers of plots feature more prominently now than fifty years ago, for example, in Robert B. Parker's Spenser novels or the Dave Robicheaux series by James Lee Burke. But from the start, the uniquely close connection between women and children has been mined to enhance the credibility of the hard-boiled woman.

An additional point is that just as

women PIs are unashamed to be moved by their attachments to others, neither are they willing to be changed by their encounters with crime and/or evil. It's true that the males of more recent vintage are more willing to admit emotional involvements, but even later models resist letting their experiences have significant impact on their self-image. There is with the male a sense that his real triumph is to come through his harrowing experience untouched, remaining the same decent ("good enough") maybe flawed, but upright fellow as when he started out. The women who face off against villainy don't even flirt with such delusions.

Physical danger points to another gender gap. Threats and damage to themselves are occupational hazards that few of these women can avoid, and while they don't usually seek out rough physical engagements, neither do they faint at the sight of blood nor run at the suggestion of pending violence. In the course of their cases they necessarily court it, that's part of their job in the genre. Threatened and beaten (although not raped), some acquire special skills, like martial arts, to even the balance against burly thugs and bad guys. Others simply endure violence when they're not able to avoid it.

None of them kills easily, but carrying a gun and knowing how to use it is part of their trade and when pressed into necessity, they'll shoot. In discussing the hard-boiled male PI as figure of fantasy, Oates suggests that, more than the gun, the PI himself represents a magic phallus to his readers. To the women, there's little magic about either guns or penises, although both are necessary.

FORERUNNERS

No matter how sudden their appearance on the mystery scene, hard-boiled women PIs belong to a tradition, being part of which imbues them with greater dimension and adds to their current vitality.

Inklings of these characters might have been noted by alert observers sixty years earlier in Anna Katherine Green's series of short stories about New York City socialite Violet Strange, who occasionally worked for an investigative agency, and in Green's Amelia Butterworth, a sidekick/helper invented to shore up the efforts of main-man Manhattan sleuth Ebenezer Gryce. Neither, however, was a real pro whose identity was primarily formed through her investigative work.

Nor, really, was Honey West, who was introduced by the pseudonymous G. G. Fickling (in reality Skip and Gloria Fickling) in 1957 in *This Girl for Hire* and starred flamboyantly in ten more paperbacks. Honey West may have been a professional PI but she was also a pin-up figure with impressive measurements, written as an exuberant and funny figure who was competent in spite of herself. Anne Francis played her in a TV series that ran for a couple of years in the mid-sixties, but at her core Honey was a woman of the fifties.

Other prototypical women PIs include Marla Trent, whose two adventures (*Private Eyeful,* 1959; *Kisses of Death,* 1962) were chronicled in paperback by Henry Kane, and Mavis Seidlitz, another pin-up PI invented by Australian Alan G. Yates (writing as Carter Brown), whose agency was in Hollywood and whose twelve slightly manic adventures ran from 1955 to 1972.

Somewhat more removed from the post-sixties class of hard-boiled women PIs but still clearly related are the women pulp writers whose characters were mostly male. Craig Rice, who was really Georgiana Craig, wrote most of her stories (from 1939 to 1967) about a Chicago trio, hard-living lawyer John J. Malone and his married friends Jake and Helene Justus, who traveled in a tony North Shore and Lake Shore Drive social set.

Dolores Hitchins is widely respected for her working-class PI novels, notably *Sleep with Slander,* which capture and hold a deep noir tone. Margaret Millar, who was married to Ross Macdonald and equal to him in talent, crafted expertly plotted tales of suspense over four decades. Other literary godmothers warranting mention are pulp mistresses Dorothy Dunn and Leigh Brackett.

VARIETIES OF INVESTIGATIVE EXPERIENCE

As edifying as a bow to their origins is a look at what the next generation of women PIs has to show. For as much as their belonging to a heritage confirms them as lasting figures of the genre, the variety these characters exhibit as a group is a sure measure of their continuing vibrancy.

The women have proven, perhaps more effectively than the men, that a PI can be as hard-boiled when far removed from an uncaring, hostile city as when operating in the dark heat of one. Kate Shugak, the Aleut PI who was introduced by Dana Stabenow in *A Cold Day for Murder* (Berkley, 1992), left her post as a D.A.'s investigator in Anchorage to move back to a homestead in the Alaskan bush where she was raised. Shugak's struggles with the expectations of her family and tribe, her personal ambivalences about her place in white and Native societies, and her attachments to a spare and demanding landscape are reflected in Jean Hager's stories about a Cherokee tribal investigator in Oklahoma, Molly Bearpaw, who debuted in *Ravenmocker* in 1992 (Mysterious). In Billings, Montana, Phoebe Siegel, the half-Jewish, half-Catholic PI introduced by Sandra West Prowell in 1993 (*By Evil Means,* Walker), finds shadowed byways in Native American traditions, in her own complex family dynamics, and under Montana's big sky.

Although a strictly defined approach to this topic would exclude any female sleuth who wasn't a licensed private investigator, the spirit of the subgenre is enhanced by a slew of female investigators for whom the P stands for a wider variety of profession.

The mean paths of twisted minds and hearts are followed by child abuse investigator Bo Bradley in the dark and effective series by Abigail Padgett. First seen in *Child of Silence* (Mysterious, 1993), Bradley, a caseworker in San Diego, is also a manic-depressive who must manage the unpredictable effects of her own illness as she probes the particularly menacing motivations of those who do damage to kids.

As hard-boiled as any in her personal nature, Kay Scarpetta, Patricia Cornwell's M.D. and high-level forensic pathologist introduced in *Postmortem* (Scribner, 1990), can't be classified easily with this group, but her exclusion is more a result of her capacity as a state official and FBI consultant. That argument applies to Nevada Barr's park ranger sleuth, Anna Pigeon, introduced in 1993 in *Track of the Cat* (Putnam), whose position within an official, sometimes bureaucratic organization prevents her from working like a classic PI but who, like Scarpetta, by attitude and chosen approaches to crime and its investigation, is an honorary member of the tribe.

It's easier for freelancers to fit into the mold. Chicago's investigative reporter Cat Marsala, introduced by Barbara D'Amato in 1990 (*Hardball,* Scribner), makes the most of her experience and research methods to probe the backgrounds of the homicides and related crimes that her stories inevitably contain. Another media-rooted investigator is Wendy Hornsby's Maggie MacGowen, who debuted in *Telling Lies* (Dutton, 1992). She works in L.A. and, like Marsala, draws on the skills of her professional training to uncover and understand both crime and criminals.

An education in law proves a substantial resource for inquiry into homicide and other malfeasance for the leads in two series from Lia Matera, both set in California's Bay Area. Willa Jansson, who appeared first in *Where Lawyers Fear to Tread* (Bantam, 1987), is a child of sixties radicals who retains her own lefty leanings and is skeptical of anything political. Introduced a year later in *The Smart Money* (Bantam), Laura Di Palma is her opposite number. Ambitious and blatantly self-interested, she also demonstrates a saving self-consciousness. New York City's Cass Jameson, whom Carolyn Wheat introduced in 1983 in *Dead Men's Thoughts* (St. Martin's), practiced for the Legal Aid Society before going out on her own. Her involvement in antiwar activity during the Vietnam War and her commitment to justice lend complexity to her dark-toned tales.

There are also, however, plenty of new, young characters who hew to the narrower line of classic noir: Private eyes who work on their own in brutal urban environments. Valerie Wilson Wesley's Tamara Hayle started down Newark, N.J.'s unfriendly streets in 1994's *When Death Comes Stealing* (Putnam). Wesley's inner-city settings and her African-American casts are sharply delineated and fresh, and Hayle is credible, troubled, tough, and resourceful. In Boston, ex-Marine Angie Matelli, introduced by Wendi Lee in *The Good Daughter* (St. Martin's, 1994), combines her respect for brute strength and weapons that kill with intelligence. Like Hayle and many of their sisters, she is both distracted and bolstered by her family's interferences with and opinions about her work.

The decade has also seen the birth and development of Janet Dawson's Jeri Howard, a practicing PI in Oakland since 1990 (*Kindred Crimes,* St. Martin's), Catherine Dain's Freddie O'Neal, first seen in *Lay It on the Line* (Jove, 1992), who plies her trade in the ripe environment of Reno, Nevada, and New York City ops Blaine Stewart, a recovering alcoholic who debuted in Sharon Zukowski's *Dancing in the Dark* (St. Martin's, 1992), and Lillian O'Donnell's Gwenn Ramadge, introduced in 1990 in *A Wreath for the Bride* (Putnam).

Mention must be made of two London PIs who give this American figure a distinct and admirable British spin. By introducing operative Anna Lee in *Dupe* in 1980 (Scribner), Liza Cody demonstrated that the daily life of a woman PI, even one who was close to antisocial and maintained a deep interest in mechanics, could be the stuff of compelling fiction. Sarah Dunant's Hannah Wolfe (*Birth Marks,* Doubleday, 1992) is introspective, frequently outraged, and unremittingly independent-minded. Val McDermid's Kate Brannigan has practiced in working-class Manchester since 1993 (*Dead Beat,* St. Martin's).

In August of 1997, Dick Lochte, a writer whose contribution to the genre grants him plenty of authority, gave high marks to four hard-boiled mysteries in a piece for the *L.A. Times Book Review,* titled "Blame Hammett." Three of the novels were written by men and featured a variation of the hard-boiled male PI. The fourth was Wendy Hornsby's latest Maggie MacGowen story, *Hard Light* (Dutton). Lochte's main point is that today's hard-boiled protagonist is personally involved in his or her cases in ways that the original models never were, a move for which he credits "a large sisterhood of sleuths." In his admiration for Hornsby's book, he describes MacGowen as a "true heroine for our times" and pulls together the particular qualities shared by the best of these characters, describing her as "a professional woman who is intelligent, feminine but tough, clever without resorting to cuteness and as resourceful as a Navy SEAL with a Swiss army knife. Long may she survive."

Not to worry—she's here to stay.

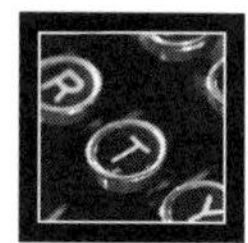

From Under Hammett's Mask

DICK LOCHTE

In the 1952 Mystery Writers of America anthology *Maiden Murders,* Ross Macdonald says of his first published short story, Find the Woman, "I suppose you could describe it as Chandler with onions. But then Chandler himself is Hammett with Freud potatoes. As Dostoyevsky said about Gogol (I think), we all came out from under Hammett's black mask."

Forty-six years later, Macdonald's statement remains valid. The shadow of the thin man is still darkening the corners of nearly all noir crime fiction.

Of today's working writers, Joe Gores is probably the closest we have to a direct line of descent from Sam Spade's father. Like Hammett, Gores writes from actual on-the-job experience; he spent a dozen years as a private eye in Spade's city, San Francisco. With that similarity of background, it's not surprising that his prose reflects Hammett's unsentimental, spare style. It is not even surprising that Gores hit upon the idea for *Hammett* (1975), a novel that is not only about the seminal author, it also seems to have been spirit-written by him.

Several other writers—all of them, I think, coming on the heels of *Hammett*—have tried to concoct fictional yarns involving that writer or Raymond Chandler, or in some cases both—with a singular lack of success. But it's not just originality that made Gores's novel work so well. That took a rare dedication to 1920s period detail and enough careful research about its protagonist's real life to qualify as a biography. Added to that is a powerful *Black Mask*-like plot—complete with essence-of-evil villain, nice girl in moral jeopardy, and sinister Mr. Big—that pushed its heroic writer-sleuth through "a corrupt city owned by its politicians, its cops, its district attorney. A city where anything is for sale." *Hammett* is, in short, that rara avis—a book gimmicky enough to attract attention and well written enough to justify it.

Even before its publication pushed him to the forefront of mystery novelists, Gores had established his credentials with strong hard-boiled tales like *A Time for Predators* and *Interface.* And he'd launched his DKA series about the sleuths who moil for the Daniel Kearny Associates detective agency. The DKA files, which began as short stories in *Ellery Queen's Mystery Magazine,* are the private-eye equivalent of the police procedural, filled with authentic details culled from the author's experiences working for their factual model, Dave Kikkert and Associates, a firm Gores helped establish. The stories, which hopscotch from character to character, are centered by Kearny, a short, stocky, notoriously unsentimental, totally professional sleuth who is the embodiment of Hammett's Continental Op. (He even comes face to face with the Op in one of his adventures.) Recent entries in the series, like *32 Cadillacs* (Mysterious Press, 1992), in which DKA is hired to locate and return an impressive number of luxury autos, all of which have been scammed by the same widespread Gypsy family, and *Contract Null & Void* (Mysterious Press, 1996), about union politics and computer chips, suggest that the hard-as-nails, bare-bones Hammett influence may be giving way to a more relaxed, humorous approach in which the professionalism of the detectives is tested by the increasing confusion and absurdity of contemporary life.

Gores, who was the first author to merit Edgars from the Mystery Writers of America in three categories (Best First Novel for "A Time of Predators," Best Short Story for "Goodbye Pops," and Best TV Episode for "No Immunity for Murder," an entry in the *Kojak* series), scores consistent high marks for every one of his books, but my favorite remains *Interface,* a yarn about a modern-day Sam Spade named Neil Fargo that is a fine example of noir writing. Critics usually mention Paul Cain's *Fast One* as being the most intense crime novel ever written. For my money, the largely overlooked *Interface* is more than its match for nonstop action and its stunning dénouement is so clean and perfect even Hammett would have approved.

In his introduction to *Like a Lamb to Slaughter,* a collection of the short stories of Lawrence Block, Gores describes a poker game held regularly at New York's Royalton Hotel during the 1960s. Its players included Block, Brian Garfield, Justin Scott, and Donald E. Westlake. As Gores tells it, in the course of one eighteen-hour session, each player sat out a few hands in the adjoining room, knocking out a chapter of a novel after reading only the last page of the chapter the previous author had penned. Finally, the writer who'd started the book brought it to a close. "An agent who regularly sat in on the game sold the novel as a paperback original for a thousand bucks," Gores writes. "The players split the pot. I don't know if the agent took his ten percent or not."

Gores's recollection of the vignette is meant as a tip of the hat to the professionalism and talent of the poker-playing writers. Both are traits Larry Block has in spades. In more than three decades he has published so many books and launched so many popular series (of such consistent high quality he received the Mystery Writers of America Grand Master Award in 1994) that it seems unlikely that he would have avoided the darker side of crime. And he hasn't. Though much of his work is breezily lighthearted (including novels about Tanner, the spy who doesn't sleep; young Chip Harrison, apprentice sleuth to the Nero Wolfean Leo Haig; and Bernie Rhodenbarr, the thief who steals to keep his bookstore in the black), several of his seriously hard-boiled stand-alone novels and the brilliant Matt Scudder series more than qualify him for the noir fiction hall of fame.

After the First Death (Macmillan, 1969), for example, has its protagonist Alex Penn waking up after an alcoholic blackout in an unfamiliar seedy Manhattan hotel with a dead prostitute on the floor. And if that isn't noirish enough for you, we then discover that Penn is a recent parolee who was convicted of a similar crime years before. In *Mona* (Gold Medal, 1961), con man Joe Marlin meets the stunningly beautiful title character and gets drawn into a very tricky murder plot.

In these and some of his other stand-alones, the line between Hammett and Block seems to have taken slight doglegs into the nightmarish alleys charted by Cornell Woolrich, whose unfinished *Into the Night* Block seamlessly completed (Mysterious Press, 1987). But in the fever-paced *Such Men Are Dangerous* (Macmillan, 1969), a well-received thriller about ex-Green Beret Paul Kavanaugh that Block supposedly wrote in eight days, the no-nonsense prose seems to have more than a dash of Dashiell. And in the Scudder series, which probably took a bit longer to write, the influences of both Hammett and Ross Macdonald are even more apparent, the former in the unblinkingly professional way the detective does his job, the latter in the brooding atmosphere surrounding the troubled sleuth.

As a New York Police Department cop, Scudder accidentally shot and killed a seven-year-old girl. He suffered a breakdown, then quit the force and turned his back on his wife and children. And he began to drink. In the early books, his guilt, his drinking, and tithing (depositing one-tenth of his unlicensed private-investigator earnings in church poor boxes) form an integral part of each story. In fact, from *The Sins of the Fathers* (Dell, 1976) to *Eight Million Ways to Die* (Arbor House, 1982), the Scudder novels are divided into three unequal parts: his guilt-based alcoholism and attempts to stay sober; descriptions of Manhattan that, regardless of its violence and craziness, make you want to pack up and go there immediately; and, finally, the exquisitely crafted crime element complete with clever wrap-up.

Eight Million Ways to Die has thus far remained the best of the series, I think, and quite possibly one of the best mysteries written in this generation. Shortly after its debut, I asked Larry what he was planning for an encore and he replied with no equivocation that it was to be the last of the Scudder books. He'd brought the character to such completion he didn't see how he could continue writing about him.

A few years later, the answer came to him. In *When the Sacred Ginmill Closes* (Arbor, 1986), he followed the example of Hammett and Chandler and cannibalized a few short stories for a novel set in 1976 New York, when the city still had no-frills bars and Scudder, a freshly guilt-ridden alky, was part of a late-night crowd of heavy hitters who went to sleep with bourbon and woke up with beer.

Ginmill, which presented Scudder with three simultaneous crimes to solve—a whodunit, a whydunit, and a howdunit—was popular enough to give the series a new lease on life. Since then, as of this writing, Scudder has sleuthed through seven more books, all of them set in contemporary times, each one moving him further away from his darker days of saloon society. Though some of these cases have taken him into the blackest of noir areas, the unlicensed detective has slowly been sending his personal demons on the big sleep. In the now-current *Even The Wicked* (Morrow, 1997), he has become as domesticated as Inspector Maigret, with a wife even more desirable than Nora Charles and a bright young African-American ward. Reading this book, which is very close in content to the classic mysteries in which detectives exercise brain rather than brawn, I was reminded of the post-*Maltese Falcon* short stories about Sam Spade that Hammett wrote for the big-pay magazines. They're fine stories. ("They Only Hang You Once" has the splendid opening line-"Samuel Spade said: 'My name is Ronald Ames.' ") But the author had pretty much finished with the character by the end of *Falcon,* and the subsequent tales don't add much. Block was able to resurrect Scudder because there were still a few more dark areas to illuminate. But as the character settles further and further into domesticity, you have to wonder what else the author may have in store for him.

One of the elements Block introduced in the post-*Eight Million Ways to Die* novels was the oddly sensitive-but-homicidal butcher boy Mick Ballou, whom Scudder befriends. Thanks to Robert B. Parker, who provided his sleuth Spenser with a conscienceless hit-man pal named Hawk, the murderous good buddy has become something of a neo-noir staple. Just as Hawk handles the wet work for

Spenser, Ballou takes some of the nastier knots out of Scudder's methods of seeking justice.

Two relatively new southern California sleuth superstars, Walter Mosley's Easy Rawlins and Robert Crais's Elvis Cole, also take full advantage of their sociopathic sidekicks—Raymond "Mouse" Alexander and Joe Pike, respectively. It's mystery critic Tom Nolan's amusing theory that Mosley may have been goofing on Parker's Hawk by naming his good badguy Mouse. More often, it's the work of Raymond Chandler that's referenced when discussing the Rawlins stories, probably because of their location. But unlike Chandler, Mosley is reconstructing the city of Los Angeles and its people not from contemporary observation but from a memory of its past. The novels are time-hopping memoirs narrated by a septuagenarian Easy who remains as consistently existential as any of Hammett's heroes.

He's a World War II vet searching for a singer in the jazz clubs of 1948 Watts in his first published book, *Devil in a Blue Dress* (Norton, 1990). The second, *A Red Death* (Norton, 1991) takes place in 1953, and involves red baiting and blacklisting. *White Butterfly* (Norton, 1992) finds the raffish hero in 1956, married, if not happily so, and on the trail of a serial murderer. *Black Betty* (Norton, 1994) picks him up in 1961, a single father of two whose impending bankruptcy forces him to take on a missing-persons case.

The murderous Mouse is a strong presence throughout the series as a sort of homicidal guardian angel on Easy's shoulder. But in *A Little Yellow Dog* (Norton, 1996), set in 1963, the author smartly shifts the situation by having Mouse get religion and hang up his gun. Not only must Easy, hip deep in homicide, fend for himself, he has to keep a watchful eye on his now defenseless friend.

Through all of his adventures, Easy continues to recall an event that shaped his life. As he first describes it in *Dress:* "[Mouse] had killed his stepfather five years earlier and blamed it on another man." Easy's involvement in the murder forces him to leave home, which in turn ups his status from an illiterate Texas teenager to a traveled and well-read man of the world. It seemed particularly clever and brave of Mosley to have his hero merely mention his epiphany without ever going into more details. But with the publication of *Gone Fishin'* (Black Classic Press) in 1997, we discovered that a complete account of Easy's defining moment had been in existence for quite a while in manuscript form. Mosley had written the short novel before *Devil,* but had been unable to find a buyer. Though the book, more mainstream than mystery, was greeted with much praise when it finally was published, my feeling is that it is considerably inferior to his detective novels. Missing are the textures and surprises and the sharp sense of place of the whodunits. And there are fewer societal observations.

All of the other novels in the series are worth any reader's time. Mosley's voice is unique, his characterizations vivid, his dialogue inflection-perfect. And he continues to take us to times and places that fiction rarely treads.

Robert Crais's Elvis Cole, in his first caper, *The Monkey's Raincoat* (Bantam, 1987), was a younger, hipper, and considerably less smug version of the then reigning king of the hill, Robert B. Parker's Spenser. Like that Boston-based detective, southern Californian Cole possessed a smart mouth, a sociopathic sidekick, and a gourmet's palate. What else did a private eye need?

Well, as Crais and the other authors of books about male detectives, Parker included, have discovered, what they needed was a life away from the case. In today's market, a sleuth as introspective as Sam Spade or as dedicated as the Continental Op would be a hard sell to a reading public that seems to prefer their private eyes to have public lives. While this has stymied some hard-boiled practitioners, Crais has smoothly opened up his series to include a personal life for Elvis that continually grows more complex. In the course of six post-*Monkey* novels, so far, he has allowed the character to mature to the point of entering a serious romantic relationship and, in the bestseller *Indigo Slam* (Hyperion, 1997), eagerly anticipating the joys of family life. Even the shadowy sidekick, Pike, has mellowed, albeit slightly. The Vietnam vet has never been quite as conscienceless as Hawk, Mick, Mouse, and others of their ilk, but he is definitely a dark and dangerous presence, though with a strong code of honor. In *Stalking the Angel* (Bantam, 1989), for example, Joe promptly blasts a proud yakuza with four rounds from a 12-gauge shotgun. When Elvis asks him why he didn't just try to wound the guy, Pike replies, "He had failed . . . He had nothing left [to live for]." But over the next few novels, Crais suggests a softer side of Joe. In *Sunset Express* (Hyperion, 1996), we discover that his life has not been as monastic as we'd been led to believe. And in "*Indigo Slam*," the author arranges for Joe to baby-sit a trio of tots, with results that are just this side of heartwarming.

One of *Indigo*'s strong subplots follows the efforts of the woman Elvis loves to move from her native Louisiana (Crais's home state) to the West Coast to be near him. The fly in the ointment is the lady's ex-husband, an oilman with far-reaching clout, who threatens to make trouble in future volumes. The former spouse notwithstanding (Joe comments that he can kill him if necessary), sooner or later, Crais may be facing the same decision that now confronts Larry Block: what do you do with a hard-boiled private eye who has found happiness?

Too much happiness is not a problem likely to plague any of James Lee Burke's dour heroes. Unlike the other crime novelists discussed here (and most crime writers in general), Burke published a string of critically acclaimed but far from bestselling mainstream novels before expanding his readership with a popular mystery series. The nonmysteries invariably featured protagonists who, in the classic noir mold, racked up more woes than wins. In *Half of Paradise* (1965), the wellborn Avery Broussard winds up in Angola Penitentiary, is paroled, then rearrested, while J. P. Winfield, a country and western performer, makes it to the top of his profession only to be cheated by his manager and lured into drug addiction by his girlfriend. Texas lawyer Hack Holland, in *Lay Down My Sword and Shield* (Crowell, 1971), is tormented by memories of time spent in a Korean War prison camp. Another country musician, Iry Paret, in *The Lost Get-Back Boogie* (Louisiana State University Press, 1987), is paroled from 'gola and leaves Louisiana for Montana, where the closing of a pulp mill turns the tranquillity of the Bitterroot Valley into a bloody battleground. It's no wonder then that life for Burke's mystery hero, Cajun lawman Dave Robicheaux, is not exactly a walk through Audubon Park.

In each of his novels, Robicheaux, a recovering alcoholic with an astonishingly rigid moral code, undergoes painful battles against evildoers, the bottle, and himself. Burke's long suit, poetic descriptions of the sights, sounds, smells, and tastes of Louisiana life, are as vivid and complete an anything Raymond Chandler ever wrote about southern California. But living in the midst of the emerald green bayous with a beautiful, understanding, intelligent wife and a sweet adopted daughter hasn't helped to lighten Robicheaux's load. He remains one terminally depressed dude. Not that you could blame him. Dave's first wife dumped him even before the start of his debut novel, *The Neon Rain* (Holt, 1987). In the second, considerably better series entry, *Heaven's Prisoners* (Holt, 1988), he leaves corrupt, bawdy New Orleans for the serenity of his native Iberia Parish, where, in quick order, his new wife is murdered and he goes back on the sauce. (Mystery lovers may recognize this as the Travis McGee Law, which states that no loved one is allowed to stick around longer than a few books. The current Mrs. Robicheaux has managed to hang on through at least five novels, but she does suffer from lupus.) In every book, Robicheaux is all but overwhelmed by feelings of helplessness and guilt at being forced to watch wealthy corrupters flourish while good men suffer and/or die like dogs. In short, when it comes to carrying emotional furniture, Robicheaux is the Bekins of detective literature.

In the course of one of his recent searches for justice, *Cadillac Jukebox* (Hyperion, 1996), Dave seriously rains on just about everybody's parade—from his wife, Bootsy, who's having a hard time living with a candidate for sainthood; to an assortment of crooks, big time and petty, who don't understand his staunch morality; to the state's governor-elect Buford LaRose and his vindictive wife, Karyn, who resent his holier-than-thou attitude, among other things. Dave and Karyn were an item back in his good-ol'-boy-drunk-and-debauched stage, and she can't quite get it in her head that's he's changed. "You're a pill," she finally says, getting the picture at last. Even his boss, the New Iberia sheriff, who treats him with avuncular affection, is moved by one of Dave's drearier comments to reply sarcastically, "God, you're a source of comfort."

There were signs in *Jukebox* that Burke may have been wearying of his hero. Two sections of the novel are presented in a voice other than narrator Dave's. Several plot elements from previous books are given a reprise-the good-bad chum out of Robicheaux's past who risks death by walking a tightrope between cops and crooks (see *Black Cherry Blues* (Little, Brown, 1989) and *Burning Angel* (Hyperion, 1995)), the movie company on location in the swamps (see *In the Electric Mist with Confederate Dead* (Hyperion, 1993)), and the smarmy politician with more skeletons in his closet than John Wayne Gacy (*A Stained White Radiance* (Hyperion, 1992)).

Like Spenser, Elvis, Easy, et al. Dave has his hatchet man and a good thing, too. Whenever his darkly humorous bad-guy best buddy Clete Purcell appears, the gloom lifts. Purcell is a funny and furious man of action who lives to break rules. He thinks the world of Dave, but even he bridles at the latter's sanctimony. "One day, you're going to figure out you're no different from me, Dave," Clete tells him. "Then you're going to shoot yourself."

One wonders if this isn't a hint of Burke's future plans for the character. At the very least, he's given him time off by creating a new series. *Cimarron Rose* (Hyperion, 1997) introduces former Texas Ranger Billy Bob Holland, now an attorney in the quaintly named town of Deaf Smith, Texas. A cousin of Hack Holland's, the Lone Star legal-eagle hero of the author's *Lay Down My Sword and Shield,* Billy Bob is a hard-drinking, fiery-tempered gent with even more on his mind than Robicheaux. He accidentally killed his partner in the Rangers, L. Q. Navarro. And if that's not enough to fill his guilt cup, he knows that Lucas Smothers, the teenaged son of the man who farms acres of Holland land, is really his own illegitimate offspring. And, as it happens, Lucas is in need of a good lawyer, having been arrested for brutally murdering his pregnant girlfriend.

Beginning, I think, with the novel *Black Cherry Blues* which won the Edgar Allan Poe Award and is arguably the best of the series, Robicheaux has been communing with ghosts. At first it was his slain wife and his father, then Civil War officers and various other shades. This mystical quality has been the subject of much criticism, which Burke either hasn't heard or chooses to ignore. The Texas series has started off with its own strong New Age elements. When Billy Bob isn't deep in conversation with the late L. Q., whose ghostly eyes are "as lustrous as obsidian," he's delving into his great-grandfather Sam Morgan

Holland's journal, hitting sections that happen to have profound bearing on his present situation.

I sort of like L. Q.'s ghost visits—they give us a pretty good idea why Billy Bob admired and respected the man. And, apart from the coincidental application of its passages, the diary seems so authentic I wonder if it might not have been written by the author's great-grandfather, whose name really was Sam Morgan Holland.

Whatever complaints I or anyone else may have about his novels, there's no denying the fact that Burke is one hell of a writer. Only the bravest novelists are willing to push style to the point of self-parody. If he steps over the line every once in a while, he's simply too talented for readers not to be willing to cut him a little slack.

Daniel Woodrell and James Colbert are two other novelists of note who write about the darker byways of my own home state of Louisiana. Neither has received the reader attention his books deserve, though both are positioned to use Hollywood to increase their audience.

Colbert scored strongly with his debut novel, *Profit and Sheen* (Houghton Mifflin, 1986), a dark and twisty tale reminiscent of books by two other men named James, Cain and Thompson. The title refers not to intangibles but to the dual leads—Daniel Profit, a New Orleans cocaine dealer, and Sheen Vicedomini, an ex-cop, who team up to take on the international drug trade. The *New Yorker* (the real one, before the British contingent took over) gave the book its seal of approval, and Charles Willeford, writing in the *Washington Post,* called it "stunning . . . if you plan to read only one mystery this season, this is the one to buy."

Some readers believed him, but not enough to make Colbert a household name. And though his next novel, *No Special Hurry* (Houghton Mifflin, 1988), was treated to equally glowing reviews, he remained undervalued by readers. *Hurry* was narrated by Tony Curbel, an innocent man serving time in prison, who is visited by an eccentric policeman with an offer he can't refuse. The cop will set Tony free in return for information about the business run by his father and his uncle, the two men responsible for his imprisonment.

The tall, gangly, unpredictable cop, known as Skinny, who refers to himself in the third person ("Skinny's pissed off now"), was too striking a creation to be confined to a supporting role, and so Colbert made him the hero of his next two novels—*Skinny Man* (Atheneum, 1991) and *All I Have Is Blue* (Atheneum, 1992). In both, the deceptively awkward but shrewd lawman, a Tulane University dropout who joined the New Orleans Police Department to avoid the Vietnam draft, and his big redheaded clever girlfriend, Ruth, serve nicely as a nineties version of Nick and Nora Charles, which is to say that they work well as a team; their life together is not precisely as idyllic as that earlier couple's, probably because they don't drink as much. Their adventures are neatly crafted entertainments that, like some of Willeford's Hoke Norris novels, manage to be both deadly serious and just an inch away from giddiness, almost simultaneously.

Blue ends with their future life together in question. And, unfortunately, there is no reason to think Colbert will be offering any further words on the situation any time soon. As the result of a friendship with attorney-novelist Andrew Vachss, whose dark fiction reflects his devotion to child welfare, Colbert was moved to follow *Blue* with a work of nonfiction, *God Bless the Child* (Atheneum, 1992), a nonetheless fascinating account of how a dedicated child welfare worker and a professional gambler teamed up to create a special center for abused kids in Mississippi.

Since then, Colbert's main fiction has been in collaboration with Vachss on an as yet unpublished novel about a group of vigilantes led by Cross, the sociopathic product of a youth correctional facility. The manuscript, "Cross:

Genesis," has been used as the source for a series of ultraviolent graphic novels published by Dark Horse Comics and has been optioned for filming by New Line Cinema. Colbert and Vachss wrote the screenplay adaptation.

Woodrell, in roughly the same timespan as Colbert, has produced a similarly small number of books, by today's standards. But they have attracted slightly more attention. Three of the novels, including the author's first, *Under the Bright Lights* (Holt, 1986), are about the Shade family of Saint Bruno, Louisiana. Rene is a police detective. His older brother, Tip, runs a neighborhood bar frequented by felons. His younger brother, Francois, is an assistant D.A. Their father, John X., is a pool hustler who is present in name only in the first two books. *Lights,* with its tale of a hillbilly hit man imported to Saint Bruno by his duplicitous cousin, has touches of Walker Percy and Faulkner and Cain and, yes, Hammett, but the bulk of it is told in a mesmerizing, unique style that proudly displays its cynical worldview.

In *Muscle for the Wing* (Holt, 1988), my favorite among the Shade titles, a group of prison-hardened white supremacists decide to wrest Saint Bruno from the control of the local Mafia. Like Hammett's Continental Op, who is forced to tread a thin line between rival gangs in *Red Harvest,* Rene finds himself in the middle of the battle—ordered by the mayor to get rid of the criminal carpetbaggers without resorting to the expense of a trial, but too moral to indulge in shotgun justice. It's a short, taut novel filled to the brim with finely etched, colorful characters and a plot that circles in on an ending that is both inevitable and eminently satisfying.

In *The Ones You Do* (Holt, 1992), Rene's dad, John X., pops into town unexpectedly after many years' absence, with a precocious ten-year-old daughter in tow and on the run from a dedicated killer named Lunch Pumphrey. John X. is the star of this show, raffish as hell, funny, charming, aggravating. But coming in a close second is his unyielding adversary, Lunch, who grills up a plate of tainted beef and watches gleefully while an unknowing associate gobbles it down. Woodrell combines good and evil, laughter and loss so smoothly and surprisingly it's little wonder his fan club includes the likes of James Crumley and James Ellroy.

It's the author's most recent off-series novel that's attracted Hollywood attention. *Give Us a Kiss* (Holt, 1996), a tale of family feuding and marijuana growing in the Ozarks, subtitled "a country noir," has been optioned by Twentieth Century Fox. *Kiss* is narrated by Doyle Redmond, a thirty-something Ozarks-bred thriller writer who's got his hopes set on a breakout book. Where the books veers away from autobiography (one hopes) is in Doyle's reason for returning home. His parents want him to convince his outlaw brother Smoke to clean up his legal problems to get the law off *their* backs. Once the brothers link up, however, Smoke convinces Doyle to join him in protecting his pot harvest from the inbred but dangerous Dolly family. The result was accurately described by novelist Annie Proulx as a celebration of "blood kin, home country and hot sex."

Will the movie be able to capture the lyricism of Woodrell's language or the oddball but honest behavior of his creations? The odds are not good. Judging by the film fate of some of the books mentioned here—*Hammett, Heaven's Prisoners, Eight Million Ways to Die*—one would have to assume that Bob Crais, who has had considerable experience in the scripting game, has good reason for stating that he has no interest whatsoever in seeing Elvis Cole on the big or small screen. With rare exception (Quentin Tarantino and David Lynch being the only two that come to mind), Hollywood seems to have forgotten everything it once knew about creating noir drama.

We should be thankful that novelists haven't.

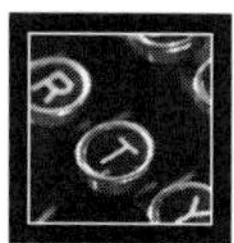

Charles Willeford:

AN INTERVIEW

SYBIL STEINBERG

If Miami is hot these days, it's not just due to the temperature and the popularity of *Miami Vice.* Miami homicide detective sergeant Hoke Moseley, who became a favorite of crime-novel addicts with the publication of *Miami Blues* and *New Hope for the Dead,* is about to reappear in a thriller from St. Martin's, *Sideswipe.* The book has been touted as the breakthrough novel for its creator, Charles Willeford—rather an ironic prediction for a man who has been writing in almost every type of genre—poetry, fiction, autobiography, journalism, screenplays, literary criticism—for over four decades.

We meet Willeford at his home in South Miami, a quite suburban neighborhood of concrete-block-and stucco pastel-colored bungalows set on well-tended lawns, very much like the fictional Green Lakes where Hoke Moseley finds himself in the new novel. Willeford, sixty-eight, is a tall man with mild blue eyes and a courtly air. He sports a bravado of a white mustache that neatly counterpoints his high, balding forehead and a comfortable paunch that suggests he shares his protagonist's fondness for beer. His conversation is studded with the same sort of specific details that invest his books with authenticity, and his sardonic humor surfaces unexpectedly.

Though his peers, notably Elmore Leonard, Joseph Hansen, and Lawrence Block, have been hailing Willeford's mastery of his craft for years, Willeford's novels for a long time earned him only a cult following. Nothing has come easy for him, a situation perhaps ordained by the dichotomy of his youthful ambition to be a poet and the reality of his enlistment in the army at age sixteen, seemingly the only recourse during the Depression for an orphan and junior high school dropout. As chronicled in the grippingly candid first volume of his autobiography, *Something About a Soldier,* published by Random House to critical plaudits last year, the peacetime army offered plenty of chances to carouse and to experience the seamy side of life, and Willeford became familiar with the whores and colorful lowlifes who could be found just off bounds of nearly every military base. As a career soldier he developed his writing skills in dozens of journeyman tasks including dashing off soap operas for the Armed Forces radio station and ghost-writing speeches for base commanders. A tank commander in the Third Army during World War II, he earned a

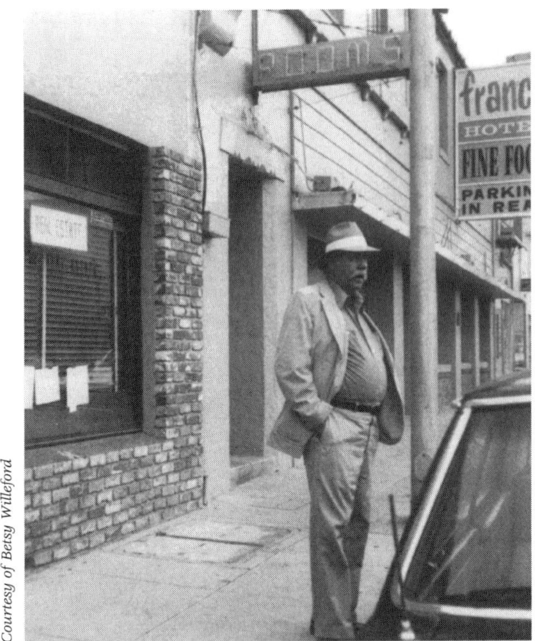

Courtesy of Betsy Willeford

Writer, Charles Willeford

number of medals for exploits he dismisses with the dry comment: "In wartime the opportunities to become a hero come every day."

The other side of Willeford's personality was expressed in avant-garde poetry. In 1947 his first collection, *Proletarian Laughter,* was published by the Alicat Bookshop Press, in a series that also featured the work of Henry Miller and Anais Nin.

"But I kept saying that I wanted to write a novel," Willeford recalls, "and one of my buddies finally said, "This is pretentious." That irritated me. I was stationed at Hamilton Air Force Base, so I drove to San Francisco every weekend and holed up in a room at the Powell Hotel until I finished a book." Titled *High Priest of California,* it was the first of what would become his San Francisco trilogy of bleak, noir novels. Acting without an agent, Willeford eventually found a publisher in Beacon Press, which issued the work in paperback in 1953. "It had two editions of one hundred thousand each and sold out," Willeford recalls, "so I knew I had readers from the first." *Pick-Up* and *Until I Am Dead* (retitled *Wild Wives*) followed. Later, Willeford was somewhat chagrined to discover that he had missed the whole Beat scene in his hotel-bound weekends. "Kerouac—I never met a single one of them," he says ruefully. "On the other hand, I had three published novels by the time I got my twenty years in." The three volumes are soon to be reissued by Research Inc. Press.

Even with his army pension, Willeford's life as a 36-year-old retiree and freelance writer was a financial scramble. Deciding to "fill in the gaps of my education" (although he had been awesomely well read since discovering Dostoyevski's works in the public library at the age of thirteen), Willeford enrolled at the University of Miami, where he carried both his B.A. and M.A. degrees, Married and with responsibilities, there were several times when he relied on his writing to supplement the G.I. Bill, once dropping out of college for a semester to produce a collection of short stories. Twenty years ago he became (and remains) a reviewer of mystery and suspense fiction for the *Miami Herald,* a newspaper that comes in for some humorous asides in his novels. And for a long time he was a teacher at area colleges.

Willeford was still writing, of course, and in 1971 he finally achieved hardcover publication with Crown's edition of *The Burnt Orange Heresy,* which critics have called the best of his noir novels. He wrote the screenplay for the movie adapted from his next book, *Cockfighter,* in which he was cast in a supporting role after the actor who was to play Judge Ed Middleton took sick. A poster for that movie, directed by Roger Corman and starring Warren Oates, has a prominent place on Willeford's living-room wall. With the kind of bad luck that also afflicts his characters, Willeford's name is misspelled. "What would you expect?" he rumbles, with the chesty laugh of a chain smoker. "You'll notice that the director's name isn't fouled up."

When he introduced the likable Sgt. Hoke Moseley in *Miami Blues,* Willeford segued into the police procedural format that seems finally to have made his name familiar to a wider audience. Since his editor at Crown, David McDowell, had retired, Willeford's agent, Jim Trupin, took the book to St. Martin's Press. Willeford was not so much searching for a detective on whom to hang a series as he was indulging in a penchant to stretch his talents. "With each novel I try to experiment a little," he says. Having previously written an "existentialist Western" called *The Hombre of Sonora* under the nom de plume Will Charles, and a fictionalized biography of the Son of Sam killer titled *Off the Wall,* Willeford wanted to see if he could write a crime novel. Hoke Moseley took shape in his imagination "the way I always do things, I write a fairly elaborate biography of my characters. I know who their parents were, where they went to school, their first love affair. That way, I don't get the chronology mixed up. Which is nice, because now if I wanted to I could go back and write about Hoke's earlier life."

In *Sideswipe,* Willeford's interest in an unconventional format led him to tell two apparently unrelated stories in alternating chapters until they intersect in a night of bloody violence at a Miami supermarket. The next Hoke Moseley thriller, Willeford says, "will be more a picaresque novel than it is a mystery. You can do a lot of experimental writing in the crime novel genre. I'm always surprised that most writers don't try to vary their stuff," he says.

Living in Miami is a plus factor in his literary gestation. The society is in flux, with an ethnic mix that makes for volatile social conditions and "a lot of conflict because everybody's got their minds made up about each other." He estimates that the population in now "fifty percent or more Latins—Puerto Ricans, Cubans, you name it—twenty percent black, with Haitians and Bajans [from Barbados] a subcategory, twelve percent Jews, and eight percent WASPs." Hoke Moseley, being macho and WASP, often makes disparaging comments about the other ethnic groups, a trait that Willeford notes should not be construed as the author's opinions. This applies also to his character's male chauvinist attitude, although Willeford concedes that "the fact that I've been divorced twice" may make him somewhat suspect. His third wife, Betsy, a columnist for the *Miami News,* seems to have modified the crustier side of Willeford's nature.

Willeford absorbs the Miami ambience as part of his daily routine when, after a morning at his desk, he goes walking in one of South Florida's enormous air-conditioned malls. In addition to exercise, the habit allows him to pick up all sorts of stuff. I check all the fashions and what people are eating, but mostly how they talk. I eavesdrop a lot." That accounts for the Visa hotline operator in *Sideswipe* who sings out "Have a rainbow day!" and the prevalence of other contemporary idioms that give Willeford's fiction its immediacy. More problematic is the source of his knowledge of the decadence and sleaze in Miami's rundown neighborhoods, which he describes with unflinching accuracy, and his straightforward depiction of the all-too-human attributes of some policemen, including Hoke, whose pragmatism puts not too fine a point on their morality. Willeford's darkly comic portrayal of eccentric but entirely convincing characters invests his novels with offbeat humor, and his often ribald dialogue is about as realistic as you can get.

Asked what he will do if *Sideswipe* confirms its potential as his breakthrough book (its selection by the Mystery Guild augurs well, as do advance reviews), Willeford says it will change his lifestyle very little. "I have plenty of money to live on," he says, although his comfortable but modest home with its cheerful Haitian and Mexican wood artifacts and wall hangings does not suggest any hidden luxuries. He'd like to find a publisher for another volume of his autobiography, already written but not contracted for. It deals with his life up to age sixteen, part of which he spent riding boxcars with other hungry drifters. Orphaned when he was young, Willeford was living with his grandmother in L.A., where she tried to support them both during the Depression. "Things were rough, so I skipped out for about a year and a half," he says. "There were hundreds of us riding those boxcars, looking for food wherever we could get it. I developed a wonderful begging technique. I was a sweet blond-haired kid with blue eyes. I'd say, 'I'm hungry' in sort of a pitiful way and housewives would feed me. Then there were transient camps that had soup kitchens, and you could always sing a hymn or two in the missions and they'd give you a meal."

Several other Willeford books are currently in the works. Black Lizard Press will reissue *The Burnt Orange Heresy, Pick-Up,* and *Cockfighter* next month. And Florida publisher Dennis Macmillan is due to bring out a volume of Willeford's literary criticism titled *New Forms of Ugly: The Immobilized Hero in Modern Literature* in April, in a limited signed edition of 400 copies. Willeford jests about the book's audience, claiming that it will sell mainly to what he calls "the shrinkwrap set. They just buy it hoping it will be valuable someday," he says.

In the same humorous vein, he mentions a dream assignment that tickles his fancy. "Larry Block said to me one day, 'Wouldn't it be great to write for *Miami Vice?* You'd write: "Sonny crawls out on a ledge . . . " Then you'd write in seven minutes of rock music—Patti La Belle singing "On the Edge." Just think—you'd have four pages right there—and you'd be paid a fortune!' "

In the last analysis, Willeford's view of life contains few serendipities. Working hard and seeing true are his verities. "I think part of it comes from being an orphan," he says. "When you're an orphan at the age of eight, you realize that you're the next one to die. Your vision of life is colored by reality rather than pipe dreams." And as Willeford knows, the gritty side of life can make a riveting read.

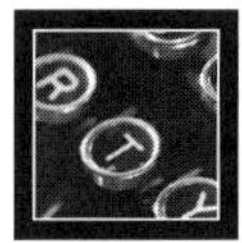

Fresh Blood:

BRITISH NEO-NOIR

MIKE RIPLEY AND MAXIM JAKUBOWSKI

First came Sherlock Holmes (so Dickens, Wilkie Collins, and a handful of dime novelists did the pioneering work, but let's concentrate for now on the bare essentials of the history of British crime fiction made easy!).

Then followed the so-called Golden Age, with Agatha Christie, Margery Allingham, and Dorothy L. Sayers, the unholy trinity of the cozy novel of detection, leading a hardy band of middle-class ladies of leisure in codifying the genre for decades to come as an unambiguous, clean-cut battlefield between good and evil in a land of blissful vicarages and passionless relationships.

Meanwhile, back in the USA, the bad boys had mutated the penny dreadful ethos into hard-boiled in the pages of the pulp magazines. But we Brits were above all that vulgarity and violence. And the stark reality of World War II isolated us even further from the new streak of noir that had taken a grip on American crime writing and cinema.

In isolation, social realist precursors like Gerald Kersh, Patrick Hamilton, John Lodwick, and a few others began laying the foundation stones of British noir with dark London novels full of dirty passion and depressing betrayals of the soul, but those by now white-haired ladies were still active and increasingly popular, and a minor wave of would-be noir British authors could only imitate, badly at that, what they assumed was the American gangster novel, and gave British hard-boiled a bad name it would take years to erase (Basil Cooper, James Hadley Chase, Peter Cheyney, Peter Chambers, Hank Janson, take a bow).

Eventually, British crime writing began making some concessions to reality as the Golden Age formulas began losing their artificial charms, and a greater attention to characterization and psychology took hold, with P. D. James and Ruth Rendell and now Minette Walters leading successive new generations of mystery authors into the arms of literary respectability.

Isolated outbreaks of hard-boiled fever would occasionally manifest themselves: Robin Cook's early novels of London bad people (before he became Derek Raymond), Ted Lewis's *Get Carter,* Julian Barnes's Duffy novels written as Dan Kavanagh, and John Milne's Jimmy Jenner adventures all spring to mind, but, generally speaking, tough, gritty crime was more often on the television screen than on the page.

But the breakthrough for what has since become a distinct brand of British neo-noir writing came in the late 1980s. Maxim Jakubowski's pioneering publishing work with his two imprints, Black Box Thrillers and Blue Murder, which revealed to the British the dark, twisted treasures of Jim Thompson, David Goodis, Cornell Woolrich, and many other stalwarts, and the opening of his mystery bookshop, Murder One, the first ever of consequence in Britain, in 1988, could be construed as influences, but the germ was already in the air.

Nineteen-eighty-nine was a good year for British crime fiction for those who were watching and waiting. The watchers were at last able to spot first novels from exciting new authors. There was Mike Phillips putting a black investigative journalist onto mean streets previously untramped in Britain while Philip Kerr put his private-eye hero onto some of the meanest streets ever—those of 1936 Berlin. Denise Danks tackled computer crime and warned of new technology to come. John Harvey created a credible ensemble cast of policemen and established Nottingham as the new crime capital of the country. Russell James gave us an uncompromising (in both style and content) view of Britain where the police seemed to be on permanent leave.

For those who had been waiting for something new to happen in British crime writing, here, surely, was confirmation of earlier signs. Mark Timlin had already launched private eye Nick Sharman on an unsuspecting south London and Ian Rankin had produced the first of his Inspector Rebus thrillers set in an Edinburgh not seen by visitors to the Fringe. In 1988, Michael Dibdin won the Crime Writers' Gold Dagger for *Ratking,* the first of his Italian Zen novels.

Something was happening.

Avid crime readers had already noticed a new direction in American crime writing. Elmore Leonard was the name to drop; James Ellroy the one to watch; Charles Willeford, Carl Hiaasen, and James Crumley were achieving cult status. The private-eye novel seemed to be sewn up by Robert B. Parker and Sara Paretsky, but readers (and filmmakers) were rediscovering their heritage and many sadly neglected exponents of noir.

The British new wave also had a noir icon in the shape of Derek Raymond (Robin Cook), a hard-hitting social novelist of the 1960s who had reemerged in the eighties as a crime writer with his bleak and uncompromising "Factory" series of novels.

And by 1990 it all seemed to be coming together. Critics had long been in agreement that while the British remained supreme at the *detective story* (and Ruth Rendell was doing amazing things with the psychological chiller), the most interesting developments in more "realistic" crime writing were coming out of America. This was something confirmed by the appearance of Walter Mosley, but perhaps now there was a domestic product that could hold its own.

Jim Huang, writing in *The Drood Review* in the U.S., identified a trend emerging among British crime writers to portray "today's Britain with an edge." John Williams, interviewed in *The Guardian,* described the new wave with basic pragmatism: "If Elmore Leonard can write about the mean streets of Detroit, there's no reason why Mike Phillips or Russell James or Sarah Dunant or whoever can't write about the mean streets of Tottenham or Holloway. After all, guns and crack aren't getting any less popular in Britain, are they?"

George Thaw, then of the *Daily Mirror,* remarked: "There is a new face to British crime writing. You might not like it, but this is the future." And in the *Daily Telegraph,* Hugo Davenport identified the new wave as "bent on dynamiting the decorous tradition of the English country house detective novel."

A handful of writers involved in this trend/reaction/new wave whatever attempted to join together to promote the new face of British crime and, of course, themselves.

They acquired a brand name—"Fresh Blood"—which was always a reflection of a fresh attitude (or bad attitude, as some said) on the part of the writers rather than on their age.

As a group, Fresh Blood was informal, based loosely in London. There was no constitution, no membership fee, no manifesto, no permanent meeting place. Members did not have to like one another; in fact, in publicity terms, it helped if a member actively disliked at least one other. There was one meeting in a pub in the West End and one dinner in the badlands of Beak Street on the fringe of Soho. Neither actually ended in violence, but legend has it they did, so print the legend.

Michael Dibdin came up with the name Fresh Blood but this shouldn't be held against him. A *Books in Print* catalogue for 1991 was produced and distributed through bookshops where we had contacts and, through friends in *Sisters in Crime,* to librarians in America. Five of the new wave—Philip Kerr, Mike Phillips, Mark Timlin, Michael Dibdin and Mike Ripley—even made it as male models in a photo shoot for GQ magazine on what the hard-boiled crime writer was wearing that year.

But that was about it, really.

Television claimed several of that first wave, radio too, for both adaptations and original scripts. At least one made it to Hollywood, two on to the bestseller lists, and one was mentioned in the same breath as the Booker Prize. Two—Ian Rankin and then Denise Danks—won the Raymond Chandler/Fulbright Scholarship to tour America. Maxim Jakubowski reverted to his fiction roots and made the giant leap back from editor to author.

There was an attempt to compile an anthology of short stories, each one starting "There was fresh blood on . . . "as a joint exercise in self-promotion. But this didn't appeal to everyone, and certainly not to publishers, who all said there were too many anthologies of short crime already and no market. Gradually, enthusiasm for the anthology faded, although almost all the stories written for it eventually found a home, and, ironically, there have probably been more collections of short crime fiction published since than in the previous decade. Finally, five years later, *Fresh Blood,* the anthology, was published.

But just as there was one distinctive new wave of writers appearing around 1988/89, there was an equally distinctive second wave of new writers emerged in 1994 and 1995. Beginning in late 1994, Stella Duffy, Jeremy Cameron, Graeme Gordon, John Tilsley, Nicholas Blincoe, Colin Bateman, and Lauren Henderson—and no doubt others—published first novels, all with a clear, individual voice and all, harking back to 1990, showing Britain "with an edge." All would become better known.

So what distinguishes these new waves of crime writing? It is not simply a more realistic approach to violence—many a traditional detective-story writer gives you the full gruesome details these days. Perhaps it is simply that these are not traditional detective stories. Few have conventional policemen or even conventional private eyes as heroes or heroines, and they often deal with far from conventional crimes. Rarely is murder at the heart of the story, and definitely not in the traditional whodunit sense.

The crime novel today is no longer a simple puzzle of detection. The authors in this collection (and others) try to show the consequences of crime in today's real world. Their central characters tend to be urban and mobile rather than rural and in a closed social circle, and outsiders (outsiders make the best observers) even if they are professional policemen. Many are young or youngish, few have responsibilities in the conventional sense, some have less morals than the villains they take on. The crimes they investigate or become involved in are often resolved outside the law. Some are not resolved at all. The characters in these stories don't realize they are committing crimes and wouldn't care if they did. They have no concept of being caught and no fear of being punished. Many crimes take place continuously and are simply accepted.

Just like life, really.

The first *Fresh Blood* anthology was, in effect, seven years in the making, celebrating as it did the new wave of British crime writing that emerged around 1989, and was then followed by a second wave of new talent in 1995.

Of that initial first flowering, writers such as Michael Dibdin, Philip Kerr, John Harvey, Sarah Dunant and Ian Rankin are now well established as top-flight practitioners of their trade. From the more recent second wave, Stella Duffy, Nicholas Blincoe, Colin Bateman, Jeremy Cameron, and Lauren Henderson have rapidly earned respect and success.

And there is already a *third* wave of new writers who have taken to crime and done so with frightening skill and aplomb. Some—Phil Lovesey, Christopher Brookmyre, Ken Bruen, Carol Anne Davis, and John Tilsley—are represented in *Fresh Blood 2.*

Certainly there is enough talent out there, plotting, scheming, observing. There is no indication that this third wave is ebbing. Check out the recent first novels of Peter Guttridge, Tony Frewin, Paul Johnston, Manda Scott, Gaby Byrne, Emlyn Rees, Greg Williams, Jerry Raine, and Jon Stock, to name but a fistful. We rest our case.

But what is fresh about Fresh Blood and how new is the new wave?

Is it a question of realism being injected into the crime story? Only partly. Even the most traditionally crafted detective story—with conventional policemen and women and, usually, a closed circle of murder suspects—can go into the most graphic detail these days. Autopsies and forensics are no longer taboo subjects and the era when victims were dispatched by a neat bullet hole between the eyes is long gone.

If there is a greater degree of realism in the new wave of British crime fiction, it probably comes in the accuracy of dialogue and the depiction of social pressures and problems in today's Britain. It is, after all, a Britain that is becoming increasingly urbanized (and paranoid!), which is multiracial and multicultural and where drugs, videos, music, and even fashion can dictate crime and the consequences of crime. Crime is an equal opportunity employer and the crime story can no longer be exclusively written to conform to any set of rules or moral guidelines.

The great American noir writers of the forties and fifties showed that crimes could be committed in fiction, as many are in life, for sad, pathetic reasons *and be successful*—though not necessarily for the perpetrator. The British detective story in its classic form has long upheld a moral code that crime must not pay, yet we all know it can and does in a thousand different ways, large and small, on personal, social, economic, corporate, and political levels.

The new wave of British crime writers recognize that crime happens. It is how people are affected by it that is interesting, whether there is a neat moral solution or not—and usually there is not. This element, perhaps, is the most realistic aspect of all.

Over fifty years ago, that brilliant crime writer and *Daily Telegraph* reviewer Anthony Berkeley predicted that the days of the pure puzzle novel—the classic whodunit?—were numbered. It would no longer be the *who?* or *how?* of crime that was important to the novel, but the *why?*

Few would dispute that he has been proved right, although few could dispute that when the puzzle element is performed by magicians such as Colin Dexter or Peter Lovesey or P. D. James, it is done magnificently well. But in the main, the modern crime novel concerns itself with motive and the psychological fallout of crime.

Where the British new wave has taken this one stage further is that not only is the puzzle element no longer predominant, but in many cases, neither is the crime.

Their stories deal with crime, of course, and are populated by thieves, murderers, and lots and lots of victims. All are, one way or another, on the edge-sometimes a very personal edge. Crimes happen to them and around them and they get sucked in. How they escape—or fail to escape—is at the heart of the matter.

Since the first *Fresh Blood* collection, two trends have emerged in crime fiction that would support the theory that a sea change in attitude is taking place.

The first is the deliberate and commendable move by many publishers to promote good fiction with a criminal element outside the straight-jacket of a fixed crime "list" or imprint or house style. With inventive design and attractive jackets, crime novels can reach an audience far wider than the mystery aficionado and come to the attention of readers who would not naturally seek out a crime shelf in a bookshop.

The themes, styles, and attitude of British crime writing are broadening, and genuine efforts are being made to market good crime stories to a broader-based audience. An audience that will, it is hoped, expand. Notable examples would have to include the stunningly presented novels of Colin Bateman, James Hawes, and Christopher Brookmyre, none of whom were specifically marketed under the soporific catchall of "crime and detection."

The newer, independent publishing houses have had much to do with this and names such as 4th Estate, Serpent's Tail, No Exit Press, and our own beloved (The) Do-Not Press now rub book spines alongside the corporate giants. Forced to rely on imagination rather than mass marketing, they have led and many are thankfully following.

The second emerging trend is a mark of the growing confidence of new British crime writers in that more and more are willing to take the risk of setting their novels in America, the spiritual home of the hard-boiled style that has influenced them.

This was once a dangerous path indeed. A British writer trying to beat the Americans at their own game would himself become fair game and British novelists attempting to write American private-eye stories have provided in the past (and not too distant past) some of the most embarrassing examples of the genre.

But within the 1990s, Brits such as Philip Kerr, Michael Dibdin, John Tilsley, Tim Willocks, Maxim Jakubowski, Christopher Brookmyre, and Lee Child have successfully, set books in America and these are by no means copycat or parodies of the home-grown product.

The authors on show in *Fresh Blood 2* were all invited to contribute stories based on their published work and general attitude to crime writing. Some might say *bad* attitude!

All human life—and quite a bit of death—is here.

Ken Bruen and John Baker, both in very different ways, show us the dysfunctional side of family life. Charles Higson and Phil Lovesey take us, respectively, into the heads of a thief and a murderer. Mary Scott and

Carol Anne Davis both offer ghastly solutions to their protagonists' dilemmas and obsessions.

Lauren Henderson and Christine Green deal, in their own ways, with the problem of unrequited love, while four contributors take the scalpel to varied types of underworld. John Tilsley adopts the cause of the rootless drifter in modern America; John L. Williams turns a compassionate eye on the underlife of the hustlers of Cardiff; Christopher Brookmyre riotously exposes the Edinburgh underworld and that of the Edinburgh Fringe Festival; Iain Sinclair takes us powerfully and surreally through one of London's criminal legends.

A multiplicity of approaches, but a surprising unity of neo-noir tone, which is likely to continue stronger than ever as the third volume in the *Fresh Blood* series is already being compiled, with more new and fascinating voices as not a season now goes by in Britain without new talent emerging. This is British crime fiction in 1998. This is British crime fiction tomorrow.

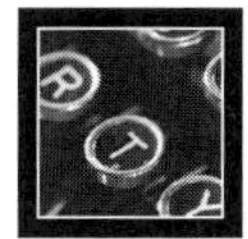

Larry Block

JAMES SALLIS

Almost thirty years ago, living in penury in New Orleans, moving from apartment to apartment, forever a scant half-step ahead of eviction, I encountered a book titled *Such Men Are Dangerous.* A friend, since dead in terrible circumstances, gave it to me. It was a short book. I read it that afternoon, then again that night, stomach grumbling with cheap chili the first time through, settling around a ninety-nine cent six-pack the second. Seldom had a book spoken so directly to me.

To me then, there at the rag-end of Vietnam, newly returned to the States from life abroad, with two Kennedys, King, and Malcolm fallen, this book seemed to be about everything important. About the incontrovertible violence at our country's heart. About the loners—mountain men, frontiersmen, Huck Finns, and cowboys—who peopled our popular mythology. About the divided selves of a people espousing Jeffersonian ideals who had murdered themselves (as D. H. Lawrence said) into democracy.

All that sounds terribly abstract and heady now as I read it over. The book was anything but. It was a hard, muscular story, trimmed down, like its protagonist's life, to basics, a kind of machine. It terrified me.

In ensuing years I'd encounter, under his own name and various assumed ones, other books by Larry Block. Some of them were incredibly funny. Others moved me in ways as complex and indefinable as did *Such Men.* From time to time I'd pick up *Writer's Digest* just to read his column. In 1981 or so I came across *A Stab in the Dark,* my first Matt Scudder, and was hooked for good. I read the rest backward, forward, backward again.

I'm not sure when I first learned the authorship of *Such Men Are Dangerous.* Certainly by then I'd read it another six or eight times and recommended it to dozens of readers and writers. But when I did learn, it was with that familiar click of recognition: of course!

With the Scudder books (echoing, again, *Such Men*'s specific effect upon me), Block hit upon a form in which city, character, and history fuse, one in which ineradicable guilt and redemptive action inform each line—creating, in effect, an engine that allowed him to say anything. Poetry of a nation, poetry of the city, poetry of the rarest kind.

Leaning over difficult tasks, we control our breathing, then, task accomplished, push back and let out a long sigh. Bernie Rhodenbarr is Block's sigh among such tasks as the Scudder books, purely commercial ventures and compulsive one-offs like *Ariel* or *Random Walk*: the other side of the coin. And the coin's that same doubloon Ahab nailed to the mast. In it we see whatever it is we look for.

Professionalism? I know of no other American writer who incorporates more fully the entire spectrum of American writing, from hack work to purely commercial enterprise to profoundly original vision.

Innovation? If the humanization of the American detective begins (as I believe it does) with Lew Archer's sleeping with his client in one of Ross Macdonald's last novels, then it continues with Scudder, and all subsequent writers of detective fiction—Grafton, Paretsky, Parker, Burke, Connelly—owe every bit as much to Block's vision as to Chandler's.

Antiheroes like those of Willeford, Vachss, Block's old friend Westlake, Dutch Leonard? They're already squarely in place with books like *Such Men.*

And then there's Bernie Rhodenbarr, who by himself pretty much created, and now defines, a whole subgenre of mystery fiction.

There are few people in literature for whom my admiration can't be expressed fully enough. Joyce. Yeats. Thomas Pynchon. Theodore Sturgeon. Larry Block.

Barthes, with his self-certain dichotomy of *écrivante* (writing for entertainment) and *écrivain* (writing as discovery), upon encountering Larry Block surely would have been left scratching his head. Not that he'd have had much chance to do so: Block's work remains safely, resolutely outside the canon.

One day, perhaps, on his way home from coffee at a midtown diner or a late movie in the village, Common Reader is assaulted and beat about the head. He wakes with amnesia, cut adrift from received wisdom, from all prior certainties, all those things he's been told are important. Lying there, he reads a novel by Larry Block—no matter which—and feels silent switches move within. Yes. *This* is the world he once knew and seeks again. *This* is literature. And so begins true recovery.

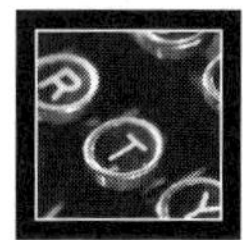

Who's in the Room

BILL CRIDER

JAMES REASONER AND L. J. WASHBURN

James Reasoner's first novel, the cult classic *Texas Wind,* was one of the first private-eye novels set in Texas. Since that time, Reasoner (who also wrote as Brett Halliday when he was doing the lead novelette for *Mike Shayne's Mystery Magazine*) has written well over one hundred novels in many genres: Western, romance, science fiction. He has written as Justin Ladd, Hank Mitchum, Matthew S. Hart, Jim Austin, Dana Fuller Ross, and Adam Rutledge, among many other names. His wife, Livia, who writes as L. J. Washburn, did a series of novels about a former Texas Ranger named Hallam, who worked as a stuntman and private eye in the early days of Hollywood. Together, Reasoner and Washburn have written as J. L. Reasoner and Livia James, and have quite likely been collaborators on some of the novels credited to James alone. They have also written a number of short stories, with most of James's having appeared in MSMM, while Livia's have been published in *Ellery Queen's Mystery Magazine.* Both writers are distinguished by their superior craftsmanship, their ability to create suspense, and most of all by their facility at weaving complex, intriguing plots. Don't-miss books: *Texas Wind* by James Reasoner and *Wild Night* by L. J. Washburn.

JOE LANSDALE

Joe Lansdale broke onto the novel scene with *Act of Love,* a stunning serial-killer novel that, had it come from a major publisher and received decent promotion, would have immediately established him as one of the top writers in the suspense field. As it happened, Lansdale had to wait a bit longer, producing in the meantime a powerful body of short fiction, including stories like "By Bizarre Hands," "My Dead Dog Bobby," and "Tight Little Stitches in a Dead Man's Back." His career began to take off with the publication of *Cold in July* and *Savage Season.* The first novel introduces private eye Jim Bob Luke, while the latter is the first appearance of Hap Collins and Leonard Pine, the characters who propelled Lansdale's career to a new high in books like *Mucho Mojo, The Two-Bear Mambo,* and *Bad Chili.* In the latter novel, Jim Bob puts in a return appearance. The Hap and Leonard novels are dark, fast, funny, profane, suspenseful, and extremely readable. Lansdale is a one-of-a-kind writer, and his books are not to be missed.

NEAL BARRETT, JR.

For years, Neal Barrett wrote science fiction novels, including the Aldair series and the extraordinary *Through Darkest America.* He has also done movie novelizations, adult Westerns, and young-adult series mysteries. But he found his true calling when he began writing mystery/suspense/comedy in *Pink Vodka Blues* and continued with *Dead Dog Blues, Skinny Annie Blues,* and *Bad Eye Blues.* Anything goes in Barrett's screwball world: a little old lady in tennis shoes who's a hit person for the Mob, a protagonist who draws bugs for a living, a novelist who writes his books on the sides of shaved dogs, and even a diorama of the Battle of Little Bighorn featuring stuffed marmots in authentic native costume. Like Joe Lansdale, Barrette is a genuine original, and his books defy classification. His plots twist and turn crazily, and his deadpan prose is both sidesplittingly funny and perfectly adapted to the sometimes very dark stories he tells. Although four of his books have the word *blues* in the title, only the last two feature a series character (Wiley Moss). Any one of the four would be a good place to begin.

JAMES SALLIS

Anyone who's looking for something new and different in a private-eye novel need look no farther than James Sallis's innovative series of novels featuring Lew Griffin, a black private investigator operating in New Orleans. The series is strikingly literary in style and intent without any sacrifice of suspense or clarity of plot. Sallis's allusive prose is so good that you can feel the humidity and taste the crawfish étouffée, and Griffin is a character like no other. The mean streets he walks are a reflection of both his own troubled mind and the troubled times he lives. There are currently three books in the series, *The Long-Legged Fly, Moth,* and *Black Hornet,* with a fourth novel due soon. Also worth looking for is Sallis's existential spy novel, *Death Will Have Your Eyes,* in which a spy comes out of retirement and goes on the road to find (maybe) a rogue agent. He finds a lot more along the way. For an antidote to bloated doorstop novels, try one of Sallis's concise and meaningful narratives.

BILL PRONZINI

Bill Pronzini has one of the longest-running and best series of private-eye novels in current fiction. All the books feature a nameless San Francisco detective, a descendant of Hammett's Continental Op, but something more besides. Pronzini is not limited by the series format; Nameless has solved all kinds of crimes, including a classic locked-room case in *Hoodwink* and a crime with its roots deep in the past in *Quicksilver,* and Nameless has faced the extremes of survival in *Shackles,* after which the Nameless books seem to have taken a somewhat darker turn. Pronzini has also done a large number of short stories, nonseries books, anthologies, and collaborative novels, including *The Running of Beasts* with Barry Malzberg. This novel is an early serial-killer novel with an especially clever plot. One of its four point-of-view characters is unaware that he has two personalities, one of which is the killer. And of course no one should miss Pronzini's affectionately hilarious tributes to some of his favorite writers in *Gun in Cheek* (1982) and *Son of Gun in Cheek* (1987).

JOHN LUTZ

For years, John Lutz was primarily a writer of short stories, some of which had extremely unusual premises. Later, Lutz began to concentrate on novels, with considerable success. His first series featured a private eye named Alo Nudger, not exactly a stalwart figure as his name suggests. Fred Carver, who operates in Florida, is a much tougher customer, and in tough, lean books like *Scorcher* and *Kiss* he shows that he can hold his own in just about any company. The books are set in Florida and evoke that steamy state's geography and characters extremely effectively. Lutz began his novel-writing career with a standalone novel, *The Truth of the Matter,* and he has continued to write nonseries mysteries and suspense novels with considerable success. The unusual *Bonegrinder* is one such book, a very well done story of a monster that terrorizes a small town in the Ozarks. And *SWF Seeks Same,* filmed as *Single White Female,* is a dark story of a young woman who advertises for a roommate and finds one—the wrong one. All Lutz's books feature skillfully constructed plots and expert pacing. Private-eye fans should look for any novel in the Fred Carver series. Others might prefer to begin with *SWF Seeks Same.*

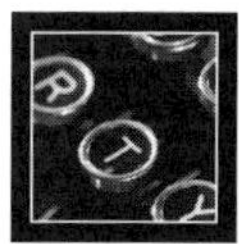

Author Notes

JON L. BREEN

Writer, Ed Gorman.

ED GORMAN

Few writers of popular fiction have practiced as many different subcategories as Gorman—pure whodunits, private-eye novels, Western-Mystery hybrids, historical and science-fictional police procedurals, political thrillers—or created as many series characters: bounty hunter Leo Guild in a series beginning with *Guild* (1987), movie critic Tobin in *Murder on the Aisle* (1987) and *Several Deaths Later* (1988), private eye Jack Tobin in six books beginning with *Rough Cut* (1985). But his specialty is a type in which series characters rarely appear: dark suspense, sometimes as himself and sometimes as Daniel Ransom, sometimes supernatural and sometimes not. His specialties are vividly captured Midwestern backgrounds, 1950s nostalgia, and a real feel for people, especially troubled adolescents and adults undergoing midlife crises. Especially notable are *Cage of Night* and *Black River Falls* (both 1996). Gorman's short stories, collected in *Moonchasers and Other Stories* (1996), are equally varied and adept. As dark and grim as his works often get, a stubborn strain of optimism about the human condition comes through. The founder of the journal *Mystery Scene,* Gorman is also one of the field's most prolific anthologists, editing the *Cat Crimes* series and the annual *Year's 25 Finest Crime and Mystery Stories.*

MAX ALLAN COLLINS

With Richard Stark (Donald E. Westlake) and Mickey Spillane as his strongest acknowledged influences,

Collins certainly tends toward the dark side in his fiction, but with humor and lightness of touch that have gained him readers from the cozy side of the wall. His earliest protagonists were criminals: professional thief Nolan, who appears in seven novels from *Bait Money* (1973) to *Spree* (1987); and hired killer Quarry, who has made five appearances from *The Broker* (1976) to *Primary Target* (1987). More recently, he has concentrated on good guys; mystery writer Mallory, of whose five appearances *The Baby Blue Rip-off* (1983) was first and *A Shroud for Aquarius* (1985) best); and Chicago private eye Nate Heller, who debuted in *True Detective* (1983) and whose meticulously researched cases (eight to date) concern such real-life twentieth-century mysteries as the death of John Dillinger (*True Crime,* 1985), the assassination of Huey Long (*Blood and Thunder,* 1995), and, perhaps most memorably of all, the Lindbergh kidnapping (*Stolen Away,* 1991). Collins has written four fact-based novels about Eliot Ness (*Butcher's Dozen,* 1988, is the best) and several TV and film novelizations. He also scripted the Dick Tracy comic strip for a number of years, directs movies, and leads a rock band in his spare time.

JAMES ELLROY

In crime fiction, Ellroy is the darkest of the dark, the noirest of the noir, the hardest of the boiled. His distinctive viewpoint is attributed in part to his obsession with an event that occurred when he was ten years old: his mother's murder, treated fictionally in *Clandestine* (1982) and nonfictionally in *My Dark Places: An L.A. Crime Memoir* (1996). While his early books, including his first novel, *Brown's Requiem* (1981), and a trio about maverick Los Angeles cop Lloyd Hopkins, beginning with *Blood on the Moon* (1984), were relatively conventional, the novels making up the L.A. Quartet developed the reader-assaulting, shock-upon-shock, almost telegraphic writing style that rivets some readers and repels others. First of the group was *The Black Dahlia* (1987) a superb fictionalization of a notorious 1947 case with similarities to his mother's death. It was followed by *The Big Nowhere* (1988), *L.A. Confidential* (1990), and *White Jazz* (1992), bringing his Los Angeles criminal history up to 1960. His most recent and even more ambitious novel is *American Tabloid* (1995), concerning the Kennedy assassination and other events of recent history. Ellroy commented in *St. James Guide to Crime and Mystery Writers:* "Dark, dense, profane, sex obsessed, emotionally complex—I hope I live up to these tags."

ROBERT B. PARKER

Parker hit the private-eye field like a thunderbolt in the mid-seventies, introducing in *The Godwulf Manuscript* (1973) Bostonian detective Spenser, a macho figure whose characteristics would recur in many who would follow: the cooking, the grudging sensitivity, the long-term serious relationship with a female professional, the violent wildman sidekick. Not quite the addition to the Hammett-Chandler-Ross Macdonald pantheon he seemed at first, Parker peaked early in the classic *God Save the Child* (1974), one of his few solidly plotted books. Many of his later appearances share two characteristics: paragraphs of description and exchanges of dialogue so beautiful you want (especially if you're a fellow writer) to frame them and hang them on the wall and plots that move in as monotonously straight a line as a desert highway. Parker's posthumous collaboration with Raymond Chandler on the unfinished Philip Marlowe novel, *Poodle Springs* (1989), and his *Big Sleep* sequel, *Perchance to Dream* (1991) are effective pastiche. The non-Spenser novel *Wilderness* (1979) is notable for suspense and characterization. A university professor before turning to full-time writing, Parker wrote a highly readable doctoral dissertation, adapted in book form as *The Private Eye in Hammett and Chandler* (1984).

LAWRENCE BLOCK

Block is among the most prolific and versatile writers of crime fiction, working in subgenres from pure suspense to private eye to espionage to classical puzzle. Though even his darkest novels and stories are leavened with humor, he unquestionably belongs to fiction noir because his series characters tend to be outlaws or outsiders: the thief-turned-spy Evan Tanner, who appears in seven books beginning with *The Thief Who Couldn't Sleep* (1966); the "criminal" lawyer Ehrengraf, a short-story character collected in the limited-edition *Ehrengraf for the Defense* (1994); the Nero Wolfe wannabe Leo Haig in *Make Out with Murder* (1974) and *The Topless Tulip Caper* (1975), both published as by Chip Harrison; the burglar-bookseller Bernie Rhodenbarr, who solved his first puzzle in *Burglars Can't Be Choosers* (1977); and his most famous character, the alcoholic unlicensed New York private eye Matt Scudder, whose career, beginning with *In the Midst of Death* (!976), continues to flourish. Long a solid pro, Block joined the greats with extraordinary latter-day Scudders like *The Devil Knows You're Dead* (1993) and *A Long Line of Dead Men* (1994). A multiple Edgar winner, including the Grand Master Award in 1994, Block was for many years a writing teacher and *Writer's Digest* columnist.

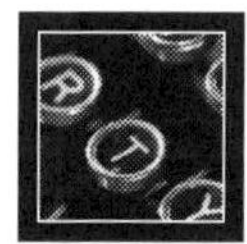

100 Authors

ED GORMAN AND LEE SERVER

90 FROM ED GORMAN

Ard, William
Hell is a City
Cry Scandal

Ballinger, Bill S.
Portrait in Smoke
The Longest Second

Bloch, Robert
Psycho
Psycho House

Block, Lawrence
After the First Death
Eight Million Ways to Die

Brackett, Leigh
The Tiger Among Us
No Good From a Corpse

Braly, Malcom
Shake Him Till He Rattles
On the Yard

Brewer, Gil
A Killer Among Us
The Red Scarf

Brown, Fredric
The Fabulous Clipjoint
The Far Cry
Knock-One-Two-Three

Browne, Howard
A Taste of Ashes

Burnett, W.R.
High Sierra
Little Caesar

Cain, James M.
The Postman Always Rings Twice
Double Indemnity

Cain, Paul
Fast One
Seven Players

Chandler, Raymond
Farewell, My Lovely
The Long Goodbye

Coburn, Andrew
The Babysitter
Off Duty

Collins, Max Allen
Quarry
Spree
True Detective

Collins, Michael
The Silent Scream
The Cadillac Cowboy

Crumley, James
The Last Good Kiss
The Wrong Case

Dennis, Ralph
Atlanta Deathwatch
The Buy Back Blues

Dewey, Thomas B.
A Sad Song Singing
Deadline

Ellison, Harlan
Gentleman Junkie
Spider Kiss

James Ellroy
L.A. Confidential

Estleman, Loren D.
Roses Are Red
Sugartown

Faust, Ron
When She Was Bad
The Burning Sky

Fischer, Bruno
The Evil Days
Murder in the Raw

Garfield, Brian
Death Wish
Recoil

Gault, Wm. Campbell
Don't Cry For Me
The Convertible Hearse

Goodis, David
Dark Passage
Nightfall

Gores, Joe
A Time of Predators
Hammett

Greene, Graham
This Gun For Hire
Brighton Rock

Hamilton, Donald
Death of a Citizen
Line of Fire

Hammett, Dashiell
The Maltese Falcon
The Dain Curse

Hansen, Joseph
Death Claims
Fadeout

Heath, W.L.
Violent Saturday
Ill Wind

Himes, Chester
Blind Man with a Pistol
The Crazy Kill

Hitchens, Dolores
Sleep With Slander
The Abductor

Homes, Geoffrey
Build My Gallows High
Six Silver Handles

Hughes, Dorothy B.
In A Lonely Place
Ride the Pink Horse

Hunter, Evan
The Blackboard Jungle
Nobody Knew They Were There

Kaminisky, Stuart
Down For The Count
Lieberman's Thief

Keene, Day
Sleep with the Devil
Carnival of Death

Kersh, Gerald
Night and the City

King, Stephen
Misery
Gerald's Game

Koontz, Dean
Face of Fear
Mr. Murder

Lacy, Ed
Room to Swing
The Men From The Boys

Lansdale, Joe
Savage Season
Cold in July

Latimer, Johnathan
Headed for a Hearse
The Lady in the Morgue

Laymon, Richard
The Cellar
Midnight's Lair

Lochte, Dick
Sleeping Dog
Neon Smile

Leonard, Elmore
52 Pick-Up
Unknown Man No. 89

Lutz, John
The Truth of the Matter
Hot

MacDonald, John D.
The End of the Night
One Monday We Killed Them All

MacDonald, Ross
The Far Side of the Dollar
The Chill

Marlowe, Dan J.
The Name of the Game is Death

Marlowe, Stephen
Catch the Brass Ring
Violence is My Business

Matheson, Richard
Someone is Bleeding
Ride the Nightmare

McBain, Ed
Nocturne
He Who Hesitates
Guns

McCoy, Horace
They Shoot Horses, Don't They?

McGivern, William
The Big Heat
Odds Against Tomorrow

Miller, Margaret
How Like an Angel
The Murder of Miranda

Miller, Wade
Calamity Fair
Kiss Her Goodbye

Mosley, Walter
A Little Yellow Dog
White Butterfly

Muller, Marcia
Wolf in the Shadows
Eye of the Storm

Packer, Vin
Intimate Victims
Three Day Terror

Patridge, Norman
Slippin' Into Darkness

Piccirrilli, Tom
Shards
Sorrow's Crown

Pronzini, Bill
The Stalker
Sentinels

Rabe, Peter
Kiss The Boss Goodbye
The Box

Randisi, Robert J.
Alone With The Dead
The Steinway Collector

Reasoner, James
Texas Wind

Rice, Craig
Trial By Fury
Having A Wonderful Crime

Sallis, James
Moth
The Long Legged Fly

Spillane, Mickey
I, The Jury
Kiss Me Deadly

Thomas, Ross
The Brass Go-Between
Briarpatch

Thompson, Jim
The Killer Inside Me
Pop. 1280

Valin, Jonathan
The Lime Pit

Westlake, Donald E.
Murder Among Children (as Tucker Coe)
Comeback (as Richard Stark)
Trust Me On This

Whittington, Harry
Backwoods Tramp
Web of Murder

Whitfield, Raoul
Green Ice
Death In A Bowl

White, Lionel
The Killing
The Money Trap

Willeford, Charles
Pick-Up
Miami Blues

Williams, Charles
The Big Bite
Man On The Run

Willie, Ennis
Game of Passion
The Work of the Devil

Wilson, F. Paul
Sibs
The Tomb

Woolrich, Cornell
The Bride Wore Black
Rendezvous In Black

10 FROM LEE SERVER

Behm, Marc
Eye of the Beholder

Bowles, Paul
Let It Come Down

Burroughs, William
Junkie

Fuller, Samuel
The Dark Page

Gresham, William Lindsay
Nightmare Alley

Highsmith, Patricia
Ripley Underground

Himes, Chester
All Shot Up

Stark, Richard
Butcher's Moon

Thomey, Tedd
And Dream of Evil

Willeford, Charles
Sideswipe

III: COMIC BOOKS

Noir, comic book style. An artist's rendering of a scene from *Raw Deal*.

Comic Book Noir

RON GOULART

Film noir flourished initially from the early 1940s through the late 1950s. Comic books, some of them, had begun exploring noir territory even a few years earlier than that. In the adventures of various tough cops and private eyes and in the exploits of such masked avengers as Batman and the Spirit, many of the standard trappings began showing up. The city by night was a frequent setting, robbery, kidnapping, and murder standard plot elements. In addition, many of the stories dealt not only with cruel and colorful villains but with civic corruption, ambiguous and often treacherous women, and with tough, cynical, sometimes wisecracking protagonists.

The comic book of the late 1930s, when our explorations will commence, was a fairly new medium. The stories and characters we'll be considering were influenced by movies, both European expressionist and Warner's gangster, by pulp magazines like *Black Mask* and *Dime Detective* and by New York itself, where just about all young comic-book artists and writers were living. Though supposedly working in a kids medium, these authors often created gritty melodramas that provided young readers with glimpses of a world that was dirtier, less honest, and more dangerous than the ones that most of them were familiar with.

Death especially was much more frequently encountered in the upstart comic books than it ever had been in the politer and more rigorously controlled newspaper funnies from which they had sprung. Adventure strips, such as *Dick Tracy, Tarzan,* and *Terry and the Pirates,* occasionally dealt in death and murder, but these weren't staple ingredients of most of the features found on the comic page.

Modern format comic books got going in the early years of the thirties, offering chiefly reprints of daily and Sunday newspaper strips. The pioneering title was *Famous Funnies* and it was followed by *Popular Comics, TipTop Comics, Super Comics, The Funnies,* and similar compilations. Late in 1934, Major Malcolm Wheeler Nicholson, a flamboyant and impecunious entrepreneur, launched *New Fun.* This was the first regularly issued comic book in America to offer only original material. The Major followed his first struggling magazine with New Comics, which also consisted entirely of new stuff. Nicholson, a former cavalry officer and current writer of adventure yarns for such pulps as Argosy, gathered together a staff of art-school students, alcoholic pulp illustrators and down-on-their-luck one-time newspaper cartoonists to fill the pages. Like the pulpwood magazines he was inspired by, the Major's new titles included a variety of story types—science fiction, Western, and, of course, detective.

Late in 1936, some of Major Nicholson's defecting staffers started *Detective Picture Stories.* Delayed by recurrent financial problems, Nicholson's own *Detective Comics* didn't hit the newsstands until early the following year. It was this latter title, however, that introduced some noir elements to comic books, The DC Company also took its name from this publication. As the title implied, every character in the new magazine was a detective of one sort or the other. Among them were Speed Saunders, a tough plainclothes cop; Slam Bradley, a tough private eye; Larry Steele, another tough PI; Bruce Nelson, yet one more tough private investigator; and Steve Malone, a tough district attorney. All of these detectives worked in big cities and subscribed to the notion that nighttime was the right time for sleuthing. In this early period, Nicholson couldn't afford to use color throughout the book and some of these nocturnal capers were printed in black and white, which obviously added to the noir look. The Major wrote some of the scripts and others were by a young lawyer named Gardner Fox. In the second year of his career, the Speed Saunders adventures were turned out by Fox and a young artist named Fred Guardineer and took on a distinct noir aura. Guard-ineer drew in a boldly outlined and somewhat diagrammatic style and was particularly fond of rendering gloomy locals and dark urban streets. He was good at depicting a wide variety of thugs, hoods, and other criminal types. His dangerous dames were always both attractive and unsettling.

Detective Comics' most successful detective made hi debut in the spring of 1939. The advent of Superman in DC's *Action Comics* a little less than a year earlier precipitated a slow-starting but now-accelerating revolution. In 1939 and 1940, hundreds of new costumed super heroes, many with incredible super powers and others simply flamboyant crime fighters, would show up in comic books. New characters and new titles hit the stands every week. Batman, the creation of artist Bob Kane and writer Bill Finger, first appeared in *Detective* number 27 (May 1939) and became an instant star. From the beginning he inhabited a grim, night world and, except for that pointy-eared costume, was similar to many hard-boiled pulp private eyes.

Batman was, as Jules Feiffer has pointed out, also a member of "the school of rich idlers who put on masks," a group that includes Zorro, the Shadow, and countless heroes of dime novels and pulp-fiction magazines. But "Batman inhabited a world where no one, no matter the time of day, cast anything but long shadows—seen from weird perspectives,' Feiffer went on to say in *The Great Comic Book Heroes.* Batman's world was "more cinematic than Superman's" and the only one that "managed to get that Warner Brothers fog-infested look." In the nocturnal Gotham City, where Batman did most of his prowling, there was never anything but a full moon in the dark sky.

While Batman, who worked solo during his first year, tangled with his share of colorful and crazed villains—Dr. Hugo Strange, The Monk, and, eventually the Joker and The Penguin—he always had time to deal with gangsters, bank robbers, and crooked politicians. And he ran into his share of dangerous dames. *The* woman in his life was a pretty, dark-haired jewel thief known initially as The Cat—she later took to calling herself Catwoman and wearing a costume. She was similar to the ambiguous and ambivalent females who populated so many of the films noir, capable of both saving Batman's life and double-crossing him. He, too, had mixed feeling about her. In most of their many encounters over the years he managed to thwart her criminal plans while, much to the annoyance and sometime amusement of his sidekick Robin, seeing to it that she eluded the law and got away.

Another inhabitant of the noir setting was The Spirit. Created by Will Eisner, he first appeared in 1940 in a weekly comic booklet insert in Sunday newspaper comic sections around the country. In 1942, he also began appearing in every month in *Police Comics.* The Spirit was actually Denny Colt, criminologist and private detective, who was apparently murdered by a villain named Dr. Cobra. But Colt decided to let Central City go on believing he was dead in order to fight crime more unconventionally as a masked avenger. Those who shared his secret were crusty Police Commissioner Dolan and his pretty blond daughter Ellen. Colt settled into a roomy, furnished crypt in the Wildwood Cemetery and used that as his base.

While employing many of the basic elements of other costumed comic-book heroes, Eisner didn't exactly turn out conventional stuff. His only concession to costume fans was The Spirit's mask. Colt wore a blue business suit, often the worse for wear after his assorted encounters with the underworld, and a fedora. Eisner was a great reader of short stories and an enthusiastic movie fan. He began trying to emulate his favorite writers, O. Henry and Ambrose Bierce, while experimenting increasingly with film approaches to layout. Eisner had grown up in New York and the look of his feature had as much to do with that as it did with the influence of Hollywood and expressionist motion pictures. He's said that his approach to lighting was due to having spent a lot of his youth looking out of apartment-house windows at night streets lit by street lamps. In a typical Spirit adventure it's raining, the street lamps are reflected on the slick pavement, and dirty water is running along the gutters.

By the time World War II was over, Eisner—resuming his feature after a stretch in the army-had pretty much abandoned traditional comic-book villains and was concentrating on civic corruption, gangster crimes, and innocents caught in the various traps the big city had to offer. He also made frequent use of femmes fatales. The three who most frequently recurred were Sand Saref, who grew up with Denny Colt in the city slum where he was born and raised; Silk Satin, who worked as an international jewel thief and spy before reforming; and P'gell, a Paris-based con artist with a "long list of husbands (all dead)."

World War II had a substantial effect on the composition of the comic-book audience. America officially entered the war in December of 1941 and large numbers of young men were called into the armed forces. Comics soon became some of the most popular reading material at post exchanges around the country. Since most of these customers were in their late teens and early twenties, they weren't satisfied with simple superheroics and crime busting. Therefore, comic books offering what later came to be called Good Girl Art increased in numbers and sales. Good Girl Art, by the way, refers not to drawings of good girls but to artwork featuring pretty girls wearing a minimum of clothing. While many of these partially clad young ladies showed up in the pages of such titles as *Jungle Comics* and *Planet Comics,* a goodly number also began finding their way into detective and costumed crime-fighter stories.

An early oasis for these girls was in the titles published by the MLJ Company, an outfit that later became the clean-cut Archie Comics publishing operation. Commencing in late

1939, the publishers began issuing a series of four monthly titles—*Blue Ribbon, Top-Notch, Pep,* and *Zip.* All four underwent changes during the war years, with *Pep Comics* turning especially dark in many of its stories. The star of the magazine was a red, white, and blue superpatriot known as The Shield. Early in 1941, some months after Batman had teamed up with Robin, The Shield added a costumed sidekick called Dusty the Boy Detective. As World War II progressed, the exploits of The Shield and Dusty grew bloodier and more violent. The Axis villains they confronted were especially bloodthirsty. There was vicious Nazi called The Strangler, an even worse Japanese known as The Fang, and a truly rotten Nazi called The Hun. The incidence of upthrust bosoms, bondage, stocking tops, and other Good Girl touches also increased. An especially nasty hero came along in Pep number 17 (July 1941) in the person of The Hangman. He got into crime fighting after his brother, an earlier Pep hero known as The Comet, was killed by Gangster bullets. The adventures of The Hangman were filled with strangling, hangings, impalings, and other methods of violent death. There was also a continuous supply of unreliable and slinky women. Among the artists who drew The Hangman's vengeful adventures were Bob Fujitani and Harry Lucey.

Lucey also illustrated the magazine's darkest and most unsettling feature. Madam Satan started in issue number 16. The dark-haired, sultry lady was employed by the devil himself and was a combination of the vamp of silent cinema and the more recent femme fatale of noir films. Sent back to earth after her death, she was assigned by the devil to "wreak havoc among mortals" by turning innocent fellows into thorough scoundrels. Her employer descried Madam Satan as having " the black, corrupt soul of a beautiful woman." Using the name Iola and donning a slinky satin evening gown, Madam Satan insinuated herself into various lives and set out to corrupt as many men as possible. A typical victim was Carl Jensen, who was lured away from his true love and was soon "completely in the toils of the creature of the netherworld, beginning an expensive orgy of merrymaking." All too soon Carl was goaded into a life of crime. "Shower me with real gifts!" Iola urged her bedazzled victim. "Steal if you must!" After beating up his own father and shooting his fiancée, Carl finally came to his senses. Here was Iola as she really was, her face a grinning green skull. Madam Satan never quite succeeded in any of her missions and she left the magazine after six issues, just as Archie Andrews entered the lineup.

Over at *Zip Comics,* Charles Brio had been drawing a superhero named Steel Sterling. The hero's origin had been explained thusly—"To avenge the death of his father, who was murdered and robbed of all his wealth by gangsters, and to avoid a similar end for himself, John Sterling devoted every minute of his youth to dangerous experiments! In one final experiment, the result of which would be success or death!—he hurled himself into a tank of molten steel and fiery chemicals! The test realized his life ambition." He emerged as Steel Sterling, "with all the attributes of this sturdiest of metals!!! As a blind to both police and underworld, Steel Sterling adopts another personality. He poses as John Sterling, four flushing private investigator and twin brother of the famous STEEL!" Biro dropped the feature in the spring of 1941 to go to work for the publishers Lev Gleason and Arthur Bernhard on a comic book devoted to the original Daredevil. His major contribution to comics was not far off.

Early in 1942 Biro and his longtime friend and fellow MLJ cartoonist Bob Wood became editors of an innovative new comic book. *Crime Does Not Pay* was advertised as "the most sensational comic magazine ever created!!!" Major influences on the genesis and evolution of the book were such hard-boiled periodicals as *True Detective, Master Detective,* and *Official Detective.* Printed on somewhat better paper than the pulps and illustrates with grainy photos of vicious criminals, blowzy gun molls, and bloody corpses, they offered breathless nonfiction accounts of daring bank robberies, brutal murders, and assorted crimes of passion. *Crime Does Not Pay* came closer than any comic book had before to emulating this particular blend of gritty reality, shoot-em-up action, and titillation. It chronicled crooks of recent vintage, such as Legs Diamond and Lepke and older outlaws like Billy the Kid. Most of the cases were packed with shooting, violence, action, and bloodshed. The sexual element was usually provided by the lady friends of various crooks and killers or by the assorted female victims of the various crooks and killers. Like many a noir movie, the magazine believed in a dark world where corruption and violence flourished and nobody, especially a pretty woman was to be trusted.

Artwork in the early issues was by Creig Flessel, Harry Lucey, and Dick Briefer. As the war progressed, some lesser artists showed up, but in the middle and late 1940s, George Tuska, who's been called "the premier crime comic artist," Bob Fujitani, Dan Barry, and Fred Kida were among those who improved the comic's looks. Biro limited himself to drawing most of the covers. He usually dealt with anticipation, showing the moment just before the hapless gas-station attendants were buried alive or just before the bootlegger got dropped in the lime pit.

Crime Does Not Pay proved to be enormously successful and by the mid-1940s was selling well over a million copies a month. Despite these impressive newsstand sales, it had the field pretty much to itself for several years. But because of the uncertain economics of the postwar period and the decline of interest in superheroes, other publishers turned to crime. Dozens of titles followed. As we'll see, much of the criticism, censorship, and boycotting that hit the comics industry in the early 1950s was inspired by the more flamboyant imitators of the pioneering *Crime Does not Pay.*

Mickey Spillane utilized many noir elements in his bet selling Mike Hammer novels, the first of which appeared in 1947. The books were rich with violence and displayed a profound distrust of the system and just about all women. Before becoming a very successful mystery novelist, Spillane had worked at writing scripts and filler stories for comic books. Late in 1942, as an unlikely backup feature in *Green Hornet Comics* number 10, he created a funny-book predecessor of Hammer in the person of Mike Lancer, "that grim-faced, gun-slinging private detective." In his one and only appearance, Lancer tracked down a murder-for-hire gang and, in just six pages, managed to kill four hoodlums. One of them he dispatches by swinging him several times against a brick wall while remarking, "And that saves the state's electric bill." Harry Sahle, who worked with Spillane at the Funnies, Inc. comic art sweatshop, drew the feature.

Returning from the service after World War II, Spillane gave the private-eye genre another try, this time calling his comic-book protagonist Mike Danger—"He backs up the law with his fists and a .45 slung under his left armpit, ready to slug or shoot it out any place, any time." Put together in 1946, the material didn't see print until 1954 in *Crime Detector.* Meantime, Spillane had changed his detective's name to Mike Hammer and written a batch of novels about him.

The private eye was often an important component of films noir-as exemplified by such movies as *The Maltese Falcon, Murder, My Sweet,* and *Out of the Past.* In the 1940s an increasing number of private detectives began to be heard on the radio as well, some of them as downbeat and cynical as their silver-screen counterparts. Among them were Sam Spade, as played by Howard Duff; Phillip Marlowe, portrayed first by Van Heflin and then Gerald Mohr; and Richard Rogue, enacted by Dick Powell, who'd been the screen's first Philip Marlowe in *Murder, My Sweet*. As the superheroes who'd dominated the first half of the decade began to lose favor in the years immediately after the war, private eyes had a resurgence in comic books. No doubt their increasing popularity in movies and on the radio had something to do with it.

Sam Spade himself had appeared in a one-shot comic-book adaptation of *The Maltese Falcon* that was published by the David McKay Company in 1946, but that didn't lead to a career in the medium. *The Sam Hill, Private Eye* comic debuted late in 1950. Hiding behind the name Close-Up, Inc. were the Archie Comics folks (formerly MLJ). Sam Hill struggled vainly to imitate his betters, namely the radio Sam Spade. Like Spade, he recounted his adventure to his pretty secretary in the form of reports and he referred to each case, as did Spade, as a caper. "I just can't figure dames!" Hill would begin, feet up on his desk. "They either love you or they hate you. They either throw themselves at you or they try to blow your head off! That's the way it was with me in this case." The magazine lasted seven issues, providing larger quantities of tough crooks, sexy dames, dark streets, and gunplay. The artist was the dependable Harry Lucey.

Other private eyes who surfaced briefly in the early 1950s included Johnny Danger, Ken Shannon, and Johnny Dynamite. Television, by this time, was taking over from radio, and several early TV Ops made it, briefly, into comic books, among them Martin Kane and Mike Barnett, Man Against Crime.

The true crime comic book began to proliferate in the late 1940s and early 1950s. Joe Simon and Jack Kerby, who'd earlier created such upright and exemplary characters as Captain America and the Boy Commandos, turned to a life of crime in 1947. That was when they were hired to turn *Headline Comics,* until them chock-full of clean-cut boy heroes, into a true crime surrogate. They also contributed *Real Clue.* A wide range of publishers were abandoning supermen and converting to crime. Among the dozens of new titles that poured forth were *Lawbreakers Always Lose, Crime Case Comics, Inside Crime, March of Crime, Wanted, Crime and Punishment, Crime Must Pay the Penalty, Crimes by Women, Fight Against Crime,* and *Murder Incorporated.* Most of these magazines made use of the noir basics—tough and cynical protagonists, ambiguous and faithless women, city streets and dark alleys, quick violence.

The EC Company—those letters originally standing for Educational Comics—had been established in 1947 by M. C. Gaines so that he could concentrate on turning out more uplifting comics than most of the ones he'd been in charge of while associated with DC. Another pioneering publisher, Gaines had had a hand in developing *Famous Funnies,* the first modern format comic book, and for DC he and his young editor had developed *All-American Comics, Flash Comics,* and *Sensation Comics.* These titles introduced The Green Lantern, The Flash, Hawkman, and Wonder Woman to the world. While still associated with DC, Gaines had put together *Picture Stories from the Bible* and *Picture Stories from American History.* As EC, he continued with these and added *Picture Stories from World History* and *Picture Stories from Science.*

After M. C. Gaines's accidental death, his son William inherited the company. EC, the letters now standing for Entertaining Comics, began to change and by 1948 was issuing such titles as *Crime Patrol* and *War Against Crime.* With Harvey Kurtzman and Al Feldstein editing and writing for him, and Jack Davis, Wally Wood, Johnny Craig, and Kurtzman drawing for him, William Gaines added *Crime SuspenStories* to his list in 1950 and *Shock SuspenStories* in 1952. These were detective fiction and not true crime and, for comic books, fairly sophisticated in content and approach. The scripts were definitely noir, also showing the influence of Alfred Hitchcock movies and Cornell Woolrich stories. There was also a James M. Cain sensibility evident in many of them. Hitherto honest men were continually being lured into committing crimes and killings by heartless blondes, the battle of the sexes often turned deadly, and there was usually a lot of rain and darkness.

Like many of the other crime titles, the EC magazines became excessive in their depiction of bloodshed and violence. The covers of both the *SuspenStories* books took to showing hangings, beatings, drug use, fatal plunges, and even decapitations. Since many parents and civic groups judged these books by their covers, this showcasing of violence was not a smart way to avoid criticism. Protests about the crime and horror magazines continued to grow nation wide—inspired in many instances by Frederic Wertham's book *Seduction of the Innocent*—and by 1955 various pressures and government inquiries had put the crime comics out of business. For the most part noir was gone from comic books, not to return, for many decades.

IV: Radio & Television

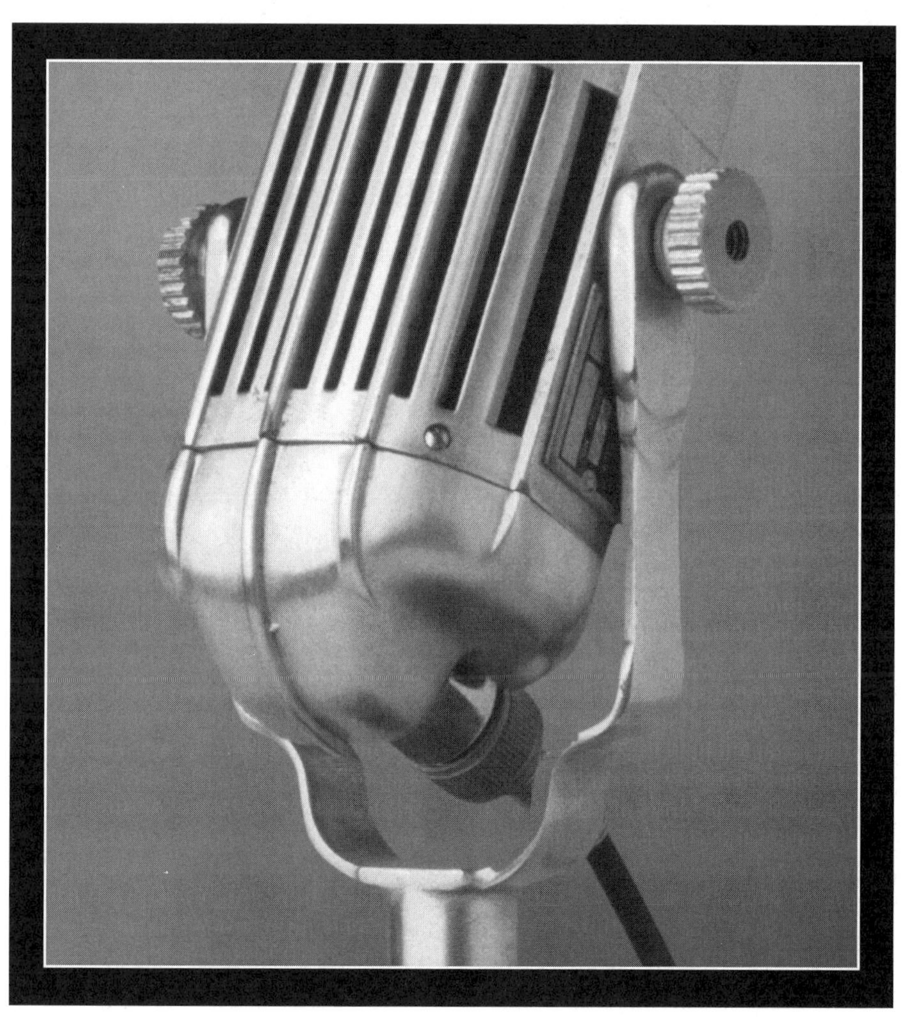

Radio Noir

WILLIAM NADEL

Radio noir is by definition film noir transformed to another medium—the medium of sound. How could the stark, bitter, brutal, dramatic world of the movies make it on radio? Only the right combination of script, acting, music, and sound effects could even begin to create that doom-laden world, one of shadows, bleakness, corruption, crime, and sharp contrasts with people on the edge of neurosis, sadism, and other seemingly unhealthy impulses.

As far back as the 1930s, radio began "experimenting" with the elements of noir. Actress-author-producer Edith Meiser brought Sherlock Holmes to the airwaves, and soon after wrote and produced *The Shadow* (then known as *The Blue Coal Radio Revue,* which featured The Shadow as only an omniscient narrator) and *Twenty Thousand Years in Sing Sing* (the reminiscences of Warden Lawes, whose tales of the most depraved of criminals set the standard for shows such as *Mr. District Attorney* and *Gangbusters*). Even though Meiser abhorred the hard-boiled school of mystery, preferring the "English" school, she would often drift very close to the world of noir. However, radio during the 1930s was a stage-like presentation, complete with full orchestras for musical bridges and even performers attired in formal eveningwear. The changes came in 1938 at about the time Orson Welles brought *First Person Singular* to listener's homes (soon to become *The Mercury Theatre on the Air* and *Campbell Playhouse*). Thus when sound films were finding their way into the noir method of storytelling, so was radio. Dashiell Hammett's novels, already subject to screen treatment, were soon dramatized. Radio writers were having a field day adapting these noiric precursors, so *Lux Radio Theatre* and the many other programs devoted to sound representation of the visual began to attempt to replicate these filmed tales and their mood. Borrowing also some storytelling techniques from the many popular radio horror shows of the time, the medium's version of the genre was beginning to develop.

Hammett unknowingly was the founder by default of this new radio category as his novel-derived series about his creation, *The Thin Man,* reached NBC on July 2, 1941. Patterned after the successful movie series, the network version featured Claudia Morgan as Nora Charles and Les Damon as Nick. Mirroring the decadent lives of Hammett and Lillian Hellman, the series portrayed the couple cavorting through life in a world of depravity, murder, spies, creeps, and criminals of all types. At a time when the movies portrayed them in twin beds, radio had them unmistakably sleeping in one. Only one thing thwarted the Charleses during their nearly ten year run across all the radio networks (NBC, CBS, Mutual, ABC)—an NBC rule that radio murders could not take place before 10 P.M. So for a brief time in 1948, Nick and Nora chased after missing babies, lovestruck prizefighters, and befuddled actors. A change in time slots returned the Charleses to their classic milieu of depravity, crime, and wisecracks, which continued until the end of the radio run.

Undoubtedly, the high point of the early 1940s was the birth of radio's most prestigious mystery anthology series, *Suspense*. From its start in 1942 to its end twenty years later, Suspense actually was the medium's "outstanding theatre of thrills." Its microphones featured many of Hollywood's greatest start acting in a gamut of dramas that ranged from scores of noir and classic mysteries to horror, fantasy, and true crime. Almost a thousand *Suspense* dramas reached the American public and they loved it. They also loved hearing if their favorite movie star could make it on the air. Some, unfortunately, did not do well in the medium, yet their efforts always were enjoyed by the listeners. "Sorry, Wrong Number" by Lucille Fletcher, a tale of a handicapped woman who overhears the plans for her own murder, was a listener favorite—and it had many re-airings. The CBS showcase for the greatest stars in the greatest mysteries, *Suspense* offered some stellar examples of Hammett, Chandler, and others of the hard-boiled-noir genre.

Suspense's only real rival for high quality, *The Molle Mystery Theatre* arrived at NBC in 1943. Not quite as high-powered, *Mystery Theatre* may have lacked the Hollywood stars, but it did have the best actors in New York radio. And it did stick primarily to mysteries and detective stories, offering the listener a veritable cornucopia of Chandler, Woolrich, Christie, and even Sax Rohmer's oriental villain Fu Manchu, until it transformed itself into a non-noir straight classic British detective show in the early 1950s.

By 1946, after several of his tales had reached *Suspense,* Hammett was again lured to father another set of radio noir detective shows. It happened that producers E. J. Rosenberg and Lawrence White had negotiated with the author to package Sam Spade for broadcast. During the nearly three years it took to bring Spade to the air, the producers discussed the possibility of an interim detective show. This apparently evolved into *The Fat Man* when a chance phrase about already having a *Thin Man* show on the air merged with a discussion of Hammett's other major detective, the Continental Op. Then on January 21, 1946, J. Scott Smart stood in front of the ABC microphones for the first time as that network's greatest noir crime fighter. Eventually called Bradford Runyon, the overweight sleuth (230 to 250 pounds) began each show with an opening speech about a certain type of lifestyle or debauchery would lead to murder or "MUR-DER," as actor Smart would pronounce it. Not your usual detective, Runyon answered to both his mother and girlfriend. Later episodes would carefully place Runyon in Foreign countries, many south of the border, where he would run into all manner of characters in script titles using the word murder. Richard Ellington held the position of chief writer, but the most memorable exploits (and dialogue) came from the supremely talented Lawrence Klee. One of the greatest of all radio authors, Klee's genius was in merging horror, fantasy, and noir into something truly remarkable. He even brought the noir touch to the serial-inspired exploits of *Mr. Keen, Tracer of Lost Persons.* Keen was a kindly old classic-style detective who would often find himself, thanks to Klee, verging into the more brutal world of Hammett-type characters. *The Fat Man, Sam Spade,* and *The Thin Man* were all just radio memories by the end of 1951, snuffed out by the hysteria concerning Hammett's blacklisting and eventual jail sentence as well as the early encroachment of television.

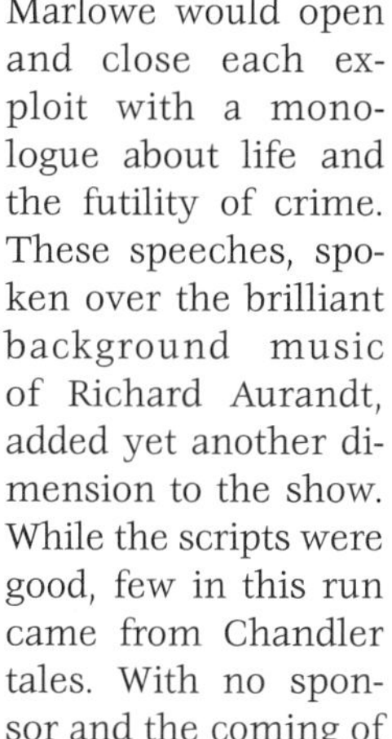

Ironically, 1951 also signaled the end of another great radio noir crime fighter, Philip Marlowe—even though 10.3 million listeners had tuned in to his adventures in 1949. Marlowe's main foe was the lack of a sponsor, but that had not always been the case. Raymond Chandler's stories had begun reaching the airwaves years earlier, also as movies done for radio, whetting the public's appetite for more tales of the prototypical gumshoe. Finally in 1947, a limited-run series replaced Bob Hope for the summer. Starring Van Heflin, these thirteen shows dramatized many if the non-Marlowe Chandler pulp stories, amalgamating their original sleuths into Marlowe. Chandler had grudgingly helped with the publicity for the show, even praising Heflin for his efforts at learning about the role of a detective. After its brief run on NBC, a year later a more streamlined, less expensive, unsponsored (sustaining) version reached the CBS microphones. Although it was very successful, *The Adventures of Philip Marlowe* only attracted a couple of sponsors, for but a brief time during its entire three-year run. Chandler himself recognized the budgetary problems and praised the producer of the show for his ability to create such quality despite the difficult monetary limitations. The Marlowe of CBS, Gerald Mohr, was no stranger to the airwaves. In fact, he was one of the medium's best. The format of the shows followed the first-person technique that now had become the noir specialty. Again, Marlowe would open and close each exploit with a monologue about life and the futility of crime. These speeches, spoken over the brilliant background music of Richard Aurandt, added yet another dimension to the show. While the scripts were good, few in this run came from Chandler tales. With no sponsor and the coming of television, *Marlowe* left the air after the summer of 1950. It returned for one last gasp as a summer season replacement in 1951. The press releases described Chandler's creation as "rough, tough—and softhearted." The hard edge had gone out of the scripts and the adventures. They were now just tales of human interest clothed in the Marlowe mold. It wasn't an actual network dictum, it was more subtle than that. Marlowe had replaced Hopalong Cassidy!

Frank Lovejoy was the ideal radio performer. He developed an ability to reach listeners like no other actor. After appearing in many shows, he finally got a gem—*NightBeat.* As Randy Stone, reporter for a Chicago newspaper, Lovejoy took a human-interest program and pushed it into the noir domain. More detective than reporter, Stone solved crimes with a flair and panache that few so-called "gutsy" shows had. Each night Stone would roam the streets of Chicago looking for that special story. Usually it was one of crime or great tragedy, and always it would be tagged with a memorable closing monologue about the people of "his" city. Then the story would be ready for printing and Stone would call for a copy boy and end the program. *NightBeat* lasted only two and a half years, yet left an indelible mark on radio.

Almost nothing has been written anywhere about *Barrie Craig (Crane), Confidential Investigator.* He began life on NBC in 1951 as a clone of the highly successful *Martin Kane* series. The leading role in both was parlayed to excellence by actor William Gargan. Gargan had left *Kane* to pursue other interests. Unable to return to the original role, Gargan slipped in as Barrie Crane until the *Kane* producers cried foul. Then Crane became Craig and the format changed, but ever so slightly. Still a noir detective, Craig also liked to deliver those ever-present opening and closing monologues. However, Gargan delivered these in a droll, almost macabre way. A better movie and stage actor than a radio sight-reading actor, the droll deliveries were actually edits of the pretaped speeches, with Gargan repeating his lines again and again. Barrie Craig shot, punched, and slugged his way through five years of cheaply but effectively produced shows originating in both New York and Hollywood. Music was supplied solely by recording, and during its last season (1955), the program suffered from the most severe budgetary constraints.

No survey of radio's bleak shows, even a brief one, can fail to include one very different and special program—*Gunsmoke.* Ostensibly an adult Western, it dealt with greed, avarice, crime, murder, and despair painted against a background of the Old West. Far more moving than detective or mystery programs, *Gunsmoke* told its often depressing tales through the viewpoint of Marshall Matt Dillon of Dodge City, Kansas, of the 1880s. No other show was ever so brutally rugged or bitter. No other actor ever carried as much weariness in his voice as William Conrad. Conrad's Dillon was superior to just about any other radio actor's performances. For nearly ten years (1952 through 1961), he did his best to defend the people of Dodge City from the worst crimes imaginable, for almost every conceivable villain managed to ride into Dodge, and into a gloriously designed radio sound pattern that has never been equaled.

By 1960 most drama was gone from the medium. The last two holdouts from the heyday years were on CBS—*Suspense* and *Yours Truly, Johnny Dollar.* Dollar was a near-noir insurance investigator who came awfully close to the genre but never quite made it. His problem was that, along with his comments about humanity, he kept a running budget on the cost of his assignment. These budgetary references diluted the noir mood and made him less gritty—a sort of detective accountant. Even he was gone by the end of 1962. Television, cost, and reality had killed off radio drama on the networks. It did not stay really dead for too long, for there were many attempts at reviving drama anthology shows, but none ran longer than a couple of years. The most unique of these was the 1973 through 1974 effort, *The Hollywood Radio Theatre Presents "The Zero Hour."* Almost exclusively noir, it was the brainchild of the young Jay Michael. A masterful undertaking guided by veteran radio actor-producer-director Elliot Lewis, *The Zero Hour* featured a variety of mystery and suspense novels dramatized in five daily episodes. Tied together with a narration by Rod Sterling, the shows offered the best of Hollywood's radio actors with a sprinkling of TV and movie stars to add excitement. Michael and Lewis struggled to get just the right mix of actors, music, and sound effects, eventually resorting to replacing modern microphones with those made in the 1940s and 1950s. When they finally succeeded, the listeners were in for a great treat. The prerecorded programs sounded terrific, and were even packaged in a two-hour format for stations that preferred a single night airing rather than five thirty-minute episodes. Unfortunately its creative success led to its undoing. Picked up by Mutual Radio, changes were made in the format so it would become just a new half-hour anthology of separate stories. It limped along for a while and then faded away. Most other efforts to revive radio drama featured some noir-type stories, but they were just pale shadows of the glory days of the forties and fifties. *CBS Radio Mystery Theatre,* the one successful revival, ran fourteen years and then closed its doors. That, however, did not signal the end for radio noir. Today, across the country, college and public radio stations are constantly experimenting with new dramas, some even noir-like. And many of the old shows continue to be replayed and even repackaged as audiocassettes and compact disks. To paraphrase Philip Marlowe's CBS opening, "Crime is not just a sucker's road, for those who follow it on radio wind up enjoying it again and again."

(Many of the programs mentioned here can be sampled by contacting the following companies:

Radio Spirits, Inc., P.O. Box 2141, Schiller Park, IL 60176;

Adventures in Cassettes-Metacom, Inc., 5353 Nathan Lane North, Plymouth, MN 55442-1978;

HighBridge Company, 1000 Westgate Drive, St. Paul, MN 55114;

Great American Audio Corp., 33 Portman Road, New Rochelle, NY 10801.)

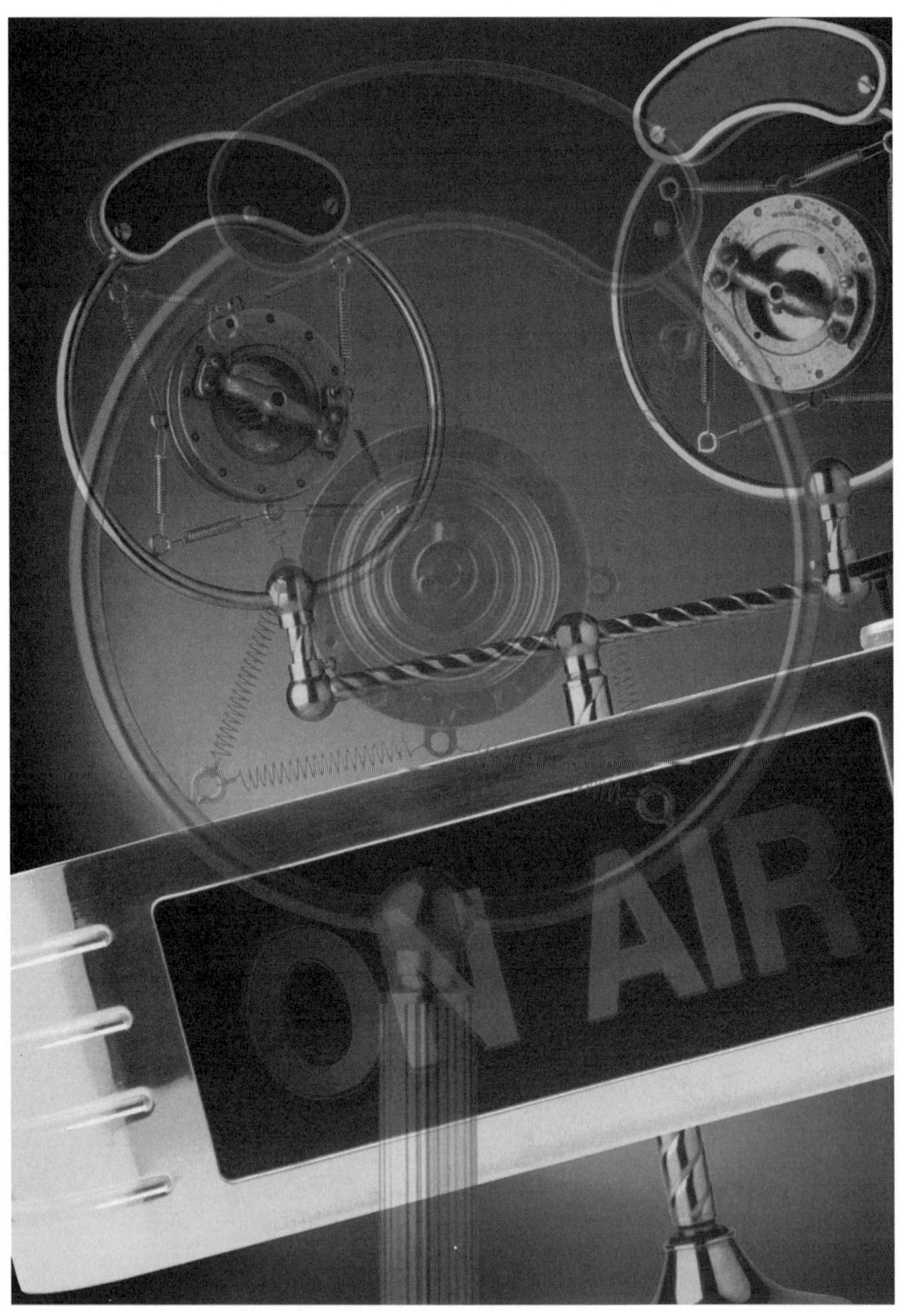
ON AIR

Howard Duff and *The Adventures of Sam Spade*

MARK DAWIDZIAK

Howard Duff, who became a star as the radio voice of detective Sam Spade, died of a heart attack on July 9, 1990. He was seventy-six. A few months before his death, Duff agreed to a lengthy interview about his involvement with *The Adventures of Sam Spade*. The actor cheerfully recounted tales of the series and his interpretation of the role.

***

The air is heavy with smoke and laughter. It is the type of Hollywood party that you might read about the next day in Louella Parsons's column. The glittering cast includes several of Tinseltown's brightest stars. Behind the mixed drinks and hors d'oeuvres, you can also find some of the industry's most powerful producers, directors and writers. Some are there to see; more are hoping to be seen.

Making his way through the clatter of conversation and cocktail glasses, young Howard Duff is feeling rather good about himself. And why not? He's earned a place at this party. Though many people might not know his face, most would recognize his name and his voice. After two years on the air, the actor's *Adventures of Sam Spade* is one of radio's hottest series.

People are even beginning to know his face. Hearing Duff as Spade during the detective show's first season, the late columnist-turned-producer Mark Hellinger had remarked, "If this guy looks anything like he sounds, we've got the right guy for our film." Pleased to see that Duff had rugged good looks to go with the rugged voice, Hellinger had cast him in *Brute Force*, a prison picture released in 1947—about one year ago. All right, so Duff didn't exactly have top billing. Okay, he didn't exactly have sixth billing, either. But it was a strong role in a strong movie with a strong cast (Burt Lancaster, Hume Cronyn, Charles bickford, and a few others capable of blasting a confident young newcomer off the screen.) Duff had held his own in pretty intimidating company. You couldn't ask for mote from a film debut, right?

Emboldened by his good fortune, Duff isn't at all displeased to learn that playwright Lillian Hellman is at the party. You don't have to be a faithful reader of Louella's column to know that Hellman is the close "friend" of mystery writer Dashiell Hammett, the creator of Sam Spade. The relationship between Hammett and Hellman is such that you put the word *friend* in quotes, even when said aloud. They are, of course, more than friends, though less than constant companions.

If anyone can claim to know Hammett, however, it is his "friend" Lillian Hellman. The opportunity is too good for Duff, who has never met Hammett. There is a question he has to ask.

Duff gets his chance when a mutual acquaintance introduces him to Hellman. The actor makes small talk while working up to the question. "Well," he thinks to himself, "the show's been on a couple of years, and we're bright and successful. Go ahead and ask."

"What does Mr. Hammett think of our show?" Duff hears himself saying.

"Dash?" Hellman replies. "Oh, I don't think he's ever heard it."

***

More than forty years after his encounter with Lillian Hellman, Howard Duff would summarize the incident in six words: "Put me right in my place." Though Hellman was unquestionably proficient at putting people in their places, she undoubtedly was being brutally honest with the actor who had achieved fame as Sam Spade. To the best of her knowledge, Dashiell Hammett did not monitor the radio life of his famous detective. Although conversations with others suggest Hammett at least sampled *The Adventures of Sam Spade,* it's fairly certain that, except as a source of income, the three radio series featuring his characters were of little interest to the mystery writer.

Yet if Hammett had given more than a passing listen to Duff as Spade, he might have been pleasantly surprised. *The Adventures of Sam Spade* may have strayed from the tone and tenor of The Maltese Falcon, but it was a detective show that seemed as fresh and different as Hammett's short stories had been to the pulp pages of Black Mask magazine. It was tough and taut and funny. You had to listen carefully, because Duff and the writers didn't always take themselves very seriously. At its best, *The Adventures of Sam Spade* blazed at a lightning pace along a fine line somewhere between hard-boiled drama and satire.

The man responsible for spinning Sam Spade from the pages of *The Maltese* Falcon into a weekly series was veteran radio editor, director, and producer William Spier. When *The Adventures of Sam Spade* premiered as a CBS Friday-night summer series on July 22, 1946, Spier was already considered one of radio's most seasoned campaigner. His credits, which started in 1929, included producing *The March of Time* and directing the CBS classic *Suspense*.

Spier, still overseeing *Suspense,* assigned the writing team of Bob Tallman and Ann Lorraine the task of cooking up weekly capers for San Francisco detective Sam Spade, hero of the third of Hammett's five novels. But who could possibly play Spade? Humphrey Bogart was justifiably identified with the character after his marvelous portrayal in director John Huston's 1941 film version of *The Maltese Falcon.* It was indeed a hard hard-boiled act to follow.

The magic seemed to be in the voice of Howard Duff, a young actor who, although only a year in Hollywood, was beginning to make a name for himself in supporting roles on major radio dramas. There was a hard edge to Duff's delivery that Spier thought would be perfect for Spade.

Until his senior year at Seattle's Roosevelt High, Duff was planning on a career as a cartoonist. Drawing characters was replaced by playing characters when he was cast in a school play. In addition to working with local theatre groups, he landed jobs as an announcer at a Seattle radio station. When the United States entered World War II, Duff began a four-year stint as a correspondent for Armed Forces Radio. He hit Hollywood in 1945.

"Bill Spier knew me," Duff recalled, "so he auditioned me along with other so-called leading men. I got lucky."

Still, the twenty-eight-year-old Duff knew he would fail if he merely tried to imitate Bogart. "I think they wanted me to more or less do a Bogart impersonation st first," Duff said. "And I didn't cotton to that. I wanted to do it in my own way. Luckily, we got by with that. Bogart did it pretty straight with wonderful touches of humor. We went a little further than that."

The Adventures of Sam Spade was an immediate hit on the CBS Friday lineup. There was no doubt that the network would find a place for it on the fall schedule. On September 29, 1946, Duff and Sam Spade moved into the Sunday-night time slot, where they stayed for the rest of their immensely popular CBS run.

During its entire five-year existence, *The Adventures of Sam Spade* was sponsored by Wildroot Cream Oil ("America's favorite family hair tonic"). The cases, referred to as capers, were wildly different, but the format pretty much stayed the same. Some fast-paced dialogue between Sam and his giddy secretary, Effie Perrine (Lurene Tuttle in the role played by Lee Patrick in the Houston film), would set up the week's caper. This usually would be the start of Sam dictating a report for Effie to type, so Duff would bounce between narrating the story and playing off the other actors.

Once Sam had hooked Effie's (and the listeners') interest, announcer Dick Joy would jump into the usual introduction: Dashiell Hammett, America's leading detective fiction writer and creator of Sam Spade, the hard-boiled private eye, and William Spier, radio's outstanding producer/director of mystery and crime drama, join their talents to make your hair stand on end with *The Adventures of Sam Spade,* presented by the makers of Wildroot Cream Oil for the hair."

Like *The Fat Man* and *The Thin Man* radio shows, *Sam Spade* loudly hinted that Hammett was in some way directly responsible for the series' content. The ploy worked. Many believed that the writer had contributed scripts and plot ideas. In truth, Hammett had no input beyond the creation of Sam Spade.

Duff and Tuttle were the series' only billed regulars, although Jerry Housner did make appearances as Sam's lawyer, Sid Weiss. Several actors—including Elliot Reid (the detective who falls for Jane Russell in *Gentlemen Prefer Blondes*), Hal March, Joe Kearns, Peggy Webber, John McIntire, and Jeanette Nolan—often appeared in a variety of roles. The Spade show was a double pleasure for McIntire. The program was one of his first regular jobs in Hollywood, and it allowed him to work with his wife, Nolan. (McIntire and Nolan would costar on *The Virginian* during the NBC Western's 1967-1968 season.) "We had kind of a little stock company," Duff said, "and as far as I'm concerned, we had the best people around at that time."

Faithful listeners could tell you that Sam's detective license number was 137596. (In the Academy Award Theatre production of *The Maltese Falcon*—aired the same month as *The Adventures of Sam Spade* premiere—Bogart gave Spade's license number as 357896.)

Ann Loraine left the series soon after its debut, and il Doud became Bob Tallman's partner in crime scripts. After the first two years, many of the writing duties fell to the prolific E. Jack Neuman and John Michael Hayes, who wrote scripts separately and as collaborators.

"Spier and the writers charted the course of where we were going," Duff remembered, "and we went in some pretty crazy directions. But we would try different things because we were on every week of the year—fifty-two shows a year. With radio, of course, you didn't have to worry about makeup and lights. You were just concentrating on the sound and the voice, so it was a simpler process than television. But it's possibly a little more interesting and challenging process for people who want to use their imaginations.

"Another thing a lot of people don't remember or don't realize is that we were doing those shows live, at least of the first four years. We couldn't record anything until Bing Crosby made it possible, because until he insisted on taping his shows, everybody thought you had to go on live. We'd do a show live for the East, and then another one later for the West. Two identical shows, each done live. All kinds of things went wrong all the time. But we were pretty good at ad-libs. We covered when we had to."

By the time the Sam Spade radio show surfaced, the hard-boiled detective hero had been around for more than twenty years. Spier thought it would be death to approach the genre in a deadly serious manner, particularly on a weekly basis. The conventions of the form were too well known. Spier stripped away the darker aspects of Spade's character and left the wisecracking humor. The spirit of his series was closer to the lighthearted lunacy of *The Thin Man* than the considerably starker nature of *The Maltese Falcon*.

Sure, there was plenty of action. The mystery might be pretty good, too. The writers, though, punched up the proceedings with bad puns, goofy non sequiturs, and outrageous situations. The result, wrote radio historian Jim Harmon in his Great Radio Heroes (Doubleday &Company, Inc., 1967), was a series "that still seems fresh and alive."

Indeed, *The Adventures of Sam Spade* anticipated many of the innovations that would win acclaim for television series of later decades. Spade indulged in the campy humor that would later become the stock-in-trade of TV's *Batman*. There was the type of straight-faced, off-the-wall lampooning that made Leslie Nielsen's *Police Squad* a critical favorite. And Duff sometimes broke the theatre's invisible fourth wall, delivering a line recognizing that his Spade was a fictional character. This device, used by everyone from Bob Hope to Bugs Bunny, George Burns to Garry Shandling, won attention for such TV series as *Moonlighting* and *It's Garry Shandling's Show*.

In one episode, Effie tried coaxing a story out of Sam: "Don't you feel like talking about it?"

"Frankly, no," Sam shot back, "but it's expected of me."

Sam once dismissed another private detective by suggesting that he "get his own program."

When Sam did start to relate the details of a caper, you could hear the clank of liquor bottle against glasses. Effie once acknowledged the bottle kept in Sam's bottom drawer by telling her boss that he should "unbourbon" himself.

During *The Dry Martini Caper,* Sam asked a suspect why she hadn't gone upstairs to get her "alibi shaped up." It was the type of cynical put-down that also would have suited Bogart's Spade.

However, not all the lines were snappy and clever. Some were just dumb. While setting up *The Bluebeard Caper,* Effie asked Sam what he was doing at the Cow Palace. "Oh, just bulling around," he answered. It was a good thing that the dialogue moved fast enough to leave such groaners behind quickly.

"We were about as hip as you

could be in those days," Duff said. "I think we were kind of ahead of our time. That's why the few shows I've listened to lately don't embarrass me. I'm always surprised if anything is successful. Even as young as I was, I was surprised. But we all kind of knew we had a great show. We thought we were pretty good. We were just happy that people agreed with us.

"Mostly, we were having a good time doing it and we were hoping that the audience was sharing in the good time. That's apparently what happened for a few years."

Almost everyone who worked on *Sam Spade* remembers it as a dizzy good time. "It wasn't labor," said Hayes, who moved to Los Angeles in 1948 and soon was contributing scripts to both *Sam Spade* and *Suspense*. "*Sam Spade* was one of the most wonderful experiences of my life. Bill Spier was an urbane, witty, and very knowledgeable guy. He was an employer and a teacher. And Howard Duff was just marvelous—very easygoing, never temperamental, firm but very professional. Lurene was a dear. She had the happiest voice. The only unhappy experience was being low paid."

Duff's Spade didn't mind tickling his own image. When Effie told Sam he was wonderful and trusting, the detective took refuge in his radio press material. "I am not wonderful and trusting," he announced. "I am a hard-boiled private eye . . . and I'm also two-fisted."

"My attitude was kind of hard-boiled and smart-assed," Duff explained, "It was a combination of good showmanship and good delivery that put it over."

Duff's Spade had a wisecrack for every occasion, which was handy because he had to deal with more than his share of bizarre characters and bizarre situations. In *The Flopsy-Mopsy Cottontail Caper*, for instance, Sam had to attend a costume party dressed as a giant white rabbit with shocking pink ears.

"We did some rather outrageous things sometimes," Duff said, "especially during the summertime when the writers were getting a little dingy. We were all getting a little dingy, So we had a two-headed guy in the shower singing harmony a capella. Other characters were almost Dickensian. Bill Spier had quite an antic sense of humor. I thought they went too far quite a few times, but it was basically a fun time for all of us."

Neuman and Hayes remember what it was like writing for the radio treadmill. "It was the opportunity of a lifetime for us," Neuman said. "Howard was a rising young star, and we were working with the happiest group in the world. I really looked forward to writing those scripts. It was wide open. You could do anything with a *Sam Spade* script. You could do tragedy, comedy, suspense, action, satire, farce. You could do high drama or burlesque, or both. That's why they were so much fun to write."

"We had a lot of double entendres," Hayes said. "We vied with each other to see how we could spice things up."

Neuman got started in radio a little before Hayes. After cutting his mystery teeth on a few *Suspense* scripts, Neuman quit his job as a CBS staff writer to devote his energies to *Sam Spade* episodes. A little later, he discovered that Hayes, also a *Sam Spade* contributor, was living in the same Sherman Oaks apartment building.

"I had been writing for Lucille Ball's radio shoe, the one with Richard Denning," Hayes said. "I moved over to *Sam Spade* because there was room to do comedy and drama and tongue-in-cheek material. Jack and I were writing scripts separately, but then we started to help each other out with plots."

Stairway encounters sometimes developed into therapy sessions for blocked plots.

"I've got a guy who's so smart," Neuman would tell Hayes.

"How smart is he?" Hayes would ask.

"Well, he graduated from Harvard at the age of nine," his friend would explain. "He speaks five languages. He has degrees from several universities. He's the recognized expert on certain codes and extinct languages."

"That's pretty smart," Hayes would concede. "Okay, what's the problem?"

And soon, the problem would be licked. It was a short and natural step to collaboration. Sometimes Hayes would write the first act, and Neuman would take over for the conclusion.

In the spring of 1949, Spier and his wife, actress June Havoc, decided on a summer vacation in Europe.

"Spier told us he wanted all of the *Sam Spade* and *Suspense* scripts for the rest of the year done before he left," Neuman recalled. "So, starting in April, John and I wrote one a day until we had the entire order finished. And you know what? It wasn't as tough as it sounds."

"We were young and reliable and very professional," Hayes said. "We were full of life and creative energy and the desire to pay the rent."

This sense of fun and enthusiasm is evident in the crisp *Sam Spade* scripts.

"One night, I went to see a picture called *D.O.A.* (a 1949 thriller with Edmond O'Brien trying to find out who slipped him a slow-acting poison)," Hayes said. "I got such a rush from its breathless pace that I went home and tried to write something that just wouldn't stop—completely breathless. I started at 11:30 P.M. and finished it at 4 A.M. Then I drove out to Bill Spier's house and left it in his mailbox. That's how we felt about the show."

The players on the *Sam Spade* team enjoyed the work and each other's company. Spier produced and directed the episodes. During his absences. Doud would fill in as director. Lud Gluskin was the show's musical director.

Dick Joy would kick things off with the familiar preamble: "The adventures of Sam Spade, detective, brought to you by Wildroot Liquid Cream Oil hair tonic, the nonalcoholic hair tonic that contains lanolin, and new Wildroot Liquid Cream Shampoo." Sam Spade was billed as "the greatest private eye of them all" and Wildroot was billed as "again and again, the choice of men who put good grooming first."

The series had incredibly wide appeal. It was an action drama for men and kids. It was a comedy for those who preferred their mystery entertainment a little cockeyed. And Duff had become a heartthrob for female listeners. Years after the show left the air, young women would stop Duff and ask him to repeat the program sign-off line to them: "Good night, sweetheart."

"There was a warmth to Howard Duff's voice that wasn't in Bogart's performance," Hayes said. Complementing Duff's smart-aleck humor was Tuttle's Effie, always bubbly and often vague. "Lurene Tuttle was one of the sweetest people you'd ever want to meet," Neuman said, "but she was about as quick as a park bench. She never understood the double entendres. She just walked right into the joke, wide-eyed as could be, which made her portrayal all the more effective."

About forty years after the series left the air, mystery fans still remember it fondly. William Link, cocreator of *Columbo* and *Murder, She Wrote,* was a Philadelphia youngster growing up on a diet of magic and mystery when *The Adventures of Sam Spade* hit the airwaves. "It was way above average," he said. "The humor was on the highest level, and Duff sounded more authentic than most radio private eyes. But it was the humor that made it special. Tallman and Doud were my favorite radio mystery writers. They went on to do *The Scarlet Queen,* a summer show that few people remember, which is a shame, because it was terrific."

Link and the late Richard Levinson

became television's most successful mystery team. They would win two Emmys, a Peabody Award, and four Edgar Allan Poe Awards from the Mystery Writers of America. Link's appreciation of Tallman and Doud is shaped by his two vantage points—that of a voracious reader of mysteries and that of a practitioner in the field.

"For me, writing a *Sam Spade* script was the easiest thing in the world," Neuman said. "For one thing, Gil Doud and Bob Tallman did such a good job of establishing the show. Another reason was that you started with character, not plot. The plot worked out of the characters. That kind of writing you look forward to doing. I'd give anything to do just one more."

What did Hammett think of all this? He apparently gave it little consideration, even though many columnsits believed that he wrote episodes and supervised production. For this reason, the *Daily Compass* expressed concern that he would allow an anti-Semitic remark to slip into one episode. Admitting that he hadn't listened to *The Adventures of Sam Spade* lately, Hammett promised to pay closer attention. The radio show benefitted from the implication that Hammett was involved, but the truth was that the writer didn't know or care what kind of Sam Spade show was being broadcast by CBS.

The money was fantastic. Producer Edward J. Rosenberg had worked out a lucrative deal for *Sam Spade* and for the development of *The Fat Man,* a series created by Hammett. "My sole duty in regard to these programs is to look in the mail for a check once a week." Hammett said. "I don't even listen to them. If I did, I'd complain about how they were bing handled, and then I'd fall into the trap of being asked to come down and help. I don't want to have anything to do with the radio. It's a dizzy world—makes the movies seem highly intellectual."

If Hammett wasn't interested in fighting for quality radio shows, he was prepared to battle for the rights to his literary creations.Warner Bros., having made three film versions of *The Maltese Falcon,* believed it owned all rights to the story and the character. The studio contended that the radio show was an unauthorized use of the character. Hammett argued that Warner Bros. had purchased only the motion-picture rights. While the case dragged on in the courts, the radio series continued.

In 1949, a New York court decided in favor of Warner Bros. However, California trial and appellate courts ruled in favor of Hammett, who realized that the outcome was important to all writers. When a Los Angeles judge finally settled the case in Hammett's favor in 1951, the decision had no financial impact on Hammett. *The Adventures of Sam Spade* had left the air.

Still, perhaps Hammett heard just enough of Duff as Spade to formulate his dislike for the show. In 1952, Neuman was trying to write a novel at the beach house he had bought a little north of Malibu. His neighbors included publisher Bennett Cerf and author William Saroyan. Parties were not uncommon, and one day Neuman was introduced to a very ill Dashiell Hammett.

"He told me he thought Spier was full of shit and he didn't thing much of the way Duff played it," Neuman remembered. "I wasn't the least bit offended. Are you kidding? I thought he was a king. He could have said anything he wanted At least once a year, I reread *The Maltese Falcon,* just to remind myself how it's done."

Certainly Hammett's opinion was not based on any week-to-week familiarity with the series. Although he boasted of not listening to the radio shows, it's difficult to believe that he didn't catch at least a few seconds of Duff's years as Spade. If so, Hammett might have instantly recognized that the interpretation was not completely faithful to his novel—and dismissed it. This is likely, and it's even more likely that Hammett abandoned the show without learning what made it tick. So Hammett probably was telling the truth when he said he didn't listen to the shows. However, his bad impression was formed, it was strong enough to jump up in a 1952 chat with Neuman.

In 1948, though, Duff and Sam Spade were riding high on CBS. "We were the number-one show of our kind," Duff said. "We were fast-moving, pretty funny, and we had some of the best writers in the business. But it wasn't all comedy. We did real heart-stoppers, too. We got down to the cases, as you have to when you're doing life-and-death situations."

Little did Duff realize that his career was about to hit a roadblock. In 1949, even though *The Adventures of Sam Spade* was still extremely popular, CBS was getting nervous about Dashiell Hammett's links with pro-Communist groups. It was the era of Senator Joe McCarthy's red-scare campaigns and the House Un-American Activities Committee's witch-hunting crusades. The Hammett connection was too hot for CBS, and network executives decide to cancel Spier's series.

NBC was willing to take a chance. The show had a tremendous following. So *The Adventures of Sam Spade* switched networks, but stayed on Sunday nights. NBC, though, didn't have the courage to stick with Duff. In his encyclopedic study, *Tune in Yesterday* (Prentice Hall, Inc., 1976), John Dunning says that Duff left the show because he "had moved on to other things." Well, the anti-Hammett sentiment has been sufficiently documented. The part of the story that hasn't been told is that Duff's name, too, was one of the 151 people listed in the infamous *Red Channels: The Report of Communist Influence in Radio and Television* (Counterattack, 1950).

Delivered to sponsors, networks, and advertising agencies, the book claimed to expose the Communist sympathizers in Hollywood. The unspoken suggestion accompanying this list was that any red-white-and - blue network or sponsor should not be associated with these actors, writers, singers, and directors.

Duff was in good company. Others listed in *Red Channels* were Hammett, Hellman, Edward G. Robinson, Orson Welles, Arthur Miller, Lee J. Cobb, Burl Ives, Zero Mostel, Burgess Meredith, Lena Horne, Leonard Bernstein, Jack Gilford, and Ruth Gordon.

On July 13, 1951, an article in *Hollywood Life* called Hammett "one of the most dangerous" Communists in America:

> Hammett is said to be responsible for selling the red banner to dozens of men and women including actor Howard Duff, alias Sam Spade. Duff is also a member of one or more red fronts, and a definite red sympathizer.

"Well, I wouldn't know if Dashiell Hammett had any affiliation with the Communist Party," Duff said. "I certainly didn't, and a lot of the people in the *Red Channels* book didn't. It was at a time when they were trying to smear liberals. It was typical McCarthy smear stuff. About all I was was a half-assed liberal. I was in Red Channels and Hammett was in contempt of court, so the sponsor and the network, showing their usual great backbone, caved in, and that was it. This is the part of the story that isn't told very much. It should be known. It was an outrageous situation. Lillian Hellman called it a scoundrel time, and I think she was quite right."

NBC and Spier auditioned all sorts of actors.

"They even auditioned Jack Webb," Neuman said. "Nobody could follow Duff."

NBC eventually settled on Steve Dunne, whom in the estimation of John Dunning, made "a boyish-sounding Spade." Even with Tuttle staying on as Effie, listeners just weren't buying someone other than Duff as Spade. A move to Fridays proved unsuccessful, and NBC canceled *The Adventures of Sam Spade* in 1951. It was replace by *Charlie Wild, Private Eye.* By then, all of Hammett's radio shows had been yanked from the air—victims of what Harmon calls "guilt by association."

"I think it was the combination of the two of us—Hammett and me—that killed it," Duff said. "They didn't want me, but they couldn't cut it with the other guy. I was a little disappointed with Bill Spier, that he would go along with someone else. But what the hell. It was a longtime ago. Bygones should be bygones. I have no regrets about doing the show. The big shame was that it should have been on television. It was just right for television. It could have naturally made the jump from radio. I'm just sorry it was truncated and didn't go on. Then there were a lot of imitations."

In fact, when Hammett died in January 1961, John Crosby wrote in the *New York Herald Tribune* that television was overrun with "imitations of imitation Sam Spades."

As for Duff, he was one of the lucky ones who survived the blacklisting. "It did slow me down for a little while," he said. "I couldn't get on the air with a sponsored show until about four years later. But it didn't bother my picture career."

He landed his first TV series in 1957. Duff costarred with his then wife Ida Lupino in *Mr. Adams and Eye.* The actor has since been a regular on five other series, including ABC's *Felony Squad* (1966-1969), in which he played a police detective named Sam Stone. There were memorable appearances in such films as *Boy's Night Out* (1962) and *Kramer Vs. Kramer* (1979).

Lurene Tuttle continued to be in demand as a character actress. She was a regular on three series: *Life With Father* (CBS, 1953-1955), *Father of the Bride* (CBS, 1961-1962), and *Julia* (1968-1970 seasons of the NBC comedy). She died in 1988.

The late William Spier did not fare so well when television invaded America's living rooms. "Bill Spier could never adapt to film or television, although he had many chances," Neuman said. "As bright as he was, he couldn't get anything on track."

Neuman, however, embraced television and became one of the medium's most successful writer/producers. There was a Neuman script on Rod Sterling's *Twilight Zone,* and he was the writer and producer of eleven pilot episodes that became series, including *Mr. Novak* (NBC, 1963-1965), *Petrocelli* (NBC, 1974-1976), and *Kate McShane* (CBS, 1975). In 1990, he was the writer and executive producer of *Voices Within: The Lives of Trudi Chase,* a fact-based TV movie starring Shelley Long as a woman with a multiple personality disorder.

Hayes turned to the movies. He wrote the scripts for two of director Alfred Hitchcock's many classics: *Rear Window* (1954) and *To Catch a Thief* (1955). His other screenplays include *The Matchmaker* (1958), *Peyton Place* (1957), *Butterfield 8* (1960), *The Children's Hour* (1962), and *The Chalk Garden* (1964). He "semi-retired" to Dartmouth College, where he teaches screenwriting.

"I don't dwell in the past," Duff said, "but I think I'm still better known as Sam Spade than for anything I've done since. It's amazing how many people remember that show. I don't think any of us thought we were doing anything spectacular. We just thought we were doing a pretty good job. And that's the way we wanted it. I know that I had a good time. That's good enough for me. I don't have to look back on it in a golden haze or anything. We found out after the period was over that we were in the golden days of radio, and we didn't even know it."

The inspiration for Jack Webb's *Dragnet, He Walked by Night,* starring Webb and Richard Basehart, photography by the amazing John Alton.

Jack Webb:

TV'S NOIR AUTEUR

MAX ALLAN COLLINS

Jack Webb's documentary-style police procedural made the primitive TV detective dramas of the early fifties (*Martin Kane, Gangbusters, Dick Tracy*) look like the silly radio melodramas brought cheaply to life that they were. Nonetheless, *Dragnet* was itself a transplant from radio—but an adult, literate, innovative radio show.

Actor/director Webb began his show-business career in radio, announcing news at ABC affiliate station KGO in San Francisco. Early on, he struck up relationships with writers James Moser (early *Dragnet* writer and creator of the *Dragnet*-like medical show *Medic,* starring Webb crony Richard Boone) and Richard L. Breen (with whom Webb did his best work, including the first theatrical *Dragnet* movie, the 1967 made-for-TV *Dragnet* revival movie, and the film *Pete Kelly's Blues*). Breen's radio private-eye spoof, *Pat Novak for Hire,* became Webb's introduction to tough-guy detection. He began landing bit parts in pictures, moving into character roles; his most famous movie role (other than Joe Friday and Pete Kelly) is that of William Holden's playboy friend in Billy Wilder's *Sunset Boulevard* (1950).

The turning point came when Webb played a lab technician in the 1948 film *He Walked by Night* (directed, in part, by Anthony Mann), a documentary-style police procedural; it not only set the tone for *Dragnet,* the term "dragnet" can be heard in the film. Technical adviser was Los Angeles police sergeant Marty Wynn, with whom Webb struck up a friendship, and the actor—after Wynn chided him about Hollywood's phony version of cops and robbers—began doing research by riding around on calls in a police car with Wynn and his partner, Detective Vance Brasher. From this, Webb picked up on the jargon of cops—"Go down to R & I [Records and Identification] and pull the suspect's package . . ."—which became not only *Dragnet*'s trademark, but Webb's; even his non-*Dragnet* work always leans on inside jargon from some male-dominated profession.

The radio show *Dragnet* emerged on June 3, 1949, at 8 P.M. in NBC's Los Angeles Studio H. CBS had rejected the show for lacking color and vitality of radio detective shows like the spoofy *Sam Spade*; and Webb only managed to get a summer replacement spot. At first he received $150 a week, for starring in and directing the show he created. But, within two years, *Dragnet* was the highest-rated show on radio.

Webb had TV in mind from the beginning, but resisted offers to do the show live out of New York, as NBC at first insisted. Only when *Dragnet* sponsor Liggett & Meyers Tobacco Company put on the pressure did NBC relent and give Webb $38,000 to shoot a pilot, "The Human Bomb," based on a previously-aired radio script (as were many of the black-and-white *Dragnets*). It was aired on December 16, 1951, as part of *Chesterfield Sound-Off Time,* the official run starting on January 3, 1952, alternating (for its first year) with the much-inferior radio-to-TV police story *Gangbusters*. Soon only *I Love Lucy* topped *Dragnet* in the ratings.

Success took its toll on work-aholic Webb, his marriage to sultry singer/actress Julie London breaking up in 1954; they had two daughters, Stacy and Liza. Julie London then married her musical arranger, Bobby Troup, who in later years became a part of Webb's stock company on the revived *Dragnet*. London went on, in 1972, to a regular role (Nurse Dixie McCall) on the Webb production *Emergency*—on which Troop also appeared (as Dr. Joe Early).

Webb's love for music—particularly jazz—was showcased in the radio, TV, and cinema versions of Pete *Kelly's Blues* (the story of a Dixieland musician in the bootlegging twenties) and in various *Pete Kelly* record albums he released over the years, using top studio musicians. He also released an album of songs, which he speaks rather than sings (a camp classic given a wide modern audience, thanks to David Letterman).

Decades before the *Star Trek* phenomenon, *Dragnet* found its way to the big screen. The 1954 box-office success was written by long-time Webb collaborator Breen and directed (of course) by Webb, who went on to direct and star in several more theatrical films (*The D.I., -30-, The Last Time I Saw Archie*). Most notable is the excellent Breen-scripted *Pete Kelly's Blues* (1955). But consistent theatrical success eluded Webb and he remained in television as a producer; finally, in 1967, he returned as Joe Friday in the made-for-television film, *Dragnet '67.*

Director Webb's handful of theatrical films reflect his dynamic *Dragnet* style, accurately described by film critic Andrew Sarris as "verbal whispering and visual shouting." Most are available on videocassette, as are a number of the black-and-white *Dragnet* episodes; many of the color episodes are available from Columbia House.

Each half-hour *Dragnet* episode follows Los Angeles police detective sergeant Joe Friday (and his partner) through a single case—a case that might span several weeks or even a year, with time between scenes bridged by the clipped first-person voice-over (apparent excerpts from Friday's police reports), which makes clear Friday and his partner are also working on other cases, like real, workaday cops.

Webb's Friday takes quiet pride in that work; and his I'm-a-cop objectivity is a mask for his compassion for victims and rage against victimizers. Officer Frank Smith (former child star Ben Alexander), on the plump side compared to rail-thin Joe, is an eccentric comic foil who, in lulls, relates to his partner the trials and tribulations of married life, which takes the edge off Frank's attempts to interest bachelor Joe in getting married. On the job, however, Frank is as no-nonsense as Friday himself.

Officer Bill Gannon (Harry Morgan), who replaces Smith in the color shows beginning in 1967, is a similar comedy-relief character, whose concerns are health related and, again, getting Friday married. In many respects Smith and Gannon are the same character, merely renamed and recast—for example, both Smith and Gannon are hypochondriacs and self-styled gourmet cooks; both are enough older than Friday to confidently subject him to patronizing advice about life. But Gannon, too, is a no-nonsense cop when on the job—though his humanity lies slightly nearer the surface than Friday's, as when the body of a drowned child discovered in a bathtub sends him rushing outside to "be sick."

The crimes depicted in *Dragnet* were often rather ordinary ones—petty theft or attempted suicide or drunk driving, not just murder and kidnapping and juvenile delinquency, although those are treated, too. Friday rarely fired his gun, but when he did, the dramatic impact was sensational, due to the show's studiously low-key tone.

That tone—actually a monotone, as director Webb worked hard to keep his stock company of actors naturalistic, by withholding scripts and having them read "cold" from cue cards—led to the show's often being the subject of parody. "Just the facts ma'am," early TV's most famous catchphrase, is typical of Friday's objective interrogation style. The individual suspects and witnesses questioned were always more colorful than the cops, who often had to steer them back onto the subject at hand.

The 1950s episodes, shot on the Disney lot, had impressive production values and noirish camera angles—shooting up through ashtrays, window rain effects, overhead shots—but when the show returned in 1967 after a seven-year hiatus, the moody visual flourishes were largely absent, with a plastic, Universal Studios look and color that managed to be garish and bland simultaneously. With Webb older, heavier, and more entrenched in the Establishment, *Dragnet* often became a virtual parody of itself, awash in antidrug preachments, dry public-service pronouncements, and embarrassing Hollywood "hippies"; however, even watered down, *Dragnet* delved into subject matter unusual for television, such as child abuse and right-wing militias. Sadly, the second, lesser batch of 1960s shows has displaced the far superior fifties ones in syndication and are the ones Webb has been judged—or misjudged—by in recent years.

After the demise of the revived *Dragnet,* Webb continued producing television series but attempts to duplicate the success of *Dragnet*—such as the popular *Adam-12* and the flop *O'Hara U.S. Treasury* (starring David Janssen)—resulted in stilted self-imitation, particularly without Webb himself in the lead. He died, much too young, in December 1982. Though he was once hailed as television's Orson Welles, Webb's death was marked with some nostalgia but little respect for his accomplishment.

The 1987 box-office smash feature-film version of *Dragnet*—an uneven spoof redeemed by co-scripter Dan Aykroyd's affectionate performance as Joe Friday's namesake nephew—testifies to Webb's genius but further threatens to make him a campy joke. The denigration of his memory in James Ellroy's *L.A. Confidential* (and the good movie made from it) further parodies and defiles this seminal noir figure.

AUTHOR'S NOTE: This article draws upon material in The Best of Crime and Detective TV *(1988) co-authored with John Javna.*

Photo by T. Hardin

Writer, Lee Server

Shadows in Your Living Room:

PETER GUNN, JOHNNY STACCATO AND THE LOST AGE OF TV NOIR

LEE SERVER

In the late 1950s, film noir was a dying genre. The venetian blinds were closing on two decades of shaow-haunted Hollywood melodramas, As early as '55 mainstream critics were deriding releases like Joseph H. Lewis's masterful *The Big Combo* as "old-fashioned" for the stylized nightmare imagery now known and loved as the look of classic noir. That look, the visualization of the 3A.M. of the soul best captured by high contrast black and white, had lost its allure to audiences and reviewers entranced by the eye-popping spectacle of Cinemascope plus color and stereo sound. The popular new processes lent themselves to the bright of day and travelogue locations, not the dark of night, rain-spattered asphalt and seedy urban warrens. Some people ignored the writing on the wall: Orson Welles (*Touch of Evil,* 1958), Robert Wise (*Odds Against Tomorrow,* 1959), and Sam Fuller (*Underworld USA,* 1961) among them, but not even these talented true believers could forestall the style's big-screen demise.

However, the history of classic film noir has an obscure postscript. Television, bastard spawn of radio and movies, gave noir a brief, creditable stay of execution, keeping the violent after-hours world alive in an assortment of broadcast series and one shots. TV's filmed programming had long fed on the leftovers of the big screen, its fading categories and personnel. And television was still black-and-white and Academy ratio., still shooting on the old hermetic soundstages. By the late fifties one could more easily find the ingredients of the classic black film in your living room after dark than at the neighborhood movie house. On any given night in this period, TV was likely to transmit one or two moody tales of crime and punishment, with their mean-streets settings, archetypal characters (tough cops and PIs, hard-boiled dames, psychos, thieves, amnesiacs, and the rest of the close-knit noir family), and familiar names before and behind the camera. The prime-time credits flashed an array of movers and shakers from feature film noir in its heyday: actors like Dan Duryea, Richard Conte, Ida Lupino, Brian Donlevy; writers like W. R. Burnett (*Asphalt Jungle*), Mel Dinelli (*The Window*), and Jonathan Latimer (*The Big Clock*); directors like Phil Karlson (*The Brothers Rico*), John Brahm (*The Brasher Doubloon*), and Jacques Tourneur (*Out of the Past*).

Film noir lived on in a slew of

anthology programs such as *Four Star Playhouse, G.E. Theater, Schlitz Playhouse, Alfred Hitchcock Presents, Suspicion,* and *Thriller,* and in (mostly) half-hour series that ranged from stark police procedurals like *Dragnet* and *Naked City* to the sexier and more ambiguous crime wallows like *Mike Hammer* and *The Untouchables.* With limited budgets and four- and five-day shooting schedules for a one hour production, television noir could not exactly compete with the sumptuous masterworks of the past, a *Double Indemnity,* a *Criss Cross,* an *Asphalt Jungle.* They were generally more comparable to the B wing of the genre, the compact, efficiently expressive low- or no-budgeters like *Detour, So Dark the Night,* or *Raw Deal.* Nonetheless, the seasoned studio talents involved gave many of these hastily shot programs strong evocative visuals and dynamic stagings. Compared to what passes for aesthetics in a present-day crime show like *NYPD Blue,* with its sophomorically artsy stuttering camerawork, the look of late fifties-early sixties filmed television is very impressive indeed.

The best example of television's devotion to noir is the case of Cornell Woolrich, masterful suspense writer and noir's founding father if ever there was one. In the forties, Hollywood made no fewer than fifteen feature motion pictures from his work, including such classics as *Phantom Lady, Deadline at Dawn, The Chase, Night Has a Thousand Eyes,* and *The Leopard Man.* In the 1950s the total had dwindled to just two films (*Rear Window* and *Nightmare*), and the writer's publishing career had declined as well. By contrast, fifties television, in anthology shows like *Heinz Studio 57, Schlitz Playhouse of Stars, George Sanders Mystery Theater,* and many more welcomed Woolrich's dark vision, bringing to the tube at least forty adaptations of novels and short stories (as compiled by Francis Nevins in an appendix to his biography of Woolrich, *First You Dream, Then You Die;* he estimated an average of one Woolrich telefilm a month during some periods in the decade). Some of these, like the Hitchcock show's "Momentum" and "The Black Curtain" and *Thriller's* version of "Papa Benjamin" have survived, while others—an intriguing-sounding production of *Black Path of Fear,* broadcast live but possibly kinescoped, and a dozen more—are apparently as lost as the director's cut of *Greed.*

While there were many veterans of the good old days of forties black film winding their careers down working in TV noir, the form was also a proving ground and showcase for simpatico new talents on the rise, neophytes who took to noir like a duck takes to cherry sauce. Robert Aldrich, who would create such late-in-the-game classics as *Kiss Me Deadly, The Big Knife,* and *Autumn Leaves,* made his directorial debut on television in 1952. His second assignment was an episode of a moody adventure series called *China Smith,* set in a nocturnal soundstage Singapore, with classic noir sleaze Dan Duryea as the ambivalent hero. The show was a perfect vehicle for Aldrich's cynical worldview and penchant for strong, Gothic visuals. Aldrich directed four half hours and then spun the series into his first big-screen film noir, *World for Ransom.* Still waiting for a breakthrough feature (which came in 1954 with *Apache* and *Vera Cruz*), he returned to TV to direct several blackish episodes of the anthology series *Four Star Playhouse.* In two of these assignments, "The Squeeze" and "The Hard Way", Dick Powell, the movies' first Philip Marlowe, played a tough-guy gambler named Willie Dante (a cross between the big screen's Mr. Lucky and another Powell antihero, Johnny O'Clock). They were stories of murder and corruption and Aldrich shot them in an elaborate, high-noir style worthy of Siodmak in his prime. The gambler character later fronted his own series,

Dante, Powell's role inherited by Howard Duff, radio's Sam Spade.

Both "The Squeeze" and "The Hard Way" were scripted by another major talent to-be shifting between features and TV as he was getting his career off the ground: Blake Edwards. The auteur of the *Pink Panther* movies put on the air what would be television noir's most acclaimed and original production, a half-hour private eye series called *Peter Gunn,* premiering on the NBC network on September 22, 1958. An astonishingly stylized creation, *Gunn* grafted pure noir iconography to a space-age bachelor sensibility, resulting in a delirious amalgam of the hard-boiled and the urbane. The title character was a suave playboy of a PI, Edwards's vision of a private detective as Cary Grant might have played him. He couldn't get Cary, of course, so he cast a journeyman Grant imitator, Craig Stevens, a slightly wooden actor who looked wonderful in expensive suits and spoke his lines with an insouciant purr. Peter Gunn was as much a creature of the night as a vampire, resident of moonlit penthouse pad, habitué of a stark jazz club called Mother's (Mother initially played by Hope Emerson, terrifying bulldyke of *Caged* and two-fisted masseuse of *Cry of the City*), where his gorgeous galpal Edie (played by the lustrous Lola Albright) warbled like June Christy to a very select audience of extras. Though it seemed a shame to do anything to muss his sleek suits if it didn't involve wrestling with Edie, Gunn did get down and dirty when a case called for it. And when things got too out of hand, Pete could always count on his friend on the police force, Lieutenant Jacoby (Herschel Bernardi), a notably understanding if irascible law enforcer. Backing the action, and as much the star of the show as Craig Stevens, was the finger snapping jazz of composer/conductor Henry Mancini, an interweaving of big-band swing and California cool, including that immortal theme, music that was bought by millions when Mancini committed it to vinyl. With its sultry after-midnight atmosphere and smoothly syncopated soundtrack, an episode of *Peter Gunn* produced in the viewer an agreeably sensuous effect, like downing two perfect martinis. Filed under the subdivision of Sophisticated Noir with the likes of, say, *Laura* and *In a Lonely Place, Gunn* was an elegant, wonderful show, still one of Blake Edwards's finest creation.

An influential show: it's distinctive elements could be detected in many of the subsequent private-eye dramas that offered similarly snazzy heroes and jazzy accompaniment (*Bourbon Street Beat, Mr. Lucky, Richard Diamond,* the aforementioned *Dante,* etc). The best of them by far, and a classic of noir entertainment in its own right, was the very hip *Johnny Staccato,* starring John Cassavetes as a bebopping pianist turned private dick ("I put my musician's card on mothballs five years ago," he growls in the echt noir voiceover, "when it dawned on me that my talent was an octave lower than my ambition"). The pilot—broadcast September 10, 1959, directed by former actor Joseph Pevney, "Shorty" from *Body and Soul*—opens cold in a smoky MacDougal Street jazz pit, Waldo's. The titles roll over screaming bebop coming from the house combo—Red Norvo, Pete Candoli, Barney Kessel, Shelly Manne, Red Mitchell, and Cassavetes sitting in on the ivories. The harsh sounds play on as Johnny slides into a booth for a business call (simultaneously necking with a hot blonde) and then heads for the cloakroom, where another platinum number hands over overcoat and .38; he hits the dark street and the story begins. From the second episode on, the opening credits were shorter and considerably more striking: an abstract hunted-man montage, frightened Cassavetes running in and out of pools of light until an abrupt and truly startling shock cut catches the star rushing the camera lens, smashing a plate of glass, and firing his gun right between the viewer's eyes. Great.

While the series was *Peter Gunn-esque* in many ways—the nocturnal setting, Waldo's rather than Mother's as the nightclub hangout, and Elmer Bernstein doing a hard-bop variation on Mancini—*Johnny Staccato* eschewed *Gunn*'s chic aura for a gritty atmosphere and some very tough, provocative story lines. Cassavetes, of course, was no Craig Stevens of the monotone aplomb. He played Staccato with a simmering hard-edged intensity, spitting lines like razors, looking at times like his character had been hitting the amphetamine bottle a little too often. The plots plundered hot topics and real- life pop culture/tabloid icons of the moment: Elvis Presley and Colonel Parker clones in a sleazy blackmail plot, a stand-in for Robert Harrison and his demonized *Confidential* magazine, characters bearing a passing resemblance to Sinatra and Chet Baker, plus a vividly drawn collection of mobsters, junkies, beatniks, and other denizens of the pre-dawn Big Apple. Some episodes were filmed on location in Manhattan, raw, hand-held footage of the star traipsing up an East Side canyon or riding the actual IRT. Episode to episode, the series maintained a consistent, highly charged atmosphere, the sense of a dark world of violence, and a city filled with dirty secrets. This was a noir creation as fully realized as some of the big-screen classics with a cast of noir veterans like Elisha *"Maltese Falcon"* Cook, Jr., Cloris *"Kiss Me Deadly"* Leachman, Charles *"Narrow Margin"* McGraw, and Eduardo *"Dillinger"* Ciannelli (as Waldo).

And for all that, there was nothing old-fashioned or retro about *Johnny Staccato*. If anything, it proved how contemporary and in-your-face the genre could still be, with timely stories and new performers who fit the style perfectly, such as Shirley Knight and the edgy, haunted-looking star himself. Cassavetes was sufficiently engaged by the show to direct four episodes, including the sensational "Murder for Credit" with noir hard-ass Charles McGraw like you've never seen him before as a charismatic, doomed crooner. But audiences didn't go for it. *Johnny Staccato* lasted twenty-seven episodes and one round of reruns, then backed into the shadows for good.

While film noir had a chance to seep into public consciousness through television, on various *Late Show* and *Million Dollar Movie* broadcasts, the medium's own contributions to the genre have never gotten a fair shake. Few nonsitcoms from the black-and-white era are ever retelevised these days, making the chances for random discoveries rare to nonexistent (though newer cable operations like Nostalgia and TV Land may eventually go rooting around in this treasure trove). The intrepid historian and noir-head must make do with the haphazard offerings of video bootleggers or the more respectable resource of New York's Museum of Television & Radio and the American Cinematheque (which revived fascinating items like the Schlitz Playhouse's "A Fistful of Love" with Lee Marvin as a Punch-drunk boxer on a surreal descent into oblivion, and Phil Karlson's powerhouse pilot for *The Untouch-ables*). For now, and perhaps forever, the great majority of television's bleakest, darkest broadcasts will remain the hidden chapter in the history of noir.

CONTRIBUTOR'S NOTES

Etienne Borgers, a French-speaking Belgian, closely followed the development of noir literature in France, his taste in everything related to the genre, from cinema to hard-boiled American authors, having been acquired since his days as a young adult. Since 1973, he has scripted a comic book series that is successfully distributed all over Europe. He now maintains a web site on the Internet—Hard Boiled Mysteries—devoted to hard-boiled and noir literature of all origins.

Leigh Brackett (1915-1978) wrote novels and screenplays in several genres, including westerns (*Rio Bravo*), science fiction (*The Empire Strikes Back*), and detective (*The Big Sleep* and *The Long Goodbye*). She won the Jules Verne award and the Western Writers of America Spur award for her fiction. She was married to noted pulp author Edmond Hamilton and edited a collection of the best of his short fiction.

Dulcy Brainard is the editor for the lifestyles and mystery sections of *Publishers Weekly,* the leading trade magazine of the publishing world. She lives in New York.

Jon L. Breen has written six mystery novels; most recently *Hot Air* (1991), and over seventy short stories; contributes review columns to *Ellery Queen's Mystery Magazine* and *The Armchair Detective;* was shortlisted for the Dagger awards for his novel *Touch of the Past* (1988); and has won two Edgars, two Anthonys, a Macavity, and an American Mystery award for his critical writing.

Max Allan Collins writes hard-edged historical detective fiction that bears more than a trace of Hammett and Chandler. Rather than just pay homage to these pulp greats, however, he puts his own indelible spin on the noir tale, with incredibly effective results. More of his short fiction can be found in *Murder is My Business, Werewolves,* and *Vampire Detectives*. His current novel series features Nate Heller, a private-eye in the 1940s.

Jean-Pierre Coursodon is a French-born film historian and critic who has lived in the United States since 1967. He has written a dozen books among which include a major study of Buster Keaton,a critical history of the Warner Brothers studios, the two-volume collection of essays *American Directors* (as editor and principle contributor), and *50 Years of American Cinema,* co-written with French film director Bertrand Tavenier. He has contributed to many film magazines and film reference books, and is the United States East Coast correspondent for the French monthly magazine *POSITIF*. He has also translated into French the autobiographies of Michael Powell and Andre de Toth.

Bill Crider won the Anthony award for his first novel in the Sheriff Dan Rhodes series. His first novel in the Truman Smith series was nominated for a Shamus award, and a third series features college English professor Carl Burns. His short stories have appeared in numerous anthologies, including *Cat Crimes II* and *III, Celebrity Vampires, Once Upon a Crime,* and *Werewolves*. His recent work includes collaborating in a series of cozy mysteries with television personality Willard Scott. The second novel, *Murder in the Mist,* was published in 1998.

Mark Dawidziak is the critic-at-large in the entertainment section of the *Akron Beacon Journal*. A theater, film, and television critic for more than twenty years, he has been a regular contributor to such magazines as *Mystery Scene, Scarlet Street,* and *TV Guide*. His published books include a horror novel, *Grave Secrets,* and such non-fiction works as *The Columbo Phile: A Casebook*, *The Night Stalker Companion*, *The Barter Theatre Story: Love Made Visible*, and *Mark My Words: Mark Twain on Writing*. A New York native, he lives in Cuyahoga Falls, Ohio, with his wife, actress Sara Showman, and their daughter, Rebecca Claire.

James Delson was a freelance journalist from 1966 to 1986, writing on film for the *New York Times Syndicate*, the *Daily News*, *Film Comment*, *Take One*, *Penthouse*, and others. He was film editor for *Psychology Today*, film and television critic for *Omni*, and conducted a monthly radio interview program for WNYC-FM in New York. Now Mr. Delson runs a mail-order business selling toy soldiers and manages his website at <www.toysoldierco.com>. He remembers his many conversations with Charlton Heston, of which the published interview was only a small portion, as being lively, intelligent, and introspective.

Paul Duncan was born at a young age, grew up, and now has the body, if not the mind, of an adult. He lives two-thirds in a house. He co-edits *Crime Time* magazine and is presently writing a biography of Gerald Kersh.

Raymond Durgnot is an author and critic who lives in London, England.

Tom Flinn co-founded the Fertile Valley Film Society at the University of Wisconsin—Madison, where he organized several film noir retrospectives during the 1970s. He was also the book editor for the *Velvet Light Trap* magazine which was edited by John Davis, his partner in Fertile Valley. Permanently addicted to film noir since a youthful excursion to a double feature that included Stanley Kubrick's *The Killing*, he is particularly fascinated by films of the late 1940s, including *Out of the Past* and his personal favorite film noir, Robert Siodmak's *Criss Cross*.

Ed Gorman's name is synonymous with some of the best dark suspense and mystery fiction being written today. His novels *Black River Falls*, *The Marilyn Tapes*, *Blood Red Moon*, and *First Lady* have all met with widespread critical acclaim and several foreign sales. He is also the Editorial Director of *Mystery Scene*, one of the top trade magazines of the mystery genre. He lives in Cedar Rapids, Iowa, with his wife, author Carol Gorman.

The work of **Ron Goulart** has its roots in many genres. His science fiction has elements of mystery, his mysteries have elements of fantasy, and almost everything is infused with wit. Under numerous pseudonyms he has written dozens of novels, short stories, novelizations, and comic strips. In 1971, he won Mystery Writers of America's Edgar Allen Poe award.

Steve Holland is a freelance writer and editor, the author of over 900 features as well as two books in collaboration with Philip Harbottle, *Vultures of the Void* (1992) and *British SF Paperbacks and Magazines* (1994). His solo book *The Mushroom Jungle* (1993) was a nominee for the Anthony Boucher award for non-fiction. Professionally he writes mostly about movies; in his spare time he researches and writes about British pulp fiction, paperbacks, and comics. He categorically denies that he hasn't slept in two years.

Stephen Hunter is an author whose articles have appeared in *Espionage Magazine*, among others. He has interviewed many authors including John Le Carré. A movie critic for *The Baltimore Sun* for 15 years, he collected his columns in the book *Violent Screen: A Critic's 13 Years on the Front Lines of Movie Mayhem*. Currently he reviews films for the *Washington Post*.

Maxim Jakubowsi is the owner of London's crime bookstore Murder

One, the world's only mystery "superstore." He is a frequent reviewer for several newspapers and journals in England, along with being an editor and publisher of several works about crime fiction, science fiction, fantasy, film, and music.

Philip Kemp is a freelance writer and film historian who lives in London. His last book was *Lethal Innocence: The Cinema of Alexander Mackendrick,* and he is currently working on a biography of Michael Balcon. He reviews regularly for *Sight and Sound,* and also contributes from time to time to *Film Comment, Cineaste, Variety, International Film Guide, Liber,* and *Metro.*

Burton Kendle is an author who lives in Chicago, Illinois.

Stephen King is widely regarded as one of the most popular authors of all time. He recently revived the serial novel with his *New York Times* bestselling six-part series *The Green Mile.* His other two novels, *Desperation* and *The Regulators,* a novel written under the pseudonym of Richard Bachman, also topped the bestseller lists. His latest work is the novel *Bag of Bones.*

Dick Lochte is the creator of Leo Bloodworth and Serendipity Dahlquist, who have appeared in two novels, *Sleeping Dog* and *Laughing Dog.* He has also been a promotional copywriter for *Playboy* magazine, a film critic for the *Los Angeles Free Press,* and a book columnist for the *Los Angeles Times.*

Gary Lovisi runs the Gryphon Press, a small press located in Chicago, Illinois. He's also the publisher of *Paperback Parade,* a magazine which celebrates the paperback era of the 1950s and '60s.

One of science fiction's most critically admired and prolific authors, **Barry N. Malzberg** was born in New York City in 1939 and educated at Syracuse University. He has written over two hundred short stories and more than seventy novels. His novel *Beyond Apollo* won the John W. Campbell award in 1970. His critical history of science fiction from the 1950s to the 1980s, *The Engines of Night,* is acclaimed for its authoritativeness. His work in the suspense field, usually co-authored stories and novels, are no less impressive.

Noel Dorman Mawer is an English professor at Edward Waters College in Jacksonville, Florida. While completing her Ph.D. at Bryn Mawer, Noel encountered Patricia Highsmith's book *A Dog's Ransom* and has since never wavered in her devotion to Highsmith's world. While publishing several scholarly articles on Shelley's poetry, Noel was clandestinely immersing herself in Highsmith—and taking notes. The notes not only resulted in the present essay, but also in the article on Highsmith in the forthcoming Scribner's encyclopedia of crime writers, as well as a book-length study of Highsmith's works which is presently in preparation.

William Nadel is a noted mystery and radio historian, as well as contributor to the soon-to-appear *Oxford Companion to Crime and Mystery Writing.* He has directed, produced, and acted in numerous radio shows as well as presented workshops and reunions featuring performers from the "classic" years of the airwaves. In addition to assisting in the writing and production of books and articles on mystery and media, he is the co-author of the forthcoming Smithsonian Historical Performances book about Sherlock Holmes, and frequently lends his talents to the editing and presentation of CD/cassette collections of celebrated radio shows.

William F. Nolan is best known for his science fiction trilogy *Logan's Run, Logan's World,* and *Logan's Search,* which detail a future world ruled by the young, where the most deadly crime is growing old. However, during his more than 40 years as a professional writer, he has produced more than a thousand short stories and non-fiction works, as well as dozens of novels, scripts, and teleplays. He has also been recognized for excellence in various genres, winning two Edgar awards and an Academy of Science Fiction and Fantasy award for fiction and film.

Gene D. Phillips, S.J., is a professor of English and film history at Loyola University in Chicago, and the author of many articles and books on literature and film, including *Exiles in Hollywood: Fritz Lang and Other European Directors In America.*

Bill Pronzini is a five-time Edgar nominee. He is, among other things, the creator of the highly acclaimed series about the "Nameless Detective." Along with his wife, author Marcia Muller, he co-edited the great mystery and detective reference work *1001 Midnights.*

William Relling, Jr. is a writer who lives in Los Angeles, California. Other articles by him appear in *The Body Snatchers Companion, Night Screams,* and *100 Fiendish Little Frightmares.*

Peter Richards is a schoolteacher in Wales. He has written criticism for a number of magazines and newspapers in Britain, the United States, and Canada, including *Film Comment, Movietone News, The Listener, The Velvet, Light Trap, Take One, Focus on Film,* and *Stills.* He was the first person ever to be elected twice to the Management Committee of the British Federation of Film Societies. He is married and has two children.

Mike Ripley is the crime fiction critic of the *Daily Telegraph* in London and the author of the "Angel" series of comic novels. He has twice won the Crime Writer's Association "Last Laugh" award for humorous crime writing.

James Sallis is an author, editor, and translator who lives in Phoenix, Arizona. His interests include French literature, guitars, and jazz. His treatise on the history of noir literature can be found in the book *Difficult Lives: Jim Thompson–David Goodis–Chester Himes.* Previously he has lectured at various writing workshops at Clarion College, and has written columns for several magazines, including *Texas Jazz, Boston After Dark,* and *Fusion.*

Lee Server is best known for his extraordinary books examining the paperbacks of the 1950s in *Over My Dead Body,* the pulp magazines in *Danger Is My Business,* and his prize-winning interviews with early Hollywood screenwriters in *Screenwriters: Words Become Pictures.*

Jack Shadoian is a professor of literature at the University of Massachusetts—Amherst. His most recent publication is *Dreams and Dead Ends,* a study of the crime film. He is a frequent contributor to poetry magazines, including *5 A.M., Lucid Stone,* and *New York Quarterly.* A chapbook of his poems, *Balcony Visions,* was recently published. He lives in Amherst with his wife and children.

Walt Sheldon (1917-1979) was an author of fiction and non-fiction whose work appeared in *Ellery Queen's Mystery Magazine* and *100 Dastardly Little Detective Stories.*

Charles L.P. Silet widely reviews crime fiction and interviews crime writers for such journals as *The Armchair Detective, Mystery Scene, Clues, Mostly Murder, The Drood Review,* and the Australian mystery magazine *Mean Streets.* He teaches film and contemporary literature and culture at Iowa State University. He is currently editing a collection of critical articles on Chester Himes.

Robert Skinner is a non-fiction writer who lives in New Orleans, Louisiana.

Sybil Steinberg is the Senior Editor for the fiction section of *Publishers Weekly.* She lives in New York.

George Tuttle, a librarian in New Orleans, is a regular contributor to *Paperback Parade* magazine. Besides doing interviews, he has also written articles on the paperback original as a medium and noir as a genre. He is currently working on an article for the *Dictionary of Literary Biography* on Arnold Hano's work as a sportswriter.

Donald A. Yates is the editor of *El cuento policial hispanoamericao* and editor and translator of *Latin Blood: The Best Crime Stories of Spanish America.* He began reading and collecting detective fiction in 1973, and a dozen years later began a long reviewing career. He has published essays on the "locked room" tradition and detective fiction in Russia, Mexico, and Argentina. He has also translated many Spanish American detective stories as well as two Argentine mystery novels, *Thunder of the Roses* by Manuel Peyrou and *Rosa at Ten O'Clock* by Marco Denevi. He has been a member of the Mystery Writers of America since 1960.

COPYRIGHTS FOR THE BIG BOOK OF NOIR:

"The Golden Harvest: Twenty-five Cent Paperbacks" by Ed Gorman. Copyright (c) 1993 by Ed Gorman. Reprinted by permission of the author.

"Forgotten Writers: Gil Brewer" by Bill Pronzini. Copyright (c) 1989 by Bill Pronzini. Reprinted by permission of the author.

"Harry Whittington" by Bill Crider. Copyright (c) 1992 by Bill Crider. Reprinted by permission of the author.

"John D. MacDonald" by Ed Gorman. Copyright (c) 1984 by Ed Gorman. Reprinted by permission of the author.

"I Kill 'Em Inch by Inch!" by Steve Holland. Copyright (c) 1998 by Steve Holland. Reprinted by permission of the author.

"Lion Books: Noir Paperback Icons" by Gary Lovisi. Copyright (c) 1998 by Gary Lovisi.

"An Interview with Arnold Hano" by George Tuttle. Copyright (c) 1998 by George Tuttle.

"Mecca Spillane" by Max Allan Collins. Copyright @ 1982 by Max Allan Collins. Reprinted by permission of the author.

"Serie Noire History" by Etienne Borgers. Copyright (c) 1997 by Etienne Borgers. Reprinted by permission of the author.

"Lew Archer as Culture Maven" by Burton Kendle. Copyright (c) 1998 by Burton Kendle.

"Fifteen Impressions of Charles Williams" by Ed Gorman. Copyright (c) 1989 by Ed Gorman. Reprinted by permission of the author.

"A Too Brief Conversation with Peter Rabe" by George Tuttle. Copyright (c) 1991 by George Tuttle. Reprinted by permission of the author.

"Dell First Editions" by Bill Crider. Copyright (c) 1998 by Bill Crider.

"Interview with Donald Westlake" by Charles L.P. Silet. Copyright (c) 1996 by Charles L.P. Silet. Reprinted by permission of the author.

"Chester Himes: America's Black Heartland" by James Sallis. Copyright (c) 1993, 1998 by James Sallis.

"Donald Hamilton" by Robert E. Skinner. Copyright (c) 1997 by Robert E Skinner. Reprinted by permission of the author.

"From Villain to Vigilante" by Noel Mawer. Copyright (c) 1990 by *The Armchair Detective, Inc.* Reprinted by permission of the author.

"Not herself Mean: Hard-Boiled & Female, Without Contradiction" by Dulcy Brainard. Copyright (c) 1998 by Dulcy Brainard.

"From Under Hammett's Mask" by Dick Lochte. Copyright (c) 1998 by Dick Lochte.

"Charles Willeford" by Sybil Steinberg. Copyright (c) 1987 by Sybil Steinberg. First published in *Publisher's Weekly,* February 6, 1987. Reprinted by permission of *Publisher's Weekly.*

"Fresh Blood: British Neo-Noir" by Maxim Jakubowski and Mike Ripley. Copyright (c) 1998 by Maxim Jakubowski and Mike Ripley.

"Who's in the Room" by Bill Crider. Copyright (c) 1998 by Bill Crider.

"Author Notes" by Jon L. Breen. Copyright (c) 1998 by Jon L. Breen.

"Comic Book Noir" by Ron Goulart. Copyright (c) 1998 by Ron Goulart.

"Radio Noir" by William Nadel. Copyright (c) 1998 by William Nadel.

"Howard Duff Remembers the Adventures of Sam Spade" by Mark Dawidziak. Copyright (c) 1994 by Mark Dawidziak. Maxim Jakubowski and Mike Ripley

"Jack Webb: TV's Noir Auteur" by Max Allan Collins. Copyright (c) 1998 by Max Allan Collins.

"Johnny Staccato, Peter Gunn, and the Lost World of TV Noir" by Lee Server. Copyright (c) 1998 by Lee Server.

INDEX

— A —

— B —

— E —

— F —

— G —

— H —

— I —